p470-472
DD
p509 H-Numan
p511

ALSO BY ABBY WYNNE

NON FICTION

How to Be Well

Heal your Inner Wounds

Energy Healing Made Easy

The One Day at a Time Healing Diary

The Book of Healing Affirmations

A–Z of Spiritual Colouring Affirmations
Spiritual Tips for Enlightenment

Energy Healing for Everyone

FICTION

The Inner Compass Trilogy

Planting the Seeds- A Book of Poetry, Short Stories and Prayers

ONLINE SELF-PACED HEALING PROGRAMMES

How to Be Well

Heal your Inner Wounds

Energy Healing Made Easy

The One Day at a Time Healing Diary

The Book of Healing Affirmations

A–Z of Spiritual Colouring Affirmations

Spiritual Tips for Enlightenment

Energy Healing for Everyone

ONLINE SELF-PACED HEALING SESSIONS

Soul Retrieval

Take Your Power Back And Be Who You Are

Healing An Aspect Of Yourself

Release The Blocks And Live Your Happiest Life Now

The Safe Release Of Grief

Healing From A Breakup

Deep Relaxation And Healing Sleep

Healing For Vibrant Health

Clearing Financial Fear And Poverty Mindset

Align Yourself In The Present Moment

Heal Anxiety And Feel Grounded In Your Life

Stop Comparing Yourself To Others And Be Who You Are

Programmes and sessions are added on a regular basis.
Abby also facilitates monthly online group healing sessions, runs Raise your Vibration Bootcamp twice a year, and offers connection through Abby's Healing Circle.

There are many ways to connect with Abby - visit www.abby-wynne.com to find out more.

THE INNER COMPASS

TRILOGY

BOOK THREE

EXPANSION

A NOVEL BY

ABBY WYNNE

PRAXIS

PUBLISHING

First published in 2023 by Praxis Publishing
www.praxispublishing.ie

Edited by Elizabeth Henry

This is a work of fiction. Names, characters, businesses, places, events, locales, and incidents are either the products of the author's imagination or used in a fictitious manner. Any resemblance to actual persons, living or dead, or actual events is purely coincidental.

Source ISBN 978-1-9163627-6-5
Ebook Edition 978-1-9163627-7-2

DISCLAIMER

There is information here delivered in an emotionally charged way that may trigger you.

This book is not for children.

The information provided in this book is designed to provide helpful information on the subjects discussed. However, **not all opinions offered here are those of the author;** conflicting information may have been delivered from time to time at the author's discretion for the purposes of contrast.

This book is not a training manual. If you wish to become a fully trained psychotherapist, Reiki practitioner or shamanic practitioner, you are encouraged to have a 'beginner's mind' and find a teacher or school in your location that is appropriate for your training needs.

None of the techniques in this book are designed to be utilised by any reader. In other words, you are not encouraged to use any of the techniques in this book with others or on yourself.

This book is *not* intended as a substitute for the medical advice of physicians. **For diagnosis or treatment of any medical problem, please consult your doctor.** The author is not responsible for any specific health needs and is not liable for any damages or negative consequences from any treatment, action, application or preparation to any person reading or following the information in this book.

If you want advice/help with your healing process, or are a healer-in-practice, **you are invited to reach out to Abby.** You can read her non-fiction books, take an online program or join a healing session, follow her on social media and more. Visit Abby's website and see what calls to you- www.abby-wynne.com

THE INNER COMPASS TRILOGY

BOOK THREE

EXPANSION

A NOVEL BY

ABBY WYNNE

For Megan, Joshua, Mya and Siân.
Keep shining your beautiful lights in the world,
and make all your dreams come true.
All my love, Mama.

'We here are pioneers, courageous lions, stepping out of the chains of our conditioning. The worlds beneath our feet are shifting and changing as fast as we are – it's difficult to keep up with it all. Above all else, we have to hold high integrity and follow our truth at all times. Know that The Truth and our own personal truth may be different. We must be able to step aside anytime The Truth proves us wrong. By doing our inner work, we keep our inner compass clear, so we can always find our way back home, wherever that may be.'

— Séamus O'Driscoll, Shaman

CHAPTER ONE

I have to go back and see Scott Taylor again. I must finish this.

Once frightened, now strong and determined, Marissa had made her mind up. She had her new armour and a sword for protection. *What else is a warrior to do?*

Walking confidently through the British Museum, she said goodbye and thank you to the Egyptian artefacts as she passed them by. She held her head high, imagining her new armour glistening beneath her clothing, nestled tight against her body as she moved. She could almost feel the hilt of the sword at her back – even though it was energetic, the sense of the solid long blade running down her spine gave her emotional support.

A golden flash in the window of the museum shop caught her attention and she stopped to investigate. It was difficult to find what had caused it amongst the many items in the busy display. Her own reflection dominated the window so she took a moment and examined herself. She looked different, poised, more in control. *I walk now as Dream-Marissa, not as Real-Life-Marissa. Maybe I always was her, and was just afraid.*

The gold flashed again, flickering in a beam of sunlight which poured through the glassy atrium's skylight. Her eye danced with it, drawn down towards the source of the golden flare. *There! That's it!* It was a solid gold ankh, about three inches long, on a golden chain. She smiled. It looked rather plain, but nonetheless it was calling her into the shop to buy it. *Simple but elegant. I need it.* At the thought, she felt prickles creep down her back and all over her arms, and she knew that it was true.

The sunlight was golden against the building when Marissa finally left the Museum, evening was coming in, and there wasn't much she could do about Scott, for now. Feeling strong, consolidated and happy with her brand-new (expensive) golden ankh around her neck, Marissa walked leisurely back towards the hotel, taking her time, dipping into Google Maps on her phone for reference. She felt peaceful inside. Nestled in between a newsagent and a phone shop she saw the restaurant she had eaten in the night before and was suddenly ravenous. *Comfort food?* An image of pasta, or pizza, then pasta again in her mind didn't excite her. *No, I'll try somewhere new, something I've not had before, something I can't get easily in Dublin.* She felt a flash of excitement and anticipation through her body and kept walking, eyes wide open for opportunities. After a few minutes she saw an Arabian restaurant. *This!*

She went straight in and, smiling, easily got a table.

The restaurant was dimly lit, unfamiliar music played softly in the background and there were wonderful smells emanating from the kitchen. She settled into her seat and looked at the menu, but didn't understand a word of it.

'Can you help me choose something?' she asked the waiter, calling him over. 'It all sounds so exotic, but I have no idea where to start.'

He smiled. 'Your first time?'

'Yes! I am from Ireland, we don't have places like this, well, not that I have found anyway!'

'Oh, interesting. I have never been to Ireland, perhaps this is why! It is my pleasure to introduce you to some of our culinary delights. What about a plate of cold mixed starters, and how about the Shwarma lamb? It comes with rice and vegetables and is very good.'

'That sounds wonderful, thank you. Can you bring a glass of wine too? Red. Thank you!'

Marissa ate slowly, savouring the warm spices and delicate flavours and textures of the food. Looking at the amount of food on the table, she felt she was at a celebratory feast. She raised her glass and toasted Isis in her mind, who nodded in return. *I don't usually drink red wine - or eat such exotic food. I like this. I* am *celebrating, I feel I have come of age or something. I have arrived. This is the real me. And I like it!*

Out of nowhere, images of the crowd chanting 'Scott! Scott! Scott!' filled her mind and she shivered. Suddenly she felt small. *Okay, maybe I've not fully arrived just yet. I can't take on everything... But I will try my best.* She drained the rest of her glass. *I drank that one a little fast! Nerves? But I know I really need to go back and see him again. If only to see how I feel around him, test my new self out. Sure what else would I be doing?*

She took a breath and slowed her mind, saw herself sitting in the audience, this time with her armour visible outside her body, her sword at her feet. The nerves dissipated quickly and her normal breath returned. She scooped some food onto her fork and into her mouth, focusing on the flavours instead of the images, which still upset some aspect of her. *It was only a few hours ago and I was really terrified. Of course I'm still upset about it. And that's okay.*

The spices and warm food were grounding and brought her back to the moment. She asked the waiter for another glass of red, and fingered the ankh around her neck as she came back to herself again. *Yes, I will go back tomorrow morning for the last session. I will stare him in the face and see what he is made of, see what I am made of too. Perhaps there's something else I can do while I'm there. If not, at the very least, I can consider it research for when I am ready. Yes, that feels right.*

She took her time, and had ice cream and a coffee to round off a most delicious meal. When she paid she left a generous tip, then went back to the hotel, picking up bath salts and some small scissors in a late-night chemist on the way. After cutting off her wrist-band and soaking in a soothing salt bath, she climbed into soft white sheets and slept right through the night.

Marissa ate breakfast quickly at her hotel, then checked out and took her suitcase with her to the event to save herself trekking back to the hotel once it was over. Her bag was stuffed full and difficult to close, which she found funny, as she hadn't bought anything new. *Besides the ankh, that is. How did I manage to bring so many things for only two nights away?*

She joined the queue of excited participants outside the venue with her printed out ticket in hand, and the cut wristband in her pocket, just in case. She felt welcomed by the people waiting to get inside; they were so bright and happy, it felt strange, as if it was a family reunion. *She pulled back from them. These people aren't my family, that's for damn sure.*

The people ahead of her were beaming with joy at having one more chance to see the master at work. *Master? Where did that thought come from? He's their master, more like.* Marissa shivered. She was standing behind a small group of four women who were all wearing wristbands and seemed to know one another. They were speaking loudly in Scottish accents. One of them turned to Marissa, smiling, wanting to include her. She noticed her suitcase. 'Hello, dear. Did you travel here too? All on your own?'

Marissa smiled. 'Yes, from Ireland. I came by myself. Did you all come from Scotland?'

'Aye, we drove down together.' The woman winked at Marissa. 'Only for the weekend mind you – we can bear it for a few days to see the man!'

The women laughed, and Marissa laughed easily along with them. Strong Celtic comradery always created an immediate connection between the Irish and the Scottish.

Ice now broken, Marissa said, 'But I thought Scott was doing an event in Edinburgh. Why did you want to come to London?'

A blonde woman replied, 'Ach, we've tickets for that one too. Wanted to see him here, though – we heard the London gigs were something else, and wow, what a day yesterday! And Marie here, she's the real groupie – she's going to both the Birmingham *and* Manchester gigs next week.'

A dark-haired woman with glasses blushed and nodded while looking down at her feet.

The tallest woman added with a grin, 'We're glad we came, even though we had to cross the border. But wasn't it out of this world? What did ya think of the afternoon session yesterday? I've never seen anything like it!'

Marissa had missed the afternoon session, having spent it in the British Museum, but smiled and nodded in agreement hoping they wouldn't quiz her on it. *What did I miss?* The whole thing felt off. She knew it was off. She gathered herself. *I need to be one of the crowd today ... blend in... I can find out more that way. Or do I say I wasn't there? Will they tell me what happened?*

Immediately she had sense that she would be considered an outsider if she admitted she had walked out. Enthusiastically, she said, 'Yes, it was amazing,' then added in a confident tone, 'Scott blew my mind.'

That is 100 per cent true, actually.

That answer went down very well with the ladies, who all agreed enthusiastically.

'I can't wait to put his work into practice with my clients,' said the dark-haired woman with a smile. She had a strength about her once Marissa engaged with her directly, and seemed genuine.

'What do you do?'

The woman made eye contact as she spoke. 'I'm a life coach. I've taken lots of courses, but it's Scott's techniques that have given me the best results. Och, that's why I'm going to the other gigs too. They're never the same – he always has something new up his sleeve. And I always get booked out after I go to his events. It's almost like people know, somehow, that I have something new to offer. These gigs always end up paying for themselves, and more besides. I do very well out of it.' She turned to the others and gave them a dig. 'Ye can slag me off as much as you like, I'll be laughing all the way to the bank!'

'Ach, Marie, you know we love you!' They all laughed again, and then the queue started moving forward.

Marissa turned Marie's words over in her mind as they got closer to the gate. *Is she selling her soul in exchange for more clients? What is the true cost of her success?*

Though Marissa was prepared to drag her cabin bag inside with her, she was glad to see they had a left-luggage service. She happily dropped her bag in, showed her paper ticket and went inside feeling lighter for it. The Scottish women had already disappeared.

Marissa took a moment to get her bearings, waiting for the familiar butterflies to fill her stomach. But they didn't come;

instead, she was filled with a deep sense of calm. She tuned into her protection, and walked gracefully to her seat. *I don't recognise myself.*

The atmosphere inside the arena was also calm. People were gathering; there were murmurings and shuffling sounds as they meandered in and took their seats, small bursts of laughter from groups meeting up in the audience, and a light crackling from the audio system, but Marissa sensed no pent-up emotion. A few roadies were on stage checking the electronics. The large space was filling up slowly.

As Marissa got to her row, she wondered what had changed. *Has he taken what he wanted already? Is that what happened yesterday afternoon?*

People had notebooks on their laps, or were on their phones. The business-like atmosphere was the complete opposite of the excitement of the previous day. *Am I in the right place?*

Marissa worked her way through her row to her seat, squeezing past a few people who were already there. She recognised a couple of them. She pulled down the lip of her chair and sat down on the tightly cushioned seat, still wearing her coat and carefully placed her handbag at her feet. *It's like a completely different planet from the one I was on yesterday.*

Even the stage was different. It looked like a counselling room, with two armchairs and a coffee table with flowers, a decanter of water and a couple of glasses. There were no flashy lights, large cinema screens, no razzmatazz whatsoever.

Well, it's not started yet. Maybe the crazy energy will appear later?

Marissa slipped her arms out of her coat and opened it out onto the back of her seat, still unsure. *I came here ready for anything, ready for a fight even. Perhaps my expectations are the problem.* She fingered her ankh and visualised her armour snugly fitting her body under her clothes.

The auditorium was filling up now. She stood several times to let people through. Then the lights went down. It was time.

Marissa sat up in her seat, eyes wide open, senses alert, ready for anything. A man wearing a white suit came onto the stage and everyone started to clap. She looked at him. Was this Scott? She didn't recognise him at all. He seemed smaller than before, quite ordinary. He smiled at the crowd, but that magical light - that draw, that attraction, that charisma - it was gone! It was just a man on a stage. But the people around him loved him all the same. They whistled and clapped as he took a bow. Scott sat down in one of the armchairs, smiled, and poured himself a glass of water.

What is going on? Part of her was relieved. She had been prepared for a supernatural fight of good vs evil. *Am I disappointed? Do I really want to fight?* She waited to feel what her body was feeling, which was, relief. *Okay, I can do this. I know I'm not ready.* She looked again at Scott, he was tapping his microphone and getting some help from one of the sound engineers. Marissa smiled. *I'm glad I came today. I needed to see this - it's very interesting, very interesting indeed. If there was a demon inside Scott yesterday, then today there isn't. Well, I can't see him, anyway. Today, this is a very ordinary man. Maybe the demon got what he wanted and left?*

Scott nodded and the sound engineer left the stage. He turned and smiled once more, and then addressed the audience. 'Good morning, my friends! It's good to see you all here today. Thank you, thank you. Aww, you're too kind – too, too kind! But we must get started, we only have a few hours together. As you can see, I have two chairs up here, as I want to show you some of my methods in-practice. I have chosen an actor to work with me so we can demonstrate as many techniques as possible in the short time we have this morning.'

The session was actually quite good. Marissa took a few notes on some clever ways to reflect things back to the client that might come in useful in her own work. But it was quite pedestrian, nothing magical, or supernatural. And then it was over. Marissa found herself clapping with everyone else, but inside of herself, she felt she had missed something. *Honestly, if this was all it was, it wasn't worth travelling all the way to London for. What is drawing them all in? It makes no sense.*

Marissa waited until most of the people cleared the auditorium before leaving her seat. She sat with the feeling of something missing, as if someone had taken a big bite out of her. In a dream-like state, she retrieved her suitcase.

Guess I should leave then. Wow. It really is over! I feel a little flat, but I guess I've learned a lot. I probably just need some time to figure out what exactly it is that I've learned.

Her flight was in a few hours, she was exhausted and didn't feel like rushing around just for the sake of it so she decided to take her time and go straight to the airport. She looked in the shops along the way, tried a burrito, had a coffee and got a few trinkets in Victoria station. All the while, though, she didn't feel fully in her body. And of course, her logical head was spinning. Something was off, something wasn't right, none of this made any sense at all.

On the plane home Marissa went deeper into the images of the past few days: Scott the day before, his eyes dark and magnetic, the crowd chanting his name; Scott this morning, a nice man with some clever psychological tricks up his sleeve that he wanted to share. Rock star vs ordinary man. It just didn't add up.

She came back to the present moment and realised she was still free from anxiety. She hadn't felt any nervousness at all since she panicked and ended up at the museum. This was new territory, and it felt good. *Let's make this about me for a while, I could do with the change of topic. I'll think about about Scott another time.*

Marissa checked in with herself – what was different? She slowed down, felt herself coming more into her body, that feeling of something missing in her chest – she went into it, breathed into it, then felt something deep within settle, and then evaporate. She felt grounded. *Grounded in the air, while on a plane! Ha ha.* But she did feel more expansive, calmer, more confident, more accomplished somehow. Definitely closer to the Marissa that she was in her dreams, only right here in real life.

That's it, yes. I know exactly who I am, and I am no longer afraid. I hope this lasts. I like it. I have a sense that it will, but I don't want to jinx it.

She paused for a moment, staying with her body at this deeper level, and it was calm. She was in a little tin box with wings, flying high above the sea, and she was calm. She smiled, and let something go. Then thoughts of her life in Dublin and her plans for the week ahead came flooding into her mind.

Oy vey! I've got Reiki clients booked in for tomorrow evening, that's so soon! Then St Mary's on Wednesday and Cabra on Thursday. And work, of course. Back to my busy reality.

She fingered her golden ankh. *Well, my ankh is real and will be a great reminder of what happened, even though I don't actually know what happened.* She remembered buying it in the museum shop and got a flash of memory around how distressed she had been at the time. *That was only yesterday, once more it feels like I have stepped out of time and space. I'm pretty sure I didn't make all this up. I do have a powerful imagination, but why would I make all this up?*

She begin to count clouds out her window as they flew past. *I must pull myself back into this reality. This week will be my first Tuesday in forever without having to go to college for a class. I want to get a degree – It will be nice to have put myself through college. I will have to remember to register with them.*

She ordered a can of Diet Coke from a passing flight attendant and made a toast in her mind's eye to the Great Goddess Isis. *Thank you for intervening, thank you for your protection, and thank you for taking all my anxiety away. Whether what happened was real or not, the more I think about it, the more confused I get. So I will stop thinking about it, for now. I'm feeling good, and long may it last.*

In her mind's eye, she imagined she saw the beautiful goddess raising a glass of champagne with a smile, in return. She needed something to do now, to make this reality all the more real. She opened her handbag and looking through it, found the gifts that she picked up in Victoria station that morning. For Amanda and Marcus, she had got some funny Pez dispensers in the shape of Disney characters. She had bought some keyrings too – a vintage Volkswagen van for Matt, one with a royal crown for her mother, a smiley emoji for her father, a Tardis for Eli and a Tinky Winky for Terry...

She giggled, imagining Terry's face when she gave it to him. *Should I go back to the shamanic classes? Oh. Wow. Maybe I should go back to the classes...* She expected her stomach to flip at the thought of it. But it didn't. She got excited instead. *Yes! I do want to go back. This is fantastic! I'll get in touch with Séamus ASAP. Oh God, I do hope all will be forgiven.* Her heart sank. *Maybe he won't let me back because I missed one...* More determined this time she remembered something Noreen told her - *If you don't ask, you don't get. So I will ask and I guess I'll find out one way or the other.*

The plane was circling Dublin, making its descent, preparing to land. Marissa packed the gifts back into her bag and put her bag under the seat in front of her, ready for landing. *I used to be so upset coming back to Ireland. I never liked coming home, but I'm excited about it now. I miss my drum and my crystals. I'll take them out straight away and let them see light and air. I want to hold my medicine bundle. Yes, it's time I reclaimed my medicine and claimed my space in the world.*

Recognisable landmarks of Dublin came into view. *There's Howth, that must be the city centre, and there, that's got to be Dun Laoghaire. Can I see Matt's place from here? That could be it!* Her heart warmed at the thought of him, maybe he was in his flat right now, seeing her plane fly over from above. *I wonder how he's doing. I didn't text him at all while I was away, and he didn't text me back.* She felt a flash of anxiety. *No, it's okay. He was just giving me some space. I needed the space too, to figure out all of this stuff. I'm looking forward to seeing him. I'll give him a call when I get settled back home.* Her anxiety lifted immediately and was replaced with excitement.

As soon as the plane landed most of the passengers stood up and opened the overhead lockers to get their bags out. Some bags had been packed in so tightly they rolled out of the hatches, some people narrowly avoided being hit on the head. Marissa stayed seated during the bustle and the beeping of messages as they came in on newly activated phones. The plane was still taxiing to its spot, but people were already calling their family and friends and totally ignoring the 'Please remain seated' lights on the overhead dashboard.

Finally the plane stopped moving, the doors opened, and the passengers spilled out. Marissa was one of the last off; she wanted to avoid the crowd. She walked swiftly through the baggage area, then through customs, and through the arrivals gate. Then she saw someone waving at her.

Is that Matt? It can't be!

Matt was coming towards her with a big smile on his face. 'Hi, love, thought I'd surprise you and come and pick you up!'

Marissa thought she'd melt into a puddle right there on the floor. She couldn't speak. Matt kissed her nose and cheeks and she dropped her bag and grabbed his face with her two hands and kissed him on the mouth.

He blushed. 'Shall we go?'

Marissa nodded. Matt took her bag and they walked together past the people and out through the main door towards the car park pay stations.

'I was worried about you,' Matt explained. 'I didn't hear from you at all, and I wanted to come and get you, to give you a hug.'

The paid-for ticket spat out of the machine, he took it and put it in his inside pocket. Turning to Marissa, he opened his arms and she stepped into them. It wasn't a good place for a homecoming hug, as people wanted to pay for their tickets, so they moved to the side, then he hugged her tightly, and she let him.

Now I really am home.

'You didn't have to come and get me,' she whispered breathlessly.

'I know. I wanted to. You left so upset and flustered, and then I didn't hear a peep. I needed to check on you, after everything that's been going on.'

Marissa smiled and pulled away so she could focus on Matt's face. He seemed younger than she remembered.

'I'm good, Matt. I feel different from before, stronger. Lots happened over there. Perhaps I didn't contact you because I am still making sense of it. I still don't understand much of it. But the best bit is that I discovered a part of myself over there, a stronger part, and I brought her home with me. I don't know who or what she is or if she will stay forever, but I like her. I need to get used to this.'

She touched his face. 'It's so nice to see you,' she said. 'I can't go to your place, though. I need to get home to Tobermory.'

'I figured that. I'll take you home to him.' Matt swept into a deep bow and said, 'Your chariot awaits, madam,'. On rising up he winked and smiled, and Marissa playfully punched his arm.

They walked to the car. Matt opened the passenger side and pulled a few bags off the seat, then opened the boot and put them in, along with Marissa's cabin bag. She settled herself into the seat, handbag at her feet. The car smelled like Matt. There was an empty crisp packet at her feet. She giggled and picked it up.

'Don't you have a bin in here?'

Matt quickly took it from her and stuffed it into the driver-side door. 'Sorry, I didn't have time to tidy up! I didn't actually plan to pick you up, it was kind of spontaneous.'

'I like spontaneous.'

Matt beamed and switched on the engine.

As they drove through Dublin, Marissa looked out of the window at the shops, houses and people.

'Do you want to talk about it?' asked Matt in a low voice.

Marissa sat for a while before answering, enjoying the silence and Matt's soft presence beside her.

'You know, one of the nicest but strangest things,' she said, reflecting on the weekend, 'was hearing my grandfather's voice strongly in my mind. It was solid and so real to me. He told me that the people who had gone to see Scott Taylor had sold their souls.' She shivered slightly upon hearing herself say his full name out loud.

Matt looked worried.

'I know, I'm processing a lot right now, it probably doesn't make any sense.' Marissa shifted in the seat so she could better face him. 'It was something he used to say a lot about people when I was growing up – people who had it easy, people who seemed to get everything they wanted without really working for it. Dad always thought it was jealousy. I never thought it could actually be a real thing.'

Matt scratched his beard as he drove. 'Yes, I guess selling your soul could be a real thing. There's so much about the world that we don't know.'

Marissa faced front again. 'I'm still working this all out, Matt. I guess I need you to be patient with me.'

'I have been very patient with you, Marissa,' he said, 'and that won't change. But I really got scared. When I saw that book, the scribbles and symbols that you drew all over it, I was incredibly worried, more scared in fact than I've ever been in my life. It was like something from a horror movie. Like you were possessed or something.' He shivered. 'I've heard stories about possession, and I think it can really happen. In real life, I mean.' He turned to look at her, cocking his head to one side. 'And now this selling your soul thing, really, it's scary as hell.'

They stopped at a red light and Matt turned to Marissa and examined her more closely. 'You do seem okay, though – now, I mean. More than before you left. Do you really think you're okay? Do you need to get some help?'

Marissa relaxed. 'I've never felt better, Matt. Something inside me has changed. It's like I've grown up or something. Solidified. It's the strangest feeling. I feel stronger now. Like I could conquer the world.'

Matt laughed nervously. 'I don't know if that's a good idea right now.'

Marissa laughed. 'No, I agree. I have to feed the cat, have a shower and call Mum first. Then I can conquer the world!'

'Seriously, Marissa, you've been through an ordeal. Maybe you should see Dolores?'

Marissa was about to jump down Matt's neck for being overprotective, but she hesitated and thought about it. *Dolores did say she'd teach me psychic protection. There'd be no harm in asking about that.*

'Yes, I'll give her a call, make an appointment. I feel good, Matt, but you're right. It really was a wild weekend, and a lot of it still makes no sense to me right now. I should make sure that I've not picked up anything nasty from being around those people, like that time I was with Cheryl Bryant.' She shivered at the memory. 'I should probably clean the energy in my flat, too.'

Matt seemed relieved. 'You do sound better. Good. I know the last time you said you'd go and see Dolores, you never did. But I think I believe you this time.'

Marissa smiled. 'Thanks for being there, for not giving up on me, I mean. I know I've been a handful these last few weeks.'

Matt chuckled. 'Few weeks?' His laughter intensified until Marissa was laughing too. When the ripples of it had died down, he said, 'Marissa, you're the biggest handful I've ever had to manage in my life. And it's amazing, and terrifying, and exhilarating and scary as hell. But I'm still here, and I hope to be here a while longer, if you'll let me.'

They were outside Marissa's flat. She unbuckled her seatbelt, reached across the centre of the car and kissed him.

Later that evening, after Matt had left, she pulled out her 'Pandora's Box' and opened it. Her heart melted when she saw all the items inside. She held them all closely to her, as if they were old friends she had not seen in a very long time. Realising how much they meant to her: her angel cards, the shamanic oracle deck, her Reiki notes, her medicine bundle and her beloved drum, she felt very emotional. *I really have missed you all.* She felt a ripple in her body, as if a part of her soul was returning to her. *This is who I am. These cards, they are an extension of me. This drum, it is my heart. I cannot hide this part of myself from myself any longer. And I have to stop caring about what others think of me. This is who I am.*

She put the card decks proudly on the coffee table, smiling, and placed her drum onto her bed.

Tobermory wound himself around her legs, mewing as she moved through the flat, gathering up all her Scott Taylor books. He followed her curiously as she put them into the tin bucket she used for ashes from the fireplace. She opened the back door and took the bucket outside, thought for a moment, then went into the kitchen and got some sunflower oil and matches. Pouring the oil on the books, she felt a deep inner resistance, as if burning books went against everything she believed in, but some part of her knew the energy from those books had to go and fire was the best way to do it. She set them alight.

It took a few moments for the flame to burn strongly, but once it did, Marissa stood there as solemnly as she had done at the fire ceremony, watching the books slowly disintegrate.

Tobermory's eyes flickered as he sat near the bucket and watched the flames with her. As the books burned the flame turned blue and green, orange violet and white. They fell into themselves and into the bottom of the bucket. Books now unrecognisable, he scampered away, satisfied that the task was complete.

Marissa watched until the books burned down to nothing, then left the tin bucket outside, as it was too hot to move. The night was cold and it was beginning to rain, so the raindrops would take care of the heat and she could clean it all up in the morning.

Coming back into the flat, she still felt the energy wasn't right, though. There was still some reclaiming to do.

She wiped the bookshelves down with a weak bleach solution, then wiped the covers of some of her books, putting the shelf to rights. She remembered.

Tobermory knew, didn't he? He knocked my bookshelf down, I remember now. He even pissed on one of my books... but it wasn't the right one! Sure how was he to know? Oh poor love! You're totally forgiven!

She giggled and felt her heart open with even more love for her feline friend, who was out in the night doing whatever it was that cats did.

Once she had finished with the books Marissa burned sage and smudged the flat. Then she picked up her drum, holding it tightly to her chest. It felt like a reunion with an old friend. She spoke directly to it.

'I'm so sorry, drum. I won't forsake you again. You are a part of me, and we belong together. I know who I am now. I will never forget.'

She drummed upon it with her fingertips, first quietly, enjoying the feeling of the reverberations running through her body, then louder, until she needed to get the beater. Then she was loud and proud, banging her drum unapologetically. *Feck the neighbours I need this!*

She whispered, 'Out, bad spirits!' and felt something lifting, so she did it again and again, saying it louder and louder until it became a battle cry. In every room she drummed and smudged with sage and chanted loudly. Then she took her drum outside and cleared the deck area and the garden. Nobody banged on ceiling or wall, nobody interrupted at all. *Perhaps nobody is home, perhaps I drove them all out, too!*

Then, when she felt her flat was clear, she ran a hot bath, poured all of her salts into it and cleansed herself, calling on the energies of the sea, the wind and rain, to wash her own energy clean.

Later, she sat in the deck area in pyjamas, wrapped in a blanket with a hot cup of tea in her hands. Tobermory appeared on the top of the wall, leapt down and rubbed against her legs, then climbed into her lap. She stroked the ruff under his neck, which was his favourite spot, studying the white streaks on his fur. *I'll never know what he did for me.*

'Thanks, baby,' she said, pulling him into her and hugging him, rubbing her face into his face. 'Thank you so much. You're a good friend to me, and I'll never forget what you did, even though I'll never know exactly what it was.'

Tobermory started purring loudly, his body thrumming like a generator. Marissa placed him gently back on her lap, where he curled into a ball and closed his eyes. Marissa stroked the circle of his back. *He's so soft. It's good to be home. It's as if I'm back from some far-off place, a journey to another dimension. I suppose I am, in essence. I went to London, ended up in Egypt, skipped a few time space dimensions, and then came home again.*

She looked at her sleeping cat and remembered the elegant animal that had been under the table as she had taken tea with Isis. *You were with me too, weren't you?*

CHAPTER TWO

Marissa was dead. Her body was hacked into three large pieces – smaller chewed chunks of flesh were scattered around the forest floor, sharp bones and sinews protruded from ripped muscle and skin. Well, she thought she was dead, then she got her bearings and realised she couldn't be dead if she was still in her body, even if her body was torn apart.

About a meter away from her she could see that an animal was gnawing on her dismembered leg. She tried to shout at the rugged, dark and hungry four-legged thing to make it go away, but it laughed at her and kept chewing.

She felt like the scarecrow in The Wizard of Oz. She breathed out, trying not to panic. If the scarecrow could be put back together then maybe I could be, too. *The creature stopped chewing, sensing her change in energy, shook itself, glared at her then ran away.*

She used the strength of her will to pull her mutilated leg back towards her body. After a moment, it started to flicker and then it shifted slightly closer.

Oh! This is like the stepping stones, asking them to move towards me so I could reach them! I know how to do this!

Shifting gears, more confident now, she used her will power once more and pulled the leg back to herself, it flew and landed with a whump! A little too strong perhaps. But at least it worked. *She looked around and drew the other parts of herself in too, then used her imagination to meld herself back together like a jigsaw puzzle.*

When the pieces of her body met each other they bound together, leaving no trace of having been severed. Almost perfect.

Marissa stood, wobbled a little, then brushed herself down and fixed her hair. She tested her limbs, all seemed okay, so she started walking. It felt good to walk.

It's not as if I wasn't going to walk again, but I do feel like I passed some sort of test.

After a short time she came to a clearing that she recognised. Deep within, nested between several smaller trees, was her dear friend, the wise old tree.

She stood there patiently, looking at him. He felt her presence and opened his large eyes slowly, when he saw that it was her, a smile widened in welcome. He yawned, and then spoke.

'Ah, there you are,' said the tree, not seeming to notice any change in her. ' I believe there are some people waiting to speak to you. Will you see them?'

Marissa nodded without hesitation. 'Yes, of course.'

The tree nodded and smiled once more, then its trunk opened, revealing the spiral staircase leading downwards. Marissa climbed in and partially floated, partially climbed down the tight spiral staircase. It was lit by small lamps with little faces similar to that of her dear tree friend. She touched the familiar walls, noticing more detail on them than she had done before.

'Jeez, things are moving very quickly now. I wonder who wants to see me?'

She arrived at a door, caught her breath, then stepped through it. There she was, by her lake, surrounded by the beautiful, familiar snow-capped mountains.

'Ah, I'm home!'

Her heart filled with joy, and she felt joy reflected back to her from the mountains. She whispered, 'Ausangate' and felt, for a moment, as if the mountain bowed towards her. This unlocked something deep within her heart and her eyes filled with tears, she became a wellspring of joy. A massive, solid wedge of grief pulled itself out and then released itself from her core. Tears spilled onto her face, she needed to catch her breath, for a moment, she was overcome by emotion.

Almost toppling over she found her footing, then heard a rushing noise from beneath the still waters. She turned to see the glorious sea serpent raising his glistening head and trumpeting in greeting, shooting jets of water up and over his head in joy at seeing her returned and whole.

Marissa's heart practically exploded with joy once more. It really hurt - sharp pains needled through it as she watched her beloved sea serpent settle back into the water. He raised his head once more, his glistening eyes turned towards her, nodding his head as he remained there, watching her, almost smiling.

She wiped the tears off of her face and shouted out 'Shall I come out to you?' Marissa's urge to wade out to hug this enormous creature was abruptly interrupted by Emelda, who appeared from nowhere and was running towards her. She stopped about two feet away from Marissa, her face tearful, wringing her hands.

'Are you okay? Emelda?'

The woman nodded. 'You came back to us. I knew you would.'

'Yes, this is my home, the place of my heart. I know it now. I'm so sorry I disappeared for so long.'

The women embraced.

As they held each other tightly, Grandmother Medicine Woman appeared and approached them, wearing all of her robes and finery. 'We knew you would overcome,' she said. 'I see the changes in you. You are coming closer to your true self. Good, good.'

Grandmother Medicine Woman held out her arms and Marissa gratefully stepped out from Emelda's tight embrace and into them. She felt her heart connect with Grandmother Medicine Woman's heart. Something beautiful and warm flowed between them and the sharp pains in Marissa's heart melted away. Her heart expanded, swollen with love.

'You go through the world with your heart wide open,' Grandmother Medicine Woman said. 'So hopeful. It will be returned when you look in the right places. Now that your heart is bigger, it can hold more love. But also more pain. You must learn to manage this.'

'I will try,' Marissa whispered.

'My turn again,' Emelda broke in. 'You hug her for too long!'

Marissa turned and hugged Emelda once more. Emelda hugged her back, then shook her, hard.

'Never do this to us again! Silly girl! Do not be seduced to the dark side. We have plenty of good things here. Everything that you need is here!'

Marissa stepped away, laughing. 'I promise,' she said. 'I have so many questions for you.'

She turned to look for her bear. She could feel his presence on the mountain, but couldn't see him. She felt a pang of remorse for having spent so long away from him, too.

She smiled and turned to Grandmother Medicine Woman. 'Will you tell me your name now?' she asked, with a cheeky grin.

The grandmother smiled. 'All in good time, my lovely. You still haven't earned that privilege yet. Come, sit down and let us have some tea.'

A small beechwood table had appeared at the lake's edge. Upon it were a small cast-iron teapot, three well-worn metal camping mugs and a basket with small, pink sugar cakes in it, similar to those Marissa had seen in the market in Cusco.

'They are not muffins,' said Emelda with a smile, 'but they are pink. Anyway, my food is better quality.' Emelda poured a hot, dark liquid from the teapot into the mugs and sat down on a cushion on the ground, inviting Marissa to sit beside her. Grandmother Medicine Woman was a little slower to sit down, although she had a chair instead of a cushion, she moved as if she had aches and pains in her bones.

Marissa held her mug in both hands. She could smell pine, clove and something deeply aromatic, like sandalwood.

'Is it true, Grandmother,' she asked, 'that those people I saw had sold their souls? And why was Scott so different yesterday to the day before? I'm still so confused.'

Grandmother Medicine Woman sipped her tea, looking out towards the sea serpent, who acknowledged her with a nod. She turned to Marissa. 'You have been on an interesting journey indeed, almost more interesting than those journeys that you experience here, with us.' She gestured to the little cakes, Marissa took one and bit into it. She felt herself relaxing at an even deeper level, she felt safe, and her body pulsed with love. The urgency she had felt a moment ago to find the answers, subsided.

'Good. Take some time to relax and rest. You won't get all of your answers here and now, and I know you have many questions, some of which have not yet appeared in your mind, but they will be revealed to you in time.' She smiled and drank again.

Marissa sat with the reverberations of the energies she was surrounded by, enjoying the company, the scenery, and a new sense of herself. She had almost forgotten what she had just asked them about.

Grandmother Medicine Woman had not forgotten. She put down her tea and looked at Marissa directly. 'To answer your most important question, yes, the selling of souls can happen, for some. They agree to sell part of themselves in exchange for something of material value. This goes *against nature. Their soul does not belong to them, and is not theirs to sell. So there must be consequences.'*

There was a hardness in the grandmother's voice as she spoke, she shook her head and looked at the ground. Her disapproval and anger cut through the conversation like a knife. Emelda wanted to break the tension, she made a silly face at Marissa, to lighten the moment. Marissa smiled, then laughed, suddenly overcome with love. She got up from the table and went to Emelda, wrapping her arms around her neck.

'I'm so sorry I pushed you both away. I don't ever want to do that again.'

Emelda allowed herself to be hugged, then hugged Marissa back even more tightly, before releasing her and looking deeply into her face. 'Did you want to do it this time, really?' she asked. 'I tried to warn you, to tell you. I knew it was not just you, there was more to it. But Grandmother,' she nodded at the wise elder, 'she said you had to learn some things for yourself. Some lessons must be experienced. Now I hope you are wiser. Like me.' She giggled, then leaned forward and poured more tea into Marissa's mug.

Marissa went back to her cushion and sat down. 'I hope so,' she said, cupping her hands around the mug, which seemed very hot. 'I do believe that I have had my eyes opened to the ways of the world.'

'Ah, but which world?' said Grandmother Medicine Woman with a smile, and all three of them laughed. It felt good.

'I know. I am still learning,' Marissa confessed. Not wanting to agitate Grandmother's anger, she said gently, 'Thank you for answering my question. It is a terrible thing. I know I have a lot to learn, and I have a better sense of how this world works, but I never would have believed it unless I'd seen it for myself.'

'Exactly,' said the grandmother, raising her mug for a toast. 'And we are here, and you are here, and he is here,' looking over at the sea serpent, 'and all is well enough for now.'

The morning sun trickled in through the spaces between the curtains and spilled out onto Marissa's bed. Marissa stretched under her warm duvet, sighed and brushed her hair out of her eyes. It was blissful having Monday mornings to herself while the rest of the world struggled to get up and combat traffic to get into work on time.

Her drum was at the foot of her bed. She reached for it and brought it under the warmth of the covers, placing it beside her for comfort. Snuggling back under her duvet she tapped the bison skin lightly. She drifted.

An hour or two later she felt a heaviness on her chest, felt a thrumming vibration through her body, then felt something wet and cold shoved onto her face.

'Baby!' she said, opening her eyes.

Tobermory was enthusiastically pushing his nose into her eye, rubbing his face on her face and making her laugh. Her hand found his body and she started stroking him. As she became more awake, she traced the white lightning bolt on his head, tracking it down to the white dots on his front paws.

She spoke to him gently in hushed tones. 'I said this to you last night, but you were sleeping. You've been through the wars for me. Thank you.'

Tobermory stopped purring for a moment and flicked his tail, then stood up on Marissa's chest, stretching his back upwards into a deep arch before settling back down on her and starting purring again.

'I suppose I'm stuck in bed for a while,' said Marissa with a grin, stroking her friend's warm fur. 'I can think of no better place to be.'

She closed her eyes once more.

Once she had had her tea and woken up properly, Marissa sent a few emails and texts.

Hi Terry, I want 2 come back 2 class, do u think Séamus would let me?

Terry responded right away:

Really? Hi! Wow! Fantastic! Wot happened? U ok?

Yeah, I'm good, we must meet up & I'll tell u all about it

Be Gr8 2 have u back - have u asked him yet?

No, not yet. Trying 2 find the words

I'm sure u'd have no problem finding words ha ha

Yeah true. I will write 2 him now

Let me kno. So happy 2 have u back!

She bit the bullet and approached Séamus next. She felt it would be better to write him an email, a text was too flippant.

Hi Séamus,
Hello Séamus
Dear Séamus
Séamus...

Maybe later.

She opened up a new email.

Hi Dolores, Marissa here. I would like to book in a session with you soon, would that be okay?

She sent that, and went back to her email for Séamus.

Séamus
I've been thinking and....
Dear Séamus, there's no easy way to say this
I want to ask you...

This is so difficult! She picked up her phone and texted Saoirse.

Hi Saoirse, hey, hope you're well.

She got a reply about two minutes later.

Yeah you?

Yeah I'm good. Better. I want to come back 2 classes.

!!

I no

Amazing!

Yeah ☺

Speak 2u soon x

An email came in from Dolores:

Hello, Marissa, of course. I have a spot free tomorrow evening at 6pm, does that suit?

She replied:

Yes, perfect see you then.

Okay, back to Séamus.

Dear Séamus,
I want to come back to the workshops
Please can I
Do you think that I could...

No, I can't do this now, I'll figure it out later. I've no food in the house – really, there is actually no food in the house. I need to do a big shop. I can't believe I let it get this bad. Wow.

Marissa did a massive shop. She had to restock everything – cat food, cleaning products, toilet roll... She even needed to buy tea bags (which she usually had plenty of in stock), as well as food. She took a taxi back to her place with all the bags and took her time putting everything away.

She cooked pasta with prawns around 3pm; it was too late for lunch and too early for dinner, but she was working that evening and needed her belly full. Fresh pasta, fresh prawns... She got a hankering for a glass of wine. *But I can't, as I'm doing Reiki tonight.* She put cordial into a wine glass instead, and raised her glass to Isis before drinking from it.

That evening Marissa took her drum with her to her Reiki room, along with all the other things she needed. The room felt stale as she entered. She felt she needed some of her cleaning products to help her, as well as the sage.

I wonder if I can get this room all to myself for the whole day. I must call the agent.

She cleared the energy using her drum and sage, then lit an incense stick, leaving it to burn itself out. The stale smell shifted, but lingered in the background. Marissa set up the plinth and got water and tumblers ready for her clients.

As she sat in stillness waiting for her first client to come, a dazzling image of Scott wearing his shiny silver suit and commanding the room, flashed into her mind. It threw her for a moment. She stopped her mind free-running and tried to consolidate the charismatic and terrifying Scott with Scott the ordinary man.

He did have some good techniques, I might even use a couple of them with clients, but there wasn't anything particularly amazing about them. Why this image now? I wonder why people think he's so good. Are they possessed? Hypnotised? Drawn in somehow? I suppose I was too... Hey, wait, maybe that's it. When he has a grip on you, you think he's a god, and when he loses his grip, he's just an ordinary man. Maybe. She fingered her ankh, which she hadn't taken off since she'd put it on. *I suppose I need more time to figure this out.*

The buzzer sounded and Marissa's attention snapped back to the present moment. She still needed to prepare, and she needed to keep her boundaries clear too, so it was important to make her client wait, even just for a few minutes.

'Hello? Yes, do come in, you're a little early, please could you wait? Thanks. There's a chair outside my door. That's great, see you soon.'

It felt good to assert her boundaries.

The first session went without a hitch and Marissa enjoyed the flow of the Reiki running through her body possibly more than her client did. She practised the heart healing and emotional healing symbols while she was working on the woman, who seemed to be sleeping, first making large symbols and empowering them, then 'sending' them into the woman's body, then she tried Dolores's suggestion of shooting out smaller symbols from her hands. That wasn't as fun to do as the larger symbols and didn't seem to have as strong an effect. Her back held out and she closed the session with the peace symbol, then poured water, turned down the music and brought the client back into the present moment.

A grateful, sleepy woman asked for business cards for her friends. Thankfully, Marissa had remembered to put them into her Reiki bag. *I must carry some in my handbag too.* She slipped some into it once the woman had paid and left.

She cleared the room with sage once more but the buzzer buzzed before she had finished. This time her client was on time. *Not much time between sessions. It would be good if I had a bit more time to clear the room.* She took a breath and answered.

'Hello there. Yes, come in.'

Marissa buzzed the door open and went to meet her next client. The woman standing at the door was very pale.

'Hello, you're Valeria?'

'Yes.'

'Come on in, it's lovely to meet you.'

Valeria was wearing colourful clothes, but beneath them she looked washed out, completely exhausted. She had dark circles under her eyes, and her long hair was scraped up into a messy ponytail.

Marissa immediately snapped into therapist mode and ushered her into the room. She helped her take off her coat and hung it up for her, then gestured to the chair.

Valeria sat down meekly. Marissa sat opposite her.

'You're here for Reiki. Have you had Reiki before?'

Valeria shook her head.

'I'll get you to lie down up there, on the plinth. All you need to do is take off your shoes. Then I'll put my hands on you or over you, and all you need to do is rest.'

Valeria shrank back. 'Oh, you're going to touch me?'

'Well, no, I don't have to touch you. Would you prefer it if I didn't?'

She visibly relaxed. 'Actually yes, I would prefer that. Thank you very much.'

Marissa sensed something had happened. 'How are you feeling?' she asked, wanting to help.

Valeria cocked her head to one side. 'Tired. It has been a very long day.' She smiled apologetically.

'Do you want to talk about it?' asked Marissa, perhaps a little too curiously.

'I didn't think Reiki was about talking?'

She pulled back. 'Oh, sorry, yes, you're correct – Reiki isn't about talking. It's just that I'm a trained psychotherapist. It must just be force of habit. But I could talk with you if you wanted. As well as give you a Reiki treatment. It could be very healing for you to have both, I'd imagine. I don't know how it would work exactly. But I just thought maybe you'd like to talk about it.'

'No, not really. I want just the Reiki. Thanks.'

Marissa couldn't help but feel slightly rejected. It was interesting after just asserting her own boundaries to find a client who's boundaries were even firmer than her own. 'Okay, no problem. Please remove your shoes.' *It wasn't me she rejected, it was the talking part.* On reminding herself of this she felt immediately better.

She softened a little, then turned the music on and helped Valeria up onto the plinth. Keeping her focus on her feet on the floor in the room where she was, she connected to Reiki, which poured out of her and into Valeria, who kept her eyes open.

I don't like that. I prefer it when they close their eyes.

Then Marissa went to touch her and Valeria winced before her hands made contact. Marissa remembered she had asked for hands-off, so she pulled away. *Shit. Sorry!*

After about twenty minutes, Marissa was more in flow with Valeria's needs and Valeria seemed more relaxed. *Maybe she wasn't ready to talk? Or she didn't know me, so she couldn't relax? I could ask her again once we finish, but that would be too pushy. I know I can help her, but if she doesn't want my help, then I can't help her. I need to learn this. Just because I can help someone doesn't mean they're ready to receive that help. Yes, that sounds right.*

Valeria stretched out on the plinth, released her hair from the ponytail and closed her eyes. Marissa didn't change anything around how she was working. She didn't want to unsettle her client.

Easy does it.

She moved to the head of the plinth to work on Valeria's crown. She felt as if the energy was blocked there. Valeria didn't seem to be receiving the Reiki as strongly there as she was through the rest of her body.

Then Marissa moved to Valeria's feet and felt an urge to draw the grounding symbol, but she couldn't remember it. Then she remembered the Reiki angels.

Reiki angels, can you help me draw the grounding symbol? Or can you draw it for me? For Valeria's feet please.

There was a subtle change in the energy flow. Marissa moved back to Valeria's head and placed her hands just above her crown chakra. There was a soft snore – Valeria had relaxed enough to go to sleep. The energy had finally shifted. *Fifteen minutes left.*

Marissa closed her eyes, settling into the session, feeling she had done all she could to help Valeria, and all she needed to do for the rest of their time together was to let the energy flow.

As she relaxed and connected more deeply to her client, images began to float into her mind. She pushed them away, as had been her practice for the last few months, then she realised what she was doing and stopped. *No, I can do this. I know she said she was coming just for Reiki, but maybe I can do more this way.* She relaxed and let go, and went into the images.

It was as if worlds were turning, spinning beneath her. She couldn't get a foothold. Time and space, dimensions ... which one was she supposed to choose? Did she even have a choice? *This is for Valeria, not for me!* The space began to settle.

She was on a farm, in a barn. The images began to solidify. Valeria was there, milking a cow. There was someone else making butter. Goats were running free and there was a smell of apple pie.

Then everything went dark.

Tall faceless people came. They were so tall; elongated and thin, they did not look human. They put shackles on Valeria's wrists and ankles and marched her outside.

Marissa hid behind a large stack of hay, watching. She crept behind the barn door and peeked outside. People were standing in a line, heads down, again, in shackles.

Marissa reached into her jerkin front pocket. Yes, she was wearing her jerkin, and her knife was there. She crept outside and found Valeria at the end of the line and cut her free.

'Come on, we have to run!'

Valeria was in a daze and not responding. Marissa grabbed her hand and pulled her away from the group, then they ran.

Tears were rolling down Valeria's face and onto the pillow. She gave a large sigh and let them fall. At the same time, a healthy colour crept back into her face.

Marissa didn't move, just kept bringing in the Reiki. Finally the flow came to a stop.

They were out of time for the session. Marissa helped Valeria sit up on the side of the plinth and escorted her back to the chair.

Valeria smiled through her tears. 'Thank you. I miss my home. I miss the sunshine. I have been in Ireland for six months and it has been very difficult for me. I have no friends, I don't like my job, I think I will leave. But at least now I feel better. I'm sorry for how I was when I arrived.'

'That's okay. As long as you feel better now – that's why you came.'

Valeria nodded. 'My country is so beautiful. My family, they are struggling for money, so I came here, as the money is good, but it's expensive to live. And the weather...' She smiled apologetically. 'Perhaps I won't stay, after all.' She smiled up at Marissa. 'You have been very nice to me. The lady at my work, she makes things very difficult. I feel like I lose my strength around her. Tonight, this has helped me.'

Marissa didn't want to go any deeper, especially as Valeria hadn't wanted to talk at all when she arrived, so she just smiled.

When Valeria had left, after making another appointment, Marissa sat in the room for a moment before packing it up.

Shackles again. I had the knife, but it was close. Who were those beings? And I forgot to wear my armour! Her heart leapt into her mouth. *Just think, if I'd had my armour I could have followed them, I could have found out where they were taking all those people to and I could have rescued more of them. I must remember that. I could try it another time.*

While walking home, she found a letter to Séamus finally starting to form in her mind. But she couldn't get to her computer quick enough before the words disappeared.

CHAPTER THREE

Marissa wrote a draft email to Séamus and sent it to herself so she could continue to work on it in the office. She had written about four different versions by this stage, and she wasn't happy with any of them. *It will never be right. But I do need to send it today.* She sat at her desk, looked around to make sure nobody was watching, then read it again.

> *Dear Séamus,*
>
> *I'm sorry for not phoning you back when you called, and for not replying properly to your email. I really feel bad about it. I don't know what happened to me, and I might never know. I got an awful fright with my client, the one I told you about, and then I got another fright when I was on the couch with you, and a really bad one again when I got home from Clifden. What I saw terrified me and I shut down. It was easier for me to pretend that it didn't happen. So I pushed it away, and when I did that, I shut you and the work we did together out too. I'm ashamed, but when I look back on it now, I see that I wasn't strong enough. Perhaps I never will be that strong.*
>
> *It has taken me ages to work through everything I've experienced and I still don't understand it all. And it might happen again. However, I have realised that I need to do the shamanic work. It isn't a case of wanting to do shamanism on a whim, as something that might be fun to do, I actually* <u>*have*</u> *to do it. Being shut off from shamanism is like being shut off from a part of myself. Without this piece of me I*

couldn't breathe, the colours of the day were gone - like being in The Wizard of Oz, *only I was stuck in Kansas. I want a colourful, magical life. It's not just about healing someone else, or being a practitioner, it's about being who I am. Shamanism is woven deep into the fabric of my being, and I suffered greatly by shutting it out for the last ten weeks.*

I have truly been to hell and back with all this. But in the last week or so, something inside me has transformed and I feel stronger now. That darkness is still out there, Séamus – I saw people who sold their souls, actually sold them, and it was shocking to me. I see them in my Reiki sessions too, and in my dreams. I feel I did that too, in a way. By shutting down, I sold a part of myself, and I couldn't live like that. I can't do it. I need my soul back and I need to help those people get their souls back too. I know I won't be able to help them all, but I want to learn what to do so I can help at least some of them break free. And I know you can teach me.

Please can I come back and finish my apprenticeship training with you? I know I missed the homework and I missed a weekend, but I will catch up if you tell me what you need me to do. I will do whatever you ask. I am willing to learn and I know I have a long way to go. I understand if I've missed too much, or if you feel you can't take me back into the group. I had to get in touch and ask you, because if I don't ask now, I know I'll always regret it.

Yours sincerely,
Marissa

I don't know, maybe 'Yours sincerely' is too formal? And do I need to say 'please' again? Or is this enough? She closed her eyes and caught her breath. She saw flickers of her landscape, the lake, the mountains, and her guides looking on approvingly, willing her forward.

She opened her eyes, copied and pasted the words into a fresh email, addressed it to Séamus and wrote 'I'm sorry' in the subject line. Then she deleted 'Yours sincerely' and wrote 'Yours hopefully' instead. She sat with it for a moment, as if she was sending Reiki into the email, into the computer, and through the internet into Séamus too, so he would be more receptive to it. She imagined him opening it, reading it and being compassionate towards her.

Enough. Just do it. She pressed 'Send'.

It only took a second for the email to fly off her screen, but she felt as if a massive weight had been lifted off her. A boot crushing her chest had been removed. She checked her 'Sent' folder and it was nestled safely in there. *It's done now. All I can do is wait.*

She felt hyper, she couldn't stay at her desk. She got up and went into the kitchen, and bumped into Sarah.

'So, you're back from London, eh? Was it everything you hoped for?' Sarah's voice was icy. She was standing by the kettle, waiting for it to boil. One finger was twirling a lock of her bobbed hair, her other hand was on her hip, and she was tapping her foot.

Marissa looked at her and for a moment she could have sworn she was chewing gum and wearing a cowboy hat.

She's still pissed off with me for not asking her to come to London with me.

She took a breath then found her brightest, most enthusiastic voice. 'Hi, Sarah, you look good today! Yeah, London, it was ... enlightening. Maybe not everything I hoped for, but I learned a lot.'

Sarah relaxed a little.

'It wasn't at all what I expected,' Marissa continued, 'but it's good that I went. It wasn't fun, but I think the experience helped me move through the worst part of my spiritual crisis.'

Sarah softened.

Marissa kept going, sensing she had made inroads. 'I feel better in myself now, much better than I've been in many weeks.'

In a flat voice, Sarah replied, 'That's great. I'm glad you've made progress.'

The kettle boiled and switched itself off with a click and they both got cups down from the shelf.

'I wonder when they're going to get the real coffee back, this instant stuff is awful,' said Marissa, trying to be jovial while heaping her teaspoon with way too much coffee and then the same amount of sugar and spilling half of it on the counter. 'Hey, I've not forgotten our weekend away. We can plan it, you and me, if you still want to?'

'Maybe. I'm not so sure I want to do it now,' said Sarah, watching Marissa wiping up the mess. Finally she had to smile. 'Look at you. Cleaning up and making a bigger mess than there was to start with.'

'Yeah, that's about right,' said Marissa, shrugging her shoulders and throwing a massive heap of paper towel coffee and sugar into the bin.

'I've a lot on right now with my management course,' Sarah continued, trying not to giggle. 'The mid-terms are coming up and I've an assessment due in.' Marissa poured the water into both mugs and managed to splash more of it onto the counter.

Sarah couldn't keep it in, and giggled at her friend. 'Do you want milk? Do you need some help cleaning that up?' The ice had broken at last.

In a warm voice Marissa replied. 'Yes to the milk, thanks. And thank you, but I think I've almost got this mess sorted.'

Sarah poured milk into Marissa's mug which brought up undissolved specks of instant freeze-dried coffee, and a lump of cracked cream floated to the surface.

'Yuck, that looks awful, I think the milk might be gone off.' Sarah put down the bottle. 'I don't think I want any now.' Then in a different tone she added, 'Marissa, you know you said you'd help me with my assignment? Could you read my essay for me?'

'Oh, sure! I'd love to. What's it about?' Marissa looked at her coffee and shook her head. 'Yeah, it does look awful.' She poured it down the sink.

'The essay? It's marketing. I'm honestly not a fan, but they want us to be well-rounded, so they cover most everything in the first year.'

"Sure, I'll read it. I don't know much about marketing too, but I can help with the grammar and stuff, if that's what you want? Just email it to me.'

'Yeah, perfect thanks. Let me know if it makes sense and all, or if I repeat myself. That would help a lot. I've almost finished it. I'm not good with essays, I hate doing them. I never did well at them in school.'

'I feel that way too, especially with college work. I'm struggling with my last assignment for the year, I've still not finished it yet.'

'That's not like you?'

'Yeah, It's been a wild few weeks.'

Sarah's resolve to be harsh crumbled away completely, and Marissa felt the softness return between them.

'Let's get a proper coffee downstairs later, hey?'

'Sounds great, let me know when you're free.' They walked to their desks, coffee-less but their friendship consolidated.

Before they went their separate ways, Sarah leaned in and said in a low voice, 'Listen, I'm glad it worked out for you in London and that you're feeling better. I *was* more worried about you than anything else. Well, maybe I was a little jealous, too. I'd love to go to London. Maybe next time if something comes up you could ask me to come with you?'

'Yes, I absolutely will – even if it's a mindfulness weekend in Limerick?'

'Er...'

'Even if it's a meditation retreat in Mayo? With no alcohol and no men?'

Sarah giggled. 'Eh, maybe not.'

Marissa sat back down at her desk and checked her emails, her heart in her mouth. No reply. *Well, of course there's no reply, he's only had a few minutes to read it, if he has even got it yet. And he doesn't sit at his computer all day, like I do. I'll just have to get on with my day and I'll hear from him when I hear from him.*

Getting on with her day proved an almost impossible task, but eventually she closed her computer and left work, early, she needed plenty of time to get the bus to the DART and the DART out to Greystones for her Reiki session with Dolores.

While she was on the DART, an email came in on her phone. Her heart leapt. But it wasn't from Séamus. It was a newsletter advertising some stuff she wasn't interested in.

I didn't realise how important this was to me. Oh dear, my inbox is just as full as the one at work, only there's so much rubbish in here, I should do a clear-out.

She focused on unsubscribing from numerous newsletters until it was her stop.

She knew the way to Dolores's house by heart now, but she hadn't seen her for weeks, and then only in the company of other people. It would be nice to get her all to herself. And there she was, waiting at the garden gate with a smile, all in green, hair up in a bun. She looked radiant.

'Hello, Marissa! Come on in! It's good to see you.'

Marissa followed Dolores through the garden, which was coming into bloom.

'Isn't the weather beautiful?' Dolores said. 'It's springtime proper now. I love the long stretch in the evenings. Here we are, come in, that's right, leave your jacket there. Perfect.'

Dolores closed the door and Marissa sat down, taking in the atmosphere. The healing room smelled beautifully of lavender, as always.

Dolores poured some water for them both and sat down too. 'Now, dear, what can I do for you this evening?'

Marissa looked at Dolores' kind face and welled up with emotion, but the words wouldn't come.

'You have been through the wars, lovie,' Dolores said soothingly. 'Do you want Reiki first and then to talk, or do you want to talk and then we can do the Reiki?'

'Reiki first, please,' said Marissa.

Dolores smiled. 'I had a feeling. No problem at all.'

Marissa took off her shoes and climbed up onto the plinth. Dolores covered her legs with a blanket and started the session. As the sun got lower in the evening sky, golden beams of light shone in through the Venetian blinds and scattered across the room.

Marissa was suddenly very agitated, her mind was racing. She talked herself down. *I'm home now, I'm safe. I'm back... It's okay, it is okay and it will be okay. I wonder will Séamus have me back...? I hope so. Breathe in and out. In and out. That's better.*

She began to relax, the Reiki took effect and her mind drifted in and out of the room while Dolores worked. It felt nice, relaxing on the plinth. She felt as if she was floating over her body, looking down on it, seeing herself there on the plinth *That's me!* She floated back into herself and imagined she was taking off her suit of armour and hanging it up in a wardrobe, but she kept on the chainmail. *Yes, that feels better.* She saw herself hanging the sword up on a wall, but it didn't seem right, so she imagined shrinking it to penknife size, and she put it into her pocket. *Yes, I'll keep the knife on me just in case. Chainmail for protection, But I don't need the armour 'cos I'm not going into battle. I feel better now.*

With half-open eyes she watched Dolores moving her fingers in the air above her, drawing symbols over her body and moving her lips but not saying anything. She trusted Dolores, she didn't need to know which symbols she was drawing.

Even when Dolores suddenly grew vampire fangs, her face changed and became red and evil, she had fire behind her eyes and looked as though she was going on the attack, Marissa knew it was her own mind playing tricks on her.

Why do I do this to myself?

She blinked and Dolores was herself again.

Why is my mind playing tricks? Could it be PTSD, or is a part of me still genuinely terrified? I ask that the Reiki energy goes to the terrified part of me to help it heal so I can move on from this and be strong again.

Dolores was finishing up now. She noticed Marissa watching her and smiled.

'Come now, all finished. Whenever you're ready.' She offered her arm and Marissa took it and sat up. The room turned a little bit, then steadied itself.

'I saw you relaxing there, taking off your armour. How are you doing now?'

'Armour – yes, I did that. How did you know?' Marissa turned to Dolores and smiled.

'You relaxed, and the Reiki went in at a deeper level.'

Marissa nodded. 'Dolores, can I ask you something?'

'Of course.'

'When you're working on somebody, do you get images from them, like you're seeing their dreams, or meeting them in a shamanic journey?'

Dolores thought for a moment. 'Sometimes, but I don't pursue it. Not for Reiki. If they come for Seichem, then I might look at what I'm being shown. But usually I feel that it's intruding on their psyche. So I continue to work and I ask the angels to send the healing for that person's highest good. But I don't engage with the images, if that's what you're asking me.'

'Yes, I think that's what I want to know. I see images a lot when I work on people, and then sometimes they tell me what they saw when they were enjoying the Reiki, and it matches what I saw! Or their body relaxes more, say, if I release something in the image. It's like I'm releasing it here, too, in their body.'

'It's very interesting, isn't it, how everything is connected? And that person probably came to see you because you are able to do what you can do. I cannot tell you not to do it, however I must stress that Reiki is a non-engagement, non-intrusive healing modality. The Reiki just flows. There is no doing with Reiki, Reiki does the doing, and the being, and the pure essence of healing. You are simply the channel. You don't need to do anything.'

Marissa thought about this. 'I saw someone yesterday, Dolores. One of their chakras seemed to be blocked, so I worked on their body to clear it. I didn't look for an image, but I did want to clear the blockage. I didn't know how to do it, though.'

'As I've said, you don't have to clear it. The Reiki will do the work.'

'Then why do I feel that I need to place my hands on different parts of their body? Or draw a specific symbol?'

'Perhaps it's the energy directing you to give that person what they need at that moment. Just be with what you are feeling.'

'But Dolores, when I feel the need to go to their head, say, and then move to their feet, how do I know whether it's me deciding I need to do that or the Reiki pulling me there?'

'Ah, but the more you do your self-practice, the more you become the Reiki, and the more the Reiki becomes you. So it no longer matters.'

'So I don't need to try and help people who come for Reiki?'

'No, you never need to try. You are already helping, and by showing up they're helping themselves. We tend to think too deeply about these things, and there's no need. Reiki is energy; you let the energy do the work.'

Marissa nodded, taking it all in. *So Reiki really isn't like shamanism then...* 'But what is Seichem and why would you engage with an image there?'

Dolores laughed. 'You really are a curious thing! Yes, Seichem is a little more, well, shall I say intrusive. We do psychic surgery as part of the sessions in Seichem.'

Marissa's ears pricked up. 'Psychic surgery? That sounds exciting!'

'It can be, but you need to be careful, and of course, fully trained, so you know exactly what you're doing. Perhaps you'd like to come to a workshop? I don't teach those as often as Reiki, but I will probably be offering one at the end of the year.'

'Sounds amazing. Yes, please! Can you let me know?'

'Of course. But all of this talking isn't telling me how you are. How are you? I did see you were emotional at the beginning of the session tonight, and I do remember all the excitement from a few months ago. I wasn't going to bring it up tonight, but I'm here if you want to talk about it.'

Marissa thought for a moment. The words she had written to Séamus echoed back to her. 'I have been through the wars. I got a little lost, I think. I let something inside me and it wasn't nice. But it's gone now, and I've come back, stronger.'

'I see you have a golden ankh around your neck. I remember suggesting to you that you get one.'

Marissa's hand automatically went to the ankh. 'Yes, I got this in the British Museum.' She was silent for a moment, then offered, 'I met Isis again.' She blushed. 'It sounds so strange, doesn't it? I wanted to get something solid and real to remind me that she did come to me, something to keep me connected to her.'

Dolores nodded. 'I understand. And it was a good idea. Sometimes we need to bring things into form, in this reality, so that we can remind ourselves that they really happened. So you met Isis again?'

'Yes, she gave me the armour that you sensed me taking off. I guess I've been wearing it ever since she gave it to me.'

'Well, warriors need to rest sometimes too. You certainly seem brighter after this session.'

Dolores helped Marissa off the plinth and back to the chair, then gave her some water. She waited until she had drunk a full glass, then asked, 'Is there anything else you want to share with me before you go?'

Marissa smiled and handed her the empty glass. 'I'm loving the Reiki, and you're right, I'll remember to keep it to just a flow of energy. I keep wanting to bring in talking, to mix it with the images I see. It's so difficult to keep everything separate.'

'I understand. I went through that too when I was starting out. You'll find your way. It's lovely to see you again, Marissa. Stay in touch and I'll let you know when I'm going to teach my next Seichem workshop.'

'Thanks for everything, Dolores. It really helps, knowing that you're here if I need you.'

'Anytime, my dear, anytime.'

On the DART back into town, Marissa looked at her Inbox wistfully. Still no reply from Séamus.

Well, if he doesn't want me back, I can do Seichem and psychic protection with Dolores. But I hope he'll take me back.

She texted Matt.

Session with Dolores was gr8, thanks 4 suggesting.

Then she texted Terry.

Hiya I wrote him & asked

Terry wrote back right away.

And? Wot did he say?

Nothing yet :-(

Oh dear. I'm sure he'll reply when he's ready. Just b patient.

Patience isn't my strong point

ha ha ha ha ha

CHAPTER FOUR

He finished his sentence midstream and turned and looked at her, fire in his eyes, wide smile, his teeth drawing down and becoming sharper until they were white fangs. She sat there, paralysed in her seat, watching him as he shapeshifted, his body bursting through his silver sparkly suit, thick heavy animal legs appearing in place of human legs. He had hoofed feet and, yes, a forked tail. He came for her, leaping off the stage with his mouth wide open, about to swallow her whole...

Marissa woke up in a cold sweat. It was 4am, too early to get up. Light from the streetlamp flickered in through the window, past the curtains she had neglected to draw the night before, as she had had a sudden flash of fear when going to bed.

My mind is still playing tricks on me, even after that lovely session with Dolores. Why am I doing this to myself?

She got up and poured herself a glass of water, then brought it back to the bedroom. She was wide awake, and felt flickers of fear lurking in the darker corners of her room. *I'm not going back to sleep just yet, that's for sure.* Tobermory shifted his position as she climbed back in under the covers. She arranged the pillows around herself so she could sit up in bed. Still completely unnerved, she took out her trusty notebook and found a pen in her bedside locker drawer. Putting down the water, she wrote and wrote until it was time to get ready for work.

Later that evening, Marissa was sitting opposite Lucy in St Mary's. The day had gone by in a haze, Marissa needed to pull herself into the session and practically pinched herself to stay awake. She focused on Lucy's face – she looked pale, dark circles were under her eyes and her hands were bunched up inside their sleeves. She couldn't look directly at Marissa. Marissa's heart opened, and she found herself suddenly awake, and fully present.

Marissa didn't want to challenge Lucy in any way whatsoever. She was just relieved that she had turned up for the session, that she hadn't died during her overdose; somehow her presence in the room as proof of her continued existence, was comforting.

She came tonight, so she must not blame me for not minding her well enough. I know it sounds silly, but I did feel responsible. The fact she's here, sitting in front of me, is kind of like a second chance. What's the word? Redemption? Isn't that religious?

Lucy still sat, saying nothing. Marissa's mind went on overdrive. *All I have to do is be here with her and listen. Or just sit here. I don't have to heal her, or fix her, just be. It's kind of nice, in a way.*

Twenty minutes passed. Lucy stayed quiet and withdrawn. Marissa was doing her best, but her patience levels were getting a workout.

Finally, Lucy shifted in her seat and smiled, shyly.

What can I say? Asking why she took the overdose isn't an appropriate line of questioning. They didn't train me for this kind of situation. But that's the old me getting flustered and anxious – what would Tori Lightbringer do? As she asked herself, she felt a shiver and tingles through her body. *It's okay, I don't need to go out and hunt down anything right now. And Lucy may be feeling overwhelmed right now, too. So let's do roads and weather.*

Marissa smiled back, and opened the session. 'How can I help you? I mean, what can we do together to make your life better?'

Marissa felt startled to hear herself blurt this out, and Lucy seemed startled too. She looked like a deer in the headlights. *I guess I should tone it down a little. I didn't realise I was this upset. It's not my stuff.*

She softened her voice. 'Seriously, Lucy, you're here. You will be okay, even if you don't feel you will be right now. You have the rest of your life ahead of you. I want to help you make, well, today a little better. Even just a little bit. Tell me what you'd like to fix.'

Lucy's lips tightened, she looked out of the window and a tear rolled down her cheek.

Marissa reached across with the box of tissues and Lucy hesitantly took one. Marissa noticed a bandage on her wrist. *Oh, I didn't know she'd cut herself too.*

'Yeah. I guess I'm not dead,' Lucy said sarcastically, sniffling and wiping her face.

The words hung heavily between them. Marissa stayed silent, not wanting to push anything.

Then Lucy whispered, 'I didn't really want to die. Honestly, I didn't.'

Marissa waited another moment before responding with, 'Thank you for telling me this.'

Lucy is still incredibly vulnerable. If I say something wrong here, might she do it again?

Fortunately, before Marissa could dig herself into an even deeper hole, Lucy started talking.

'Lookit, I know what I did, and I'm sorry for it. I won't do it again. I promised Ma and Da. That's a promise I intend to keep, not like the others I've made.' She tucked her tissue awkwardly into the sleeve of her hoodie, revealing her bandage once more.

'They told me you had taken an overdose. But did you cut yourself too?' asked Marissa, then kicked herself. *What is wrong with me today? It's like I'm not in control of what I'm saying. I need to back off.*

'Yeah, I did,' Lucy admitted. 'And it's really sore. It's turning purple too, all the way up to my elbow, even though I didn't go that far with the blade... Guess it was just as well I didn't know how to do it right.'

She smiled, and Marissa smiled back.

'I'm really glad you didn't know how to do it right,' she said, 'and I'm really glad you're here tonight, even if you don't want to talk. That's okay, really. You don't have to talk at all. I'm here just to sit with you, if that's all you're able to do right now.'

Lucy nodded. After a moment she said, 'Thanks. It sounds mad, but I think that helps. Knowing I don't have to talk, I mean.'

Marissa nodded. 'Yes, we don't have to do big work every time, or any time in fact.'

But in the silence all her questions came flooding in: *Why did you do it? What was going through your head? Why are you here and not in hospital? Did you actually think you would die? Why did they say it was an overdose when it wasn't? Or was it both? What did it feel like?*

She pushed the thoughts away, adjusted herself in her seat, breathed out and brought her focus into the moment. *It doesn't matter. I don't need to know, and if she wants me to know, then she will tell me.*

Lucy smiled again.

'Da told me it was a bloody awful stupid thing to do.'

A moment passed.

Then she added, 'And he didn't even text me back. Not Dad. Peter, I mean.'

'You're still in touch with him?' *Oh no, maybe I shouldn't have asked that.*

'Well, I text him, but he doesn't reply. Well, he did once, a while back, to say Happy New Year. He sent me a picture of fireworks – you know, one of those videos that someone drew. Not real fireworks. Anyway, I told him, while I was in the hospital, that I was there. What I'd done. But he didn't text me back.'

Marissa nodded.

'He doesn't care about me.'

'Maybe it was too much for him to think about? To understand?'

Lucy laughed. 'Or maybe he blocked me from his phone, more like.' She scratched her head. 'But I think about him all the time.' She looked away.

The silence closed in upon them again. Marissa looked at the clock. It was getting close to the end of the session. *No point opening any big cans of worms this late in the day, but she needs reassurance.*

'Peter doesn't sound like he was good for you, from what you told me in our first session. He hurt you before. Maybe it's time to stop giving him permission to hurt you.'

Lucy looked up curiously. 'But I've not seen him in months... How could he still be hurting me?'

'Maybe he's not actually hurting you at all, not now anyway. Maybe it's you wanting him to respond to you that's opening you up to being hurt again. By texting him, then wanting him to reply, when you know that he won't.'

Lucy shook her head, but said, 'Yeah, maybe. Well, he did reply, back at New Year...'

'But not since then, not even when you were in hospital.'

Lucy was silent for a while, then in a broken voice said, 'No. Not even when I was in hospital.'

Marissa left silence between them to honour this realisation before saying, 'I know it's hard.' Then she added, 'Did you officially break up?'

'Kind of. Well, I told him my Da said I wasn't to see him again. And he did leave – he moved to the UK. Took his boat with him and all. So yeah, I guess it was officially over. But we never said goodbye, not properly.' She shifted in her chair, then turned to Marissa and asked, 'Marissa? Why do I keep thinking about him? Wanting him to come back? That's why I did it, really. I thought he'd care about me enough to come back. But he didn't even answer my text.' She started shaking. 'How could anyone not answer a text like that?'

Then the tears came.

Marissa had to suppress the urge to rush over and put her arms around her. She was so small, so vulnerable. Her sobs increased; Marissa being a witness seemed to give her the permission she needed for an emotional release. She began bawling, loudly.

Then there was a knock at the door and Mary R. stuck her smiling face around it, expecting the room to be free for her session. She took one look at Lucy and her smile dropped away. She looked at Marissa, wide-eyed.

Marissa mouthed, 'Come back in twenty?'

Mary nodded her head, looking very serious, and closed the door quietly behind her. Marissa couldn't help but feel that she would be standing guard outside.

It took some time for Lucy to gather herself. When her sobs subsided, Marissa said, 'You mightn't think it, but crying is good.' She offered Lucy another tissue.

Lucy blew her nose noisily and wiped her face again. 'I do feel a little better, I think,' she said, a small bit of colour appearing in her cheeks.

'You know, we are well past our session, but we can go over time a bit, as I want to help you with this. Can you stay a little longer? I have an idea for you.'

'Okay,' said Lucy, straightening her hair and adjusting her top. Marissa could see the bandage peeking out under her sleeve.

'There's a technique that I've used before,' she said, 'called the two-chair technique. We can try it here, if you want to. Then once you know how to do it, you can do it yourself anytime you want to.'

Lucy nodded her head.

Marissa had a flashback of this method not working somewhere. *Was it with Cliona? It's got to be worth a shot with Lucy. Yes, I'll try it again.* She cleared her mind of the memory, stood up and moved behind her own chair, gesturing down to the cushions there.

'Okay. Imagine Peter is sitting in this chair.'

Lucy shivered.

Marissa continued, in a gentle tone, 'You know he's not really here, it's just the Peter that's in your mind, the one you can't stop thinking about. Your idea of Peter, not the actual Peter. But doing this gives you the opportunity to talk to him as if he really *was* here. You can say all the things you want him to hear – get it all out there, instead of holding it all in here.' Marissa gestured to her heart.

'Ah, I see. Like playing pretend? Should I say it now?'

'Yes, a little like playing pretend. And we don't really have a lot of time, so maybe pick one thing to say to him now, then you can say more yourself, on your own, yes?'

Lucy nodded and turned to the empty chair. 'Peter,' she started, then blushed. 'This is silly.'

'Pretend I'm not here. It might help if you imagine you can actually see him. Can you see him?'

Lucy shook her head.

'What would he be wearing?'

'Jeans and a sweatshirt. And those runners he always wore, and he'd have his hair all mussed up.'

'Imagine him sitting here. Can you?'

'Yes. Okay, I'll try it.' Lucy faced the imaginary Peter in the chair. 'You didn't reply to my text. I tried to kill myself and I told you, and you didn't reply.'

Tears welled up again, she looked at Marissa for support. Marissa nodded, so she continued.

'I feel so alone, so lonely, lost without you.' The tears started falling, but they were more controlled as Lucy continued to speak. 'You treated me like shit and you still treat me like shit. Like dog shit on the sole of your shoe. Who wouldn't text back someone with a message like that? How dare you! I don't want to feel like this anymore. I am worth more than this as a person.'

She looked shocked, hearing herself say the words.

Marissa felt proud of her, watching her break through some barrier in herself and find strength in herself again.

'Good work,' Marissa said, very aware of the time, and wanting to stay with this success, rather than dig deeper into the inevitable emotional pain that was simmering not too deeply below the surface. 'Now it's time to swap around. You need to come over to Peter's chair and sit in it, pretend to be Peter.'

Lucy looked a little shocked. 'Why?'

'Well, it might be good for you to hear what he would say in reply to you.'

'Eh, okay, I'll try it.' Lucy swapped chairs.

'Good. Now you are talking *as* Peter to you, Lucy. What would he say in response?'

Lucy hesitated.

'Remember what you said he was wearing? Now you're wearing it... You're sitting in his body too – you have his face, his arms and legs. Look at your feet, you're wearing his runners, because you are him. What do you want to say to Lucy? She just tried to kill herself. She sent you a text telling you. Why didn't you reply to her, Peter?'

Marissa willed the energy in the room to stillness and said a small prayer that something positive would happen for Lucy.

Lucy's face changed, became neutral, then she looked at the empty chair opposite her, and spoke as Peter. 'Lucy. Girlo. You knew I was bad for you. I told you that right from the start. You didn't listen. You wanted me to be someone I wasn't and I'm still not that person. It's better for you if I don't get in touch. You know you should listen to your dad. Go back to school, get your diploma. Make something of your life. You deserve better than me. It's finished between us.'

Lucy's face softened and she sat there in silence. Marissa took a breath. *That was powerful.*

'Wow,' said Lucy, standing up and shivering. She danced a little, as if shaking something off her body. She took a breath. 'You know,' she said, 'I could almost hear his voice, his actual voice, saying that to me.'

She looked at Marissa, who gestured for her to return to her original chair. She didn't want to sit in her own, not with Peter's energy in it. *Lucy must have felt that too, that's why she shook it off just there.* She clapped her hands and imagined the energy was gone, vaporised.

That feels better.

She faced Lucy. 'Well, even if it wasn't him, there is a part of you that wants you to hear what you said as him. It came across very strongly and I think it's very good advice: "Go back to school, get your diploma, make something of your life."'

'Yeah, he did come across, didn't he?' Lucy looked surprised. 'That didn't sound like me, that's for sure. My life isn't over, but my time with Peter *is* over.' She blew her nose again and smiled. 'There is a lot of stuff I could do, I suppose.'

'What would you *like* to do?' asked Marissa.

Lucy blushed. 'I've always wanted to be a primary school teacher.'

Marissa smiled. 'I really think you could do that. You'd be great with kids.'

'Really?' said Lucy, brightening and pulling her sleeves down over her bandage.

'Yes, really. We really have to finish now, though. Mary R. is going to come back in again in a minute.'

'Back in? She was here already?'

Marissa smiled, 'Yes, while you were crying. Guess you didn't see her.'

Lucy froze.

'Hey it's okay,' Marissa said quickly. 'Mary R. is a good one. She'll look after you.'

'Yeah,' Lucy nodded. 'She already is. I just don't like people seeing me crying. But I guess it's okay.'

'You'll be okay, Lucy. I believe in you. I think you're much stronger than you realise. And we can work together to help you get the strength and stamina you need to do whatever you need to do so you can become a primary school teacher.'

'I'd like that.'

Lucy got up to leave. Marissa stood up too and walked her to the door. Lucy held out her hand as if to shake hands. Marissa took it gently and just delicately held it so as not to hurt Lucy's aching wrists.

'Thanks,' whispered Lucy. 'I feel better. Much better. Maybe I'll try that talking technique again when I'm on my own. But I think I've said everything I need to say to him.'

Marissa smiled. 'It's there for you if you need it. You'll probably have more to say to him in a day or two, so know you can always use it. And tell yourself that you've really spoken to him so you lose the urge to text him again. Then you can really begin healing.'

'Healing. I like the sound of that. Thank you.'

No sooner had Lucy left than Mary R. bounded in, deep concern showing on her face.

'I waited outside till you were finished. Is she alright?'

Yes, she's a good one. Marissa nodded. 'Thanks so much, Mary, for giving us that space. She really needed it.'

'No bother at all. I've been worried about the little mite.'

'She's stronger than she looks. I reckon she'll be fine. She just needs some time. Now then, come in, sit down, let's make this about you now. What do you want to talk about tonight?'

But hang on. Marissa shifted in her seat. She felt sticky from emotion after the session with Lucy and she didn't want to do Mary a disservice by staying caught in it. *Argh, how to wash this off myself?* She imagined herself walking to her lake and jumping into it. Cold fresh water washed away some of the heavy emotion. She shivered. *That's better. At least I can focus on Mary now.*

Mary was pacing the room. She scratched her head, looked thoughtful for a moment, then rubbed her hands together, as if she was gathering her thoughts. It was a crisp evening but Mary was wearing a white vest T-shirt, a dark grey waistcoat and combat trousers. Her arms were muscular. Marissa hadn't really noticed them before. There was a tattoo of a heart with a knife going through it on one of the biceps. Marissa couldn't read the name that was inscribed beneath.

'Okay,' Mary said. 'I saw what you did with Lucy. That was great. Thanks, like.'

Marissa nodded, wondering when Mary was going to sit down.

'I think you're a good one,' Mary continued. 'I can trust you, I mean. And, like, we've had a few sessions, but I feel I've not actually told you anything. About me, I mean. My past.' She looked Marissa in the eye, as if wanting her approval.

Marissa knew she was being tested again – Mary was standing high above her, she was sitting down. She held Mary's stare, but said nothing. *Mary wants some sort of validation – to see if I'm up to the task perhaps?*

'And?' she asked after a moment, still holding eye contact.

'Well, I'm kind of ready to talk some more.' Mary plonked herself down into the chair, legs wide, feet flat on the floor, and folded her arms, leaning forward, almost into Marissa's face only for the coffee table in between them.

Marissa would have been threatened by this posture, but after getting to know Mary over the last few sessions she thought it was funny. Keeping her laughter to herself, she sat back in her own chair and crossed her legs. 'Great,' she said. 'Let's talk.'

'Great,' said Mary, pulling back a little, unfolding her arms and smiling. 'Just checkin' you were still with me, like.'

'I'm with you,' said Marissa, smiling.

Mary nodded, then relaxed. 'Good, good,' she replied. 'Hey, I read a book since I seen ya last week, one on gardening. It was good. It didn't take me very long to read it. And they seemed happy with me. Think I'll put that *Moby Dick* back in the library. That was a good idea you had.'

'Glad to hear it. Yes, choose books to read that you like, instead of books you think someone else would like for you to read. It's a much better idea, and you're much more likely to finish them then.' Marissa shifted in her seat again, then added, 'So, what did you want to tell me?'

'You're not lettin' me get away with nothin' tonight,' said Mary with a large grin.

'Ha, ha. Now, Mary, you don't have to tell me anything if you don't want to, remember?'

'Yeah, I remember. But I want to. Tell you. I'm just tryin' to find the words, like.'

'I understand. I know it can be difficult.'

'Okay, here goes.' She took a deep breath. 'Me ma, she was an addict. Crack. She was out of it most of the time. Wasn't easy livin' with her. Me da, well, he wasn't around much. When he was, he'd cuff me with the back of his hand, like. So I kept quiet around him. I ran away a lot. Kept goin' back, though, needed to check on her. Ma, I mean. She always needed someone to mind her. I got sick of it, though. I knew it wasn't my place to mind her. She was my ma, for God's sake, I was the child. Anyway, one day...'

Marissa stayed silent to give her space.

'One day, me ma, well, she overdosed. Like Lucy did. Only she really did it, I mean. Lucy, she didn't do it right. She cut herself too, did you see?'

Marissa nodded her head.

'That Lucy, she made an arse of cuttin' herself too. Anyway, my ma, she didn't plan to kill herself, I'm pretty certain of that. But it just kind of, well, happened. I wasn't there, I had run away, but I came back that night and found her there, dead.'

Marissa was looking at Mary for signs of emotion, but none were coming. She seemed to be relating the story quite matter-of-factly.

'Foamin' at the mouth,' she continued. 'It was awful. I called the neighbour in. She sorted everything out. I was sixteen. But I couldn't help but think if I had been there...' Mary drifted off, then she came back. 'Anyway, that scare with Lucy brought it back for me. A little bit. She's a flippin' eejit, Lucy.'

'I can see why you would think that.'

Mary rubbed her hands together, winked at Marissa, then said, 'So am I okay, Miss Marissa? Like, satisfactory?'

'I don't know what you mean.' Marissa was genuinely puzzled.

'Well, did I do good – tellin' you, I mean?'

'There's no test, Mary, or judgement here.'

'Were you waiting for me to cry or something? I guess that's what I want to know.' Mary's face flushed a little and she added, 'Is it normal to tell you something this, well, horrible, about me own ma, and not be upset about it? *Should* I be cryin' or summit?'

Marissa took a moment before answering, 'One of the most interesting things that I have learned in my training, Mary, is this: there are no shoulds. It is what it is. You feel what you feel. Or don't feel. You are here, you are talking to me – that in itself is enough. I have no expectations of you being emotional or not, I just want to meet you where you are. Get to know the real you. Don't put on a show for me. Anyway, I'll know if it's fake.'

'Ah, you'll know, will you? How will you know?' Mary raised both eyebrows in an exaggerated way to accentuate her question.

'I'm a witch, and I know things.'

Mary cracked up. 'Miss Marissa, I had a feeling about you, for sure. Miss Marissa the witch!'

'Mary, don't go telling the others now. They might get scared of me and all, especially after you doing such a good job convincing them to come and see me.'

Mary winked. 'Don't you worry, Miss Marissa, it will be our little secret.'

'See you same time next week.'

After Mary left, Marissa got up and stretched. Loretta hadn't shown up for her session, and it was probably just as well as she had run over with Lucy, and had given Mary the full hour. It was time to go home. She blew out the candle and put the chairs back in a more neutral setting. Then there was a knock at the door.

Marissa opened it. There was Audrey, in a white hoodie and bleached blue jeans, looking much more casual than she had been when Marissa had met her the first time.

'Hi! Come in!'

'Hello, Marissa, I was working late and noticed from the book that you were still here, so I thought I'd pop up. Were you about to leave? Do you have a few minutes?'

'I ran over time with Lucy, so Mary and I ran over too. I had a feeling Loretta wouldn't come, and she hasn't, so I was just about to leave. I'm happy to stay, if you want to talk.'

'Ten minutes for a quick catch-up?'

'Sure!'

They both sat down in the counselling chairs.

'How are you getting on?' Audrey asked. 'I wanted to check in with you because of Lucy. I know you're still in training and probably haven't experienced anything like this before.'

'I'm doing okay, thanks. I think Lucy has made some progress. She did come tonight, and she did talk to me, after crying. I am able to tell you that without breaking a confidence, aren't I?'

'Of course, although this isn't a full-on supervision session, it's more about you. Do you feel out of your depth? I know I should have asked you before, but it's been crazy busy in the office. Do you want me to move her on to someone more experienced?'

'Honestly, I don't know, Audrey. I felt we connected tonight, and we did some work together too, which seemed to help. If you feel she would be better with someone more experienced, I guess that's fine with me.'

'I think I'll ask her, then, how she feels about working with you. I'll remind her that you're still in training, see how she feels about continuing and let you know if there's any change.' Audrey got out a small notebook and pen and wrote something down. 'Well done, by the way, really jumping in at the deep end. That's what happens, though, it's unpredictable. Hopefully more rewarding than frustrating! Anyway, how else are you finding it here? Is there anything you need?'

'I think I've settled in now,' said Marissa. 'It took a while, though. Mary R. has been looking after me.'

'I've heard her telling the girls to come to counselling – she's a great ambassador for you now! Well done there. So, all good then?'

Marissa nodded.

'That's what I like to hear.'

Audrey stood up. 'Hopefully in the next few weeks we'll have a full hour of supervision together, when you've got ten sessions done. Make sure you schedule that in with Bronagh. I need you to keep on top of it for me, if that's okay.'

'Sure, I will. Thanks.'

'Good stuff. I know Loretta was having difficulty with the crèche, so that's why she wasn't here tonight. I'll make sure that's sorted for her next week, so no more excuses then. See you again soon. If you need anything in the meantime, you know you can contact me via the office.'

After two buses home in the rain, a very tired Marissa lit a fire, made a hot chocolate and settled onto the sofa. She looked at her phone. *Matt, I said I'd call you, but I'm all talked out. I'll text you instead.*

Hi love I miss u. can we get together soon?

Her heart leapt to see the little bubble showing him writing back.

Hi! Want 2cu 2 but not free till weekend ☹

☹ aww ok.

Let's go out Friday and do something fun. Stay at mine?

Ok gr8! nite

nite x

Heavy-hearted and suddenly missing Matt, Marissa checked her emails for the one-hundred-and-eleventieth time that day, and noted there was still no response from Séamus. She put her phone aside with a sigh and reached into the shelf under the glass on her coffee table and pulled out her pack of oracle cards. Tobermory wanted to see what she was doing. He came over, took one look at the cards, then lost interest and curled up in a ball beside her on the sofa. She held the cards in her hand for a moment, breathed, then opened them, spreading the entire pack face up on the table.

Why did I hide these from myself? They're so beautiful.

The fire was crackling as it came to life. The smell of smoke filled the flat and Marissa got up and put a couple of briquettes on top, then sat down again, admiring the artwork on each card, particularly her favourite cards – Bear, Bison, Swan. She then pulled them all together, shuffled and drew a card from the deck. *Phoenix – Rising up from the ashes.*

Nice. Yes, I suppose I kind of did rise up from the ashes today with Lucy. That was so powerful. I'm glad I could help her. She seemed much stronger when she left, and she has a purpose now to focus on. I really hope she will be okay.

She opened the angel cards and looked through the pack. The artwork was more familiar now and she felt comfort coming from the deck. She shuffled the cards and drew one. *Uriel – You are loved.*

Matt might love me, but I miss him. He feels miles away.

As she stared at the image of Uriel, she felt a warmth encompassing her whole body. She shifted in the sofa, stretching out and taking up more space, softening in herself. The warmth intensified, became electric. It was a wonderful feeling.

Uriel, are you here? Is this you?

She felt a wave of bliss move through her, filling her with peace.

Thank you. Angels are real. I will never doubt it again.

CHAPTER FIVE

The patter of heavy rain outside on the window was comforting as Marissa woke up under warm covers and slowly pulled herself into the day. This time her dream had been slightly different. She hadn't been eaten or dismembered, and it hadn't been about Scott, either. (The images from London were thankfully beginning to have less of a hold on her.) This had been a puzzle dream, the kind of dream she loved, where she was trying to put the pieces of something together. Like her stepping stone dreams at the lake, but this one was more intricate and complex. The energy of the dream clung to her body as she switched off her alarm and moved about her room, getting her day started.

She was becoming worried about Séamus. Anxiety started to eat away at her insides, consuming what was left of her dreamscape and she gave it the space it demanded, like a puppy wanting her attention. As it took hold, her thoughts began to spiral.

Maybe I really messed up when I left and he's so angry with me he won't have me back. She became emotional. If I don't finish my training, I'll never be a shaman... If I can't do shamanic work, how could I help my clients properly? She caught herself. Hey, wait, I'm doing 'what ifs'. I've got to stop doing that. She took control of her mind. *If I don't get invited back to Séamus's training, then I'll just have to find some other way to learn what I need to learn.*

That felt much better, more solid, more like the person she wanted to be.

The workday was slow. Every minute felt like ten. Eventually it passed, though, and Marissa was on the bus travelling to Cabra. She finished her sandwich and bag of popcorn, brushed the crumbs off her hands and got off at her stop.

She was a little early, for the first time since she had started there, the door to Room Three was closed. She was just about to open it when she realised there were people talking inside. *Someone's in before me?*

She stood outside listening, trying to hear what was going on. It sounded as though there was another session taking place in there. She looked at the time: she still had ten minutes before Niamh was due. She went to the bathroom and washed the popcorn smell off her hands, realising that all the counselling rooms were busy. *I suppose we're coming to the end of the academic year and everyone needs their hours. It's great, but I'd prefer to have the room to myself.*

She got back to the room just in time to catch the door opening. Two women were standing there saying their goodbyes, one in a coat and one not. The woman in the coat pushed gently past Marissa and left. *She must be the client.*

The other woman spoke. 'Hi, I'll be out of your way in a moment.'

She was in her mid-forties and wearing a skirt, a cardigan and flat shoes. She disappeared into the room and a moment later she came out again with a coat and a small black handbag over her arm.

'It's all yours,' she said with a smile.

'Thanks,' replied Marissa, and she went inside.

The room felt wrong. The energy was damp, as if someone had been crying in there. Marissa put down her bag and felt inside it for her Saint Germain aura soma bottle. Pouring two drops into her left hand she rubbed her hands together, then ran the energy through her aura and relished the tangy smell and the calmness it instilled in her. She waved her scented arms through the air, trying to break up the damp feeling. It wasn't shifting.

The buzzer sounded. It was Niamh.

But the room isn't ready! I really do wish I had my own place. Oh well, I guess it goes with the territory.

Marissa pulled herself into the moment and buzzed Niamh in. It only took a few moments for her to appear at the door. *Here we go, another night on the hop. It gets so intense so quickly at times.*

'Hello, Niamh, it's good to see you this evening. Come on in.'

Marissa rearranged the chairs and lit her favourite candle as Niamh hung a wet red raincoat on the back of the door.

'It always seems to be raining on a Thursday night!' said Marissa, gesturing to the chairs.

Niamh smiled, chose a chair and sat down. 'I think it's been raining all week!' she said, fixing her hair. Niamh had a large handbag with her, Marissa remembered she had arrived last time with lots of shopping bags. Just then a phone rang inside her handbag.

Niamh blushed. 'Hang on.' She rummaged through the oversized bag taking more time than was comfortable and eventually pulled out her phone and changed a setting.

'Is that off now, not on vibrate?' Marissa asked. 'I don't want us to be disturbed during your session time.'

'Oh, yes, of course.' Niamh dipped her hand back into the bag, switched off the phone this time, then put the bag on the floor by her feet.

Marissa took a breath. She had settled into the room now, dismissed the damp feeling and was able to focus completely on Niamh. But she couldn't let the phone thing go just yet.

'I'm wondering, Niamh, how you got on with the homework, but first I want to ask you why you're not offering yourself the full hour here?'

Niamh looked shocked. 'What do you mean?'

'Well, with your phone on, someone could interrupt us – interrupt *you*, I mean. It's your time for yourself. By having your phone on vibrate, it could still be an interruption.'

'Oh. I didn't think of it like that...'

'I just want to point out that you're not giving yourself time for yourself. If you don't switch the phone off, I mean.'

'Point taken.'

'But there's something else. I'm wondering, do you ever switch your phone off at all?'

Niamh smiled. 'Of course I do. Yes, when I go to bed.' She nodded to accentuate her response.

Marissa mimicked her nodding, then caught herself and stopped. She pulled herself back into the moment.

'How does it feel when you switch off your phone?'

Niamh shrugged her shoulders. 'I don't know. Quieter?'

'Can I ask you to go deeper with this? In the moment that you switch off your phone, what does your body do?'

Niamh thought for a moment. 'Actually, I think my body relaxes a little bit.'

'Are you tense all the time? I know you've come to work on reducing your anxiety levels, so this is probably going to help with that, having this conversation, I mean.'

'Okay. Maybe I'm tense all the time, yes.'

'Do you think your phone makes you tense?'

'I've never thought about it before.'

'Well, it's off now, so just sit with it for a moment. You're here in this room with me and your phone won't be ringing, or vibrating, for a whole hour. What does your body say to you about this?'

'I don't know, honestly. Maybe I'm a little anxious anyway, because I'm here. With you.'

'Can we sit for another minute with this? Tell your body that the phone is off now.'

Niamh thought about it. After a moment she said, 'Actually, yes. I think you're right. Something in my body is a lot calmer now because the phone is off.'

Bingo!

'So. How was your week since I saw you last? How are your anxiety levels?'

Niamh shifted in her chair. 'The week was okay, and my anxiety levels kind of the same. But the mindfulness exercise helped. I like the one with my hands, it's beginning to calm me down as soon as I start doing it.'

Marissa smiled. 'That's wonderful. I'm delighted to hear it. You're beginning to condition a new response.'

'What does that mean?'

'The more you do something, the more your body gets used to it. It takes time in the beginning to build up that trust – it's like you're programming yourself. For example, if you persist with the practice, your body learns that when you do the mindfulness exercise, you will relax. The more you repeat it, the earlier your body recognises it, and it starts to relax earlier and earlier in the process, until it becomes a conditioned response. Of course, it takes time for this to sink in thoroughly. And it's less usual for this to be something deliberate, something you're aware you're doing, I mean. We usually slide into patterns and reactions – they happen out of habit rather than us programming them in. We forget that we can take control of our thoughts and steer ourselves in a direction that is healthier for us. By deliberately creating a new response, and repeating it often, you train yourself into that response being your new reaction, instead of something that's harmful or hurtful. Or something that causes more anxiety.'

Hey, that sounds great! I should do that more often too. Marissa was beginning to get used to speaking words of wisdom during healing sessions and hearing them for the first time along with the client.

Niamh appeared to be taking it all in. 'That's really interesting. Should I keep going with it then?'

'Yes please, and let me know how you get on, if your body starts to respond earlier. It means that you will be more in control of your physical response.' A moment passed, then Marissa asked, 'Is there anything in particular you'd like to talk about tonight?'

Niamh replied enthusiastically, 'I do like the sound of being more in control of my responses. Maybe there are some other things I could do to help myself? The anxiety was still pretty bad this week. The mindfulness did help, like I said, but overall there hasn't been a massive change.'

'Okay. If you don't mind, can I bring up your phone again?'

Niamh looked worried.

'I mean, you've just admitted that it causes you stress. So it's something we could look at. If you're not turning off your phone here, do you keep it on all the time? I have a sense that when your phone is on, you feel you're "on duty", "available" to the world? Does that sound right?'

'Perhaps,' said Niamh pensively. 'I'm not sure.'

'If you're taking time to relax but leaving your phone on, if your phone is causing you stress then you're not really able to relax fully. Do you agree?'

'I guess so.'

'Yes, okay. Anxiety builds up over time, so you need to make time for it to, well, for the levels to properly drop. Can we try to find the root cause of why your phone increases your stress levels? Good. When your phone is on, who are you expecting to phone you?'

'I don't know. My family probably. Or my best friend. I can't think of anyone else. Work doesn't call me after hours.'

'So if it was your mother phoning you, and your phone was off, what would happen?'

After a moment Niamh replied, 'She'd leave a voicemail?'

'So you'd get the message?'

'Yes.'

'Or she'd text you?'

Niamh seemed more confident now. 'Yes.' Then she shrank. 'But she doesn't like being ignored. By me, I mean.'

'I don't think anyone likes being ignored. But just because they want your attention when they want it doesn't mean you have to give it to them. It also doesn't mean that you care for them any less in that moment in time.'

'Okay,' Niamh said slowly. 'Seeing as we were talking about conditioned responses, I see now that I'm conditioned to be available to Mum whenever she needs me.'

'That's great, that you can see it! Well done.'

Niamh looked very uncomfortable with her realisation. 'So what do I do?'

Marissa thought for a moment. 'Well, you don't have to become completely unavailable, but you do need to claim back some space for yourself, so your anxiety levels become more manageable.'

The room was silent for a moment while Niamh digested this.

Both women began to speak at the same time, then stopped, and smiled. Niamh said, 'Go ahead. What were you going to say?'

Marissa smiled again. 'What if you turned your phone off for one hour each day, to take an hour for yourself? Whoever wanted you during that hour could leave a voicemail or send you a text message, and you could get back to them once your hour was over.'

Niamh digested this. 'That sounds so simple, I know it does, but still there's a part of me that's having difficulty with not being available when people phone me. Particularly Mum. But taking time for myself isn't ignoring them, is it?'

'Of course not. You're practising self-care. What if you framed it for yourself that way? You're taking an hour for self-care, as opposed to doing something selfish, or ignoring other people. I'm wondering whether you've been ignored? In your life?'

Niamh nodded. 'I was excluded in school. Bullied. Left out. It was awful.'

Marissa took a breath. 'So your mother demands your full attention whenever she wants it, and you feel you also need to be always available to the rest of your family and friends, in case they feel you're excluding them.'

'Yes, that sounds about right.'

Marissa let the room go silent for a moment.

Niamh said, 'But I'm not ignoring them, or excluding them, not really, if I'm taking an hour for myself. An hour of self-care.'

Marissa smiled. 'Exactly. Self-care isn't selfish, because you need it. Selfish means taking more than you need, at the detriment of someone else. You're certainly not doing that by taking an hour off to get a rest. If I was your friend, I'd understand. I wouldn't feel excluded, mostly because I'd know you'd contact me when you were ready to. I know I've been upset before when people don't reply to me, but that's usually after a day or a couple of days, not after an hour.'

Séamus, please write back to me!

Niamh smiled. 'Yes, I guess an hour isn't such a long time really.'

'Can you think of how you felt when it took an hour or more for someone to reply to you?'

'You're right, it wasn't that bad. I didn't even notice it took that time, actually.'

'Okay, let's go one step further with this then. Pretend you're on your own and you've turned off your phone, just for an hour. How do you feel?'

'Anxious, but I'm reminding myself that they can leave a message and I'll talk to them when my hour is over. And that it's only an hour, it's not really a long time at all for them to wait.'

'You're worth the wait, Niamh. Don't forget that.'

Niamh smiled. 'Yes, I suppose I am.'

'We are coming up to time now, I want to make sure you're going to be able to practise this during the week between now and our next session. Do you think there's any other reason why you feel that taking an hour for yourself might be difficult?'

'What if they *really* needed me? Like in an emergency?'

Marissa was silent for a moment.

'I'm wondering if you feel like you're on stand-by all the time, in case there's an emergency?'

Niamh thought about this. 'I'm not sure.'

'Being on stand-by creates a lot of anxiety and stress. It affects your body. This could be part of the reason for your high anxiety levels.'

Niamh nodded.

'Okay, I want to ask you this – is it realistic to believe that there is always going to be an emergency?'

Niamh laughed. 'That's childish!'

'So, it's a little child part of you that believes that – now I'm not judging you, I promise, but you need to hear it like this – a little child part of you believes that you need your phone on all the time so that your mother can reach you whenever she needs to, so that the other people that you care about don't feel you're excluding them, or in case you're needed in an emergency. And if you don't do this, then you're being selfish. Would that be correct?'

'I've never thought of it like that, but yes, I suppose you're right.'

'Do you think if you switched your phone off for, say, just one hour a day, you'd get a break from this, and your anxiety levels would drop?'

'An hour still seems like a long time, though.'

'How about half an hour to start with?'

'Yes, I could try that.'

'Great. So that's your homework. Starting tomorrow, switch your phone off for a half-hour each day, with the intention to build it up to an hour in the future. Okay?'

'Okay.'

'You could try fifteen minutes first, just to ease yourself into it. And keep doing your mindfulness exercise, so it becomes second nature.

'Second nature, I like that!'

'Wonderful. Well done, Niamh. That's our session for today.'

Niamh smiled and reached into her handbag, pulled out her phone and switched it on. It beeped several texts and messages in different tones. She shrugged her shoulders, smiled apologetically, got her coat and left.

Marissa stood up and moved around, stretched and almost immediately the buzzer sounded. It was William. Their fourth session together, and he was still having nightmares. *I need to remember that I'm his counsellor, not his shamanic practitioner. But I would love to be able to do something to help. Oh! Maybe I'll wear my armour?* She got a full-body shiver. She closed her eyes to visualise putting it on, but she could hear William approaching, so she speeded up the visualisation and smiled as he appeared in the doorway.

'Hi, Marissa, good to see you.' William brought the cold and wet into the room with him. His hair was damp and a sheen of water on his forehead had coagulated into drops, which were trickling down his face. He helped himself to a tissue from the box on the table and wiped the raindrops from his face.

'April showers,' Marissa said, happy at his familiarity. He hung up his coat and she gestured to the chairs. 'Which one?'

He smiled at her and chose the one he always sat in.

'How could I have guessed?' said Marissa, smiling again and sitting down in her usual chair. She had become very fond of William. She looked at him more closely. He was pale and drawn, and looked older than his age. *How could he have aged so much in a week?*

She tried to keep the concern from her face. 'How have you been since I saw you last?'

William shrank a little, and when he answered, his voice was weak and low. 'The dreams, I thought they were improving, but they're getting worse. And it's taking longer for me to lose the feeling of them. In my chest.'

This seems like a setback, oh no! But they did say in college that sometimes it got worse before it got better.

William didn't offer anything more, so Marissa said encouragingly, 'Please tell me about your dreams. If you want to?'

William looked very uncomfortable. He shook his head. 'I don't like to talk about them. They're getting very graphic now. Dark, nasty. Actually, I'm a little ashamed too.'

'Ashamed? Why?'

He blushed and looked at the floor. He shifted in his chair, crossed his long legs then uncrossed them again. Then he looked up, catching Marissa's eye. 'Do you remember I told you that sometimes I'm hurting people in my dreams?'

She nodded.

'Well, it's been happening again. I was putting someone in chains the other night, pulling them tighter and tighter around them. They were crying out, like I was torturing them. I was so glad it wasn't me being put into chains that I pulled harder.' He shifted around uncomfortably. 'I don't know, it was like the person I was in the dream was someone else. It wasn't me at all.'

Marissa said nothing, not wanting to break his flow.

'Marissa? This sounds weird, but do you think that we can be inside someone else's dream?'

She took some time to answer. 'That's a really good question. I've never thought about it before.'

'I would never do such a thing to a person in real life – it goes against every bone in my body. But I've had this same dream three times since I saw you last week. *Three times.* I'm almost afraid to sleep in case I have it again.'

He looked pleadingly at Marissa, needing some relief.

'I don't know what to say, Will. I don't have an answer for you. All I know is that there are some things in the world that are stranger than we could ever understand. I suppose from what I know of the shamanic journey, and Reiki healing, we *can* go into other people's consciousness. So it is possible, I suppose, that we might be able to find ourselves inside somebody else's dream... Maybe we will never know. What do you think?'

The colour was returning to William's face. 'I don't know. It's refreshing to be able to talk about it with you, in a way. It really helps that you don't think I'm crazy.'

'I've never once thought that you were crazy.'

'Thanks. I suppose I'll have to think on this a while longer.'

It has to be something energetic. So shamanism would probably help him more than psychotherapy would.

Marissa had an idea. 'I'm remembering what you told me in our first session together. You said that you'd seen a healer, someone who'd tried to get you off your medication.'

William nodded.

'You said it was worse than psychosis, what happened. That you got really sick from it.'

'Yes, I thought I was going to die. Which was strange, seeing as I had tried to kill myself a couple years before. I'll never do that again, that's for sure. One way to know whether you want to die or not is to be in a situation like that.'

'I'm wondering, William, when did these dreams start? These particular dreams?'

He thought for a moment. 'About a year or so ago.'

'So it wasn't the healer that has triggered them?'

William thought for a moment. 'No. I did have bad dreams around that time alright, but they weren't like this – the texture was different, if that makes sense? They were about him and what happened with him. They stopped eventually.'

'Oh. Okay. We can rule that out then.' *Unless it created a weakness that was later exploited?* 'Do you have any idea what it might have been that may have triggered these current dreams?'

Silence filled the room.

Marissa added, ‘It might be something to think about, to get the answer to. I find that once you start asking questions, you usually find answers.’

‘I think I see where you’re going with this,’ said William. ‘If I figure out what started the dreams then maybe I can remove myself from it?’

‘Yes, step away from it. Clear it from your system, so to speak.’

He definitely looks more like himself now. So whatever we are doing, it’s helping.

‘This is scary,’ William admitted, ‘because you’re saying that these dreams may not be mine. They might be those of something I’ve connected to. Maybe they *are* someone else’s dreams. But in a way it’s also kind of refreshing to think that my mind hasn’t created something that awful. That was my biggest fear – that something so cruel had come from me. I don’t know how, though – the dreams are like no movie I’ve ever seen, no book I’ve ever read.’

‘I feel that there’s something else going on here,’ Marissa said reassuringly. ‘I suppose if we were to stick to traditional psychotherapy, it would be the case that everything in your mind had come from your mind. But then, there’s the transpersonal. Jung said that there is a collective consciousness, where we all pool our consciousness and unconsciousness together. So maybe you connected to something dark in the collective consciousness, maybe because you did try to kill yourself, or because what happened with that healer led to some kind of weakness. Maybe, somehow, some dark energy saw that weakness and was able to get in.’ She sat bold upright in the chair. ‘William, what I’m going to say to you may sound strange, but it could really help. I think you could benefit from seeing a shaman.’

‘A shaman?’

‘Yes, it’s a type of healer.’

William shivered. ‘I saw a healer before, remember? It was a total disaster.’

‘Yes, I know, but one bad healer doesn’t mean that all healing is bad, or that all healers are bad. If this is what we think it might be, you could be connected to something that isn’t yours, and it could be really important for you to disconnect from it. I have done some training in shamanic healing and I think a good shamanic healer might be able to help you with this.'

William shivered. 'You've given me a lot to think about. I won't say "yes" right now, because I've had bad experience in the past. But I hear what you're saying and I'll keep it in mind. I don't want dark energy in me, and these dreams are dark, that's for sure. I'll try to remember when they started, what I was doing at the time, in case it helps.'

'That sounds good. We can keep working on this if you like. This is our fourth session together, so we have two more. I can put in for another six if you want them.'

'Can we decide next week?'

'Of course. It's time now. Thanks, Will. I know that was difficult to talk about. I do appreciate your honesty.'

William stood up, got his coat and held out his hand to Marissa. They shook hands.

'Seriously,' he said, 'I came here tonight not expecting to make any progress. At least I feel now that I can talk about this with someone, and that there may be some things we can try. Thanks.'

Marissa had a few minutes before Aisling's session to properly clear the energy of the room. She was relieved, as Aisling had been so fragile during the last four sessions she didn't want her walking into any dark energy that William might have inadvertently left behind. She closed her eyes and connected to the Reiki light. She felt the energy come rushing into her body so quickly it was like a reunion between old friends. She smiled at the feeling. It was so good, her body relaxed and she felt centred and present.

I can't believe this is session five already, I hope Aisling feels able to talk to me tonight. She did seem stronger last week, but it's good for me to sit with someone like this. It teaches me patience. Patience helped me a lot with Lucy, I suppose sitting in silence with a client is another skill that you don't really learn in college, but learn from experience, if at all.

She drew the emotional healing symbol over both chairs, the power symbol in the middle of the room, and the mental clarity symbol over her own chair.

Please, Reiki angels, can you fix the symbols for me? I can't quite remember them perfectly yet. Thank you!

The buzzer buzzed. Marissa pressed the button and clapped her hands one more time to clear the space. She closed her eyes and checked the energy of the room one more time.

There was a soft knock at the door.

Aisling was as pale and drawn as usual, she was a slight woman who looked much younger than her age. *Not really substantial, as if she isn't here at all. You'd not notice her in the room.*

'Hello, Aisling, do come in.'

Aisling quietly entered the room and hung up her coat, Marissa gestured to the chair she had prepared for her. Aisling sat down. *Right into the symbol. Perfect.*

Marissa sat opposite her and took a moment to imagine herself absorbing the mental clarity symbol. They sat together in silence for several minutes. When it got too much for her, Marissa broke it.

'How have you been this week?'

'Okay, thanks.'

'How can I help you tonight?' *I don't want to push her. I have to be gentle.*

Aisling seemed distant, as if the wellspring of emotion that she had been emptying with Marissa as a witness was, well, empty. Normally at this stage of the session she would be crying. Tonight she wasn't, but she wasn't offering any information either.

Marissa took a breath to centre herself.

'Shall we talk a little bit tonight? Are you able to?'

Aisling nodded.

'Is it still raining outside? I noticed your coat was dry.' *Roads and weather, always a good place to start.*

'No, it's stopped now.'

'Do you have far to come?'

'About a ten-minute walk.'

'Walking is great. Do you like walking?'

Aisling nodded again.

I need a way in, something to open the conversation. Could I ask her about her dreams? 'Aisling' means dream...

'Do you remember your dreams?'

Aisling recoiled and turned even paler. *Jeez, that was the wrong thing to ask. Or maybe it wasn't...*

Emotion welled up in Aisling's face. Tears formed in her eyes. Marissa let her cry, offered the tissue box and sat holding the space for her.

I can't leave it like this though, she's so emotional. Maybe I could connect to her energy and see what is going on. Yes, I could do that. I've not been working shamanically with anyone for a long time, but I'm ready to do it now.

Marissa lightly closed her eyes, kept some of her awareness in the room with Aisling, then took the rest of herself lightly into a journey.

Down, down, down, through the building, through the earth, the rocks and stones. She landed with a bump on the forest floor. She picked herself up and brushed herself down, then walked off to find her beloved tree. Upon seeing him, Marissa's heart opened.

'Dearest friend, I need your help. Can you show me what is going on with Aisling? Why is she so sad?' Why haven't I thought of doing this before? I should do it for all of my clients!

The tree stirred and opened its eyes. 'Hello again, it is good to see you once more. You want to find out about Aisling. How interesting. But I was expecting this. Are you ready?'

Marissa smiled.

The tree bowed to her, then gestured to its lower branches and Marissa went over to them. Two large branches melded together and became a platform, then turned downwards, like a slide. When they touched the ground a portal opened, going further down. Marissa climbed up into the branches and let go. She went down, down, down the slide. It was like a DNA helix spiralling down and down. She couldn't see what was around the corner but she trusted the tree and allowed herself to go wherever it was taking her.

She was spat out at the bottom into a very dark room. It felt musty and dusty and she couldn't see anything. Then a small orb appeared, radiating a soft golden light. It bobbed around her, as if delighted to see her, then it flew over to the wall, illuminating shelving running from the bottom of the wall to the top. Each shelf had many little jars crammed together. They appeared to be glass jars with lids.

Marissa was silent, taking it all in. As she got her bearings, she felt as if she was in a kitchen pantry. She walked through it, exploring. Shelves upon shelves with jars upon jars, different-sized jars, all with lids, all of them dark...

But what does this have to do with Aisling?

The small golden orb rose and flew quickly to a shelving unit which was behind several other shelving units, all of them stocked to the brim. Marissa followed it, noticing how heavy she felt. Her limbs were heavy, as if she was underwater. The orb pressed itself against one of the jars and after a moment, Marissa could see a tiny light shining inside the jar. She peered into it and saw a tiny person. The light was dim. She looked again, peering into the glass.

That can't be! *Yes, it was. Aisling was inside the jar. Marissa felt sick.*

She stood back from the wall and gathered herself, then she looked into another jar. Yes, there was another person inside it. She didn't know who this person was, but that didn't matter. She looked into another jar, and another, and another, and inside each jar there was a person. Some of them saw her and started banging on the glass from the inside, weak lights lighting up inside the jar as she looked at it. Some lights were brighter than others, as if the little people were shouting from the inside, 'Help me, help me get me out of here!' but Marissa couldn't hear them. Others didn't notice her at all. They had lost hope. Aisling was one of those.

What do I do? Oh God.

Suddenly Marissa felt herself being lifted up by the scruff of her neck. She flailed about, arms and legs struggling, but to no avail. She had no power in her body, she was a gnat and whatever had her was a giant. She was deposited into an empty jar and the lid placed on top of her and screwed on tight. There was nothing she could do about it. Now she was one of them, inside a glass jar. The jar was placed on a shelf and whoever or whatever it was that had done this to her, was gone.

Back in Cabra, Marissa's body had stiffened and her breathing was short and sharp. Aisling was still crying.

I'm trapped! Oh no! What do I do? Great Goddess Isis, please come and help me. I'm so sorry, I didn't realise, I didn't know. How stupid am I.

She sank to the bottom of the jar in despair. Now I know why Aisling is so sad – her soul is trapped here inside a jar. And now mine is too! What am I going to do?

'Please, Goddess Isis, please come and help me.'

There was a tapping on the jar. Marissa jumped in fright. Tap, tap, tap.

Marissa looked at the creature outside that was making this noise. It looked distorted. Was it a bird? She wasn't able to really see it from inside.

Suddenly the jar was moving. Marissa reeled. There was nothing to hold onto.

The jar moved again, to the edge of the shelf, then it fell, taking Marissa with it, and smashed on the ground.

Marissa stood up, surrounded by oversized shards of glass, and tried to breathe. She could see her rescuer now. It was a large bird with very strong claws for feet. It looked like a hawk, but she wasn't sure about bird identification. It stood there, then cocked its head to one side, looking at her as if she was an idiot. She did indeed feel like one. It spread its wings – then there was a ruckus approaching.

Marissa heard a voice inside her mind: 'Get on the bird's back, for God's sake, girl!'

She ran over to the bird and climbed up to sit behind its head. Two strong feathers stood out on its neck. She grabbed one with each hand.

The bird rose up and flew out of the door and into the night.

As they gained height, Marissa felt the heavy feeling rolling away from her and she could move her body freely once more. Moonlight illuminated the scene. Marissa looked down and saw a large castle with a moat and large turrets. She shivered.

'Thank you, bird, I am so grateful. I really thought I was trapped in there.'

'You are indeed an idiot, girl, Luckily for you I wasn't busy and I heard your cry for help.'

'Isis? Is that you?'

'Of course it is, didn't you call me? But I can't be making a habit of this. You have to be more careful in future. Why are you going to a place like this with no protection? Where is your armour? What are you thinking? You are crazy, crazy, crazy! There is real danger here.'

Back in the office in Cabra, Marissa's body had relaxed a little. Her breathing was almost back to normal. Aisling was still crying, but the tone had changed.

They were far away from the castle now. Stars were twinkling in the sky, the bird was skimming the surface of a lake, moonlight was shimmering in the water and Marissa was becoming more relaxed.

'I'm so sorry. Thank you so much for rescuing me. You're right, it was totally stupid thing to do. I had a client, and I wanted to see what was wrong with her, and I just went to see without thinking.'

'Without protection too. Very bad, Tori, you must never do that again. Always wear your full armour.'

'I promise I will never forget again. What was that place?'

'The fortress of the enemy, the enemy's lair. You must go back here one day, when you are ready. But not tonight. Now go to your client and remember I won't always be there to rescue you.'

Marissa was deposited briskly back into her body. She landed with a crash in the healing room, her head spinning from all that she had seen. Aisling looked depleted and as if she wanted to sleep. It was late, almost time for the session to end. The candle on the table had gone out. *Strange, that's never happened before.*

Marissa took a few moments to orient herself back in the room, then closed the session, helped Aisling with her coat, closed the healing space and went home, getting off the bus a little early so she could walk it all out. She had a lot to think about.

She stopped off at the chipper to buy a bag of hot crispy chips with a good helping of vinegar and salt. She found it helped her bring her focus more into the present moment. She ate as she walked home, going over the images in her mind.

I thought I had put on my armour when I saw William. Maybe I hadn't put it all on correctly? I did speed things up a bit. And that place, all those lost souls in jars, it's awful. Are they really in there? How many of them are there?

I need something to ground me here, to keep me in this world. I could lose a piece of myself on those journeys... Well, that's how it feels. I wonder if it's an actual thing, losing a piece of yourself? When those people sold their souls, is that where their souls ended up? Ooh! Maybe that's it! Wow. And the energy of that place, it felt so familiar, like I'd been there before. Maybe in a dream? I've been having lots of crazy dreams lately.

She finished the chips, licked the salt off her fingers and stuffed the paper bags into a bin as she passed. She kept walking.

Since I decided to continue my apprenticeship, everything seems to have accelerated. I hope I can keep up with it. Isis, thank you. You saved my life, my soul. I will be forever grateful. I know I have so much to learn.

She fingered the ankh around her neck. *I really have to be more careful.*

CHAPTER SIX

The sun came into the room, waking Tobermory. He was hungry. Marissa had to wake up and feed him. Right now. Didn't she know how important he was? And it was bright outside, so it was definitely time for breakfast. He climbed up onto her bed, sat on her chest and stuck his cold wet nose into her eye until she woke up and looked at the time with a sigh.

'Tobermory, it's 5am.'

Tobermory followed her dutifully to the toilet, winding around her legs and brushing up against her to the extent that she had difficulty walking.

'Tobermory, it's so early... Okay, I'll feed you, then go outside and play, okay?'

Marissa had slept well, despite the events of the previous evening. She was still tired, so once she had closed the back door, she climbed back into her warm bed to doze until her alarm went off.

She turned on her side. Then she turned onto her other side. Her mind went back to the room with the jars, and poor Aisling stuck inside one of them. *So many people there too – who else was in there?* She knew she had to do something about it. She'd be more careful this time. And wear her armour. Yes. That was it. She had to rescue Aisling, she couldn't leave her like that one minute longer.

She stretched out, lying on her back, flexed her toes and brought her awareness down into her body. She was calm. *I am going to do this and I will be successful. But I need my armour first. And I need to put it on carefully. Where is it?*

She visualised herself at the lakeside. It was quiet and the waters were calm. She walked beyond the lake to a spot she had been to before and found a door, with no building attached to it. This must be it. *She stood there for a moment, then touched the door and it opened.*

She went inside, down several flights of stairs and into a corridor. At the end of the corridor was a small room with an open door. Her armour was laid out on a table inside, along with her chainmail suit. Her sword hung from a silver grip on the wall.

She examined the armour carefully, checking to make sure it was intact. She shrugged off her pyjamas and stepped into the chainmail, allowing time for it to shrink to fit her body snugly. Then she placed her armour on top, piece by piece, taking her time. She fingered the ankh around her neck before putting on the chest plate.

She hoisted her sword down from the wall and sheathed it behind her back. And there was her helmet, shiny and new. She put it on her head and felt the armour changing and becoming exactly the right size for her body. It felt strange, even though the armour was comfortable and light and she could move easily, it was unfamiliar. But she had it on properly now.

How was she to get back to the room with all the jars in it? It had reminded her of a storeroom, or a pantry. I hope nobody is going to... No, that doesn't bear thinking about! *She felt the need to get back outside.* How did I get there last night? *Thorough the tree. Yes, of course, that was it.*

She climbed up the stairs, went back through the door and was outside again, by the lake. The door glimmered in the mist from the lake, then disappeared. She noticed the glistening head of the sea serpent watching her as she found her bearings, then walked into the forest grove.

I have everything I need right here. I have grown. This feels good! I am powerful and strong. This is who I truly am.

She strode confidently into the dark forest, walking on crunchy needles, following the direction of her heart. She could almost smell the wet earth as she strode onwards. She soon came to her beloved tree.

'Hello, my tree, I have come to meet with you again.' She bowed.

The tree opened its sleepy eyes. 'Greetings, lovely Tori, it is good to see you. It has been a while.'

'But I was here only last night!'

What did it call me? Tori! *Her whole body felt electric. Tori! She was Tori! She was the lightbringer, bringing the light into the dark places. Yes! Of course! She knew this to her core, she could feel the reverberations of it right through her body. She smiled. Joy rippled through her armour and it lit up.*

'Tree, my dearest friend, all of these years together and we are still here.'

'Yes, indeed we are,' said the tree, now wide eyed and paying her its full attention. 'Now, my dear, what can I do for you today?'

'Take me to the place with the jars, the place where Aisling is. Where Marissa went last night.'

The tree nodded and started to open. Two of its lower branches knotted together and twisted around each other to make a platform, a portal opened in the forest floor and the branches unravelled and unfurled themselves through it, seeming to continue for eternity. No slide tonight. *Tori-Marissa had to navigate her way down, to climb and crawl, to manoeuvre her body over knots and bumps in difficult twisted branches.*

Just when it was becoming tedious, the ends of the branches smoothed out and she was able to lie on them and slide the rest of the way down. The slide deposited her into yet another forest.

She stood and got her bearings. This forest didn't feel like the one where her tree resided; this one was darker, it felt ominous, as if someone was behind the trees watching her, but she wasn't scared. Her armour glistened softly in the darkness as if to emphasise that she had brought the light with her.

She started to walk, not really knowing where she was going. Then she remembered the small golden orb of light and how it had helped her when she had been there before.

'Is there anyone here that can help me find Aisling?'

It didn't take long. Three small soft golden orbs flew towards her. They looked how you would imagine fairies would look, if they were, indeed, fairies.

'Can you show me that place, the place with the jars where Aisling is?'

They fluttered, as if they were discussing it with one another, then moved away from her, spiralling round one another as if in agreement, then circling back to her as if to encourage her to follow them. So she did.

They led her deeper into the forest. Soon she saw a log cabin with a low light inside and smoke coming from a chimney. The door was ajar and the little orbs went inside. Tori followed them.

The room was warm and a bubbling cauldron was hanging from a wooden beam over a fire. The orbs seemed jittery and excited, spinning circles around each other, drawing Tori deeper into the cabin. She followed them, taking a quick look inside the cauldron as she passed. There was a thick, dark viscous liquid in it that looked like tar. She shivered, ripples of light moving through her armour, and moved quickly on, following the orbs into a narrow corridor which went downwards, bending around and changing direction, then up again. They stopped in front of a door. Tori opened it and she was outside. Now she was standing on cobblestones. It was daytime and she felt she was getting closer to where she wanted to be.

She looked around her. Am I inside a castle? Is this the castle I saw in my other journey?

The orbs were harder to see in the daytime. She craned her neck and strained her eyes but no, there they were, over there! She ran, following them, and they moved quickly thorough a market and a manicured garden, another courtyard and then to a large door in a heavy, tall stone wall. Tori looked up to see the top of it, and it was clear that it was a castle wall.

'The back door of the castle?'

But the orbs didn't answer her. The door had a heavy metal bolt pinning it closed, but it was on her side, so she could open it. She struggled, trying to pull out the heavy handle, then she realised that she could lift it instead of slide it – she put all her weight behind it and released it, then the door opened. The orbs seemed more urgent now, they led her down another dark corridor and she had to move fast to keep up with them. Her heart was beating heavily, she knew she was very close.

It was a labyrinth. Left and right and left again, Tori couldn't keep track, she just had to trust she would find her way out when the time came right. The orbs came to a halt in front of an unobtrusive wooden door. She pushed it forward and it swung open heavily. When she went inside, she felt a sudden heaviness, just like before, as if she was suddenly under water. This must be the place.

And it was. Looking around, she could see the shelving, and many jars, with lights inside, different vibrancies, flickering. So many of them, such pain, languishing, loss. Grief was everywhere, she felt sunk, depressed, without hope. It's got to be a trick or something. This emotion will floor me if I don't snap out of it. *She girded herself and summoned all of her strength.* I am going to do this and I will succeed. *She whispered to the orbs, 'Show me where Aisling is, please.'*

All three orbs circled around the jars as if looking, then all of them settled on one jar, which was on a very high shelf.

Tori went over to it but she couldn't reach this particular jar. I need a ladder or a step, something to stand on ... Ah, look. *There was a small step ladder over in the corner. She went to it and pulled it over. It made a loud noise and her heart jumped.* Oh dear, that will call attention to me, that's bad. But I can't leave her here.

She deftly climbed up the step ladder and reached up to the high shelf, grabbed the jar that Aisling was in and carefully slid it out from the shelf. It was about the size of an ordinary jam-jar. She looked into it, knowing she didn't have much time. And it really was Aisling, looking small and helpless, sitting on the glass floor of the jar with a blank look on her face. Tori held her breath and screwed open the lid; it came off easily enough. Aisling's body shifted, then dissolved into itself, collapsing and rolling, it began turning many colours, then it lifted out of the jar like the essence of something potent and powerful, and grateful. It unrolled and stretched, then spun around, raced around the pantry as if it couldn't believe its good fortune, then came back to Tori, shot out of the door, and was gone.

She breathed out. That's it? Is she free now?

Tori looked inside the jar. It was empty. That must be it! *She smiled.*

Nobody was coming so perhaps they hadn't heard the ladder moving, and there were so many people here, she had to keep going, she couldn't leave them all trapped.

She reached for the next nearest jar and looked into it. Inside was a young man, he wore very old fashioned clothing, it reminded her of something straight out of Charles Dickens. She opened the jar, again, the shape of the person's body dissolved into itself, tumbling into different different colours and shapes. She shook the jar and the essence of this man fell outwards and into the room. Once it realised it was free, it seemed to leap for joy, racing around the room like a bright orange firework going off, then it shot straight out the door and was gone.

She tried another one, she didn't even look at who was inside, she opened the jar and the essence inside was green, and the next one was red. Another one was blue, then green again, and then she felt a kick in her side.

Marissa's body in the bed spasmed.

Tori fell off the ladder, dropping the jar she had been holding which smashed as she hit the ground. Whatever was in it got away quickly.

My armour? Why can I feel this? She felt another kick. This one was harder, right on her spine. It jolted her and the pain ran through her body and shot up to her head. Her ears were ringing now and she had fallen on her leg, it was twisted.

Marissa's body in the bed twisted up and the ringing in her ears brought her right back to the bedroom. She tried to go back into the journey, but she couldn't, she'd been kicked out of it, literally kicked, and she couldn't return, however hard she tried.

A spasm of pain wracked her whole body and the ringing in her ears was becoming unbearable.

It's only a journey. I didn't really go anywhere, did I? I made it all up. I'm fine.

She pulled herself up into a sitting position, but moving was incredibly painful. It felt as though knives were digging into her bones, fire licking up her nerves. She tried to focus on the room. But her body hurt. It hurt like hell.

There was a scratching at the window, Tobermory was looking in, wanting to come in, but Marissa couldn't go to him, not just yet.

Then her alarm went off for work. *Shit!*

She reached to switch off the alarm, but moving felt like knives cutting deeply into every part of her body. She wanted to cry. *Okay. I'm spasming up. But it's just my body being silly.* She held her breath and switched off the alarm, then reached for the bottle of water by her bed, each movement of her arm feeling like broken glass. She lifted the bottle to her mouth and drank. The water was flat and tasted awful, but she drank it anyway. It wasn't cold, but it felt wet going down her oesophagus and into her stomach. The texture of it helped her come more into the moment.

I can do this. I can get up. She lifted her hip up off the bed and – *ohmygod, I've never felt anything like this.* Fire and ice, knives and broken glass and electric shocks all at the same time. She had to lower herself back down once more. She broke out into a cold sweat and was panting with the pain.

She looked at the clock. It was a quarter past eight. Had it really taken her half an hour to sit up? She was going to miss her bus. Heck, she wasn't going to be able to get to work at all. *Damn, damn, damn.* She reached for her phone (*ow ow ow*) and texted Sarah.

My body is so sore, its spasmed up, it could be a virus. I don't think I'll make it in today sorry

Yeah, that sounds okay. She sent it.

Sarah texted back right away, as she always did.

Oh no, you're hardly ever sick, will u go see a doctor?

If I feel better I'll come in l8tr

Ah jayzys Marissa, its Friday, take a sick day and I'll see u Tues. Get some rest, text me l8tr.

It felt strange to see her name there in the text message. Marissa. She was Tori, wasn't she? *Getting confused.* No, she was Marissa. Tori wasn't real.

Right. I really need to get up.

She pulled herself up again. It hurt too much to move further, but now she didn't have anywhere to go in a hurry, she could take her time. She lay back down and closed her eyes. Her head was spinning from the pain.

This can't be real, can it?

When she woke up, it was ten thirty. She stretched. It hurt. But not as badly as before.

Maybe this is passing now. It would be great if it was passing.

Her bladder was full, really full. She had to go to the bathroom. She summoned all of her strength and sat up in bed. Her chest tight, her back aching like nothing she had ever experienced in her life, she swung herself out of bed and placed one foot on the floor. It felt as though knives were going through the sole of her foot. She had read a story when she was a girl, *The Little Mermaid*, in which when a mermaid got feet, it hurt her to walk. *Now I know how that feels.* She had no choice, though, she really had to go to the toilet now. She put her other foot on the floor and dragged herself to standing. *Yes!*

Hissing out her breath through her closed lips helped somewhat. *Now one foot in front of the other – no, wait, take the phone with you just in case. Just in case of what? I don't know, but I might need it.*

Okay. One foot then the other foot. She moved like the Tin Man – she couldn't bend her hips and each time her foot hit the floor, excruciating pain shot up her legs and into her hips and lower back.

She made it to the toilet and delicately sat down on it, grimacing through the pain. She did her business and flushed. The relief was immense, but only in her bladder. Her whole body was throbbing now, and she felt that familiar heaviness. *Wait, is that from the journey? Maybe I am really trapped there. Maybe I'm in a jar now too? Oh my God, what am I going to do?*

First of all, she had to get back to bed, she needed respite from the pain so she could think more clearly. She stood up delicately, held on to the doorframe and pulled herself out of the bathroom. She took one step, then another, and then she fell. She landed on the floor on her side. The pain was unbearable. She started to cry. This was excruciating, it was the worst pain she could ever imagine. She couldn't get up. She had to get help. Matt, Matt would help her. She would phone Matt. But the phone had fallen out of her hand and was just out of reach. With all her strength, she scrabbled for it with the tips of her fingers...

Yes! Thank God. She dialled.

'Hello?'

Oh God, I thought I was phoning Matt. 'Séamus? Is that you?'

'Marissa?'

'Yes! Oh my God, Séamus, I need help! I can't move, I'm on the floor.'

'What happened?'

'I was in a journey, I don't know, I think I'm still in there. I was kicked out of it, literally kicked in the back, and now my back is spasming and I'm on the floor. It's been hours. I'm in so much pain. Can you help me?' Her voice was cracked and faint.

'I'll be right there. What's your address? Grand. I'm not too far away – for some reason I felt the need to go to Southside today. I'll be there in about a half an hour.'

Marissa hung up the phone and cried again, then realised she wouldn't be able to answer the door while lying on the floor. How could she let Séamus in? Anyway, did she really trust him after what had happened in Clifden?

I'm in my pyjamas too – I look a mess. And what the hell happened there? How did my phone phone Séamus instead of Matt? I only just put his phone number in there in case I needed to follow up on the email... But maybe he was the right person to phone. Matt would just dodder about and tell me to make an appointment with Dolores. Or make me go to the hospital. No! This is connected to my journey, and I need someone who will know what to do. And if Séamus can't help, he'll know who can...

She took a breath. Could she possibly get up and answer the door? And maybe brush her hair and put on a cardigan?

She *had* to get up to get the door, at the very least. There was nobody else around. Matt was at work now and he didn't have the keys anyway; the only person with keys was her mother. She certainly wasn't going to be phoning her. She had no choice, she had to stand up.

She breathed in. *Ouch, that hurt so much.* Her ribs were digging into her, squeezing the oxygen out of her. *But I can stand it. I have no choice.* She imagined herself as Tori. *Pain means nothing to Tori, she could do this. Oh yes, she could do it.*

She needed something to lean into to push against to help her stand up. *The coffee table? Yes, that would do it.* There it was, not too far away. She reached out her hand and gritted her teeth. White pain flashed through her body, but she could reach the table with a little effort. She wiggled her hips and inched her way across the floor until she had a better grip on the table top. She waited there for a few minutes for the pain to abate. Once it had reduced to a more manageable level, she pushed down into her two hands with all of her might and used the table as a counterbalance to bring her body to standing. But she faltered and fell back down onto the carpet again, this time onto her backside.

She gritted her teeth as the pain flashed through her. *Breathe. He'll be here soon. I have to try again. Ready, steady. No.*

This time it will work. It has to. Yes.

She rolled onto her side, then hauled herself up, using the coffee table once more. She was hunched over, hands still using the table for support, but she was up off the floor.

The sofa next. I can get to the sofa. Small goals, small do-able goals.

Marissa slid one foot clumsily towards the sofa and put her weight on it, then flung the other one out. It came crashing down, sending flames of pain up her leg into her hip and lower back, and she saw stars and thought she was going to faint, but no, she was okay, she could do this. She put her weight on that foot and then hoisted the first leg. She felt as though she was moving a pile of bricks, but she was moving it. Teeth still clenched together, she was moving.

The sofa! She threw her arms out onto the back of the sofa and was able to get hold of it. She hugged the sofa and pulled her hips and legs towards it.

What do I look like?

She laughed at how ridiculous this all was. She'd been fine last night, she was always fine, this never happened. Now it had.

She was almost at the door now. Her body felt like two tonnes of bricks – no, three tonnes. It wasn't her body at all, this was a joke, she had stepped into a movie, one of those 'choose your own adventure' books. *This can't be real life.* The pain in her body said otherwise, she felt as though her bones were breaking and she was walking on broken glass, but she had to make it to the door.

He'll be here in a few minutes. Oh my God! Séamus will be here, in my flat, and I'm in my pyjamas and I can't even stand up on my own. That man will be here, that man I was so afraid of. What did he do to me that time? Stop it! I have no choice. This man will be able to help me. He has to.

More pain flashed through her body and she saw stars again. She stopped and held onto the sofa, panting and sweating, but at least she was still standing up. An image of Séamus flashed through her mind, her on the sofa, paralysed, him leaning over her. What did he do to me? I said stop it! This is much worse, so much worse, and if he can help me, well, I'll do anything. Anything at all. He's on his way anyway, I can't stop him from coming. Shut up, mind, focus on what I need to do! I have to get to the door. I need to open it. The wall – yes, I could use the wall.

Marissa manoeuvred herself so she was facing the wall and flung her arms out once more, shifted her weight and fell forward until she felt the strength of the wall under her hands. *Good. I've got this now.*

She shifted her legs again, shuffling tonne weights on each leg as she got to the door.

And then she was there. There was a soft knocking and a voice right outside.

'Marissa? It's Séamus.'

His voice so tender, so warm, how could she have doubted him?

'Can you open the door?'

She reached up, her arm all knives and fire, unlocked the latch and turned the knob. The door opened inwards, Séamus pushed it and knocked her off-balance. She was falling again.

He rushed in and caught her before she hit the floor.

CHAPTER SEVEN

When she woke up, she was lying on the sofa, still in her pyjamas, with one of her throws over her body. Séamus was on his hunkers down on the floor beside her. He was whistling something through his teeth, he was burning something in his hands...

She looked at him and panicked.

'Shhh, it's okay now, it's okay. Close your eyes. I'm here now.'

Marissa closed her eyes and drifted.

Everything was fuzzy, she was in an in-between space, gold and blue and white and dark and light. She could hear Séamus's voice singing – yes, there it was, his voice, the only solid thing she could find. She followed it, scraps and bits and pieces of her, tatters in the wind, laundry on the line on a crisp spring day, bits of fluff from dandelions and petals on the wind... She was floating, drifting... His voice, so beautiful, was pulling her in. *Follow the voice. But why? Why should I go back? It's so peaceful here – nothing to do, nobody to look after, nobody to explain yourself to...* She saw her mother's face, her father upset, and Matt, her beloved Matt, and so much to do, so much still to learn – no, she had to go back. Had she drifted too far? No! There it was, the song of life, the glue that sticks everything back together, that song, that melody... there! She willed herself to it, and met herself on it, and bumped into pieces of herself in it. She melded to other pieces of herself, connecting and reconnecting, weaving golden threads back and forth, forth and back, being woven back together by that song, back and forth, forth and back, stronger and solid and solid and stronger, and with a thump and a bump and a whump, she was suddenly back in her body on the sofa in her flat in Dublin with Séamus.

'There you are,' he said. 'Thank God. I thought I'd lost you for a moment. I was really worried there, genuinely. You're some challenge, Marissa. Keep me on my toes. It's a miracle you're still here. You must have some god's favour. What were you doing to be torn to pieces like that? Anyway. First things first. Can you move your body?'

Marissa opened her eyes. She felt the sofa beneath her and really felt heavy in her body. Then she remembered the pain, the excruciating pain throughout the whole essence of her being, and she was afraid to move. It was too soon. Fear of the pain rippled through her. But she couldn't spend the rest of her life on the sofa.

Start small, start small. Small steps. She wiggled her fingers – yes, that was okay, that was working, and it didn't hurt. Then she moved her whole hand, then her other hand and her arms. *Thank goodness, it doesn't hurt!* Lubricated with life-force energy, all of her joints were articulating smoothly.

What a relief!

She could hardly believe it, but *hang on,* she shifted her pelvis, *no, no pain now.* No pain in her back, or her shoulders, no pain at all. She was back to herself again. She sat up slowly, just in case, swung her legs onto the floor, keeping the throw wrapped around her for warmth.

Séamus looked up at her. Then he looked at the sofa, as if to ask her permission to sit beside her.

'Yes, please sit down,' she said, rubbing her eyes as if waking from a deep sleep.

Séamus stood and stretched, then sat down beside her, knees bent, hands on his knees as if studying her. He had on black jeans and a white shirt with a black waistcoat, his hair was in a sliver plait down his back. His denim jacket was thrown over the side of Tobermory's armchair.

They were both silent for a few minutes, then they both started to speak at the same time.

'That was some...'

'Thank you so much...'

They looked at each other and smiled.

'Thank you,' Marissa whispered. Not quite humiliated, but definitely humbled.

Séamus stood up and rubbed his hands together the way he'd done back in the workshops, when he was teaching the group. 'Have you any tea at all?' he asked.

'Oh yes! Of course! Let me...'

'No, girl, I can stick on a kettle. I'm not such a Neanderthal, I can do that much. Take your time.' He went into the kitchenette and filled the kettle from the tap and switched it on. 'That was something else. Something else entirely. Don't think I've ever seen anyone that... Anyway. Tea first. Yes. Tea.'

Marissa gathered herself. She got gently up off the sofa, testing her body, hesitant in case the pain came back again, but it was okay. It was clear. She stumbled into the bedroom, found her cardigan, washed and dried her face quickly and came back out again, scraping her hair back into a messy ponytail.

The kettle switched itself off and Séamus poured out two mugs of tea and let them brew for a moment or two. Marissa got some biscuits and milk, and brought them out to the table and sat down again. Séamus brought over the mugs.

'Sugar?' he asked, going back to the kitchen

'Sorry, yes, there on the shelf by the window. That's it.'

He put two spoons of sugar into his tea, stirred it and came back to the sofa and sat. They held their mugs in their hands and were silent.

'You were in absolute bits,' Séamus said after a while. 'Torn to bits, flapping in the wind. What the hell were you doing?'

Marissa took a breath. Part of her couldn't believe that Séamus was here in her flat with her, part of her was in denial that anything was happening or had happened at all, but another part knew he was here, and she was here, and she was lucky to still be here. She pushed the smaller part of herself aside and allowed the heat of the mug in her hands to bring her into her body and into the moment.

'I went to rescue a client,' she said slowly, 'from a psychotherapy session. She was trapped in a jar on a shelf with lots of other jars on shelves with other people inside them. I saw her there in a journey last night. I was upset, I needed to get her out. So I went there again this morning to set her free. It wasn't the same as last night, Séamus, the journey was longer, it was much more difficult to find her today. But I got there, I found her and I let her out.'

'What happened next?'

‘Next, yes. Then I let someone else out. It was easy to release them and they seemed so happy, so I released someone else, and someone else after that. This sounds so ridiculous, Séamus.’

‘Yes, perhaps it does, but it’s also very real. What happened next?’

‘I got a kick in the back. I felt it here, in my body, here in the flat. And then I was kicked out of the journey, I couldn’t get back into it, and I was in pain. So much pain.’

Séamus nodded. He drank deep from his mug.

Marissa stayed silent, not wanting to muddy the waters between them any further than she already had.

Then Séamus said, ‘You can’t go messing with dark energy, Marissa, especially when you’re not trained and you have no idea what you’re doing.’

‘You’re right, you’re right, and I’m sorry.’

‘You don’t need to say sorry to me, I’ve not taken you back yet, remember. But you *do* need to *be* genuinely sorry. Spirit is everywhere. It is watching you.’

Marissa blushed and looked down at the carpet.

Séamus was silent. His face was tight, he was inside himself, working something out. Then he looked at Marissa directly.

‘I got your email. I read it several times. I knew someone would leave and someone would come back to us this year, but I didn’t think it would be you leaving and you coming back. If I take you back, that is.’

He placed his index finger under Marissa’s chin, raised her face and looked her in the eye.

‘If you want to come back, Marissa, you have to promise me you will never do anything like this by yourself again. You always need someone at your back when you are fighting dark forces. You went into a dangerous lair on your own and anything could have happened.’

‘I know. I wasn’t thinking straight.’

‘Damn right you weren’t thinking straight. Lucky for you I was close by. Lucky for you, you had your phone near you and you phoned me. Lucky for you they didn’t kill you there and then.’

'Yes, I suppose am lucky.' Her voice quivered as she spoke and tears formed in her eyes.

Séamus's voice became very hard, then. 'Haven't I taught you anything at all, Marissa? There is no such thing as luck. You called this experience to you. You must take the learning from it, because you've obviously been given another chance.'

The tears were falling now. She couldn't stop them, couldn't hide them from him.

His voice softened. 'It's some hell of a ride you're on, sister.'

She sniffed and wiped the tears off her face with her cardigan sleeve. He reached for the tissue box and offered it to her. She took one gratefully and blew her nose.

'Let's knock this on the head right here and now, shall we? Put you out of your misery. You've had enough torture for one day. Yes, you can come back. It was always on the cards.'

Marissa brightened immediately. 'Really? Thank you, thank you!'

'Yes, really. No more messing around, though. This is serious work and you have to catch up. You have a lot to do. We're meeting at the Monastery in three weeks' time – that gives you three weeks to do six weeks' worth of homework. You've handed me your essay already – that email was spot on. Better than what most of the others came up with.'

She blushed again.

'I will email you with the rest of what you need to do for me, and but don't start today. You'll need the rest of the day to recover from this. Check in with the group and they'll help you catch up. Hopefully you've not burned too many bridges there.'

Marissa shook her head.

'Good. I'll make a move now. You obviously need some time to think about what you've done. Spirit has witnessed your promise to me. Make sure you keep it.'

Marissa closed the door behind him and stood there, the events of the morning reverberating through her body. Her flat was silent. She could easily convince herself that nothing had happened and get on with her day. But that was the old Marissa. Séamus's empty cup was on the coffee table beside her own, proof he had been there.

He never hurt me. She ran that through her mind several times, checking with every inch of her body, making sure it felt completely true. It did. *Séamus is a good man; he was genuinely helping me in Clifden. How could I have doubted him? And he just saved me from the most horrendous pain, put me back together again. How could something in a journey have such an impact in real life? What is real life anyway?*

Suddenly she felt sticky and hot. She needed a shower, she needed to change, she needed to text Terry and Saoirse. She was going back to the classes!

She looked at the time: 12:40. *I have a lunchtime appointment with Olive. I could make it if I hurry. I need the hours.*

She scrambled - showered, changed, grabbed some toast and ran out the door, incredibly grateful at how easy and fluid her body moved without feeling any pain.

By the time she was standing outside Olive's house, pressing the buzzer, it was 1:05 and Olive was waiting for her.

'Good to see you, if a little late.' Her tone wasn't disapproving, just a little impatient.

'Hi, Olive.'

Olive was all in green today; even her tortoiseshell glasses were green. Her hair was in a bun and she was draped in a light summer shawl. She let Marissa in and they walked together through the small courtyard into the glass room where she held her client sessions. Marissa appreciated the colours, light and sensations of being in the garden, bringing herself into the moment, slowing down her thoughts as she sat in her usual chair.

'You're looking very casual today. Are they doing casual Fridays at work now?' asked Olive as she sat in her own chair, opposite Marissa.

Marissa looked at her jeans and dirty sweatshirt, it was all she could find in a hurry. She smiled. 'No, actually, I took a day off for myself today.'

Olive smiled. 'Ah, good to hear that. Would you like some water?'

Marissa nodded. Olive poured some water from the decanter into a small glass and handed it to Marissa. The plants had grown and were taking up more space, but it was beautiful in the little sunroom. *Like being in the glass house at the botanic gardens.*

Olive looked closer at Marissa, she took her glasses off and looked at her again, tilting her head first to one side, then the other.

'There's something different about you,' she said. 'You seem ... taller? More present. Now, are we going to spend the session pussyfooting around your issues today, or can we get straight into them? I have a feeling you have much to tell me.'

'Yes, you're right, a lot has happened. And I don't want to be avoiding issues anymore – my own issues, I mean.'

'Hmmm... Good. You've been in London since I saw you last. How did that go?'

Marissa had to take a moment to orient herself in space and time. London felt so long ago.

'London. Ah yes, it was wild, Olive. I see now how little I've shared with you. And you gave me all the hints that I was able to – the shamanism book, the one I've not even really read yet. I can talk about everything with you, Olive. I don't need to hide myself.'

'Why of course, you always could, but I do realise how difficult it can be. And we all think that we are being judged all the time. I believe you judge yourself and what you want to say before you open your mouth, and that stops you from speaking. But I'm here to help you, not judge you. Don't forget that.'

'I need to fix this,' Marissa replied, looking down into her glass. 'I've made so many mistakes. I've kept too many things inside myself. I do need help working things through. I will talk more about it with you, if you'll let me.'

Olive smiled. 'I've never not let you talk, dear. It's always been you that was holding yourself back. Why? I don't know. These are your sessions, for you to talk about whatever you want. That includes not talking, if that's what you are choosing – I can't make you talk to me. But if you do talk, do want to share, then perhaps you will learn something just from hearing your own thoughts outside yourself. Or perhaps I might have something to add to them that will help you also.'

'I know.' Marissa looked up. 'I say that to my clients all the time and I never hear it when I'm with you and you're the one saying it.'

'Well, perhaps you have heard it today. And maybe you will understand then, when your clients don't hear it when it comes from your mouth.'

'It's strange, isn't it? How we expect people to hear what we are saying, but we don't really listen in return.'

'Indeed. Well, dear, there's always more to learn. And it's true, when we don't want to hear something, we just don't listen to it. Whether we are in denial of what it is that's being said, or we're just not ready to hear it yet. Now,' Olive wrapped her shawl around her, even though the room was warm, 'London.'

Marissa smiled, feeling affection for this kind and clever woman who had been there in the background, waiting patiently for her to warm up to her. It had certainly taken her long enough.

'London. Yes. Let me tell you all about London.'

Marissa left Olive's feeling much lighter. *Strange, when I felt much heavier after Séamus helped me. I'm happy with both.* Her heart was singing the song of life. The sun was out, and her body felt so good because it wasn't in pain. She hadn't realised how much pain a body could be in, and she promised herself to be grateful for every day she wasn't in pain.

She had told Olive almost everything – London, Scott, Isis, the ankh, how it was so ordinary on the Sunday, her clients, getting muddled up between shamanism, Reiki and psychotherapy. And the journey. She felt brave telling her, but she did. She even told her about Séamus coming to put her back together again.

Olive had listened to all of it, just as Dolores had, as if it was a retelling of a normal week in someone's life. And that was exactly what Marissa needed, because, well, it had been a week in her life. It was her sort of normal. The words Olive had said as they finished their session were still reverberating through her body.

'Some people choose to get up in the morning, go to work, come home, drink wine, watch tv, then go to bed. And they do it all again the next day. They choose to save money for a big house, a nice car or a holiday. Their life passes by, each day the same as the next. And that's okay, sometimes that's all they can do, or it genuinely is all that they want. But then, there are people like you. They grab life with both hands and shake the hell out of it until the lies drop away so they can see it for what it really is. They extract the magic and wisdom out of every moment, find the colours buried beneath the grey. They demand more – more from themselves, more from their lives, and more from other people, too. That's challenging - you open yourself up for disappointment, but also for a deeper level of joy. When you live truthfully and authentically, with integrity, the quality of your life is, well, it's more than going to work and coming home and going away for two weeks a year. It's a life worth living, a well-lived life. Well done, Marissa. I knew you were a girl after my own heart.'

Marissa got the bus home and spontaneously got off a few stops early, in Dublin city centre. She had nothing particular to do and nowhere in particular to be. It was Friday afternoon, Matt was still at work and there was plenty of time before their date that night. *That doughnut shop, and a stroll in Stephen's Green. I'm alive, and I'm not in pain. I'm going back to Shaman School! Olive doesn't think I'm an idiot and I'm doing something that I love. I'm grabbing life with both hands. I got my magic back!*

Sitting on a bench with a delicious doughnut and a cup of strong coffee, she savoured the flavours of the moment, watching the people walking past.

I wonder which ones are the ones that grab life with both hands? They all look so pale and disinterested, no, wait, there, that's someone bright and smiling, yes. And there! Yes, that woman there, and that man, they have a look about them like they demand more from life, too. But does it matter? Maybe it doesn't matter. What was it that Séamus said? Spirit is everywhere, it is watching you. Spirit knows who you are. She shivered. Spirit knows me, probably better than I know myself.

Fingering the ankh around her neck, she remembered Séamus saying earlier, 'You must have some god's favour.' *Oh, I certainly must.* She smiled and felt warm all over. Closing her eyes, she connected into her lake, her mountain, her bear, her guides. Yes, they were all there, close by. They seemed relieved, happy to see her happy, willing to help if she needed help. Her angels too. She was going back to the apprenticeship.

Shit! I need to get cracking on the homework – three weeks to do six weeks worth of work, that sounds like so much. I hope Séamus sends it to me soon! And I have to finish my essay for the diploma too, and get that sent in. I've still got Ronan's essay to read, and Sarah's too. And I haven't even told Terry and Saoirse I'm coming back yet!

Breathe.

She'd be seeing Matt soon, and she hadn't seen him in almost a week. She relaxed at the thought of his smiling face. *First things first.*

CHAPTER EIGHT

'You seem like a totally different person. I mean, I know it's still you and all, but I've never seen you this happy.'

Marissa had stayed the night at Matt's place and they were having brunch in one of the cafés in Dun Laoghaire. She always slept better when she was with Matt; her dreams were more settled, she felt safe when he was around. She enthusiastically cut into her scrambled eggs.

'I know. Long may it last.'

Matt raised his cup of tea in a toast. 'Long may it last indeed.' He smiled. 'So, what do you have planned for the weekend?'

After telling Olive everything, Marissa hadn't felt the need to burden Matt with it all, and she didn't want to spoil his delight at seeing her so happy, so she hadn't mentioned anything about Aisling, or the journey. Or about Séamus being in her flat. But she had told him that she'd heard back from Séamus, which *was* true, in a way, and that he'd accepted her back into the apprenticeship.

'I need to contact Terry, and Saoirse to find out what the homework is, and maybe meet up with them so I can catch up. I want to read over my college essay one more time, too. I'm pretty sure it's finished. And I've Ronan's essay to read. I've the whole weekend to get this all sorted out, though. How about you?'

'Sounds like a lot of homework stuff.' He looked down at his plate and spoke, cheeks colouring while he said, 'My sister and her daughters came over from England last night. I was hoping you'd be free later on so you could meet her.'

'Oh!' Marissa stopped eating and put down her knife and fork. 'Your sister? Wow, yes, I would like that. When and where?'

Matt mopped up some of his egg yolk with a piece of toast and ate it, then started to butter another piece before answering. 'They're staying with my uncle and aunt in Lucan. I didn't fancy a trek out there, didn't really want to see them at all, actually, but Gwen said she'd leave the kids at home and come into town specially to meet me for dinner. She wants us to start afresh, renew our relationship. I guess I should try, I couldn't really say no to her. I'll be happier going if you come too.'

Marissa didn't want to push anything, this was new territory, she decided to tread delicately and take it at Matt's pace. 'How old are the children? Girls, you said?'

'Yes, all girls. Six, eleven and fourteen.'

'Fourteen, that's practically grown up.'

'Yeah. I haven't spoken to them since they were little. Like three or four years old. It would be nice to see Gwen, to try again. Life really is too short. I've missed so much.' Matt wiped his plate with the last bit of toast and finished it off.

'Do you want any more?' asked Matt, pointing to Marissa's almost empty coffee cup.

'Yes, thanks. Why haven't you told me about them before – Gwen, and your nieces, I mean?'

Matt ordered another round of coffee and some more toast for himself.

'Dunno, really. You've always seemed so preoccupied with your own stuff. Always fighting something, working through something.'

'Hey, don't make this about me. It's not my fault you don't have a close relationship with your family.'

'Sorry. Yeah, you're right. Okay, well, I didn't feel that I wanted to tell you anything about myself.' He blushed again, and cleared his throat. 'The truth is, I don't like talking about myself. I get awkward in it. And there never seemed to be a right time. But it's different now. We're different now.'

Marissa frowned.

'Hey, it's cool, don't get upset. We've only been together a short time, you and me. You can't know everything about me all at once, hey?'

'Okay, I'll let you off this time. But I'm upset to hear that you felt you couldn't talk to me.'

'Well, like I said, that was then. You're more receptive now, you feel softer. And yeah, tonight's a good time for you to meet my sister. And for me and her to try again. Just don't ask us too many probing questions about family stuff, okay? Don't go and turn into a therapist, please? We had enough of that about ten years ago.'

'Sure.' *Curiouser and curiouser.* 'Matt?'

'Hmm?'

'I'm sorry things were difficult. With us, I mean.'

'I stuck around. You're worth the effort.'

Marissa blushed. 'Okay, I'll take your word for it.'

James didn't think I was worth it, Matt does. Am I that difficult, really? Maybe I am.

She looked up at Matt, who was smiling at her, and smiled back.

'Dinner's at eight, I choose a place on Camden St. Does that work for you?'

'Sure. I'll head back to my place now and get some work done. I'll meet you at the restaurant later.'

Perhaps we passed a test of some sort. It feels as though we've been tested, that's for sure.

They walked back to Matt's place so Marissa could get her bag. They snuggled into each other and held hands all the way. In a low voice, Marissa asked, 'Hey, do you want to stay over with me afterwards then?'

'I was hoping you'd ask.'

'I love you, Matt. You're worth it too!'

He shoved her and she shoved him back, and they laughed.

'We're a right pair, so we are.'

Marissa was on the DART heading back into Dublin City Centre when the email from Séamus with all her homework came in. Included was his official invitation to re-join the class:

> *It will be good to have you back, but you do need to catch up. Time is tight – we meet in less than two weeks. I'd teach*

> *you the extraction process myself in a catch-up session, but there isn't enough time. Perhaps you can get your classmates to show it to you and we can discuss it in Clifden together to make sure you're clear on it. In the meantime, you've got a lot of work to do. And you need to settle the balance of your fees. I know you can do this.*

Yes, I can do this. She glanced at the homework list, and then at the balance of fees due. He hadn't charged her for the missed workshop, but he had added in a small fee for coming out to her house. *Fair enough. Yes, I'm happy with that.*

She replied right away without hesitation, the small screen and little keys on her mobile phone didn't stop her expressing herself fully.

> *Thank you so much again. Yes please, I'll be there. I wouldn't miss it for the world. And thanks for helping me yesterday. I don't know what happened. I feel so much better today, and I know I still have a lot to learn. You're right, it was stupid. And I'm so glad that you were able to help me. I'll sort the fees out in the next few days. See you in Clifden in two weeks' time!*

That's it. Done. I'll study the requirements list, and see them all in two weeks' time. Can I get it all sorted by then?

She looked at the list again. The main work she needed to do was make five new medicine stones and learn the new extraction process, plus she had to do three chakra-cleansing and clearing sessions with family or friends.

It's not like me to be so behind. But she knew could create more medicine stones herself by journeying into each stone to find a guiding spirit and gift and blow the gift into the stone. She'd need to ask her friends for help with the rest. She might manage to fit one or two sessions in around the classes when they met next time. *I'll do as much as I can. I can only do my best.*

The rest of the requirements were a little easier to sort out, or so it seemed. She needed a pendulum, preferably one made of quartz. *What's that for? I'll get one at the Angel Shop.* She had to learn how to fold her medicine bag properly. *I still can't remember how! Where's that video of Brigid? I'm pretty sure I deleted it. I'll have to ask Terry to send it to me.* She had to know the entire prayer off by heart. *Well, that's not too hard, I already know most of it.* And she had done the essay, tick. *Yay!*

The workshop coming up was the fourth direction, the last in the series. After this, they would be able to work on family and friends, but not see official clients. *A little like Reiki Level 1, I guess.* If they wanted more, they could join for the advanced certifications. *I have a feeling I'll be there.*

Thinking about all the work she needed to do, she almost missed her stop on the DART. She walked to the bus stop, head full of homework, and the bus came almost at once. Soon she was walking along her road and letting herself into her flat.

The first thing she did, once she'd fed Tobermory and aired out her living space, was dig out her medicine bundle from her wardrobe. It was easy to find – on top of her pile of (mostly) black clothing, it was the most colourful thing in there. *Besides my orange top, my wardrobe hasn't really changed that much, has it?* She reached for the bundle, drew it out and cradled it in her arms for a moment before sitting down on the bed. She held it close to her as if it was a teddy bear. She hadn't reconnected to it since she'd taken it out of the box, and she felt bad about it. *But it is what it is, I suppose.*

Apologetically, she fingered the pattern on the cloth. It was a bundle of pleats and creases, it didn't look like a tight medicine bundle at all really. She really did need to learn how to fold it properly. She buried her nose deep into it regardless, hunting for any trace of Peru. Going beyond the musty smells of the box and the wardrobe... *Ahh, beautiful.* There it was – a faint aroma of musk, citrus, sage and fire. It took her right back through space and time to Peru. Colourful memories of the night with the medicine woman flooded into her mind like a river that had been dammed, one that was overfull and now gushing through her body, releasing everything, washing all the layers of her being clean. It felt good. She lay down on her bed, clutching the folded cloth to her heart and closed her eyes and went to visit the landscape in her heart.

She walked along the lakeshore, there was her dear friend, waiting for her.

'Emelda!'

They embraced, and then Emelda frowned. 'You have been a foolish, stupid child. It was a reckless thing to do, to go looking for that woman like that.'

Marissa was silent.

'You have much to learn,' Emelda said, raising her voice. 'I would slap you for your stupidity only you have suffered enough. You can see now, it is not sufficient to put on your armour and just go. Armour does not make you a warrior, it is there for a reason. For protection. To protect you.'

'But I...'

'Stop it!' She caught herself getting emotional, and toned it down. 'Marissa, Marissa, Marissa. You have a good heart. I know it is in the right place. But that was a wrong place for you and very wrong to go there alone.'

'I understand. I won't do it again, I promise.'

Emelda nodded her head, lips still tight with anger.

'Séamus said the same thing to me.'

'Did he now?' Emelda's harsh face cracked into a knowing smile. 'Well, maybe he isn't so bad after all.'

Marissa regained her sense of self after the shock of being shouted out. She smiled back. 'You knew all along, didn't you? That he never hurt me that time. Why didn't you say?'

'Sometimes you need to learn things for yourself.'

'I really did get him wrong. He's a good man and he's taking me back. So I will become a shamanic practitioner.'

'You got him wrong – what else are you getting wrong, eh? It's important for you to slow down. You're moving too quickly, you're full of impetuous youth, and you're entering dangerous waters.'

'You're right. I'll slow down.'

'Easy for you to say, yes? Not so easy to do. You will have to prove yourself to me with that one girl.'

'I understand. I will try.' Marissa remembered having a similar conversation with Olive.

'So, you'll become an Irish shaman now, eh? As well as the other type that you already are. You just remember who you are, eh!'

Marissa laughed and hugged Emelda. 'I thought the healing work we are doing was from your land – isn't that right?'

Emelda shrugged her shoulders. 'The work belongs to everybody now.'

'It's good to be back with you. You always give me so much to think about.'

'Maybe, yes. You be careful. I am watching you. As you have seen already, I cannot always help you.'

Marissa opened her eyes and turned on her side, holding the bundle close to her stomach. It felt good to lie down, to process everything that was happening. *Stillness. Yes, I remember Olive telling me I needed to be still. Now I understand why.*

After a while she rose, laid the bundle down on the bed and opened the leather thong holding it all together. She delicately unwrapped the folds of cloth to expose what was within: a little heart-shaped stone and a silver bear. *Pieces of me, they do feel like pieces of me.*

She lifted her little stone, her only medicine stone, small yet loyal, patiently waiting for her, and turned it around in her hand, looking at the place where it had broken. *It was when Zaad worked on me and healed my heart that the stone turned into a heart shape. I remember it now. How could I have walked away from all of this magic?*

She lifted the bear too, looked at his face and remembered her own beloved Bear. She was filled with love. She imagined him there with her, then she felt a deep sense of wellness. All was forgiven. She forgave herself. *That's what I needed to do. Yes.* Then the tears came.

When they abated she noticed a white feather had fallen onto her arm. She reached for it, plucked it out of her sleeve and turned it in her fingers with wonder. *Where did this come from? It's too big to be from the duvet. Is it from my pillow? No, it's too big for that, too. Angels? Yes, the angels are here!*

She sat up quickly, still holding the feather, but she couldn't sense any other change in the room. If angels were there, she couldn't feel them.

Thank you!

She placed the feather gently into the centre of her medicine bundle with the bear and the stone. *It is a medicine bundle, after all. And angels are part of my medicine.* An image of Emelda flashed through her mind, standing by the lake nodding her head, proudly. *I'm not that stupid really, am I? Maybe more enthusiastic than stupid.* Her thought sounded out to her in the accent that she attributed to Emelda. *But I thought I said that to myself, not that she said it to me?*

That brought to mind something that she hadn't thought about in-depth yet. *I see myself mimicking clients in session, and now I am mimicking Emelda. What is that about?*

It was mid-afternoon. She looked at the homework list again. *I'd like to do something today to check it off. I'll feel better later, knowing I've started the work. I need to contact the group and ask them if they'll be able to help me. I'll do that bit now.*

She got out her phone and wrote an email:

Hi, everyone, it's me, Marissa.
I'm coming back! Sorry for all the messing around. I had a spiritual crisis and needed some time, but I'm feeling much better now. I have a lot of work to catch up on, and I hate to ask, but I need some help with it. I have to make five medicine stones before the next workshop and learn the extraction process. I know, it's a lot to ask in such a short time. If any one of you is able to help me with this, I would be most grateful.
Looking forward to hearing back from you,
xx Marissa

No, that's a little formal, like work, but it will do. She sent it. *Okay, what's next?*

She emailed Terry and Saoirse:

Hi, guys, I guess you got the email I just sent.
Could either of you teach me the extraction process? Please? I know it's been messy between us, and I know this is a lot to ask, but I'd really appreciate your help. And your patience.
I'll get cake?
Lots of love, xox M

Okay, now I've got time to do one of the medicine stone journeys, then shower and change for the dinner with Matt and Gwen. I wonder what Gwen is like. Is she like Matt? Will she tell me more about their family? It could be very revealing.

She turned her attention back to the room and her medicine bundle and the work at hand. *Okay, I need a stone and I can do a journey. A stone that means something to me.* She looked lovingly at her lapis lazuli, still beside the bed. *No, I can't use that, that's my crystal from Matt, it's not for my medicine bundle. And anyway, Séamus said a stone, not a crystal.*

She got up and walked into the living room. There on the mantelpiece were three stones that she had on display. She had picked up two of them the day she was skimming stones with Matt at Greystones. The third stone was one she had found on the beach in Lima. She picked it up and held it in her hand. It was a strange shape – dark, long and skinny, sort of like a boomerang. That was why she had selected it. Holding it reminded her of when she had picked it up; Sarah had been swimming in the sea and she had been too hot to sit still, so she'd wandered down to the water's edge to watch. She'd noticed the stone amongst the other, more ordinary-looking stones. *That's me, not an ordinary-looking stone. Maybe that's why I chose it. A stone from Lima would be perfect for my bundle.*

Journey into the stone. Get a gift, bring it back and blow it into the stone. That's what he said.

She checked her notes.

And find a guiding spirit. I wonder what that is? Okay, there's no time like the present.

She found her headphones, plugged them into her phone and found the drumming track that she had prepared all those months ago. She was ready!

She held the stone in her hand and stretched out on the sofa, sitting up so she wouldn't fall asleep. The drumming track played. It took a while for her to tune into it. Then she remembered she had to travel into the stone. *How do I do that?*

She imagined herself getting very small, shrinking into herself, into her heart. It seemed to take a long time. Then she saw herself moving from her heart across her body, down her arms, into her hand and into the stone. It was dark there. *Of course it's dark, silly! It's a stone!* She giggled. *Focus, Marissa, focus.* She flexed her toes.

There was a scratching at the window. Tobermory was looking in, scratching at the place where the window opened. *Use the cat flap in the door you silly cat.* He insisted. She got up and let him in, and got back onto the sofa to try again. Tobermory ran around the flat chasing an imaginary mouse.

Marissa looked at the time. *I can do this. I'm just looking for a distraction.* She became very agitated. *I was so relaxed earlier, why can't I do this now?* Tobermory had stopped running and was cleaning his long legs, looking at her disdainfully. *Well, if you hadn't interrupted me, I'd be finished by now.*

She shook it off. It wasn't working. She took off her headphones, put her phone on charge, put the kettle on, then went outside. The sun was low in the sky and time was ticking. Sitting in her deckchair facing the sun, stone still in her hand, watching the light flicker through the leaves, she felt bereft. *There must be some other way to get into this stone and find out about it.* The sun was warm on her face. She cast her mind back to the beach on Lima once more.

She was standing there, on the beach, watching the sparkles on the surface of the water. She looked down. Her feet were covered by the lapping waves. It was beautiful. She saw the long, curved stone there, half-buried by her feet. She knelt down and picked it up.

There was an electric shock and it turned to her and started to speak.

'You never asked my permission to bring me to this cold, hard land. I loved the sun, the sky, the sea.'

'Oh! I'm so sorry, I never thought...'

'Humans! That is what is wrong with people – they think they own everything. And they never think of anything but themselves! You took me from the place I loved and never asked if I wanted to go with you.'

Marissa opened her eyes and looked at the stone in her hand. 'You're right, I never asked you if you wanted to come home with me. I'm sorry.'

She thought about all the other times she should have asked permission and hadn't. Remorse flooded in.

'I will remember to do that in the future with anything else that I come across in nature.'

She felt something tight inside her soften. She imagined herself small. It was easier to do it this time, maybe because she had just done it. She seemed to be drawn straight into the stone this time and found herself in a cave by the sea.

'I wanted an apology. I thank you for that.'

A beautiful pale woman wearing a light kimono-type shift placed her hands in prayer position and bowed to Marissa.

'I am so, so sorry,' Marissa said. 'I didn't think. Yes, you're right – humans, we don't think like that. And it isn't right. You have taught me a lesson.'

The woman smiled. Is she Japanese? *Her hair was in a dark black bun behind her head, held by long golden sticks. She was smelling peach* blossoms. Maybe Chinese? Strange! The stone was from Lima.

'Who are you?'

The woman giggled.

'Are you the guiding spirit from the stone?'

She giggled again and shook her head. Then nodded her head. 'Yes and no. I am the Goddess of Mercy. You are forgiven. Nice to meet you, Marissa.'

The pale woman placed both of her hands over her heart and bowed. Marissa did the same.

'The stone has forgiven you also and would now be happy to be part of your medicine.'

Marissa's heart lightened and she smiled.

'I will go now, so you can talk to the stone directly. I am sure we will meet again.'

The woman disappeared, leaving behind several delicate peach-coloured petals.

'The Goddess of Mercy. Beautiful.'

Marissa gathered the petals up and they formed a ball of light in the palm of her hand. In her other hand was the stone. She looked at it. It was darker now.

Blow the gift into the stone. Maybe this ball of light is the gift? I will blow it into the stone now.

She lifted her hands and carefully blew the ball of light across one hand and into the stone in the other hand. There was a flash and a sparkle for a moment as the energy appeared to enter and become absorbed by the stone. The stone radiated light briefly, then settled and buzzed in her hand. It felt alive now.

Nothing else was happening. Do I stay? Are we finished? Is this a medicine stone now?

The stone turned in her hand and spoke to her in the same voice as before. It seemed to have a face now – two dimples in the side were eyes, and its mouth was a nick that Marissa hadn't noticed before.

'I will be honoured to be part of your medicine,' it said. 'I represent the connection you have with your lineage, the line of great ancestors in South America that you do not remember in this lifetime. But we are here, and will always be here if you need us.'

The stone turned back into a stone again.

Tobermory was running around the courtyard and the sun had moved away from Marissa's face. She opened her eyes. She was cold. Her hand had tightened around the stone and it took a little more effort than usual to open it up.

She examined the stone. She hadn't really done this before she chose it, so she didn't know what she was looking for. The dimples and nick that she had seen in her journey weren't present on the surface of the actual stone itself. It looked like an ordinary stone. *No, wait.* It was heavier than it had been, weightier, more substantial.

Marissa got up and stretched and went inside to place the stone in the medicine bundle with the other stone. *That's better. Two stones, a bear and a feather. Thank you again.* She folded the bundle gently, wrapped the thong around it and tied it. *Not exactly right, but neater than before.*

She placed it on her pillow. Matt would be over after the dinner; it was wonderful she didn't need to hide things like this from him. Now it was time for tea, and a quick shower and change.

CHAPTER NINE

Gwen's energy was soft and welcoming, just like Matt's. She seemed much younger than him, as well as being younger in age. Her hair was more blonde than red, and her face was similar to his, but less round. She had green eyes that drew you in and a laugh that lifted your spirits. *Why aren't they in touch more frequently? She's great!* Lithe and stylish, she wasn't intimidating, and she was very funny, too.

'You may not have been in touch for a long time, but you both ordered the same thing,' Marissa observed. 'I guess you're more alike than you realise?'

'Perhaps,' said Matt with a twinkle in his eye, 'or perhaps we both just fancied the spaghetti.'

They all giggled.

Gwen talked about her children, Hazel, Rebecca and Charlotte, and a pony farm they lived next door to, where they were helping to look after a rescued donkey. The children liked to feed it carrots each day. 'It makes life a little more difficult on the school run, but it's worth it to teach them how to look after an animal.' They had no pets; Gwen's husband didn't let them.

Gwen married her father. That's what Matt said, anyway.

Not knowing enough about their father, Marissa wasn't able to agree or disagree. She wondered he was like. Matt had mentioned that he was a smoker and had had a heart attack, which was why Matt had given up smoking. Neither Matt nor Gwen had a good thing to say about their dad, he came up in conversation only in passing and Marissa could see how uncomfortable Matt was around the subject. She was about to offer something to them that might help, but Matt must have realised, as he warned her with a glare across the dinner table. She remembered he had said, 'No therapy.' She was his girlfriend, not his fixer-upper. She stayed silent.

'So, what do you do for a living, Marissa?' asked Gwen, once the waitress had taken the plates away.

Matt doesn't want me to mention therapy... I can't say I'm a therapist then? Feels like I'm treading on eggshells tonight.

'Erm, one of the things that I do is work for a software company, I'm assistant to the company director.'

'Ooh! That sounds interesting! What type of software do they make?'

'Mostly training programmes, office securities and encryption processes. The encryption and securities are so complicated, they had to go into making training programmes so our clients could learn how to use them! But they found themselves good at that, so they're branching out and creating training programmes for other things too. They're setting up new training division, and it's almost becoming more successful than encryption and securities.'

Matt said, 'I didn't know that, it sounds really interesting. What types of things do they offer training in?'

'Anything really, from bespoke systems to basic software systems, and they're thinking of doing the ECDL as well – that's European Computer Driving Licence.'

'Driving licence for computers? That's funny!' said Gwen.

'I know, they could have come up with a different name for it I supposed. The EDCL idea is brand new, they've only just started putting together the materials, and they might not go ahead with it. In my work, I mean. I don't usually talk about my office job, I tend to leave office stuff in the office.'

'I understand,' said Gwen, nodding her head. 'Many of my friends are doing well in their jobs. They tend to make careers out of them and leave their children in the crèche. I could never do that.'

'I think you *are* a career girl,' said Matt to Marissa. 'You're making your own career.'

'I suppose I am, in a way. I never thought of it like that before.'

'You said it's only one of the things that you do?'

Marissa looked at Matt. He nodded.

'Yes, I'm training to be a... a healer.'

'Oh! That's much more interesting than computers.'

Marissa noted that Matt liked how she said that. *See, I didn't mention therapy at all!*

They ordered coffee.

'What kind of healing?'

'Reiki and Shamanism, and a bit of talking.' Matt's energy levels flickered, but Marissa continued. 'I think we need to talk about what it is we are healing, so we understand it better. I've been studying for a few years now, I'm nearly qualified, and I'm probably eventually going to leave the office work, and set up as a healer full time.'

'Shamanism, that sounds scary. Matt? You said you were doing Reiki?'

'That's right, that's where we met, at a Reiki workshop.'

'Oh, how romantic! I like that!'

Matt reached out and held Marissa's hand. She squeezed it and they smiled. *Perhaps it was another test? I hope I passed it.*

'I really should get back to the children,' Gwen said. 'I have to get up at the crack of dawn for the flight home tomorrow, and it's so difficult getting the girls up and ready so early. I think we should pack tonight. Matt, you should come over to the U.K. and visit us sometime. Bring Marissa. Meet the children again. They're much bigger now!'

'Yes, I know they're much bigger. It would be nice to get to know them.'

'There's plenty of space in the house – you could stay with us.'

'I'll think about it, Gwen, but if we do come over, we'll get a hotel. I'd need my own space. I'll call you a taxi now – it will be quicker for you to get back to Lucan that way.'

After they had packed Gwen off in a taxi, they went back to Marissa's flat. Matt was quiet and seemed downcast. *Did seeing her bring up unwanted memories of his childhood? What can I do?*

'Would you like some Reiki?'

Matt accepted, and then went straight to sleep. She looked at him and was grateful to have him in her life. *The mysteries will untangle themselves over time.*

The next morning was Sunday, and Matt still wasn't his usual happy self. Marissa made breakfast for them both and they sat eating in silence.

Eventually Marissa said, 'I know you don't want to talk about this, or share your family stuff with me, but maybe you could do me a favour and I could help you in return?'

Matt muttered grumpily, 'What do you mean?'

'Well, you know I have a ton of homework to do for shaman school?'

'Uh-huh.'

Marissa cleared her throat. 'Could I do one of the cleansing and clearing sessions on you? Maybe it will help you feel better. We could do it here, I mean, if you want to. And the best thing is, for you, you don't even have to speak to me, or tell me anything in fact. It's just energy work.'

'Let me think about it.'

They took their tea outside. Marissa found the second deckchair and they placed them together facing the sun with a little stool between them for the mugs. *It's so nice here, just the two of us, no pressure.* But Matt definitely wasn't himself. *What memories did Gwen trigger in him? Oh, it's so difficult not to pry.*

'I don't have to speak about what happened?' he asked. 'In your session?'

'No, you don't need to tell me anything. And it will really help me, I have so much to do before the workshop. Please?'

'Okay.' He smiled. 'If it will help you.'

Marissa's heart opened as she felt Matt relax a little bit more.

'I usually feel strange after being with my family,' he admitted. 'That's why I try not to be with them very often. Maybe you understand now why I haven't introduced you. It's not about you at all.'

'I *was* wondering about that. I did feel for a while that you were ashamed of me, didn't want them to see me. But after a time, I realised you genuinely didn't want any contact with them. I can see it in you now, you're so tense. It's okay, Matt, we each have our things. This is yours. You've certainly seen *my* stuff from close up!'

He cracked a laugh. 'Yes, I certainly have. Tell me a little bit about your homework and the process you want to try with me.'

Marissa described the chakra-clearing process and Matt seemed more comfortable with it.

'Let's do it now,' he suggested, 'I don't like feeling this way, I want to enjoy the rest of the weekend. And if it shifts because of your work it would be wonderful.'

'Great. Let me prepare myself and the flat, and then I'll call you in.'

Marissa left Matt outside and went into her living room. Suddenly, healing Matt seemed like a big and important task and the room needed to have exactly the right energy.

The prayer! I'll open space. Of course! I need to do that. And sage, and maybe some aura soma too. She got her medicine bundle and placed it on the coffee table to help her gather her thoughts. Then she hunted out the complete text of the prayer from her notes and found the instructions Séamus had sent for the chakra-clearing process and reread those too. With each instruction she felt the process solidify inside her. As the pieces appeared, she organised them in her mind, like Tetris bricks in a wall, until they fit together perfectly. She had it.

I've not done a process like this in a long time, but it's Matt, so it will be okay, but it's Matt, I want it to be right for him. No going off on tangents, no rescue missions, just healing.

With her intention straight in her mind, she pushed the coffee table out of the centre of the room and stood there, facing where her phone compass had told her was North. She read out the prayer, changing direction with each verse, the words becoming stronger as she said them out loud, their energy rippling through her body, the energies she invoked rippling through her flat.

When it was over, she stood in silence. *Yes, the flat feels better now, more able to hold the process.* She lit her large pillar candle, found a brand new bundle of dried white sage from her supply, set it alight using the flame from the candle, and smoked the room. She mashed it out on the draining board of her sink, and placed it beside her shamanic medicine bundle on the coffee table. *That should be part of my medicine too. It felt right.*

She got the duvet off the bed, folded it in half and brought it into the living room, spreading it out on the floor with a few pillows for support. She put her angel cards and oracle cards beside her medicine bundle for support. She got her lapis lazuli too, and the quartz point, just because why not? Her drum was ready on the sofa too, if she needed it.

I have made an altar! All my friends are here. She looked around her, feeling whole and happy. *This is who I am. It feels good. Now, do I have everything I need?*

She looked around again. *Flowers would be good. Maybe next time. This will have to do.*

'Matt?'

There was no answer.

She went to find him. He was sleeping in the chair with the sun on his face. She kissed him softly until he woke up.

'Love? Are you ready now?'

He smiled. '"Love." I like that. Yes, I suppose I'm ready now.'

He got up heavily from the chair and walked slowly into the living room. 'It seems different in here.' He looked at Marissa. 'You seem different. Like you're wearing a headdress or something.'

Marissa smiled. 'Come here and lie down. I think we can manage this if all you do is rest. I can do all the work myself.'

Matt shrugged his shoulders and Marissa helped him get comfortable on the floor, with pillows under his knees and head and a light throw over his body. He closed his eyes.

He really doesn't feel good. Okay. This will help.

Marissa automatically was drawn to use Reiki. *Why not?* She connected to the Reiki light and drew some down into her body, then placed her hands on Matt's crown, then his shoulders, chest, hips, knees and feet.

He definitely seems more relaxed now. Now for the process.

She ran the energy up and down his spine which was easy to do because she had already relaxed his body with the Reiki. He flexed his legs and stretched out a little more, and began to snore lightly. She kept going, mapping his energy body onto her physical body. Wham! It felt as though a hole had been bitten out of her stomach. *Wow, no wonder he was shaky.*

She let go of the body map and had to make an effort to shake it off of herself before she felt ready to continue. She felt for Matt's sacral chakra, unwound it as per the instructions and let it spin for a time, then closed her eyes. She imagined her drum holding the space for her. *Lub dub, lub dub, lub dub. Why didn't I do this when I went into the stone yesterday? No wonder it was so difficult. Oy! Never mind.*

The moment was lost. She gathered herself and started again. She set the intention out loud to focus in a more refined way.

'Please bring me a healing gift for Matt that will help him feel better. Thank you.'

Lub dub, lub dub, lub dub. Her heartbeat slowed down, her body pulsing to the rhythm of the heartbeat of the world. Matt hadn't moved. He was peaceful. It was safe to go.

She started climbing down the branches of the tree to go to the Lower World, but was soon caught in a thicket of cobwebs, sticks and thorns. She had to carefully extract herself and watch every step, every handhold, going down and down. It never seemed to end.

Finally she jumped down out of the tree and landed on a path, still in the forest. She plucked some stray sticks and tattered webs off of her body, and then started to follow the path. It led her to a cottage, one that looked like it was straight out of the Hansel and Gretel *story.*

There were lights on inside and she could hear laughter. Looking through the window Marissa saw a small boy and an even smaller girl jumping up and down, clapping their hands with excitement. Their mother had baked a cake and was putting it on the table. Marissa could smell the warm sweetness and it almost made her hungry. Then there was a loud bang and everybody froze.

'Quick, upstairs, under your beds.'

The children dashed out of the room just as an angry man entered the house shouting at the top of his voice.

Marissa was transported upstairs. The young boy – Matt? *– was shaking with fear, his arm tightly around his sister, as they dove under a bed in a young boy's bedroom.*

The noise of shouting and clanging of saucepans was coming from downstairs. Matt, if it was Matt, was trying to reassure Gwen, if it was Gwen. Marissa could see that the boy was terrified himself, although his brave face helped his sister feel safer.

After a time, which seemed like forever, the shouting stopped. The sudden silence was almost worse.

A woman's voice called out, 'You can come out now.'

Gwen moved to go and Matt dragged her back in under the bed with him.

'Let me go first. They did this before, remember?'

Gwen placed her finger on her eye as if remembering.

'Exactly,' said Matt with a shiver.

Yes, it definitely was them.

The images were sharper now, they weren't in a forest anymore, they were in an ordinary house on an ordinary street. Marissa was watching from above as Matt wiggled out from under the bed.

'Shh, stay there, I'll check first and come back for you if it's safe.'

He stood at the door, alert for any sign of danger. Marissa could feel his fear as he stepped onto the landing, then slowly down one stair after another.

Gwen shuffled out from under the bed and stood at the door, watching her brother from a safe distance.

He got to the bottom of the stairs, then slowly opened the kitchen door. His mum was there, hunkered down and picking up broken bits of something. She looked pale and drawn, tears were running down her cheeks and her face was red and swollen.

Matt turned his head to look at the table. He looked about six or seven years old. The plate with the cake on it had been smashed, a hefty chunk of cake seemed to have survived and was on a new plate, the rest of it was broken and thrown all around the floor.

'You okay, Ma?' Matt asked hesitantly, double checking nobody else was there before entering the kitchen.

'Yes. He's gone, love. It's okay now. I'll be grand. And look, there's still some cake left!'

Matt got the sweeping brush and started to help her clean.

The images faded.

The gift! Don't forget the gift!

She was back in the cave from her journey the day before. The Goddess of Mercy was standing there, smiling at her. Marissa had a heavy heart from the images she had just seen, casting her eyes on the Goddess was a massive relief. She took a moment, then remembered the greeting. She placed both of her hands on her heart and bowed to the goddess.

'Hello. It's nice to see you again.'

The woman smiled. The most delicate peach scent filled Marissa's senses.

'I am Quan Yin. That is my name, yes I am the Goddess of Mercy. But you can call me Quan Yin. Here is a gift for you, for your Matt.'

She held out both of her hands, and inside them was a small bird. It was beautiful. It chirped and flew out of her hands and around the cave.

'Little sparrow,' she said.

Marissa nodded.

'Open your hand. It will come to you,' Quan Yin said encouragingly.

Marissa held her hand open and the bird flew around the cave a little longer, then settled onto it. Then it turned into a ball of golden energy.

"Thank you, beautiful goddess. I appreciate your help.'

The goddess bowed, the images dissolved, and Marissa was back in her flat.

She didn't have time to process what she had seen, or question if it was real. She felt the energy in her hands and, like a sparrow, it was chirpy and light and it felt as though it wanted to fly away. She cupped her hands together to contain it, then placed them over Matt's sacral chakra. After a moment, she placed her lips over her hands, opened her fingers slightly and blew the energy into his body. His body spasmed in a jump, but he didn't wake up.

Marissa waited a moment. The energy had gone in, most definitely. She closed the chakra as Séamus had shown them. Then she decided to use more Reiki to help seal in the process, and when she had finished, she closed the space the way Dolores had showed her. *I love this. Blending everything together makes so much sense to me.*

She stood up and left Matt still asleep. She stood in the middle of the room and felt the energies moving around her. She could sense angels, and there! Yes! There was Quan Yin, in her flat. Her new friend. She placed her two hands on her heart and bowed in the direction she felt the goddess was standing. She felt a ripple of pleasure go down her body, and something heavy lifted from her chest. She smiled. *Time to close the space.*

She found her notes and read the closing prayer, turning to each of the directions as she read, shutting them down. She needed to learn this prayer off by heart, too. The healing was done.

As soon as the last direction had been closed and thanks been given, Matt woke up with a stretch and a yawn. He reminded Marissa of *Bagpuss*, a television show she used to watch when she was little. He reached out and put his hands on his stomach.

Marissa went over to him. 'When Bagpuss wakes up, all the mice on the mouse organ wake up too.' She smiled. 'Hello sleepy guy, how are you doing?'

He blinked and smiled at her, and her heart did a tumble, he looked so sweet.

If that really was a slice of his childhood, no wonder he doesn't want to talk about it. Poor Matt, only a small boy and looking after his mum and his sister. Brave little Matt, no wonder it was second nature for him to look after me. I hope I can look after him. He deserves it.

Tears formed in Marissa's eyes just thinking about what he must have experienced. She knelt down and kissed Matt's face over and over again. He kissed her back and they embraced. She carefully helped him up and onto the sofa.

'Wow, such an outpouring of love!' he said. 'Thank you. I'm not sure how I feel, but that was strong. Thanks, Marissa. I think I'll need some time with this to figure out what it is and what it means.'

'So will I. Matt?'

'Yes?'

'I love you. I want to mind you and always be there for you.'

He blushed.

'Now. More to the point,' Marissa stretched, 'I've got some of my homework off my plate now, thanks to you, so I'm not feeling so overwhelmed. The weather is beautiful and I've got some old bread for the ducks in Stephen's Green. Do you want to go and get some fresh air?'

'Sounds like a plan.'

Matt didn't want to leave, and Marissa was happy to be in his company. After their walk they brought food back to the flat, put music on and Matt read a book while Marissa caught up with her essays. It felt free and easy to be together. He said he felt much better that evening over dinner.

'Can I just check something, in your energy field?' Marissa asked.

'In case you didn't do it right?' His teasing tone made her blush now.

'No, I just want to see...'

'Yes, of course you can.'

Marissa mapped his energy onto her own. It was quicker to do it now; it felt sharper too, as if she was wearing Matt over her own body and her body indicated to her where the imbalances were instead of her having to feel them deeply and extricate them from her own.

She quieted her mind. *Silence. No big gaping hole in my stomach. It seems much softer now, more manageable. Maybe that's what came back, the missing bit.*

She opened her eyes and disconnected from him, his face growing fuzzy in the candlelight. *So romantic. He's lovely and he loves me, and I'm helping him.*

'Well, am I in once piece?'

Marissa raised an eyebrow 'Hmm, now I don't know about that, but it does seem as if a big piece of you came back to you.'

Matt thought for a moment. 'Yes, maybe that's what feels different. I feel more together. It feels nice. Thank you for doing that for me.'

Marissa smiled.

'If that's what you're planning to offer to the world, then I'm supporting you all the way. You could do a lot of good helping people like this.'

'Sounds like a plan!'

CHAPTER TEN

Matt left Marissa's flat early to get across town to open up the garage. Marissa rolled into the empty space where he had slept and felt a sweet ache in her heart. *It really does feel like he's taken a piece of me with him, though. I wonder if I can get it back. I got a piece of him to come back last night, it shouldn't be too dissimilar?*

Before they went to bed the night before, Gwen had texted Matt to let him know she'd got home safely. She asked if they could stay in touch more often. She'd also asked for Marissa's number and whether she could text her, too. Matt had agreed that it felt good to get closer to her.

Marissa brought her awareness into the day. She had time to do more homework, she wanted to make another medicine stone, finish off her essay for college and do some light housekeeping. Matt *was* lovely, but the place always seemed messy when he left. It was also Reiki Day, well that's how she was coming to think of her Mondays, especially when she had bookings. She had two clients booked in for that evening. Deciding to start her sessions at 6:30 to give herself time to set up the room gave her a sense of peace.

Actually, I've the whole day free. I could be seeing people in the afternoon, too. It really is annoying to have to wait till Sam leaves before getting the room. I wonder if I can find another room, or get the room for the whole day... Maybe there's another room in the building free on Monday afternoons. What did Matt say? 'If you don't ask, you won't get.'

She sent a quick email to the letting agent to find out the situation in the building, just on the off-chance, and noticed that she had received a few replies to the email she sent to the shamanic group. Her friends sounded enthusiastic about her coming back to the class and many of them wanted to help. *Jenny and Stephanie – yes, that sounds great, I'll defo take them up on it. Finn? Maybe.* In his reply he'd said:

Yeah, I've been there myself, not sure if it was for me. But as you know, I'm back in it again, but I'm doing it for real this time, second time around. Would love to help.

That's three. Zaad hadn't replied. *Well, I've worked with him already. Maybe I need to do this with one of the others.*

Terry said he wanted to teach her the extraction technique, but he was on a photo shoot in Marrakesh. He'd be in Dublin the following weekend, staying with Bruce, who was also on the photo shoot. *Okay, we'll need to do the work in my place then if we want space and peace!* Marissa laughed, remembering Bruce with the pink jacket from their dinner. *Yes, he did take up a lot of space, both in terms of his personality and his physique.*

Saoirse had written too and was genuinely happy about Marissa's return. Marissa could feel it in the energy between the words she used. *Nice. She really was upset for me. I'm so glad we didn't fall out over her tracking me down.*

After emailing each other back and forth, Terry and Saoirse agreed it would be better if they explained the technique to Marissa together, in case one of them got it wrong or forgot a part of it. So they invited themselves back to her flat the following Sunday. *That's in six days time.* Marissa wrote back:

I'll get cake! Thank you so much. You are both angels.

They asked her to get a pendulum before they met so they could show her how to use it. *A trip to Dun Laoghaire? I guess I could try to squeeze it in but my week is already so full...* She looked at her diary: it was just as well they were able to come that Sunday, the workshop was the following weekend! *Cutting it fine, but there is just enough time to get it done.*

After cleaning the flat and finishing her essay for college – *Just one or two more things to add* – she had a couple of hours free before it was time for Reiki. *I can do the journey for my second medicine stone. After that, I'll have three. So satisfying to tick these things off my list.*

She set up the room, opened her medicine bundle and lit a candle. She had chosen two potential stones for this exercise, one from Greystones beach, the other from her garden. She held them both in her hands, as if they'd tell her themselves which one she should use. Then she remembered her journey. *Oh! I should ask their permission! I forgot!*

She closed her eyes and became aware of the stones in her hands. *I would like you to be a medicine stone in my medicine bundle. Would you like to work with me?* She heard a chorus of 'Yes please' in her mind and she laughed. *Both of you at once! I never knew stones could be so enthusiastic! I suppose I really do have a lot to learn.*

She looked at the homework notes again. She needed a black medicine stone for the next workshop, and the stone from her garden was kind of black. That decided it – she'd have both of them, *Seeing as they're both so enthusiastic and all,* but the garden stone would need to wait a little longer. *What is time to a stone? Will it even realise?* She found a small jewellery pouch that she wasn't using and put the black stone into it for safe keeping, then placed it gently into her open medicine bundle with her bear, the feather, and her other two stones.

Now for the work at hand. She sat down and examined the stone from Greystones. It was red-brown, more like terracotta in direct sunlight. *Not local then.* It had called out to her from the sea of grey stones that made up Greystones beach. There had been an issue with coastal erosion and at one point tonnes of stones from a quarry had been poured onto the beach, so there were many there that weren't local.

I wonder where you're from.

Marissa looked at the stone. It seemed slightly porous – was it a stone at all? She heard a 'yes' within her body, so she decided to go with it. *Because it is just a journey, I don't need to open sacred space. Or do I? I wonder what would happen if I did? It's an opportunity to recite the prayer again, and I do need to learn it off by heart. What's the harm?*

She found her notes and opened them at the prayer, tuned into the energy, connected to the directions and opened up a sacred space in her flat. She liked the feeling she got when the space was open.

Such calmness – no, 'serene' is the word. Serenity, yes, that's the right word. Now I've to go find a guide and a gift to blow into the stone, and then it will be part of my medicine.

She lit a candle for support, then went to get her headphones to listen to the drumming track. As she put them on, her body recoiled, as if remembering how agitated it had become the last time, so she left it aside. *Just going with my eyes closed and no background drumming then. Okay, I can do that.*

At the thought of her drum, she urgently needed to be touching it, so she ran into the bedroom and retrieved it, placed it by her side and ran her fingers over the tight animal skin surface. *Okay, I'm ready. Let's go.*

Lub dub, lub dub, she listened to her heartbeat, took her awareness within and sank down into her body.

She was in a marsh. The air was damp, the sun hot, and the colours around her were mostly greens and blues. As the images settled she could see she was walking along a marshy riverbank. There were tall rushes there, taller than she was, crickets and frogs chirping. Her feet were damp and the waters were dark.

She stopped walking and peered through the rushes to get a closer look at what was going on around her. People were working, dark-skinned people wearing thongs and head coverings. Some had sandals, some were in bare feet. They were very busy at the riverbank, working the mud through some sort of sieve, pouring it into buckets. Behind them was a half-finished pyramid. Ooh! Marissa's heart leapt with joy. Egypt!

In her flat in Dublin Marissa fingered the ankh around her neck, but she held her focus in the journey.

Marissa came slowly out from the rushes and walked cautiously towards the pyramid, not wanting to disturb anyone.

'You're a little too conspicuous dressed like that,' said a soft male voice from beside her.

Marissa turned and saw a gentle-looking man by her side. He was dressed in a white linen tunic and long white linen trousers. 'Can we fix this quickly?'

Marissa nodded, not sure who he was, but agreeing with his sentiment. She was wearing her black jeans and a sweatshirt, exactly what her physical body was wearing back in her flat.

The man lifted his arm, pointed at her discreetly and encircled his finger as if casting a spell.

Marissa looked down at her body. She was wearing a white tunic and pants, similar to his. 'Nice job!'

'Thank you. I am Thoth. We met before, only that time I had the head of a bird. I prefer to don my human clothing when outside, it's less conspicuous. Discretion is very important in my line of work.'

A connection to Isis, and yes, the Great Goddess had said that I would be working with Thoth. How exciting!

'Nice to meet you again.' They continued walking.

'Over there, from the river, that's where they get the terracotta,' Thoth said. 'They take wet mud out of the river and partially dry it in large vats, then shape it into plates, vases, mugs and bowls, into anything we want. Then it hardens in the sunshine, and to finish it we put it into the fire. After that, we can paint it! It's wonderful. I've been working on some statues, you can make a mould and pour the mud into, or you can shape them with your hands when the clay is still wet, and carve in the finer details as it dries. I like to make little people with the heads of animals – dogs, cats and birds.' He gave Marissa a wink.

She smiled. She really didn't know what to say to him.

'Isis told me to come and meet you,' he explained, 'and now seemed like a good opportunity. You can call on me to learn the deep wisdom of the mysteries of the universe. If that's something you're interested in?'

'Actually yes, I am very interested. And I do have a question, if it's not too much trouble?'

'Go ahead.'

They found a shady spot under a tree by the river and sat down, watching the people all around them. It was a nice space, not a market as such, but people were busy on the dusty streets, making things, selling things, laughing and doing business. There were people working clay and draining barrels of water on the side of the river. A woman was cooking over a small fire, wrapping meat in some sort of bread and giving it to the workmen.

Marissa turned to face Thoth. He had a kind and gentle face. Someone so important and wise is talking to me! This is incredible.

'Why me? I think that's my question. Only part of it, I mean. Tori. Tori Scarlett Lightbringer – who is she?'

The name felt difficult to say, even though she wasn't actually saying it out loud, she was saying it in her mind in full for the first time. The question suddenly became urgent, so she asked it again, with more confidence this time. 'Who is Tori? And why does Goddess Isis think she is me?' and then she remembered a missing jigsaw puzzle piece with a full-body shiver. 'And why did I think I was her, in one of my journeys?'

Thoth smiled. 'Isis did tell me you'd be curious, and sometimes difficult. Alright, yes. This is not a simple question to answer. How shall I put this? Tori is you and you are Tori. You meld into each other. At the lower soul level, no insult intended, you are Marissa, living in Ireland. Ah yes, Ireland. What a wonderful place. You live there, doing your work, meeting your friends, yes? But even so, Marissa feels small at times, does she not?'

Marissa nodded.

'Tori, on the other hand, is a higher aspect of you. She lives across space and time, can jump universes and timelines, go to other planets and dimensions. You are a fractal of her, similar in a way to the whole of her, but not as, say, comprehensive. Queen Isis told me that you have awareness of her. That is remarkable - do you, truly?'

'Two times that I can remember, when she has been near – Queen Isis, I mean. Queen or Goddess?'

'Both Queen, and Goddess.'

'Ahh okay. Yes, I felt myself as both Tori and Marissa when I was with the Goddess. But that time when I journeyed for Aisling, when I went to the... That time, that was the only time I felt that I actually *was Tori.'*

'You were interfering in that journey, no wonder you felt like you were her. Tori is renowned for causing trouble, she's a rule breaker as well as a light bringer. Although her interference at the best of times is well intended, it is still interference, none the less. When you break the rules, sometimes the rules can break you.'

Marissa shivered and looked withdrawn.

'I'm sure you meant no harm. However you still have much to learn. Which is why I am here! I have a sense about this. Your teacher, Séamus? He is a good man. He felt the draw I placed upon him to visit an obscure bookshop in the south of Dublin, so he was close to you that day when you needed him. He was rewarded with an esoteric book that he would not otherwise have discovered, and of course, by being in your presence also.' Thoth winked.

Deliberately ignoring the last part, Marissa asked, 'You know Séamus?'

'Ah yes, many a shaman walks with me, for I am the original shaman. I am Thoth, also known as Hermes Trismegistus, also known as the Great Wizard. I am the stem from which the branches, leaves and flowers pour forth. But without the stem, all the other parts are nothing.'

Marissa took another look at this gentle, mild-mannered man who was claiming to be an all-powerful being. It just didn't add up.

Thoth laughed. 'I can choose my appearance. Does my avatar's face not please you?'

'Avatar? No, it's not that, not that at all.'

'Appearances can be deceiving, dear Marissa. An avatar is how I appear to you, but it is only what I choose to show you, and may not reflect the truth of who I am. This is another lesson for you perhaps. Are you satisfied with my answer?'

'Oh, yes. Yes, a fractal. I will have to look that up to understand it better. You have given me much to think about.'

'Good. And yes, do your research. You must compare from many speakers, many teachers, to separate the wheat from the chaff in your mind. Of course you can trust everything I say, implicitly.'

Marissa laughed, it was obvious that he was joking with her. She felt free and easy with him, and he laughed with her, the light behind his eyes glimmered with the promise of multitudes. There was definitely more to him than his current avatar revealed.

'Now,' Thoth said, standing up and brushing down his clothing. ' You need to continue your work and I must get on with mine.' He looked at her, straight on. ' I offer to be your guide for this medicine stone, so you feel more connected to me. I know humans need something in physical form to remind them that spirit is real. You need a gift, yes?'

Marissa was beginning to realise just how immense this being of light actually was. She stood up and brushed herself down too. I can't assume anything. And there I was in awe of Goddess Isis, when this man is possibly twice as powerful.

'Thrice as powerful, my dear. That's why they call me Trismegistus. I am at your service.'

He gave a deep bow, throwing his arm across his stomach like a magician on a stage. A tall black top hat appeared in his left hand and a black magic wand with white tips appeared in his right. He waved the magic wand over the hat, and then held the hat out to Marissa.

'Dip your hand inside my hat and pull out a gift for your medicine stone.'

Marissa hesitated, then cautiously dipped her hand into the hat and pulled out a white rabbit by its ears. She laughed. The rabbit dangled in her hands and she grasped it by its body.

'A white rabbit means so many things,' Thoth said. 'Lightness, fluffiness. Don't take things so seriously. Also, all rabbits know the secrets of the mysteries. You would never think so to look at them! But why? Because they go down their little rabbit-holes to find them. And, if you're not careful, they will take you down there with them and you will become trapped. Marissa, look only for the answers that you are ready for. Otherwise, you may grow too large and become trapped somewhere you cannot get out of!' he laughed, then added seriously, 'It could be your downfall.'

The images melted away and Marissa was back in her flat, aware of the energy of the rabbit in one hand and the solidity of her stone in the other. She felt as if she had travelled a long way, the images had been vivid and clear and Thoth's presence had been very strong beside her. He seemed close to her still, even now, here in her little flat. *In my little life.* She repeated what he had said to her, to make sure she wouldn't forget it. *He is an avatar of Thoth, and I am a fractal of Tori. So much to learn!*

She took a moment to get her bearings and bring her awareness properly back into the room, and into the moment. *Feet on the floor, hips into the chair.* Her head was groggy, filled with information, then a huge tiredness washed over her. She wanted to sleep. *Do the work first,* she reminded herself.

She gently lifted the rabbit energy by its ears and placed it over the stone, but it wasn't going in, though. Something like the repulsion forces of a magnet seemed to be pushing it away. It just wouldn't connect with the stone at all. Then she saw a small hole in the stone so she placed the rabbit energy over it, then the energy was sucked into the stone through the hole and was gone with a snap. It took Marissa by surprise. The heavy feeling lifted and she became wide awake.

She examined the stone. *Has it changed colour?* No, it looked exactly the same as it had done before she began. But she wasn't that familiar with it, would she really notice a change or a shift in it? *Maybe not.* She had to trust that she had done what she had set out to do. She heard a voice inside her head say: *And not get sucked down a rabbit-hole!*

Ahh. Rabbit energy, sucked down a rabbit hole in my rabbit-hole-terracotta-Thoth-stone from Egypt. Well it's from Egypt now, that's for sure!

She stood and stretched, then looked down at her medicine bundle. Bear, feather, heart-shaped stone, curved Lima boomerang stone and now a terracotta Thoth stone. *I like Thoth. I'm grateful that he is one of my guides, and very happy I can put his energy into my medicine.*

She folded her bundle, a little neater than the last time she did it, tied the thong tight, then looked at the time. Although a nap would be wonderful she had to get going and prepare the room for Reiki. Her clients would be arriving soon.

CHAPTER ELEVEN

She was lying on the forest floor. Ah yes, this is the dream where I'm dead and all the parts of my body are scattered around on the ground and I put them back together. I remember!

There was an animal watching her, hidden by the trees, bright eyes staring, but she wasn't afraid. She reached her hand out, but there was no hand, nor was there an arm. She lolled her head from side to side. It really was most unladylike.

Am I just a head this time? Where is the rest of me?

She looked around, but she could not turn her head. She closed her eyes and sensed her body was strewn all around her on the forest floor. There were many more than three heavy chunks this time. Her heart fell, but then rose again to the challenge.

Right then, I have to put myself back together. But where do I start?

Before she could begin, however, a large black four-legged creature stepped out of the woods. It looked like a large, very old wolf. It stared down at her, blood rippled on its mouth, saliva dripped down its jowls.

'What do you want from me? Is it you that keeps doing this to me?'

When she spoke to it, it looked her directly in the eye, whimpered, then turned into a dog, wagged its tail and ran away.

Strange.

Marissa woke up and bleary-eyed, went on autopilot for her morning routine, and made her way into work. Tuesday felt strange without college to rush over to at the end of the day. She had nothing lined up to do that evening, but Matt had said he'd come over around 9pm and stay the night. Instead of focusing on her tasks, she daydreamed about organising herself so that she'd have her homework done before the final workshop.

But I still have to find two more clients for my chakra-clearing process – it's all very well deciding when I'll do it, but with whom? And, feck, I still need to catch up on my psychotherapy hours. Maybe I'll take all summer to do my hours. But that would mean I wouldn't get the diploma till later this year! But it would take the pressure off... Oh No! I need finish my hours sooner than that to be able to apply for the degree. She sighed out loud, surprising herself. She looked around, nobody seemed to notice.

I'm wasting my time at work when I could be getting all of my real work done. Guilt crept into the pit of her stomach when she remembered Noreen's generosity towards her. This work was real work too, just not the work she was most interested in. Still agitated, she looked across the room at Sarah's new office. The blinds were semi-closed, but she could just about make out Sarah at her desk, head down, reading something.

This is the work Sarah's come alive with - she really has done an amazing job, finishing night school with honours and now getting full board approval on her project. She's moving up in the world, and quickly, too. Impressive woman, hiding her light for so long. And so different from who she was when we went to Peru. Oh! Maybe I'll ask Sarah if she'll be a client and do the chakra-clearing process with me? Then I'll only need one more person! That's a great idea. I'll ask her at coffee, if she's around. Or I'll email her, yes maybe I'll email her once I finish this job.

Marissa's mind then floated to her Reiki room, she still hadn't heard back from the agent about the extra hours on Monday. *Maybe I'll write to them again? No, get a coffee, settle down, finish this spreadsheet. Hold it all together, Marissa, no need to get scatter-brained.*

She laughed at herself. This time a few months ago she'd been anxious for a completely different reason. *Funny how things change so quickly. Terry is flying to Marrakesh today for his photo shoot.* She looked up the weather in Marrakesh. *Wow, that's hot! Who will be my second person? Eli didn't like Reiki, I can't ask him to do this, it's much more intense. Or can I? I wasn't in a good space when I worked on him the last time. And he does owe me a favour, or three... I'll think about it.*

She emailed Sarah.

Hello, Ms Managerial Lady, are you free sometime for a healing session with me? It's not Reiki this time, though, it's shamanic healing.

The answer came back right away:

Ooh, that sounds intriguing, what is shamanic healing?

Marissa smiled as she typed a quick reply:

It's different from Reiki, it's difficult to describe it. It's a little more pro-active, I will take a look at your energy field, clear away blocks to your energy centres, then go on a shamanic journey for you and bring you back an energetic gift, which will help your energy flow.

Ooh, anything to help my energy flow! Will that help my workflow too? Thanks for asking!

It might do, if your energy is in flow, everything else flows better too. That's what my teacher said anyway! But when could we do it? I'm free tonight, or next Monday evening?

Tonight is good - Where?

My flat? I have all my stuff there. We could get dinner together too. Matt's coming over at 9, so as long as we are finished the healing work before he comes, you can stay as long as you like.

Oh, I get to meet him again! Sounds great.

The afternoon at work wasn't so bad after that. Knowing that she would be making progress with her homework list, Marissa was better able to push her thoughts away and focus on the work at hand. But it still felt strange to be at her desk on a Tuesday past 4.30pm.

Sarah showed up at her desk at ten to five in a short pencil skirt, her growing bob scraped up into a tiny ponytail. Two long strands of twisted hair covered her face. She looked quite demure.

'I declare the working day to be over,' she said. 'Shall we get some food? There's a Mexican place down the road that only just opened last weekend. I'd love to try it. Shall we go?'

'Sounds great. My treat for you going out of your way for my homework!'

'But you're working on me, that's not fair. Let's go Dutch.'

The girls got back to Marissa's place around 7pm. It wasn't ready for a healing session, the air felt stale from being closed up all day. Marissa opened the back door and a blast of fresh air came in. Tobermory stretched and leapt off his armchair, brushed against Sarah's legs and started to purr.

'Oh, hello, kitty cat, you're so pretty!'

Tobermory walked a circle around Sarah as if showing off how beautiful he was. Marissa laughed.

'I need a few minutes to arrange the room before we can do the session. How are you feeling?

'Okay. I'm a little hyper, though, after all that food. Didn't your burrito look great? I must order one of those next time. We should go back there again, take everyone – how about an office night out? I'll ask Noreen. I'm sure it will go down well with the gang, and we can try the Margaritas!'

Sarah couldn't settle. She walked around the flat, examining what was in the kitchen, looking at Marissa's books on the shelf and playing with Tobermory.

Marissa decided to have her lie on the sofa for the healing process, rather than on her duvet on the floor. She got a few throws together, and a candle, and laid her medicine bundle and drum on the coffee table for support.

'I think I'm ready now,' she said, lighting the candle.

Sarah shivered. 'I don't know if I am. It sounded like a good idea earlier, but I'm a little anxious now. What are you going to do to me?'

Marissa smiled. 'I suppose it does sound a little scary, shamanic healing. I was scared of it myself, and some of it still is scary at times.

But it's very powerful and real, and it can really help you with how you're feeling.'

'Can it get rid of my anxiety?'

'Depends what you're feeling anxious about...'

'Well, promise you won't say anything to anyone?'

'Yes, of course. Anything you say to me here is between you and me, and I won't tell anyone, unless of course I think you're going to do harm to yourself.'

'Harm to myself? No, I would never. Hey, that girl, is she better now? From your sessions. Where are they ...? Oh yes, the women's refuge.'

Marissa smiled. 'She's doing much better now, yes, and I know it wasn't my fault. Thanks again for your support with that, but this is about you, not about me.' *It's funny how people so quickly turn something around if they want to avoid a topic.*

'Okay. So shall I lie down on the sofa?'

Shit! I have to open space.

'Do you mind waiting a moment while I open sacred space? It's just a prayer I need to say, before I do any work' *I guess it could be a poem, or an invocation, or all three. Maybe for people that don't like the idea of a prayer.*

Sarah smiled, sat down and crossed her legs at the ankles, not still, but rocking her body softly. Marissa noticed her agitation seemed to be amplified.

I'll see if I can do this silently. Marissa got the prayer out and read it quietly to herself. She was becoming very familiar with it now and practically knew it by heart, but she wanted it in front of her just to be sure.

'Good. Ready to go.' She turned her full attention to Sarah. 'So you said you want to work on releasing anxiety?' *I'm not sure if we've actually applied this process to a specific issue, but maybe they did it in the workshop I missed. I'll go with the flow of this and see where we end up.*

'Yes.' Sarah's voice was a little shaky.

In a gentle tone Marissa asked, 'Do you know what the cause of your anxiety is?'

'I think it's mostly coming from thinking I'm not good enough.' Sarah tucked a stray hair behind her ear, looking a little lost.

But then something changed. Marissa saw a resolution in her face, a determination to confront her anxiety head on.

I hope I can do her justice.

Sarah composed herself and took a breath. 'At work. I get anxious now that I am a manager, but more lately, since I have more responsibilities. Did I tell you they're going to ask me to be in charge of the ECDL project? It was my ideal, the ECDL, but managing it feels too much too soon.'

'I know you can do it though, you're doing such a great job already. You're a much better manager than I could ever be, a better manager than many of the others, in fact. You're a natural.'

Sarah blushed, and seemed to relax a little bit. 'But I feel so unsure of myself at times, and I've made so many mistakes.'

Some of the wisdom from Marissa's Scott Taylor books came tumbling into her mind. *Oh no! But wait, don't push it away. If it's good, it's good. I can take the learning and leave the dark energy out of it.* Marissa felt something inside her strengthen.

'Mistakes are how you learn. As long as you don't chastise yourself for a mistake, and chalk the learning up for next time, then you can benefit from it. It might even have happened for a reason.'

Marissa felt good sharing that. She was making peace with Scott. *No, not with him, with myself for falling so hard for him. I forgive myself for that. I didn't know.* Something lifted from her heart and her stomach unwound a little bit. *Ooh, I felt that. I didn't know I was holding it in my body.*

She hesitated, just in case there were any repercussions from going into Scott territory, but nothing happened. *Maybe because I didn't say his name? No, all good.*

Sarah was still sitting with her words. 'Yeah, okay, that makes sense, though it's hard to do, my 'inner critic' is quite harsh. And on top of that, I'm pretty sure that Mr Browne, on the board of directors, is watching my every move. So he'll see any mistake I might make - it's really freaking me out.'

'Mr Browne? Which one is Mr Browne... Ah yes, Noreen told me about him. She said he's always looking at people of promise. If he's taking an interest in you, it could be a good thing.'

Sarah's eyes widened. 'People of promise? Really? I thought he just fancied me! That makes me feel better.'

'Not thinking you're good enough is based on your confidence levels. It's – hang on a minute, sorry about this.'

Marissa went through her notes again and found the description of the chakras and the drawing of the human body with the chakras on it.

'Ooh, what's that?'

'A diagram of the energy centres, the chakras. Séamus said they discovered them back in India in ancient times. Anyway, each energy centre is connected to something and I just want to see which one is for self-confidence. Ah, here it is. The solar plexus chakra.' Marissa pointed at the diagram.

'The stomach?' asked Sarah. 'Makes sense, I get anxiety a lot in my stomach. Oh, but there's me eating too much taco! It was delicious, though. Will a full tummy affect the healing?'

'I shouldn't think so. This is for the energy body, not the physical body. We can go easy though, and if it's uncomfortable, tell me, okay?'

Sarah's stomach growled. She smiled and said, 'Okay. Hey - will this make me more confident? If so, then it's worth it, even if it is uncomfortable. I'm tired of second-guessing myself all the time.'

'This healing is supposed to remove all the energetic blocks around your issue,' Marissa admitted. 'But how effective it is, I guess, depends on you and how ready you are for it. I do think that changing your thoughts around self-confidence will really help. You can frame stuff differently. For example, knowing that Mr Browne is watching you because you're a person of promise instead of thinking that he wants to see you fail changes something in you, even though the situation has not changed.'

'Framing stuff differently – okay, instead of thinking it's the worst possible scenario...'

'...don't take it personally. Exactly! I want to weave the energy work with psychotherapy, I need to learn how to do it for Reiki but it looks like it would come in very useful with shamanism too. I suppose if you were to keep thinking the same way after any type of energy work, it wouldn't be as powerful a shift as it would be if you shifted your thinking, too. That makes sense. I'd be interested to hear from you if doing both does make a difference.'

'I'll try it, and of course I'll tell you.' Sarah smiled.

Marissa smiled in return. 'Thanks, that means a lot to me. Okay, back to business.' She read from her notes. '"Solar plexus – above the belly button, self-esteem, confidence, responsibility and personal power."'

'Personal power. I like that. I'd love some more of that. Can you get me more of that?'

'I'll do my best. I'll need you to lie down on the sofa, but then all you'll need to do is rest and relax. I'll be working on you or above you, You might feel hot or cold – I have a blanket here if you need one. I'll be blowing the energy that I get for you into your solar plexus. That could feel weird.'

Sarah giggled.

'Can you take off your shoes please and lie down?'

Marissa helped Sarah settle, covered her legs with a blanket, then proceeded with the body mapping. As soon as she started, something twinged in her right shoulder. She made some space in her mind to connect to Sarah's energy body. *Right hip feels weak? Is that right? And there's a pulling in my lower back, okay, and a lightness in my stomach, not as much as there was for Matt, but yes, it feels as though there's something missing. I'm feeling I'm more in the right side of my body than the left side. Doesn't feel like me at all!*

She looked at Sarah, who was wide awake and smiling up at her.

Might as well ask her.

'Do you have a pain in your back?'

'Not right now, but when I have to stand for a long time, yes.'

Marissa nodded. 'Do you have anxiety now?'

'A little. You're quite scary standing over me like that, Ms Shaman Medicine Woman!'

Marissa softened. 'Okay, Ms Amazing Manager Woman, I think I know everything I need to know for now.'

She released the energy and shook herself free of Sarah's body map. But then when she went to place her hands on Sarah's crown, Sarah stiffened. *Maybe there's more to this than I realise. I'll connect to*

Reiki. That will help her relax a little.

Marissa closed her eyes for a moment, drew down the Reiki light and felt it flowing through her shoulders, down her arms and out through her hands. She moved to Sarah's feet, knelt on the floor and placed one hand on each of the feet under the blanket.

'That tickles!'

Sarah laughed, then seemed to relax.

'Better?'

'Yes. Actually, I feel much better.'

'That's good.'

Marissa moved to Sarah's head and placed both hands on her crown, hunkering down on the floor once more. Sarah did seem substantially more relaxed.

Can I run energy on her spine from here? It's quite uncomfortable working at this angle. Marissa visualised the quality of the energy coming from her hands changing and light and fire rushing through Sarah's body, going up and down her spine.

Sarah jumped as if she'd got an electric shock.

'Sorry! Too much?'

Sarah nodded.

Marissa softened the intensity and Sarah relaxed once more.

I have to be careful with this.

After a moment or two, Marissa sat cross-legged on the floor facing Sarah and leaned over to open her solar plexus chakra. It didn't feel right, she couldn't feel the chakra at all. She leaned in to get closer, to it, yes, she was right, it seemed that there was nothing there at all. *So strange! How can a chakra just disappear? Well, Sarah doesn't seem upset. Guess I'll just continue.*

Marissa's back strained as she hunched over Sarah's body. It's so uncomfortable working like this, I should buy a stool. Or get my plinth for when Terry and Saoirse come on the weekend. Yes, that's a good idea. Okay, back to Sarah. Does she really have no solar plexus chakra at all? Or maybe it's so tiny I can't sense it. Ahh, that must be it. It really does need some help then.

She switched position using the sofa as support, and sitting cross-legged on the floor with Sarah behind her and her drum on her lap. She tapped the bison skin with her fingertips.

Tap tap, tap tap, *lub dub, lub dub...*

'Whatcha doin?' Sarah sat up.

'Oh! Sorry, I never said. I'm going on a shamanic journey now to get your energy for you. I just need the drum to support me while I go.'

'Oh, okay. I didn't know. The sound was weird. Kind of nice, though. I like your drum. I didn't know you had one.'

'Shh, you're distracting me!'

'Oh sorry!' Sarah giggled and lay back down again. 'Don't you need some drug or something to go on a journey?'

'No, just my drum. Sssshhh!'

Sarah flexed her legs and wiggled her toes. Marissa couldn't help but laugh.

I am setting an intention to get the energy that Sarah needs to reactivate her Solar Plexus chakra so that she is confident and strong in her sense of who she is.

Lub dub, lub dub. *There it is now.* Lub dub, lub dub. *I have it.* Lub dub. *I hope Sarah stays quiet.* Lub dub. *Family and friends are much harder work than people I don't know, ha, ha.* Lub dub, lub dub.

She was flying. Oh, this is nice! *Flying over an ocean of water.* Am I some sort of bird? *She ebbed and banked in the breeze and adjusted her height, then went higher. She could see the frothy tips of waves beneath her and there – there! Her sea serpent! In the sea!* Of course! But how did he get to the sea from the lake? *Still, there he was, rollicking in the surf.*

She flew down to get a better look at him. He recognised her at once and raised his head and roared, a loud sonic roar, like a trumpet. It boomed out across the sky and reverberated through her whole body. It was a blast of power, she felt freer as a result, as if he had blasted off caked dirt from her wings. She stretched them out. No, she wasn't a bird, her wings were large and translucent. She wobbled then, loosing her balance, forgetting how to fly. Thankfully she was coming up to a small island , she focused on the beach and landed ungracefully on all fours, like a cat. Her wings had dissolved. The beach was made of crystal sand, turquoise and pink, various grades, winking and sparkling in the sunshine. It was stunning.

Marissa turned to the sea and looked at the beautiful face of her friend. His friendly eyes shone. If sea serpents can smile, then he's certainly smiling. *She smiled back and sat down on the beach, looking out towards the sea.*

Sarah. Energy. What do I need?

There was a beautiful shell on the sand by her feet. It glistened and she felt compelled to pick it up, but she turned it over instead. It had white and cream whorls and the inside was a ripe, delicate pink. Is this the gift for Sarah? *A crab scuttled out of the shell, leaving it empty.* Just as well I didn't pick it up right away then!

Marissa knelt down, got the shell, held it up to her ear and listened. She heard a woman's voice from far away, singing a familiar song.

'Hush, little baby, don't say a word, Mama's gonna buy you a mockingbird, and if that mockingbird don't sing, Mama's gonna buy you a diamond ring.'

It was a sweet voice, soft and lilting. Marissa moved the shell away from her ear and it faded away, she could hear the sea once more.

There, in the waves, she thought she saw something moving. It was coming closer, but then it stopped. She strained her eyes to get a better look. Not the sea serpent this time no, it was a woman!

As she approached the sandy shore, Marissa could see her better. She had long, red hair and was semi-naked. She was waving at her. Was she standing on some sort of shell? The Birth of Venus? It can't be!

Marissa stood there and waved back, wondering if she was making this up.

The woman was not coming any further in. She beckoned to Marissa to come into the water and join her. Why not?

Marissa stepped up to the surf and got her feet wet. She could see now that there was no shell at the woman's feet, she was half in the water and half out. Marissa approached her, as soon as the water touched her body she shivered, The woman dove deep below the waves, flicking a large shiny tail – It's a mermaid! – *down deep beneath the surface of the sea. Marissa followed, a tail appearing behind her, propelling her downwards, and quickly too. It felt amazing, similar to flying.*

She followed the mermaid past a kelp forest lit with hundreds of tiny lights, and into a cave. She didn't know if she could talk, or even breathe. She touched her neck and found she had gills, so she tentatively took a breath. Yes, it was fine.

'You are finding your way,' the mermaid said, more as a voice in Marissa's head than one spoken out loud. 'Good! Your friend will find her way too. She must know that she is allowed to be strong and feminine at the same time. In balance it can work well. She must learn how to set good boundaries and to ask for what she wants.'

She offered Marissa the conch shell.

Marissa took it, and the images faded away.

Sarah was sleeping, snoring lightly. Marissa felt a little discombobulated after the intensity of her journey, she took a moment to centre herself in the room, then blew the energy of the conch shell into Sarah's solar plexus chakra. After thinking for a moment, she added Reiki on top of the newly found energy, before closing the chakra. She tested Sarah's body, there was heat from the solar plexus, it seemed to be back and at full strength. Marissa poured Reiki in to each of Sarah's other chakras, then tested them all to see were they all at the same power and strength. It took a few minutes longer, but she felt that it completed the healing. She knew when it was done. She sealed up Sarah's aura and sealed her in with golden light.

That was beautiful, and I'm so relieved that Sarah's got all her chakras working again. I wonder is this a common thing, to have chakra's so out of balance? She looked at the time. *It's getting late. Matt is coming soon. I'll make us some tea, that will refresh us both.*

While Marissa (deliberately noisily) organised the cups and things for tea, Sarah awoke, stretched out on the sofa, made a soft moan, then opened her eyes. The kettle switched itself off - Marissa poured two mugs of tea and brought them to the table while Sarah pushed herself up into a sitting position.

'Do I smell camomile tea?'

Marissa smiled. 'Yes, it's camomile, I think you've had enough stimulation for today.'

'Thanks mum.' She stretched again, and cupped the mug in both hands. 'Wow, that was strange, and amazing, and weird. What did you see? On your journey?'

'First things first. How do you feel?'

'Taller? I don't know yet how I feel. It wasn't like the Reiki you gave me before. I do feel a little weird. But not in a bad way.'

'Have a drink, take your time.'

'Have you any biscuits?' Sarah smiled, and tried a sip of it. 'Ooh, it's too hot.'

'I'll get an ice cube for it. Yes, I've got digestives, or Hob Nobs.'

'Hob Nobs please! An ice cube would be wonderful – even two of them. What a good idea!'

Once Sarah had her ice cubes and her biscuit, Marissa spoke.

'It was a very different journey – different from anything I've seen before. I needed to check that I wasn't making it up! It was so vivid, beautiful, sparkly and light. Lots of light! Yes, very beautiful.'

She started to relate it to Sarah, and when she mentioned the song, Sarah stiffened.

'My mother used to sing me that song,' she said. 'There was a time when I was small, I don't remember exactly, but she told me that I wouldn't go to sleep unless she sang that very song to me.'

'So I wasn't on the wrong track then.'

'But what does all this have to do with self-confidence?'

'The mermaid said that you could be feminine and strong, that you would learn how to set boundaries and ask for what you want.'

'That's wonderful. But what does the song have to do with my self-confidence?'

'Only you can answer that,' said Marissa, taking a sip of her tea. 'Maybe we won't find out tonight, it could come to you later. I remember Séamus telling us in class that we are only seeing a small part of the picture, just a fragment, and it might not mean anything by itself. But when more of the picture is revealed, then suddenly it will all make sense.

'Okay. Well, I trust you, and I don't feel bad. Just emotional, and maybe just a little groggy.' Sarah put down her tea, stood up and wiggled her hips. 'Still working!' She put her hands on her hips and said in a funny accent, 'Got to take care of the merchandise!'

'Merchandise? What do you mean?'

'Well, I've got a good body, it will get me places... Aah, now I understand.'

'You're going plenty of places without needing your body to take you there. What do you understand now?'

'Mum, you heard her singing... She used to treat me like I was a pretty thing with no brain. So that's what I thought I was – a pretty thing with no brain. Give me a diamond ring cos all I'm worthy of is getting married to someone rich. I'll never get rich off my own bat. It's not true. So not true.'

'Especially not true right now, look at what you're achieving, and what you're about to achieve.'

'Yes, I know, I'm quite proud of myself. A whole new training division, just because of me!' She sat back down on the sofa. 'Mum used to say that, about merchandise, it was a catchphrase in our house when I was little, but I didn't really understand what it meant. I do now. No, you're right, I'm not merchandise. I'll never say that again.'

'I'm glad to hear it.'

'Yes, so am I.'

'I wonder, does that explain the triple dating thing? Your determination to find a man? I thought it was interesting that you've made it a choice – career or dating, why not both?'

Sarah thought for a moment. 'I think yes, the two are connected alright. The mermaid in your journey said what, exactly?'

'Something about setting good boundaries, and asking for what you want. I think you can have it all, Sarah, if you decide that you want it.'

She nodded her head. 'It's really strange that I got up and did that wiggle and said that thing just now. It has been years since I've done that.'

'I guess the energy is working its way through you,' Marissa said. 'Maybe it's something you're letting go of as part of your healing process.'

'Maybe. I'm glad it's you here and not someone else. I know you won't tell anyone else any of this.'

'Of course I won't. I'm excited for you, Sarah. This is new territory for you.'

'Yes, I think it is new territory. That sounds good.'

'Well, if this was a psychotherapy session I'd get you to remind yourself that you can have it all, and tell yourself that often, instead of telling yourself that you can't do a thing, or aren't clever enough. Because you really, truly are.'

'I like that. Tell myself that I can have it all.' Sarah turned to Marissa with a wide smile. 'I'm learning as I go, and I'll make mistakes, but it's going to be okay.'

'Exactly,' said Marissa nodding her head. She raised her mug of tea. 'A toast, to your best life ever. Starting now'

Sarah giggled and the girls toasted and drank.

'It sounds so simple and so easy, doesn't it?' said Sarah. 'I've heard what you have just said to me a hundred – no, a thousand – times before. But this time it really means something. It's as if I'm hearing it for the first time – actually hearing it instead of just going, "Yeah, yeah, yeah," in my mind.'

'I guess you have to be ready before you can really hear something at a deeper level.'

'I guess so.'

Sarah sat back on the sofa and Marissa got up and put away her drum and medicine bundle, but left the candle burning. She sat down beside her friend.

'You're breaking new ground too, Marissa,' Sarah said. 'I'm proud of you, figuring it out. I think you're right, we have to do the psychotherapy part with the energy part, otherwise you'd have just given me some energy and I wouldn't have known what it was, and I'd have left here, continuing to, how did you say it? – frame my situation in the same way.'

Marissa smiled. 'Yes I think so too. Frames are so important.'

Sarah raised her mug again. 'To frames!'

They toasted once more.

'Jokes aside Marissa, you're a natural healer, and a good one at that. I think I've said that to you before. Are you ready to hear it this time?'

'Ha, ha, Mrs Pot.'

'Ha, ha to you too, Mrs Kettle.'

They embraced.

Then there was a soft knock on the door.

'Matt! Yay!'

Sarah laughed. 'I love it that he makes you so happy.'

'He makes me? I think we make each other happy.'

Marissa opened the door and Matt was standing there, overnight bag over his shoulder and flowers in his hand, leaning in trying to hear what they were talking about.

Marissa blushed at the flowers and whispered, 'Sarah's here.'

'I thought I heard voices alright.'

'Don't mind me, I won't stay too long,' Sarah interrupted. 'It's nice to see you again, Matt.'

'Sarah! Lovely to see you too. Don't rush off, unless you need to go somewhere.'

Matt came in and Tobermory went over to him, wrapping himself around his legs and tangling himself up in his feet. Matt had a padded lumberjack shirt on, with a white T-shirt and jeans. He managed to make it to the bedroom to put his bag down without falling over the cat, then he picked him up, brought him over to the sofa and sat down on the edge of it, stroking Tobermory all the while.

'Ooh look at Tobermory, letting Matt hold him like that – he doesn't let me!'

'He likes me better than you,' said Matt with a wink.

'Sarah was just helping me with my homework,' said Marissa.

'She did a session on, too,' said Matt, 'looks like we both survived Marissa the Shaman.'

'That sounds weird,' said Marissa, 'I don't feel like I am a Shaman, I'm just getting my homework done, thanks to my two best friends.'

'Gold star for you!' said Sarah, raising her almost finished camomile tea.

'Oooh, nasty!' said Marissa with a smile.

'Well, it is funny. You love ticking things off your lists – you would have made a great manager.'

Matt got up, went to his bag and brought back a six pack of beer. 'Beer, anyone?'

'Maybe later, thanks,' said Marissa. 'I've just been working. And Sarah really shouldn't for 24 hours after the energy work.'

'Aww, you needed to tell me that up front!'

'Would it have stopped you?'

'Probably not.'

'No bother, so.'

Matt put Tobermory on Marissa's lap then got up again, put the cans in the fridge, opening up one for himself. Tobermory leapt off Marissa and stretched out on the rug, then rolled over and showed them all his stomach.

'So cute!' said Sarah. 'Wish I had a cat.'

Matt came back to the sofa and squashed himself in between the two girls, can in hand. 'This is the life,' he said, kicking off his shoes and putting his feet up on the table in front of them.

'Eww!' Both girls cried out in disgust.

'Right, so, let's watch a movie. Where's the remote control?'

CHAPTER TWELVE

Sarah stayed till 11pm the previous evening and they had all really enjoyed one another's company. Marissa was sleepy after finishing a long day in the office, she slumped in her window seat on the bus going out to the women's refuge. Spring was spilling over into summer, tulips were making way for peonies and roses. It stayed bright up to nearly 9pm at night.

Marissa's routine for the refuge included changing out of semi-formal office wear and into something more casual, before leaving work. Her slacks and jacket were stuffed into a bag which slung over her shoulder, even while she sat. Sticking her hand out of an oversized hoodie sleeve, she turned her lapis lazuli egg in her fingers, feeling an ache in her heart. She was missing Matt.

The bus was getting closer to her stop now and she had to go downstairs to the door. The stone egg was too big to stuff into her denim pocket but she wanted it close to her body, so she stuck it in one of the large zipped pockets in the front of her hoodie and closed the zipper with a sigh. The bus speeded around a corner, Marissa used its momentum to swing herself around and down the stairs, managing not to lose her balance when it came to a standstill.

After alighting on the street gracefully, she walked unhurriedly towards St Marys. After all this time she was more familiar with the neighbourhood, she knew the drill with the door, and clients were actually showing up.

Funny, though, that they're turning up now, when I'm not worried about it. It will take as long as it will take to get my hours done. Are they showing up because I'm not worried, or am I not worried because they're turning up...? As long as they're doing well, and feeling like they're making progress, that's more important to me than clocking up the hours.

I think that Reiki helps with everything. Especially me, I'm much calmer when I use it. It made such a difference to the shamanic session with Sarah last night too. Maybe I'll suggest it to Lucy? Reiki and psychotherapy, Reiki and shamanism, why not? It does relax you ... and when you're relaxed, you can do everything better. Yes, it could be just right for Lucy, especially if she doesn't feel like talking.

The centre was busy. Marissa went up to her designated room, rearranged the table and chairs to how she liked them and lit a candle. She sent a few moments connecting to Reiki, and used her hands to fill the room with light. *I'll open sacred space, too. Why not?* She took out her phone and used the compass to figure out where North was, then recited the prayer quickly by heart. *Got it! Yes!*

Looking around the room, it felt a little empty, on the clinical side. *What the heck.* Drawing more Reiki down into her body, she lifted her arms and drew large spirals and shapes in the air, placing the Reiki symbol for emotional healing in the centre of the room. She empowered it and made it bigger and bigger until it filled the entire room, then she imagined it bursting, like a balloon filled with water, just bursting and spraying itself everywhere. She giggled, it was fun, and the room felt better then.

She sat down. *I need to tell Lucy what Reiki is before I offer it to her.* She started going over her explanations of it in preparation.

Lucy, however, had other ideas. Ten minutes later she still hadn't arrived. Marissa practiced Reiki on herself while she waited, wondering if she was going to come at all this week. *So strange, I thought we were making some real progress together the last time we met.*

At twenty-five past the hour there was a knock on the door.

'Come in? Oh. Hi Lucy.'

'I'm so sorry I'm late, I fell asleep.' Lucy was dishevelled and stressed, and genuinely looked upset. She wore her usual ensemble of a dirty sweatshirt and jog pants. She had slippers on instead of runners.

Marissa wasn't angry with her in the slightest. *I usually would be wound up waiting so long, perhaps the emotional healing symbol was for me! Ha, ha.*

She smiled at Lucy who was still standing at the door, waiting for permission to come in. 'It's okay, Lucy, these things can happen. Do come in and have a seat.'

Lucy closed the door behind her, smoothed her hair out, and sat down in the chair opposite Marissa, crossing her legs.

'How have you been?' Marissa asked, adjusting her position so she could sit up straighter and look at Lucy a little better. 'I'm sorry, but because you're late, we won't have our full hour today.'

'That's okay, I understand. I'm feeling a little better, I guess. Very tired and I'm still emotional, but that thing you did with me last week, talking to Peter, I don't know, it seemed to help a bit. Can we do it again?'

'Sure.'

Mary came into the room at her allotted time, not a moment too early and not a moment too late. She was standing tall and looked all-business. The sides of her head had been freshly shaved, making the slicked-back hair on the top of her head seem longer. Her combat pants and white T-shirt were freshly ironed.

She sat down in the chair opposite Marissa, rested her elbows on her knees and her tight-lipped face in her hands and stared directly at Marissa, unblinking.

This most unlikely entrance and awkward pose were quite disconcerting. *Is she angry at me? Or just playacting? Anything goes with Mary.*

Marissa smiled softly. 'Hi, Mary, it's good to see you again. How are you doing this week?'

Mary sat back in the chair, crossed her legs and folded her arms, continuing to stare at Marissa, looking at her up and down very intensely. She still didn't speak. Then she stood abruptly and approached her, hands on hips, cocking her head to study her at a closer angle. She walked completely around Marissa's chair and stopped right in front of her, looking her dead in the eye.

'Mary? What's going on?'

'Just checkin' to see what a real witch looks like!' Mary cracked up, slapped her thigh and sat back down again, still laughing. 'I gotcha! Ha, ha! So funny!'

Marissa felt her cheeks go red hot. *I shouldn't have said anything last time!*

'I see you didn't bring your broom and cauldron with you tonight! Ha, ha!'

Marissa sank into her chair, deciding to take the joke as well meant. It *was* slightly amusing, she had to admit.

After she had composed herself, Mary's face became serious once more. Then Marissa stuck her tongue out at her and she cracked up again. It felt good and easy between them.

Marissa tried to open the session a second time. 'Are you going to tell me how you are this evening?'

'I'm in good form. Did you notice, I got me some new clothes! And a haircut too. Don't I look swanky?'

'Yes, you do look very well today.'

'Why, thank you, Miss Marissa.' She took a little bow in the chair, then continued with a grin. 'I have some news. I had an interview two days ago and it went great, I knew it when I hung up the phone. Then I found out this morning I got the job!'

'Oh, Mary! That's wonderful! Well done!'

'I'm proud of meself!' Mary cocked her head to one side then to the other and did a little wiggle in the chair. 'Yeah! It's gonna be great.' Then her face fell, and she added, 'But it's not in Dublin.'

'Oh?'

'It's in Mayo, in an adventure centre. They want me helpin' with boats and kids and stuff. Doing some groundskeeping, cutting back trees and rescuing lost sheep, taking the dogs to the vet, that kind of thing.'

'That's fantastic, and sounds right up your alley,' said Marissa, smiling. 'I can see you doing that and really enjoying it too.'

'Yeah, I think I can too. I'm excited. And I get me own cabin as part of the job, so I can move outta here. And there's another job going, if Becks wants it.'

'Becks?'

'My bestie. Becks. You've not met her 'cos she's not here.'

'You've not mentioned her, either,' said Marissa.

'Yeah, fair enoughski. Anyways, I've known Becks years, she's great with kids. Better than I am. She could come with me and live in the cabin and we could, you know, save up for a car and stuff. It's only for the summer, the job. She's still thinkin' about it. They want me there right away, to get ready for the end-of-year school trips and the like.'

'That sounds really exciting. I'm so pleased for you.'

I guess we are finishing up together then, before we really got started. Oh well, that's the therapist's life. Marissa couldn't help feeling disappointment mixed in with genuine happiness for Mary.

'I used to work on a boat for a while, me,' Mary added, 'so I got boat skills. Hey, I can even teach knots and stuff. They said I could, if I wanted to, 'cos nobody else there was doing it, or had even thought of it!'

'You know knots?'

'Oh yes, and sailing, and fishing. They do all that stuff there.'

'And you told me you had no skills!' *More last-minute big disclosures!*

'Well, that stuff comes so easy to me and feels second nature, it doesn't feel like real skills. I thought the chances of me gettin' a job on the boats was slim to none. I never thought of an adventure centre. That Audrey,' Mary rubbed her hands together, 'she's amazin' – she found the ad and made me call them right away.'

Marissa smiled. 'Well done, Audrey! So, when are you going?'

'I'm takin' a few days to get my stuff sorted here, then heading up on the train on Friday. Hey, I guess this means I won't see you again.' Mary's face fell for a moment, then perked up again. 'So, yeah. Wow. This is goodbye so. Thanks for everything. Really, I mean it. It's been good. I learned stuff from you. I think it helped me be more confident, and you told me I could focus on what I liked, even though I thought it always had to be difficult. This job will be something I like, so it will be easy, unless the kids drive me mad, but sure, if they do, they do.'

‘I’m truly happy for you,’ Marissa smiled again. ‘and you’re right, life doesn’t have to be difficult. You have great skills, you just didn’t see it that way before. You and your friend Becks will have an amazing time.’ She cocked her head to one side, imitating how Mary had sat only moments earlier, then, drumming her fingers on the arm of her chair, she said, ‘Maybe you could convince a few of the others here not to be afraid of counselling before you go?’

Mary smiled, clicked her fingers together, then said, ‘Sure thing, Miss Marissa, your wish is my command.’

They both laughed.

‘You’ve got a great attitude, Mary,’ Marissa said encouragingly. ‘You’ll do just fine, as long as you keep believing in yourself, and I feel that you will. Before we finish here, though, I’d like to give you something to think about, if you’d be up for listening to it?’

If I ask her to listen and she says she will listen, then will she actually hear what I’m going to say? After the discussion with Sarah the night before about listening and not hearing, Marissa felt she had to call attention to bring in Mary’s focus.

‘Eh? Alright, Miss Marissa, do tell.’

‘Don’t think so little of yourself. You’ve had a hard life, and a difficult upbringing, in fact it seems you brought yourself up, but that isn’t who you are, it’s just what you’ve experienced. You should be proud of yourself. You’re still here, you’re strong and determined, and you have some very good friends. You’re loyal and clever, and you care a lot about other people. It shows, Mary, it really does.’

Mary sat in silence, taking it all in.

‘Ha, ha, Mary, are you speechless?’

‘Won’t be the first time, Miss Marissa. But really, that’s a lot of good stuff you’re sayin’ about me. It’s kind of hard to hear it.’

‘I know. That’s why I asked you to listen – so you *would* hear it. You’ve certainly heard every nasty thing that anyone has ever said about you, so I’d like you to hear some nice things that I’m saying about you to your face. The difference between the nasty things and the nice things is that the nice things are *true* things, and you know it. You do, don’t you?’

Mary blushed.

'Ha! You blushed!'

Mary's scarlet cheeks became a deeper shade of red. 'Ah, you're just takin' the piss out of me now.'

'No, not really. Well, maybe a little bit! But mostly I'm emphasizing the good things about you. It fascinates me how we're wired not to hear them as easily as we hear the bad things.'

She could see from Mary's eyes that she was losing her now; there was only so much good stuff a person could hear, if they weren't used to it.

I'd better pull back. 'Mary, I know this new job is a perfect fit for you. I'm really delighted for you and I'm going to miss you. Take all the good things, go to Mayo, and have a fabulous time.'

After Mary left the room it felt quiet and empty. Marissa's last client of the night was Loretta, she had missed several sessions already and Marissa didn't hold out much hope that she would turn up. Around five past the hour there was a hard knock on the door. It opened and much to Marissa's surprise, Loretta was standing there, pale and drawn.

'Come in, Loretta, have a seat,' said Marissa, trying not to sound too enthusiastic.

Loretta walked in heavily as if she was carrying many bags of shopping, but her hands were empty. She sagged into the chair. She had black circles under her eyes, her hair was scraped back into a messy ponytail and she had stains on the shoulder of her blue sweatshirt.

'Sorry I missed last week. Ava was sick and I couldn't leave Barry in the crèche, he was awful clingy. Audrey said I couldn't bring the kids to these sessions.'

It had been three weeks since Marissa had seen Loretta, but somehow what they had spoken about that first day flowed back into her memory. The longer she looked at Loretta, the more she remembered.

'Are you still not sleeping?' she asked.

Loretta smiled pitifully. 'I'd give my eye teeth for a good night's sleep at this stage. If it's not Barry Jr wailing and kicking in the night, it's Aaron having a nightmare, or Ava puking her guts up. Well, that was this week, anyway.' She shrugged her shoulders, noticing a stain on her shirt. 'That was Barry about five minutes ago, sicking on me in protest at my leaving him in the crèche.' She got a tissue and wiped herself down. It made no noticeable difference, however. She sighed. 'Parenting. Why does it have to be so hard?'

'It does sound like hard work. I think, though, that it's the most important job in the world.'

Loretta sank back into her chair and closed her eyes. 'Yeah, well, it's fuckin' hard. Especially as I'm doing it all myself. And I worry about fuckin' up the kids the way my parents fucked me up. I worry a lot about that, actually.'

Marissa blinked for a moment. She was focusing on Loretta, connecting with her energies, and she had phased out for a moment, as if she wasn't in the room with her. She brought herself back in and blinked again. *Still here.* She still heard the echo of Loretta's last sentence in her mind, so she came back to it. 'Would you like to talk about that with me now, tonight, or is there something else you wanted to talk about?'

'Actually, there is something else, if that's okay?'

'Of course.'

It started happening again, the phasing in and out, as if Marissa went somewhere else yet was still in the room at the same time. She pressed her feet into the floor and brought her awareness more into her body. But something was going on, it became difficult to stay alert.

'It's Barry,' Loretta was saying, 'the children's father. My ex. Well, my husband. We're still legally married. He wants to see the kids and I don't want them seeing him. They're used to being away from him now, they've settled, well as much as they're gonna settle, anyway. If they see him, it will upset them. They cry a lot after being with him, see, they act out all angry and such. It takes so much energy out of me. I don't know what to do about it.'

'How do you feel about it?' It sounded stupid, but Marissa didn't know what else to say.

'Besides exhausted? Angry. How dare he! He'll probably show up anyway no matter what I say and take the kids out in his flashy car. Buy them ice cream, take them to the amusements, or to the fun park. Then they'll be crying for hours afterwards, saying they miss their daddy and it's all my fault he doesn't live with us anymore, and I'll be the one who'll have to clean up the mess. And that fucker will get away with it.'

Marissa was phasing out again, the room was going blurry and she saw images of Loretta in her mind that didn't match Loretta's physical presence. There was a collar around her neck and shackles around her wrists. *Wait a minute! This again? Of course, I saw these on her before, too, but I convinced myself that they weren't there. They still are there. Oh my God! What do I do? She's here for counselling...*

'What do you think I should do?'

The question pulled Marissa back into the room; she tried hard to pull her head out of the images and back to what she could see with her eyes, right in front of her, but it was difficult. She smiled weakly with effort.

'Loretta, I was hoping you wouldn't ask me for advice. I can't give advice, it's not in my remit. I can listen to you, ask you how you feel...' As she spoke it became easier to focus on the issues in Loretta's mind. 'Maybe I could remind you that even though you and Barry don't get along, he still is the father of your children...'

Marissa was able to take a breath while Loretta thought about this. Did I say something wrong? Will that make her angry? At least I'm a little more grounded now.

Loretta sighed. 'Feck, yeah, he is. I know.' In a softer voice she said, 'He's a right bastard though, but yeah, as much as I hate to say you're right, he is their da. It's not their fault he's their da.'

Thank God. Okay. Maybe we can make some progress. 'Would they be upset with you when they're grown up, if you don't let them see him now?'

'Jeez, I don't know. Right now it really doesn't suit me at all. I'm so angry with him I don't want to give him what he wants so easy. Or at all, even.'

'I understand. You're really frustrated with him, it feels like you're doing all the work and he's having all the fun.'

'Fuckin right it does. Yeah, that's it exactly.'

'Doing the right thing is always more difficult. I'm not judging you here Loretta, I just want to open it out so you can see the options, and not just what you want, but what is best for the children, too. To help you make the right choice, but ultimately it is you that has to make that choice.'

'Yeah, fuck sake. You're right, of course you're right.' Loretta sighed, 'It's not about whether it suits me or not. Good cop, bad cop, with the kids. I'm always the bad cop. I need to cop on to myself and say "yes" and let him see them. But I'm just so tired of all of this.'

While Loretta was talking, Marissa imagined a part of herself standing up and walking over to the Loretta that wore the collar and shackles. The images seemed to hold, she stopped phasing in and out, and found herself able to multitask. Marissa imagined the collar was made of old leather. She pulled out a very sharp silver knife from her pocket. *Why not?* Carefully, she cut through the collar. It came off in her hands and the energetic Loretta could breathe better.

Back in the counselling room, Loretta was waiting for Marissa to reply to her. *Whew, this is challenging, I'm working with her energy and her brain at the same time!* Marissa began to enjoy it. She looked at Loretta who was now rubbing at her neck with her fingers. *Wow! Wow, wow, wow! She must have felt me release the collar - but I can't say anything about this, it's too crazy. I'll just keep going.*

The echo of Loretta's last sentence still hung in the room and Marissa picked up the thread of it.

'I hear you, you're exhausted Loretta, the kids are full-on for you. I don't know enough about this though, I need to remind you that I'm still a trainee counsellor. But even if I was fully trained, I still couldn't give you advice. This is very important, especially as your children are involved.'

'Fair enough. What would you do though, if you were me?'

Marissa smiled. 'But I'm not you, so I can't answer that in a way that would be helpful to you. I'm just suggesting, perhaps you should look at it from the children's perspective before making any firm decision. Think about the long-term scenario as well as the short term.'

'Fuck yeah, but it helps to get it out there, to talk to you. I don't tell anyone else this stuff.'

'I'm glad I can help, even if it's only just to listen to you. Look, I know you're feeling many emotions right now, but we can deal with those emotions here, in this room. Then maybe you will feel a little clearer in yourself and you won't react from the emotions anymore. That will help you be better able to handle the day-to-day. Maybe you'll even feel stronger to handle the situation because you've told someone else what you're going through.'

'Yeah. I was feeling alone in it all. And the kids drive me up the walls keeping me short on patience doesn't help at all.'

'I'm sure it doesn't. You're handling a lot by yourself. Perhaps you need to talk to someone else too, someone who knows about the legal stuff? Get some professional advice. Maybe from a solicitor?' *She still has those shackles on.*

Marissa had lost the image, though. She couldn't get back into it. It was gone. *She does look less pale now, though. I have done something to help at least. Maybe if I see her again, I can get those shackles off her.*

'Ah, yeah,' Loretta said. 'I guess I could do that. They have one here, a solicitor, thank God. I could never afford one, but she's free. I've heard some good things about her. Didn't think it would come to this...'

'Maybe it's not as bad a thing as you think.'

'Maybe. It just seems strange, you know, making it more ... official, like.'

'You're in here – it seems pretty official to me already.'

'Yeah, I know. Maybe part of me has been hoping it'll work itself out. But I know it won't. He'll never change. And anyway, if I don't let him see the kids, he might do the same thing himself, talk to a solicitor. I don't want him gettin' the upper hand on me.'

'Sorry I can't be of more help.'

She won't know what I did to her energy, I wonder what will change because I released her neck. I wonder who bound her neck in the first place... And why?

'No, you are helping, actually. I liked what you said about reacting from emotions. I didn't realise my emotions were taking over. I feel a little calmer now. It's nice to talk to another grown-up about grown-up things. And the idea to get some help from someone else is a good one too.'

'I wonder, seeing as it is so full on with your children, as you've described to me already, do you think it's a good idea to get some space away from them? Just for a few hours on a regular basis. It might help you manage what's going on a little better. You'll have more patience for them, too. Just a suggestion.'

'Okay. Maybe I'll put them in the crèche and then go for a walk, just on me own. I'm usually at class, or busy doing something else, when they're at the crèche. So yeah, that could help too. Thanks, Marissa. It's late now, got to go pick up the babbies and get them to bed. See you next time.'

Marissa stayed in the room after Loretta had left, trying to make sense of what had just happened with the energetic images and her real-life physical reaction.

I guess it was multitasking of sorts. That knife was cool. I'd wonder though, if Barry took the kids, then she'd get space from the kids, and he'd get to see them at the same time. That would kill two birds with one stone, it's kind of obvious really. But I'm not sure if I should be the one to suggest that. Anyway she's gone now. I suppose she has to come up with that idea herself, it's not up to me to spoon feed her.

She felt good about the night's work. Lucy was making progress, Mary had a new job, and Loretta, well, she might get a better night's sleep. Tonight, at least.

She stood in the centre of the room closing the sacred space. She imagined the violet flame rushing through the room, burning away all the emotional energy that had been released there that evening so that the room was left as empty as it had been when she got there. *I wish everyone thought to do this for everyone else, it's more hygienic this way.*

She blew out the candle, switched off the light and went home.

CHAPTER THIRTEEN

Marissa was trapped inside a jar on the shelf of a pantry of a grand castle. There was bustle and hustle around her as many workers were preparing for a large banquet.

'Help me! Help me!' she cried, tapping on the glass, trying to get someone's attention. But nobody saw her, nobody heard her, nobody even noticed her. They were laughing, running around in the kitchen, totally preoccupied with their baking and cooking.

She looked around but she couldn't see any way out. The lid was sealed, shut.

'Isis? Thoth?'

No answer, no bird to crack the glass, no luminescent orb came to visit her. She shrank down and crumpled into a heap on the bottom of the glass. Tears started down her cheeks. She was alone. Nobody was coming to rescue her.

She woke up in a sweat. *It was just a dream. It was only a dream. I didn't really go there, I'm not really trapped, it's all okay.* She grabbed up Tobermory and held him tightly to her chest until her heartbeat slowed down, and she was able to get up and get going with her day.

Whoever was in Room Three in Cabra was still in there and it was coming close to 6pm. Niamh would be arriving soon and once again she had no time to create a healing space and clear the energy. She looked at the time on her phone for the third time. *I need my own place, full time, I don't like sharing. That sounds so childish. Yeah, guess it is. But it's also true. Relax, it will be fine. I need some unconditional positive regard for myself here.*

She shifted her weight from one foot to the other and looked at her phone again, then the door to Room Three opened and the two women from last week stood there chatting.

One of them noticed Marissa. 'Oh, sorry! We will be out of your way in just a moment.'

The therapist said goodbye to the other woman, who left, then the therapist went back inside to get her things. Marissa followed her in.

'It's great here, isn't it?' The woman said. 'The people are lovely. Nice to meet you, I'm Frances.'

'Hi, I'm Marissa. Yes, I like it here too.'

'Do you have Mr Blakemore for a supervisor? I've heard he has been quite sick.'

'Oh? Yes, I do. I haven't heard from him in a while. He's sick?'

Frances nodded. She got her coat and was about to leave when the buzzer sounded.

'That's my client,' said Marissa. 'I'll phone the office tomorrow and find out more.' She scratched her head and added, 'I'm sure I'm long overdue a supervision session with him.'

'I heard he was in hospital,' Frances said as she put on her coat. 'That's why I haven't met him yet. But maybe he's out now. Lovely to meet you, have a good evening.'

She left hurriedly and Marissa pressed the buzzer to let Niamh inside.

I hope he's okay. Guess I've been so busy I forgot about Mr Blakemore. Oh dear. I'd better clear the room and get it ready for the evening's work.

Niamh was already standing at the door, waiting to come in.

'Hi, Niamh! Good to see you. I just need a moment or two – the people before us took longer than usual. Would you mind waiting outside just for a minute?'

'No problem,' Niamh replied in a tired but cheery voice.

'Thanks,' said Marissa, surveying the room.

She moved the chairs. Frances hadn't lit a candle, so she found one and lit it. She needed to spray the room, again it felt quite damp. *Wonder what they talk about that makes the room seem damp?* She got the room spray from her bag and sprayed once in each corner and once in the middle of the room. The lavender scent was almost overpowering. *Too much! Oh dear! Never mind. Nothing much more I can do right now.*

She went to the door and invited Niamh to come inside.

'It's not raining today!' said Niamh with a smile as she came in and sat down in the chair. 'It's even a little bit warm. See, no coat!'

That's interesting. Marissa sat down in the opposite chair. *Even her handbag is slightly smaller than usual. Feck! I haven't open sacred space. Wonder if I can do it now, quickly, in my mind?*

Marissa felt a ripple of confirmation through her body. She concentrated and then said the prayer in her mind, on fast-forward, getting through each verse quickly. It felt different doing it like this; she noticed that each verse felt different as she sped through it, as if each had an energy of its own that she was invoking. *Of course! That's what it is – I'm invoking energies. Why didn't I realise that before? I wonder what's the name of that alchemy process – ah yes, distillation. I wonder, can I distil the energy of each verse and not say the words at all?*

Niamh was smiling, patiently waiting for her to begin the session.

'Sorry, Niamh. One day I will have my own room, so I won't have to clean up after the person that was in before me.'

'The room looked pretty clean to me,' said Niamh in a puzzled way, 'and it smells good, too.' She smiled.

'Energetically cleaning up, I mean. I'm working with the energy of the room.'

'That's interesting. I didn't know that was a thing.'

'Yes, very much so. Have you ever walked into a room and felt there had just been a fight in there, or there was someone who had been crying, but there was nobody there?'

Niamh thought for a moment. 'One time I remember my parents had a particularly bad fight in the kitchen which lasted all evening. I went into the kitchen later that night cos I was hungry and wanted some toast. I was young, around Six years old, I remember I was starving. Maybe they didn't make me dinner, yes, that's why I was so hungry. I snuck in, worried that they'd be angry with me for being out of bed. It was so weird, it felt like they were still in there with me, still shouting at each other. It freaked me out a little. I kept checking behind me, just in case, but they weren't actually there at all. I thought it was funny afterwards, like being in a pantomime – "They're behind you!" But they weren't. I always wondered about that.'

'That's it exactly, yes. I think emotional energy hangs around in spaces longer than people do, leaving behind an echo of what has happened there. And counselling can bring up deep emotions for many people. So difficult emotions are left behind in a counselling room, and then the next client comes in. Or the next therapist!'

Marissa changed the tone of her voice. 'I don't want you, or any other client of mine, to walk into a cloud of emotion that the person who was in here before you left behind. It's not fair. Depending on how sensitive you are, it could affect you, and our session together. I'd rather have the room clear for you, so we can focus on what you need and not on what the emotional energy brings up in you.' *And it's not fair to me either. All counsellors should be taught this, so they can clean up properly after themselves. Maybe one day they'll realise this is a real thing and important.*

'That makes sense, but you never hear about it anywhere.'

'I know. I suppose because we can't see it, or have a way to measure it, it doesn't seem that important. One day perhaps science will catch up. Anyway, let's turn our attention to you, and your session with me here. What would you like to talk about tonight? How have you been this past week?'

'Hey, I turned off my phone!' said Niamh proudly, waving it about, then putting it into her handbag.

Marissa remembered the homework she had given Niamh the week before. 'Well done, you! Was it difficult to turn it off during the week?'

Niamh's proud beam quickly dissolved. 'Well, actually, yes, it was. Harder than I expected. I had a lot of trouble doing it, so after the first few days I just stopped trying. Sorry.'

'No need to say sorry to me, Niamh. You tried, and that's a good start. You can tell me anything, and we'll work it out together. It's not like school, where you get marks for doing your homework. We can look at what was so difficult about it, if you like.'

'Oh. Really? Okay.' Emotion filled Niamh's face. She looked wistful for a moment and turned to look out of the window. Marissa could see that she was thinking about this, making a decision whether or not to talk about it.

Eventually she turned back to her with a resolve in her eyes. 'Yeah, you're right. I *would* like to sort this out, and you've been great, so I know it's okay to talk to you and be honest about it. So, during the week I noticed something about myself and my phone. I didn't like it, but it's like I can't help myself.'

In a compassionate voice Marissa said, 'That's great, though, that you noticed. You might have been doing whatever this thing is for a long time, and not realised. You need to be able to see something before you can change it.'

'True. Okay. I'm a little embarrassed saying it. It's like I've been bold and am expecting to be told off.'

'You know that's not my job, to tell you off. I'm here to support you. I suppose we are so deeply conditioned from childhood, it's difficult to shift gears into adulthood! Take your time. Why were you expecting to be told off – did you feel that you'd been doing something bold?'

'Yeah, it felt like being on the phone was being bold. That's it! I felt much better when the phone was off, but I still couldn't help myself.' Niamh looked awkwardly around her as if to reassure herself that nobody else was listening. 'It feels good to be bold sometimes.'

'You're an adult now though, you get to set the rules for yourself.'

Niamh laughed. 'yeah, and it's much cheaper now to make a phone call than it was when I was small.'

'For sure.'

'I guess that's just me being silly then?'

'No, I wouldn't say that. We don't experience a formal shift into adulthood, where it's clear that the rules have changed. And there are many aspects of ourselves that stay quite young, you've heard of the inner child?'

'yes, of course'

'So I guess as the grown adult, we need to tell our inner, children, that we get to make the rules now. It sounds funny doesn't it, no wonder we don't do it. Maybe that would help though, to give yourself permission to be the adult in your life?'

'That's an interesting idea, yes, I like the sound of that. I give myself permission to be the adult in my life.'

Niamh's permission statement sounded apologetic, as if she didn't really mean it. *How can I help her be stronger in that?* Marissa imagined a small child, growing up quickly, then stepping out from underneath their parents, to be on an equal grounding with them.

'Niamh, see yourself stepping out from underneath the authority of your parents, so that you're all standing together, on the same level, as equals. You and your parents are adults, and each of you get to choose how to live your own lives, instead of you remaining submissive to them, even in your mind.'

'That sounds obvious, but I suppose I've still been feeling like the child in that relationship. You're right, I'll say it again. What were the words again?

Marissa repeated the statement, and Niamh said it three more times. 'I give myself permission to be the adult in my life.'

The last time Niamh said the affirming statement, it sounded significantly stronger.

'Well done, I think this is a big thing. You sound like you believe it this time!'

'I do.' Niamh did a wiggle in the chair, as if affirming a newfound pride in herself.

Marissa smiled. 'Back to your phone though, I'm wondering, was that all that you noticed?'

She hesitated, and then spoke. 'Actually, there was something else I noticed too.'

Marissa waited for her to continue, which she did.

'I noticed that not only do I have trouble turning off my phone, I have trouble being away from my phone. Like, if I leave it in a different room, I need to go back and get it, so it's beside me at all times.'

Marissa nodded.

'I was wondering about this. It doesn't seem healthy - I mean, once I realised what was going on, I annoyed myself! At one point I even asked myself, "What would Marissa say?"' She giggled. 'I imagined you asking me, "What is in your phone that's so important that you can't leave it in the other room?" Now I don't know if you would actually say that, but I heard you say it in my mind, in your voice. It was funny! And then I had to answer the question. So it was good, too.'

Marissa smiled. 'Yes, I probably would have said something like that! So, what did you say back to me?'

Niamh relaxed. 'I realised that it wasn't about phone calls or texts. That's what we spoke about last time. It's more than that. I'm on Twitter, Facebook, Pinterest, and some other apps too – news apps, stuff like that. I keep picking up my phone to look at them, to see what I'm missing.'

Marissa remembered something she had heard about recently. 'Is this a fear of missing out?'

'Maybe. Yeah, seems like that. I was wondering for a while if I was addicted to it. I guess I want to know if my friends liked what I said. Or to see what my friends are saying... That sounds like a fear of missing out, doesn't it? I'm not really afraid though, if I miss something, I mean. And it's not so much about what's going on in the world. I don't look at the news apps so much, not really, now that I think about it.'

'Okay. That's a lot to have figured out in just a week, Niamh. Well done for doing all this work.'

Niamh brightened again at the praise. 'Thanks, Marissa, you really helped, even though you weren't actually there!' She smiled. 'The thing is, once I noticed myself doing that with my phone, picking it up to check stuff all the time, I noticed that I wasn't really reading any of it, just looking at it. Looking through it, like I was looking for something, but I didn't know what it was. And when I did find something, something I thought I was looking for, I wasn't actually that interested in it.'

'Yes, that does sound strange.'

'Yeah, isn't it? I feel relieved just telling you about it. I was thinking there was something wrong with me.'

'I'm sure there isn't anything wrong with you. I need to do some more research on this, but I do know they design the phone to make you want to use it more. And fear of missing out is a real thing. Maybe you're burnt out from it? Or you have turned it into a habit that you do on autopilot, and now it's so ingrained you're going through the motions without being present to it. You don't even realise you're doing it, until you catch yourself.'

'Oh, that's interesting. Yeah, that could be something.' There was a pause, then Niamh added, 'It gets worse at night-time. Now that you said that, about it being a habit, rather than me doing it deliberately, that's really interesting. Because every time I close an app and put my phone down before I go to sleep, I remember I haven't looked in the other app and I pick it up again and open that one. It's very tiresome. I find that I can't settle easily for sleep, I keep picking the phone up and not really enjoying it, or knowing why I'm doing it.'

She looked pleadingly at Marissa. 'God, that sounds awful, doesn't it? It's like I don't control my own actions. I wonder how many other people do this too. I didn't even realise I was doing it until I caught myself this week. I've probably been doing it for a long time now. I don't want to be a slave to my phone – shouldn't my phone be working for me and not the other way around?'

Marissa took a breath. *Wow. That's big, and everyone could be doing this too. Slave to the phone. I wonder, being a slave, is that shackles and binds again? Would I see something in Niamh's energy field like I did with Loretta last night, if I tuned into her? It would be worth investigating whether the connection between Niamh and her phone is energetic. But do I need to ask her permission? We did mention energy earlier. Why not tell her what I want to do? I'll take a risk.*

'Niamh, this might sound strange to you, but I don't think it's any stranger than what you've just told me. You know how I said before that I needed to clean the room before you came in? What if we needed to clean your energy, too?'

Niamh began to look anxious.

'Hey, it's okay – we'll figure it out together, yes?'

'Okay.' She calmed a little.

'It does make sense, if you've never cleaned your own energy, there could be something in your energy field that's irritating you. I could take a look at your energy right now, if you let me, and see if there's something there that I can clean up for you.'

'Oh! Will it hurt?'

'No, it won't hurt. I'll just take a look.'

'Okay.'

Marissa tuned into Niamh's energy. It felt very messy and scattered. It reminded her of a solar system with lots of planets spinning in circles, only with Niamh they were all going in different directions, at different speeds. It felt hectic, chaotic. Marissa even felt herself becoming ungrounded. She couldn't see Niamh for all the clutter around her. Then she had an idea.

'Niamh, would you mind getting your phone out of your bag? I want to see what your energy looks like when you're holding it.'

Niamh reached into her bag and picked up her phone. Nothing changed.

'Should I turn it on?'

'Oh yes, that's a good idea. Please.'

Niamh turned the phone on and or a moment there was a judder in the energy, then several texts came in. Niamh looked apologetic, but Marissa smiled at her, so she relaxed.

After a time, it appeared as if the phone was sucking Niamh's energy into itself. Marissa watched for several minutes, trying to figure out what was going on.

'Shall I turn it off now?'

'Yes, please turn it off. Thanks.'

Niamh turned the phone off, and to Marissa, it was as if someone had switched off a noisy radio that had been playing in the background. There was a moment of relief in the room, but Niamh's energy still felt very chaotic and cluttered. She put the phone back into her bag.

'Fascinating,' said Marissa, not realising she was saying it out loud.

'What?' asked Niamh in a slightly panicky way.

'You have a lot of clutter in your energy – you know, like a very messy room filled with lots of things. Like a bedroom, if you spilled the entire contents of your wardrobe onto the bed and the floor. You would definitely benefit from having your energy cleaned up a little bit. And there's something strange happening when your phone is on, but I can't see exactly what it is, because of everything else that's around you. But it does seem that your phone is taking some of your energy from you.'

Niamh shivered. 'Oh dear. What do I do about it?'

Marissa looked at the clock. They had twenty minutes left.

'I'm very aware that this is a counselling session and not an energy healing session,' Marissa said carefully, 'but I'm also learning energy healing, and I guess we can do that too, if you give your permission. Would you let me? Then I could try to clean up some of your energy for you, and maybe it would help clear up your thoughts too. And then you could do the same homework as before – turn off your phone for an hour – no, a half an hour – every day. What do you think? You might find it easier to put your phone down, even put it in another room, after doing this. We won't know until we try it. It's new territory for me too. But I really feel that it will help you.'

Niamh perked up. 'Energy healing sounds interesting. Is that like Reiki? I've heard of Reiki.'

'Yes, it is Reiki, and shamanism, that's what I'm learning. I know shamanism sounds scary, but I think it can really help people.'

'Okay, let's try it,' said Niamh. 'I really don't know what else I could try. It's like my willpower has been worn down and I haven't any left. I just give in to the urges and then I get upset at myself for giving in. It's a like an addiction would be, I imagine. Or going on a diet! I went on a diet once. I found that very difficult too.'

'This would be a phone diet, and yes, I imagine it could be difficult. Give me a moment to figure out how to do this, if that's okay?'

'Yes, of course.'

Marissa closed her eyes. A consultation with her guides was long overdue.

Emelda? Grandmother? Bear? Are you there? How can I help Niamh?

She saw herself standing by the chair, placing Reiki hands on Niamh's head. *Okay! I'll try that, thank you.*

She stood up and went over to Niamh. 'I'm going to do some Reiki on you. You don't need to get up, I'll just place my hands on or over your body. Is that okay?'

Niamh nodded, freezing up a little bit.

'It won't hurt, I promise.' Marissa smiled. 'Can you uncross your legs and arms so the energy flows through you better? That's it, thanks.'

As Niamh relaxed, Marissa stood behind her chair and connected to Reiki. It flowed it down into her body, into her heart, up her shoulders and down her arms to her hands. She felt it flowing down her spine too, her hips, legs and feet. She grounded herself into the foundations of the building and her energy filled the whole room.

Niamh seemed much more relaxed now. *And I haven't even started yet.*

Marissa placed both of her hands on the crown of Niamh's head. She tuned into Niamh's energy field and visualised the clutter there, but there was too much. *Just one layer of it, please.* It became clearer then. She was able to imagine some of the chaos dissolving, the speed of the many different-sized 'planets' spinning around Niamh slowing down and shrinking.

She stood there for about five minutes, while Niamh's breathing levelled out and became even and calm. Then she imagined Niamh's energy field expanding, pushing all the clutter further away from the centre, even pushing some of it out of the room. That felt better.

Where do I go next? Marissa checked in with her guides and saw herself in front of Niamh with a hand on each of her knees. So she moved around the front of the chair and knelt down, placing a hand on each of Niamh's knees. Niamh seemed to come into her body at a deeper level. It was as if her energy settled and slowed down. She felt more substantial.

Marissa stayed in this position for a few minutes then she felt that there wasn't much else to do. They only had five minutes left before the next client was due. Si she stood back from Niamh and visualised her being surrounded with golden light.

Niamh looked much better than she had done when she arrived – her face was softer, her eyes lighter, and she had more colour in her face. Marissa sat down in the chair opposite her.

'That was lovely,' Niamh said. 'Have you finished?'

'I think so. I've not done this like this before. I just want to take another look at you to see what your energy is like.'

Marissa unfocused her eyes and saw Niamh's energy field was calmer, and the Niamh in the middle of it all was much larger, and smiling.

'You know how you said you didn't have much willpower to stay away from your phone? How you felt burnt out? I think you've got some of your energy back now. So it should help you with anything you want to do.'

'I do feel as though more of me is here now. It's a strange feeling. I wonder if this will help my anxiety levels too?'

'You know, I do think that it will. When you're small, ordinary things seem so much bigger, I suppose, so when you're bigger, they're the same size, but you can handle them better. Yes, I do think this will help. I'll be interested to know how you get on this week, Niamh, and I'm looking forward to seeing you next time.'

Niamh got up and stretched, then brushed down her clothing as if removing dust. 'I do feel different. Heavier in a way, but lighter too, and definitely much calmer. Thanks Marissa, I hope it works!'

Marissa had a few minutes before William was due in. She used sage to clear the room, really working it into the corners, to make sure the energy was fresh and ready.

If Niamh has more energy freed up because of the healing I just did she'll have more energy to put into her will power, no matter what she chooses to do with it. That makes so much sense! Emotional healing is accelerated by energy healing! It's so interesting, I love this! I do have to blend all of my skills together to get the best results. Oh! Emotional healing! I could draw the Reiki symbol for William, that might really help him.

She put out the sage bundle by grinding it into a mug until it stopped smoking. Then Marissa visualised the emotional healing symbol in her mind, imagining lots of little emotional healing symbols filling the room from her hands, flying into every nook and cranny. *I usually make one big one. This is new. Interesting. I like it, though.*

The buzzer sounded.

William walked slowly up to the room, taking more time than usual. Marissa stood by the door, waiting for him. He nodded to her as he came in, went straight to his usual chair and sat down heavily.

Marissa looked him up and down as she took her seat. If he was a light, he'd be a flickering tea light at the end of it's life, instead of a strong spotlight, or the lighthouse that he had the potential to be. He'd lost weight since they had started working together - his cheekbones were protruding, his neck was skinny. His skin was pale and drawn, he looked sick. This was their fifth session together and Marissa didn't feel as though they'd made any progress at all.

'How are you doing today, William?' she asked, feeling quite concerned for him.

'Will. I asked you to call me Will, remember?'

'Oh! Yes, sorry, I do remember, I suppose I think of you in my mind as William. Sorry about that.'

'That's okay.' William clumsily crossed his legs and shifted his position in the chair. He took a deep breath, and let it out as a sigh. Marissa left the space open for him to start the session.

'I've been thinking about what you said last week, about going to see a healer, or a shaman.' His discomfort was obvious. 'You know I don't want to do it. But I'm so worn down, Marissa, I think I really may have to do it. I have to do something – the dreams are getting worse. It's like they're coming after me. I'm having two or three of them a night...'

'Oh I'm sorry to hear that.'

'Yeah, it's not easy. And I don't want to go to bed, now, and when I do go, I'm trying not to go to sleep. But that's next to impossible.'

He stretched out his long legs on the floor in front of him and looked as though he wanted to go to sleep right then and there.

'I don't know what to say that will help fix this,' Marissa said. 'And you're right, I've not really been able to help. Maybe I could give you some Reiki tonight instead of us going around in circles talking? It could help you settle a bit, and then perhaps you'd sleep better tonight.'

William shook his head. 'I don't want you to come near me. I'm feeling on edge. I'm very sensitive right now – everything is bothering me. I'm thinking of going back on the meds. I really didn't want to do that, it's so disappointing, but I could be close to paranoia, or a psychotic episode... I can feel it, bubbling away in the background, like a volcano about to erupt. That scares me. I'd just feel more comfortable if you stayed away from me.'

Marissa really wanted to do something to help, then she remembered her Reiki 2 skills. 'Actually, William, I could give you Reiki from here. I wouldn't have to come over and place my hands on you or be near you at all. They say one hour of Reiki is like getting a full night's sleep - shall we try it? If it doesn't feel good, you could let me know and I'll stop doing it right away. What do you think?'

William shrugged his shoulders. 'Okay. I'll try anything.'

Marissa remembered Dolores taught her how to use her leg as a surrogate for a client. She crossed her legs and shifted her position so she could place her hands comfortably on herself. *William looks shattered. I could do a journey for him too, to see if there's anything I can help him with energetically.*

He was closing his eyes now.

Marissa connected to the Reiki and drew the opening time and space symbol in her mind. Then she mapped William's energy body onto the leg closest to her. The Reiki flooded out from her, like a fountain bubbling over. It was so fast and strong she had to ground herself to contain it.

'Rest and relax in the chair,' Marissa told him. 'I'm here. I'll send you the Reiki, and at the very least you'll get some rest.'

He was already nodding off.

After a minute or two the energy flow settled down and Marissa positioned her hands over the surrogate map on her leg where William's first chakra would be. The first chakra, the root, the connection to the land, to the ancestors, to tribal, primal fear. Her leg was like a vortex, sucking in the Reiki, but she didn't feel it going into her leg. *It must be going straight into William.* She looked at him the whole time she was working, he was looking more relaxed, but there wasn't any other obvious change.

I could check his energy and then do a journey for him.

She unfocused her eyes and asked if she could see what was going on. After a moment she saw that there was a collar around his neck, and his arms and ankles were shackled. Her heart sank. *But no, wait, there's more...* He had rocks and boulders around him and they had shackles too, and chains, and they were attached to his neck collar. *He's dragging rocks and boulders by his neck?*

She waited for the image to make more sense but none was forthcoming. She closed her eyes and saw it in her mind's eye more clearly. They weren't rocks and boulders, they were other people. She almost jumped out of her chair. *This matches everything I had seen in my journeys – people chained together. I had been one of them at one point, hadn't I? You couldn't make this stuff up!* She started to get panicky thinking about all the people that were affected, all the memories of being shackled herself.

No, I'm here, and I need to help William. I have to be strong. She held her composure and pulled her awareness back into Room Three. *Now, Tori would just jump in, but I'm Marissa in this lifetime, and I am not going to do anything stupid. Well, not deliberately, anyway. Think, Marissa, think. What do I do?*

She heard her inner voice say, 'Free him. Free William.'

Okay. I will try. But first I need my armour. She brought her awareness into her own body, down into her heart, while still working on William through her leg.

She was her small room by the lake where she had found her armour waiting for her before. She got her chainmail suit off a hanger which was on the wall, and put it on, then took her armour out of a glass case that was hanging on the wall and put it on too. Everything shrank to fit her perfectly and felt light and easy to move in. Good.

She brought her awareness back to the room in Cabra. William had his eyes closed now and his breathing was soft and even. She imagined herself standing up from her chair and walking over to him to free him. The images weren't as clear as they had been when she had done this with Loretta, they kept fading in and out. *I need to get help. Archangel Michael, Archangel Haniel, Archangel Metatron, please? Will you come and help me?*

She didn't notice anything for a moment, then she had a strong sense of sweeping great energies entering the room, powerful beings holding space for her. 'Thank you,' she whispered under her breath.

Now what? Emelda and Grandmother Medicine Woman might know. I have to take this slowly and delicately.

She imagined she was bac at her lake and then she was there. William was there too, on the stony ground by the lakeside, bound so tightly by his chains that he couldn't stand up. The others weren't there, it was just him and Marissa. But Marissa felt safer to work here this way.

'Let me help you,' Marissa said with great compassion in her voice, coming over beside him. She knelt down and started to untangle the chains but the more she got them untangled, the more they tangled back up again. William was writhing with discomfort.

The chains began snaking around her own wrists of their own accord. They slid off her armour though, but still became caught on her hands and wrists. She jumped at their touch, as if she had got an electric shock, and stood quickly back, rubbing her wrists and reprimanding herself for jumping in again without thinking.

Then something started to change, the chains became actual snakes, coiling and wrapping themselves all over William – so many snakes, so many kinds and colours it was difficult to see him underneath them.

Emelda was standing beside Marissa, tapping her foot. 'You bring him here, with all of this ... mess,' she said.

'I didn't mean to, I just wanted to come to you to get some help, or advice. He just appeared here with me.'

'Hmm, the energies here are better for healing though. It is a different frequency. I see the chains have turned into snakes. We can deal with snakes. Chains not so much.'

Emelda rolled up her sleeves, put her hands to her mouth and whistled loudly. There was a rushing from the lake and the great head of the sea serpent appeared. Water drops glistened off his large silver and blue scales as he trumpeted his hello. There was something different about his face; the blues were deeper, some of the scales looked like they were infected and were beginning to peel back from his body, and he had some sort of a skin growing over his left eye.

'Speet on him, my love,' shouted Emelda to the sea serpent. She turned to Marissa and added, 'Looks like it is coming to his time.'

'Time?'

A large thick jet of yellow spit shot out from the serpents mouth and covered the lump of writhing snakes that William had become. The snakes fell away very quickly - some burning from the acid spit, some went on fire, and some escaped, but most of the rest of the snakes disintegrated into a dark red powder as soon as they hit the water. The lake dissolved the powder swiftly and soon there was nothing left.

William! *He was black, burned to crisp - he had turned into an unrecognisable twisted statue of himself.*

Emelda studied him critically. 'He has very little life-force left. This is very bad. Very, very bad indeed. But we can help.'

Marissa had seen overcooked ducks hanging upside down in the window of a Chinese food market once, more bones than meat. William reminded her of them.

Back in the counselling room in Cabra, William let out a soft moan. Marissa's heart leapt, and she snapped out of the journey to check if he was okay. He had fallen asleep, but he was struggling with something. Marissa realised that she had been so preoccupied with the journey that she had stopped giving him Reiki, so she brought her awareness back to the surrogate map of William on her leg, moved her hands upwards slightly and sent Reiki to his whole body, instead of just one part of it. After a moment, William seemed to settle. Marissa waited for another minute, then closed her eyes and went back to the lake.

Emelda was looking William up and down. Then she looked at Marissa. 'What are you doing? Is working, look, his colour is coming back to him.'

It was – the brown sticky burnt colour was dissolving and William was plumping up again, untwisting, looking less bony and more like a person than a statue.

'Keep doing it, what you are doing. Reiki? Yes, I like this Reiki. I never use. Maybe I will learn!' She nodded her head and rubbed her hands together with approval.

'Thank you, Emelda, Oh thank God it's working.'

'Me, I do nothing, it is he you need to thank.' Emelda pointed to the sea serpent, who was standing guard over the scene.

Marissa smiled at him. 'Thank you so much, beautiful friend.'

The serpent nodded his head, one of his scales looked like it was about to fall away. He disappeared gracefully into the water.

'Go now, go back to your place and keep doing that Reiki. It is very good.'

Marissa took another look at William. He looked human again. She brought her awareness back into Room Three.

William's breathing was steadier now and he finally had some colour in his cheeks. He was sleeping soundly.

Marissa looked at the clock, they still had some time left. She decided to let him sleep and continue with the Reiki. *Is he still tied up, though? Or did the serpent eliminate everything? It was strange, the chains turning into snakes... I wonder why that happened. Show me William now. What is going on with his energy now?*

She unfocused her eyes and allowed William's body in the room in front of her to show her what was going on. He still had cuffs around his wrists, cuffs on his ankles and a collar around his throat, but they weren't connected by chains, and the heavy boulders had gone. *Were they really people? No, I don't want to think about it. Can I cut the collar off? I can't leave him with it on, I have to try.* Marissa imagined herself touching the collar around William's neck. It popped open and fell off into her hand. *Oh! That was easy? Did I really do it?* She touched the cuff on one wrist. It also popped open and fell off. *Wow.* She did the same to the rest of them.

Still dozing, William stretched his long legs out and arms up and took up more space in the room. There were fifteen minutes left for their session, but Marissa felt the Reiki was slowing down and she wanted to give them some time to talk together before he had to leave. Marissa closed off the Reiki, removed the surrogate map from her leg and visualised herself sealing William up with gold. Just as she finished doing this, he opened his eyes.

Marissa smiled at him and brushed the map off of her leg once more, just to make sure they were properly disconnected.

'I think I got a better sleep just now than I've had the last three nights.' William said, stretching again. 'Could I get some water?'

'Of course!' Marissa smiled with relief and poured some from a carafe into a tumbler for William. He drank it all in one go, asked for another and drank that too.

There is more colour in his face for sure. He looks so much healthier now, like he has come alive again.

'Hopefully you'll get a good night's sleep tonight too,' said Marissa as she took the tumbler back from him, 'but there are no guarantees, I guess.'

'Thanks. That Reiki was good, I feel I'm alive again.' William stretched and wiggled his fingers, stood up and touched his toes and sat down again. His eyes were brighter. He wasn't a flickering tea light anymore; he wasn't a lighthouse either, but at least he was brighter.

You'll never know how close to not being alive you may have been. 'I'm so glad you feel better. I actually do Reiki on Monday nights in a different venue, if you want to come to me for a whole session sometime.'

'I might do that, thanks.'

'William? I mean Will? This is session five of six. I don't know if you want another cycle, seeing as they've not really been helping you.'

'If I did, I think I'd come to you for Reiki instead of talking. No, the talking isn't helping with the dreams, and they're so horrible, I don't want to talk about them at all.'

'Will you come back next week? For your last session? So we can see if the Reiki helped at all? I could do some more Reiki with you then as well. If you come to my other room I'll have to charge you – I need to pay rent there – so you might as well take advantage of coming here.'

'Yes, that sounds good. Thanks, Marissa. I'm so sleepy now,' he yawned, 'but in a good way, not in a wrecked kind of way.'

Marissa gave him her business card with her email and phone number as he was leaving. 'Just in case.'

'Thanks.'

Marissa had ten minutes before Aisling was due. The energy of the room felt heavy, she needed to clear it, and clear her head too. She clapped her hands, ran some St Germain Aura Soma through her hands and through the room. Then she opened the door to let the air in, went to the bathroom and washed her face, then went downstairs to the kitchen to get some fresh water and to wash the glass that William had used. There were more people than usual milling around the centre, it was busy in a nice way.

She went outside the front door to breathe in the fresh night air, then made her way back upstairs to prepare the room for Aisling's last session of her cycle. She started to get nervous at the thought of seeing Aisling after what had happened the previous week.

'Nothing needs to happen tonight, Marissa,' she said to herself. 'It will be okay.' An image of the sea serpent with his sickly scales flashed in her mind. *I hope he's okay – what is going on with him? Does he need some Reiki too?*

The buzzer rang then, interrupting her thoughts. Aisling bounced into the room, happy and bright with a big smile on her face, a total change from how she had been in all of their previous sessions together. Marissa couldn't help but see how different she looked – buoyant and happy. The room had improved with the air, there was still a touch of the heavy energies there, but they were manageable compared to how they had been just a few minutes ago.

'Hello, Aisling, you look wonderful tonight. How are you doing?'

Aisling sat lightly in the chair that Marissa had been sitting in. Marissa liked the change in perspective that came from changing chairs. As she sat down in her own chair she noticed a soft glow around Aisling and took a moment to still the rush of joy that came tumbling into her body.

'Hi, Marissa,' Aisling said brightly. 'I'm doing so much better. I don't know what happened last week, but I woke up on Friday, the day after we met, and I felt different. Really different. It was as if some part of me had returned from a long holiday somewhere. I don't know how to explain it without sounding crazy.'

'That's okay, Aisling, it would take an awful lot of crazy to make anyone sound crazy to me.'

CHAPTER FOURTEEN

It was the weekend. Well, it was almost the weekend. Fridays always had a much more relaxed air about them and the office was a fun place to be. There was just enough work to keep Marissa occupied and her weekend plans were made so she knew she'd be good on the homework front. Sarah had a date that night, they spent their lunch together outside in the sunshine, chatting over which outfit Sarah should wear, and reminiscing about disastrous dates they'd had in the past. When they packed up their lunch to go back inside, they embraced and laughed, knowing that they'd never make most of their past mistakes again.

'I do feel different about dating now Marissa – yes, you're right. Maybe it was a good thing that I didn't have a boyfriend for the past while. Finding my feet in work was complicated enough without having to work on relationship stuff.'

'I think though, that when you really want to find a man, it's kind of harder to actually, well, you know, find one that's good. Or one that treats you well, where the relationship works out. Or even find one at all.'

Sarah nodded her head. 'It's like you and Matt, you weren't even looking for someone when he showed up. And me and Vincent, so funny how we connected up. I've known him for years but I never knew he was interested in me.'

'I hope it works out for you, he sounds great.'

'I don't plan to, as you said, "cut off a part of myself" so I can put his needs and expectations ahead of my own. Not this time. Not ever again!'

'I have a feeling though that this time it will be different for you.'

'You do? What do you mean?'

Sarah put her rubbish in the bin and they stood outside the front door of their building, as was their habit, to draw out their lunchbreak a little bit longer before going back inside. Sarah nodded hello to a group of people as they passed by, high-ranking people she wouldn't have associated with before. They didn't really acknowledge Marissa, but she didn't mind. Instead of getting upset, she felt pride rising inside her for her friend. *This is Sarah's world, not really my world anymore. I'll be going to Clifden this time next week. That's what excites me, and she loves what she's doing here, so it's right and proper that she gets in with the management crowd.*

Sarah was still waiting for her to reply. 'Well?'

'Oh, sorry! I got a little distracted there, thinking about Clifden next weekend, how I'm doing what I love, and you're doing what you love here. Aren't we doing well!!'

'Yes, and it's Friyay too, but please tell me what you meant when you said this time will be different?'

'I don't know, it's just a sense that I have about it. I can't really explain it.'

'Hmm. Okay, I won't hold you to it, but it's nice to hear it.'

Sarah went back to her desk and Marissa went back to her own, head full of plans for her homework catch-up effort.

I need to finish these tasks for work though, I'm off on Monday, and it would be great to come in Tuesday and have all these little things off my plate for next week, especially as I'll be focused on getting all my shamanic homework done. It's all planned out, I hope it all works out the way I've planned it! Right then, sort this out, then Matt and a pint, and a movie!

The next day, Marissa and Matt went to brunch with Marissa's parents. She loved how easy they all were with each other now, and how easy it now was to show up at her parents' house with her non-Jewish boyfriend.

They walked with linked arms on the way over, enjoying the warmth of the day and admiring the gardens that were coming fully into bloom.

'It's almost summer now,' said Marissa as they walked. 'I love summers best.'

As they walked past the main street of Rathmines towards Portobello, they could hear activity behind open gates in one of the buildings at the top of the road.

'Ooh, Matt, look, it's a market! I've never seen one here before!'

'It must be one of those new pop-ups. Let's go in and take a look!'

'We could get some cake for brunch, if they have any. Mum loves it when I bring something with me.'

The pair looked at all the stalls that were packed tightly together, selling breakfast and coffee, crèpes, fruit and vegetables, jams and breads and other baked goods. Marissa and Matt browsed, buying fresh oranges and raspberry scones, enjoying the banter and picking out people who looked as if they were still hung over from the night before.

'Mmm, you can't beat a breakfast roll, sets you up for the day,' said Matt looking on longingly as someone bit into a freshly served buttery baguette heaped with egg, bacon, sausage and a hash brown. 'That looks amazing. I fancy one myself right now actually.'

Marissa playfully whacked his arm. 'You can't! You'll spoil your appetite for brunch.'

He cocked his head at her. 'I could you know, and eat brunch too.'

'Then you'll smell like bacon! Dad won't like that.'

'How will he know?'

'He just knows.'

Marissa dragged Matt away from the food to the back of the market, where some of the stalls were selling books, antiques and craft items.

'Look,' Matt said, 'they have incense. Do you need some?'

The stall Matt found was packed with trinkets, incense, sage sticks, meditation and yoga CDs (second hand and new) and had boxes of small crystal tumble stones. Handmade dreamcatchers hung from tall poles, feathers flapping in the soft mid-morning breeze.

'I could do with some sage, I'm running low – oh look, frankincense, that sounds interesting. I'll try that too. And there's a green stone! I needed one for my medicine bundle. And there! A red one! I'd given up on finding those! Thanks Matt! Just what I needed for next weekend. Perfect! Oh look! Pendulums!'

Marissa felt a rush of excitement and relief.

'Oh, Matt, I really need one of these for next weekend. I didn't think I'd find one – in fact I didn't even know where to get one! I was going to try the Angel Shop, but I didn't see any in there the last few times we went. Of course I wasn't looking for them specifically, but oh, what a stroke of luck!'

As soon as she heard herself say that, Marissa remembered what Séamus had said about luck. *Oh. There's no such thing as luck. So the universe must have heard my call for a pendulum and has given me an opportunity to get one. I think I understand now. Thank you.* She had a sense of a gentle, yet strong masculine presence around her. *Thoth?* She felt an acknowledgement. *Thank you!*

She ran her eyes over the selection of pendulums, wondering which one was meant for her. *If the universe has brought these to me, then one of them is supposed to be for me. But which one?*

The pendulums were in all shapes and sizes, and once she looked at them in more detail, it became even more difficult to choose. Some were brass triangles, some had elaborate crystals glued to them, some were metal and some had carvings. She kept coming back to one; it was quite plain, but had a very clear terminated quartz crystal as its main element. She picked it up.

'Well, you could ask the pendulum if it's the one for you,' suggested the woman at the stall with a smile.

'Oh, you can do that? I didn't know,' said Marissa.

'Yes, sure. Ask it to show you a "yes" first, then a "no", then ask if it wants to work with you.'

Marissa picked up the quartz pendulum and held it in her hand. *Hello.* There was a small ball of rose quartz on the end of the long silver chain that was attached to the crystal.

'It's beautiful, isn't it?' said the woman. 'Here, I'll show you how to do it.' She picked up a different pendulum, one with a black crystal on the end, and held it loosely by the chain so it dangled down towards the table. 'Like this.' She held the ball at the end of the chain in the palm of her hand.

'Show me a "yes".'

She held her hand very still, yet the pendulum began to swing in a small clockwise circle. The woman grasped the crystal, pulled the chain taut and started again.

'Show me a "no".'

The pendulum slowly swung anticlockwise.

'Wow,' said Marissa, wondering if it was really happening, or if the woman was controlling it.

'Then you ask your question, which is: "Do you want to work with me?" Go on, have a try.'

Marissa copied the woman, held the chain and the rose quartz ball as still as she could and asked the pendulum to show her a "yes". She noticed that as she did this, some part of her willed the pendulum to move in a clockwise motion. It did. She grasped the chain and pulled it taut until the crystal was still, then she asked for a "no". She tried her best not to will the pendulum to move anticlockwise. It didn't move at all.

'Ah, this one likes you,' the woman said. 'It wants to teach you how to use it! Look, your "no" is standing dead still. It could be different next time – ask for "yes" and "no" every time, in case it changes. Now you can ask your question.'

Marissa looked at the crystal and asked, 'Are you my pendulum? I mean, do you want to work with me?'

She let go of her need for an answer and tried not to will anything at all, and the pendulum began to swing clockwise. She smiled. 'Looks like that's a "yes". Thank you.'

Rose was delighted with the fresh scones and oranges. The little house looked sparkling with a new coat of paint, a new kitchen and a new hall carpet. While she was finishing off the preparations, Bernie took Marissa upstairs to show her the new shelves and the wardrobe that he had installed in the main bedroom.

'Well done Dad, it looks great! Didn't know you could make stuff like this.' Marissa touched the wood, it wasn't perfect but it was hung up straight, all the edges matched when it closed and it was certainly functional.

'Used to want to be a carpenter when I was at school, a chippie, they called it.' Bernie smiled wistfully.

'And then?'

Bernie shrugged. 'The family business. Sure you know that already.'

'Well, you're not worried about money now, maybe you could do some more of what you love?'

'Yeah, maybe I could.'

All the anxiety within Marissa was gone. She was no longer worried about her parents turning on her the way they had when she was with James, but the memories of it still echoed through her body. She reassured herself that all was well, and breathed into the feeling of discomfort until it lessened and became background noise. It was refreshing to sit at a table with the people that she loved, without fear or anticipation of argument.

Bernie asked Matt's advice on some new upholstery he was thinking of getting done for Rose's new-to-her car, and Matt became animated as they discussed the options, while Rose fussed around clearing the table and pouring the coffee. *It's like I've stepped into a different dimension where everyone is nice to each other! Can I trust it? Is it real?* Marissa wanted to ask her pendulum, so she dug deep into her handbag, pulled out the small pink parcel and unwrapped it. A shaft of sunlight caught the edge of the crystal and shone through it to create a rainbow that danced on the white tablecloth.

'What's that, dear?' asked Rose, her eye caught by the light that glimmered in Marissa's hand.

Marissa smiled. *I still can't get away with anything, so it hasn't completely changed, which is good.* 'It's a pendulum, Mum. You can ask it a question and it answers with a "yes", or a "no". I just bought it at the market this morning, where we got the oranges. I wanted to look at it while you guys were talking about cars.'

'Oh, it's pretty. You can ask it a question, you said? Ask about Eli's baby – will it be a boy or a girl?'

Marissa thought for a moment. 'I suppose I could ask. I'm not taking responsibility, though, if I don't get it right!'

She looked at the crystal. 'Okay, pendulum, please can you show me a girl?' She held her hand still, trying to think of nothing, and the pendulum began to swing clockwise.

'Interesting.'

Rose sat down beside her, watching with avid interest.

'Now show me a boy.'

Again Marissa held the pendulum very steady, and the silver chain quivered, but the pendulum didn't move. *Like the "no" from before.*

She ran her hand down the silver chain and held the crystal in her hand, like the woman at the stall had done.

'Thank you. Now show me, is Eli going to have a boy or a girl?'

She dangled the pendulum again. There was no movement for a moment, then it began to swing clockwise.

'Girl!' said Rose. 'How wonderful! I'll get some pink wool and knit her a cardigan.'

'Mum! I told you, I've not done this before, it could be wrong.'

'No, no, I've had a feeling that it's a girl, and this confirms it. How fun!'

'Marissa, love,' her dad said, 'will you go through that suitcase before you go? I want to clear out the attic.'

'Sure, Dad. I can do it now.'

Marissa put the pendulum away and followed her father up to the small attic. They manoeuvred the suitcase through the access hatch and down to the upstairs landing, and Marissa opened it up to find photographs and trinkets from her childhood.

'Matt! Come up! I want to show you a photo of my grandad!'

Matt trundled up the stairs, belly full and satisfied, and sat down with her on the floor.

'Look, there's me with Eli on the beach, that was when we stayed in Brittas Bay, and look, there's me as a baby!'

Matt laughed and reached for a small woollen cardigan with colourful speckles of red, blue, green and yellow. 'Did you wear this when you were small?'

'Yes. I even think I remember it! I think Noreen bought it for me. She was always giving out about how you could only get baby clothes in pink or blue and she wanted something a little different.'

'Noreen from your work? You've known Noreen a long time then.'

'I think she's known me longer than I've known her!'

After saying goodbye to Rose and Bernie, Matt and Marissa went to Marissa's Reiki room to get the plinth for her session with Terry and Saoirse. Matt brought it in and leaned it up against the back wall, then got his stuff to go. It was almost 5pm.

'Hey, woman, will I see you this week, before you go to your workshop?'

'Oh. Probably not.' Marissa's heart fell. 'I miss you when you're not around.'

'I miss you too. You're too far away from me, though, to just pop over for a kiss...'

'You'd do that?'

'I just might. Got to keep you on your toes! Here, kiss me now before I go.'

They embraced and Marissa felt his warmth up close, and didn't want to let him go. *I know he loves me but I don't want it to hurt when we're apart anymore. Especially as it's going to be so long this time. I really don't want him walking away with a piece of me if that's what's been happening.*

Matt pulled away and was about to leave.

'Matt?'

'Yes?'

'Can you wait for a moment?'

'Okay.'

Marissa pulled him back close to her and placed her hand on his heart. *If I have any energy of mine here, inside Matt, can I take it back? Will my energy come back to me, please?* She waited, then felt a subtle shift of energy.

Matt's shoulders softened. 'What are you doing?'

'I'm just making sure you don't walk off with a part of my energy.'

'Oh, that's interesting.'

'Yeah, I miss you a lot when you're not around, maybe sometimes too much. And I really want to be able to focus on my work, the shamanic work. So I don't want to be pining for you.'

Matt cocked his head on one side. 'You pine for me?'

'Sometimes, yes it feels like that. I wondered if it was because, well, it sounds stupid, but if it was that I gave you a part of myself and I was actually pining for that.'

'No, that doesn't sound stupid at all. It makes sense, actually. Here, let me do it too. What do I do?'

Marissa took his large soft hand and placed it on her heart centre. The heat from his palm radiated straight into her chest and she felt tension leave her body.

'Now ask for your energy to come back to you.'

Matt whispered the worlds, then he jumped like he got an electric shock, and then he smiled and they both laughed.

We are figuring this out together. I'm lucky – no, not lucky, blessed – and grateful, to have such a wonderful man in my life.

Chocolate Cake, fresh strawberries, cream, a new pouch of freshly ground coffee and an anxious Marissa waited for Saoirse and Terry to arrive that Sunday. Marissa didn't quite know how to repay them for doing this work for her. The cake was an extravagance she knew, but it was a small gesture compared to what they were planning to do today. She knew they were nervous about teaching something they had only just learned themselves. And it had been a long time since she had seen them, so she was feeling a little nervous about that, too.

At 10:55 the doorbell rang. Marissa jumped up and opened the door to be greeted by both of them together! Seeing their happy faces washed away all of her anxiety.

'I'm so happy to see you both. And you got here at the same time! Come in, come in.' She ushered them both in. 'Wow, Terry, look at your tan, and your hair! It's so different like that!'

Terry looked like he stepped out of a Duran Duran video - he was wearing a shiny black plastic jacket, tight black leather trousers and a bright blue shirt and his hair had been dyed black. It was in a classic mullet - long on top and behind, and short on the sides, and a tiny plait that went down to the middle of his back. With his tanned skin, he looked totally different.

'Hello, dear,' he said, giving her a kiss on the cheek. 'Yes, it's me, I know, crazy isn't it. And both of us arriving at the same time! Isn't that funny? I met Saoirse on the street. She was walking from the bus stop. Of course she didn't recognise me! My taxi driver thought I was Simon whats'hiz name from that band? You know who I mean. Anyway. He couldn't find the right road – imagine that! I thought taxi drivers were supposed to know all the roads. I suppose it isn't London, though, is it, they don't need the knowledge in Dublin.' He put down his bag and turned to look Marissa up and down. 'Oh, Marissa darling, it is so good to see you.'

He opened his arms with a smile and they embraced, then Marissa stood back to look at him again, blinking to get her head around the transformation.

'I know,' he laughed, twisting some of his long hair around his finger. 'Black – strange for me. And hair extensions, they went all out this time! I didn't have time to sort it out – I need to visit the stylist so he can take the extensions out. He was doing an eighties theme – I had to wear shoulder pads! Imagine! I'm not a fan of the mullet myself but I thought I should wear the clothes for impact, until I get my hair sorted out. The tan, though, it's almost completely natural, and I'll keep that for as long as I can.' He giggled.

Saoirse laughed too, stepping out from behind him. Her face lit up to see Marissa and they embraced. Saoirse was dressed similarly to Marissa herself, in jeans, a T-shirt and a hoodie top.

'It's really good to see you,' Marissa said. 'Both of you. It's been too long. How are you, Saoirse?'

'I'm good. Yeah, he does look totally different doesn't he! How are you, more like? And you're coming back? Wow! What changed your mind?'

'I'm good too, and so so happy to be coming back. I'll tell you more about why later. Do you want coffee or tea? I have cake, but I thought we could have that later if you like. Or we could have it now?'

'Darling, I would kill for a glass of water if it isn't too much trouble.'

Marissa looked at Saoirse and smiled. 'I guess Terry needs a few days to come back to himself after being with models for a whole week!'

Saoirse laughed.

'Yes, darling, I suppose I do,' Terry agreed. 'They are quite difficult to be around. And Morocco, well, it's hard to come home, I love it there, I had so much fun, especially this time. They rented a whole Riyad just for us! We had so much fun on the roof at night, looking at the stars. And they had snakes and scorpions for the shoot! I was terrified, but I did what I had to do! And the food.. Oh my! So much food, we had our own cook. Just as well, some of the girls were so fussy... Anyway it was lavish. But now I'm home, and it is just us and I will try to be more hu-*maine*! Ha, ha. But first I really would love a glass of water, if there's one going?'

'Water too, please, Marissa, if that's okay?'

'You're both easy guests!'

'So, did they renew your contract at the museum?' Marissa asked Saoirse while she was getting the water. 'I remember you telling me about it when we met at the National Gallery that time.'

'Oh yes, they actually did. Such a relief. And even better, I got a three-year contract, so that's an end to my stress for a while. I got a small salary increase too, but it means I can get myself a new laptop.'

'That's so great, I'm really happy for you.'

Marissa put the three glasses of water down on the table and they all sat down. Saoirse and Terry sat beside each other on the sofa, Marissa sank into Tobermory's armchair and looked at her two friends with a heart full of love. Tobermory was outside, sleeping in the sunshine.

'So here we all are! A toast – to the gang coming back together again!' said Terry with joy in his eyes.

They clinked glasses.

An hour later they were still talking.

'And I couldn't believe that he did that!' said Terry in between mouthfuls of chocolate cake. 'I mean, come *on*, he knew that Bruce and I were together.' He froze. 'Oh. My. God. Oh no! That's slipped out. I didn't mean to tell you!' He did a double-take, quickly looking around the room as if checking who else might have heard him. 'Oh well, I suppose I couldn't hide it forever.' He sighed, recovering a little too quickly.

Marissa and Saoirse put on mock upset faces for him, and then they all giggled.

'Okay, okay,' said Terry, putting down his cake and brushing the crumbs off. 'So you already guessed it I suppose? Well, now you know for sure me and Bruce, we have a thing. It's been on and off, mostly off. And staying together in that little Riyad, well, we couldn't help ourselves.'

Saoirse pretended to look concerned. 'Why didn't you want us to know about it? And would you like a napkin? You've got chocolate all over your face.'

Terry took the napkin, wiped his face and said 'Gone? Good. Well, Marrakesh is a special place for Bruce and me, it's where we got together the first time, I think it was about three years ago. We were drinking one night by the pool in this gloriously expensive hotel, the sun was going down and it was so romantic. 'There's something special about Morocco, when you put your feet on the soil there, it's almost like it says to you "You're free to do anything you want, it's all good." It's like an invitation to care less about what people think, or to be careless, either or, depending on your sensibility. Of course Bruce pretended it never happened when we got back to Ireland. That's why it's so difficult with him.'

He filled them in on the details of his turbulent relationship with Bruce, but after the third time of hearing about the designer clothing that Bruce had been gifted by one of his exes, and how he and Terry would fight over which of them looked better in leather jeans, Marissa looked at the clock. As much as she really did love Terry, she was concerned that she wouldn't get to learn the extraction technique. Terry was catching a train to Cork that evening and they'd already been chatting for almost two hours.

'Hey, guys, I love you both to bits and I hate to interrupt, but you've been here now for ages, and I don't want Terry to miss his train. Can you show me some of the extraction work that you guys did with Séamus?'

'Oh, shit,' said Terry, 'I'm sorry. I've taken up so much time, but I can't help it. I'm full of the joys of living, and I've missed you girls so much. We've just got so much to catch up on! All you need is love! And a pee! I'll be right back.'

He got up, did a twirl around the room, then went to the bathroom.

Saoirse laughed, then found her handbag and reached into it and pulled out a sheaf of papers. 'I had a feeling I'd need to bring these. Here you go, take them. You can read them when we've gone. Just in case we miss something.' She put them into Marissa's hand. 'My notes from the last workshop. Everything we covered is in there. Give them back to me next weekend.'

'Wow, really? Thank you, so much!' The pressure Marissa was feeling around learning the process was alleviated. *I didn't realise it was stressing me out so much! Maybe it was Terry that was stressing me out...*

'Saoirse, did you know about him and Bruce?'

'Kind of. I did some work with him on love and relationships at the last workshop. He said that he was sort of seeing somebody then, on and off, but he wouldn't tell me his name. I think he loves keeping secrets.'

'I hear you both gossiping about me!' said Terry, emerging from the bathroom and smoothing his hair back. He laughed. 'I forgive you both. I'm happy, and once I get my hair back to normal I'll be much happier. I'm glad that you know about Bruce and me. Friends are just as important as lovers.'

'Bruce is a real babe,' said Marissa with a grin.

'You've met him?' asked Saoirse.

'Yes, over a rather wild dinner a few months ago, with Matt. Now, guys, please can we do some work? Otherwise I'll be having a panic attack coming to the workshop.'

It was funny hearing herself say she'd be having a panic attack when she knew that this time it wasn't going to be an issue. Terry stopped in his tracks and looked worriedly at her.

Marissa burst out laughing. 'A *metaphorical* panic attack, not a real one this time, I promise.'

'Thank God! Now, you're right. Let us do the extraction! I will extract your pain from you, whether you want me to or not!'

'That sounds awfully painful.'

'That's what I thought too,' said Saoirse, 'but actually it was quite relaxing. I found it very good when Liz did it on me.'

'Oh, Liz! How is she?'

'She's much more settled in herself now. She's been much more relaxed since the second workshop,' said Saoirse. 'Something has shifted in her, maybe because of the work that she has been doing around her baby.'

'Oh, don't talk to me about Liz and babies,' said Terry. 'Please. I don't have any more patience for that woman. She drives me demented.'

Saoirse laughed. 'Come on now, she's not that bad. Not like before, anyway. And we're going to see her next weekend, so you'll need to up your patience levels.'

Marissa said, 'If you decide you don't like her before you go, then you most probably aren't going to give yourself any space or time to accept her for who she is.'

'Yes, Terry, give her some space,' Saoirse urged. 'Give her another chance. She was much better the last time I saw her.'

'Like I *know*,' Terry sighed and flung one arm across his forehead in a mock-dramatic pose. Then he said, 'I'm just tired. It's the jet-lag talking and I'm missing my lover.'

'The extraction?' said Marissa, trying to maintain a business-like composure. 'Please? What do I need to know?'

'You're tired, Terry. Let me work on you, to demonstrate,' said Saoirse.

'Oh, yes, good idea.' Terry turned to Marissa. 'Remember Séamus was talking about energy and how it flows around your body and how some can get stuck and stagnant? Well, this process is about pulling out the bits and pieces of energy that get stuck. Look, I'll show you how to do it. Do you have a pendulum? You need to learn how to dowse for stuck energy first.'

'Yes, you need a pendulum to find the stuck energy,' said Saoirse, 'because it's not necessarily in a chakra. Here, I brought mine.' She got her medicine bundle out from her bag.

'Oh! I'll get mine too,' said Marissa. 'I brought my plinth home as well, just in case we needed it. It's over there. I'll set it up now so we can use it.'

'Oh yes, that's a great idea.'

Marissa set up the plinth while listening to Terry and Saoirse discuss how to use a pendulum, and their different ideas about what stuck energy is. She threw a blanket on top of the plinth and got a couple of pillows.

'I'll lie down on it first then,' said Terry, heaving himself up onto it, and lying down. 'Is that okay? I'm still jet-lagged!' He kicked off his shoes and they fell in a heap on the floor.

'Of course it is!' said Saoirse, moving the shoes out of her way. She opened her medicine bundle, Marissa peeked inside. Inside she had six stones and a small pouch. She shook out a purple crystal pendulum.

'Oh! How beautiful!' said Marissa, trying not to get upset about the number of stones that Saoirse had. 'What's the crystal?'

'Amethyst. It's for wisdom. I thought it would be a good one to have.'

Saoirse showed Marissa how to dowse for stuck energy over Terry's body. She was holding her pendulum differently from the woman in the stall. 'So this is a "yes", and this is a "no". See? He has some stuck energy here. It takes a while to get used to it, but I love the pendulum. It's like the drum – I think you need to get to know it, have a relationship with it, then it will speak to you.'

Terry lifted his head. 'I'm still here, you know!'

'Ha, ha, you're the demonstration model now.'

'Always the model!' Terry sighed dramatically. 'Well, I'll just close my eyes then. It's quite comfortable up here.'

'Thanks, Terry! So, I imagine a "yes", then it shows me a "yes",' Marissa took her turn, holding her new pendulum by the bead on top of the chain this time, willing it to move in a clockwise direction, 'but is it showing me what I want to see instead of what's actually there?'

'I wondered that too,' said Saoirse. 'I suppose you have to be detached from the outcome to let it show you what's there, instead of what you want to see, or what you think is there.'

'So that means you don't want to see anything at all. That's difficult.' said Marissa.

'I think if you know what's there in the first place you don't need the pendulum at all,' said Terry with his eyes closed and a cheeky grin on his face.

'Maybe,' said Saoirse. 'So then you place the pendulum over the body and ask it where the stuck energy is, like this.'

'Ah, yes. Okay.'

'So let's say we found some here. Terry, you've got some stuck energy here.' Saoirse was at Terry's upper chest.

'That must be from Marcel. While we were away, he was so jealous of me. He wanted Bruce, and Bruce wasn't having any of it. And on top of that, I got all the best shots, it really put him off his game. It wasn't my fault, but it was so funny. I could see daggers in his eyes...'

'Well, maybe he stuck an energy dagger into you then, 'cos I'm picking up a lot of energy right here, now that I've tuned into you,' said Saoirse, turning to Marissa. 'Are you picking it up too?'

Marissa tuned into Terry's energy field. She tried with the pendulum, but it felt awkward and in the way. 'I think I'll do it the way I usually do, just using images in my mind.'

She breathed in and out, relaxed and unfocused her eyes, then turned her attention to Terry. She ran her hand up and down his energy field without touching him.

'I can see lots of small intrusions. They *could* be little daggers, but they're more like arrowheads. That's what I see, flint arrowheads.'

Terry scoffed. 'Marcel *is* primitive, that would be just like him – arrowheads of jealousy. I can see him now, sharpening his arrows. But honestly, I didn't notice them. He isn't that powerful. But go ahead and remove them, it's good practice for Marissa!'

Saoirse showed Marissa how to remove one, then Marissa took out the next one, then soon they were taking them all out. Terry wriggled on the plinth each time and both girls giggled, he was just so funny.

'I certainly feel more mobile, and not as tired as before,' he said.

'Now to end the healing, said Saoirse, you need to ask your pendulum if you've finished.'

'I think I'll ask my guides,' Marissa replied. 'Then let's compare notes.'

'Sounds good to me.'

After asking, both seemed satisfied that they had finished Terry's session. He hopped off the plinth and said to Saoirse, 'Your turn now.'

Saoirse got up on the plinth, also forgetting to take off her shoes. Realising, she kicked them off and Marissa moved them over beside Terry's shoes.

'Now I'll show you how it's really done!' said Terry with a grin.

Saoirse shook her head. 'Jaysus, you're in top form today, Terry!'

Terry took a small pouch out of his jacket pocket and shook out a golden pendulum with a golden chain. The metal bob was inscribed with symbols.

'Pretty!' said Marissa.

'Yes, isn't it? It's Egyptian – look, there's a sacred scarab, and the eye of Horus. I love it. I got it in Marrakesh.'

Terry and Marissa dowsed over Saoirse's body. Both of them kept coming back to her heart chakra.

'There's something here in your heart, Saoirse, can we work on it?' asked Terry in a more formal, therapeutic tone.

Saoirse stiffened. 'What have you found?'

'I don't know,' Marissa said. 'Can I look at your energy field?'

'Yes.' She sounded reluctant.

Marissa mapped Saoirse's field onto her own and immediately felt something large and damp around her heart.

'I'm not sure if this is stuck energy, it feels as if it's still active and moving, but it's heavy and slow. Like grief.'

Saoirse's lips tightened and her eyes glazed over.

'Oh, darling, are you okay? What happened?' asked Terry, putting his pendulum down and patting Saoirse's arm. 'And there I was talking about me all morning, and I never asked about you.'

'It's nothing really.'

'You can tell us, it's okay, we won't tell anyone if you don't want us to,' Terry added.

'No, it's not that, it's just that I'm not sure I'm ready to talk about it yet.'

'Well, I can relate to that,' said Marissa. 'That's okay. Shall I give you some Reiki while you're here? It might ease the grief a little for you, and you don't have to talk.'

Saoirse nodded and a tear ran down her cheek and onto the pillow.

Marissa connected to Reiki and drew it down into her body, then she stood at the top of the plinth and placed her hands on Saoirse's crown. Terry sat patiently on the sofa and watched quietly, which seemed like an effort. Marissa focused on Saoirse, and after a few minutes something loosened and Saoirse seemed a little more relaxed.

'Did something happen?' asked Terry.

'Yes, something happened.'

There was silence. Marissa kept working, the heaviness loosened around her own heart and Saoirse's breathing became easier.

'I think you've been carrying this for a while,' said Marissa, disconnecting the body map.

Saoirse nodded.

Terry came over and examined Saoirse using his pendulum. It didn't seem to upset her. She smiled at him.

'It's the anniversary of my father's death,' she explained in a voice so small, it sounded like a whisper. 'I always get upset around this time of year, especially today.'

'Oh, darling, I didn't know. That's awful. I'm so sorry,' said Terry, genuinely upset.

'It's okay. It happened a long time ago, I was only fourteen. It's been the worst thing to happen to me in my life, though. That's kind of why I'm doing the shamanic work. It's strange, I went to a psychic medium to talk to my father and the whole session ended up being about me and how I was a healer and how I needed to be learning all this stuff... I was so disappointed with her, the medium, because I just wanted to talk to my dad. Well, I suppose she was right, and all these years later, here I am.' She shivered.

Marissa brought her a blanket, which she took gratefully.

'Did you talk to him? Your father, I mean? I hope you got your money back,' said Terry, 'I hate it when they do things like that.'

'No, I didn't get my money back, the medium said there was no guarantee. Which I suppose is fair. I didn't hear anything from him. It just wasn't meant to be.'

'I suppose it is fair,' said Marissa, really thinking about it. 'But you probably were very disappointed all the same.'

'Ah, it was okay. I survived it. Anyway, he died today, twelve years ago. I suppose my body remembered.'

'He's always in your heart, but your body, wow, that's amazing really, when you think about it,' said Marissa.

'Yes, I know. I've heard about people who get physically ill when anniversaries come around and they don't relate the two things to each other. Or they become accident prone and hurt themselves, and it makes them slow down and think.' Saoirse sat up slowly, brushing the last of the tears from her face. 'Can I use the bathroom?'

'Of course!'

She got up and went in.

'I hope she's okay,' said Terry. 'How awful to lose your father so young. Oh my God, look at the time! I've really got to go. I've to head back to Bruce's place to get my suitcase and do the long goodbye before the train. Or I'll get the later train... yes I think I'll do that. Hey, it's been great to see you and I'll see you both next weekend. Can't give you a lift this time, I'm afraid, my sister has the car.'

'That's okay,' Marissa said. 'I can get the bus.'

Terry put his pendulum back into the pouch and pocketed it, 'We both will have to get the bus!'

Saoirse came back from the bathroom, looking refreshed.

'Got to run, darling,' said Terry, hugging her and then Marissa. 'Look after yourselves and I'll see you both next weekend! Byeeee! Oh, and thanks for the cake!'

He was out of the door and suddenly the flat seemed very quiet.

Marissa turned to Saoirse. 'Are you in a rush too? Or do you want tea? Are you really okay?'

'Not in a rush, and tea would be lovely. I'm okay. There's a supermoon today, so I'm probably feeling more emotional than usual.'

'It must have been hard for you to lose your father. I'm so sorry.'

'He was killed in a car accident, so it was all of a sudden. Yes, it turns your world totally upside down, changes your idea of what life is and how it all works. It took us all by surprise, and a long time to come to terms with.'

Marissa filled up the kettle and switched it on, took the cups they'd been drinking from earlier and stacked the plates by the sink.

'How are things going for you?' asked Saoirse. 'It was difficult to get a word in edgeways with Terry today, he was so chatty. I love him to bits, but he does take over the place at times.'

'I'm good. Happy to be joining you next weekend. No, "happy" isn't the right word. Relived. Excited. Feeling more like myself now,' Marissa said as she poured the tea. 'Hey, how are you feeling now?'

'Much better, thanks.'

'Let's take our tea outside and sit in the garden.'

It was a little chilly in the late afternoon, but the change of scene, the quietness of Terry's absence and the hot cups of tea made up for the thick clouds in the sky and the lack of sun.

'So tell me,' Saoirse said, 'what made you change your mind? Why are you coming back to the classes?'

'It's who I am, shamanism. I know I probably shouldn't have left in the first place, but I guess I had to go all around the world to come back again and remember who I was. That sounds just like Dorothy from *The Wizard of Oz*, doesn't it?'

'Yes, actually, it does,' agreed Saoirse, cupping the tea with her hands. 'It's the hero's journey. I've been reading about that. You have to leave home to learn something, so you can come back again, different. Better. With a gift for your community. We can get too comfortable in our familiar lives; something has to make us uncomfortable, dislodge us from our reality, so that we feel the urge to make that journey. Maybe that was your spiritual crisis?'

'Yes it was a crisis alright. I wonder sometimes about the hero's journey, though. If we didn't have the contrast, the difficulty, then we would never make that journey – like you, here, learning healing because something awful happened to you.'

'I think that way too. My father's death has been a great teacher for me. I went to another medium a year or so ago. I didn't want to say in front of Terry, I know he has a problem with healers because of the bad experience he had.'

So many people have had bad experiences with healers, it's a little like playing Russian Roulette...

'Anyway, this one did connect to my Dad, and she said that my father agreed to die like that, suddenly, when I was young, because it put me on the path that I'm on now. It was difficult to hear, and I still don't know if I believe it. But it is what it is.'

'That's interesting. Did your dad speak to you through her?'

'No, but I wasn't as disappointed that time. I heard from my grandmother, and my great-aunt, his mum and sister. They told me stuff about him that I didn't know. She could have made the whole thing up, only I mentioned something in passing to Mum who got a surprise to hear it. She had forgotten. So some of it was true, anyway.'

'I have a lot to learn,' said Marissa, 'spiritual work is more complicated than I expected, and from what I've seen, the quality of the work seems to depend on the person you're dealing with.'

'Séamus says that all the time. Well, he did in the workshop you missed. The importance of doing your own inner work, to be the best that you can be, the clearest channel. What did he call it? The hollow bone. Be the hollow bone so you can channel clearly.

Something like that anyway. I'm feeling much better now. I guess when healing is good, there's nothing like it.' Saoirse finished her tea and stretched out in her chair.

'I hope that more people are having good experiences with healers than bad ones,' Marissa said.

'Someone said to me once that they thought they were supposed to have a bad experience because it pushed them to learn more things about themselves. It's a fine line I guess - out of bad things can come good things.'

'Out of the dirt, the flowers grow. What doesn't kill us makes us stronger. Maybe, I don't know, it is a fine line that's for sure. It makes me upset when I hear about people being treated badly by therapists and healers. I have a client that had a very bad experience with a healer, he's so traumatised from it still that he won't go to another healer because of it. And I think he really needs to. Anyway. Can I dowse you again before you go? Just to check your energy is okay? And for practice!'

'Sure.'

Marissa dowsed Saoirse's energy field, and it felt much better. She helped her get her coat on.

'Thanks so much for everything,' Marissa said, hugging Saoirse at the door. 'Take some time for you this evening, to be with the grief, yes?'

'I suppose I should, okay. Thanks for saying that.'

Saoirse left, but a moment later she came back. 'Marissa? You said you were seeing Finn tomorrow night?'

'Yes, that's right, he's coming over to help me play catch-up. Why?'

'Listen, I like Finn, but there's something dodgy going on with him. I just thought I should tell you.'

'How do you mean? The girlfriend and messing around thing?'

'Yeah, but there's something else. Not sure if I can put my finger on what it is, exactly. Just be careful.'

'I've got Matt on call if I need back-up. Anyway, he's never tried anything on with me.'

'Okay, but keep your eyes open.'

CHAPTER FIFTEEN

She was on the forest floor, her body torn to bits. There were dark eyes watching her, glowing red from behind trees in a dense thicket.

Argh, I've been here before. I remember.

Marissa took stock of her situation, then willed the broken bits and pieces of her body to come to her, but this time they didn't move. They didn't even flicker from her attention and intention.

Oh. *She sighed, tired from her efforts.* Okay, not that way then.

She lifted herself out of her body and floated above the mess of blood, guts and broken bones. Her body was unrecognisable. She wove her way around the bloody mess, seeking for something, some way to put herself back together. It seemed impossible. But I feel alright.

She willed herself forward, up and out of the clearing, past the thicket and beyond, but there was a pulling, a tugging, so she stopped and just hung there for a moment, then she felt herself being reeled back in, back over the thicket, back to the clearing, and back to the mess on the ground.

I can't escape this, but I can't seem to put my body back together. How do I heal this?

Marissa woke late. It was May Day, a relatively new Bank Holiday, so the whole country had a day off. She was hoping to make a medicine stone with Finn that afternoon, and she had two clients that evening in the Reiki room.

Me, working on a Bank Holiday, who would have thought! And always two clients, never three? Maybe two is enough though. I wonder, do we only get what we can handle? I remember someone said that to me before. Who was that? I don't remember.

Lying in bed and looking over in a slightly disconcerted way towards the plinth, which was still set up in the living room, she caught herself fretting over how to move it to her healing room by 6pm. *Maybe I'll take a taxi. Or maybe Finn will have a car. It will be fine, there's no need to worry.*

Marissa was still processing her dream. If willing her body parts together wasn't working, yet she was tethered to her body, then there was something she was missing. She knew it was just a dream, but she also knew it was a teaching dream. She had to solve the puzzle. *What if I don't figure it out?*

Her stomach did a flip. *This dream has really upset me. Wow. These dreams are probably more important than we know. I'll persist and I'll figure it out, just like I figured out the stepping stones.*

Slightly reassured, she rolled over, reached for her phone and sent Matt a Good morning sweetheart text. She checked in with herself around Matt - she wasn't feeling as bereft as she had been, but she still felt an ache deep in her heart, and a heaviness around her chest.

Imagining Matt there beside her, she saw herself placing her hand on his heart again, gently pulling her energy out of his chest. Something in her body shifted and eased, but it still wasn't right, it still felt tight. She saw herself taking his hand and placing it on her own heart, she immediately softened. Then she offered him any energy of his that she might have taken from him. She felt something tight leave her upper chest, and the ache dissolved away. Matt smiled in her mind's eye, and she smiled back in real life. Then she released the images.

Wow, powerful! Was that really him here with me?

Before she could explore that any further, Tobermory wound himself around her on the bed, pawing and mewing to be let outside.

'Okay, love, time to get up. Let's get the day started.'

Marissa spent several hours poring over her final assignment one last time before sending it off to college. She sent Ronan his essay back too, with a few comments, then she needed to switch off her computer. It was good to get those off her plate.

She still had some time before Finn was due, so she read over Saoirse's notes from the workshop that she had missed. When the doorbell rang, she didn't hear it and it rang again. She jumped up and got the door.

'Oh! Finn! You're early. Sorry, I was busy reading the catch-up notes! Come in!'

Finn stood at the door awkwardly, holding a bunch of flowers and wearing a crisp white shirt, a waistcoat, and matching freshly-ironed trousers.

What's the story here? He looks a little overdressed, maybe he's going somewhere after here?

'Erm, hi, Marissa. Thanks for asking me over.'

He took a step into the flat and Marissa moved in behind him and shut the door, ushering him towards the sofa. *Or shall we sit outside? I need to figure out what's going on here. He does know I have a boyfriend, doesn't he?*

'Would you like something to eat?' she asked. 'I've not had lunch yet. I can make you a sandwich, if you like.'

'Here, these are for you,' Finn said, handing her the flowers.

She shuddered. 'Oh! Thank you.' Brightening up she said, 'But *you*'re doing *me* the favour, coming here today and helping me with my catch-up work.' *Saoirse did say there was something off. I do need to keep my guard up after all*. 'I'll find a vase. Hang on.'

Marissa poured water into a vase, took the packaging off the flowers and arranged them in the vase too, then placed them on the coffee table. They were yellows and whites, really good-quality flowers, they radiated sunshine.

'Thank you. They're really lovely.'

Finn blushed.

'You didn't say if you wanted lunch?' Marissa continued, 'Do you want a sandwich? I've got tuna, egg or chicken.'

'Thanks, yes please. That would be great. Tuna.'

'Okay. I'll be a minute – can you go outside and open out the other deckchair? We can sit outside. Here's a sponge to wipe it down – it gets covered in snails and stuff.'

Finn went outside and Marissa put together two tuna sandwiches and some crisps. She took the sandwiches outside and placed them on the wall, then came back with two glasses and a bottle of cold lemonade from the fridge.

Finn was sprawled in the deckchair, his open body language was way too open, long legs wide, as if inviting her to take him. He smiled at her, expectantly.

Marissa sighed. She sat down adjacent to him and turned to speak directly to him.

'Look, Finn, I'll knock this on the head now. I really like you, and I'm very grateful for you helping me out today. I've got a boyfriend and I'm very happy with him. You won't have any joy trying it on with me, so don't even go there.'

'Oh,' Finn said, crossing his legs, his face registering a slight disappointment. 'No, I didn't mean anything, no harm intended.'

'Good. Glad to get that sorted. Can we be friends? You're a lovely guy and I would like to get to know you better.'

'Sure.' Something in Finn seemed to visibly relax. He took a bite out of his sandwich then, and smiled. 'Good sandwich. Hey, you know, it's impossible to get parking around here. I might have to run out later and get a new parking ticket.'

'Oh, Finn, you have a car? Could you give me a lift to my healing room with my plinth when you leave? I've been wondering how I'd get it there. You would really be a lifesaver.'

'No problem, but I'll have to leave at 3 o'clock, I'm helping my cousin set up for a gig tonight. He's working in Vicar Street and someone let him down for tonight at the last minute. Helping him means I get to go free, though, so I'm minted.'

'Who's playing?'

'Kodaline. I tried to get a ticket for them, but it was sold out, so it's so cool that I get to go as a roadie!'

Finn tucked into his tuna sandwich, smiling with delight, packing in the crisps too. He looked like a little child, and Marissa really did like him. *I wonder why he felt he needed to make a pass at me... He seems so much happier now that we have cleared that up.*

'Have you heard their latest album?' he asked. 'It's in the charts.'

'No, actually, I haven't even heard of them! I'm crap when it comes to music. I will defo check them out, though.'

'You should! I have a CD of theirs in the car – I'll lend it to you. Bring it back to me on the weekend, or whenever.'

'Thanks! That's very nice of you.'

'No problem! I like introducing people to new music. Have you heard of Bell X1? They're great too. And the Villagers?'

'Actually, I think I might have heard something by Bell X1...'

' "Pinball Machine"? Yeah, I thought so, everyone's heard that one. It's really good, isn't it? You should listen to the lyrics, they're deep.'

'Finn, I never would have known you liked music this much. You always seem to keep yourself to yourself in the workshops.'

Finn blushed and looked at his feet. 'I guess it takes me a while to warm up to someone, and then there's the, well, you know, sex thing. It's good to clear that with you.'

"Sex thing"? Oh, maybe I shouldn't ask. 'Well, I'm looking forward to us getting to know each other better.'

They took the empty plates and glasses inside.

'Just put it all in the sink, thanks,' said Marissa. 'I'll wash up later.'

'No bother at all, I'll do it now.' Finn quickly washed the plates and glasses and stacked them on the draining board. He looked at his watch. 'Can I use the bathroom? Then I need to run out and top up my parking ticket, and then we can do the shamanic work and I won't be distracted!'

While he was gone, Marissa got the flat ready and opened sacred space. Her medicine bundle was out and open, a candle was lit, the room smelled of sage and her drum was at the ready, just in case.

She had left the front door ajar so Finn let himself in, then closed the door behind him. His waistcoat was gone, over his shirt he wore a fleece hoody instead. He looked much more comfortable in himself.

Finn looked around her flat approvingly. 'Smells great in here! It actually won't take very long to help you make your medicine stone. Do you have a stone?'

'Yes.' Marissa reached for the stone from Greystones beach, and handed it to Finn.

'This is what you want me to use?'

'Yes, please.'

Finn looked at the plinth, and Marissa kicked off her shoes and climbed up onto it, smiling. She lay down and pulled a blanket over her legs.

'Shall I start?'

'Yes, I'm good to go.'

'What is your intention for this work? What medicine do you want to put into your stone?'

'Oh. Well, I think anything that's in the way of me being a good healer. I really want to do it right, to help people as best as I can.'

'Okay, that's great.' Finn closed his eyes, mapping Marissa's energy onto his own. 'Your stomach, it feels a little squelchy. Is that just the tuna and lemonade?'

'Ha, ha, maybe. Actually, it was off this morning, so maybe this is for my stomach. Thank you, Finn.'

'Okay, great.' Finn thought for a moment, nodded his head, then placed the stone on her stomach. He opened up her solar plexus chakra and ran energy through her body for a moment or two.

I can really feel that! I really do want to let go of anything in the way of my being a great healer. Ooh, that sounds a little cocky. But it's true, I want to be a great healer. So please can I let go of whatever is in the way of being confident as a healer and put that into my medicine so I can use it to help others? Thank you.

'What are you doing?' asked Finn. 'I'm meant to be doing this for you, not you doing it for yourself!'

'Oh, you can tell?'

'Of course I can! Don't worry, I can do this, I don't need you to do it. Ye of little faith.'

'Oh! It wasn't like that. I do think you're able to do it, I just wanted to go deeper...'

'Ha, ha, I was only messing!'

'Oh, that's a relief. I guess because we're getting to know each other better, I felt safe with you to go deeper. I really do want to clear everything in myself so I can be the best I can be.'

'You're very determined,' Finn commented. 'I've seen it before in you. You really must have had some battle to step away from the workshops and then to come back to them.'

'Yes, it did feel like a battle, a battle between good and evil. I guess I got in the way of it a bit. But I'm here now, and thanks for helping me.'

'So, will you let me do the journey for you now?' Finn looked at her with his head cocked to one side, looking like a young pup wanting to play. 'Please?'

Marissa laughed.

'What's so funny?'

'That's twice now I've seen your inner child come out to play. It's beautiful.'

'Shhh, let me work!'

Marissa tried not to squirm on the plinth while Finn closed his eyes and went on a journey for her. She breathed and relaxed into it, feeling energy move through her. There was definitely something happening in her body, but she wasn't sure what it was.

After about ten minutes, Finn opened his eyes. He was holding something carefully in his hand.

'Ooh, what is it?' asked Marissa impatiently.

'It's a pink rose. Now let me give it to you and we can talk in a bit.' Finn blew the energy of the pink rose into the stone. He smiled. 'It seemed important to get it all in.' He closed Marissa's chakra, sealed up her energy field and helped her get down from the plinth.

'A pink rose? What was that about? Can you tell me?'

Finn smiled. 'Yes of course. I went down a rabbit hole, that isn't my usual way into a journey, but I went with it. I found myself walking down a corridor, it felt nice in there though, like it was a hobbit house, underground. Very homely and sweet. I walked into a kitchen with a family, the woman was pouring soup out with a ladle from a large bowl for two children and a man who were sitting at the table, waiting to eat. The house felt very relaxed and happy. I kept walking, past the family, and into a darker place. I felt red eyes watching me from the sidelines and it was a little creepy.'

At the mention of the red eyes, Marissa shuddered, but she held her tongue, wanting to know what else Finn saw on his journey for her.

'Then I found myself in a clearing. There was a delicate pink rose growing there, on a grassy mound. It was the only one, there was nothing else around it. A shaft of sunlight like a spotlight shone down upon it and it glistened, sparkled, like fairies were around.'

'Oh! How lovely!'

'It was quite lovely. I looked around but nobody else was there. I thought that must be the medicine for you, so I checked, and got a yes. Next thing I knew, it was in my hand, and the light was still there, in the rose. Then everything spun around me like a vortex, like water going down the plughole in a bath and I went along with it. I was spat out in a white room, like a laboratory. It was so weird. There was a man working there, doing an experiment. He was wearing a white coat.'

'Thoth?' she asked

'Who?'

'Thoth, a very wise man.'

'I don't know if it was him. He turned around and looked at me and smiled, then turned into a wizard, then he was gone. And I was back here.'

'Wow. That sounds like Thoth to me. He's been in my journeys before. What do you think it means?'

'I'm not sure. It certainly had something to do with alchemy – that experiment was complicated. And the wizard reminded me of Gandalf from *The Lord of the Rings*.'

'Oh I love that story!'

'Yeah, me too. I had to read *The Hobbit* at school. I really hated that book, but when the movies came out, I went and read it again, and it was brilliant. I'm really excited about the next movies. But how has Peter Jackson managed to make three movies from *Lord of the Rings* – those books are huge – and then another three movies from such a little book as *The Hobbit*?'

'No idea! I guess we'll have to wait and see,' said Marissa, bringing her awareness back into the room. 'Thank you so much

Finn, that was very strong, I felt the energy through my body and I don't usually feel it as strongly. You're powerful!'

Finn blushed for the second time that day.

'Oh, I need to fold up the plinth. Are you sure you can drop it into my Reiki room for me?'

Finn looked at his watch again. 'Yes. If it's not across town, that is?'

'Just a few minutes up the road.'

Finn put the folded plinth across the back seats of his beat-up Ford, and Marissa hopped into the front and told him where she needed to go. It was easy and free between them now, she felt comfortable with him.

When he pulled in, there was nowhere to park.

'I'll hop out and get the plinth,' said Marissa. 'Just put on your hazard lights, won't be a minute.'

'Hey I can hop out too, hazard lights work miracles here you know.'

'That's okay, I can manage. It's nice to help, and nice to have a new friend.'

'Hang on,' Finn reached across Marissa and opened the glove compartment, rooted around and pulled out a CD. 'Kodaline, for you. Have a listen and let me know what you think.'

'Thank you, I will. See you on Friday!'

'Yeah! Looking forward to it.'

Marissa pulled the plinth out of the back of the car, closed the door and waved as Finn pulled away. *Nice guy. He doesn't come across in the group as easy and relaxed, and as clever. We needed to break the ice or something. It's always good to face things up front. I like him much more now.*

She put the plinth back under the stairs, as Sam needed to use the room first, then went back home to have a rest before her evening sessions.

When she got back to her Reiki room later that evening, she was a little early. Sam wasn't in the room, so she went inside. *It must be because it's a bank holiday. Shite, I could have set up earlier. Never mind.*

She heaved the plinth inside and took her time setting up the room. And then she put on her Reiki playlist and sat in silence as the smell of sage filled the space. She closed her eyes.

She was at the lake. She could see the serpent struggling in the water, so she went up to the water's edge to see if he was okay. His glimmering scales were not as bright as usual and he was covered in slime. He looked terrible. He couldn't see out of one eye, and there was a strange eggy substance covering most of his head and going all the way down his long neck. He flicked his tongue at it, but he couldn't reach it. He was trying to wipe it off and seemed quite upset.

'Oh my poor lovely friend! Can I help you?' Marissa asked. 'What's going on?'

The serpent flicked his tongue at her, made a wailing sound which almost broke her heart, then he disappeared into the water. Marissa wanted to cry.

The buzzer buzzed and snapped her out of her journey. The pain in her heart was very strong, but she had somebody new coming for Reiki, Gráinne, so she had to be fully present and on duty. Trying to push her feelings aside, she went to the door.

'Hi! You're Marissa? I'm here for the Reiki.'

'Yes, that's me, come on in.'

Marissa walked a very excited Gráinne down to her healing room. They sat down.

'My friend got me this session,' Gráinne said. 'She thought it would be good for me, but she never told me what it was – what is Reiki?'

Marissa took a breath and looked at Gráinne who was smiling brightly with enthusiasm and excitement to try something new. She seemed very nice, had long curly tangled red hair and wore a pink cardigan and a cream coloured woollen skirt.

Marissa explained what Reiki was. As she spoke, she felt the sadness within her wane. Gráinne had lots of questions about Reiki. Marissa started to feel like she was giving her a lesson on Reiki, rather than actually practising it. *That's not what I'm here for. Maybe I'll teach it one day, but not today.*

'Shall we try it now?' she asked. 'It's better to experience it than to talk about it. Please, kick off your shoes and hop up here on the plinth. You can close your eyes if you want to, relax and let the energies do the work.'

Gráinne complied, and as soon as Marissa placed her Reiki hands on her, she fell asleep.

While she was working, Marissa sensed a blockage beside Gráinne's heart. *I'd love to have my pendulum here, it would be a great chance to practice, especially as I've just learned extraction. But I'm doing Reiki, not an extraction. Maybe I should extract it anyway... What do I do? I hate leaving her with this blockage in her heart, I wonder if...*

She placed her Reiki hands above and below Gráinne's heart and flowed Reiki in with the intention of loosening and releasing the blockage. *This isn't intrusive, it's just me placing my hands.*

It wasn't shifting. She moved to Gráinne's feet and then brought the Reiki up her whole body back to her head. Gráinne was still sleeping, snoring lightly.

Okay, I'll try one more thing, as we are running out of time.

Marissa stood at Gráinne's head and imagined she was also standing at her feet. She placed her actual hands on Gráinne's head and her etheric hands on her feet at the same time. Gráinne shifted position then stopped snoring. Marissa pulled back, Gráinne's breathing settled, so Marissa continued her experiment.

After a few minutes, Gráinne stretched and flexed her feet, then Marissa sensed a 'Pop!' and the blockage in her heart eased a little bit. She let go of the image of herself at Gráinne's feet and placed her hands on Gráinne's heart. The blockage was still there, but it was much smaller now.

Gráinne opened her eyes and smiled. 'I feel much better now, thank you. Are we nearly finished?'

'Yes, it's almost time. Just a few moments more.'

Marissa closed the session, helped Gráinne to her feet and gave her a glass of freshly poured water.

'I feel so much lighter,' said Gráinne with a smile, taking a big drink.

'It seemed you let go of something big which was around your heart.'

'Yeah, my heart has been very heavy for a while. My sister's boyfriend was killed in a traffic accident two years ago and I've been very upset about it, even though he wasn't my boyfriend. Now my sister is in love with a new man and I'm having a hard time accepting it. Like I think she should be still grieving and all. But it's been two years, so maybe it's me that's grieving and I should let my sister do whatever she wants.'

'Everybody, I suppose, has their own way of grieving. Maybe you needed to grieve too and it's been prolonged because you've been looking after your sister?'

'Yeah, actually, that makes sense. Thanks for that. Hey, where can I find out about the different levels? Of Reiki, I mean. It's great.'

'Try the Reiki Federation Ireland website, if you want to find a teacher.'

'Don't you teach it?'

'No. Maybe I will in the future, but no, not yet.'

The room felt bigger after Gráinne left . She had only been there a short time, but she took up a lot of space. Marissa cleared the room with sage and clapped in all the four corners to clear the energy. She got her St Germain and was waving it through her own energy field when the buzzer sounded. It was Valeria, coming for her second Reiki session.

Oh I remember - Valeria didn't want me to touch her the last time. I wonder how she's going to be, tonight.

Valeria was much calmer in her demeanour than before. Her hair was scraped back into a ponytail and she wore track suit pants and a sweatshirt. She smiled on seeing Marissa and walked briskly into the healing room.

'Hello, Valeria, it's good to see you again.'

'It's very good to see you too. Isn't a Bank Holiday a great thing! I love having a rest today. And then I get to see you!'

Marissa smiled.

'I got such benefit from coming to see you that I wanted to see you again.'

'I'm so glad, and its wonderful to see you more relaxed. Well, shall we get started? You don't need to talk to me if you don't want to. You're welcome to get up on the plinth when you're ready, and lie down and relax.'

'It's okay, you can touch me this time. And maybe I talk a little bit too.'

Valeria kicked off her runners enthusiastically and got up on the plinth. 'Since I saw you my family's farm is doing much better, somebody came and bought all the butter for the farmers market. They were asking for cheese, too, but they had none ready so they are busy with the orders now. I don't feel as stressed as before, like I am not carrying them as much.'

Farm? Of course, yes, they have a farm – but did she tell me they had a farm? I don't remember. Marissa put a blanket over Valeria's legs, and opened the session. Valeria stretched out, then closed her eyes. She worked her way down Valeria's body, hands-on this time, instead of hands-above. When Marissa placed her hands on Valeria's stomach she felt as if she was falling. She closed her eyes and steadied herself, but she still felt as if she was falling, falling down through Valeria's body, falling through the plinth, falling through the earth, falling right down into the centre of the Earth.

This is strange and I don't like it. Am I being taken on a journey? It feels as if I'm being pulled somewhere. She thought she felt a presence beside her and she opened her awareness to it. In her mind's eye, it was a little girl wearing a pretty white dress with red embroidery. She had dark curly hair and she was radiant and happy.

Enthusiastically, the little girl said, 'I take you to my homeland. I show you where I live. I show you all the beauty, the places that I love. I want to show you, come with me.'

Then they were falling together. Marissa felt giddy, and out of control, she managed to stay calm but just as soon as the anxiety began to kick-in, they stopped. Then they were pulled sideways, it was like being on a fairground ride. This reminds me of the Wurlitzer in Funderland, only this time I didn't choose to get on it, and I can't seem to get off. No more! Angels, help me! Bear?

Suddenly everything stopped. Instead of being pulled, Marissa found herself standing on an escalator, still holding the little girl's hand. She looked down at her curly hair, the girl still seemed very happy. Marissa could stay there and just allow the escalator to take her with it. It felt much better than being pulled, so she decided to stay with it. The little girl saw that Marissa wasn't going to leave, so she ran up and down the steps as they moved forward.

They came to a large opening at the top of the stairs. The little girl said, 'Come, visit my home,' and held out her hand. Marissa took it and stepped into a bright place.

It took her a few moments to get her bearings. The little girl was leading her by the hand to a bright beach beside a sparkling sea. it quickly transformed into a colourful marketplace and transformed again into a large cathedral, where people were gathered in groups. It was some sort of festival. There was singing, and sugar cakes and oranges were laid out in large dishes on a table.

Then she was in an old house with a woman in the kitchen, cooking. She looked very sad.

Okay, enough, enough. This is too much, too fast. I don't want to see any more.

Marissa pressed her feet into the ground in her healing room and tried to pull herself out of the journey. Her head felt foggy. It wasn't working.

She slipped back into the images of the room with the sad woman, then said, 'Thank you,' and retraced her steps, growing larger in her mind as she gathered all the pieces of herself from where she had been, and finally managed to bring herself back into the room where she was.

Jeez, that was crazy.

Valeria was still resting. She had a smile on her face. About thirty minutes had passed, leaving them halfway through the session.

I'm not letting that happen again. Nobody can pull me into their journey without my permission. What the heck was that about? I need to check it out.

Carefully, slowly, Marissa made her way to her forest to visit her beautiful tree. Her bear was standing there. She ran to him and embraced him, feeling his strong arms around her. It was a relief to feel back in control of herself again. And she had not seen him in a very long time.

'It's so good to see you!'

Bear grunted. She looked up at him, he had a twinkle in his eye. He shuffled his feet as if dancing, and her heart opened.

The tree slowly raised the eyelid of one of his large eyes, and then the other, and he smiled. Yawning he said, 'Good for you. Always ask for stability and strength. Do not give away your boundaries or your energy to anyone.'

'I don't understand – what just happened?'

'That little one, she's very strong, but she never trained. I think she was so happy you could help her that she wanted to show you her homeland without asking you first. She misses it and she is out of balance. Tell your client how to access her homeland through the journey. She might become more balanced in that way.'

The tree sent an image to Marissa to show her what to say to Valeria.

Marissa nodded her head, gave thanks and returned to the healing room.

Valeria was enthusiastic either way. 'Oh! Yes I would like to hear your message for me.'

'Okay. Well, while I was working on you, a little girl came and took me on a journey through the centre of the Earth. We came out on the other side, to visit what I think was your homeland.'

'I was dreaming of my homeland while I was there on the table,' Valeria said. 'How does that work?'

Marissa smiled too. It was going to be okay. 'My spirit guide told me that everybody's always connected and you're never too far away from anyone, even if you're on the other side of the world. I think you miss your homeland, yes?'

'Oh yes, very much. I was remembering the beach, and could almost hear the music that my father plays every Sunday outside the church.'

Marissa described the images that she had seen while she was journeying. Valeria sat bolt upright in her chair, fascinated.

'That is amazing. And it must be true, because how else could you know about the sugar cakes? The place you saw, it sounds exactly like my homeland. Can this is really be true? How can I do this?'

Marissa said, 'My guide said that by going through the centre of the Earth in your mind's eye you can connect to any place and go visit anyone you like, energetically. As long as you come back to your body the same way that you went.'

'But energetically? What does that mean?'

'It means your body doesn't go, but your energy body does. You may be able to actually feel it - the energy of your home. Or imagine giving your parents a hug and a kiss, if that's what you'd like to do, or spend some time at the beach. Just make sure you come back the same way that you went – through the Earth and back out the other side. Then back into your body, wherever you are, so that you don't...'

Don't... Marissa had a flash of the images from her dream, her body dismembered on the forest floor. *Ah, we can break up into many pieces energetically. We need to be put back together again.*

'Just try not to leave a piece of yourself there.' Her heart skipped a beat. 'There was a little girl with me. Maybe it was a piece of you that you left behind? She didn't come back here to the room with me...'

'Oh, can you describe her?'

'She was small, had long dark curly hair and she was wearing a pretty white dress with red flowers.'

'That could be my sister. She had dark curly hair, I even think I remember that dress. I had blonde hair, so it was not me. Can you believe it? Look, my hair is so dark now, but when I was small, I had blond hair, so maybe it's a piece of my sister. Maybe she came to Ireland with me. She was on the phone to me the other night, crying because she missed me. Maybe you took a piece of her, back to her?'

Marissa felt immediately relieved. 'That could be it. Yes, that's probably what it was, I brought an energetic piece of your sister back to her. Wow, it's amazing how this happens. I'm so happy you enjoyed the session, and I feel I learned a lot from it myself.'

Valeria paid Marissa and said, 'I will most definitely come back for another Reiki session with you.'

'Erm, that wasn't exactly Reiki that we did...'

'That's okay. I liked it, whatever it was!'

Marissa closed the space, put everything away and folded up the plinth and put it under the stairs. *Yes two sessions are plenty for one night. I don't think I could handle another one just now.*

She took her time walking back to her flat. She had to process everything that had happened that day. She felt as though she had packed three whole days into a single day. And it was only Monday.

CHAPTER SIXTEEN

Marissa stood at the photocopier watching the paper move in and out of it. She'd been there twenty minutes already and had at least another hour to go.

It's good to have something mindless to do when I've got a lot to make sense of. That extraction process... So interesting, yet I feel Terry and Saoirse didn't show me all of it. There's got to be more to it than that.

A page jammed. Marissa opened the back of the machine, located it and pulled it out, then closed the machine and pressed the 'Copy' button for the tenth time that day. Taking out the ream of finished copies to make room for more, she placed them on the table beside her, only half paying attention to what she was doing.

An image of the sea serpent flashed through her mind. She had forgotten about him. *Poor thing, what's going on with him? I wish I could help.* She closed her eyes for a moment and imagined *herself back at the lake, but the images were foggy, rippling in and out. The noise of the photocopier had blurred the lines and she wasn't able to stay, or go. She could get a sense of him there, still struggling, but she couldn't 'land' there.*

Noreen's in the office today, I have to stay present in case I'm needed. *Oh, here's Tim!*

Tim had several files in his hand to photocopy. He took one look at Marissa and turned to leave.

'Tim, hang on, you only have a few files, and I've still got heaps to do. Go ahead.'

Marissa cleared the photocopier and moved aside to let Tim use the machine.

'Are you sure?'

'Yeah. I'll be here for ages yet, so you might as well.'

‘Thanks!’ Tim opened the lid and placed his paper on the glass.

‘How’s your girlfriend?’ asked Marissa with a cheeky smile.

Tim gave a knowing smile in return. ‘We are doing good, thank you. It’s still a secret from the office, though.’ He put his finger to his lips.

‘Why?’

‘I’d rather keep my work and personal life separate.’

‘That’s fair. But has Sarah tried to fix you up with someone else?’

‘After the Christmas party, I don’t think she’ll try that again.’ Tim winked, then collected his photocopies from the tray and stood aside for Marissa to take over once more. ‘Cheers, Marissa.’

He was about to walk away when Marissa said, ‘Tim, hang on, I have a question for you. I know you used to play Dungeons and Dragons. Do you still?’

He nodded his head.

‘Do you know anything about serpents? Sea serpents, I mean? They’re kind of dragon-like.’

Tim broke out into a wide smile. ‘It depends on the universe you’re working in. In some realms, sea serpents are related to dragons, in others, there’s a fine line between sea serpents and actual sea dragons.’ His shoulders dropped and his face softened. ‘But not always. And it’s not really Dungeons and Dragons intel. Sea serpents, you said?’

‘Yes.’

’A sea serpent can be a juvenile form of a dragon. Like a larval stage. Like frogs and tadpoles. Like I said, it depends on the universe you’re in of course.’

‘Interesting. Different properties in different universes?’

‘For most things, yes. Sea serpents don’t feature very often, it’s usually dragons that are more common. And the mythology that dragons hatch from eggs, I don’t believe it myself. But, that universe thing again, it depends on where you are. For example, in *Game of Thrones*, dragon eggs can lay dormant for hundreds of years and then hatch out of fire. I guess in fantasy, anything goes. Mostly when I’ve come across sea serpents, they've been unapproachable. They lay low, they're often hidden. It's rare that anybody sees them at all.'

'So you're saying sea serpents can change into dragons?'

Tim nodded. 'Possibly. They say, when it happens, they form a type of shell around themselves, like a cocoon. They're in there for a while, then they hatch out as dragons. A bit like caterpillars becoming butterflies. There's a series of books by an author called Robin Hobb that features the whole process of sea serpent metamorphosis. The people in that universe turn the husk of the cocoon into magical objects, small ones like necklaces that speak the truth, and big ones like ships that come alive and speak. I'd love to see one of those in real life. Imagine – a ship that's alive, that's what they're called, live ships. Super books, each one of them. There's a new one coming out next year about dragons, the fourth one in the series. I recommend them all, even the ones that aren't about the ships.'

Marissa felt somewhat relieved. Her sea serpent was possibly going through a metamorphosis. And she always loved something new to read.

'Thanks so much! I'll check the books out for sure.' *And I'll visit him again to make sure he's okay.*

'Why do you ask? Are you playing D&D yourself? I thought serpents were incredibly rare, not really recommended for beginners.'

'No, I don't play. A sea serpent came to me in a vision, a dream, and it looked like it was in pain. I just wondered if there was something I could do for it. If I have the dream again, I mean.'

'Do you have lucid dreams?' Tim asked excitedly. 'You know, when you're aware you're in the dream, and have control of yourself and can change the course of events? You just said you could do something for the sea serpent, if you had the dream again.'

'Yes, lucid dreams, I guess I do have them. Quite often, in fact.'

'That's amazing. I've wanted to have them for ages. I even took a class on lucid dreaming once, but I kept sleeping through the night. So disappointing! I've been thinking of going on a dream retreat – there's one coming up in Scotland. I didn't know *you* could lucid dream – you've inspired me! Maybe I'll go then.'

'Yes, do! Go, and tell me all about it when you come back!'

Tim went back to his desk with a skip in his step.

Lucid dreaming and Tim, who would have thought? I guess many people hide their interest in magic in case people think it's weird. I wonder who else in the office is interested in this stuff? And sea serpents turning into dragons! Magic everywhere, and in the most unexpected of places. Does this mean I'll have a dragon for a guide now?

She got a shiver just thinking about it.

Sarah was at her desk looking through her emails when Marissa dropped the finished photocopies bound with spiral binders onto her desk.

'Thanks, really appreciate it.' She was preoccupied, winding a stray lock of hair around her finger as she focused on the screen.

'That's what I'm here for – you're doing the manager thing and I'm just the office girl,' said Marissa quietly, moving away to leave her to it.

'Hey!' Sarah turned around. 'You're not just the office girl, you're my friend. And a very good healer too. Since you did that work on me last week, I've been feeling so much more confident. And when they finally officially asked me to lead the ECDL project, I said "yes".'

'Wow, Sarah! Go, you!'

Sarah smiled, stood up, took a bow, and sat down again. 'Noreen was delighted as well. She asked John to shadow-supervise me, but so far I've not had to ask him anything. I've made a few decisions myself on how to lead the project, and so far it seems to be working out. It's good to know he's there, though.'

Marissa beamed from the doorway at her friend. 'You're amazing. I'm so glad to have helped you shine.'

Sarah blushed, 'I don't know about that.'

'Well, I think you do, and I'm proud of you,' Marissa said.

'I'm proud of you, too,' Sarah replied. 'Look at you, making your dreams come true too. We must organise that weekend away. Let me get my calendar. Oh dear, I've got so much on right now, it won't be till later in the summer. I hope that's okay.'

'That's perfectly okay with me, I have a lot on too. Let's wait until we are both free to enjoy it without being preoccupied. Did I tell you - I'm going back to my shamanic training this weekend? I'm so excited!'

The phone rang. 'That is wonderful,' Sarah said. 'I've got to get this, sorry! We can do coffee tomorrow morning, if you're around. I want to hear all about it.'

'Sounds great. Go for it.'

It was raining. Marissa grabbed a ready-meal on her way home from work and heated it up in the oven. Jenny was coming over that evening; it was Marissa's last shot at getting the shamanic homework done before the weekend.

Jenny tonight, then Cabra and St Mary's, and then Clifden! Yay! I'm so glad Jenny can come over to help me. I've not seen her since the last workshop, and that's almost ten weeks ago. Ten weeks.

There was a slight chill in the air and the flat felt slightly damp, as it had been raining all day. Marissa turned the heating on, even though it wasn't cold outside, and burned a scented candle to freshen up the air. At 7pm on the dot, the doorbell rang.

Marissa opened the door to see a slightly damp Jenny standing there. It was strange to see her out of her usual context. Jenny smiled, and Marissa smiled back, then invited her in.

'Hi! Jenny, it's really good to see you. Thanks so much for doing this.'

'No bother, sure I wasn't doing anything else this evening.'

Jenny entered the flat, put down two large bags and a handbag, and took off a heavy woollen cardigan which was damp from the rain. Marissa took a look at her: jeans, brown curly hair, large crystal pendant – yes, this was Jenny. She took the cardigan and hung it on the back of the chair so it wouldn't loose its shape as it dried.

Jenny smiled, then hesitantly reached out and hugged Marissa. Marissa hugged her back. *There. It feels better now.*

'It's good to see you again,' Jenny said. 'And I'm glad you're coming back.' She pulled away to look at Marissa, then looked at the flat. 'Wow, this place is great! Do you have a garden too? Can I see it? It's stopped raining now.'

'Oh great! Yes, of course.'

They went outside. Raindrops covered the deckchairs, which were still out from Finn's visit, but now the sky was bright, the air was balmy, birds were chirping, and they could hear the sound of children singing clapping songs down the street. It had turned into a lovely summer's evening.

'Oh, look at those rose bushes, they're just about to blossom! I should really do something with my garden.' Jenny peered into the flowerbeds, examining everything and commenting on how lovely it all was.

'Thanks,' Marissa said. 'Michelle loves flowers. She lives upstairs. We grow sunflowers together every year. She starts them off in pots in her flat. We're trying some early ones this year. Look, they're small but powerful, as she says! I don't know if these will grow very tall, though. It's still a little cold. Michelle rarely comes outside, but she loves seeing the sunflowers from her window. Last year they got up to eight feet tall!'

'I'd say this was a real sun trap,' said Jenny, noticing the position of the setting sun. 'You could probably grow anything in here, I think. You should get some borage, it makes great tea. The flowers are great too. They're said to give you courage. And the tea gives you psychic abilities!'

'That sounds fascinating,' said Marissa, genuinely fascinated.

'Yes, I know. I tried growing it once. The flowers are so beautiful and bright, but the tea tastes awful,' she grimaced, 'unless you put a lot of sugar and honey in it.'

Marissa laughed. 'Did you notice any difference in your psychic abilities?'

'Actually, I did. It was almost as awful as the tea! I heard every spirit in the house. It went on for weeks, too. It was fun at first, of course, but after a while I just wanted them to leave me alone. Yeah, if you're ultra-sensitive already, like me, maybe it's not such a good idea!'

'Speaking of tea, would you like some normal tea?'

'Sounds great, thanks.'

They took their mugs outside and Marissa wiped down the deckchairs. The sun was golden now. It really was a very pleasant spot, even when it was damp.

'I bet you come out here a lot,' said Jenny, settling into the chair, her hands wrapped around her mug. Marissa brought out a plate of chocolate digestives and Jenny took one. Marissa did too, then settled into the other chair.

'Yes, I love it here. Maybe one day I'll have enough money to be able to buy the place from the landlord. It does feel like it's my home.'

'But don't you have a boyfriend? There wouldn't be enough room here for the both of you, and a few babies too.'

'Oh! Well, I didn't think of that.' *Am I going to have babies with Matt? Oh God I'm not ready for that. She did say she was quite psychic though.*

'Maybe you'll be able to buy the whole building! You'd have plenty of room then! But there's plenty of time for all that!' Jenny dipped her biscuit in her tea.

'Are you doing a reading on me? I'm certain I'm not pregnant right now.'

'Maybe. I don't know where that came from.' Jenny turned to study Marissa again. 'You've changed since I saw you last, Marissa. Your energy is much bigger, brighter even. It seems like you have expanded quite a bit, you're taking up more space.'

'Well, I have changed, that's true.'

'Why did you give it up? Was it because of the dark energy you mentioned? Is that what scared you away?'

'Yes, it put me into a real spin. I went into crisis for a while and had to shut it all down. But I'm much more myself while I'm doing this work. It's like I couldn't breathe without it, and now I've got an oxygen supply.'

Jenny seemed satisfied with that answer.

After a moment Marissa said, 'I remember now, you saw some too, didn't you? Dark energy. Around the same time.'

'Oh yes, I see it a lot. I've always seen it. It's a part of our lives, I think most people switch it off because they don't want to see it. But we have to accept it. We don't need to take it on, though, or engage with it. That's what I've been learning. Every time I saw it, I'd think I had to clean it up, but I'm not strong enough most of the time.' She sipped her tea. 'The work I've done with Séamus has really helped me with that. Though I have a lot more to learn. That's really why I wanted to do the apprenticeship. I've been seeing spirit for many years, and it can be overwhelming.'

'There's a lot I don't know about you,' Marissa said thoughtfully. 'Funny how we didn't become closer during the workshops.'

'Well, we move in and out of each other's lives as we need to. Timing and energy are connected. There's lots of time for us to get to know each other better. And maybe you weren't ready to hear what I have to say. Now, should we do some work? It's getting late.'

'It's usually me that's the timekeeper!' Marissa laughed. 'Yes please, let's do the work. And thanks again for coming over. I need to get a stone, though, before we start. I was going to take one from here, from the garden. Give me a moment.'

She went over towards the magnolia tree, looked amongst the stones there and found one that she liked. It was a pebble, white and nondescript, but it came from her garden, and that was the energy she wanted for her medicine bundle.

Hello, stone, will you be my medicine stone and work with me? You will? Thank you!

They went inside and left the plate and mugs in the sink.

'I had a plinth here yesterday,' Marissa said apologetically, 'but I had clients last night and needed to take it back to my Reiki room. Would you rather I lay on the sofa or the floor?'

'Reiki room! You're seeing clients now for Reiki?'

'Yes. I've just started really, I'm still getting the hang of it, but I do like it. I hope to see them for psychotherapy there too at some stage, and maybe even some shamanic work.'

'Ah, that's great.' Jenny smiled. 'Yes, you're stepping into your power. Lots still to do, of course. Let's work on the floor. It's easier for me to do this kneeling down, otherwise I might hurt my back.'

Marissa had her duvet and a pillow at the ready. She laid them on the floor and got another pillow and a throw as well.

'Let's open sacred space,' said Jenny. 'Which way is North?'

After they had said the prayer, Marissa lay down.

'What is your intention for this medicine stone?' asked Jenny.

Marissa had been thinking about this all day. 'I want to be able to access my inner magic,' she said, confidently.

'Okay then! Nice.' Jenny connected to Reiki and started a treatment.

Marissa recognised the energy. 'Oh! That's Reiki! Thank you, it's lovely.'

'You're welcome. I think shamanic processes are more effective when you relax the client with Reiki first. I can keep going, if you like. You do seem very tense.'

Tense? Am I? I didn't think I was. 'Okay, thanks, if it isn't too much trouble.'

'No trouble at all.'

Marissa shifted her position, got more comfortable, then closed her eyes.

She was flying through a dark night. Stars were glistening in the sky and the moon was almost full. Her arms outstretched, she banked and dove through trees towards a castle, a tall dark castle which rose from the surrounding landscape. There were several large windows that had lights inside them. She was drawn towards one of them.

She landed on a turret and looked in. It was a large bedroom with a four-poster bed, portraits hung on the wall in elaborate frames and there was a dressing-table with many items laid out upon it for a man. The window was slightly open, there was a light breeze and she could smell a musky scent wafting towards her through the window. Her head was spinning from the exhilaration of flight. The images were so vivid she could hear her own breath as it slowed. She knew where she had to go.

Armour? Did I put it on? Yes.

Tori moved swiftly through the open window, through the bedroom and out into the corridor. She kept moving.

There were smaller portraits hanging on the corridor wall. She thought she recognised one of the faces, so she went over to take a closer look. Scott Taylor! Oh my God! *And there was another one.* Martin? That can't be Martin? My lovely Martin? *She shivered and walked to another.* Is this Cheryl Bryant? What is this place?

She wanted to get out of there fast, but something pulled her back. William, is there a portrait of him here too?

She ran up and down the corridor, looking at the portraits, becoming frantic. She didn't find William, but she did see an unfinished portrait. The face was flickering in and out. It looked so familiar... Who is that?

'Marissa! Stop it! We have a mission here, you're interrupting me...'

'Sorry, Tori, I didn't mean...'

'Why are you here?? Well, we'll have to work with it. Now shhh, stand back and let me do what I came here to do.'

Tori moved swiftly past the other images in the corridor, looking firmly ahead of her. She went down two staircases and came out into what could have been servants' quarters. The corridor here was plain and the rooms were sparse and simple: two single beds to a room and a plain wooden wardrobe between them. Some rooms had windows and some had not.

Tori went into one of them. There was a girl on the bed dressed in a dirty white nightgown, curled into a foetal position on top of the sheets. She held her hands over her ears, she was writhing in agony.

'There now, it's going to be okay. I'm here.'

Tori reached for her belt pack and felt for a small purple glass bottle with a liquid in it. She released it from the belt, carefully opened the stopper and held it to the girl's lips, forcing her to drink some of it. The girl stopped moaning, unfurled her body and went to sleep quickly.

The girl in the other bed was watching every move. 'Can I have some of that too?' she asked, nodding towards the bottle.

Tori went to her and poured a few drops onto her tongue.

'Thank you kindly, miss,' said the girl. She lay down on the bed, gathered the covers over her and went to sleep.

Tori left the room, went into another, and did the same with the occupants of that room.

'What are we doing?'

'Shhh, Marissa, let me work. You shouldn't be here, remember?'

After she had visited each room in the corridor, Tori found the stairs once more and went down one more level.

This place was dark, close and dense. The energy was heavy and sticky. Tori walked to a heavy, dark wooden door at the end of the corridor, opened it and went into a room full of cases and shelves – shelves filled to the brim with glass jars with lids on them.

I know what these are! thought Marissa, trying not to disturb Tori. She received an affirmation in the form of a grunt as Tori looked through the shelves. She took a torch from her belt pack and scanned each jar, but there were no labels, and the jars were so dusty the light didn't seem to make any difference to her search.

She used a finger to rub the dust from one of the jars and a soft light glowed from inside. Once it had appeared, the jars on either side of it began to glow with a faint yellow light too. This started a cascade effect, and soon the whole room was alight.

'We don't have much time. Ah, here we go. It's this one.'

Tori plucked a jar from the shelf and pocketed it. The lights in the other jars began to fade, and the room became dark once more.

Marissa's heart fell. She knew inside each jar was a soul, a trapped soul with no hope of getting out. She wanted to stay there and sing to them, to tell them they hadn't been forgotten, and to release them if she could. But Tori walked swiftly to the door, looked left then right, then left again, then started creeping back the way she had come, up the stairs, past the servants' quarters, up more stairs and back through the corridor with all the portraits.

The bedroom door was closed.

Tori took some kind of lock pick from her belt pack and opened the door with a quiet click. She could hear activity inside –laughter, the clinking of glasses, men's voices.

Tori crept silently into the room and hid behind a curtain. She glanced at the window she had come through, calculating her chances of getting out without the people seeing her.

Slowly she crept along the wall, keeping to the dark places. The men, three of them, wore medieval style outfits you'd imagine a prince in a fairy tale would wear. They toasted small glasses with a dark red drink in it and *laughed, then one of them said, 'Let me show you,' and they followed him through a door into an ante-chamber.*

Now, *thought Tori, and she ran for the open window and climbed deftly through it and out onto the turret, into the night air.*

Someone was standing there, waiting for her.

'Almost finished now,' said Jenny, 'I'll use Reiki to close, then I'll blow your gift into the stone.'

Marissa was reeling. *Did Tori get away? She must have got away.* She tried to go back into the images, but they were gone. She felt her stomach sicken and a weight press down on her chest. Whatever Jenny was doing didn't seem to help. She sighed. She couldn't do anything. Hopefully whoever was waiting for Tori was no match for her. *And all those souls in all those jars... What to do about them?* She tried to bring her awareness back into the room and saw Jenny blow into the white pebble from the garden that had been sitting on her chest during the session.

'It's a strange gift that I got for you,' Jenny said, 'but things are often strange to me. It's not for me to decide. I suppose a medicine bottle is good medicine. I thought it was too literal, though. Maybe I made it up?'

'What did it look like?' asked Marissa, taking the stone into her hand and sitting up. She felt as though a part of her energy was stuck in the journey. *But I'm not in pain this time, so that's good.*

'It was small. Like a perfume bottle, I think. Purple. With a stopper. Nice, actually. I wouldn't mind one like that myself. Medicine for your magic. Magical medicine!'

'Thank you, Jenny.'

'I didn't see much in the journey, but there were lots of angels, some fairies too, we were in a pretty forest, it really was quite beautiful. Oh yes! A white rabbit gave me the bottle for you. That seemed important.' Jenny looked at her. 'Are you sure you're okay? You don't look so good. The Reiki was supposed to help you relax, but you seem tenser than before I started.'

Marissa shrugged her shoulders, feeling despondent, needing to know if Tori was okay, yet wanting to appreciate the gift of her new medicine stone at the same time. It really was a lot to process.

'A good night's sleep will help,' said Jenny firmly, helping Marissa to her feet. 'Spiritual work isn't always pretty. Sometimes it opens up something that's painful, needing to be cleared.'

Marissa opened her medicine bundle delicately and looked at its contents. She added the new stone to it. It was much more substantial now: she had five stones, a bear, a feather and a pouch with her new pendulum, and another pouch with the black, red and green stones that she was saving for the weekend workshop.

'Nice bundle!' Jenny said. 'I love your bear. You got it from Brigid, didn't you? You've almost caught up with us all now.'

Marissa smiled, trying to shake off the strange heavy feeling.

'Oh, is that the time already?' Jenny said, looking at the clock. 'I'd better be going. I've an early start in the morning.' Then she paused and looked at Marissa again. 'No, there's definitely something wrong here.'

'I'll be okay, go. Sure, like you said, after a good night's sleep I'll be fine.'

'Let me know tomorrow how you are?'

Marissa saw Jenny to the door, then wrapped a blanket around her shoulders and went back outside. The garden was cold and dark. She shivered, then folded the chair Jenny had been using and leaned it up against the wall. She sat in the other one and replied to Matt's Goodnight text, not mentioning that she wasn't feeling so good.

Tobermory mewed and wrapped himself around her legs, then climbed up onto her lap. He was checking her. *He's only done this twice before, when I was in shock, after that thing. I wonder what this means?*

She stroked him. He still had the white flash across his face and white spots on his front leg, but that was all. He'd been spared further colour changes.

Or bodyguard hits. He's such a good cat, protecting me. Maybe I'll need him again. Maybe I'll have to go back there and release those poor souls. If Tori is okay, that is. Who was waiting for her? Oh God, I'm too scared to go back there alone, after all that pain that time.

She lifted her cat up to her face and nuzzled against him, drawing comfort from his presence. He started purring and her heart softened slightly. After a few moments he indicated with twitching tail that he would prefer to be back on her lap as before.

Sleep crept up Marissa's legs and through her body, and she dozed off. Then she woke suddenly with a flash of inspiration: *Tori! She got away!* She felt better then. She got up and went inside, and tumbled into bed still in her clothes.

CHAPTER SEVENTEEN

Marissa woke in a cold sweat. *William! The flickering portrait was of William!*

Sitting up in bed she rubbed her eyes and tried to recall the dream images that were already dissolving.

I really have to do something to help him. A sudden physical flash of physical pain reminded her. *I can't do this on my own, though. That's what Séamus said: 'Don't do this alone.' I need to get some help. But from where?*

She lay back down and turned on her side, looking out of the window. There was still time before she needed to get up. She sighed. *I'll visit my sea serpent and see how he's doing.*

She checked her alarm was still set, then, closing her eyes, willed herself to the lakeside.

It was foggy and difficult to see anything. The lake was covered by a cloud, the mountains had faded into it and she couldn't even see their snowy caps. She knew she was in the right place, however. The ground was still her stony beach, and she could feel the strong presence of her mountain behind her even though she could not see it.

'Emelda? Grandmother Medicine Woman! I need you! Please come and talk to me. I want to ask your advice. I need some help. Please?'

She paced the shore, but nobody came. Then she saw a white rabbit appear.

'You!'

It hopped from one foot to another in a cartoony way, flicking its ears. It was cute and funny and after a few hops, it made her giggle. It obviously wanted her attention, she walked towards it then it turned its back on her and hopped away.

Follow the white rabbit!

She followed it and it turned away from the lake, towards a forest, then it was gone.

Marissa started to run to catch up. There!

There it was, hopping along casually to make sure she was still following. It stopped for a moment by a tree, then went inside it.

Marissa went to the tree and found a hole near the ground.

It didn't go in the tree at all, it went down a rabbit-hole!

Carefully, she climbed in after it. A slide took her down and down and spat her out into a dark place lit by torches.

Hieroglyphs on the wall. Egypt! Pyramids! *Marissa touched the ankh around her neck.*

'It's a pity you don't do that more often in your real world,' said a masculine voice off to one side of her. 'It might keep you on the straight and narrow.'

She followed the voice and found Thoth sitting at a table with books and measures, doing accounts. He put down his pen and looked up at her.

'We are here to protect and teach you. I've been expecting you for a long time, but you haven't come.'

'The white rabbit? Was that you?'

He nodded. 'White rabbit medicine. The rabbit, then the medicine. Yes, that was me sending for you with a warning from the Great Goddess. Sit down.' He gestured to a chair which appeared at the other side of his desk.

She sat.

'Tea?'

A tea set for two appeared on the table. He waited a moment, then poured a light coloured liquid out from the teapot into elegant China cups, which looked quite out of place with the rest of the scene. He lifted his cup, drank in the scent, and then sipped.

'It's not quite as powerful as the elixir you came across last night,' Thoth said with a grin.

Marissa wasn't ready for her tea just yet. 'Tori. She's okay? What happened to Tori?'

'Tori is fine. She's been doing this for a long time and is well able to handle it. But you, you're a novice.'

'But I thought I was her last night. I'm so confused.'

'You are an incarnation of her, but you are not fully integrated with her. She does what she does while you go about your own business, and

sometimes you merge, and, like last night, you split. Your dilly-dallying caused her much distress. Thankfully she was able to get away.'

Marissa hung her head then sipped her tea, full of remorse.

'I know you couldn't help it, and yes, those people were who you thought they were in the portraits. There's not much you can do for them at this stage.'

Marissa looked up. 'Martin? I thought he was free of the demon? And William? Was that him in the unfinished portrait?'

'Martin currently has an opportunity for atonement, which is an unusual situation, thanks to you. Well done, by the way. But plenty of damage has been done to warrant his face on that wall. It's up to him, now. And as for Will, well, he is not lost yet, he's quite the fighter. He must do it for himself, though. As must we all.'

Thoth sipped his tea again. 'Perhaps you can help him get stronger. Evil is a nasty, difficult business. You must learn contract law and be very clever in order to work with it and come away unscathed.'

'Contract law?'

'It's an art form. Art at its finest. But that's what you have me for, for now. Next time you find yourself on one of Tori's missions, it would be best if you just rode along with her instead of pulling her away from her task, yes?'

'Is this a scolding?'

'In a gentle way, yes, it's a scolding.'

Feeling slightly better, Marissa asked, 'Were there souls in those jars? And who was in the jar Tori took? Why couldn't she take more than one? Can she free them?'

'So many questions, young Marissa. But I have only one piece of wisdom to impart to you today.'

She nodded. 'Contract law?'

'Perhaps. Or perhaps it was something else. You decide.'

'I don't understand.'

The images faded away and she was back in her bed. *So frustrating!*

Sarah and Noreen were having an issue with the recognition of qualifications.

'There is absolutely no point in offering ECDL if they're not going to accredit us as a provider,' said Noreen.

'You're right Noreen, I'll get Marissa to help me put together the application.'

It's quite interesting working on this new project, and it makes the day go faster.

After work, Marissa caught her buses out to St Mary's.

I miss Mary R already. She'll be in Mayo by now, I hope she's having a ball. Hey, I wonder if I'll have someone new today. And Lucy might finally try Reiki. I remember how Dolores showed us in Level 1 how to do a chair session. Perhaps I'll ask if I can try that with her. And Loretta...

She remembered cutting away the collar from Loretta's neck in her previous session. *I wonder how she got on this week, if that made any difference. I wonder if she'll even show up for our session tonight...*

Marissa quickly calculated how many client sessions she had done and how many she had left to do before she qualified for her diploma. *Not enough. I'll be working all through the summer at this rate, and I still won't have enough hours. I'll need to get access to my own room earlier on Mondays.*

She pulled out her phone and emailed the letting agent, asking if there were more hours available.

I'll need to make a website, and post some adverts, as well as the business cards. I've been putting that off for a while now, too. I wonder why.

She had no clients booked in except for Valeria, who had been so delighted after the last session that she had block booked Marissa three weeks in a row.

I'll sort it all out next week, when I get back after the workshop.

Feeling practical, Marissa made a list of everything she had to do.

At least the bus trip has been useful, even if nobody shows up tonight.

After being buzzed in, Marissa got a hot cup of instant coffee from the canteen and made her way to the therapy room with a few minutes to spare. She settled in, lit a candle, then stood up and felt agitated. She fingered the ankh around her neck. Images of her dream – *Or was it a journey?* – flooded in as she touched it. *Ah, was this the piece of advice from Thoth? What a strange piece of advice. What now? I'll open sacred space. At least it will make the energy of this room nicer to be in.*

She was still saying the prayer out loud when Lucy knocked and came in. She stood by the door watching Marissa, who decided to keep going, even with Lucy watching. When she had finished, they both sat down.

'What was that, miss? It's lovely.'

Lucy looked much brighter. She still had a bandage on her wrist, but it was smaller, and the bruising was yellow now. Her eyes were wide and she had colour in her face. It was nice to see her looking stronger.

'You don't need to call me "miss", it's "Marissa".'

'Oh yeah. Sometimes I think I'm back at school in here. Some of them treat you that way anyway.'

'Well, you don't have to do that with me. And the prayer, it's a sacred prayer for opening a healing space. I thought it would make the room feel good to work in. Not that there was anything wrong with it before I said the prayer.'

'I pray all the time myself,' Lucy stated. 'I find great comfort in it. The Lord's Prayer and the rosary, mostly. But I like the sound of your prayer too. I'd never heard of it before.'

'It is a beautiful prayer, I love it. It's from the native peoples of the world, calling on the energies of the world to support them while they do healing work.'

'Not from the Bible then?' Lucy was suddenly very interested.

'No, it's not a Christian prayer. I don't know if it belongs to any religion at all, to be honest. Perhaps it's the religion of nature – The Bible of Earth, Sea and Sky.'

'I like that.' said Lucy, nodding her head. 'I always feel better when I'm outside. Nature is the best healer, that's what I read in a book one time. It stuck with me, but I don't really know what it means. What do you think it means, Marissa?'

Marissa thought for a moment. 'Well, nature doesn't want to fight you, it doesn't criticise you or offend you. It's never personal, if it rains, it rains on everyone, not just you.'

Lucy giggled.

'It takes you as you are, and if you sit there peacefully, you feel more at peace.'

'True. That makes sense. And the sea, I love sitting by the sea.'

'The sea is a wonderful place. Emotional, like we are, I suppose. Big strong waves, just as we have big strong waves of grief, or happiness.'

'But how does that heal us?'

'Maybe we heal when we see ourselves better, and we see ourselves better when we go to nature because she is the same for everyone.' *Yes, that makes sense to me too!*

'That makes more sense than what I read in the book that I saw. You should write a book, Marissa.'

'Maybe I will one day. I certainly read lots of books, so why not?'

Lucy smiled.

'So, Lucy, what did you want to talk about with me tonight?'

'I feel good tonight, Marissa. I'm still sad, but I learned how to knit this week and I think I'm almost ready to go back into the real world. Maybe when I finish my scarf.

'That sounds good, then you can wear it for support.'

'I'm making it for my Mam. But I could make one for me, too.'

'Did you try that exercise with Peter again?'

'I didn't need to. I think I'd said everything I needed to say to him, and I don't mind so much now not hearing back from him. Something inside me isn't stormy anymore. Like nature. It's a calmer day in here.' She patted her heart. 'It's still raining from time to time, but it's soft gentle rain, not a harsh storm.'

'I like this, weather comparisons. Well done, Lucy, and I'm very glad you're feeling better, if a little damp.'

Lucy grinned.

Maybe it's best not to do Reiki with her, it might bring up something and she seems to be managing just fine right now.

'Okay then. Let's talk about what you'd like to do when you get out of here and start to create a new life for yourself.'

'Well, I was thinking of going back to school...'

The room was quiet when Lucy left. *It was refreshing to see her so animated and interested in her future.* Marissa stretched, got up and cleared the energy ready for the next person. She looked at the time. Loretta could either show up or not, depending on her mood and whether she had a space for the children in the crèche.

At about ten minutes past the hour, there was a knock on the door. Loretta came in looking dishevelled as usual, but there was new life behind her eyes and colour in her cheeks. *Today is a good day!* Her hair was in a messy bun and she was wearing a grey tracksuit. She sat down in the chair opposite Marissa and crossed her legs.

'Hi, Loretta, it's good to see you. Glad you could make it. How are things with you this week?'

After a moment, Loretta answered, 'Well, I managed to get one or two nights' sleep, which made a big difference. But Barry Jr has another tooth coming down and he's been terrible cranky the last few days. I thought he was finished with all of that! He's quite a handful when he's cranky. And Barry senior, their da, well, I managed to speak to him. I think we've come to an arrangement now. You were right – he's their father and I do need to let them see him. It wouldn't be right for the kids not to know their da.' she scratched her nose, then added, 'But I want it to be on my terms. So I said he could see them on the days that I picked. He was real nice about it, surprised me. He even said I deserved a break from the kids. He agreed they were a lot to manage. He said he'd take all of them, even the baby.' She looked at the floor, and kicked her top leg. 'It means I can do a few things for myself when they're not around. So it could end up being a good thing for everybody. The kids too, I suppose.'

'That's great, Loretta, well done. You must be happy?'

Loretta smiled. 'I'm too tired to be happy. I almost want him to take them today so I can sleep. All I want to do is sleep. But it's good, isn't it?'

'Yes, and I understand about the sleep.'

'Have kids?'

Marissa shook her head.

'Naw, you don't understand then.' Loretta laughed.

'Fair enough,' said Marissa, smiling.

'So, once I catch up on my sleep, which could take a while, I can start to make some plans for my life,' Loretta said, sitting up straighter. 'I've not been able to before. The kids have taken up all my time.'

'That's really great,' said Marissa, wondering inadvertently if having a collar removed energetically had helped Loretta find her voice with Barry. *I suppose you could take these things literally. Or maybe it's just a coincidence. I will never know. But either way, something has improved for her. And that's really why she comes to see me, so that's good.*

'So, Loretta, what would you like to talk about tonight?'

'It's funny, Marissa, I haven't been able to see the forest for the trees, so to speak. But now that Barry will actually help instead of hold me back, God willing, I'm wondering what I can do to create a better life for myself. Of course it still remains to be seen if he shows up and does what he says he'll do. I still don't trust the fecker. Still, I've got to give him a chance. For the kids' sake. I'd like him to give *me* a chance too. Treat others how they would treat you, right?'

Marissa nodded.

'Yeah, so I'd like us to talk about what job I should get, stuff like that.'

'Sorry, Loretta, I'm not trained to do that, I'm not a guidance counsellor and I can't give you career advice. But I can certainly listen to what you have in mind and reflect it back to you so that you can get your head straight around what it is you would like to do, based on the information that you already have.'

'Yeah, Mary kind of said that to me. I miss her. Heard she's doin' great in Mayo. She's a good kid.'

'Oh, that's good to hear.'

'Yeah, she deserved a break. Hope she has a very happy life. Anyway, as far as advice goes, I didn't expect you to have a college prospectus or anything like that for me. But maybe college is something I might do in the future, when the kids are older. Right now, my hands are tied with them.'

Hearing those words, Marissa remembered that Loretta had also had shackles around her wrists. *Maybe I should look at her energy while she talks to me and see if there's anything else I can do to help.*

She let Loretta talk while she unfocused her eyes slightly and allowed herself to peer into her energy field. She felt a tightness in her hip and realised that was coming from Loretta's hip. *I must be body mapping. Oh, how interesting! I suppose when we do this, it's difficult to keep the boundaries clear. I must make sure I disconnect properly.*

Allowing Loretta's energy to map itself onto her in a more detailed way, Marissa felt a tightness around her own wrists and hands. She looked at her lap and saw that she herself was shackled now.

She looked at Loretta and couldn't see anything different about her. *Maybe I've mapped the shackles onto myself, too. Does that mean I can take them off?*

She tried to move her hands but felt the energetic binding around them. She visualised herself in her mind so she could get her shamanic knife, but of course, her hands were shackled and she couldn't do it.

Ooh, a puzzle. I love puzzles. How can I unshackle myself?

She thought for a moment then imagined she was wearing the jerkin that had the pocket knife in it. The pocket was open and there was her shiny knife sticking out of it. She was able to reach it with her mouth. It was unsheathed, of course, just like in the movies, *very convenient.* Although if this was real life, it probably would have cut through the jerkin pocket and possibly cut Marissa, *but I'm in control of this, to some degree.* In her mind's eye, with her knife in her mouth, she managed to cut the binding between her hands. Then, she was able to take the knife in one hand and use it to cut the cuff of the shackle around the other. She released her hand, then cut open the other cuff.

She sheathed the knife and put it back in her pocket, and in her mind she gathered together the energy that had created the shackles in the first place. As she gathered it, it became very dark and sludgy. She imagined the violet flame on the floor beside her feet. She pushed the dark energy over her knees and it fell into the flame and was gone.

In the room, Loretta shifted her body at that exact moment. She stretched out her arms, flexed her fingers and stretched them outwards, turning her wrists clockwise and anticlockwise while she spoke about how her grandmother had made her mother go to secretarial college, and how her mother had hated it so much she had refused to send her own children to college, even though they wanted to go.

Marissa looked at her body to see whether there was anything else that she could free. She checked her throat: the collar was still gone. She thought that she felt something in her back between her shoulder blades that was causing constriction in her chest, so she visualised herself stepping out of her own body and walking around behind herself. She took the knife once more and carved gently and carefully around the constricting energy, releasing it, pulling it off and rolling it into a ball. Then she went back around and sat back into her own body and put the ball into the violet flame.

Is it just my imagination or is Loretta sitting up taller now?

The energy of the conversation had changed. Loretta was talking about how she loved to grow different flowers and plants and maybe that was something that she could study and become good at. Marissa agreed with her. She was multitasking now, as Loretta was wanting feedback. So she visualised her own energy field disconnecting from Loretta's and released the body map so that it disconnected from her completely.

She felt the pain in her hip lessen.

'But I couldn't do gardening for a long time,' Loretta was saying, 'particularly when I was pregnant with Aaron, because I had awful pain in my hip. I guess it was like a premonition of how much the kids would take from me.' She laughed.

A pain in her hip. You couldn't make this stuff up. It's just too crazy. I wonder, is there something energetic causing it that I can fix?

'What happened to your hip?'

'Oh, it's always been sore. I think it's from carrying the children – well, it is *now*, anyway. The sore one is the hip I use to rest my elbow on when I have a baby in my arm. You've never seen me carry the children, I always have them in the crèche when I come here, but normally while I'm carrying one of them, one of the others insists on climbing up me. They're getting much too big for it now.'

Maybe it's just a sore hip.

Before Loretta left, Marissa imagined a golden waterfall of light washing them both clean of any energies that had been released during their session together, and she made sure they were completely disconnected from each other.

Loretta looked tired but happy when she left, determined to bring something new into her life and much more confident about the situation with her ex-husband.

It was time for Marissa's next client. Unexpectedly, right on time, there was a knock at the door.

'Come in!'

Marissa really appreciated the client sheet she got in Cabra; here, she didn't know anything about who was coming next. She was just grateful that they showed up, whoever they were.

'Hi, I'm Sorcha.'

'Hi! Nice to meet you. Come in.'

Sorcha came in and chose a chair. She was about twenty-five, average build with long straight dark hair, wearing blue jeans and a dirty white hoodie top. She smiled apologetically.

'What would you like to talk about with me tonight?' asked Marissa as she sat in the other chair.

'My boyfriend. I was talking to Lucy, and she told me how you'd helped her get over Peter. Maybe you could help me too?'

'Sure. Tell me about him.'

CHAPTER EIGHTEEN

Marissa was dead. Her body was scattered on the forest floor in many pieces. She remembered being here before, and her heart sank. The devastation this time was worse than before. She waited, hesitantly, in case there were dark hungry animals lurking in the forest, but there was nothing.

Okay, maybe they've already gone. I have to try something. What can I do?

She lifted herself out of her macerated body so she could look at the situation from a different angle. All of the hacked and chewed parts of her body were in different states of degradation. Some of them looked healthy, and others looked as if they've been totally destroyed. She delicately picked up one of her hands and as she did, it melted into her energetic hand, glowing for a moment, then disappeared into her. It was gone!

Oh! I wonder...

She went to one of her feet. It looked okay. She stepped into it and again it glowed for a moment, then dissolved into her. She felt more solid now.

There was a rustling in the thicket and the dark hungry animal came out with wild eyes, pointed teeth and saliva dripping down its jaws.

'Wait your turn,' said Marissa sharply. 'You can have what's left when I've finished.'

The animal whimpered, then sat, panting, waiting for her to finish.

The work was quite disgusting, but Marissa managed to salvage as much of her body as she could, then she allowed the animal to eat the rest.

'What comes from the forest goes back to the forest,' she heard from behind her. She turned, and saw that her tree was watching her.

'You're here? I didn't see you here before.'

'No, you did not see me, of course. You had to put yourself back together first, my dear. Well done. You have left behind what you no longer needed, what no longer served you, and you have become whole once more.'

'I thought I was dead.' The words just slipped out, sounding strange, but there had been some part of Marissa that had been really worried by these dreams.

'Some part of you has died, yes. It is some older part of you. But you have salvaged what you could and let go of the rest, and so you are renewed. It's all part of the journey, dear,' said the tree, yawning. 'Sometimes we have to go deeply into the dark places to find the pieces of ourselves.'

'And you say the tree told you that?'

Olive adjusted her wrap. Marissa nodded. She had trekked across town from work in a taxi during her lunchbreak. It was a warm day and hot in the sun-room, yet Olive still wore a pashmina. This one was pink, ashes of roses, the colour suited her. Marissa couldn't recall seeing her in it before. Olive also wore pale pink tortoiseshell glasses and a darker pink long cotton skirt with a kick-pleat. She looked good.

Marissa continued. 'Yes, the tree told me that, he's very wise, my tree friend. It felt good to solve that puzzle.'

'It doesn't feel to me that you've finished completely with that one. Dismemberment is a difficult lesson to learn. I remember when I learned it myself. Not quite in the same way as you, it wasn't as ... graphic.'

Marissa giggled. 'I'm excited, Olive. Now that I'm not pushing my journeys away, I'm learning so much. And it's having a positive impact on my clients, too.'

'What do you mean?'

Marissa blushed, catching her unintended disclosure. She had to tell Olive something now that she had blurted it out. *Why not tell her?* 'Well,' she took a breath, 'it's seeping into my therapy sessions – the energy work, I mean. It's almost as if I'm journeying for my clients while I'm in the session with them. I see images, get information... It *has* been helpful so far.'

'So far perhaps, dear,' said Olive, looking more serious, 'but you must be careful to set good boundaries. I know, I know, it's difficult to keep these things separate, but as long as you're working in the system, you must stay in the system.'

‘Oh, yes, I know, and I do.’ *Most of the time, anyway...*

‘Well that’s enough about that then. Please keep it that way. On another note, have you had any movement towards getting some psychotherapy clients of your own?’

Marissa was relieved at the change of topic, yet this one wasn’t going her way either. ‘The letting agent for my healing room, in Rathmines, she wrote back to me and told me that Sam, the man before me, has the hour in the room I use booked and paid for until December.’

‘Oh dear, how disappointing.’

‘I know. Unless I move to a completely new place, I’m kind of stuck.’

In a pointed tone, Olive asked, ‘Exactly how may sessions do you expect to be able to do in one day?’

Marissa thought, and counting on her fingers she said, ‘I suppose I could do six or seven, if I started at 11.’

‘Is that something you could sustain? It could lead to burnout. I’m talking from experience. I had to give up therapy for a year, several years ago, for that very reason.’

‘Olive really? I didn’t know.’

‘Well how could you know unless I told you?’ Olive took off her glasses and cleaned them with her pashmina, then put them back on again with a smile. ‘Yes, I was ambitious, I do see myself in you at times. That’s why I want you to listen to me. For what is the point of my learning if I cannot share it? We always talk about self-care in these sessions, Marissa, and I don’t see your continuity. That is what worries me the most about you at present. Self-care is a practice that must be maintained.’

Marissa’s face fell. ‘Yes, you’re right, I’ve not been doing anything bar the occasional Reiki self-practice.’

‘And only when you remember to do it, which is not when you may actually need it. Marissa, you have to keep a schedule, you must put your self-care sessions in your diary. At least once a fortnight you should organise something for yourself to nourish you and replenish your soul. And you really must spend some amount of time every day in silence. ’

'It seems like a chore.'

'If you decide it's a chore, then it will be one. When in fact, it is quite the opposite. You might think it eats up time now, my dear, but you will thank me for it in the years to come, I promise you. You must look after yourself.'

'Yes, okay, I'll give it a go.'

'I hope so.' Olive looked at her notes. 'It could simply be a half day off, you know, just walking somewhere in nature, or drinking coffee and reading a good book. It doesn't have to be something spectacular or expensive. Just time for you to come back into yourself.' Olive made a note in her notebook, then tucked it away again. 'And how are you getting along with your boyfriend – Matt, isn't it?'

'He's so lovely.' Marissa softened, resolving to do better with her self-care. 'And easy-going. We love each other's company, he gets on well with Mum and Dad, and Eli asked if they could go drinking together, just the two of them, which is unusual. But I liked it. Carol is due her baby soon. Actually, Eli's friend might have a room for me. He's mentioned it before...'

'And are you finding time for stillness?'

'Erm ... does watching TV count? Though I've not been watching it as much lately. I've started listening to music a little bit, but I guess I've been scrambling to get everything ready for tomorrow. I've had a lot of homework for Séamus to catch up on.'

'That most certainly does not count as time in stillness, Marissa.'

'I'm only pulling your leg! Seriously, Olive, can't you see when I'm telling a joke?'

'No, I can't.'

'I'll make more time for stillness after this weekend with Séamus, I promise. But I've got too much to do first!'

'You don't need to promise me anything, you need to do it for yourself. That's always the way. But you'll know when you start burning out. Is there anything else I should know about before we finish? We are just about at time now.'

'Yes, there is something I wanted to ask you about. What does contract law have to do with evil?'

Olive looked completely taken aback. 'My dear, at five minutes to the hour, you ask me that?' She smiled and wrote something down in her notebook, then turned back to Marissa. 'I've not heard it put that way before, how very interesting. You really are multitasking. Stillness, child, take time out to be still. And we can talk about this another day.'

Marissa quickly ate her warm (and now squashed) egg sandwich in the taxi back to work, as she was somewhat concerned about leaving an eggy smell in the car. It was a quick and rushed lunch, and a quick and rushed afternoon as she needed to leave slightly earlier than usual to make it over to Cabra for supervision. *Olive, now Mr Blakemore, then three clients, plus work. I can see why Olive's concerned about me doing too much, but I am getting it all done. I feel just fine. Wonder what she meant when she said that I'd know when I start burning out?*

Later that day, in what felt like the blink of an eye, she was sitting in Mr Blakemore's office. She slowed her breathing down, trying to bring her awareness out of her work day and into the room where she was. She needed a moment to catch up with herself. *One squashed sandwich for lunch and nothing at all for dinner. Oh well, I'll get chips on my way home. Yes! That's a great idea.*

She observed Mr Blakemore. He looked pale and drawn in dark brown cords, a cream shirt and a purple tie. He also looked very formal, if a little awkward, reminding Marissa of the phrase 'a fish out of water'. His hair was brushed over to one side, a little too much, it was thinner than before and his glasses needed cleaning. *I wonder if he's married? He needs someone to look after him. It must be difficult to be sick and be on your own.* Someone had been in and cleaned his office, but somehow, it still felt dusty.

'Hello Marissa, it's good to see you after such a while.'

'Welcome back, Mr Blakemore. The office told me you were only starting back today.'

'Yes, that's right.'

They were sitting in their usual chairs, but Mr Blakemore couldn't seem to settle. He uncrossed his legs, stood up slowly and walked over to his desk, opened the drawers, then closed them again. He looked around the room.

'I think the girls in the office must have moved my stuff around. I can't find your file, Marissa. Can you fill me in on how you've been getting on in my absence? Who are your clients at the moment?'

'I've just finished with Aisling. Tonight is William's last session, and I am also seeing Niamh.'

'Ah yes, William. I knew his father. Lovely man. How is he doing?' Mr Blakemore went back to his chair, sat down and crossed his legs again, his brown trouser leg riding up as usual to expose white flesh and purple socks that were almost the same colour as his tie.

His socks match his tie today. Marissa tried to keep her focus on the topic at hand. 'Honestly, I'm not sure how William is doing. I feel we've made little progress, but he doesn't want another cycle.'

'That's a pity, that's a pity. I'm sure you've done your best. Perhaps he would be better suited to someone else? A man, perhaps? You could ask him tonight if he wants to do another cycle with a different therapist.'

Marissa was taken aback at the thought. *Me, unsuitable for William? How?* Mr Blakemore was looking at her, still waiting for her to answer. With a heavy heart, she answered, 'Yes, I suppose I could.'

'Good, good. He doesn't have to, and he may not want to, but it's always worth a try. Chemistry is important between therapist and client. Sometimes, try as we might, the chemistry just isn't right.'

I'm pretty sure that's not the problem here. Marissa felt herself getting upset and angry, taking it personally, feeling that there was something wrong with her. *No, stop it. Therapy isn't about me, and there could be something to this. I have to stop feeling I know everything and I can help everyone. I don't and I can't.*

'We can't always help everyone, you know,' said Mr Blakemore, apologetically, looking kindly at Marissa. 'I'm sure you're doing your best. Don't take it personally. Therapy isn't about the therapist, and sometimes the relationship just doesn't work out. Now, who do you have starting with you tonight?'

'I'm not sure,' said Marissa, 'I've not had a chance to look at the client sheet yet.'

'Ah, here it is,' said Mr Blakemore with pride, standing up and pulling a file out from under the cushion of his chair. 'Ha! I must have put it there earlier, knowing you were coming in! Your file.' He opened it and pulled out a coffee-stained sheet of paper. 'Kevin. Yes, that will be interesting. Nice man. I know his son.'

Marissa laughed. 'You know everyone, Mr Blakemore!'

Mr Blakemore chuckled. 'I've been around a long time, yes, although this past scare – well, it's over now. And I'm quite alright,' he added in a reassuring tone. 'As far as knowing everyone, perhaps not. But I have met quite a few of our local community. It's good to be able to help them, and I'm happy they're availing themselves of our services. Now, Marissa, I won't keep you any longer. You've a full night ahead of you.'

When Marissa arrived upstairs, Frances was still in Room Three and Niamh was waiting for her, standing in the corridor, wearing a short bright yellow dress with a white cardigan on top, and carrying a small backpack-style handbag with roses on it. Frances smiled at Marissa apologetically, knowing that it was after the hour, and left quickly.

'Do you need a minute?' Niamh asked knowingly.

'Actually, yes, a minute inside to prepare for you would be great, thanks,' said Marissa. 'One day I'll have my own full-time space and there won't be any of this messing around,' she added under her breath.

Niamh heard her. 'Oh, how wonderful, that sounds perfect for you! I'll wait outside until you're ready.'

Oops. That's nice, though. I like her.

Marissa went inside. There it was again, that damp smell. But the walls were dry, the ceiling clear. There was nothing tangible to explain it.

'What is going on with this dampness?'

Marissa lit the stub of a candle and used it to set her sage stick alight. *Just enough candle to get through three sessions, it will be fine.* Soon her sage was smoking. She wafted the smoke into the four corners. After a moment, the damp energy lifted, it felt better, so Marissa opened the door and invited Niamh inside.

As she had settled into the chair she always sat in, Marissa asked, 'How are you this week? You seem happy. And I love your dress, very summery.'

'Thank you, I do love it too. I have something good to report to you this week!'

'Great, do tell me.'

'I've been able to keep my phone off for one whole hour every day since I saw you last week! And on the weekend, I even went without it for an afternoon, and I didn't miss it!'

'I'm delighted for you!' Marissa smiled. 'What was the difference?' She cast her mind back to their last session together, but so much had happened since then she was having trouble remembering what they had done.

'You did Reiki on me, remember? I think it really helped.'

'Ahh yes! I remember now, you sat in the chair and I put my hands on you.' *I also cleared up some of the clutter she was carrying inside her energy field. Which wasn't Reiki. Now I remember.*

Niamh nodded. 'Well, I liked it so much, I organised a whole session of Reiki – you know, the full hour. It was marvellous.'

Marissa's heart fell. *She's my client, but she saw somebody else? She could have come to me! She took a breath. Maybe not. Ok. I have to stop being so possessive. It's like Mr Blakemore just said. Twice in a row now. I guess I need to listen, and hear what is being said.*

Niamh was still talking. 'I think it really helped. I felt a lot calmer after it. And I was so happy to be able to switch my phone off.'

Who did she see? No, I don't need to know. And it's good, really, that she feels better. Stop being so self-centred, Marissa. Bring it back to the now. Breathe.

Niamh was looking at Marissa as if she wanted a gold star for the work she did.

Marissa pushed away the hurt which still sat in her heart. 'So, what else can I do to help reduce your anxiety? That's what you came to me for in our first session.'

'It's so much better now, and you've shown me so much, I'm much happier and I can manage the anxiety that I have now, probably for the first time in my life. In fact I don't even know if I need the next two sessions. Don't they give you a cycle of six? We can finish up tonight. I'll let someone else take the rest – they probably need them more than I do.'

She's not getting away from me that easily. 'Actually, don't be so quick to finish up with me,' she said. 'I think now that you have your anxiety in hand, it might be a good time to talk about the possible deeper underlying issue.'

Niamh looked shocked. 'But there isn't one!'

'Maybe it's just not obvious.' *Maybe that's why she didn't want to come to me for Reiki. If there is one I will certainly find it.* 'You can stop counselling now if you want, just because you feel better. But the issue you're managing is more than likely a symptom of something deeper. Usually, you need to feel stable before you can talk about deeper issues. Do you want to try talking a bit tonight and see what comes up for you? If we find something then we can transform it together, and you will feel better for longer. And if we don't uncover anything, then sure, I'll tell the office to cancel the rest of your cycle.'

Niamh looked thoughtful.

'It's okay, we can take it slowly, and if you're uncomfortable with anything you can tell me that, too.'

'I suppose it is an opportunity to go a little deeper, and I know you now, Marissa, so I guess I don't mind telling you stuff.'

'Okay. Good. Now, tell me about the relationship you have with your mother. What's it like?'

Niamh's lips tightened immediately and she went pale. *Good call, Marissa.*

'Take your time, there's no rush.'

Niamh took a breath, then willed herself to continue. 'Yeah, you're right, there's something there for sure. Sometimes I wonder which one of us is the mother. Honestly, she needs me to look after her, she can't do anything by herself.'

'Give me an example?'

Niamh thought for a moment. Sitting in silence for a little while allowed her to regain her composure. 'Well, last week there was a problem with the tap in the kitchen. She lives by herself, Mum, and the tap, it wouldn't shut off. So instead of calling a plumber, she phoned me to ask me what to do. The place was almost half flooded and she was calling me! And then the time before that, when her car wouldn't start... Me again. What do I know about cars? There's lots of stuff like that, where she calls me instead of looking after it herself. I know she *knows* what to do. I suppose it goes back to when I was small.'

'What happened when you were small?'

'Dad left us, and Mum took to drinking, so I had to look after us. Me and my two sisters, and Mum. They're twins, three years younger than me. Mum would start drinking in the morning and be drunk by the afternoon, and then sleep all evening, and then drink again at night. So I made the dinner, got my sisters bathed and put them to bed, and got us all up for school, that kind of thing.'

'That's a lot of responsibility for a child.'

'Yes, much too much for a nine-year-old. I was nine. I didn't know what else to do.'

Marissa thought for a moment. 'I suppose it's difficult to put that down – the responsibility, I mean. Do your sisters still contact you too, looking for help?'

A tear rolled down Niamh's cheek. She took a moment before she could answer.

'It's complicated. I'm kind of in the middle now. They said Mum was a bad influence and they didn't want anything more to do with her. They will see me, but not her. They've tried to make me choose, them or her, but I can't choose. I can't leave Mum on her own.'

'That sounds very difficult for you.'

'Yeah. It is. Mum talks about them all the time, blames me sometimes for their behaviour. And they talk about her too. They want to know how she is, but they pretend that they don't. They have each other, so they don't need me, but they still call me when things go wrong. Yeah, it's difficult. It's like I'm their surrogate mum, and Mum is my child too. And I'm not able to relax around any of them. It *is* hard.'

'Niamh, when I did Reiki on you last week, I did a little more than just Reiki. I worked on your energy field and I found a lot of energy in there that didn't seem to belong to you. I thought you might be interested to know this. It's like you've taken on everyone else's problems, emotional energies, things like that.'

'Yes, sounds like me alright. Why didn't you tell me this last week?'

'I wasn't sure what it was until just now, listening to you. I'm still in training, I'm learning shamanic healing as well as Reiki, and psychotherapy at the same time. It can be a little confusing. But I've told you now. I think it would be useful for you to learn how to stop taking on others' energy and carrying it for them.'

'Okay, it would be worth a try. It is really draining – I'm almost at my wits' end. How do I do it?'

Marissa thought for a moment. 'I don't know for sure, but I have an idea. Your situation, it reminds me of a phrase – "carrying someone else's baggage". How about imagining you're putting that baggage down, instead of picking it up? Start with your mother's. Can you see how many bags you're carrying for your mother? Use your imagination and see - if her emotions and her troubles were bags, that is.'

Niamh closed her eyes for a moment. 'Yeah, actually, I think so. Wait a minute, I've got two suitcases, a backpack and some shopping bags. That's crazy!'

'Yes, it is a lot. Can you imagine you're putting them down now?'

Eyes closed, Niamh looked deep in thought. 'Yes, okay, I've put them down.' She wriggled her shoulders with relief, as if she had actually put heavy bags down on the ground.

She didn't even know that she did that! Marissa smiled.

'Can you imagine yourself walking away from the bags now?'

'Actually, that's really hard. It feels like I have to mind them, stay with them. Even though they're not mine.'

'How old is your mother?

'She's sixty-three.'

'Okay. Do you think she made her own decisions and lived her own life the way she's chosen to live it?'

Niamh opened her eyes. 'Well, I don't know. Maybe. I suppose so.'

'Really think about this. See her as the adult that she is. She's made her choices, whether she's aware of them or not. Now it's your turn to be the adult. What are you choosing?'

'I'm choosing not to carry all those bags for her, that's for sure.' Niamh shivered.

Marissa ignored it and continued. 'Take a step away from the baggage, just one step.'

Niamh waited a moment before answering, 'It's still too hard. Maybe I need more Reiki to do it, like I needed for the phone.'

Marissa shrugged her shoulders. 'I don't have time tonight to give you a full session but you could come and see me in my Reiki room.' Then she added, 'Or you could go back to the person you went to last week, if you liked her.'

'It was a man, actually, and yes, I did like him.' Niamh's eyes lit up.

Aah, see, it's not competition with you. Let it go now.

'We're almost at the end of the session, Niamh. What's going on with the bags now?'

Niamh closed her eyes again and concentrated. 'The bags are still on the ground, but I still can't walk away from them.'

'At least you're not carrying them anymore, that is progress.'

Niamh looked brighter.

'Do you want to come back next week and do some more work on this?'

'Yes, I really do. Thanks for making me stay, Marissa.'

'No problem. I'll set you some homework if that's okay? Every day, visualise this scene, by asking yourself how many bags you're carrying for other people. We haven't looked at your sisters yet, but it doesn't have to be your mother's or your sisters' energy, it could be anybody's. See if you can put the bags down. And if you can, see if you are able to walk away from them. You might need to experiment with it – someone else's bags might be easier for you to walk away from than your mum's. See how you go with it, keep a note of what you've learned, and we can talk about it again next week.'

'Thanks so much, I actually do feel like I put down some heavy bags.'

It had been an intense day and a long evening, and it wasn't over yet. Marissa had an urge to text Matt in the few minutes she had in between sessions.

Hi Love, miss u. Just saying hi.

She was rereading it when the buzzer sounded. It was William. Her heat leapt into her mouth and suddenly she remembered her journey, all the information flooded back into her mind.

What am I going to do? I don't want him to be a portrait on a wall in that horrible place!

She forgot to send the text, buzzed in William, switched off her phone and put it into her bag, and stood up just before William knocked at the door.

'Hi,' she said, letting him inside and looking him over. He appeared to be in the same condition as the previous week, still not good, but no worse. *That's something at least.* 'Come in.'

He was already in, hanging his light jacket on the back of the door while whistling through his teeth.

'Which chair would you like?'

'I don't care. I almost didn't come tonight.' He stood with his legs apart, looking at Marissa. She could almost hear the song 'Should *I stay or should I go?'*

She wanted him to stay.

'Well, I'll take this chair then. You don't have to stay if you don't want to, but I'd like you to, if you're able.' She felt a flicker of anxiety and wondered if William was bringing any bad energy in with him. *If he's flickering in and out in the portrait in my journey, then some part of him is evil, isn't it? Or is it? Was Cheryl Bryant evil? Truly? Or was she just captured too, like the souls in the jars in the basement?*

William sat down awkwardly in the other chair.

'I'm afraid to ask you how you are tonight, Will,' Marissa said, feeling low-level anxiety lap at her ankles.

He smiled weakly. 'I'm crap. Worse than I was before I started. Who told me to come to counselling? It hasn't helped at all.' Then, looking at her face, he said, 'Oh no, I didn't mean – I didn't want to upset you, it isn't you, it's just that nothing has improved, I feel worse in fact, but I know it's not *your* fault. I didn't expect you...'

'It's okay, I hear you, I understand,' Marissa faltered. 'And this is our sixth session of six, so you don't have to come back for any more. You don't even have to stay tonight if you don't want to.'

'No, I'll stay,' William said. 'You're nice, and it's been nice to talk about this. I suppose knowing that someone else knows what I'm going through – well, even just a little bit of what I'm going through – has helped. Just a little bit. So I should take all that back. I'm sorry. I just thought that I'd defeat the bad guy in my dreams and be the king of the castle by now, instead of still being trapped in a basement somewhere.'

Marissa felt a cold flash through her body. *King of the castle? Trapped in a basement? He must have some inkling of what's going on. What do I say? How do I approach this? Thoth – Thoth told me to help him help himself. Yes, that's it – I can't do it for him, but I can help him do it. But how?*

William was waiting.

'You said that I only understood a little bit of what you were going through, so do you want to tell me more? I know you don't want to tell me about the graphic quality of your dreams, but there must be some other things you can tell me about.'

William thought for a moment. 'In the dream, there's this half-man, half-beast type creature there. He seems to be the one in control, making me do bad things. I managed to escape him the other night. I was aware of what I was doing and I ran away, but they caught me again. It was so frustrating.'

'You're aware that you're in your dream while you're dreaming it?'

'Yes.'

Lucid dreaming – what Tim was talking about the other day. And we can change the quality of our encounters if we are aware of them while we are dreaming them! Let's go with this.

'Do you ever try to do anything different when you're in the dream? Instead of letting the dream just play itself out, like a movie.'

'How do you mean?'

'Some dreams just play themselves out, unfold around us, as if we are in them just watching what happens. It's like the dream is trying to teach us something, or we are in a dream, trying to make sense of something, and we have no power to change things. But in other dreams, we are a character in the dream and we can decide what happens next. What we do, next. It's a lucid dream. I think you told me before that you were in a dream once and they wanted you to do something horrible to someone and you refused to?'

William winced. 'Yes, sometimes I'm able to hold my ground, other times I'm doing what they want before I realise, and last night I ran away, but they caught me.' He thought for a moment. 'You're right, though. I remember being aware that I could run away, and then doing it... It felt good too, to make a choice in the dream. You could be on to something.'

Marissa remembered flying above the treetops looking down at the castle. 'You know in a dream, it's still a dream, right? So you could do anything – you could fly if you wanted to, instead of running, or you could make yourself really small and go down a rabbit-hole, or you could turn into a cat, and run up a tree!' She sat up taller in her chair, excited. 'They wouldn't find *you* then, because they'd be looking for William...'

'...and not a cat! Brilliant! Why didn't I think of that? I could turn into a bird. I love birds. I could turn into a bird and fly away, far away from them, and they wouldn't be able to catch me then.' William smiled. It brightened up the whole room. He had beautiful energy when he smiled.

Marissa was smiling too. She felt good about this idea and seeing William light up warmed her heart.

'I really hope this helps,' she said, thinking it out. 'I wonder, William – Will, I mean – what if you practised turning into a bird in your mind, when you were awake, so it was easier to do it in your dream? I mean, you'd need to practise it a few times so it came naturally to you.'

William started laughing. 'This is the best counselling session I've ever had! Practise turning into a bird! You're right, though – yes, I do need to practise it. I take it all back, Marissa – these sessions have been useful after all.'

Marissa flushed. She really wanted to stay on track. She wouldn't see William again more than likely, and she wanted to give him as much help as she could in the few minutes they had left. She brought the focus back to the job at hand. 'What bird do you want to be? It would probably help if you were to pick one now and stick with it, so you weren't confusing yourself when you are in the moment.'

'Oh, a crow or a raven, definitely,' William said, with certainty. 'They are powerful birds, very clever and strong. Not rare birds either, so I could just fit in with all the other crows and ravens and it would be easier to hide. If I was going to be something wild and colourful like a hummingbird, or large like an albatross, I would stand out a lot more. And owls, they don't fly as fast. Well, I don't think they do, anyway.'

I like this change of tone, he's quite chatty. He must know a lot about birds. 'I'm not sure about owls either, but I think being a raven or a crow is a great idea. They seem to be powerful, and strong, as you say, and they can fly fast. Would you like to visualise yourself turning into a raven now?'

'Sure, why not?'

William closed his eyes and Marissa unfocused hers, focused on his energy field and saw in her mind's eye that there was something moving there, something dark. Was it bird energy? She wasn't sure, but she felt that if she touched William, she would get an electric shock. It was as if there was a force-field around him that kept her away from him. That was okay, though. He had to do this for himself.

He opened his eyes. 'That was strange. But I think if I do it a few more times, I will be able to do it faster. Shrinking my arms into wings, my head into a bird's head, that was easy.'

Marissa could visualise him doing it as he spoke.

'Shrinking my body into a bird's body, easy too, but my legs, they're so long. Shrinking them into bird legs? But I can do it!'

'Yes, I know you can do it. Maybe don't do it one body part at a time, but all at once?'

'That could work. Yes. Yes! You know what, Marissa? Next time I dream that dream, I won't even wait for something bad to happen, I'll just turn into a bird right away and get the hell outta there. Maybe I'll even have a good dream then. It would be fun to dream about flying high above the trees. Yes, I'll look forward to that.'

Marissa smiled. 'I'm so glad I could do something to help you tonight.'

'I'm glad too.'

'Will, this is our last session, but if you want to take me up on the healing, if you want to come to my room in Rathmines for shamanic healing, or for Reiki, then here's my business card. It's totally up to you. I have to say that I'm in training still, so it could be better for you to see someone who is fully qualified.'

William shivered. 'You know what, Marissa, I'll try the bird thing, and if that doesn't work, I might just give you a call. But if it does, then you've helped me enough for now. I just want an easy life. I don't need bells and whistles, just a few good nights' sleep a week and not to feel like I'm being eaten away by life.'

Eaten away by life. Wow, there's an image.

William stood up and got his coat, then turned back to Marissa. 'I know it's early, but I'm ready to go now. I don't want to talk anymore. Hey, it was good meeting you. Thanks for everything.' He held out his hand.

Marissa stood, then hesitated, remembering the electric shock. *No, that's not there now.* She grounded herself through her feet, shook his hand confidently and was almost surprised at its softness.

'Thanks, Will, it was good to meet you too.'

He left and the room was emptier without him. And Marissa's heart felt a little emptier too.

Another client finished up with me. William, Martin, Cliona, Margaret, Mary R... I get close to them, get to know them and like them, and then I never see them again. I know I'm not supposed to like them, but I do. I wonder, has Cliona had her baby yet? Is she still with Brendan? Is Martin going jogging? Is his mother still driving him crazy? Has Margaret managed to keep her difficult thoughts away? Did Becks ever go to Mayo? I guess it's a therapist's job to help people over a slippery patch in their lives, not to know how it all turns out for them. And I have someone new starting in fifteen minutes. This is intense.

She was grateful for the time alone to sit in stillness. *Olive, you'll be proud of me. Now I'm beginning to understand why doing this is so important.*

The buzzer sounded. Marissa snapped back into the present moment, then looked at her client sheet. Kevin, age sixty-five. She let him in.

Marissa got off the bus a few stops early and got herself a portion of crispy, salty chips. It was late. The sun had gone down a half-hour before and it was dark except for the flickering of the street lamps and the usual tinge of orange light pollution in the sky. She walked the rest of the way home, enjoying the taste, the crunch and the salt. She stood, finishing them, then threw the empty bag in the bin and turned onto her street, licking the salt off of her fingers. There was a dark figure sitting in a dark car on the dark side of the street outside her flat.

Hang on, I recognise that car!

'Matt! Oh my God, you didn't?!'

'I did!'

He got out of the car and embraced her. She fell into his arms.

'I was going to text you. I even wrote the text, but never sent it!'

'I think I felt it. What time was it at?'

'Probably around seven.'

'Yes, that's when I decided I was coming out to see you. The weekend would have been too long a wait. You smell like chips! Yummy! Can I stay over? I've got work in the morning, I'll have to leave extra early...'

'You're mad!'

'Mad about you!'

She unlocked the door and they tumbled into the flat all arms and legs, pressing into and kissing each other.

'I'm so glad you're here. It's too late for tea, do you want a glass of wine or something?'

'A glass of you would be preferable!'

'Matt!'

CHAPTER NINETEEN

All was still. The moonlight glimmered on the surface of the lake, accentuating the faintest ripple, giving away his position. Far below the surface, very far below, was a dark shadow, vaster than anything Marissa had imagined, for she had never seen his full size.

With a splash, the tortured serpent's head rose up above the waterline. He moaned and thrashed and wrestled with himself. Both eyes were now covered in slime; a thick viscous substance, which also covered most of his face, ran along his neckline and curled around his belly and his fins. His fine, beautiful fins, that seemed useless when it came to scraping off slime. But his gills were not covered. He could still breathe, for now anyway, even though he could not see.

He no longer cared. He thrashed in impatience and agitation, wanting it all to be over, struggling and wrestling with the caked substance.

Then the lake had enough of him. The waters gathered, pushing him upwards, a large funnel, ending in a spout, flinging his long, worm-like body out into the air. Marissa watched, heart in mouth, fascinated and as helpless as he, seeing her majestic friend thrown out of his home.

He tucked his small limbs tightly into his body as he rose higher, the funnel of the water propelling him upwards, his long, large, seven-finned tail, useless. Marissa could see it was also caked in the dark, sticky mucosal substance.

Suddenly, the water pulled back and he was suspended in mid-air, just for a moment. He was elated, he felt power in his belly thrusting through his body, he roared and convulsed uncontrollably as his body started falling, and then, just when he least expected it, there was a large POP! From the middle of his shoulder blades, rudimentary wings unfurled like sails on a ship held by masts as thin as twigs on a tree.

Oh no, they'll never hold him up!

The sails were as thick as the wings of a dragonfly, and there he was, the size of a house, as big as a castle. How could such tiny wings hold such a majestic creature in the air?

Instinctively he spread them anyway, using all of his will and all of his might, buzzing, flapping, not finding any rhythm as his body twisted in the air, trying to stay alight. He was too heavy, too awkward and ungainly. Resigned to his fate, he flipped in the air, twisted most ungracefully and fell with a massive splash back into the water.

He knew he had failed, but for those few seconds he had felt invincible, and those few seconds had given him the strength he needed to continue. He would fight no longer, wherever he was going with this process, he would surrender to it.

He dove deep, deep down to the bottom of the lake, down to an old cavern there. Dragging as much seaweed as he could find inside it, he sealed himself up, sealed himself into the darkness. He ate some of the seaweed, then covered his aching body with the rest and slept.

CHAPTER TWENTY

The early morning sunshine crept across the bed. The two lovers lay in a heap of arms and legs, surrounded by covers, while somewhere beside them, a cat purred.

Marissa yawned. 'I'm so glad I took today off. I wish you could stay here for longer.'

'I've got to go to work, you know I do. Are you sure you're going to be okay?' Matt turned and smiled at her, but his eyes betrayed his worry. He was still hesitant about her going to Clifden after her previous episode.

'I'm totally over it, Matt, I promise. Really, don't worry about me. I've seen Séamus since last time, and I know he's on my side, I'll be surrounded by friends, it'll be perfectly okay.'

He caught her out. 'What do you mean, you've seen Séamus?'

Marissa blushed scarlet and felt a trap door open in the pit of her stomach. *Shit. No, I don't want him worrying before I leave.* She held his gaze, feeling the heat in her cheeks. 'I've spoken to him, I mean. Seriously. It's all good.' She found her resolve. 'And he's let me come back, hasn't he?' *Hopefully he won't need any more than that.* 'Even after all my messing around...'

Thankfully, Matt looked at the time and hopped out of bed. 'I have to get up now, to get to work before rush hour.'

He stretched, rubbed his eyes, then looked at Marissa.

'You're a grown woman, you know your strengths and weaknesses, so I trust you're okay if you say you are. I have to stop feeling like I need to mind you all the time. But I just don't know if I could stomach another event like before. I suppose I'll just have to wait and see.'

'Honestly, Matt, I'm much more prepared now, and I have some good friends on the spirit side too. I'm protected. And I won't do anything stupid.'

Matt shook his head. 'I hope not.'

He was in and out of the bathroom in a flash. He threw on his clothes and came over to kiss her goodbye. He knelt by the bed and stroked her hair, just looking at her for a moment.

'Hey. I've got to go.' He kissed her. 'I'll let myself out. Have a great time and I'll see you when you get back.' They kissed, warmly, then he pulled away.

She heard the door click closed behind him and she was alone. She felt as if he'd taken a part of her heart with him. It felt torn in two. Tears welled up inside her. Their conversation was unfinished, there was more to say, and she wanted to tell him everything, but she didn't have time. She didn't even know what it was that she needed to say. She ached all over, not wanting to fall into the never-ending a pit of longing in her stomach. She turned over in bed, catching her breath, and stroked the pillow he had slept on, drinking in his scent.

Tobermory leapt off the bed, breaking the atmosphere.

'Silly cat. Silly man. Now I'm upset, and I wanted to be happy going away.'

He didn't mean to upset me. He's just worried about me, that's all. Why does it feel like we're fighting now?

Unable to go back to sleep, she dragged herself out of bed and made tea. Wrapped in her cardigan she went outside, brushed debris off her deckchair and sat down, mug in hand, still feeling bereft. She listened to the birds.

Not much I can do about this now, I guess. I could pack, but my train isn't for ages. The sun was bright and the birds were busy with their babies, it was a stunningly beautiful day, a total contrast to how she felt inside. *Why can't I shed this heavy feeling?*

She fetched her phone.

u left me with all of your worry, and I feel heavy in it.

She read back what she had written. *That's exactly it. I don't want it. And I don't want to feel like this anymore.*

She imagined herself standing outside the door of Room Three in Cabra, knocking. She got the door and looked at herself. '*Come in, which seat would you like?*' She giggled and something in her heart eased.

In her mind's eye the image melted away and then there was Matt, beautiful and soft, standing there, smiling at her. *I love you so much.* She placed her hand on his heart and asked for her energy to come back to her. She immediately felt a shift, the torn part of her heart felt sore, yes, but a mending kind of sore, instead of a ripped one. The relief was palpable. But she was still left with the heaviness.

It's Matt's worry, not mine. She drank some of her tea which had cooled significantly, showing her how long she had been sitting there. *I don't want to take his pain to Clifden with me, I want to have fun, and learn and grow... It feels strange to let it go, like baggage, just like I said to Niamh. But it isn't mine, and it will get in the way of my work.*

She imagined herself carrying Matt's worry, but it didn't feel like shopping bags, more like stones - big, heavy, solid stones. *I guess his worry means he loves me? If he didn't love me, he wouldn't be worried. Or maybe this is more than just about me.* She looked at the stones. *Thanks for showing me what Matt always carries, but I don't think either of us need to carry you anymore. Can you go now?* They started to shrink and she began to feel lighter. But some of them were still there. She waited a little longer but no, they remained. She imagined herself making a little man out of them and placing him under the magnolia tree in her garden. She looked at the imaginary little stone man in her mind's eye. It even looked like Matt.

Maybe he left a piece of himself here, too.

Knowing this confirmed his love for her, and that helped her feel lighter, too. After about ten minutes more she felt much more solid in herself. She decided not to send the text and saved it into her drafts folder. *I'll send him a picture when I get out into the country, even a picture of myself smiling. I don't usually do that, but he might like it.*

Terry and Marissa planned to meet at the train station in Galway and catch the bus to Clifden together, then hitch a ride with Stephanie for the rest of the way. It was going to be an amazing weekend.

Marissa took a long hot shower, left a thank-you note and some money for Michelle with Tobermory's food, and started packing her backpack. She couldn't seem to fit everything she wanted to bring into it, but she didn't want to take her suitcase, as dragging it around was such an annoyance.

What can I leave behind? That heavy cardigan? No, even though it's warmer weather now, it's great as a blanket, and for outside at night. But it's too hot to wear it. I could just carry it? But I'm carrying my drum, and my handbag too. Whatever about Niamh and all the shopping bags, I'm going to end up taking loads of bags with me!

She remembered she had an old schoolbag. Once she'd dug it out and emptied it out, she found she was able to fit her drum inside, and her medicine bundle too. It had a pocket with a zip on the front of it and a side pocket which she could use instead of her handbag. She stuffed all of her daytime things into it.

Yay! That saves a lot of trouble. She looked at her travel items, two bags and a cardigan seemed very reasonable for a weekend away.

I don't need to take my wellies, most definitely not in May, anyway. I remember how upset I was the first time when I packed walking boots instead, then thought I needed them so badly when it rained. I had to buy some in Galway, and after all of that, I didn't even wear either pair. It's funny how I got in such a tizzy going that first weekend, and now it's not a bother at all. Look at how much I've changed.

I do need my raincoat, though. Where the heck did I put it? Oh dear. Oh, there it is, behind my wardrobe. How did it get there? Maybe I've not changed as much as I thought I have, ha, ha!

She stuffed the raincoat into a side pocket of her backpack, then found her notebook from the last workshop. It still had fresh pages so she decided to take it with her, even though it had some very strange doodles and scrawls inside of it since the last time. *Slipper socks for inside the Monastery, toiletries, extra underwear and a complete change of clothes ... what else?* The jewellery pouch with her new stones ready for the work, and the pendulum, all tucked nicely into her medicine bundle, were packed into the schoolbag with her drum. She had to double check they were still in there, which meant unwrapping the bundle and wrapping it back up again, but it was good to know for sure.

Then she was ready. And the heaviness had almost completely lifted. She checked the little man statue under the tree in her mind's eye, it was starting to look like a Buddha. She smiled, thinking of Matt as Buddha. She said goodbye to her cat and left her flat for another adventure.

The train station was relatively busy. It was Friday and many people would take a half-day to get home early for the weekend. Marissa got her ticket, found the train and got on board. It was about half-full, and there was no sign of any of the others. *I don't know who else from the group would be getting the train. Anyway, I'm here now, and I have a book, some music and a sandwich. I think a few hours of a journey alone will do me some good.*

She found a window seat and settled into it. Not too long after, the train pulled out of the station and headed towards Galway.

It felt good to get out of the city, leaving behind the energy of lots of people living closely together. Marissa felt as if she was not only carrying Matt's energy, but the energy of everyone living in her building, everyone on the street where she lived, and all the energy from her client sessions, too. *I've had so many sessions this week. I don't want to take that energy to my weekend away. This weekend is for me, not for them.*

She imagined she was in a white room. She put all of the bags and rocks and things that she was carrying down on the floor, then stepped out of the centre of them and looked at the mess on the floor. *Ooh, where did they come from? I thought I got rid of all of it. I feel icky. I'll take a shower!* She imagined herself taking a cold shower, washing away the residue of everyone's energy. *Much better.* She started to sort out the energy she was carrying. *This is Dad's, and this is Mum's, here's Eli's and, wait, it's Sarah's! Wow, so many people's energy. There's Dad's again! And Matt's, and Valeria's. I wonder why I have her energy in my energy field! Strange. I'll get the violet flame onto it.*

As she burned the energy in the white room in her mind, her body on the seat in the carriage on the train relaxed significantly. She felt her shoulders soften, her arms and hands relax and her stomach loosen. It gargled, and she giggled.

What am I keeping any of this cruddy energy for, anyway? Burn it all!! Soon everything in that white room bar herself was consumed by the flames, licking purple and lavender, orange and dark green. She saw herself step into the purple fire and open up her body, allowing the flames to burn away everything inside her that needed to go.

Marissa felt significantly lighter, something in her chest had opened up. She stretched out in the seat, feeling more expansive. A shaft of sunlight came in through the window and shone down upon her. She smiled. *While I'm here working on my energy field, is there anything else I could do to improve it? To prepare for the work ahead? Maybe I'll visit my guides.* She shifted the image of the white room into the lakeshore.

They were all there: Emelda, Grandmother Medicine Woman, Bear. No, not quite all – there was no sign of the sea serpent. My serpent! I forgot about him! *Marissa reached out for him and found an emptiness inside.* Where is he? Is he okay?

She turned to her guides in a panic. 'Emelda, Grandmother, where is the serpent?'

Emelda answered. 'Ah, he go through his time now. Metamorphosis. He in his cocoon cave. We are very lucky to be witness to this, very lucky indeed, for it is only once in eight hundred years this happens. Eight hundred! I have known him since he was a baby.'

Marissa felt some sense of relief at Emelda's nonchalance. 'Will he become a dragon?' she asked curiously.

'Yes, he will. But what kind of dragon he is? We will only see when he hatches out.'

Her relief was unmistakable. 'How exciting! I was worried about him.'

'He knows this,' the grandmother said. *'He took great solace from your visits. You came many times. What? You don't remember? You come here in your dreams every night. Sometimes during the day too. Aah, you think you remember everything you dream about! Silly girl.'*

She smiled.

'And more,' added Emelda. 'You think we only see you when you come and visit us? We are always with you. Every thought, every deed, we

know you inside and out. We see your heart and we know if you are good person.' Emelda raised her eyebrow in mock contempt. Then she laughed, she couldn't hold the mask for very long. But it triggered something in Marissa nonetheless.

'So you saw that I didn't tell Matt about Séamus visiting me that time.'

Emelda gave the grandmother a playful dig with her elbow and they both giggled. 'Ah yes, we think you very clever, very funny. You have good sense of Matt, he would not like that at all.'

Marissa looked wistfully at the water.

'He knew you were worried,' said the grandmother, gesturing towards the sea serpent. 'He thanks you for your love.'

Marissa felt deeply touched, then she realised what had just been said. 'You watch me all the time? You listen to my thoughts? How can that be? Do I not get any privacy at all?'

Emelda laughed. 'No, of course not, not even when on toilet! Privacy! What is that? Spirit knows nothing about privacy, and everything about you. But if you have nothing to hide, then there is no problem, yes?'

Marissa grinned.

'That boyfriend, anyway, I see he put spanner in your heart.'

'Spanner? Well, he is a mechanic...'

'No, I serious. Look there.' She pointed to Marissa's heart. There was something dark and heavy inside.

'Shall I take it out for you?'

'No, you will do no such thing,' said the grandmother. 'The child must do it for herself if she is to learn anything.'

Marissa smiled, but was worried now that she saw this intrusion.

'You learned extraction, didn't you?' said the grandmother. 'So, extract.'

'But this is different.'

'Different how? Extract the energy that is solid and stuck.'

'Stuck? I thought he just put this into me.'

'You are right, he did put it in just today, but now you must remove it, so you can learn.'

'Okay.' Marissa dug into her chest with her nails to pull it out, but it hurt.

'Not like that!' said Emelda. 'Silly girl!'

Marissa smiled. 'Yes, I realise that.'

'You will figure it out, said Grandmother Medicine Woman. 'You did ask what else you could do to improve.'

'I did indeed,' said Marissa.

The train shuddered to a halt at Limerick Junction snapping Marissa back to this reality. People got off, people got on. Marissa opened her eyes. She put her hand on her heart. Yes, there was something there. *A spanner. A spanner in the works.*

Someone came and sat beside her. She felt encroached upon. She shifted in her seat, feeling pushed up towards the window.

I must extract this energy from Matt. So strange that he would do this to me. Is he angry? Or jealous? I don't know. Maybe it's his worry. I should text him.

She picked up her phone again. The draft was still there: you left me with all of your worry, and I feel heavy in it. It felt satisfying in a way, to read it again, but she had shifted that energy, so she couldn't send it now. And she didn't want to dump on him, either.

She deleted the draft and wrote instead:

> Hi Love hope ur having a good day. I'm in Limerick Junction already, train is busy 4 a Friday. I'll send u a pic of the monastery when I get there. Love you xx

It felt strange, almost the opposite to how she was feeling. Too nice, too friendly. It was as if it cost her a part of herself to send it, but she sent it anyway, then sat back in her seat and closed her eyes again.

The train pulled out of the station for the final leg of the journey. Her phone beeped and she jumped. It was Matt, replying with a single 'x' and nothing else.

Well, that's rude! Her body stiffened. *That's decided it then. Blast him. I have to extract this spanner thing in my heart. Maybe I'll do it the way Terry and Saoirse showed me, on my body, instead of in a journey space.*

She put her hand on her heart. Nobody was looking, so she connected to Reiki and flowed some energy into herself. She started to feel better almost immediately. She was still cross, though, so she texted back Matt back: xx. *That's shorthand for 'fuck you'.*

But then he texted back right away: xxx and it made her laugh. It was okay between them, she was making something out of a thing that wasn't even there.

Her body softened.

She wanted to open her heart chakra and take the spanner out, but she didn't want people to see her doing it. She lifted her hand from her heart and motioned to open the chakra. She felt something loosen in her chest. She reached in with etheric hands, rooted around, found something hard and pulled it out.

Suddenly, something heavy flew straight into her heart. It felt like a whack in her chest. Then something else flew in, something sharp and pointy, and something else that reminded her of pellets from duck shooting. *Oh no! What's going on?* Marissa became breathless. She closed her heart chakra quickly and then realised what she had done.

I opened my heart chakra on a train filled with people, without protection. I suppose I deserved that. What have I picked up?

Her heart hurt now, physically hurt. It was tight and sore. She looked around her. Everyone looked exactly the same, as if nothing had happened at all.

I think I understand now what Dolores meant about Reiki being non-intrusive and Shamanic healing being intrusive.

The train was pulling into Galway. Everyone stood up to get their bags and leave, phone calls were being made, the train became busy with activity. Her chest was tight, she stood up taking short, shallow breaths. She had trouble reaching for the bag over her head.

'Here, let me,' said the man who was sitting beside her, and he reached up with ease and got her bag down for her. 'Have a nice day,' he said.

Maybe it was his pain that I took onto myself. Well, I hope he appreciates it.

Marissa staggered out onto the platform with her backpack and schoolbag, her cardigan in her hand and a whole lot of energetic clutter in her heart. The lessons had already begun, and she wasn't even in Clifden yet.

Slowly, Marissa dragged herself to the bus stop. Her body felt like lead and every step set off a twinge in her chest. The hot sun pounding down on her head didn't help. *At least it's not as bad as that time back in my flat. I wish I knew what Séamus did then so I could do it to myself now. No, this is different...*

She delicately sat down on the wooden bench to wait. The Clifden bus wasn't for another half an hour and there was no sign of Terry. Her stomach growled. *I'm hungry, but it's such an effort to move, maybe I'll go without lunch.* Her stomach growled again.

She looked around. It was busy. People were boarding the bus for Dublin. Across the road an old woman wearing a headscarf was dragging a shopping basket behind her, stopping every few moments to take a rest. *She looks eighty-three. If she can walk around and do stuff, particularly in this heat, then I can get up and get myself a sandwich, for God's sake.*

Marissa hauled herself up and shuffled back along the road to the newsagent's, went in and bought a sandwich and a can of Club orange. It felt like a feat of strength to bring her haul and her bags back to the bench. She nibbled gratefully on the sandwich and swallowed a mouthful of fizzy orange, but her chest hurt as it passed through it on the way to her stomach. *What the hell is going on?*

She closed her eyes and brought her awareness down into her body. It was like going into a dark cave filled with weapons of war. Sharp objects were everywhere, threatening to pierce her. In her image, she started to cry, loudly, then to wail. She heard a soft voice in her ear: 'Are you okay?'

She opened her eyes. It was Terry.

'Marissa, you're crying!'

Indeed, her face was wet with tears.

'Terry! I'm so glad to see you! I picked up something nasty on the train, some energy, and I can't shift it. Can you help me?'

'Of course! Hang on. Move up a bit so I can sit beside you.'

She shifted up and he squashed in.

'Oh, Marissa, how the hell did you do this to yourself? You're all twisted up! I don't want to map this onto me.'

She could feel his full-body shiver as he pushed her energy field away from his.

'Right,' he said, 'let's get you sorted out.' He put his hand on her knee and closed his eyes, and she could feel something in her body relax immediately. Her chest began to loosen and soon she was breathing normally.

'Thank you,' she whispered gratefully.

'Not done yet, hang on,' he said, eyes still closed, concentrating hard.

She felt something slither away from her neck, and suddenly all the tension she was carrying was gone. *It's gone!* She turned to Terry, threw her arms around him and gave him a big hug.

'Thank you. so much. Wow, that was bad.'

'It was really bad, my girl, what the heck did you do to yourself? No wonder you were crying.'

'I opened my heart chakra on the train.' She was embarrassed to admit it, but yes, that's exactly what she had done.

'What!? That's a crazy thing to do.'

'You don't have to tell me twice,' she said. 'Lesson learned.'

Hearing those words, she got an ice-cold shiver up her back. *Why? What did I say? Weird.*

She looked at her friend. Terry's hair was blond again, white blond, and short. He looked more like himself than he had a few days previous. He was wearing a blue denim jacket and jeans; with his hair, slim figure, slight tan and piercing blue eyes, he was stunning to look at. He smiled at her and she squeezed his hand.

They were calling people to the bus. Marissa stood up and shook her body out, feeling much better.

'You look amazing. Where did your tan go?' she asked, as she and Terry got in the queue.

'I washed off what wasn't real. This is the real me,' he said, smiling at her.

They boarded and found two seats together at the back.

'Did you talk to Stephanie? About a lift?' asked Marissa, as they settled into the seats.

'Yes! She said she'll meet us in Clifden, outside the newsagent. This bus ride is an hour and a half – what a pain, eh? I much prefer being independent. I'd save up for a car, but I just don't seem to be organised enough.'

Marissa smiled. She was still trying to understand what had happened to her, how she could go from feeling perfectly well to feeling terrible to feeling better again so quickly. *I wasn't perfectly well, though, I had a spanner in my heart. According to Emelda, anyway. Has that gone now too?* She got a full-body 'yes'. *Oh, Terry, you took it out for me!*

Terry was peeling a banana and making quite a show of eating it.

'How are you and Bruce getting along?' said Marissa with a giggle.

He giggled too. 'It's good. Of course he gets incredibly jealous whenever I go away without him. I hope he doesn't throw some kind of fit while I'm away this weekend.' He opened his eyes wide. 'Oh, that Marco had better stay away from him while I'm away!'

'Are you sure he's the jealous one?'

Terry scoffed and finished the banana, rolled up the peel and put it in the front pocket of his bag. 'Moi? Jealous? I'm not the type! Except maybe when it comes to Marco. I know he's had his eye on Bruce for some time. Must have been that swimwear shoot we did last year, and Bruce's insistence that we keep our relationship a secret doesn't help.'

As Terry nattered on about Bruce, Marco and Marrakesh, and something that had happened at a dinner party by the pool, Marissa faded out a little and went into her heart, double-checking that it was okay. *Has the spanner really gone?* She got another full-body 'yes'. Terry had extracted it while he was working on the rest of it. She sighed with relief.

Irish Buses are not prepared for hot sunny weather. After what felt like three long days, the bus finally pulled into the terminus on Clifden Main Street and they tumbled out onto the street, sweaty, with their bags in tow. Feeling the cool breeze on their faces was a much needed relief.

‘Terry! Marissa! Hi!’

They turned and saw Stephanie waving at them. She had her hair in large whorls up on her head and was wearing a long gold and black short-sleeved tunic with a golden fringe, over blue jeans and sandals. She looked radiant.

‘Marissa! You’re really back!’

Marissa’s face lit up. ‘Stephanie! Oh, it’s so good to see you!’

They hugged.

‘Terry! You look amazeballs!’

‘Group hug, group hug!’

‘Are you ready to go?’

Marissa felt a flush of excitement at the thought of the gang getting back together. They walked towards Stephanie’s car, then Marissa had a thought. ‘Hang on, do we have enough chocolate and treats to keep us going for the next few days?’ She smiled a cheeky smile.

‘Actually, we could get some supplies. Great idea,’ said Terry.

They went into the small supermarket and filled up a basket with sweets and treats. Terry stood for a long time in front of the alcohol section. ‘We shouldn’t, but it would be fun. It is our last weekend together as a group – we should have a party.’

‘Last weekend. Wow.’

‘I don’t know if alcohol is a good idea with the work we’re doing,’ said Stephanie.

‘You’re not supposed to drink with Reiki.’ said Marissa.

‘Oh, I know that,’ said Terry, ‘but one shot of something, a toast, wouldn’t hurt.’ He grabbed a naggin of Irish whiskey and brought it with him to the till, along with six Club Milks, four packets of Tayto and a packet of Kimberly. ‘We can dedicate it to the ancestors. Anyway, we don’t have to do it, but we can’t do it if we don’t have it.’ He winked and paid, then buried the whiskey deep in his bag.

They clambered into Stephanie’s car and rolled all the windows down for fresh air. Marissa sat in the back seat, all the bags of shopping were on the floor beside her, and her backpack, Terry’s rucksack and her old schoolbag on the opposite seat.

‘How have you been since I saw you last?’ she asked Stephanie, once they got on the road.

'Work has been very busy,' Stephanie replied, 'and very boring. Is it this right way? Yes, this is it, I recognise it now. I know I said I wasn't going to give up my job but I'm not so sure anymore.' She indicated then took the turn, driving away from the little Galway town.

'I get quickly bored by spreadsheets and money talk. I don't know what happened to me but I don't think I have the patience to stay there forever.'

'We all change when we do healing work,' said Terry in a lilting voice, 'and we can't predict in which direction we will go. There's no way of knowing, which way we are going...'

'As long as we don't get lost on the way to the Monastery,' quipped Marissa with a similar lilt. Stephanie laughed and Terry frowned in mock disgust, stuck his tongue out and then laughed too.

'I suppose it's better to be honest with yourself than pretend something is working when it isn't.' said Marissa

'You're right, I think it was already a problem even before I came to these classes. I just see it better now. Life would be so much easier if I could continue to ignore how I am feeling. I don't know how people do it – work in jobs they don't like for years and save up for holidays, just two weeks of fun.'

'I don't know either. And is it really fun if you know you're going back to work at the other end of it?'

'That's why they say "Back to the grindstone", because it's a grind,' Terry said.

'I don't want to live like that,' said Marissa. 'I've rented a healing room for a few hours on a Monday, and gone part-time. I hope to build it up to a full day of clients.'

'That's impressive,' said Stephanie, seriously impressed.

'Our Marissa has Reiki 2 now, too. She's been busy for a dropout!' said Terry, opening his packet of Kimberly. 'Anyone want one?'

Marissa took one, Stephanie shook her head. Terry took out three, folded the packet up and put it back in the bag.

'Ha, ha! I'm not a dropout, I just left for a while, but I'm back now. Oh it's been ages since I had one of these! Thanks Terry.'

'Welcome. But Hunnie, you are a dropout. It's funny, I didn't expect you to leave, I thought it would be Finn, or Jenny. Or Liz! But Séamus did say in our first workshop someone would leave and someone would join us. Ha!'

'I guess Séamus was right,' said Stephanie, 'even though it was Marissa both times.'

'Spirit never gives you all the information,' said Terry, still munching his biscuits. 'Sure that would be like watching a movie and reading the script in advance – you'd know what was coming next. Where's the fun in that?'

'Ah, but if you knew, would you do it differently?' asked Marissa, brushing the last of the crumbs off her top.

'But if you were doing it differently because you knew,' said Terry, 'then that would be part of the script too, wouldn't it?'

'I guess. I never thought of it like that before.'

'I've always wondered,' said Stephanie, 'about fate and destiny. It sounds like this is what we're discussing. How much of our lives are fated to go in a certain direction, no matter what we do. Like dying - being fated to die in a car crash but it doesn't have to be a particular car crash. Destiny, that's a little more flexible, I think. We can be destined for great things, but those great things could change, depending on what we choose.'

'That's a really good way of explaining it,' said Marissa. 'I get very confused about the difference between the two. Fated to meet someone and marry them - whether you are destined to get along well and have a good marriage or not, is up to you.'

'Yes, that sounds about right.'

'So is the script fate, or destiny?' asked Terry.

Stephanie and Marissa both looked at him in confusion.

'Oh dear!' he said with a smile. 'Well, maybe it's not that simple after all.'

They arrived at the Monastery.

Stephanie pulled the car up to the house and switched off the engine. They sat for a moment in the car, in silence. There didn't seem to be any other cars around.

'Looks like we're first,' said Marissa.

They got out of the car and took out their bags, and went to the front door. The door was locked. Puzzled, they checked and double-checked the time. It was close to 5pm.

'The workshop starts in an hour, surely the doors should be open by now?' Marissa asked.

'Maybe it's another test. You know, the universe testing our calibre. Do we really want this?' said Terry in a cheeky voice, but Marissa could hear the uncertainty in his tone. They glanced around for the others, still no sign.

'Yes, we do want this,' said Marissa, firmly. 'So let's just sit here and wait.'

They sat on the warm grass in front of the house with their bags. The sun was lower in the sky now and not as harsh as it had been earlier that day. Terry lay down and used his rucksack as a pillow. Marissa closed her eyes and listened to the birds, feeling glad that she had eaten the sandwich earlier.

The crunching noise of gravel under wheels eventually reached their ears as a car wound its way around the long driveway. It was Finn's car, Marissa recognised it from the other day. He pulled in and parked beside Stephanie's car, and he and Zaad got out, both wearing jeans and tee-shirts, both looking very happy to be there.

'Hello, roomies!' said Terry, waving at them without getting up.

They laughed and waved back.

Marissa smiled at them both, Finn her new friend, and Zaad. She hadn't seen Zaad in a long time, he looked slimmer and taller, somehow. He smiled back at her and his face lit up, he really was very good looking.

The boys came over, bags in tow. Finn carried a brown leather jacket over his arm.

'Hello!'

Marissa was about to stand up when Finn sat down comfortably beside her, and Zaad on the other side of him.

'Hi! How have you been? Where are the others?' Finn was much more comfortable around Marissa, it showed in his body language. She felt relaxed around him too. It did feel as though they could be friends.

A small blue car came up the drive then, driven by a smiling Jenny, with Liz in the front and Saoirse in the back. *The gang is back together*. They parked beside Finn and poured out of the car, coming over to join the group on the lawn.

'Why is the door still locked?' asked Liz with a frown as she sat cross-legged on the grass, leaning on her rucksack. She looked good in a black vest-top and denim shorts, she had a tan and her hair was growing out of a pixie cut.

'Your guess is as good as mine, my love,' said Terry, with his arm over his eyes so he could see her through the sunshine. 'Should have brought my sunglasses. Wonder if it will stay this hot for the whole weekend?'

'Marissa, it's good to see you back here again,' said Zaad in a low voice.

'And you, too,' she replied, looking at her friends. They had all changed, but somehow they all seemed the same. It was difficult to put her finger on what the difference was.

'Yeah, the Famous Five are back together again,' laughed Jenny. Her hair shone golden in the sun, it rippled down her shoulders. She wore a blousey short-sleeved top over a long blue dress, and sandals.

'Only we're more than five,' said Finn with a grin.

'Well, yeah,' said Jenny, tucking a strand of hair behind her ear. 'I knew that!'

Saoirse was grinning from ear to ear. She looked very relaxed in casual jeans and a white tee-shirt and runners, and she wore cream coloured tortoiseshell glasses. She smiled at Marissa, who smiled back at her. No words were needed.

'I'm very hungry. I hope they have a dinner for us soon,' said Stephanie.

'Me too,' said Saoirse. 'I just hope that they have remembered the vegetarian option for me.' She looked at Marissa. 'They forgot again last time. I had to have toast for dinner one night, and some potato from the top of the shepherd's pie.'

'I don't believe you!' exclaimed Marissa. 'That's surprising, at this stage.'

'I know,' agreed Saoirse, 'you'd think by now. Especially as there are more vegetarians about these days. I brought some cereal bars just in case.'

They talked of roads and weather, concerts and current events. Everyone was in high spirits, looking forward to whatever the weekend ahead would bring.

Terry stood up. 'I call for a toast on this auspicious occasion.' He raised an imaginary glass. 'To a very good weekend with very good friends, and no drama, or crazy crazy.'

'I second that,' said Jenny.

'Sounds good to me,' said Finn.

'Me too!' said Stephanie.

Everyone raised imaginary glasses and drank, and cheered. Then Terry ran around the house, laughing and flinging his arms around like a five-year-old wanting to be an aeroplane when he grew up. His joy was contagious; soon they were all playing a game of chasing. They fell breathlessly onto the lawn, they had given up waiting to be given entry to the house and were just enjoying their own company. It felt good.

The unmistakable, battered black BMW that Séamus drove eventually appeared. The group watched as it chewed its way up the gravel driveway and parked up against the wall, beside Stephanie's car.

There was an older woman with Séamus. *That must be Mrs Mahon, who looks after the house.* Sure enough, once she got out of the car, they could see she had the keys, and she let them all inside.

CHAPTER TWENTY ONE

It was a warm evening, so the fire wasn't lit. The sun was still bright; shafts of light fell across the room in wide beams through tall windows, motes of dust dancing within, giving the appearance of smoke. Bellies full of tea and biscuits, love and laugher filled the heavy room. Everyone was here – later than expected, yes, but here all the same. Their main meal wasn't ready yet, so they were going to have it later. The workshops were always a grand exercise in letting go of expectations, and they wanted to make the most of every minute of this last one.

They lounged casually across sofas and armchairs in anticipation of whatever the evening would bring, yet there was a slight tension in the room. Saoirse sat on a cushion on the floor in the front and Marissa was squashed on a sofa between Jenny and Terry. Séamus stood at the window, looking outside, perhaps waiting for the right moment to captivate the room. But they were his already. He looked resplendent in black jeans and a sky-blue shirt, his silver hair woven in a long plait down his back. His hat was on his head and he was sporting a black leather waistcoat.

I've missed this, I really have. I'm so glad I'm back.

Séamus turned, took off his hat and took a deep bow. The crowd yelped as if stunned by a taser, and then the laughter came, spilling over everything. Séamus's stoic face broke into a smile, then a large grin, and then he laughed along with them. All tension was broken; everybody was welcome here, this group was a home away from the home they never had. He strolled through the group and made his way to the stool, hanging his hat on a hook on the side of the fireplace.

'Ah sure 'tis great to be here with yiz all once more.' He waited for the crowd to settle down, then gestured towards Marissa.

'Marissa, Marissa, Marissa. Welcome back, sister. We missed you. You've been all the way 'round the world and back again. The hero's journey – anyone know it?'

The group nodded, but nobody wanted to speak first.

'Ah, yes, you go all the way around the world to come back again as a different person, bearing gifts, holding knowledge. A part of you dies, a part is reborn, you may look the same but you are not the same. It takes something huge, massive in fact, to get most people up off their asses to take that journey.' He looked around the room, grinning a cheeky grin, and he got his expected response of giggles and laughter.

'I kid you not, this is the inner work, the shadow work, the growth work that we all must do, if we truly are to walk along the red road, the healing path, the shamanic way.' He began walking around the room in his usual fashion, their eyes locked onto his every move.

He continued talking. 'The road is the same, no matter what you want to call it, but it winds differently, in different directions for different people. And all it is, is the road from your head, to your heart. Only a few inches, yet, it can be the longest journey somebody could ever make in their lifetime. Amazing.'

He stopped walking and smiled at them all. 'All of yiz have taken that journey, I see it in ye, and many of yiz will take it again, and again and again as you peel away the layers of yourself and your conditioning, to find the truth.'

He raised his head and looked around the room, studying everybody. 'I'm proud of yiz all for gettin' this far. Hey! Don't let it go to your heads! No, keep that ego of yours at bay, for a good healer knows they are not the ones that do the healing.'

'So. Let us begin the work of this, the last of our apprenticeship workshops together. We are in our final direction. There's a lot to do this weekend, and we can't have no messin'! Sorry, lads!' He aimed that comment particularly at Finn and Terry, who both laughed.

'As ye can see, already we are behind schedule. So we start now with questions and answers, anything that might have come up for yiz personally and through the homework since the last workshop. Then we will do a short exercise outside, before the sun goes down, then start into the new work, where I will go deeper than before. This is an ending and a beginning. We step out of ordinary reality and into a liminal space where anything is possible. Be mature in your outlook, discerning in your choices. You're stepping up a level after this weekend, but that is no excuse to be stupid.'

He walked around the room, rousing the group's emotions.

'We will both live and die this weekend, yes, we will die to ourselves and that which we know, and be reborn as the healers that we are becoming. The theme of this weekend is death and rebirth. Putting back together the pieces of ourselves so we can step into a new world and a better life. I will be teaching yiz a soul-retrieval technique, how to get back the pieces of your soul that left because of a trauma, either in this lifetime or in previous lifetimes. We will go on a death journey tonight, tomorrow we will be working our medicine bundles, and we will have a fire ceremony tomorrow night, then Sunday we will close it off.'

'Know that this is not an ending, it's just the beginning. Everything yiz are doing here is a taste of how much deeper yiz can go. I'll be running the advanced apprenticeship later in the year if you want to step further down this road with me.'

Finn and Stephanie's hands went up and Séamus held both his arms out to the group to stop them. 'Whisht! Now, before anyone else asks me anything, we need to open sacred space together. There'll be time for questions after that. Let's make this a sacred journey from start to finish, yes?'

Everyone nodded and stood up, gathering drums and rattles. *Those look great, I want to get a rattle – where did they get them, I wonder?*

'Pay special attention to the words in the verse of the fourth direction – that's the focus of our journey this time,' said Séamus as he led them into the prayer.

Marissa solemnly said the prayer aloud with the others, all turning to face each direction as they addressed it. When they came to the fourth verse, she was struck deeply by every word:

> *Great Spirit of the West, direction of death, of the sunset,*
> *of powerful medicine that goes beyond this lifetime.*

Teach us to live better lives, to be unafraid of death, to lift off the heavy chains that hold us back, support us as we transform our darkness into light, and help us bring that light to others.

After calling in Mother Earth and Father Sky, they held the last few moments in silence until Séamus gestured to them all to sit down.

'Now, we begin. Have yiz any questions? How did yiz get on with the homework? Let's use the talking stick and go around the room. Tell me how you're doing.'

He handed the stick to Saoirse who sat on the floor in front of him. She took a moment to collect her thoughts.

'Hi, everyone. I'm doing good. I had some trouble with the journey work, but then I realised I was trying to control it. I wanted to see only what I wanted to see, and not what was directly in front of me. I'm still having some difficulty with it, but I'm aware of what I'm doing now. I think that was big learning for me.'

'Well done, girl,' said Séamus. 'It's something many people don't work on, one of the main problems that healers have – separating themselves from the journey, letting go of what they want as the outcome.'

Saoirse looked at the floor. 'Thanks, Séamus. I'm also not good with praise. The work of the South, that we did last time, it was profound for me. To allow myself have beauty in my life, to feel beautiful...' she blushed, 'it's something I've only done on the outside. I never thought about the inside part before. I'm still working on that, too. I'll be back for more work with you.' She reached behind her and offered the stick to Stephanie, who was sitting behind her on the sofa.

Séamus laughed. 'Not so fast, girl, you've not told me about your clients. And you've still got to get through this weekend before you decide you're coming back – dying to yourself is no easy task.'

Saoirse brought the stick back to her centre.

'Yes, okay. The client work was difficult. I had trouble finding family or friends who would do it. Thankfully, I could work on a few of the group. I didn't get it all done.'

Séamus nodded his head. 'Better to be honest. Thank you, Saoirse. It can be difficult when your family tribe is not your soul tribe.' He turned to the group. 'Yiz all have an additional space of time to get your last works in to me. I know this year has flown by in a rush. I haven't got to teach you everything I wanted to, either. What came up is what we went with, as it was important at that time. Spirit knows best. Every workshop is different, every apprenticeship group is different. As time passes the energies change, the work changes, and I change along with it. Being honest with you is important – I'm changing and growing along with you.' He turned back to Saoirse. 'Don't want to get stuck in the mud. When we let go of what no longer serves us, this can mean letting go of stuff that we love deeply, too. It's not easy. Anyway. Do you have any questions for me, young Saoirse? We might as well cover it all in the one go.'

'Actually, yes. How do you know if you've got all the energy out during an extraction?'

Séamus nodded, addressing the whole room as he answered her question. 'Hmm. You don't. Setting the intention to do as much as you can do that day is helpful, then you focus on that, instead of trying to heal the whole wound in one go. You never heal the whole of it anyways. As long as you're alive, there's always more to heal. Healing's in layers, remember? Only some of it might be ready to go, or the whole thing might pop out easy, or nothing at all. Remember, it's a learning process. The wound needs to teach the client something, therefore something is unfinished, unlearned, if it doesn't heal. The client may be refusing to listen, or to let something go. As I said, it's not easy work. You can always take a step back at any time in the process and ask, "What's in the way of my client healing this?" then see what comes of it. And for your own personal work, you can always do a journey on what is in the way of your own healing, too. They call it a block, but by calling it that, I think you solidify it and make it seem unsurmountable.'

'Oh, I didn't see it that way before. It's a good idea. Thank you.' said Saoirse, writing it down. Most of the others were taking notes too.

'For sure,' Séamus went on, 'we often obstruct our own healing work through fear of being healthy. Most people don't know what vibrant health looks like, so being well and healthy can be scary. Most of us relate better to being sick, incapacitated, not able to function at our best. Fear of the unknown stops us in our tracks, so it's important to ask what exactly is in the way of our own healing process, so we can heal that too.'

Marissa wrote this down verbatim and underlined it a few times.

'Thanks, Saoirse. Now. Stephanie's turn.'

Saoirse handed the stick to Stephanie, who held it for a moment, then lit up the room with her smile. 'I can't believe seven weeks have gone past so quickly. Seven weeks of having difficulty sitting at my desk in my work, not wanting to do my job. I am changing, Séamus, and it is your fault!'

Everyone laughed, including Séamus.

'No. I know it's not your fault,' Stephanie continued, 'you just inspire me to be myself. You must get this a lot, people saying this.'

He nodded. 'Yes, I do. We fool ourselves into a life we don't enjoy, because it is expected of us. But we are the mavericks, the movers and shakers, we are the ones that change the world. How can you expect a lion to stay happy while chained to an office desk? But not everyone is a lion, remember that. There is a place for everyone, but we have to find our place, not fall into one because we were told to, or we think it's right. Thinking something is right and knowing it are two completely different things. So, tell me, Stephanie, how did you get on with the homework?'

'It was strange,' Stephanie said slowly, 'because I'm changing. I was interested in my clients in a different way, as if I was actually helping them, making a difference. Before, I was just doing this for myself and I wasn't worrying so much about the clients, but now I find myself caring about them more. Being gentle with them, wanting them to feel good, really wanting to help them.'

She continued. 'Yes, I worked on my childhood friend, and it was beautiful. She let go of something deep, and she cried afterwards. I cried with her. I know it was probably not a good idea, but it was very beautiful and healing for both of us. Thank you, Séamus, for teaching me this extraction process. I think her life will be different now because of what we did together, and mine certainly will never be the same again. I have a question for you.'

Séamus nodded.

'You say we shouldn't work with family and friends when we are a practitioner, yet our homework was with family and friends. Why was that?'

'You're learning, and you feel safer with family and friends, but yes, this is a good question. Professionally, it's a safety issue for both you and the other person. As you have expressed, working with someone you know can create emotions for both of you, and in a professional setting this is not ideal. Also, because of your assumptions around people that you know, such as thinking that you really know them, you might not be able to see the whole story. Or you might not want to. Or they may not want you to see a part of them that they themselves are not yet ready to see, or admit to. What you see cannot be unseen and it could, in actuality, jeopardise your relationship.'

'What do you mean?' asked Finn, wanting more.

'You only see the side of the story that they give you, which is not necessarily the truth. It might be difficult for someone to admit they were lying, or withholding information to a friend, as telling a friend something deeply personal may affect the friendship. When you work with a stranger you are not friends with them, you won't see them in a different context, nor they you, so it is easier for them to disclose deeply personal information. It's cleaner that way.'

'Ah, that makes sense. But why did we work with them for our homework?'

'Because they're more forgiving if you mess up?' suggested Séamus with a smile, 'also, it's good for you to let people close to you know what you are doing, what you can do. And it's a confidence builder. But only for a short time. I agree, but it is a little bit of a choice between a rock and a hard place.'

Stephanie nodded her head. 'Oh yes, another thing - is it possible to pick up bad energy from the other person?'

'Stephanie, Stephanie, Stephanie! What have I taught you? There's no such thing as bad energy, it's just energy. Don't label anything – labels carry heavy energy, and they can solidify, and become true. It boils down to frequency, and resonance. What resonates with you and what does not. You're correct, because when you see your family or friends in pain, it's more likely that you'll try to carry their emotional pain for them so they feel better. And yes, it is possible that it is more likely you'll take on heavy emotional energies when it comes to working with someone you know. Another reason not to do it, once you are on your feet. But you can still do it with a stranger, too. Which is why you need a daily spiritual hygiene practice, especially if you're working in practice. Good question. Do you have anything else you want to share or ask?'

'I'm good, I'm a little nervous about death, but everything you do with us makes me a little nervous!'

'Everyone laughed.

'It's not the easy path,' Séamus agreed. 'If it was...' He paused, looked at the room, then everyone chimed in together, '...everyone would be doing it!'

'Well done, Stephanie, you will find your way with your work and with this work, and learn how to balance it all. Thank you.'

Séamus brought his hands into prayer position and bowed. Stephanie bowed back, then handed the talking stick to Liz.

Marissa looked at Liz. There was something softer about her, her hair was longer, her face less severe. She was still taut, tight and muscular, but she had a soft glow around her that hadn't been there before.

'Hi, Séamus. It's great to be back,' she said. 'Some of my yoga students wanted to be shamanic clients, so I had no trouble finding people to work with. I loved the journeys we did, especially when I visited my soul tribe on another planet. That was very meaningful for me, knowing that I belonged somewhere, even if not here. That's what I've been missing all my life.'

That sounds amazing, I did miss a lot.

'I've no questions, not at the moment, but I'm sure I'll think of something over the course of the weekend. I'm interested in hearing how the others have been getting on. I'm happy to be here, and I'm really looking forward to our fire ceremony tomorrow night.'

'Good stuff,' said Séamus. 'Yes, it will be a good one.'

Jenny was next. She was a little dewy-eyed and shy. 'I'm a little overwhelmed right now. The energy in the room is very strong and there are a lot of, well, beings here with us.'

Everyone wanted to hear more, they craned in and a hush fell over the room.

'Just like Stephanie, I'm becoming more comfortable being myself. So I want to tell you all, I see Spirit. I've always seen it. I'm not afraid of it anymore – that's the biggest change for me, Séamus, since our last workshop. It was something you said that triggered this in me – it ate away at me for a week or two, and then something popped or broke open inside me, and I stopped trying to fight it. Being myself is more important than what people think of me. And, I can see Spirit and say hello to it, in whatever form it takes, without needing validation from others as to whether it is really there or not. I know it's really here. I see the angels now all the time, because I allow myself to. It's quite beautiful.'

Séamus nodded his head. 'That's a big thing, Jenny. I'm not gifted myself that way, but we all have our own gifts, and the more we open up to them, the stronger they can become. Like muscles we work out in the gym. One gift can lead to the opening of another. Go gently, child – you say you're overwhelmed. Take a step back often, you can ask them to phase out a little so you grow with it. You don't need to jump right in all the way, all at once.'

'Thanks.'

Zaad was next, he was relaxed and open as he took the talking stick. He crossed his arms on top of it like a wise elder sitting by the fire, taking his time to speak. 'Hello, everyone. Hi, Séamus. This seems a common theme for us all. If you had told me when I signed up that I would change this much, I probably wouldn't have signed up. But I am glad that I did. Very glad.'

He waited a moment, composing his thoughts before continuing. 'I have been having trouble in my, real life, if you can call it that. My home life. Yes, that's better. I never fit in completely before, but now I feel I've totally changed my shape and I don't know where I am supposed to be. It is more difficult than not fitting in at work. Not fitting in at home means there is nowhere to go to rest. It feels like growing pains. I see myself as a caterpillar deep in the metamorphosis state. I don't know when I will emerge from my cocoon, but I hope that I will, eventually. I am looking forward to it because it is very uncomfortable in here.'

Oh, like my sea serpent. I wonder how he's getting on. Perhaps we are all going through a similar change.

'Maybe the work we do this weekend will help with that,' suggested Séamus, gently. 'We will be clearing blocks and realigning our energies, and of course the soul-retrieval will be powerful ingredient to add to your medicine tools, but it will also return to you a piece of yourself that has been missing. It's a coming home to yourself.'

'Something else came up for me during the break between our classes,' Zaad said cautiously. 'It sounds silly, because it was in a movie but it has plagued my mind. I have been having dreams, even nightmares, about it. It is about dimensions and dreams, changing the course of world events. I am very confused, and I think a little disturbed. How does the movie *Inception* relate to the work we are doing?'

Ooh, I've not seen that movie, but I heard some amazing stuff about it.

'You think it is silly, but it isn't,' said Séamus. 'Movies speak to our subconscious mind, and themes and messages are embedded in many of them. I make a point of watching many of them to learn what is being disclosed to us. It's interesting how much was revealed in that particular movie, in such a hidden way. They go into the dream space to talk to their target, to plant an idea, don't they?'

Zaad nodded his head.

'Then they go into another dream space within the dream space, and I believe they go into another one there too – a dream within a dream, within a dream. Is that right?'

'Yes, that is correct.'

'Without getting too deeply into magical thinking you can do a similar thing in the shamanic landscape, through the journey. The journey is you, going into the subconscious, and the dream is the subconscious coming into your awareness. It's the same landscape. As you all know, how we interpret it is different, depending on our filter and how we see the world. Imagine you go on a journey within your journey. That's your dream within a dream. But in the movie they do this for nefarious reasons. With journeywork, the premise is always healing.' Séamus scratched his head. 'You could probably go on numerous journeys within journeys, however I don't see a reason why you would need to.'

Zaad smiled, obviously relieved. 'Ah, of course, that explains it. I went on a journey for one of my homework people, and in that journey I went into some kind of trance and went on another journey. It was as if the me in the journey had to find something at some deeper level for them. I didn't understand it. Now I know why that movie stuck in my head – my mind was trying to explain it.'

'In the quantum field,' Séamus said, 'which is the field where our consciousness resides, everything is connected. Remember, our human mind is not able to comprehend everything that exists, and can distort it for ease of understanding. We make time linear so we can keep track of it, and we layer landscapes of our subconscious in a chronological way, but we are neither linear nor chronological. Confusing, isn't it? Console yourself with knowing that you don't need to know everything. As long as you come back from a journey the way you went, then you should be okay. Simple is easier, so I wouldn't make a habit of going on multiple journeys within journeys, in case you can't manage to come back whole.'

'I don't know if I can control that,' Zaad said thoughtfully. 'When I was in the journey, it kind of happened by itself. It was only that one time, but it stuck with me, and I wanted to ask you about it.'

'Interesting stuff. The world is changing, and we are changing too. There are plenty of changes afoot.' Séamus looked deep in thought.

'What about planting an idea?' asked Terry, 'I saw that movie too – could you use the shamanic journey to make someone do something they didn't want to do?'

'Of course you could. But we must choose not to do that. That's the nefarious reasons I spoke about. It's also why we must do our shadow work. If, on the other hand, you wanted plant an idea through a journey for therapeutic reasons, I suppose it would be a similar thing to hypnosis. Hypnotherapists plant a script in someone's consciousness for something, like stopping smoking, or losing weight. The script can take hold, or not, depending on the person's sensibilities.'

'I saw a guy hypnotise someone once on a night out. He convinced the guy that he'd lost his pet leprechaun, and made him knock on everyone's door on the way home from the pub, to ask them had they seen it.' Terry said, and everyone giggled.

'Hypnosis is never something to be taken lightly. Having the power to mess with someone's mind goes against what is true and good. I never took to hypnotherapy either,' Séamus continued. 'The credibility of the practitioner should always be questioned. And, as far as the method goes, I believe a script is an instruction to override bad programming, but it's better to get into the circuitry and reprogramme what isn't working than place something like a band-aid into it. Anyway. Enough about hypnosis. Back to Zaad's topic. A journey within a journey is what we must do for deep extractions. It's an advanced technique. I will be teaching it in the Autumn, if you care to join me.'

'While I think about it, as we are discussing time and space, logical and illogical, chronological and the quantum field, did you know that last year, the Mayan calendar came to an end? Did any of you follow that? We haven't spoken about it here yet. People thought it would be the end of the world, but then they were laughing, saying, "See? We're still here! What did they know?" A little bit like that Y2K thing. However, Y2K was man-made, and the Mayan calendar was from Spirit.'

Some of the faces registered understanding. *I love how we talk about this stuff.*

'When Spirit speaks, you listen, but know that you can't take it literally, not always. Something gets lost in the translation. Our world, our physical reality, did not end. But something else did. A way of being? A stream of consciousness? Something in the quantum field? Perhaps we cannot feel it yet, we can only wait and see what will unfold. Just as we will die to ourselves this weekend, something died in 2012, exactly what it was, we do not know. It was a cosmic moment – the world as we know it, died somehow. The changes will reveal themselves to us in time.' He took a breath. The energy in the room was very intense.

'Like I said, I teach what is here, right now, what is needed in the moment. We here are pioneers, courageous lions, stepping out of the chains of our conditioning. The worlds beneath our feet are shifting and changing as fast as we are – it's difficult to keep up with it all. Above all else, we have to hold high integrity and follow our truth at all times. That means no planting of ideas in anyone's subconscious mind, for fun, or for any reason. Know that The Truth and our own personal truth may be different. We must be able to step aside anytime The Truth proves us wrong. By doing our inner work, we keep our inner compass clear, so we can always find our way back home, wherever that may be.'

The room took a few minutes to digest this while Zaad carefully handed the talking stick to Terry.

'Well, that's a hard act to follow,' Terry said with a smile. 'I always wondered about that prophecy – it didn't seem like nothing to me at the time. Anyway, I want to talk about myself now!'

After filling everyone in on his state of well-being and his homework endeavours, Terry asked, 'Séamus, I was having some trouble with my pendulum. I'm sure it's spinning one way and then another, and that has nothing at all to do with my "yes" or "no". What do I do to fix it?'

'Hmm. Are you holding your mind in stillness while you dowse?'

'You're supposed to do that?'

After the room had stopped laughing, Terry gave the talking stick to Marissa. She looked around the room and then at Séamus.

'In your own time,' he said with a gentle smile.

'Oh, yes, sorry. I'm just so happy to be back. To be home.'

Everyone was smiling and the love spilled over and washed away any doubts or fears that Marissa had. She smiled back. *I am back. No more hesitation or questioning why.*

'Well, I guess my homework was doing all the work I needed to do to be able to come back to you all again. It's been thirteen weeks since I was here and I've been working the whole time. Though maybe not to Séamus's curriculum. It's certainly been the pathway the universe held for me. I've seen so many clients, mostly for psychotherapy. I've done Reiki level 2, and have been finding it difficult to sit with psychotherapy clients and talk without putting Reiki hands on them. And lately, I've been using journeys a lot with my clients, even psychotherapy clients, to help them. I think there's something I need to figure out – a way of blending energy work with talking work that's much more powerful than either one of them alone.

'I don't have a specific question, Séamus, I'm still catching up with the group. I'm just grateful to be here. Everyone in the room is asking my questions for me just now. I'll do my best to keep up this weekend. I just need one more medicine stone to be caught up with my bundle. Maybe someone will help me out with that during one of the breaks?'

'Sort it out during dinner,' said Séamus. 'I'm sure you'll find someone who will be happy to help. All is well, all is in balance. Thanks, Marissa, your honesty around your way of working with clients is refreshing, and I'll be interested to see what you come up with in your research around techniques. It's good to have you back. Now, last but not least, Finn?'

'All good, sir,' said Finn, taking the talking stick from Marissa. 'Personally, I'm having a little trouble with my love life, as usual, but other than that...' he winked at the group and they giggled. His tone changed. 'The homework was tough, but I just about got it all done. I'm still working my way around extractions. But the chakra-clearing process makes sense to me now and I can do the whole thing without my notes. Something seems to have gelled with me, I feel more solid in the work. And I even managed to find a green and red stone for this weekend. Small ones, not boulder sized!' Everyone laughed.

Séamus smiled. 'Well done, Finn. You've made great progress, I can see it. I'm sure if you keep going the way you're going, your integrity will attract the right girl to you. Eventually. Now, do you have a question for me?'

'Yes. Can we get some food? I'm starving!'

'Ha, ha! Right, folks, yes, let's take a dinner break, then we can start into the new work.'

CHAPTER TWENTY TWO

It was fish pie for dinner and it was worth the wait, or else it tasted extra delicious because they were so hungry. There was a veggie bake for Saoirse, so everyone felt that their needs were being met, for the moment anyway.

Marissa helped herself to a large portion of pie, took extra peas, then sat down at the table. Everyone was in great form, chatting about everything from football to music, Séamus's outfit and the holidays they had planned for later in the year. Marissa didn't say a word, she just listened to it all, tuning into the energy of the group, tasting the food in her mouth. Her senses were heightened, and she was enjoying simply being there, surrounded by her friends.

She had the same bed as before in the room with Saoirse, who hugged her tightly for the sixth time before she sat down at the table to eat.

'I'm so relieved I won't be alone this time,' she said. 'Last time I was so freaked out by the spirits, I took my duvet and slept on the floor in the room with Stephanie, Liz and Jenny.

'The spirits came back?'

They never left! Séamus didn't ward the rooms last time, he wanted us to do it. I believe I didn't do a good job.'

'Do we need to do it tonight?'

Saoirse chewed a crispy bit of potato from the top of her vegetable bake. 'Yes, we do, most definitely! In fact, last time the girls said we should all do it together to make sure that we get it right this time. Thanks for reminding me! I must remind them.'

'Anything for a good night's sleep,' said Marissa, spearing some peas with her fork, 'and much preferable to being woken up by ghosts!'

'So, are you going to tell us the real reason why you dropped out?' said Finn curiously.

Terry gave him a whack.

'I don't mind, Terry,' smiled Marissa. 'I guess yes, I should tell you all why I left. I don't see why not at this stage.'

Everyone stopped talking, some of them stopped eating and they all looked at her with avid attention. She held the room. She took a breath.

'I had an encounter with dark energy. A ... demon. Well, that's what Séamus *and* Dolores called it. I suppose if angels exist, then demons have to exist too.'

There was a quiver in the energy of the group as they let it sink in. Marissa kept talking over their murmurings. *It's now or never.*

'What I believe, is that a demon stepped into one of my psychotherapy clients through a crack in his psyche. My client was schizophrenic.'

There were shocked looks when she said 'was'.

'No! He's okay, nothing happened to him. He's just not my client anymore.'

Visible relief from the group.

'Anyway, the demon found me through him, during one of the psychotherapy sessions. I think he came looking for me here, in the last workshop, and it really scared the living daylights out of me.' She paused. They were all listening intently. 'He came to my flat then, through a dream, and found me there, too. He was actually, really there, in the room with me. That was the worst bit. I can tell you about it now, but when it happened, I couldn't talk... I actually had PTSD from it. I didn't even know that was a thing. It took months for me to... Well, anyway, I don't think I was okay even then, when I thought I was okay again. I couldn't keep myself together, so I had to push all of this stuff away, as far away as I could, so I could put myself back together.'

Marissa had tears in her eyes as she looked at her friends, soaking up their compassionate silence.

Then Saoirse broke in. 'Oh God, that makes so much more sense now,' she said. 'No wonder you got upset with me when I just turned up at your work that evening. And I thought you were just being prissy or something.'

'No. Not prissy. My mind had associated all of you guys and the shamanic work with the demon, so I needed some time to figure it all out. To get my head together.'

'And I thought *I'd* had some strange encounters with dark energy,' said Jenny with a shiver, 'but I've never met one of them, not like that. I don't know what I'd be like if I did. Are you okay now? Did he hurt you?'

'He didn't hurt me, but he did speak to me. Directly. I was paralysed with fear. Or he paralysed me, so I couldn't run away. I wasn't sure which. I was paralysed here too, with Séamus, that time when I was alone with him, remember? And I thought it was Séamus doing it to me, I blamed him. But Séamus is okay, he would never hurt me. I know that now.'

Her friends looked as though they were putting their pieces of the story together with hers, to make sense of it too.

'And I made that joke about Séamus having the hots for you!' Terry looked genuinely remorseful. 'I'm sorry, I didn't realise it was such a big thing that had happened. I was upset you wouldn't tell me about it. Then I thought you didn't like me anymore, or I had done something wrong. I understand now. I'm sure I'd not be able to talk about that either.'

Marissa suddenly wasn't hungry anymore. She put down her fork and looked at all her friends. Zaad had a look of great concern, as if he wanted to rush to her and protect her.

She sighed. 'Guys, I'm okay. I've had a few more experiences since then, but I'm stronger now. I haven't told you about London and what happened there... That was only three weeks ago. That's when I realised that I need to learn more. So I asked Séamus if I could come back to the workshop.'

'It's great he took you back – he's been known not to, especially if you've missed classes,' said Terry.

'What happened in London?' asked Liz, leaning in. She had stopped eating too.

Finn looked at his watch. 'I don't want to spoil the fun, guys, but Séamus was expecting us at the front of the house five minutes ago.'

'I'll tell you everything later, I promise,' said Marissa standing up with her plate. 'We'd better get back to it now.'

The group cleared the dishes in a sombre mood, digesting the new information as well as their dinner.

The sun was about to set. Séamus took them outside, deep into the forest at the back of the Monastery. He spoke to them in a whisper, they had to really focus to find his voice.

'The universe is speaking through me, whilst you're with me, showing you the way. But I'm just one of many guides you may have if you choose to continue to follow the path of your heart. What I tell ye is not the whole of what yiz may need. You must to listen to the breeze, the trees, the water, the Earth. This exercise will open a door for you, but you need to step through it yourself.'

'Now, lads, Shh! Listen. Underneath everything runs the fabric of the world... And running through that, is the heartbeat of the world. Listen, can you hear it? *Lub dub, lub dub, lub dub...* It's not the birds, or the rustle of the breeze through the leaves on the trees. No, it's not that. Listen, listen deeper, shh!'

'I never realised a forest was so noisy,' said Terry, and there was a giggle.

'Now come on, lads, this is serious work,' said Séamus, trying to pull the group together.

With great effort, Marissa pulled her energy out of the conversation they had at dinner and into the moment, into the forest, and felt her body get heavier. She focused on the forest floor. The incessant hum of midges, the crunching of sticks and the crackling of leaves beneath feet were distracting. For a moment the sun got into her eye, it was golden. And then it was gone. After a few minutes something shifted and the group settled, became more present in their circle, and she became more present, too.

Yes, Terry's right. Forests are very noisy places. I never noticed it before.

'Ah, 'ere you all are now,' Séamus said with a smile in his voice. 'Let's try it again. Listen. There it is now, *lub dub, lub dub, lub dub*.' He started to sway to the rhythm. 'Can you hear it?'

The group started to sway too, mimicking Séamus but not really understanding what they were doing.

'Okay, lads, find your tree and do that exercise I told you about.'

Each of them found a tree, bowed to it, and asked its permission to work with it.

Placing her hand on her tree, Marissa felt her heart open as she connected, hearing the 'Yes,' feeling the stillness. She allowed her energy to flow into the tree, then upwards, looking up above her head, travelling and spinning a little as she got her bearings, her energy moving to fill the trunk and rise right up to the top of it. She felt much taller now. It was as if a part of her had travelled away from her and was having an adventure on its own. She could see what it was seeing as it moved up to the canopy then sat there for a moment.

Am I making this up? It's so real. My body is down here, yet I can see the sky!

Her energy moved over the canopy, looking down at the forest, looking down at them all, her friends, each of them, in their own way, connecting to other trees. She could feel the joy, warmth and happiness of their fellowship.

Then her energy shot back down through the trunk of the tree. *No! I'm not ready yet!* But still she kept going down, through the trunk, right down to the soft moistness and warmth of the roots beneath. Her heart opened even more as she connected to the root network and shot outwards to the ends of the roots...

I'm home!

Pftttttt!

She started and was pulled right back to her body, a cold sweat breaking across her brow.

'Sorry, lads,' said Finn. 'Couldn't help myself. Had to be done.'

The moment was broken by more giggles.

'I guess it's better out than in,' said Stephanie with a smile.

Burp!

'Who was that?' asked Terry, his voice giving him away.

'Let's try again,' said Liz, 'but please, Finn and Terry, keep your expressions of gas a little quieter, please.'

'That's gas!' said Terry, and they all cracked up.

Marissa took a breath before reconnecting to her tree. She looked around. *It's so peaceful here, how could I have thought there was a darkness lurking? It's beautiful. Just a moment more.*

Lub dub, lub dub, lub dub. Marissa closed her eyes and pressed against her tree, then felt someone's shoulder brush past her. There was a whisper in her ear. 'Good to have you back, sister, it's good to have you back.'

'Right folks please! That's enough messing about. Let's go back into the room, it's time to die.'

Séamus's drum was on the floor by his stool, the fire was lit and the heat was beginning to fill the cold gaps in the air. It was late, and it was dark outside. Nobody minded the hour, they had nowhere else to go, this is what they came for. They all took their seats. Jenny squeezed in between Liz and Zaad, Marissa sat on the armchair beside them and Saoirse plopped herself back on the cushion at the top of the room. Finn and Terry sat together on the other sofa.

'We're on the naughty step!' said Terry.

Séamus clapped his hands together. 'Right, folks. Can I have your full attention please? Tonight yiz will join me on a journey. So you'd better not doze off now, after eatin' such a grand meal and being so especially grounded and all. I know yiz enjoyed journeying to your soul-family the last time. That was nice and pretty, but this one's not gonna be as nice. Or as pretty. The theme for the weekend is death and dying. Death as the end of who you were, dying to yourself, letting something go so something new can come in. Let me be clear, we're talking about leaving this Earth plane and finding out what happens next. I'm going to invite you to venture where you haven't been before – to The Land of the Dead.'

Everyone took a breath. He had their full attention now.

'I know many of yiz have religious beliefs. Grand, grand, leave them at the door. We are here to dismantle our beliefs and break apart the structure that was created to keep us contained, for we cannot grow when we are inside something tight and rigid. We must die to who we were, and also die to who we think we are, so we may be reborn as our best selves.'

He gave them a moment to digest this.

'It all sounds grand, doesn't it? If you're afraid of death, you will never live. I say this again – if you're afraid of death, you will never live.'

He spun on his feet in the middle of the room.

'Never leave the house. Never take a risk. Never try to fly. Shamans don't live like that. We need to clear that fear tonight.'

There was a genuine fear in the room now. The tension was electric.

This work we do,' Séamus continued, 'is the path of non-attachment. We cannot attach ourselves to anything, because we have to be able to let it go at the drop of a hat. When we cling to something, it cannot die, and we cannot die to it, or to our idea of it. And it stretches us thin and takes us out of where we're meant to be. It distorts the natural order of things. We have to let go, of everything.

'Don't be afraid, you won't be dying physically tonight. That's the plan, anyway. Some teachers would have you out at midnight digging your own graves under the light of the moon, then make you spend the night in them. I find there's too much messin' about with that. The monkey mind takes over, agitated by discomfort like cold, wet clay, or strange sounds, like the hoot of an owl. Many don't get the benefit of the journey, as they're too distracted to travel. Although this balmy May night would be an ideal time to try it if you were so inclined. I'd rather be with you here, holding space, watching over you as you go and come back, deliberately receiving specific information in a much more targeted manner. There's nothing wrong with either approach, mind you. This just happens to be mine. But if you fancy spending the night in a wet clay bed, you're welcome to take your pick of the shovels in the back and go and dig yourself a grave when we finish here.'

Finn laughed. 'No chance, mate!'

'That's what I thought,' said Séamus with a grin. 'Still, tonight we die. Position yourselves for the journey ahead.'

There was bustle as people got up and found a space to sit in. Marissa choose to sit upright, leaning back against the wall for support, with a pillow beneath her outstretched legs for comfort. Others were doing similar, except for Terry, who stretched out on the sofa with a large pillow under his head.

Séamus turned off the lights and Marissa realised candles had been lit around the room. They gave a soft glow, and the fire flickered, its warm golden light spreading into the room.

'Let us go then, you and I,' Séamus said, 'while the evening is spread out against the sky.' He started to drum. '*Lub dub, lub dub, lub dub, lub dub*,' said the drum. '*Lub dub, lub dub.*'

Marissa was overcome with emotion on hearing Séamus's drum once more. It filled her with a sense of beauty and joy. She was home, this is who she truly was, this drum, this beat. It filled her heart, her eyes, her ears, her mind.

'*Lub dub, lub dub*,' called the drum, 'it's time to fly, to journey, to travel. Come with me, come, *lub dub, lub dub*, come with me and find out where you go to when you die, *lub dub, lub dub*, no need to fear, you are surrounded by love and all is well. Forget what they told you, forget what you know, you know nothing, *lub dub*, you are empty, an empty vessel, a hollow bone, *lub dub, lub dub*, you are free, free from your body, free and go now. Go, fly, go...'

Marissa was running. She was in the forest, running fast, from what? Wolves? She had four feet, four legs – was she a wolf? Running through the forest, through the night... Yes, wolves! It was dark, so dark, and she was free. This felt so good. She could go even faster, faster, if she wanted to, but she followed the pack – no, the pack followed her, she was ahead, in front, she knew where she was going.

Out to the clearing and stop! What was this? Broken bones? Bits of flesh strewn around the forest floor? A leg? An arm? She sniffed at it; the scent was familiar. There was a torso, and a decapitated head. It's me! My dream! I was in this dream before! Torn to pieces, that's me!

Suddenly she was on the ground in pieces and the wolves were looking down at her, salivating. Helpless, unable to move, a hand over there, a leg over here, and her head lolling on the ground, she looked up at the nearest wolf. But I've done this work! I've done it already! No! This can't be right!

The wolf's saliva came down in thick gobs, trickling onto its fur. All this meat, fresh meat on the forest floor, what a feast! Other wolves started to eat, devour the meat, the blood... Roar! The leading wolf grew twice as large as the others and roared directly at them as if to say, 'This feast is mine. Go now, leave me, find your own prey, your own dinner.'

The other wolves ran away whimpering. The large wolf ate Marissa's hand, devouring it in huge chunks, spraying flesh, blood and saliva everywhere. He came to Marissa's helpless head and looked at her in the eye, then swallowed her whole. There was nothing she could do.

It was black inside the wolf.

Am I dead? But wait, I can still hear the drum...

The drum! *It was calling her,* lub dub, lub dub, lub dub.

She moved towards it, then ran towards it. Am I the wolf again? No, I'm running faster than a wolf. Wait, I'm flying. Flying!

Soaring up and up through the branches, she flew up to the clouds, up to the moon.

Wow, oh, wow, the moooon.

Lub dub, lub dub, *higher and higher now, looking down at the land below, the forest, the trees.*

And there it was. A castle. A beautiful, tall, strong castle made of heavy blocks of stone, its turrets and towers gleaming in the moonlight. She could see a courtyard, high walls and a large moat. She soared and swerved and turned towards it, willing herself to land on a turret. I was here with Tori! Am I Tori now? Or Marissa? Or a bird? But wait, I'm not supposed to be here, am I? Surely this isn't where you go to when you die. Oh no, did I set an intention for this journey before I started? Or did I just go where my heart took me on the wings of the drum? Oh dear, I should have set my intention...

She was on the turret now as herself, not as a bird, and not as Tori. She got her bearings for a moment.

I wonder, could I go down to the basement and release a soul from a jar? Just one? Or maybe two?

She crept carefully through the open window. There was nobody there. She recognised the bedroom from before; it was the same one! Now she could get a better look at it. There was a large four-poster bed in the centre with curtains around it, a walk-in wardrobe to one side and a cabinet with a crystal decanter, tumblers and some sort of drink in a bottle beside it. That's where the men were talking the last time. There was also a dressing-table with toiletries on it and a large leather stool with a lavish outfit laid out on it. A man's room, a very well to-do man's room.

Marissa crept out into the corridor. She was a little anxious now, but she wanted to find the portraits on the wall.

And there they were. A large portrait of Scott adorned by a large, elaborate golden frame. She peered at his likeness. He had a big evil grin on his face, slightly bigger than a normal grin, scary and distorted. The longer she looked, the more it felt as if he was looking back at her and laughing. She felt like he winked at her and her heart flipped. The whole thing, it just wasn't natural, it was terrifying yet captivating. She had to look away.

There, beside it, was a smaller portrait, one of Martin, in a plain wooden frame. He looked bleak and sad, depressed, the way he had when she had first seen him. Her heart fell. Has he gotten to him again?

Beside Martin was a silver-framed portrait of Cheryl. Marissa skipped past that quickly, having seen her distorted face too many times already in her mind.

Next there was another wooden frame, but this time there was just a blank canvas inside. William? Marissa peered forward and spotted a long, elegant black feather wedged in between the picture frame and the wall. William! Yes! He got away! He turned into bird and he got away!

Her heart expanded. With a wide smile on her face, she touched the feather. It glistened from her touch, then dissolved in her hand.

Then suddenly she heard the drum again, felt it pulling her back. Lub dub, lub dub, lub dub. She couldn't go any further. Lub dub, lub dub, the drum dragged her back along the corridor, lub dub, back into the bedroom, lub dub, back out through the window, lub dub, lub dub, onto the turret, lub dub, and up into the sky again.

She flew on the wings of the drum, she had no choice, but she didn't mind, William was free and that was all that mattered. She was a bird now, a strong white bird with large heavy wings, flying up and up and up towards the moon and stars, the large moon that was smiling down upon her.

The closer to the moon she got, the larger her wings became. She went higher and higher, lub dub, lub dub, then she flew right past the moon. She touched the edge of it with her wing tip, banked then flew past *the planets, the stars, going higher and higher. Here was the sun, such a big, blinding light, so beautiful.* Lub dub, *she flew past the sun,* lub dub, *touching it again with the tip of her wing. It didn't burn her. And there, just beyond the sun, was another sun, this one larger, dazzling, so much bigger, a thousand times brighter than their own little sun, so bright it was white, a white powerful strong sun, calling her in.* Lub dub, lub dub, *she flew straight into the large white sun. She wasn't flying now, she was the sun, the white light, and then she was the sky, the stars, the cosmos, the atoms, all of it, she was all of it, expanding, flowing, flooding back to Earth, flowing back as light, as rain, as a waterfall, as the wolf, the bird, the fox, the rabbit, the blade of grass, all of it, the earthworm and snail, the rock, the tree, she was the tree, she was the earth, she was the diamond in the dirt, she was a new-born baby, she heard the baby cry, and she gasped for breath and cried out too, and then she was back in the room.*

The drumming had stopped. Marissa started to cry.

Jenny ran over to her. 'Are you okay? You screamed. Oh gosh, you're crying, hang on I'll get a tissue.'

In a quiet voice she replied, 'Don't go, hold me, just for a minute.'

Jenny scooped Marissa up in her arms and held her, tightly. Being held was reassuring, and the love coming from Jenny was palpable. After a moment, Marissa was able to gather herself back into the room. Jenny released her, holding her loosely now, looking at her with concern.

'Marissa cries' she said, 'that must have been some journey.'

'Yes, yes it was. But I'm okay.' She pushed herself up and sat up.

'I was just born. I was a baby, crying. That was me, crying.'

'Okay. Yes, that's good. You're okay.' Jenny seemed relieved.

'Wow, there was so much.'

'Did you see it?'

'What?'

'The demon?'

Marissa shivered. 'No. No, I didn't see it.'

'I was worried because we'd just talked about it and sometimes when I talk about something just before going on a journey, I see it then. I didn't see much just now. I think I was worried about you the whole time.'

Marissa was more present now. She reached for Jenny and pulled her in and hugged her. 'Jenny, that's the sweetest thing. Thank you so much. But you don't need to look after me, I can look after myself. Promise.' She let go of Jenny and looked her in the eye. 'This is your weekend too, you're not here to mind me, you need to do your own work. Promise me you will do your own work.'

'Okay, I promise. Maybe it felt easier to look after you than to do my own work. That's fair enough. Yes, you're right.'

The lights came back on.

Marissa smiled. 'I think I need some tea.'

'Tea sounds good. It's late, but let's have tea anyway.'

Séamus had gone.

Is that it for the evening session?

'It's nearly 11 o'clock, can you believe it?' said Terry, rubbing his arms. 'Wow, that was one hell of a journey. I can't even talk about it. I need tea first.'

Everyone had tea on their mind. Saoirse was already in the kitchen, waiting for the kettle to boil. Liz was putting biscuits on a plate.

'My head is wrecked,' Saoirse said to Marissa as they poured out the tea.

Zaad brought the milk over, Jenny got the sugar.

'Biscuit anyone?' said Finn, sitting down with them.

They were silent for a while, sitting with the energy of their journeys.

Marissa broke the silence. 'Don't forget we have to ward the rooms before bed.'

'Good call,' said Stephanie, joining them. 'I need my tea first, though. That was a wild one.'

'What did you see?'

'I was a drop in the ocean, then I was the ocean, then I don't know what I was. It was beautiful.'

'I think I was a butterfly, but I don't quite remember.'

'I became the drum. The heartbeat, it was my heart. I was at the centre of the world. I actually started crying during the journey, that had never happened to me before.'

'That was incredible. I was on a spaceship and saw other planets. I was given a medal – there was a ceremony and everything.'

Everyone drank their tea and looked at one another and smiled. They had had an incredible experience, one they would never, ever forget, a life-changing vision to carry in their hearts, no matter what. They finally knew, really knew, that they knew nothing, yet they had touched something transcendent, divine. Something that encompasses us all. Love. Divine Love. Pure, unconditional love. And all that love is right here. That's what they learned that night. Love is everywhere and right here, all the time. All you have to do is let it in.

CHAPTER TWENTY THREE

They stood as a group in the corridor in the centre of the building, where Séamus had done the warding the last time.

'I remember how to do it,' said Jenny. 'I've been doing it a lot at home. It's been working, too.'

'Okay then, you lead,' said Terry, 'but we all need to do it.'

Jenny drew the symbols on each wall, the floor and ceiling. Marissa had forgotten the symbols, but she watched Jenny and followed her movements.

Then Jenny said the banishing prayer.

The banishing prayer, I forgot about that. I have to make sure I write that down and learn it.

'Done!' said Jenny. 'But if you want to be certain, you could do your bedrooms too. See you in the morning, I'm only fit for bed now.'

It was almost midnight. Marissa put on her pyjamas and brushed her teeth while Saoirse made up her bed and waited for the little sink to be free.

The girls got into their separate single beds. The glow of the moon fell across them through the half-open curtains. It was their habit now to leave them that way.

'The moon was full almost a week ago, but it's still so bright,' said Saoirse. 'I love it here, it's so peaceful.'

Marissa laughed. 'You wouldn't know it was peaceful with all of us making so much noise together.'

'Ah, but it's different kind of noise. I don't know why, but it doesn't disturb me as much as living in a city does.'

'Cities are quite noisy, busy places, aren't they? All those people, but they don't interact that much. I like how people on the road always salute each other, once you leave Dublin.'

'Or Galway! It's as if once you get into a town that has more than a certain population, you forget to be nice.'

'Maybe you can just hide better that way.'

'Are you saying that people basically aren't nice?'

Marissa thought for a moment. 'No, I don't think that's the case. If you said hello to everyone you met in a city, you'd be so tired, you'd get nothing else done. So it's not really practical. Maybe that's what it is.'

Saoirse giggled. The room was silent and they both shifted in their beds, trying to get more comfortable. Marissa was wide awake.

'Marissa?'

'Yes?'

'Was it awful? It sounded awful.'

'Yes, it was awful. And it still is, at times.'

Saoirse sat up. 'Still is? You mean it hasn't gone?'

Marissa felt nauseous at the turn of the conversation. 'No, it hasn't gone. Can we not talk about it now? Not when I'm trying to go to sleep?'

'Shit. Sorry. Didn't mean to...'

Saoirse tossed and turned, and Marissa couldn't get easy now either. She sat up in bed and reached for her cardigan, then swung her legs out and put on her socks and shoes.

'I need to get some fresh air, it helps me settle,' she said.

'I'll come too,' Saoirse said, putting her own shoes on and throwing a blanket around her shoulders.

They walked quietly down the corridor, not wanting to wake anyone, then went downstairs and out of the front door.

Marissa walked up and down the gravel path outside the large house until her nausea settled. *Not anxiety this time, nausea. I don't know if that's better, or just different.* She remembered her ankh and her hand flew up to it. The solidity of the gold beneath her fingers calmed her and she felt centred again.

'Sorry, I shouldn't have brought it up,' Saoirse said, full of remorse.

'Hey, it's okay, I guess it's fascinating, it's just that I'm in it and you're looking at it. It's a little different when you're inside it.'

There was a noise behind them and they both jumped. Turning, they saw Terry and Finn.

'Couldn't sleep?' asked Terry with a smile.

Marissa nodded.

'Zaad is out like a light. Finn and I were talking and didn't want to wake him, so we thought we'd come outside.'

'Difficult to sleep after a journey like that,' said Finn.

'Yeah, totally,' agreed Saoirse.

Marissa looked at Finn. Something was different about him. There was no tension there, none at all. He was peaceful, serene, glowing. Ironically, he was quite attractive.

They walked slowly around the house together, stopping by the fire pit. Marissa kicked some stray bits of wood into the centre of the pit.

'I loved the fire ceremony we did at the last workshop I was on,' she said. 'I kept returning to the memory of it to keep myself sane. It was an anchor for me.'

'It sounds really scary, Marissa, what you went through,' Finn said. 'You're stronger than we gave you credit for.'

Marissa didn't look up, and she ignored the comment. *I don't want to know how weak or pathetic they thought I was for dropping out. They got it totally wrong if that's what they thought.*

After a moment she said, 'There are people trapped there, you know. The demon, he traps souls in jars, and keeps them. I don't know why. I was seeing it in my client sessions. He has hundreds of them, thousands even.'

'What do you mean?' Finn asked. 'Thousands of souls trapped in jars? Where?'

Marissa blushed. 'In a castle. I know it sounds like a fairy tale, like something I made up, but he has a castle, that's how I see it anyway. There's a room in it, like a basement room. It's near the kitchens, I think. I've been there a few times now, but I'm not exactly sure where it is. I guess I need a better map. It sounds ridiculous, I know. But I was there tonight, during our journey.'

'Souls in jars, that sounds just like The Soul Cages. I was always haunted by that,' said Terry.

'Soul Cages? What are those?' asked Marissa, feeling a tightness in her chest.

'In Irish folklore,' said Terry, 'they're where the Devil keeps the souls of lost sailors, in lobster pots. Well, they say it's a merman, but I've always felt it's the Devil, because sometimes he causes the ships to sink on purpose. Then he captures the souls of the sailors and keeps them in the cages. It's hard to know with folklore, because nobody really writes it down. Do you know the story? My grandmother told me it when I was young.'

'No.'

'I know it,' said Saoirse. 'I thought it was a merman though, not the Devil.'

'Is that it?' asked Marissa. 'Does anything else happen?'

Terry spoke. 'There's a human, he is invited to dinner at the merman's house, and he finds the cages in the kitchen. In the basement, I think. That's what reminded me of it. He goes back one night to turn over the lobster pots and free the sailors' souls.'

There was an urgency now in Marissa. 'What happens then?'

'Nothing,' said Terry quietly. 'He doesn't see anything at all, and the Devil who has them trapped doesn't even know that they're gone. I always thought it was a strange story, but it haunted me when I was a kid. I felt there was more to it, something they weren't telling us. But just the idea of it, captured souls in pots, it made me sick to my stomach. I had nightmares about it for years.'

'Yeah, it's disturbing,' said Finn. 'And very familiar. I'm feeling strange myself right now, hearing it.'

'Nevertheless, the human did release the souls and set them free,' said Terry more brightly.

'*I* set some of them free,' said Marissa slowly.

They all turned to her in astonishment.

'What happened? Tell us! Do tell us!'

'One of my clients, she was trapped in a jar in a room, I don't know if she was in the castle, but anyway, somehow I ended up going to visit her on a journey. I found her jar and I set her free. Well, Tori did.'

'Who's Tori?' asked Saoirse.

Marissa didn't care anymore. *Why keep anything else a secret from them at this stage?*

'I think Tori is a part of me, or I'm a part of her. I don't know. Sometimes I turn into her in my visions, my journeys. Sometimes it's like we are two people in the same body. I'm still figuring it out. Anyway, I released my client. The woman in the jar. I could see her soul when I set it free – it was so beautiful, a light, dancing with joy. It sparkled and twisted and turned like a firework, and then it was gone.'

She was silent for a moment, they held onto her every word. 'So many of them there, sitting there, in the jars. I felt awful about it, so I released another one, and it did the same thing, danced with joy, like a firework, and then disappeared. I opened another one, and another, and then...'

Her body winced with the memory of the pain. She felt lightheaded and needed to sit down. She moved towards the house and leaned against the wall for support. Everyone followed her, waiting for her to tell them more.

'And then something awful happened – I was kicked out of the journey, like I actually got a kick in the back. Back in my flat, I couldn't move. The pain was the worst thing I've ever felt.'

'Like a psychic attack?' asked Finn.

'Maybe, yeah, I don't know. It was so bad, so strong, the pain, that I was on the floor crying. I couldn't stand up, I didn't know what to do. Then, somehow, I phoned Séamus.'

Finn, Terry and Saoirse were looking at her, holding their breath.

'He came to my flat and he took the pain away. I don't know how he did it. Then he gave out to me, of course he did, he was so angry. I think I gave him a shock, too. Anyway, once he calmed down, he said I could come back to the programme.'

"That makes more sense to me now,' said Terry. 'He doesn't let people back in without good reason. There's the reason.'

Marissa nodded. There were tears in her eyes as she spoke. 'So many souls are still trapped there that I'm drawn to go back and release more. I've been back since.. then, and I was just in there, in the castle just now, when we journeyed together. I wanted to go back and set them free, set them *all* free. But Séamus, he was so angry at me for going on my own.'

She looked at the others. They looked back at her. Something dawned between them. But they said nothing.

A moment passed.

'Well, we could all...'

'Erm, maybe...'

Finn spoke the loudest. 'How many souls do you think are there?'

'Hundreds, if not thousands. I don't know – every time I go, the room seems bigger.'

'I'll come with you. We can go together.' Finn really meant it. 'I know I'm supposed to help you do this.'

'I'll come too,' said Terry. 'Maybe that's why I've been haunted by that story. This could be something I have to do, too.'

Saoirse didn't look so sure.

'You don't need to...' Marissa said to her, then she looked at the two boys. 'You guys, you don't have to either.'

'I know,' said Terry, 'but I used to dream I was the human, travelling down to the bottom of the sea to release those souls, to upturn those cages. I think I released a few of them, but I got caught sometimes. I don't know if it was real or a dream. Now I have a chance to do it for real, I want to do it. It's like I'm meant to do it. I'm in.'

'I'm in too,' said Finn. 'Let's go now!'

Oh. My. God. This feels too much. Too soon. I need time to think about it.

'I'm not sure, I'm so tired, and it's so late... And I don't think we should go right away. Especially after that last journey.'

'But we have all weekend... Shall we do it tomorrow night? After the fire ceremony?' Terry started dancing with anticipation.

'Can I think about it?' said Saoirse.

'I need to think about it,' said Marissa. 'None of you have to come with me.'

'But I want to!' said both Terry and Finn at the same time.

Marissa turned to Saoirse. *I guess this is really happening.* 'You can keep sketch for us. Okay?'

The boys agreed and Saoirse looked relieved.

Marissa looked at all three of them. 'I don't think we should tell the others,' she said. 'They'll all want to come and that would be too messy. I still need to think this through. And I have to stay focused, it's dangerous there, we can't risk getting caught. I was caught at one point too ... one time.' She looked up at the sky, and touched her ankh. 'I was put in a jar and had to be rescued. It was dangerous, and very scary.'

'Who rescued you? Séamus?' asked Saoirse.

Marissa smiled. 'No, it was the goddess Isis. She came to me as a bird, smashed the glass, and I climbed up on her back and we flew away. She was angry at me for doing it. Just like Séamus was. So we really can't tell the others. But I know that I'll be going back there, and it *would* be great to have back-up.'

The boys solemnly nodded their heads.

'I like to feel useful, and this seems important,' Terry said.

Saoirse put up her hand with a question and they laughed. She blushed. 'This question is important! You know how we all had different experiences in our journeys earlier? To the same place? Well, how are we, I mean you, all going to go into the same journey? How can you go to the same place – together, I mean?'

'Oh! I didn't think of that,' said Marissa. 'Wow, that's a good question. Maybe we need to think this out a bit better.'

'That's fine with me,' said Terry with a yawn. 'I certainly don't fancy being in excruciating pain, so we *should* make a plan. Let's sleep on it. We can chat during breakfast tomorrow.'

'Sounds good.'

They all headed into the house.

'Until tomorrow then.'

They slept.

CHAPTER TWENTY FOUR

The warding had held, nobody was disturbed by spirits, and after the excitement of the day before, they all slept deeply. Saoirse had forgotten to set her alarm and she and Marissa were late for breakfast. The boys had been and gone. They got their toast and tea in a hurry and took it into the front room, where Séamus was already at the helm.

Marissa glanced over at Finn and Terry. Both of them looked frustrated. Terry pointed at his watch and mouthed, 'Where were you?'

Marissa shrugged her shoulders, then mouthed back, 'Talk later,' and took her seat.

As she settled down she felt something electric running through her body. She wasn't sure what it was, or whether it was a good thing or not.

'Morning, ladies,' Séamus said, raising an eyebrow. 'Good to see you made it to class. Please take a seat. Right, folks, let's get started. Finally! Ye have three medicine stones to make today. Let's talk soul-retrieval. Can anybody tell me what a soul-retrieval is?'

Everybody put their hand up almost at the same time.

'Yes, Finn?'

'Soul-retrieval is when you retrieve a piece of your soul.' He grinned, as if this was so obvious it had to be wrong.

'Yes, correct and on the button. Well done,' said Séamus.

Finn raised his hands as if to tell a crowd to stop clapping him, and they weren't, so he grinned and quickly put his hands down.

'Soul loss,' said Séamus, 'and soul retrieval. Soul-retrieval is when you get a piece of your soul back, soul loss is when it leaves. Now, can anybody tell me what happens to make a piece of your soul leave?'

The room was less enthusiastic about answering this one. Marissa put up her hand tentatively.

'Marissa, yes. Let's hear your dulcet tones.'

She blushed as she answered. 'I suppose, during a trauma, a piece of your soul can leave and not come back?'

'Yes,' said Séamus. 'Correct. What else could cause a piece of your soul to leave? Anybody?'

Everyone was silent now. Marissa thought back to the day before, when Matt had left early in the morning and she felt as if a piece of her heart had left with him. She raised her hand again.

'Séamus, I'm not sure if this is soul loss, but can another person take a piece of your soul? Like, somebody you love? Can they walk away with a piece of you?'

'Yes,' said Séamus. 'Spot on. Well done. Your soul can leave with people, or you can give it away to a person, or a thing. You can also loose it in a specific place. We will look at all three of these. When it's a place where something happened, you need to travel back to that place across time and space, get the piece that was left there. When it's a person, you travel to that person, have communion with them, and do a soul exchange, because more often than not, you have a piece of their soul too.

'When it's a thing, it's not as straightforward, though. What type of thing could have a piece of your energy?'

There was silence for a moment.

'A doll?' suggested Jenny. 'Like a childhood teddy or something like that?'

'Well done, yes. What else?'

'A photograph? Didn't the Native Americans hate having their photograph taken because they believed it would capture a piece of their soul?'

'Very good, Terry. Yes, also possible. To be honest with you – and sure, aren't I always honest?' Séamus waited for the acknowledgement before continuing, 'we really don't know if this is true. Does a photograph really capture your soul? Does your birth certificate really sell your soul? Do you give away a piece of your soul with every contract you sign, every deal that you make, every cake that you bake? They don't call it a mort-gage for no reason. Anyway, that's another discussion for another time, where pints are involved.' He gave a cheeky wink.

'Name two more things that could have a piece of your energy.'

'Your mobile phone!' shouted Stephanie. *Of course!*

'One more... come on lads, I know yiz can do this!'

Marissa thought about how anxious she was when she handed in an assignment in college, when she was there the first time around. *Not so much this time, interesting.* 'A college thesis?' she offered.

'Brilliant. Yes, a project, or a piece of art, a piece of writing. Something you literally put your heart, and soul into. I knew an artist who had trouble selling her paintings for this very reason.'

Lots of people nodded at the realisation of this.

Séamus went on. 'Okay then. What about a place? Where could you have lost a piece of your soul, and that piece of your soul still be haunting it?'

'A graveyard?' suggested Terry, thinking he was on a roll.

Everyone laughed.

'It's a little different. That's psychopomp work. We do work with the dead in future workshops. But in a sense, yes, you could leave a piece of your soul there, if someone you loved died and was buried there, and you were grieving for them and kept returning to the gravestone. Anywhere else?'

Stephanie put up her hand. 'My old school. Where I was bullied in the yard. Every time we drive past that school, I get nervous, then I feel sick. Thankfully, it's not very often.'

'Indeed, very good, yes, and your body must know it well, if it still holds a charge for you. If you take that piece of your soul back and heal the trauma around what happened to you in that yard, then your school yard will just be a school yard, and the power it has over you will be gone. Then you can drive past it and feel nothing.'

'Glory be the day,' Stephanie said.

'Anyone else?'

'A church?' suggested Jenny.

'Yes, depending on the circumstances. Anywhere that something traumatic happened, there could be a piece of your soul lying there waiting for you, some part of you that got a shock – your childhood home, your school, a car, if there was an accident, the disco where you got your first kiss. Yes, even something like that can cause soul loss. How? Well, a piece of you wasn't expecting it, a piece of you thought it would never happen and got shocked that it did.

'Know this – what's traumatic for you may not be traumatic for someone else. And the other way round, too. So please, do not judge. Some people come away from accidents just fine, others are scattered to the four winds. When pieces of your soul leave there is less of you here, less of you to deal with what is going on for you in your day-to-day life. With less of your soul here, you can become disempowered and anxious. Like driving a car with an empty petrol tank, you just know you won't get to where you want to go without breaking down. That's why it's important to get your soul pieces back. It's empowering to be whole. With a tank full of petrol you know you can drive anywhere you want.

Everyone nodded in agreement.

'On a practical note, we're going to work with all three areas of soul loss – people, places and things. Start thinking about you - from where, what and whom would you like to retrieve the pieces of your own soul. You might need to talk it out a little with your shamanic practitioner,' he gave a wink, 'to hone in on what the person, place or thing may be. For the first session, stick with the place or the thing. We will look at how to work with the person in more detail after lunch. Working with people is more complicated, no surprise there.'

'We are going to imbue the last three medicine stones with the energy of the lost soul pieces before you absorb them into your energy field, so that these missing pieces become part of your medicine. After this, your medicine bundle for the Four Directions will be complete.'

Marissa still needed to find somebody to do one more homework medicine stone with her, then she'd have the six she needed to be caught up with the others. She looked across room and Liz caught her eye. *Liz said she'd help me with the catch-up stone. She pointed to her bundle, then gesticulated towards Liz who* nodded in acknowledgement. They smiled at each other. It was all good.

Séamus went on. 'Some people think of the soul as a solid thing, your soul is in your body, animating it, giving it life. But your soul floats around your body too, and it travels away from it. It could be more true to say your body is inside your soul. Your soul is fluid, like water, just as we can't tell a single drop of water from another drop, we cannot tell apart the pieces of your soul, one from the other. As you saw last night, we don't have all the answers, we can only learn as we go. And sometimes the information changes too, depending on where we are sourcing it from. So, whether your soul is like a jigsaw puzzle with missing pieces, or the pieces of your soul meld together like water droplets in a stream, we will never know. But we do know that we have different bodies - an energy body, an emotional body, a mental body and a physical body.'

'Last night your spiritual body went on a journey to where it came from, and where it goes to when your physical body dies.' Séamus sighed. 'Unfortunately, some of ye could not leave your thoughts behind, so yiz had colourful and interesting images that had nothing to do with the dying process, and everything to do with how exciting and interesting your personalities are. But hey, that's part and parcel of who yiz are, and I know yiz all got what yiz needed last night. And yes, it was spectacular and beautiful, not to play it down by any means, as it's all connected, like the particles of water are connected in a stream. When you take this massive essence that is you in your wholeness and squeeze it into a tiny little physical body – yes, that's right, Finn, don't laugh now, but your body is tiny compared to the size of your spiritual being – there have to be some parts that don't fit into it. So you could imagine you spill out of yourself from time to time, and leave pieces of yourself behind as you go.'

Ahh, like the Disney princesses leaving sparkles everywhere they walk. What a lovely image. But then wouldn't you need all those sparkles back?

'Your first exercise is to retrieve your soul essence from a place or a thing. I'll go through the technique in detail now, so get your notebooks out. Imagination is key, but so is permission – and remember, you're bringing these soul pieces back home, so all the work you've done up to now is a very important part of the process. If your home is a mess, they won't want to stay around for long.

Séamus described the soul-retrieval process with the group until he was sure that they knew what they had to do. It was an amalgamation of all the work they had already done - a combination of the chakra-clearing process, an extraction, then ending with going on a shamanic journey to retrieve the soul piece. It all came together quite beautifully.

'Any questions?'

The room was silent, everyone was eager to get working.

'Right. Go get started then! Find a partner, and off you go!'

The group looked to one another to partner up. Marissa went straight over to Liz, wanting to grab her before anyone else did. 'Let's go to my room,' she said, 'as it looks as though Saoirse and Stephanie are going up to yours.'

'Sounds good to me,' said Liz grabbing her cardigan and bundle. They went upstairs to Marissa's room, cleared some space to work, and placed blankets and pillows on the floor for the client to lie down on. There was a candle on the mantlepiece, Marissa lit it for support.

'Shall I work on you first?' Liz asked, getting comfortable on the floor. 'We can get your new medicine stone sorted too, if we have time.'

Liz opened her bundle. Marissa saw that she had nine stones, two small velvet pouches, some unpopped pop-corn, a bracelet made of what looked like some berries, and some silver trinkets – an angel, eagle, jaguar and something else, Marissa couldn't quite see what it was.

'Liz! Wow – what a bundle. But nine stones? I thought we only needed six for this weekend? Where did the other ones come from?'

'I worked over in Sedona for a while and bought some crystals while I was there. They helped me through a very difficult time in my life and they felt important to me, so I thought I'd put them in with the other stones, have them all together. It's felt much better since then. I actually had more stones than these at one point. Anyway, as Séamus says, our medicine grows and changes as we grow and change. This just feels right for me, for now.'

Marissa opened her bundle. She had been so proud of catching up, yet suddenly her collection seemed paltry compared to Liz's. She opened her jewellery pouch with her four new stones, the red, green, and black, and her last homework stone.

'I could do the chakra extraction process for you now,' Liz suggested, 'then we could do the soul-retrieval process. Then you'd have two stones done before lunch and you're ready to rock. How do you feel about that?'

'Really?' said Marissa, her heart lifting with relief. 'Thanks! That would be amazing. I know we're tight for time, I want to make sure we get your stone done, too.

'It will work. Let's see how we go,' Liz said.

'Okay, thank you.'

'How about we open space together, we can do the work, then close it together when we're done, instead of doing each time we swap over,' suggested Marissa.

'Perfect.'

Liz stepped into practitioner and her demeanour changed. 'What do you want to work on? Where did you lose a piece of your soul? And what would you like to be extracted?'

'Oh, my goodness,' said Marissa. 'That's a lot of think about all of a sudden. I get so focused on doing the work, I never think about what I want to heal in myself. I suppose the last time that I knew I'd lost a piece of my soul was when Matt left for work the other day. I definitely want to learn how to stop doing it, though. I was sad all day after it happened and I really don't think there was a good reason to feel sad. But we haven't covered that type of soul loss yet.'

'Why don't you pick something else, then?'

'Okay, sure. Give me a minute. Maybe you could help me figure it out?'

'Sure. But I know what you mean, about feeling sad all day for no reason, when a man leaves. I need to learn how to stop doing that too. Maybe it would help me make better choices around men.'

'You're having a difficult time with your love life?'

'Oh, absolutely. Definitely. Do you remember I told you that my husband and I broke up after the death of our baby? Well, I've never really been able to let somebody into my heart after that. I suppose part of me is deeply wounded. I feel very reluctant to start loving again.' She looked very sad. 'I think I have to move out of my house,' she added. 'I'm stuck in the energy there, that's where everything happened.'

Marissa took one look at her and said, 'I can see you are filled with emotion, and while it's active in your energy field, we should take advantage of it. Let me do your soul-retrieval for you now. Then you can spend whatever time is left working on me and we'll just do as much as we can.'

'Oh, would you? That would be great,' said Liz. 'I'll get out the stone that I want you to use for me.' She pulled out three – a green stone, a red stone and a small yellow stone.

'Which stone do you want?'

'I don't know. Séamus never told us which ones to use, what each colour was for. But this is about love energy, and green is the colour of the heart chakra, so I'll use the green one. Would that be okay?'

'Yes, absolutely.'

'Give me a moment to go over the technique that Séamus gave us.' Marissa looked quickly over her notes. 'Yes, I think I have it. Now, if you'd like to lie down here, that would be great, and you can put the green stone on your heart.'

Marissa started to work. She opened sacred space, used the pendulum to feel for intrusions in Liz's body and she dowsed over the heart chakra. After doing some work on her energy field, she was ready to try doing her first soul-retrieval.

'Liz, can you connect into the part of you that's aching?'

Liz nodded.

'Good. Now I'm going to go on a journey for you to find your missing soul piece.'

Marissa closed her eyes, mapped Liz's energy onto her body and went inwards.

Everything faded. She found herself in a grassy meadow with a happy family having a picnic. Everyone was laughing and lots of food was laid out. There were children wearing pretty white dresses laughing and playing with hula hoops and chasing one another. Someone threw a ball into the air. There was a pond nearby, ducks were quacking, and everything was beautiful.

'But I'm here to find a missing piece,' said Marissa, puzzled.

Suddenly it was if a page had been turned. The picnic picture disappeared and everything went dark.

'Oh my goodness, where did everything go?' Marissa shivered, feeling an evil presence, a sense of dark energy all around her.

And there in the centre of the darkness was a large red scorpion. Tail up, standing at attention, ready to fight, it reminded Marissa of how Liz had been the very first time they'd met – on guard, ready to fight or sting.

The scorpion looked at Marissa and Marissa looked at the scorpion.

What's going on? Is this scorpion the soul piece?

She waited. Well, this is a journey, and the scorpion can't hurt me. It's not mine, anyway, it's Liz's pain.

She got down on her hunkers and looked at the scorpion more closely. 'Are you the soul piece for Liz?'

The scorpion came a little closer and twitched. It seemed cross and was quite uncomfortable to be around, but Marissa stayed with it a little longer, then it eased.

'Okay, well, I could take you back for Liz,' she said to it, 'then maybe then we could see if you wanted to stay around.'

She reached into her pocket and pulled out a square of blue velvet cloth with drawstrings sewn into it. She laid it down on the ground and the scorpion walked onto it. Then she drew the strings, enclosing the scorpion inside a bag. It shrank a little bit and she was able to pick up the bag and hold it delicately in her hands.

She brought her awareness back into the room. Liz was lying there with her eyes open.

'Did you get it? Did you get it?'

'I think I did. I'm not sure if it's right, though. It's a scorpion. Does that mean anything to you?'

Liz said, 'I hate scorpions. They terrify me. I used to think the worst thing in the world would be to be stung by a scorpion.'

'Have you ever met a scorpion in real life?'

'Yes, actually, while I was over in Sedona, during one of the camp sessions. It was getting dark, we had been hiking and we got lost. It was quite scary actually, we didn't know if we'd make it back to camp at all. We turned the wrong corner and we were in a scorpions' lair. The place was filled with them. It was the worst thing I've ever experienced in my life.' Liz thought for a moment. 'Actually, no, it wasn't, it was the *second* worst thing. The worst thing was losing my baby.' Tears formed in her eyes.

Marissa said, 'I think the scorpion *is* probably yours then. It feels like a very strong medicine. If you can survive that experience, you can survive anything. And when you lost your baby, you lost a big piece of yourself too, which is understandable. Perhaps it's taking on the shape of a scorpion to remind you of your inner strength, that you can face your worst fears, and survive. Are you ready to welcome this piece of yourself back into your heart?'

'Oh God, that's really hard! Beautiful, but difficult!'

'Can you love a scorpion?'

'I really don't think so.'

'Could you try to if it was yours? A piece of you...?'

'I know I have to do it. Scorpion medicine for my medicine bundle. I already experienced the worst thing, so I don't have to experience it again. And here's the strength I get from healing the worst pain I ever felt in my life. Yes, it makes sense, Marissa. I'm ready now.'

'Wow, that's a great way to see it. Well done.'

Marissa placed the energetic bag with the scorpion in it onto Liz's stomach. 'I think it's probably better not to put it straight into your heart, I don't know, it doesn't feel right to do that. Maybe you need to get used to feeling it first, and it can move into your heart by itself when the time is right.' Marissa shivered. *It's just so creepy thinking of a scorpion going inside someone's heart. I know it's just energy, but...*

Liz said, 'It's not too terrible. Maybe I could soften to it.' She relaxed. 'Okay, but what do we do with the stone? It's on my heart, and the scorpion is on my stomach.'

'Séamus said to place the stone in such a way that it absorbs the energy. But maybe I still have some of the scorpion energy in my hands. I know, hang on...' Marissa gently picked up the stone and blew into it, so it imbued the scorpion essence. Then she gave it to Liz, who placed it on her stomach instead of her heart. That felt better.

'Okay, that's good. Perhaps think this is not supposed to be for my heart, after all.'

Marissa opened Liz's sacral chakra and the scorpion energy dissolved into her body almost instantly. Liz shuddered, then her whole body convulsed.

'Ouch! That stung,' she said.

'Well, it was a scorpion!' laughed Marissa.

Liz laughed. 'Yes, that's true. It was a scorpion. And I'm happy about that. It fits. Thank you very much, Marissa, this has been very interesting.'

Marissa closed off Liz's chakra and sealed up her energy field. Something still felt a little off, though. 'I feel you're out of balance. That energy did bring up a big trauma for you, although you handled it very well. Would you mind if I gave you some Reiki?'

'Thanks, that would be lovely.'

Marissa connected to Reiki, and brought it down through her body, and into Liz, placing her hands on Liz's head and then her feet. After a few minutes, everything felt like it was in it's right place.

'That feels much better now, thank you,' said Liz

'Let me just check your chakra again. I'll use the pendulum and dowse to make sure everything is complete. Yes, all done.'

Liz got up, stretched and did a yoga pose.

'Can I give you a hug?'

Wow, that's unusual. I never thought she would ask that.

Marissa received the hug gracefully.

'I know you're worried about catching up,' Liz said. 'I saw you looking at how many stones you had in your medicine bundle, but don't be worrying. I think you've got all your medicine already inside you.'

'Thank you, that feels nice to hear.'

'Now, do we have time for a quick drink of water? Then it's your turn.'

Liz went off to get water for them both. *She wouldn't have got water for me before, she used to make it all about herself. How she's changed. This healing work is really profound.* Marissa cleared the energy around the blankets and pillows from the work she just did with Liz, so that it would be clear for her own session. By that time, Liz had come back with the water. They both drank.

'What would you like me to do for you first? Your medicine stone or your soul piece?' Liz asked. 'You've had such a lot going on, you've probably lost quite a few pieces of your soul over the last few months.'

Marissa went inwards to think. 'Yes, it's too soon for me to be working on anything to do with what's been going on. In fact, I'd rather not mention that at all right now.'

'Oh, I totally understand that. That's fine. I just wanted to help you figure out what we could work on together for finding a soul piece and doing an extraction.'

'Hmm,' said Marissa, thinking, 'I always find it so difficult to choose something.'

'Let's take a step back,' said Liz. 'What part of you asked for the dark energy to come to you in the first place? We could heal that. If you want, that is.'

'What do you mean? I didn't ask for any of this!'

'No, I know you didn't, not consciously, but the dark energy wouldn't have come in the first place, if you hadn't attracted it. You could look inside yourself and see what it is in you that did that. It might be interesting. Don't think too much about it - I think you get too cerebral sometimes. You're a psychotherapist so you spend a lot of time working with thought patterns, whereas I'm more interested in energy. That's what yoga does – it opens up the body, releasing stuck energy. So, if you focus in on whatever energy it is in you that attracted the dark energy *to* you, instead of trying to analyse it, then we can dowse for that in your body, and I can do an extraction on it.'

'Oh, I think I understand what you mean now. It's difficult to think that I attracted the darkness in the first place, but I suppose I must have done, in a way. So, thank you, this sounds as though it'd be very useful. Okay.'

'Excellent. So you lie down there and allow me to do the work.'

Marissa lay on the bed they'd made up on the floor and Liz went into a meditative state. Then she picked up her pendulum and held it in the palm of her hand, breathing into it.

I've not seen that before. Liz is connecting to her pendulum before using it. What a good idea! The stronger the connection and relationship with the pendulum, the easier it would be to use it. I must try that!

'I'm ready to work on you now.'

Liz dowsed Marissa's body for the energy that needed to be extracted, starting at the crown of her head and moving down towards the root chakra. Back to the head, back to the root.

'It's in your crown and it's in your root. I'm not sure what's going on there.'

'Well, I do have two stones – we could do both at the same time.' *That would give me two medicine stones. That would be brilliant.*

'I think that could work,' said Liz, 'and I could take more time doing this and go deeper for you. Yes, okay. Do get me the stones from your medicine pouch.'

Marissa rolled over onto her stomach and took out the jewellery pouch, shook out two stones and gave them both to Liz.

'Which one for your head?'

'I don't mind. Why don't you choose?'

Liz put a red stone on the top of Marissa's head and a white pebble down on her root chakra. It kept falling off.

'How are we supposed to keep it on your root chakra?'

'Dolores, during Reiki, said that you can put your fingers on the inside of somebody's knee and send Reiki to their root chakra from there.'

'That's right, I remember they're connected. So why don't I put this on the inside of your knee?'

Marissa rested one leg out towards the floor and Liz put the stone on the inside of her knee. Liz did some work on Marissa's chakras, ran energy and opened up her energy field, ready for the soul-retrieval.

'Now, I'm going to go on a journey for you. All you need to do is rest and relax. I'll come back and blow the energies into each stone, because I'm doing two, or it might be two journeys, I'm not sure yet. Either way, I'll let you know when I've finished. Why don't you just focus on your breathing and relax while I work?'

As Liz journeyed for her, Marissa could sense her energy. She had a very strong presence, solid and reassuring. *Of course, she just got some scorpion energy, scorpion medicine. Maybe it will help her find what attracted the dark energy to me.*

After a few minutes Marissa found her body relaxing at a deeper level. *What's going on with my root chakra anyway? Maybe I'll go into it and find out while Liz is working.*

She imagined herself getting smaller and smaller until she was able to travel down and into her body, right through it to the root chakra. It was dense and damp with a thick and heavy energy. She was in a tropical jungle that was very familiar, and there was her medicine snake!

'It's good to see you here again, it has been much too long. However, you are meddling in things that do not concern you. I must warn you.'

'Oh, Sachemama, beautiful medicine snake, it's so good to see you. What meddling?'

'You are interfering with other people's destinies.'

'I don't understand.'

'Destinies – what they are supposed to live out in their lives. You are changing too much, too many things.'

'What is this about? My shamanic work?'

'No. The shamanic work is very good, very good indeed. This is not about that.'

'Is this about the people that are trapped in that castle, then? Is this about William? I thought he'd got away. Did he not get away?'

'Everything is not always your business, woman. Relax. Slow down. This is what I want to say to you. You are not here to save everybody.'

The large snake coiled around herself as she spoke, slowly weaving in and out of figures of eight on the ground. 'Perhaps it is your destiny to do some work with this, but sometimes it is for the other person to decide what they are choosing. You are always in too much of a hurry. For you, everything is urgent. It is not urgent. Remember, divine timing is not your timing. Remember, you step out of space and time when you do this work. Remember, you could be living many lifetimes all at the same time. You could be interfering in your own destiny in another timeline, another lifetime!'

She was a big tangle of snake now, she unfurled herself gracefully and straightened herself out, raised her head and looked Marissa dead in the eye.

'Most important. I want you to slow down.'

'Okay.'

'Listen to me. Like I say. Be slow.'

Marissa was overcome with love. She threw her arms around the snake's neck and gave her a hug.

The snake looked startled. 'It is not common for someone to hug a snake. Thank you. You're unusual, Miss Marissa Tori Rosenthal. You're doing good. Aside from this, keep going. Give my regards to my brother, the sea serpent.'

'He is a sea serpent no more. I think he's turning into a dragon.'

'Already? His change time? Aah, yes, you could be right. That's right! Time for celebration! It's all good. And I appreciate your visit here. Take this apple.'

Marissa laughed. 'A snake, an apple – what a cliché!'

The snake laughed, 'Yes, I know, you get the joke. I have something else to say now: be careful who you trust. Distinguish between what is true and what is the false self; it will tell you that untrue things are true.'

'Thank you.'

'Remember this truth also – sometimes an apple is just an apple!'

Marissa could feel Liz doing stuff around her head. She slowly climbed out of her root chakra and saw that Liz was blowing something through the stone and into her open crown, and she felt something cold slithering through her entire being, filling up her skeleton, lighting up her bones. And then she felt something unlock in the back of her neck and it was as if something had been loosened and released, and then she expanded, outwards and outwards, as if she was growing wings. She was breathing much more easily now, her chest was clear and her breathing was deeper than before.

'That looks a lot better now,' said Liz, nodding to herself.

'What was that?'

'That my dear, was a key.'

'A key?'

'Yes. A key to something. I don't know exactly what, whether it was to wisdom or to a box or to something that was locked. I reckon a key is always good, but don't hold me to it, just in case!'

'Thank you. So did you do the root chakra too?'

'Yes, I've done that one. I think you missed it. You were sleeping.'

'What, what did you blow into my root chakra? No, don't tell me,' said Marissa, 'let me guess.'

'Okay, but I have a feeling you won't guess.'

Marissa said cheekily, 'Was it an apple?'

Liz started to laugh. 'How the heck did you know that?'

'Lucky guess? No, really, I was down there with my medicine snake and she gave me an apple. So I just guessed you got one too.'

Liz sat down facing Marissa and crossed her legs. 'I have a message for you, that came with the soul piece. The apple was given to me the way you give an apple to your teacher. Learning a lesson. I'm not sure if that was to do with why the dark energy was attracted to you, or if it was a personal lesson, or if you are supposed to be teaching a lesson, but it's connected to your root chakra. That's tribal, primal survival, so it's a lesson I feel around good and evil. I think the apple is medicine rather than a soul piece. The soul piece I blew into your crown chakra. Yes, that's what it was.'

'Wow, okay. What was the soul piece?'

'It looked like a child, a little girl. She was spinning around and around in circles, smiling and laughing. She drew stars in the air and told me that she liked to fly in spaceships.'

Marissa smiled. 'That sounds like me when I was about three or four.'

'Yes, she looked around three or four to me. Your magical child, she's come back.'

CHAPTER TWENTY FIVE

It was lunchtime. After closing space and clearing the energies of the room, Marissa and Liz went to the dining hall to eat. They didn't realise how hungry they were until they saw all the sandwiches made with fresh batch bread, and steaming cups of tea and coffee. Marissa gave Liz a hug and thanked her, then helped herself to several sandwiches and a cuppa. Liz went over to join Zaad, Jenny and Stephanie, and Marissa noticed Terry, Saoirse and Finn were sitting at a table together, so she joined them.

'Are we still on for what we said last night?' asked Finn in a quite tone.

'Yes, I am, totally,' said Terry.

Thinking about what her medicine snake had just told her, Marissa said, 'I don't know. Maybe this isn't such a good idea, after all.'

So little time to process what's going on, it's like running a marathon. And she says it's not urgent, so let's leave it for now.

'Are you having second thoughts?' asked Terry. 'Because I've been thinking about how we could all get into the same journey, and it does sound like it could be very fun.'

'Go on?' *Well, that does sound fun.*

'It requires careful planning, we should do a few trial runs. What do you say?'

'I suppose there's no harm just trying it out,' said Marissa. 'At least we'd know then, if it was even possible.'

'Exactly. So let's try it before you decide we shouldn't do it. Seeing as we don't even know if we *can* do it. I think we should try it right now,' said Terry, looking around to make sure nobody was listening in. 'Let's do something silly, or small, just for fun. How about I imagine a place and see if we can all go there together and see the same things?'

I really don't know if we could do this... Oh! I remember, Cliona and her coyote! We both saw the same thing at the same time. Maybe it will work!

'That sounds like a brilliant idea!' said Saoirse, 'I want to try it too!'

'Okay yes, let's try it now, a practice run, go somewhere safe. Sounds good,' said Finn, while chewing and smiling at the same time.

Terry pushed his empty plate away and closed his eyes. He looked like he was concentrating. 'Okay, I've got it. This is where we're going. I'm in.'

Finn sat patiently, then he got agitated. 'Terry, where are we going?'

'Can you not just guess?' Terry had a mischievous smile on his face.

Marissa didn't like the messing around, and she was conscious of the time. 'If it was a guessing game, we could end up anywhere! You've created a specific place. Let's see if we can all get there.'

'Okay, okay. I was just trying to keep it light,' Terry said. 'I'm at a fairground with a carousel and a big circus tent. Now. Can you come to me?'

Marissa looked at him and tried to tune into his energy. She mapped his energy onto her body and imagined herself melting into it.

She found herself standing on a grassy field. The grass was newly cut, a perfect height, and the sky was big and blue, with several white fluffy clouds. Behind her was a large, very colourful circus tent that looked a little like the Taj Mahal. Ha, ha! Of course it would!

Terry was standing beside her with his arms crossed and a large grin on his face. He was wearing a tight-fitting gold suit and a tall top hat. The ringmaster of the circus!

'Okay, Terry, I think I've got you. Can you see me there?'

'I can feel you here, not so sure about there, though. What do you see?'

'I see you, and a large circus tent, which reminds me of the Taj Mahal. It's very colourful and stripey!'

'I suppose you could say that. Yes, close enough. That's actually brilliant.'

Back in the dining hall, Finn was grimacing as if constipated – his face was tense and his eyes were squeezed tightly shut. Saoirse looked like she was sleeping. Marissa in the journey saw an orange kite appear in the sky, flapping in the breeze.

'Can you see a kite?' she asked Terry.

'What? A kite? I didn't put it there. Hang on, I can't see a kite, but I can see something faded, moving in the sky. I think it's a bird.'

'Look,' said Finn, more relaxed now, 'I think it's me.'

Marissa looked at the kite again, and saw that it was a bird, and it was flying towards them. It didn't seem to be able to control its speed and it crashed onto the ground, turning into Finn and knocking both her and Terry over onto the grass.

All three of them snapped out of the image.

Clumsy, yes, but amazingly, we were all in the same place, even if just for a moment.

'What was I wearing, Finn?' asked Terry. 'What did you see?'

'Something gold? With something on your head – a hat? But it was hazy, weaving in and out of focus. I'm not sure if I did it right.' He laughed.

'That felt too easy,' Terry whispered to Marissa.

'Yes, maybe. But are you sure that we were doing it? How do you know that we actually were all in the same place and not making it all up?' asked Marissa.

'Hmmm, this is going to take a while, particularly if you don't have faith. I have faith. What about you, Finn?' Terry was unusually self-assured.

Finn grinned. 'I was a kite. That's a type of bird.'

'Ha ha!' said Marissa, 'I saw a kite! But it was made of cloth, flapping in the breeze. On my second look it turned into a bird.'

'So funny!' said Saoirse, but the disappointment showed on her face. 'I was trying really hard, I was, but I didn't know how to get in.'

'It was funny seeing you both there,' Marissa said. 'But Finn, why didn't you show up as yourself?'

'I don't know. A bird just felt like it would be more fun. And I've been reading about birds, a kite just came into my mind.

Anyway, why do I need to be myself? I think I'm hardly ever myself when I journey.'

'Interesting,' said Saoirse. 'I wish I was there. What did you do?'

'I mapped Terry's energy,' said Marissa, 'because he was the one setting the location.'

'Oh! I didn't think of that, what a good idea!'

'Okay, then maybe we need to decide exactly where we're going before we go, so we can map onto the person who sets the location. It might also help to decide what shape we're going to be, and tell each other first, so we're able to recognise each other.'

'Oh, what fun!' said Terry, clapping his hands together. 'I do like a challenge. I think this could be could be quite good. Even if we don't get any of the souls released, it's interesting to try meeting up in a journey! I'm up for this.'

Marissa had a sinking feeling. *I'm not so sure now, myself. All of our good intentions might come to nothing. Or even harm. But they mean well, and I can't go alone. So maybe we should pursue it for a while. Sure we might not get anywhere with it anyway.*

The gang at the other table got up to go. 'Time to get to class. Come on, guys.'

They left their plates by the kitchen sink and quickly manoeuvred themselves into the front room, sliding into whatever seat was available.

Séamus was waiting for them. 'Yiz are all back again. Good stuff. How was the morning's work?'

After an animated question and answer session, it was time for Séamus to give them their next set of instructions.

'This might be the most useful piece of work yiz ever learn from me. Once ye know how to do it, ye can do it anytime yiz need to.'

He once again had their avid attention. He was sitting on his little stool at the top of the room, wearing his hat, usual jeans, and a bright, crisp, sky blue shirt that set off his eyes. He leaned in and said in a low voice, 'Yiz have heard about energy vampires?'

They nodded, wide-eyed, not wanting to interrupt his flow.

'Well, they're real. They exist, and, they feed off your energy. Your soul energy. They take your personal power from you and keep it for themselves, as food. This technique will teach yiz how to get your personal power back. Once you keep taking your energy back, it stays with you, naturally. Like training a dog to stay, instead of having it walk off with just anyone. Once you have a good relationship with your energy, and you do this technique regularly, it's more likely your energy will stay with you. And these feckers may just leave you alone! And, as ye grow stronger in this, your energy will come back to ya quicker if it does leave, and it will learn not to go with other people as often, just for the sake of it.'

Séamus leaned back and raised his voice, giving them all a fright. 'But! There's always someone that gets away with it!' He leaned back in and whispered, 'Only because you let them.'

He gave them some space to absorb this information.

Stephanie put up her hand.

'Stephanie?'

'Why would I let someone do that to me?'

'Aren't you already?'

She thought about it. 'I'm not sure...'

'Well, let's start with your manager at work. How do you feel when he comes into your space?'

She thought for a moment. 'Yeah, okay. I shrink a little and feel smaller than I was when he wasn't in my space.'

'Exactly. So you become subservient, he being an authority figure. Do you ever get back to your full size when he walks away? Do you even notice?'

Stephanie scratched her head. 'I suppose I can't really answer that, I never thought about it before.'

Séamus got up and walked around the group. 'Now. I'm not saying your manager deliberately takes a piece of your energy, nor am I saying that all managers take their employees' energies, either.'

Sarah would never...

'But what I am saying, is that we have a tendency to give our energy away to a superior, an authority figure. We become like a little dog, rolling onto its back, completely submissive. This is what's fundamentally wrong with society. Nobody is superior to us, we all have the same value. It's our idea that someone is more important than we are, that takes our power from us, and we give it to them, because we think we have to. Some people just get paid more than we do. Some people get keys to lock up and open up a building. That's all. There's nothing superior about them, not really. Unless you think a stronger dedication to the grindstone is a superior trait?'

They giggled and relaxed.

'I do it myself,' Séamus admitted with a shrug of his shoulders. 'Sure, it's years and years of conditioning. It's beaten into us. I'll tell yiz, on my way here, driving up from Dublin, I was stopped by a Garda car. Scared the livin' shit outta me!'

Everyone laughed.

'And I'd done nothing wrong! I wasn't speedin', my tax was in date, yet I was shivering in my boots. What the fuck was that about? Why did I automatically give a piece of my personal power away and get so small? Because of the same thing – we think they are more important than we are. They hold authority – the authority of the law. You need to know what law you live by, that's vital. I remembered, and by the time the Garda came over to my window, I had got hold of myself. But I'll tell ye, I was still shakin' for a while afterwards.'

He got up and stretched his body out, and walked over to the window, looking outside for a moment. Then he turned and faced them once more.

'Thing is, we don't always respond to these things as ourselves. We can react from the collective energy, go back into our conditioning, our mindless thinking. It's a survival mechanism. People talk about the "fight or flight" response, but they forget about freeze. This is the freeze response. Freeze, and hope the fucker goes away.'

Everyone laughed again.

'You've got to become the master of your responses, and that includes the conditioned ones. That Garda, he was just telling me my indicator light wasn't working. But I automatically assumed I was in trouble for something. Just like being back at school, hey?'

Zaad put up his hand. 'I find this happens to me all the time. I always assume the worst. While growing up in Ireland I looked so different from everybody else, people would attack me. A lot. But now, there are so many others here who look less Irish than I do! But my body still remembers and still responds that way. You say it well, Séamus. Shrinking – yes, that's exactly what I do.'

'It's good for you to know this, Zaad, know thyself is the best weapon on the block. And you're exactly right in how you said that – my body remembers and still responds that way. It took a lot of conditioning to create that response, and a lot of damn hard work to uncreate it.'

'I think you're right about my manager. I do lie down on my back and expose my belly to him, energetically I mean. I can see it now,' said Stephanie. 'Pandering. That's the word that comes to mind. Maybe that's one of the reasons why I find it so difficult to be at work right now.'

'Well, once you start using this technique, it may become easier for you to stay there, if that's what you decide to do. And your manager may even notice something different about you because he won't be able to get your energy so easily. It can be a subtle change, you sitting obediently instead of lying belly-up on the floor, provided you're not putting your hackles up and growling at him. We've all done that one before. Subtle is better.Know that you've got sharp teeth and can bite, but you choose not to.'

He took a breath. 'Remember what happens when you heal? You send ripples out to the world, and some people don't like that. They don't like to see you looking better than they do, feeling happier and stronger than they are. Most people identify themselves through other people's pain, and when you're not in pain, they don't recognise you, or themselves. Funny, isn't it, how doing your own healing work can put someone else out so much. But are you here to satisfy their needs, or are you here, on this planet, to grow? What say you?'

Terry put up his hand.

'Yes, Terry, m'dear?'

Terry beamed. 'I say that some people will never grow and always be resentful of anyone who is healing and growing, but that's not a good reason not to do your work. If that makes any sense!'

'Perfect sense, and it's perfectly true. Anyone else want to say anything?'

Marissa spoke. 'I can't imagine not wanting to get better myself, but I think that's my personality. I'm always trying to improve something. I suppose some people use their pain to create a comfort zone that is familiar, and it can be less scary to stay in a familiar pain than to step into the unknown.'

'Exactly,' said Séamus, 'and it's not just your manager that wants you to be subservient, you get that in families, too. Sure, isn't that where we learned it? And they learned it too, it was handed down over many generations. Who are the primary authority figures in your lives?' He scanned the room. 'Saoirse, you've been very quiet this weekend. What say you?'

Saoirse piped up. 'Yes, Séamus, you're right, I have been quiet. My father died twelve years ago this week, and I always get sad around this time of year. I guess he was a primary authority figure in my life.'

Everyone could see the grief in Saoirse's eyes as she spoke about her father, even her glasses couldn't hide it. Séamus said quietly, 'Sorry for your loss, girl. Time means nothing in matters of the heart.' He turned to the group. 'Our fathers, and our mothers, too, are primary authority figures. How our parents held us, disciplined us, sets us up for dealing with any other authority figure we encounter in the world. If we shat ourselves every time our dad got mad at us, then anytime a Garda car pulls us over, it's a conditioned response to do the same thing. Or anytime our manager tells us we made a mistake, or we get a letter from An Post looking for the TV Licence money.'

Saoirse smiled with the others, so Séamus knew she was okay.

'So,' he continued, 'what does any of this have to do with soul-retrieval? Everything! I'll tell yiz. When you take that piece of energy back that you inadvertently gave away, you're retrieving a part of your personal power.'

'What's the difference between personal power and a piece of your soul, Séamus?'

'It's difficult to tell the difference – and honestly, as I'm always honest with ya, I can't tell the difference, not really. It's all life force, innit? All I know is that soul-retrieval is about taking back an aspect of yourself that was frozen in time, due to some trauma or other. And your personal power can be taken from you by dominating forces; boyfriend, girlfriend, mother, father, teacher, manager, garda – whomever.'

He started walking around the room, becoming more passionate. 'You give away your power when you're submissive. When you think someone is superior to you. But your personal power gives you the strength you need, to do the things you need to do. And the things you want to do. Without it, you're exhausted and drained. With it, you are motivated and excited by the possibilities of life. Your soul pieces are your creativity, your hope and dreams, your belief in beauty and truth, and they're your ability to know you need to tell someone to fuck off. Your personal power is what you need to actually tell someone to FUCK OFF!'

The jumped. The room reverberated from his voice.

'Yes, I see it so clearly - you need power do things, you need power to take back the larger soul pieces that you've lost. Your soul pieces are your inspiration, your power is what you need to put behind whatever it was you were inspired to do. The power of your will. Will power. You need power to will things into being.'

'Ahh, But of course, you're once again caught between a rock and a hard place when you are powerless, hey. Gettin' started is most often the hardest part. And it's one of the biggest mistakes many healers make when doing soul-retrieval. You've got to be strong enough for those beautiful soul pieces to want to stay with you. They need to feel like you have the power to look after them, appreciate them and protect them.'

The room fell silent. Séamus let them absorb the new information, it seemed he was absorbing it too. Then he continued in a quieter tone.

'You can take that piece of your soul back that you gave to your lover because you wanted them to love you. You can take that piece of your soul back from the sick person who took it from you because they were jealous of you being well. You can take that piece of your soul back from your co-dependant mother who fed off you because she didn't have a life and was jealous of yours. You can take a piece of your soul back from anyone who has ever taken a piece of your soul from you, if you know how to do it, and have the power to do it.' He paused. 'Shall I tell ya how?'

Grinning, he stood there, waiting to see their reaction.

The group was salivating like a pack of hungry dogs wanting to bite into fresh meat that was right there in front of them, waiting for the command to eat to roll off of their master's tongue.

Séamus faced them, prolonging it for as long as he could.

'Aah, look at yiz all. I'm so proud of yiz, and how far yiz have come on this journey with me. All of ye are amazing.'

'Aww come on, Séamus, tell us! Come on!'

He laughed. 'See, yiz are giving me your energy too, aren't you? Wanting to know what I know, you're giving it to me as an exchange, thinking it's fair an' all. And if I wasn't a good man I'd be lapping it up right now, soaking in it, basking in fact, absorbing your good energy. I'd be using it to keep myself young and beautiful.'

He did a little jig and everyone laughed.

'Sure look at me, amn't I beautiful enough, already?' Séamus bowed, then laughed. 'I don't need your energy, thank you all the same. But for some spiritual teachers, gurus and even celebrities,' he winked, 'your power is their life's blood. Energy vampires, the lot of them.'

Images of the audience at the London event flooded Marissa's mind. *Scott Taylor, that's exactly what he was doing – soaking up everybody's need for him, taking that energy from them. Then, when he had them weak and wanting, he'd bind them to him. I think that's how he did it. This is so interesting, and interesting that Séamus is talking about it so openly. I wonder do other teachers talk about this, too?*

'And so good at taking it too, many of them. Real vampires don't hide in daylight. They hide in plain sight. You never know who they are, until you start hunting them down.'

Marissa felt eyes on her. She scanned the room and saw Terry and Finn were looking right at her. She could guess what they were thinking. *We will be hunting for souls. Not for the demon, no. We are just freeing souls.* She tried to send that message to the boys, but she didn't know if they received it. *But maybe they sent that message to me?* There was too much going on in the room and they had never tried telepathy before. *I'll just have to say this to them up front, make sure they know. We're not vampire hunters. I hope they don't get any crazy ideas.*

As if mirroring her thoughts, Séamus said, 'We're not hunting vampires today. Or any day. It's too messy a thing, sometimes dangerous, and there are too many of them. They're everywhere; you'd be sickened if you could see them all. No. We are just making ourselves unavailable, taking our energy back, and changing our vibrational frequency so they can't find us anymore. No longer in plain sight, for them. We will change the way we taste, we will become sovereign in our very being, and we will solidify our essence so they can't break into our field. Sound good?'

'Yes! Oh my God! Yes!!'

'Good. Now, here's how you take your client's energy back from a person. It's so easy, I don't know why everybody isn't doing it. Ha, ha! Of course I do – sure they don't want you to know! Your client and you talk about who the person is, then you need to get them to visualise them, so you can connect to them through your client. Then, the practitioner will go on a journey to that person and ask them kindly for the energy back. Then take it, say "Thank you," yes really say that, always with grace and gratitude, it elevates our frequency. Then bring the energy back to the client, cleanse it, then gift it to them as you have been doing already.'

'It sounds straightforward, but it isn't always. I'm sure you can imagine the person you travel to might not necessarily *want* to give the energy back, so you might have to be a little more, shall we say, subtle. So you get a hint of the flavour, density and frequency of the energy of your client, then you can strip it from the person, collect all of it and bring it back to your client. And often, the client doesn't know who has their energy, so you might need to journey blind. Or, it might not be the person that your client thinks it is. All part of the fun of it. But don't forget, before you give the power that you've retrieved back to your client, you must clean it – because who knows where it's been.'

'To lay another layer of complexity onto this – we all take energy from each other. This doesn't mean that everyone is an energy vampire. It just means you could be insecure in a relationship and need to hold on to a piece of your loved one. So you can ask your client if they're holding on to any energy from the person that they feel took their energy in the first place. There's no shame in finding out you've been holding onto someone's energy, like a comfort blanket. But once you know, you must give it back to them. It's much better to keep everything clean.'

'So, scan your client's body for any energy belonging to the person they've chosen to work with, bundle it up with you and take it on the journey to their person. Then you can offer it in negotiation, if the person won't give you back the energy, offer an exchange. See? Makes good sense. Then everybody is happy.'

'It takes practice and confidence. And medicine stone, yes. You want the stone to remind you of how strong you are when you are in your power. So bring the stone with you for the ride, and when it's all done, map your new powerful body onto the stone, to create a memory point. Then take the map off your stone and it becomes part of your medicine. You've got two stones left, each of you, yes?'

They nodded.

'Right. Questions?'

Jenny put up her hand. 'You said we could do this for ourselves? But you only described how to do it for a client. How would that work?'

'I'll tell you later, once you have worked this technique with your client and are familiar with it. Okay? Good. Now go find someone you've not worked with in a while. We do one exchange now, and one after dinner, and then it'll be time for the fire ceremony. Dinner will be ready from 6 to 7:30. Go in when you're ready, help yourselves, then find new partner and get back to work. I'll meet you at 9 at the pit. All good?'

There was a resounding: 'Yes!'

'Good. I'll see yiz later, so.'

CHAPTER TWENTY SIX

Stephanie walked over to Marissa. 'We've not worked together in a long time. Do you want to do this with me?'

Marissa brightened, 'Yes, I'd like that very much.'

'Liz is working in my room already...'

'And Saoirse in mine.'

They looked around them. then spoke at the same time.

'How about here?'

'What about this sofa?'

Marissa shivered at the thought of lying down on the sofa again. 'Here is fine, but can we work on the floor?'

'Perfect. I have a throw upstairs. I'll go and get it, if you get us some pillows and water.'

They organised themselves behind the sofa, using the back of it to lean up against.

'I think space has already been opened in here,' said Stephanie, 'so I feel we don't need to do it, what do you think?'

She opened up her medicine bundle beside Marissa's.

'Oh, may I?' She touched Marissa's fabric. 'It's so unusual. It's beautiful.'

'Yours is beautiful too, said Marissa admiring the turquoise and blue fabric of Stephanie's medicine bundle. 'I don't mind you touching it.' She was happier having caught up with the others. Her medicine stone collection felt more substantial, now.

'I don't know if the colour is really me,' Stephanie said. 'I was thinking I might carry something from my ancestors. I mean to say, I'm Irish, born here, lived here all my life, but my grandmothers on both sides were from Africa – one from Namibia and the other from Zaire. It's the Republic of Congo now. I believe that the families were enemies, so my parents are peacemakers! They never met each other, my grandparents.' She touched Marissa's Peruvian cloth again. 'But you're not from Peru, so I suppose wherever resonates with you is good, you don't need to actually have family there.'

I feel as though I do have family in Peru, though, if a mountain counts as family.

'I feel as though I am from Peru. Some part of me feels very deeply connected to it. That's why I chose this cloth. Or the cloth chose me – that's what it felt like. My grandparents are Irish, but their parents were from Russia. They came to Ireland to make a new life for themselves.'

'So did mine. I understand what Zaad feels at times – I also had trouble at school when I was young, but it wasn't too terrible once I made some good friends. I'm still friends with them even now!'

Marissa became aware of the time. 'We had better start working, if that's okay?'

'Oh yes, of course! I always lose track of time. So, are we to do a soul-retrieval from a person? Or is this a power-retrieval? I suppose the method is the same. Do you know who you want to take your soul back from? It sounds so funny, doesn't it? As if my father would deliberately take my soul from me. I don't think he would dream of it.'

'I don't think Matt would deliberately take my soul from me either – I just gave it to him anyway. So I'd like to take it back from Matt.'

'From your boyfriend? that sounds like a good idea. So maybe I will do my father then. Perhaps I'll get a boyfriend once I get my soul piece back!'

'You're single?'

'Yes. I like it that way – too much baggage from too many men – but I'm getting older now and I think I'd like to have a relationship, maybe a baby, who knows? I feel something needs to change in my life right now, whether it's my job, or being single. I was made for more than I am getting out of life. Maybe I want to put some more of myself back in to get more out!'

'So getting your soul back is a good place to start. Do you want me to guide you first? Then you can do me.'

'Okay!' Stephanie smiled and shook out her ponytail. Many long plaits loosened and swung free, then settled, and she seemed softer.

'It's too uncomfortable to lie down with it up,' she explained. 'My hair, it's the bane of my life. Thankfully I've found someone good in Camden Street who knows how to plait it the way that I like.'

'Your hair is amazing – it's so beautiful. Here's a pillow. Are you comfortable now?'

'Yes, very. Thanks.'

Marissa looked over her notes. 'Okay, we are going to get your soul piece back from your father. Let's set our intention that this will be gentle and kind, and loving.'

'That sounds good to me.'

Stephanie closed her eyes. The tassels on the fringe of her gold and white tunic fell across her body and onto the floor, rising and falling with her breath.

Marissa took a few minutes to tune into her. *This feels wrong, I can't just do it like this. I need a candle or something.*

'Stephanie, I'm just getting a candle. I need to burn some sage around you.'

'Okay!'

Marissa took a small tea light from the hearth and her sage bundle from her handbag. *I think I should keep some sage in my bundle too.* She lit the candle, then lit the sage, and ran the smoke up and down Stephanie's body.

'Mmm, that smells good,' said Stephanie, still with her eyes still closed.

'I couldn't tune into you. I felt there was a lot of energy debris around you. It seems better now.' Marissa crushed the sage bundle out against the side of the saucer the tea light was resting in. She turned to Stephanie.

'Okay, I need you to think about your father, feel the connection that you have with him.'

Stephanie nodded her head.

'Good! Okay, now I will scan your body for your father's energy,'

Marissa unfocused her eyes and waited a moment, then could sense a blue and yellow energy around Stephanie's body, particularly around her hips and stomach. She gathered it up, drew it to her in a ball and saw that it was caught in a spider-web construction which was gathered in Stephanie's heart. She tugged at it, but it was fixed tight.

'Ow! What did you do?'

'I'm taking the energy of your father from you, but it's stuck in your heart.' She tugged again.

'Ow! I don't like that.'

What if I left some of it behind? If I disconnect her totally from her father, will that affect their relationship? I don't want to cause any trouble.

Marissa thought for a moment, then loosened her grip on Stephanie's father's energy. It settled down, leaving a light cobweb-like structure on Stephanie's body, but the rest of it came away in her hands.

'Okay, some of this energy just doesn't want to go, so I'll leave it there.'

'That's fine with me!'

'I'll cleanse this energy first, then journey to your father.'

Marissa visualised the blue and yellow energy becoming brighter in her hands. It expanded. She closed her eyes. She couldn't get a reading on where to go to find Stephanie's father, so she went to her old familiar friend the tree.

'Hello, tree.'

She wanted to fling her arms around it, but held herself back, not wanting to lose Stephanie's father's energy.

The big wise old tree opened one eye, saw it was Marissa, and opened both. Its wide grin infused Marissa with love and joy.

'Ah, my friend, it is good to see you again.'

'And you.' Marissa curtsied and giggled. 'I need to find Stephanie's father, to give him back his energy. And to take back Stephanie's energy.'

The tree raised an eyebrow. 'Ah, yes. Good. Come on inside.'

The door at the side of the tree opened, and Marissa entered. She was expecting a slide downwards, or steps upward, but there were neither. Instead, there was a corridor with a highly polished floor. She stepped onto it and walked forward until she got to the end. She was in a large, cold room with tall windows and a view of a beach. There was a dining-table at the window with cutlery and plates on it, it was set for a meal. It had white linen, yellow flowers in a centrepiece and there was a man sitting there eating on his own. He was dark-skinned and had neat short hair and a moustache. He was wearing a grey suit and black leather shoes, and there was a briefcase at his feet.

Marissa approached him hesitantly. He didn't seem to notice her, so she cleared her throat to get his attention.

He looked up from his food.

'Ah yes, leave it there.' He pointed to an empty wooden fruit bowl on the table.

Marissa looked at him. Does he know what this is? Does he know who I am?

'Well? what are you waiting for?'

Marissa felt like a serving girl. She quickly dropped the ball of energy she held into the fruit bowl, where it shifted and moved, swirled and ebbed. The yellow and blue didn't mix; it was like looking at oil and water, yin and yang.

Marissa stepped back. The man continued to eat.

'Sir?' Marissa said. 'May I have Stephanie's energy, please?'

The man gestured nonchalantly to the briefcase by his feet. 'That should suffice,' he said, finishing his breakfast and reaching for a newspaper which was on the table. He kicked back his legs, opened the paper and, with a satisfied grunt, started to read.

Marissa stood there. She couldn't see his face, as he was behind the newspaper. She looked at the briefcase, then picked it up and walked away from the table, back the way she had come, back into the forest.

The door in the side of the tree closed. Marissa put the briefcase on the ground and realised it had a lock on it. She looked at the tree in puzzlement.

'How am I supposed to open this?'

Marissa came back to the room and saw that Stephanie wasn't asleep.

'Stephanie, what's your birthday?'

'Oh? It's 14th April.'

'That was quite recent! Happy belated birthday! Now hang on, I've not finished the journey yet.'

Marissa went back to the tree and the briefcase on the forest floor. She put in the numbers 1404, tried the briefcase and it opened.

'Phew, that was a good guess,' she said.

Inside the briefcase was a swirling energy. It was dark green and fuchsia pink, and like the father's energy, the colours didn't mix.

Marissa watched as the briefcase sank into the forest floor and disappeared. The energy hung in the air in front of her. It had grotty black bits in it and looked quite dirty.

Marissa connected to Reiki right there in the journey and brought the light in. It was beautiful! She could see the light clearly, it was white, but had colours in it, and little golden speckles moving through it. It shot out though her hands and went straight into Stephanie's energy. Wow, this is amazing! Why haven't I done this before?

The tree was watching her closely as she placed her hands around Stephanie's energy and allowed the Reiki light to diffuse through it. The grotty bits started to gather together, then swell, then burst, like small fireworks going off. Some were like balloons, others were like streamers. Each time one of them burst, the ball of energy got bigger and brighter, until it was quite substantial. It was light now, and moving fast, and Marissa was pleased that she had cleansed it.

'Thank you, my friend,' she said to the tree as she gathered the energy in her hands. She leaned over to the trunk and gave it a kiss.

Then she walked away slowly and came back into the room.

Stephanie was sitting up. 'What did you do? What happened?'

'I have the energy here, in my hands.'

They looked, but of course in this reality, they couldn't see anything.

'Where is your medicine stone?' asked Marissa.

'Here it is,' said Stephanie.

'I took the energy to your father from your hips and stomach, so I think we should put this energy there, to make up for that. Keep the stone beside you for support.'

Marissa ran energy through Stephanie's body to warm it up before opening the chakra. Stephanie wiggled her hips and couldn't lie still. She laughed. 'I apologise, I get like this when I'm excited! It used to drive my father crazy.'

If he was anything like that man I just met, I imagine that it would.

'I remember you did this when we did our first demonstration. You said you weren't doing it on purpose and I didn't believe you.'

'Maybe you do now!'

'Can you settle enough to let me finish the work?'

'I'll try.'

It took some visible effort on Stephanie's part. Marissa laughed and so did Stephanie. She became more relaxed then, and Marissa was able to place the energy onto her body. Stephanie stopped wriggling almost right away. She stopped dead, and it was a bit of a shock for both of them.

'Can you run the energy again?' Stephanie asked.

'But I don't need to... Okay, why not?' Marissa placed one hand over Stephanie's head, the other at her root chakra and ran the energy.

Stephanie didn't wiggle. 'How strange!' she said. 'That's new. What did you see?'

'Hang on, you need to map your body to the stone, and I need to close the chakra first, then seal your energy field.'

Stephanie and Marissa did their work, then both of them sat cross-legged on the floor, Stephanie still holding onto her new medicine stone.

'Tell me!' said Stephanie.

'Okay. First I took the energy from you that belonged to your father. Then I took it to my guide, the wise tree that I always visit.'

'Ah, your axis mundi.'

'Yes, that's right. It let me through a portal, only I didn't go down or up, I went straight in. It was strange. I don't think I've done that before.'

'Because my father is here, he is still alive, so you were in – what do they call it? – the middle world. You didn't need to go down, or up.

'I see. Yes, that makes sense. Thanks.'

'What was my father doing?'

'He was eating breakfast alone at a big table. The room was very fancy, but cold, no warmth. I don't mean temperature.'

'Yes, I know what you mean, exactly.'

'There were big windows and I could see the sea outside, but he didn't seem interested in it.'

'Yes, that sounds like him.'

'He thought I was a maid!'

'Ha, ha, yes, that's definitely him.'

'I left his energy from you in the fruit bowl, and he gave me a briefcase. It was locked. I needed a numeric code.'

'Aah, that's why you asked me for my birthday.'

Marissa smiled. 'Yes, and it worked. Your energy was beautiful but small, and when I did some healing on it, it grew.' Marissa described the fireworks and the balloons.

'That is amazing.' Stephanie said. 'I always felt that I drove my father crazy whenever I was happy. "Too happy, always too happy," he would say to me and hush me down. I was never allowed have a party in the house, I never could have my friends around. Around him I always had to be quiet and still. I loved him so much that I wanted to kiss and hug him like my friends did with their fathers, but he wouldn't have it.'

'All those times you couldn't celebrate with him, couldn't express your love, you were losing pieces of yourself. Maybe each firework was a party that you couldn't have.'

Stephanie had tears dripping down her face. 'I am happy, Marissa, not sad. My father is still very much alive, but I have never felt joy the way I knew it was possible to feel it. That is why I came here to do this shamanic work. I think all the work I've done has led me to this point.' She got up and stretched. 'I'm ready now for my joy to come back, and my father had it in his briefcase waiting for me! Thank you so much for helping me take it back. I think my life will be so much better now.'

Marissa was so happy for her friend.

'It wasn't as if I didn't have friends,' Stephanie explained. 'But not being able to invite them to my house made me feel very bad. I was afraid to go to their house, in case they wanted to come to mine.

I stopped going to my friend's houses after a while, it just became easier. I know I missed out on a lot of fun.'

Marissa stood up too and together they cleared the space.

'I know the energy that came back was joyful, but it still feels heavy here, can we work somewhere else for me?' asked Marissa.

'Of course!'

Marissa clapped her hands to clear the heaviness and then realised that there were two other people working in the room too, up by the window.

'Sorry!' she whispered and looked around for somewhere to move to. 'I guess we need to stay in this room after all.'

'How about in front of the fireplace?'

'Sounds good.'

They moved their medicine bundles to the hearth and Stephanie looked at her new medicine stone for a moment before putting it into her bundle. 'I have one more stone to go!' she said, 'but I don't care, I got my joy back and that means everything to me! Thank you, Marissa, again.' She gave Marissa a hug. 'I find these weekends so intense,' she went on, 'the pace of them – we get through so much and we have to keep going! I need to take a few hours off to make sense of everything! Oh well, I am ready for you now. Are you ready?'

Marissa nodded her head. 'Yes. I want to feel more independent from Matt. I don't like missing him so much when he's not around.'

Stephanie arched an eyebrow. 'Perhaps it is good, though, to miss him? You love him, don't you?'

Marissa smiled. 'Yes, I do. Very much.' She saw him in her mind's eye and felt the familiar ache in her heart.

'So it's natural to miss him, isn't it?'

'I suppose so, but I get very sad. I don't like that.'

They arranged the throw and the pillows so Marissa could lie down comfortably. She had brought the candle over too, in its saucer, and placed it carefully on the hearth.

'Now you can lie down,' said Stephanie, 'and I will run the energy, then scan your body for energy belonging to Matt. May I have your medicine stone? It needs to be here beside you for the process. You can hold it if you want to?'

Marissa relaxed and closed her eyes with her stone loosely in her hand. She felt her body letting go of tension as Stephanie worked around her. The image of Matt was still strong in her mind. She smiled and relaxed, then allowed herself to feel how much she loved him. Her heart opened, liquid love burst out of it and flowed like warm milk over her body. Something in her shifted and she felt better.

Didn't know that I didn't feel good. Maybe being away from him, I feel like I'm on hold or something. Like I'm holding my breath until the next time I see him.

Then Matt's face changed shape, and turned into James. Marissa froze. Her body stiffened. Stephanie, already on the journey, didn't seem to notice.

I should be able to relax with James, he has no power over me anymore. She remembered throwing the stone out to sea in Dun Laoghaire in the rain, saying how she was now available for life. *Funny how Matt is from Dun Laoghaire! I wonder if he picked up my stone! Maybe he heard me saying that! Strange how these things happen. Perhaps there is more synchronicity going on than we realise.*

She focused back on the image of James in her mind. It had shifted into him with a wife and three babies. He looked hassled as he packed them into the car. They were going somewhere. She took a closer look at him. He looked tired. *I honestly do wish you well, James. I want to be happy, but you have to make your own choices so that you can be happy. I've already let you go, but maybe there's some energy here that you need. Did I take some of your energy without realising it?*

'Now then,' Stephanie said, 'I am back and I have energy for you.'

Marissa reluctantly broke away from her thoughts and pulled herself into the room. Stephanie placed a ball of energy over her heart chakra. Marissa lay still as Stephanie blew the energy into her body. She felt cold for a moment, then she felt like herself again. Her stomach clenched, then relaxed. She felt a tightness in her jaw, then that released too. Stephanie was still working on her, closing the chakra and sealing off her energy.

'Now, you are finished. How do you feel?'

Marissa sat up and rubbed her eyes. 'I don't know yet.' *I don't feel that much difference. But my heart does feel better, thinking of Matt. Maybe I have more work to do with James?*

'Are you sure that Matt isn't married with children? I saw a man like that – that is where I went to get your energy back – but I don't think it was from Matt.'

'Oh. I saw James too, my ex-boyfriend. It must have been him that you went to.'

'Yes, perhaps that is what it was. Your ex-boyfriend, then. I took back his energy to him. You had a lot of it around your shoulders and your heart, Marissa. Maybe you didn't know this? It's good for you to clear it away. He didn't seem to have as much for you as you did for him! Always relationships are imbalanced. Maybe that's why I've been so reluctant to have one.'

'Thanks Stephanie, I've learned something from this. Maybe James and I will always be connected, whether we want to be or not. When I saw him in my mind, he didn't look very happy, but that could be me. If I was saying this to a psychotherapist, they'd probably say I was projecting my own feelings onto him. Maybe I want him to look unhappy because he didn't pick me. But honestly, I don't mind now. It's nice to have the energy cleaned up, though, especially if I had some of his energy. Maybe that's his happiness going back to him, like yours coming back from your father.'

'Maybe. I find this shamanic work fascinating, but if I think too much about it, my brain hurts. Map your new energy onto your stone, and then we are finished. Good! I want to get some fresh air, I need some space to think about my father. Maybe I'll text him to say hello. I wish it could have been different between us.'

'I guess you can't change somebody's personality, only how you see them in your mind. Thanks, Stephanie, it's been a pleasure to work with you.'

They hugged. Stephanie went outside and Marissa went upstairs to get her phone and text Matt.

> Hi love I'm having fun, learning a lot. Miss u maybe see u tmrow night?

No reply. He must be off doing something fun.

Marissa texted her dad.

hi Dad, just wanted to say I love you and Im glad you always let me be myself at home.

Her phone rang right away. It was her dad.

'What's this about, love? Is everything okay?'

'Hi, Dad! You didn't need to call me. I'm okay, everything is fine.'

'What's the text about?'

'I'm on a personal development weekend and someone here has a difficult relationship with her dad. It just made me appreciate you more.'

'And so you should! I won't keep you then. Glad you're okay. Have fun and see you soon.'

As soon as she hung up, a text came in from Matt.

miss u2 love, cu tmrow xx

CHAPTER TWENTY SEVEN

The dining hall was laid out with food, ready for people to help themselves. Roast potatoes, vegetables, Indian curry or vegetarian lasagne, water, and coffee cake for after. Liz was already there, heaping food onto a plate. Marissa picked up a plate and did the same.

'Potatoes with everything,' said Liz. 'Potatoes and lasagne, potatoes and curry – but no rice! At least they have something veggie on the table.' She prised up a few of the roast potatoes looking for hidden, crunchy skins. 'I love the burnt bits!' She putting a few of them on her plate, got some water and pointed to a table. 'Join me?'

'Sounds good. Yes, see you in a minute.' She put a slice of cake on her tray, got some water and took the lot over to a table.

'It's quiet in here, the others must still be working,' Liz said, looking around.

I was hoping to meet Terry, Finn and Saoirse here. Wonder if they're still in the middle of their sessions.

Zaad and Stephanie came in and got food, then joined Liz and Marissa at the table.

'Hello there! How's the work going?' asked Liz.

'It's good, thanks,' said Stephanie enthusiastically 'We've just finished two sessions, a really interesting process.'

'I enjoyed it,' said Liz.

'You like cake?' asked Zaad with a puzzled smile, looking at Stephanie, who was eating her cake before her dinner.

'It's a celebration!' she said, swallowing some and smiling. 'Marissa helped me with something big, so I felt like cake for dinner. It felt appropriate to mark the occasion!'

'I wanted some chocolate earlier and I didn't bring any,' said Liz, looking disappointed.

'Oh, you should have said something – I have some upstairs!' said Marissa, ready to leave the table and get it.

'No, it's okay, I don't want it now, but when I did want it earlier, I really wanted it. It was so weird, like chocolate had power over me, wanted me to be at its beck and call.'

'I haven't experienced that before,' said Zaad, 'but I can have thoughts that keep coming back to me, telling me something I know isn't true. Like you wanting the chocolate, the thoughts have power over me. They keep telling me the same thing over and over, even when I want them to go away. It's most annoying.'

'Yes, that happens to me too,' said Marissa, 'I find I have to focus on something else to get them to quieten down. A mindfulness exercise is good for that.'

'Which one do you use for that?' asked Stephanie, brushing cake crumbs off her clothing.

'Oh, well, I remind myself where I am, what I'm doing, what I see, what I hear. All in the present tense of course. Thoughts usually are not about what is going on right now, so it's always useful to bring yourself back into the present. Then you have a chance to ground yourself, calm down, and you realise that you weren't really in control of your thought's after all.'

Zaad asked, 'Interesting. I will have to try that next time. Oh, Marissa? Can we work together for the next exercise? It has been a long time since we did, and it would be nice to end the workshops with you, seeing as we began them together.'

'Oh, yes! What a lovely idea. Thanks for asking me.'

'We can go up now, if you've finished, to my room. There is space there, it's all set up and ready.'

Marissa put her plate away, and just as she and Zaad were leaving the kitchen, Terry, Finn, Saoirse and Jenny came in.

'Oh, there you are,' Marissa said, trying to keep the disappointment out of her voice. 'I was hoping to see you a little earlier.'

'Helooo there, lovely scrummy ones,' said Terry. 'I'm starving. Oooh, look, my favourite! Roast potatoes!'

'It's vegetarian!' said Saoirse with delight, inspecting the lasagne.

'It looks as though we've finished now, and you're only getting started,' said Marissa.

'Well, never mind, we can chat after the fire ceremony. I have a feeling we'll be busy until then,' said Finn.

Marissa left with Zaad, leaving the others deep in conversation. She followed him up to the bedroom, which looked as though a tornado had hit it.

'Just a minute, please,' Zaad said, blushing, and went in and tidied it up a little. He looked more relaxed when he returned. 'It's safe to come in now. It was Terry and Finn making a mess. I am not as messy as them.'

Marissa laughed and went inside. The room felt familiar to her. She remembered the last time she had worked with Zaad and how beautiful the session had been. She smiled at him and he smiled back.

'Marissa, there is something I want to tell you,' he said very seriously.

Oh no!

'I like you. Very much. I thought about you a lot after I met you. But I have met someone else and she is my girlfriend now. I thought it would be important for you to know this before we worked together. Maybe it will release a tension between us so that we can trust and enjoy the sensations of what we are doing now, without feeling that there is something more behind it.'

'Oh! Okay, good to get it out in the open. Thank you. I have a boyfriend now too, but I was thinking about you a lot too, after we first met. Funny how you felt that as well.'

'Life is funny this way, isn't it? If I had never told you, you would never have known.'

'I know! I wonder how many people meet and like each other like that and never tell each other and then miss a chance to be together.'

'Well, I don't know if we missed a chance to be together,' said Zaad thoughtfully. 'I felt you weren't ready for a relationship. You told me about your fiancé leaving you, so I wanted to wait until you were in a better place. But then I met Izzy. She is so beautiful and kind, and Muslim too – my parents liked that before they liked her! Ha, Typical! Izzy means "powerful" and "strong", and I know that she is the woman I am going to marry. So I am glad that I listened to my instinct and didn't say anything to you when we met. It's better this way. It has worked out well, hopefully for us both.'

'It *has* worked out very well. I'm happy for you.'

'Good. Now, let us work! What do you want to work on?'

Marissa thought for a moment. 'Séamus wanted us to do a person, place or thing. I did a person with Stephanie just now. That was clear-cut. But when I worked with Liz this morning, it wasn't so clear to me which it was, a person or a place. So I don't know what to do now.'

'Can you tell me a little more?'

'Sure. Liz had the idea to clear what in me was attracting the dark energy to me. You remember what I told you about at dinner last night? So we did a healing on that.'

'What was the energy you received?'

'I think I stepped out of time, I can't remember, and it was only this morning. Oh yes! I got an apple for my root chakra, and a key for my crown chakra.'

Zaad thought for a moment. 'I think that we should work on a place then, specifically. As it would help balance you. You've looked at what in you was attracting the dark energy, so we could go to a place where you lost a piece of your soul because of the dark energy, so you can get that back.'

Marissa's hackles stood up.

'I can see you're worried,' Zaad said quickly. 'Don't worry. I'm the one that's going there, not you. So it will be okay, and you'll feel stronger afterwards.'

'Oh yes, of course. That sounds good.' Marisa was visibly relieved. 'Can I sit up then, while you're doing it, so I don't go on a journey myself while I'm waiting for you?'

Hey hang on, where is Tori? I thought I was stronger than this. And any soul piece I get back will be a good resource for the rescue work I will be doing later with Terry and Finn. Maybe I need this soul piece back, because without it I feel I can't do it. If I get back all the soul pieces I lost while being afraid, then I won't be afraid anymore, I'll be stronger and freeing the souls will be more successful. I have to do this! Of course I must!

Zaad looked worried. 'Marissa, we don't have to do this now if you're not ready.'

'No, I am ready, and you're absolutely right, I do need to do this. I think I trust you more, because of our conversation. I will lie down as normal. Thanks for being there for me. Let's do it.'

They both opened sacred space. Then Marissa lay down and Zaad ran energy through her and dowsed her energy field. 'It is your solar plexus, your centre of power, that's where we need to get the energy for.'

He got down on his hunkers beside her.

'Good, that sounds right,' she said, smiling up at him.

'Now I will go and get it. Get your stone out, yes? Good. You stay here.'

Zaad shifted his position, sat cross-legged and closed his eyes.

Marissa closed hers too, holding her stone lightly in her hand. *I want to make sure I get all of my energy back. Show me where Zaad isn't going so I can get it back from there, too.*

An image formed in her mind. She was somewhere bright, with lots of old white buildings.

London!' I'm in London, in the queue for Scott Taylor's big event. Let me see my energy please.

Golden sparks around her body turned into balls of light that looked like fairies, they were hovering all around her. She imagined she had a basket on her arm and she started to pick some of the golden sparkly balls out of the air and place them into it. When they were inside the basket they merged together and became more substantial.

She got to the front of the queue and became nervous. I don't like this. I want everybody gone now please, and I'll just take my energy back from the place.

Everyone disappeared.

Marissa walked inside. The stage was there, the main hall lights were on, but thankfully, nobody else was there. She walked through the rows and rows of seats and found the one she sat on. She looked around it and found more of the golden energy, and put that in the basket. She flipped the seat up and attached to the bottom of it was more golden energy. She gathered up all of it, then asked, 'Where else do I need to go?'

Her heart led her to the stage. Oh, that's strange. *She climbed up on it and looked towards the auditorium.* Wow, so many people were here. Such a big venue. I wonder, did they all leave parts of their souls here too?

She asked if she could see, but she saw nothing.

Someone was standing between the rows of chairs. It was Emelda. Marissa's heart lifted to see her.

'Emelda! It's you!'

'Marissa! it's you! Ha, ha, of course it is me.'

Marissa got down from the stage and went to her. 'Why can't I see all of the other souls from the other people who were here?'

'Because he took them. That was what he wanted, wasn't it?'

'Does he have some of my soul too?'

Emelda nodded her head. 'Not a big amount, but any amount is too much.'

'So there's a part of me in a jar in that terrible place?'

Emelda nodded. 'Not much, but there is a jar with your name on it, yes.'

They took another look around the arena.

'Thank you, Emelda. I always appreciate your honesty.'

'You want to hear the truth, don't you, so I always say it. Anyway. What are you doing here girl without your armour? Silly child. Always forgetting your protection!'

'Oh God! You're right. How could I have forgotten?'

With a plonk, Marissa landed in her body. She still felt as if she had the basket on her arm. She felt childish having forgot her armour, she needed to shake off that feeling. She sat up and saw that Zaad was working with a ball of light, manoeuvring it between his hands to place it over her solar plexus chakra.

'Zaad?'

'Yes. It's good, I got your energy for you.'

'I got some too.'

'Oh? Okay! If we both got some, you must have lost a lot.'

'I'm not surprised at that. And my guide said that this isn't all of it. Zaad, can I put the energy I got with the energy that you got, so we can clean it together?'

'Good idea.' Zaad stopped what he was doing and Marissa gently pushed the energy ball she was carrying into his hands. He thought for a moment.

'Different type of energy, but still yours, yes?'

'Maybe? Where did you get my energy from?'

'I went to visit my medicine snake. She knows everything – you remember, you introduced me to her. I've been working a lot with her, she's wonderful. She took me to a little room with two chairs and a small table. Nothing else there but a lot of your energy. It was sitting on a chair crying, waiting for me. It seemed so happy to see me! I took it – you, I mean – and we went to another place. I think it could be your bedroom, I don't know. In the bed, there was energy, a lot of it, that was yours. I picked it all up, and put it in a bag. So I have a bag of energy and this part of you in the small room. Then there was one more place...' Zaad closed his eyes. 'I remember now. It was a very small room with no window and no furniture but a mirror. It was a moving room, with doors! It felt very strange.'

'Hmm, maybe it's the elevator at work? I had a panic attack in there one time.'

'Yes, that makes sense. I honestly had no idea what that place was!' Zaad was laughing. 'The elevator! Well, bless me! That's exactly what it was. I always wonder if I am getting it right, the journeying, but it makes sense to my clients. That's the main thing, that's what I do it for, anyway. Good. So we are here now, and here is all this energy. Marissa, you lost a lot of soul, didn't you?'

'Yes, I did.' *I wonder how much more is still missing. Maybe I'll get Terry and Finn to help me get it back. Yes, that's what I'll try to do tonight. I definitely have to do it now.*

'Okay, Marissa, I've cleaned your energy, it's time for me to give it back to you. Can you lie down again?'

Marissa felt a little nervous at the prospect of getting all this energy back at the same time. Zaad took a moment to centre himself, then he blew the energy back into Marissa's body.

She didn't feel any change at first. Then it was as if someone was standing on her, actually standing on her body. She shifted, as it was uncomfortable, and the pressure left, but the weight remained. Her shoulders felt heavy, her hips pressed into the floor and her legs felt like they weighed 1,000 tonnes each.

Zaad was smiling at her. He offered her his hand to help her up. She took it and he hoisted her up. Her head felt heavy too. She felt like a baby trying to lift its head when its neck isn't strong enough.

'Are you okay, Marissa?'

'Yes, it just feels very strange. I feel heavier.'

'Ah, that is interesting. Can you map this onto your stone? Then it's done. Good. Are you ready to stand up? Maybe it will help if you walk around a little bit and wash your face? I know Izzy says that's good for her when she feels she needs to take a break from something.'

'That would be good, yes. I'll go and wash my face, take a drink and come back, then we can do your session.'

'Oh yes, I forgot – of course, it will be my turn then. Great. See you in a few minutes.'

Marissa walked out of the room. The sensation of walking was unusual and strange. *It's as if I don't recognise my body.* It felt as though her feet had lead weights attached to them.

She went into the bedroom and splashed cold water onto her face. She enjoyed the sensation of rubbing it dry on the towel, even though the towel was dried out and rough. It felt real, she was here, much more present in the moment than before.

If I feel this heavy, there must have been a lot of energy coming back to me. Was there? She had a sense of a 'yes' from inside herself. *I didn't realise I was so, well, empty...*

She had a sudden flashback of being in her flat trying to lift herself up to get the door for Séamus, then being in the bed with the demon standing at the foot of it, then in the courtyard, shivering, wrapped in blankets after all the terror she had experienced. *Yes, I suppose I have had a lot of trauma lately. It's so strange how I got used to living without all of that energy. All of those parts of me were gone, and I didn't seem to notice. They're back now. This is wonderful.* She wanted to give herself a hug, then she welled up with emotion. She had never felt that way before. It was strange, to want to hug herself, but she was so happy to have the pieces of her soul back. She wrapped her arms around herself and hugged herself for a moment. *That's nice. It's going to be okay. I will get the rest of my soul back and I will be whole again. Then I can do it for other people, too.*

She looked in the mirror. She looked older, wiser somehow. She noticed the beginnings of wrinkles around her eyes. *Not for today, not going there! Soon I'll be looking for silver hairs, eek!* She fixed her hair and went back to the boys' room to find Zaad.

He was waiting patiently for her with a smile.

'Hi, Zaad, I'm here to facilitate some healing for you now. What would you like us to work on?'

Zaad took a deep breath. 'I see you being brave, Marissa, and it inspires me to be brave also. So, I want to get my soul pieces back from the place where the worst thing in my life happened to me.'

Bullying at school, no problem. Let's do it! Marissa waited for him to say what was on her mind. What came next surprised her.

'I was eight years old. There was nobody at home but my uncle, my father's little brother. I think he was about as old then as I am now. I know he knew better. I believe there is no excuse for what he did.'

Zaad's face filled with emotion.

Shit, I'm the practitioner here, I'd better get into motion.

'Zaad, you don't need to tell me if you don't want to.'

'I have never told anybody. But you're a counsellor, Marissa, you may have heard this sort of thing before. And if you have not, then you will hear it. Because it happens a lot. I want to tell you so that you will journey for me and bring back the piece of me that I lost because of him. I think it would be better if I say it out loud, then I know at least one other person in the world knows. And I will heal this, because I find that sometimes with Izzy, I switch off. Or I become disgusted with her and I lose my cool, shout and hurt her. I don't want to do that anymore, Marissa. I want to be her man, a proper man, with nothing to be ashamed of. So I will tell you.'

Marissa connected to Reiki and infused herself with light, then radiated it out into the room. She visualised herself drawing the symbols for emotional and mental healing, saw them activate and then put both herself and Zaad inside them, sealing them with golden light so that they wouldn't be disturbed during the healing and he could go as deeply as he wanted into it without fear. *I don't care if we're late for the fire ceremony, this is much more important. It will take as long as it takes.*

Zaad talked, and cried, and told Marissa how his uncle had abused him many times, over many years. He breathed shallowly as he was speaking, and Marisa could see that talking about this was very stressful for his body, the memories rekindled the fear, and after a while it appeared as if he was close to a panic attack. *I need to do something to help him slow it all down, to get him back to his centre.*

Zaad stopped speaking, his breaths coming in short, sharp gasps. Marissa breathed with him, copying the speed and frequency of his in-breath and out-breath. He didn't notice; he was caught in a flashback of some kind. Marissa reached for his hand and held it, flooded the Reiki into his body and began to slow down her breathing, willing him to slow down his too.

It worked. He began to match her breathing. She kept pace with him for a while, then slowed her breathing even more, and he matched her once more. They kept this slower pace, and then Marissa reduced the time between their breaths one more time, until Zaad's breathing returned to normal.

'Thank you,' he said.

'I can see this is very emotional for you,' Marissa replied. 'I am glad you told me, and I promise you I will never tell anybody else about any of this.'

Zaad smiled gratefully. Marissa could see the fear, panic and tension were still in his body, but his lips were soft, and his eyes looked like those of a child needing to be held after a terrible nightmare.

'I can go and get your soul pieces for you now, without needing to know anything more.'

Zaad nodded, his face full of emotion. Marissa helped him lie down on the floor, fluffing the pillow under his head, keeping the physical contact between them so he knew that she was still there, that nothing had changed between them.

He began to relax once he lay down, but his hand had become clammy, so Marissa let go of it and wiped the sweat onto her jeans, then covered him with a blanket and placed her hand firmly onto his arm, with the blanket there between them.

'Where is your medicine stone?'

'Over there, on the bed. Yes, that's the one. Thanks.'

'Good. Now I'll run energy and dowse your body.'

The chakra Marissa needed to work with was his root chakra, so she placed the stone there, on top of the blanket.

'I'll go on the journey now. Zaad, you just rest here.'

'Okay. Thank you, Marissa.'

'No need to thank me, Zaad. Thank you for doing this. It's big, important work for you and I'm honoured to be the one to help you.'

Marissa closed her eyes. She felt Zaad still needed the contact, so she kept her hand on his arm. He was breathing more easily now and seemed more at peace, but still fragile.

Marissa made herself very small and entered her heart space, then found her tree. The tree bowed to her, smiled and opened, and the stairs led down and down and down to a tropical rainforest.

Waiting for her was a large, two-headed, yellow and brown medicine snake hissing at itself in a menacing way, as if each head was ready to attack the other with pure venom.

Shocked, she said sharply, 'Sachemama? is that you?'

The snake turned, both heads fierce, looking as if it was about to attack her, now. She backed away a little, holding her hands out defensively.

The snake pulled back, then out of both mouths it said, 'Yes, it is I. And it is you, Marissa.' It shrank and the heads merged into one.

'Why are you split like that? And attacking yourself?'

'There are two sides to every story. Two sides, and only one is true, or perhaps neither is true. Each side thinks it is the true side, but who knows what is true?'

Marissa was silent.

The snake hissed, 'He must let go of the stories he tells himself, all of them. He is evenly split – he will split himself apart. He needs a stronger soul piece to weld himself together. We will find it, but you must give him this message. He needs to stop doing this to himself even after the soul piece comes back, or he will destroy that, and himself.'

'I will tell him.'

'Good. Now we will go to seek his soul essence.'

Marissa became small and the snake became large, so large that it rose up and opened its mouth and swallowed her whole.

Everything went black. She opened her eyes and for a moment saw just blackness, then she could see light, feel heat and smell everything. She was the snake, weaving and undulating through the forest, over sticks and roots, past trees and vines and flowers, heading for what was calling to her.

Here! This is the place!

She wound herself around herself and swallowed her own tail and was consumed and – pop! – she was in a small room in a standard three-bedroomed house on an estate in Dublin. Everything was sepia, brown and white, no colour anywhere. There was noise from the street, the sound of children playing. She followed her heart and went upstairs. There was a small boy crying on a bed, curled up into a foetal position. Zaad?

He looked up at her, sucking his thumb. He said he was eight when it happened, but this boy is younger. Is he the soul piece?

The boy got up from the bed and rummaged under it, then pulled out a small train set. He smiled, picked it up and handed it to Marissa. He can see me! He held her hand as the scene changed and an older boy appeared in the room. This boy looked closer to eight years old. He sat on the floor, crying quietly and banging his head off the wall.

'Zaad?' asked Marissa. She wanted to go to him, to protect him. This is terrible! How can he do that to himself?

The boy saw her. Without a word, he got up, ran to her and embraced her. She held him. He pulled out a watch from his pocket and gave it to her. A train and a watch. Boys' things? Or soul pieces?

Both boys holding Marissa's hands now, they all stood still as the scene changed again and an older Zaad was there, looking about thirteen. He was clenching his fists, rubbing one of his hands, and he had a bruise on his face and a black eye. He wasn't crying, though, he was looking satisfied. He saw Marissa and the two boys with her and smiled.

She smiled back. 'Are you okay? she asked him.

'It is you! I knew you were real!'

'Yes, I'm real. Are you a soul piece for Zaad?'

He nodded. The two younger versions of Zaad ran to teenage Zaad and embraced him.

'Come back with me then, all of you,' Marissa said, 'and we can return you home.'

The middle boy looked at the bigger boy. 'Are you me, only big?' he asked.

'Yes. And he never does that to you again. Not after what I did today.'

The middle boy smiled. The youngest boy climbed into the arms of the thirteen-year-old and held on to him like a limpet.

Marissa put the train set and the watch into her pocket and offered both of her hands. Teenage Zaad held baby Zaad tightly up to his chest and took one of Marissa's hands. Eight-year-old Zaad took the other, then she connected to her heart, not quite knowing how to get them back to adult Zaad.

'Help us get back to Zaad.' Marissa said this in her mind, so that the boys wouldn't be afraid.

A small hole appeared in the wall of the bedroom, then it grew. They could see a forest on the other side of it. When it was big enough, all of them stepped through the wall and suddenly were in the forest. The scene became full colour, but the boys remained sepia toned; stark in their browns and whites against the lush forest, they looked like paper cut-outs, only they were three-dimensional. The two small boys were enthralled by the colours of the forest, large red hibiscus flowers beckoned, along with green grasses and colourful vines. A golden monkey swung past, a toucan squawked. The younger boys wanted to reach out and touch everything, but the older boy was a little hesitant, not sure if it was safe.

'You will be okay,' Marissa reassured them. She led them through the forest, letting them explore a little bit, the younger boys squealing with delight when they saw a baby elephant.

Marissa's heart guided her back to her tree. She was feeling more confident with each journey that as long as she connected to her heart, she would find her way home.

She led the boys into the tree trunk, and they went up the staircase, the boys becoming more transparent as they got closer to the top of it.

They all tumbled out into the room. Of course Marissa couldn't see the boys anymore, but she could most certainly feel them.

'Zaad, I have three soul pieces that are aspects of you as a boy. They're here in the room with us. They're ready for you to welcome them home.'

Zaad was a little groggy.

'Here,' said Marissa, 'have a drink of water.'

He sat up and drank.

Should I blow the boys into Zaad? It feels strange to do that. But they have to merge with him somehow.

She looke*d at Zaad. He was more present now.* 'These soul pieces need to merge with your body. I think like me, you lost a lot more of your energy than you realised.'

'Yes, I know. I'm pleased we have done this big work together, Marissa, it means a lot to me.'

'The older aspect of you, the teenager, he recognised me. And the others seemed to know me, too.'

Zaad sucked air in through his teeth and shook his head with realisation. 'Ah. Yes, that explains a lot. This is crazy! I used to have a dream of a kind lady who looked after me. She had dark curly hair like you do. And I felt I knew you when we first met. So crazy! But probably the reason.'

'Hey, we're not done yet!' Marissa laughed. 'We can talk about this later. Right now we have three boys here who need your attention.'

The three beings of energy in Marissa's mind's eye appeared to be standing to attention. *Oh! Maybe this is how we do it. Rather than blowing them into the chakra, he must give them his attention.*

An image came into her mind of Zaad giving each of the boys a hug. *Ah, they will merge through his heart, through his love for himself. How beautiful.*

'Okay, Zaad, this is a different process from the one Séamus taught us, but I need to go with it because it feels right to me. I hope that's okay?'

'Yes,' he said. 'Shamanism is working with what is right in front of you – isn't that what Séamus says?'

'Oh yes, they're right in front of you, that's for sure. I think they want to hear you tell them that your life is okay, that it turns out well.'

Zaad turned to address the energy. He seemed weak after all the emotion, but there was a brightness in his eyes as he spoke.

'Hello, my beautiful soul pieces. I want to tell you that my life is good. Look at me here, learning how to do shamanic work. And best of all, I have a beautiful lady who loves me, and I am going to marry her. So I am loved, and you are loved too.'

Marissa felt emotion welling up in her as tears came into Zaad's eyes. She closed hers and could sense the three aspects of Zaad, his soul parts, were emotional also. In her mind's eye she saw them holding Zaad. Zaad's open heart was like a waterfall of emotion. They were all crying now, openly, as each of the aspects of Zaad stepped into his body and became him once more.

It took a while for them all to settle down.

'Wow. That was powerful,' Marissa said.

'Yes, my head is spinning,' said Zaad. His face was glistening with tear tracks.

'I have to ask you to do one more thing, just hold your medicine stone, and map your body onto it, then clear it, like Séamus said. So you get your medicine.'

Zaad held the stones and did the work with his eyes closed. He opened them. 'Done.'

'I need to close the space, and we need to get to the ceremony. I think we will might just about make it on time.'

They packed up the room. 'I feel very different now, Marissa, as if a piece of my heart has come back to me. It is difficult to describe.'

'I think just leave the words for now and enjoy the sensation. It will probably settle as you sleep tonight and you can see how you feel tomorrow.'

'Yes, that's a good idea.'

'Oh, I almost forgot – at the beginning of the journey I met Sachemema. She was so angry! She had two heads and she was attacking herself. She almost attacked me! She told me to tell you to stop doing that to yourself. Do know what she meant?'

Zaad blushed and shrank into himself a little. 'Ah yes, I know exactly what she meant. I must stop tearing myself apart with conflicting thoughts. I will try my best. Do we have time for you to tell me about the soul pieces you found? Where did you find them?'

'In your bedroom, I think.' Marissa described the room.

'Yes, that sounds like my room in the old house, the one we lived in before the one we have now. I was very glad to leave that place. Well, I now have person, place and thing. That's good!'

Marissa smiled. 'Yes, it's very good. These soul pieces were you then. I couldn't tell how old the youngest one was, maybe three or four. He wanted to give me a train set.'

Zaad's smile was so wide Marissa could see his teeth. *He's going to be okay, thank goodness.*

'Aah, my train set! I loved that train set!'

'I still have it here,' said Marissa, laughing softly while pulling the energy out of her pocket. 'I'm glad you remembered to ask me that!' She passed it to Zaad, who cupped it in his hand.

He laughed. 'It looks a little different from how I remember it.'

'Ha, ha! I think that energy is for you, a gift for your medicine – wait a moment, maybe place it in your body? Where does it want to go?'

'Right here, in my heart, with the others.' Without hesitating, Zaad placed his hands on his heart and allowed the energy to be absorbed into his energy field.

'Beautiful. Then I met you again, you were older, maybe eight. You ran to me and hugged me, as if you recognised me. Then you gave me a watch.'

She felt for that energy and held it in her hand.

'I wonder what that was,' Zaad said thoughtfully. 'I don't know.'

In a lower tone Marissa said, 'The eight-year-old you was banging his head against the wall.'

'Oh.' Zaad shrank. 'Yes, I used to do that. How strange that you saw me do that.'

'Well, I am getting your soul pieces back, so that could be how you lost some of your soul.'

'The watch! I remember it now. It was my uncle's watch. That first time ... he gave it to me. I don't want it.'

'So what should we do with the energy?' Marissa opened her hand. 'Maybe we have to let it go?'

'Yes, I want to.'

'Can you forgive yourself for taking it? The watch?'

Zaad looked as if a lightbulb had lit up in his mind. 'Yes! That was the problem – I thought it was all my own fault. He gave me the watch and then wanted payment for it, but I never wanted that watch... I banged my head because I was blaming myself.'

'So forgive yourself for thinking it was your fault.'

'It was not my fault. It was never my fault.' Zaad took a breath, closed his eyes and went deep inside himself.

After a moment he said, 'Marissa, I think this will take some time to do, but I will work on it.'

She really wanted to fling her arms around him and give him a hug, but they hadn't finished yet. 'Then lastly, I met you as a teenager.'

'Ah.'

'You had a black eye and a bruise on your cheek. It looked as though you had hurt your hand, yet you seemed happy.'

Zaad smiled again. 'Yes, that must have been the day I punched my uncle in the face. Hard. He didn't touch me again after that. He stopped calling at the house, too, and I rarely saw him. I have not seen him in many years. I can keep it that way.'

'I thought as much,' said Marissa. 'You looked like someone who punched above their weight but left an impression.'

'I certainly did. He didn't expect it and I think I might have broken one of his teeth. My hand really hurt, but I didn't care. The pain felt good, it reminded me of my power.'

Marissa waited a moment before saying, 'Look, you have nothing to be embarrassed about or ashamed of. You really don't. You were very young, and you are right, he should have known better.'

'Yes, you are right. I've been very hard on myself.'

'Ah, that's the snake then, you attacking yourself over this.'

'Yes.'

'Well, she says it's time for you to stop, or you'll tear yourself apart.'

'I will try my utmost to stop. But I think it may take some time. Thank you so much, Marissa, the woman of my dreams! Can I give you a hug?'

It sounded funny to hear him call her that. 'Of course!'

They hugged. Then they said the closing prayer together, both of them smiling with every word of it.

'Oh no!' Zaad said, looking at the time. 'The fire ceremony started a quarter of an hour ago! Oh no!'

Marissa turned to him and smiled. 'Oh well! This was so much more important. I'm so glad I could help you.'

Zaad smiled back, brightening up the room.

'Seriously, Zaad, this work with you was much more important than any fire ceremony. Izzy is lucky to have you. I'll get my drum and my cardigan and see you at the fire.'

CHAPTER TWENTY EIGHT

When Marissa arrived at the fire pit, the sun was going down. Her head was still full of the work she'd just done with Zaad, and the work that he had just done, with her. She found him and stood beside him, joining the others, who were also basking in the afterglow of the evening's energy work.

Séamus had lit the fire and it had taken. Long sticks were warming up the heavier logs, which were just starting to catch fire. He had his hat on; he looked like a Master of Ceremonies through the flames on the other side of the bonfire. He nodded at Marissa and began to drum. *Lub dub, lub dub, lub dub.*

Someone let out a whoop, and then the others picked up the rhythm with their own drums, *lub dub, lub dub.* There were lighter tones of gourd rattles being shaken, and the beats of the different-sized drums became the heartbeat of the world. *Lub dub, lub dub, lub dub...*

Marissa tuned into the fire, tuned into the energy, tuned into her heart. It was different from the last time. The air was lighter, the energy more expansive, everyone seemed more mature, more whole, more present.

Séamus picked up the pace of the drumming and the group followed. Whistles and shouts soon died away and all that could be heard was the drumbeat, the rattles and the crackle of the fire as it cut into the heavy logs in their centre and split them open, burning away all the pain, all the resentment of the world, burning away the jealousy, the anguish, the fear. There was nothing but the flame, there was nothing but the fire. The flame and the drum and the heartbeat of the world.

Séamus abruptly stopped drumming. The others took a few moments to come out of their drumming trance, then they stopped too and stood listening to the hiss of the wind through the trees behind them, the crackle of the fire as it burned in its full strength, the flapping of nocturnal wings in the dark sky above them. Stars were twinkling in the black sky. There was no moon.

Séamus spoke above the crackle of the fire. 'We stand here under Father Sky, on the breast of Mother Earth, on this night, to celebrate our rebirth. To celebrate our coming into service to you, Great Spirit. For we are one and we are all, we have died and we are reborn. The old parts of us, the scared parts, the frightened parts, the small parts, they know now that they are not alone. We have taken back our power, taken back the parts of us that have left due to fright or trauma, and we stand here with this fire as witness, pledging our allegiance to truth, our allegiance to the way.'

There was silence as everyone resonated with these words. Then Marissa shouted to the sky, 'Yes!' It broke the tension, and the others whooped and catcalled, whistled and yelped with joy.

Then they became quiet again and Séamus spoke once more.

'Put your drums down and choose a stick from the ground nearby.'

Everyone left, got a stick and came back.

'Now contemplate what you are letting go of, what work you did, what you wish to leave behind you, what parts of yourself you are allowing to die and to dissolve away, and blow them into the stick. Then place it onto the fire to be transformed.'

There was silence.

I suppose my fear of being myself, of hurting someone's feelings if I speak out and they don't understand me. I no longer want to cut off a piece of myself for somebody else, just so that they can feel more comfortable around me. Yes, that's exactly it.

Images of Marissa's mother flashed in front of her eyes, then her father, Uncle Lou, Aunty Naomi and her cousins.

I am myself and I honour myself and I will be true to my heart.

She remembered giving herself a hug upstairs, just a few moments ago. Then she blew into the stick, feeling something inside her stomach dislodge, feeling something in her chest release. She blew again, and then she blew into the stick all the nights she had spent crying over James, all the times she had hidden away at school, all times she held her tongue, all the things she hadn't said but longed to say, she blew away the yearning to be seen for who she truly was, and not who they wanted her to be. She blew, blew for the girl that waited to be brought home to her real family, blew the ache to belong somewhere, anywhere... And as she blew she realised she was home, she did belong, she belonged to herself. She felt herself growing taller, she felt her energy expanding outwards. She blew the last of all of her pain into the stick and let go of everything that was in the way of being the best that she could be.

She was silent. Empty of her pain. And then she made a pledge. 'I am of service to spirit. I am a healer. I claim my space in the world. I am here. I dedicate my life to truth and love. I offer myself to you, Great Spirit, to go wherever you need me to go, to heal whoever you send to me for healing, to open my doors to the world and to offer myself as your vessel of light.'

Where did that come from? It sounded great, and yes, I meant every word that I said.

She stood and looked deep into the fire. She didn't notice anyone else around her. The others didn't impinge upon her experience. They were all going through their own process too.

And then, as if she had been pushed, she moved forward with her stick, and everyone took a small step backwards and held hands, closing the circle while she stood close to the flame. It roused her emotions to feel that the group holding her so well.

I forgive myself for turning my back on who I am, for closing myself off to the magic that is all around me. It was always there. Never again. Never will I do that again, and I will not attack myself for doing it. I will never attack myself for anything ever again.

She breathed in the smoke, it caught in her throat and she coughed. She washed herself in the smoke, cleansing her energy field. Then she blew one more time into the stick and carefully placed it into the flames.

Goodbye, old me; hello, new me. Same me.

She stayed there for a moment, watching it burn. The fire was hot on her face but she didn't mind. Then it was time for someone else. She stepped back, the circle of hands opened and she joined it.

Saoirse stepped forward a moment later, and Marissa joined the others holding space for her, just as they had held space for her. And so they went around the circle until each of them had had their turn at the flame.

It was late then, and the fire had shrunk to half of it's size. They all stood silently, watching the flames being licked by the breeze, or was the breeze licking the flames. It was hard to tell. And it didn't matter.

Séamus spoke sombrely. 'Well done. Good work, every one of you. We have died this weekend to ourselves, and we are now reborn, and becoming whole. There is one more thing to do tonight before we close this fire ceremony. Unlink hands, please and enlarge the circle, take one step apart from each other. Good.

'Now, connect your awareness to the extremities of your energy field.

'Good. Unfurl yourselves out to your full size. You are in Clifden, in Galway, there is nobody else here, there is plenty of space for you to be here, plenty of space for you to show yourself to yourself. And we are not intimidated by you, we are not afraid, so you can show yourselves to one another now. Turn to your neighbour and show them how big you are, how big you can be!'

Marissa imagined she grew three, no, four times her size – no, six times! She turned to Finn, who was beside her, and spread her arms wide. He grinned at her and did the same, and they laughed, then turned to the person on the other side. For Marissa, this was Zaad, and he looked so happy and free. She had never seen him like that before.

The whole group wove in and out of one another, keeping the circle, laughing, meeting one another for the first time, remembering how they had known each other for lifetimes.

The fire was almost down to its ashes. They were sitting on small stones encircling the fire pit, watching the flames dwindle. Stephanie, Liz and Jenny had gone back to the house, as there was a chill in the air. Zaad yawned and stood up, stretched and took his leave also. That left Terry, Finn, Saoirse, Marissa and Séamus.

'You'll guard the fire?' asked Séamus, standing up and pounding his chest. 'Someone needs to stay until it goes out completely, to ensure that the energy work we did tonight is completely transformed and diffused.'

'Yes!' said Terry. 'Absolutely.' Marissa and Finn nodded.

'Good. I've an early start. I'm going to see a man about a dog before we start class in the morning.' He winked at them.

'Night, Séamus,' said Saoirse.

'Sweet dreams.'

He left.

'Always the man of mystery,' said Terry with a giggle.

They watched the fire sink down into itself. There was barely a flame now, just glowing coals. It was getting close to midnight. But none of them were ready for bed just yet.

Marissa looked up to the sky and saw a shooting star. She grabbed Saoirse, 'Look!'

'It's a UFO!' said Terry. 'Look, it's moving back in the opposite direction.'

Marissa squinted, but she couldn't see it.

Finn said, 'Look, there, another one!'

'Whoo hoo, here we are, come and get us and take us home!' laughed Terry.

'There's so much going on up there that we'll never know about,' said Marissa. 'What if aliens are watching our every move? What if we're like a reality TV show to them?'

'Ha, ha! Brilliant!' said Saoirse. 'I've never thought of it that way before.'

'What if we are the aliens and they're the owners of this planet? What if we're just one big experiment?' asked Terry.

'Like in *The Hitchhiker's Guide to the Galaxy*!' said Finn, enthusiastically.

'Yes!' said Marissa. She turned to him and asked, 'You've read it too?'

'Yes, I've read them all. I've read lots of books like that,' he said, 'I love sci fi. I've just never admitted it before. Cool guys don't read books, well they didn't in my school, anyway. After this weekend, I don't care. I like who I am, and I don't want to hide anymore.'

'You're a cool guy Finn, you don't need to try to be one. You just are one.'

'Thanks, that's nice of you to say.'

'I mean it though. But I know what you mean about not wanting to hide, that's what I was doing too at the fire – letting go of the part of me that hides. I hide in case I scare someone away,' said Marissa.

'Me too!' said Saoirse. 'But I'm afraid I won't be able to do it in real life. I still am so worried I want everyone to like me.'

Everyone turned to her.

'We do like you, Saoirse!'

They all leaned in towards her and fell on top of each other, giving her a group hug. She squealed with delight and they all laughed.

'Well, I'm not worried about hurting anyone's feelings,' said Terry, sitting back down on his stone.

'We know, and that's what we love most about you,' said Marissa as she sat back on hers, and they all laughed again.

Then there was silence.

'So here we are,' said Terry, and then he added quietly, 'I wonder, could we try again?'

Marissa hesitated. 'I was afraid you'd ask.'

'Yes, I am asking. I really think we could try again. Those soul cages are still there somewhere, and the souls need us to rescue them.'

Marissa felt a twinge of nausea. She remembered Emelda telling her there was a jar there with her name on it. She shuddered.

'I'm in,' said Finn, brightly.

'You're not too tired?' asked Marissa, shaking off the feeling.

'I'm wrecked, but I could try it,' said Saoirse. 'You seemed to get somewhere with it at lunchtime and I felt left out. I think I'd like to come, too.'

'Okay.'

The fire shrank into itself again, the last of the embers went black and smoke rose from the ashes.

'We aren't on guard over the fire anymore,' Finn said. 'Do you want to do it here? Or go inside?'

'Here is kind of cool, with the spaceships above us and all.' Terry laughed. 'It might be fun. And it isn't *that* cold...'

'Okay!'

'Where shall we go?' asked Marissa, 'Shall we do a practice run?'

Finn looked at Terry, who looked at Marissa.

'No,' said Terry. 'Let's do it for real. And because you know where it is, Marissa, you have to anchor us in.'

'Oh. Okay.' *This all seems very fast.* Marissa's hand went up to touch her ankh. *I'll go as Tori.* That felt better.

'Okay,' she said. 'I am going to do this journey as Tori. She's a warrior who looks like me, only she's taller and fitter, and she'll be wearing a suit of armour. It's thin armour, I guess it looks a bit like a catsuit.' *That feels right.*

Terry and Finn nodded. Saoirse shrank a little.

'I'll be a bird,' said Finn. 'I liked being a bird.'

'Okay,' said Marissa. 'Terry?'

'Why, I'll be myself of course!' said Terry, raising an imaginary top hat.

'Ha, ha! So you'll be The Fool, then?' joked Marissa.

Terry blushed. 'Well, The Fool is the one who always tells it like it is, so perhaps I am he,' he said. Then he winked to save face.

'Not a bad character to be,' said Saoirse. 'You have beginner's mind, you can see things for what they are, and you aren't afraid to call out the bullshit.'

'Well, I'm calling you out, dear,' said Terry. 'Are you coming or not? You have to be all in or not in.'

'I'll come,' said Saoirse, 'but I'll be an animal too. I think a cat.'

'Okay, good. Marissa, where are we going?'

Marissa took a breath. 'Let me take a moment to get there. I'll describe it to you then and you can come and find me. But first I need to be in the middle of the group, so I can anchor you.'

They rearranged themselves on the cold, dry ground so they were more comfortable, Marissa in the middle. She closed her eyes and went inwards.

I am Tori, in full armour, under a full moon, sitting high up in a tree, near the castle. I'm looking over the moat and I can see the turret just outside that bedroom window.

She focused on the image and willed herself there, projecting her essence through her mind into the scene, until she felt that she had landed.

'Okay, I am here. In a forest, under a full moon, in a tree beside the castle where the soul cages are in the basement.'

Easiest to call them that; even though they don't feel like that, they know what I'm talking about. She kept her focus on the scene.

There was a rustling behind her and a yellow bird landed on a branch. It was quite small and kept flickering in and out, like a TV station that wasn't tuned in properly.

Marissa reached out her hand and touched Finn, who was sitting beside her, then the bird came in more strongly. *Wow, that worked!*

'Hey, guys, if you can touch me, maybe you can anchor to me better.'

They adjusted their positions so that each of them could put a hand on her.

Terry appeared on the branch beside her, in a white fool's outfit, dangling his legs in the air. His face was painted white and he had a large black diamond across the centre of his face, with painted red diamonds over each eye.

'Very conspicuous,' said Tori-Marissa. 'We're supposed to be sneaking in, remember?'

'Oh yes, I got a little carried away,' said Terry. His outfit transformed into an all black one, but the face paint remained the same.

'Much better,' said Tori-Marissa.

'Your armour is pretty snazzy,' said Terry, admiring it. It wasn't quite black, but it wasn't quite red either. The colour was somewhere in between.

'Who are we waiting for?' asked Terry, looking at the little bird. 'Is that Finn? He's rather small, isn't he?'

'Yes, I think it's him, alright.'

'He can't talk to us?'

'He's a bird! Ha, ha!'

'I kind of like him like that.'

Finn-bird opened his wings in a threatening way and Terry laughed and flicked the air in his general direction.

There was a scraping noise and a mewing, and two cats appeared. One was large and black, like a jaguar, and the other was a small tabby kitten.

'Two cats?' said Tori-Marissa. 'Which one is Saoirse, and who is the other one?'

The jaguar moved in the branches and caught the moonlight, and Tori-Marissa could see a white streak that ran across his face and over his ear.

'Tobermory! You're here!'

The jaguar looked at her as if to say, 'Of course I'm here, are you stupid or something?'

'Who is Tobermory?' asked Terry. 'Is that your cat from your little flat?' He giggled.

'Actually, yes, it is,' said Tori-Marissa.

'Well, he's some tiger in journey world, isn't he?!'

'Yes, he is. He's amazing.'

The jaguar rippled with pleasure.

'And there's sweet little Saoirse kitten. Nice to have you here too.'

The kitten went to Tori-Marissa and mewed to be picked up. She picked it up and held it to her chest. It was very small, like a new-born. She looked into its eyes and saw Saoirse.

'You know you don't have to do this, and I can see you don't really want to. Why don't you stay at the fire and make sure our human bodies don't get eaten by wolves'

The kitten perked up at this and – pop! – it disappeared.

'I knew she didn't really want to come,' said Terry, picking at his nails.

'Right,' said Tori-Marissa, 'I guess we're all here now so. Let's go.'

'Really?' said Terry. 'Can't we stay here? Only kidding! Yes, let's do it.'

'Give me a minute to figure out how we get in.'

'You really planned this well, didn't you?' said Terry.

'Shh!' said Tori-Marissa, thinking.

The turret is out of reach, as we aren't flying. Maybe there's a way in from the ground? I did get inside once from the ground, didn't I? From a servants' entrance around the back.

'Okay, we'll scout around the outside walls and see if we can find a back-way in. The jars with the souls in them, the soul cages, as you call them, are in a basement near the kitchens, so the servants' entrance might be the best way.'

Tori-Marissa remembered a journey where she was in a forest and entered via a cabin in the woods... Was that the same place? I don't know. Maybe there's more than one place? Well, we are here now, let's see how far we can go together.

They scrambled down the tree, the jaguar and bird much more elegantly than the two humans. Once on the ground, they started running towards the castle, the moon lighting their way. Finn-bird flew in the sky ahead of them and Tobermory was in front. Terry was obviously excited and happy to be there.

This really is fun, it's amazing to all be here together.

Tori-Marissa caught up with the jaguar and ran beside him, then reached out and stroked his back.

'Hello, my friend, I didn't expect you to come. How did you know I was here?'

'I had a feeling you would do something like this at some stage,' rippled Tobermory, 'It was just a matter of time.'

'You are talking to me! This is incredible!'

'We are in this world, not your world – of course I can speak. You just never asked me before. And my name is not Tobermory, although you often call me that.'

'I'm sorry. Tell me then, what is your name?'

'I might tell you, I might not. Names have power. Let us keep our focus on this for now.'

They reached the castle walls which were as tall as a house. Finn-bird flew over the top of them and scouted around, then came back and changed direction.

'Follow the Finn,' said Terry with delight, and started running after him.

Tori-Marissa and Tobermory went with them, and soon they were around the back of the castle.

Finn-bird shot off in a different direction.

'What is he doing?'

Then he came back and beckoned for them to follow, so they did, even though it pulled them away from the main castle wall. They went through a thicket of hedges and came to a small cabin in the woods.

Marissa's heart lifted. I recognise this! Amazing!

Finn-bird didn't want to go inside. He stayed by the door.

'Do you want to wait for us?'

Terry, Marissa and Tobermory crept into the little cabin.

'It's not a good place for a bird,' whispered Terry loudly.

They carefully ducked their heads to avoid a low beam, there was hardly any room in there for a large jaguar. They worked their way carefully to the back of the cabin and there, on a shelf, were some smashed jars and some open jars, but none of the closed jars had any souls inside.

'They were here!' said Marissa. 'This is where I was yanked out of the journey,' she added with a shiver.

'Ah,' said Terry, examining the empty jars, 'maybe he moved them as this wasn't a safe place anymore, seeing as you were here and all.'

'Yes, good point. I would have done the same thing.'

'So we need to get into the castle then. But why did Finn bring us here?'

There was a noise behind them, voices.

'Somebody's coming! Quick!'

By the fire, Terry jumped up and squealed, snapping Marissa out of the journey. Saoirse jumped too.

'Are you okay, Terry? What happened?'

'Oh, it was wonderful! We were all there, it was so real, so amazing. Oh Marissa, that was amazing! I didn't know we could do this. We have to go back right away!'

Finn yawned.

'You couldn't talk as a bird, could you?' asked Marissa.

'No, I couldn't,' said Finn with another yawn.

'Why did you take us to the cabin?'

'It leads into the castle. I could see that from the air, but you have to keep going further in. Why did you come back?'

'There were voices. I guess Terry got a fright and snapped out of the journey, and pulled us all out of it.'

'I did not get a fright! Your cat bit me!'

'Tobermory? He wouldn't do that!'

'Why was Tobermory there?' asked Saoirse.

'I have no idea,' said Marissa, thoughtfully.

'He's some tiger,' said Terry laughing. 'That cat has another life as a tiger in those woods.'

'He's a jaguar,' said Marissa, 'But I knew him in Egypt in another life. I could hear him talking to me.'

'It's very late,' said Finn, 'and we have an early start in the morning. I think we should call it night. Maybe when we all get home, we could do this again.'

'Yes, I think that's enough excitement for one day,' Marissa agreed, relieved but sad at the same time.

'Goodnight.'

'Night.'

'Sleep tight.'

'Don't let the bugs bite.'

'Night, John-Boy.'

'Okay, okay, enough already!'

Saoirse and Marissa went back to their room, trying to be quiet in the corridor so as not to wake the others. It was after 1am. There were several texts waiting for Marissa from Matt, asking how she was and if she was okay. She didn't want to reply in case she woke him up.

She brushed her teeth, washed her face and fell into bed.

Saoirse just went straight to bed in her clothes.

'Don't you smell like the fire?' Marissa asked her.

'Yes. I don't mind it. It's kind of comforting in a way.'

'That was incredible, but you really weren't comfortable being there, were you?'

'I didn't know if I was doing it right.'

'But you were there, you were a cute little kitten.'

'I thought I was, alright. But I could hardly see you or Terry, and I couldn't see Finn at all. So I thought it would be better if I didn't get in the way.'

'That's fair enough.'

'There was a dark presence there too. I didn't like that.' Saoirse rolled over in bed.

'What do you mean?'

'Big and black, watching us.'

'Oh, that must have been Tobermory. He came with us as a jaguar.'

'Yes, you were saying. How fun! But no, I'm not talking about him. Something else, dark, like I said. And big. Watching us from the shadows. I don't think I want to try it again.'

Marissa turned over with a sick feeling in her stomach. *We're okay, we all got out of there in one piece. Didn't we?*

CHAPTER TWENTY NINE

Time had passed, however, it was difficult to tell exactly how long he had been here. The sea serpent stretched out, but found he couldn't move. He remembered he was caught in a tight space, the discomfort and agitation was immense as he rippled his will through his body pushing and stretching, with no result. It was as if he didn't have a body at all. He opened his eyes and saw nothing, the darkness surrounded him completely. He knew then what it was, and why, but he couldn't help but feel afraid. Images of powerful ancestors came to him, spoke to him, reassuring him that he was safe, on the path, that he would make it through this dark time. They soothed him, then disappeared.

He tried once more to shift his position, but again, nothing. He was in containment, in a small space, and not in control of his body whatsoever. He roared with irritation, and eventually fell asleep.

The early morning light came in through the half-open curtains, crept across the bed and snuck under Marissa's closed eyelids. She turned. The bed felt different from her own bed, smaller, lumpy... Ah, yes, she was in Clifden. She stretched out, opened her eyes and reached for her phone, which was on the floor. It was almost 7am. Matt wouldn't mind her texting at this hour. She read back the texts he had sent her the day before, then replied.

> hi love we were up late with the fire last night, its going great can't believe today is last day. Ill b getting 3pm train so i'll b in Dub @ 5, got 2 feed cat so going home, ur welcome 2 come visit if u want, love Mxx

As she pressed 'Send', she hoped with all of her heart that he would turn up at her flat later that evening. She turned over the other way to say good morning to Saoirse, then got a surprise: Saoirse wasn't there. Her bed looked slept in, though.

Must be in the toilet. But what if that dark energy she talked about took her in the night?

She was bolt upright now.

That's ridiculous...

Then the door opened and Saoirse came in, wrapped in a small towel, hair wet, with a smaller towel in her hand. She looked vulnerable without her glasses, Marissa didn't recognise her for a moment.

'Jeezuz, there you are! I didn't hear you leave.'

'You were sleeping. I needed a shower to get the smoke out of my hair.'

'For a moment I thought you had been taken!'

'By whom? Oh. No. Not a peep during the night. I slept well. How about you?'

'I had mad dreams. I felt as if I was in a tight shell, like a nutshell, and couldn't turn around. I couldn't move, but I was really agitated. So weird. My dreams are predictably unpredictable these days.'

Marissa rubbed her eyes, trying to wake up.

Saoirse smiled and sat on the edge of her bed, using the second towel to dry the ends of her wet hair. 'These towels are shit,' she said.

'Well, it's not a four-star hotel, not even a two star.'

'Or a one star!'

'I guess we didn't come here for the towels, or an *en-suite*.'

'True enough. Glad I got to the showers early, I don't like other people around when I wash.'

Saoirse wrapped her hair in the towel, then turned her back to Marissa and got dressed quickly.

'What are we doing this morning?' asked Marissa, splashing water on her face. She got dressed, too.

'More soul-retrieval work, I think, then we have to close the space. Oh yes, we learn how to do it for ourselves this time. How useful! Can we arrange a get-together up in Dublin, do you think, with the gang? I don't think I'm ready to say goodbye to the group today.'

'Yeah. Defo, we should meet up. I don't want to say goodbye to anyone today. I feel like I'm only just back and it's over already.'

'Well, you kind of are, and it kind of is.'

'I know.' Marissa's heart fell. 'Well, at least I can keep working shamanically, not like the rest of you having to switch it all off for your "real jobs".'

'Hey! I love my real job,' said Saoirse. 'Working in a museum is fun, especially when they bring in new artefacts. And I've realised I can journey into them when nobody is looking and find out the story behind each of them!'

'Ooh! That does sound fun! I'm much happier working with people, although they do exhaust me from time to time.'

'I'd imagine so. Are you coming to get breakfast?'

Saoirse was dressed in bleached jeans and a white sweater. Her damp hair was down around her face and her round tortoiseshell glasses gave her an intellectual look.

'You're not so glam this time around,' Marissa observed. 'You were all into your pink boas and wedge shoes once. You're much more practical now.'

'Yeah, I know. I guess I realised I don't need to impress anyone. I certainly didn't want to be impressing Finn!'

'He's okay. Have you noticed he's different?'

'Yes, actually, now that you've said it, I don't feel jumpy around him now.'

'Yes, he's softer, there's less urgency around him. As if some tension has left him. Must be the soul-retrieval.'

'I think we're all different, except maybe for Terry.' Saoirse winked. 'Are you ready? Let's go downstairs.'

A few minutes later, they were downstairs filling their plates with breakfast food. The others came in, looking sleepy but happy.

'What a fire ceremony!' said Stephanie. 'I loved it! I could have danced all night!'

'It was amazing,' agreed Saoirse, as she put some bread into the toaster.

Finn was already at the table. Marissa put her porridge and honey down beside him and went to get some tea.

Sitting back down at the table, she quietly studied all of her friends. Liz's eyes were bright and alive; she looked radiant. Jenny was animated, putting honey on cereal and describing the fairies that she had met when she went on a journey. Zaad was relaxed and at ease with himself. He caught Marissa's eye and smiled, and she smiled back. Everyone looked radiant, vibrant and alive – beautiful. Marissa smiled and absorbed it, as if every moment was precious liquid that needed to be appreciated, like a fine wine or an expensive perfume – something exquisite, to be cherished for your whole life.

'What's got into you?' asked Terry as he sat down opposite her.

'Look at everybody.'

'What do you mean?'

'Well, look. Everyone is so beautiful.'

There was a hush. Everyone stopped talking and looked at one another.

'Can you see it?' Marissa asked. 'You're all glowing. You're alive, really alive, bright. If you were lights, you'd all be lighthouses. Amazing.'

'Aah, yes! I see it,' said Jenny. 'I understand. Our soul pieces came back and we are whole again.'

'We're doing more soul-retrieval today, though, 'said Liz, 'so we might not be completely whole yet.'

'But we are certainly more whole than we were, that's for sure,' said Marissa. 'I thought I was whole until a large soul piece came back to me yesterday. It hit me like a ton of bricks, I'm still getting used to it. I thought I was fine before it arrived, I'm certainly feeling much more substantial than I did. It's difficult to put into words - I don't know, how much of us is here now? How much of us never comes down to our bodies? I guess we will never know, but there's certainly more of our soul energy here than there was before.'

'True,' said Liz. 'I do understand what you mean. We are a rather good-looking bunch, aren't we?'

Everyone looked at everyone else in appreciation, then suddenly it felt strange and uncomfortable. They went back to eating.

'Hey,' whispered Finn to Marissa, 'I went back there last night, in my dreams.'

Marissa's hackles went up. She continued to eat, but she turned to Finn to indicate she wanted to know more. 'And?' she asked, with a little trepidation in her voice.

'It was amazing. I was flying. I was bigger than the bird that I was the first time. A different colour too, I think. It's like I'm getting a hang of it! It's so fun! I flew up high this time and was able to see the entire castle. It's in the shape of something familiar. I don't have the word for it – I'll draw it.'

Finn drew intersecting lines with the back of his spoon on the table.

'A swastika?' said Marissa, shocked.

'Yeah. It kind of looked like that from the angle I was at. Could have been completely wrong, though.' Finn rubbed the table as if he was rubbing out what he had drawn.

'Wow,' said Marissa, a cold shiver going down her back. 'So strange, there's so much we don't know about the world, so many things that we don't understand. Like that symbol, I've heard it's originally from Tibetan Buddhism.'

Jenny's ears pricked up at the mention of Buddhism. 'Buddhism?' she said, 'What about it?'

'I was just saying to Finn how the swastika used to be part of Buddhism. It's interesting and strange how a symbol can be turned completely upside down to change the meaning behind it.'

'Yes, that was always a weird thing, I thought,' said Jenny, 'but then you need to remember they love symbols.'

'Who is "they"?' asked Marissa, her curiosity now well and truly piqued.

'Why, the cabal of course.'

'Cabal? Who are they?'

Jenny looked around to see how many people were listening in, but nobody was, but she continued in a low voice regardless. 'They are the bad guys, they run everything, and keep hidden. But one day they won't be able to hide anymore. Then people will understand and take their power back from them and finally be free.'

'I don't really understand.'

Jenny smiled. 'I don't really understand either, I'm still figuring it out. All I know is that this has been going on for millennia, but it has to end. It just has to.'

'How do you know about them?'

'My parents. My dad actually, he was in the Masons. I overheard him talking to Mum about why he wanted to leave. I wanted to know more, so I did some snooping around, but I couldn't find much information. I'm still looking into it.'

'Not just a pretty face then,' said Finn with a smile.

Jenny slapped his arm, then picked up her breakfast things. 'I didn't know you were listening. Hey, we've got to get going, the first session starts in a few minutes.'

'Shit, yes. Come on, guys, I can see Séamus is back.'

They left their breakfast things at the back of the dining hall and filled into the front room, sitting anywhere that was free. They all felt much more at ease with each other than they had ever been.

Séamus was looking out of the main window as they came in. He turned to see them and smiled. They smiled back at him, and the room filled with warmth and love. Blue jeans and cowboy boots today, with a white shirt, and his hair was down, it spread out over his shoulders in waves of silver and white.

'Jaysus, would you look at yiz all!' he said. 'Yiz are so beautiful! All of yiz look different, more whole, there's more colour in your faces. Yiz all found some lost soul pieces, I reckon!'

They beamed.

'What a lovely way to end this apprenticeship. The focus of this weekend was death, but it's the death of the old way of life. We all died to ourselves, and today, reborn, look at yiz, whole and ready for the rest of your lives! Stand up, all of yiz, take a bow! Come on, I mean it!'

They all stood up, slightly hesitant, then giggles abounded as Stephanie first, then Liz, then everyone else made a deep bow or a curtsey to one another.

Jenny put her hands in prayer position, turned towards Séamus and bowed her head to him. 'Thank you, Séamus, it's just been amazing. I don't think my life will ever be the same after this time with you.'

Everyone else did the same, then they all clapped, and clapped one another! The atmosphere was electric.

Séamus put his hands out to calm everyone down. 'Oy! We're not finished! We still have some work to do today, as well as to close off space later on and close the workshop. I have some things I need to talk to you about, and I want to teach you one more thing today. So please, sit, sit, sit.'

Everyone was smiling as they sat, Séamus included. Then he stood up again and walked up and down the room, banging his drum a few times to tone down the energy. His hair was splendid in the sunshine, Marissa had never seen him wear it out of his plait, it kept catching her eye.

'*Lub dub, lub dub.* Shhhh, there you go now. Good, good, good.' He turned and faced the group, his teaching tone was activated. 'Now, duty of care – what is it?'

Marissa put up her hand. 'Looking after your client, making sure they're safe and that they won't have a breakdown when you're not around as a result of the work that you've done with them.'

'Good. Very comprehensive answer, Marissa, and from you, I expected nothing less! Duty of care is care for your client, yes, but it's also care for yourself. When it comes to energy work, you have a duty to be at your best, in your best state of reference. Your energy needs to be clear, your mind sharp and focused, and you need to be completely present to your client. Not picking up your own stuff and throwing it at them, telling them they need to heal something that is yours. So, what then do you, as a practitioner, need to make your utmost priority?'

'Sleep!' said Terry, and everyone laughed.

'He's not wrong!' Séamus said. 'If you're exhausted, you'll miss some detail that could be vital. So, yes, well done, Terry. What else?'

'Listen?' asked Zaad.

'Yes, good. Listen to your client, but also listen to yourself and your own intuition. What else?'

'Self-care,' said Liz.

'Yes,' said Séamus, 'But be more specific. What is self-care, Liz?'

'Well, personally, I do yoga as well as teach it, I get massages as well as give them, and I eat well, go for walks and make sure that I take time off so that I don't get resentful of my clients.'

'Spot on!' said Séamus. 'Becoming resentful of clients, or not wanting to see them, is a sign that you're not in the right place, that you need space for yourself. That's self-care. Give me another example, anyone?'

'Not getting the phone!' said Saoirse with a giggle.

'Yes! Totally. Just because you have a phone on you doesn't mean you are obliged to answer every call that comes through. Remember that. What else?'

'Not taking someone as a client if you don't want to work with them?' suggested Stephanie.

'Good, can you tell me more about that?' said Séamus.

'I told my friend about the work I am doing here with you, and that I had homework to do. She offered herself as a client, and I felt, "No," but I said, "Yes." I should have listened to myself, and not done it. It was a total disaster.' Stephanie's tone hinted that she didn't want to go into details about it.

'Yes, listen to your inner "no". That's vital for self-care. Your inner compass, your inner navigation system, it gets sharper and more accurate, the more you listen to it. You do yourself a disservice if you ignore it. Well done, Stephanie. But nobody has said the most important thing that you need to do as a practitioner. I'm still waiting.' Séamus looked directly at Marissa when he spoke and she got shivers.

Not go on journeys and cause trouble with darkness alone and uninvited. She didn't say that, but she did feel pressure to say something. *The old reliable, here goes.*

'You have to do your inner work, so that you can know who you are and be able to tell the difference between yourself and your client. So you can leave your own stuff outside the door. And to make the time to do your personal healing work, so that you don't get triggered by your clients and become emotional. And don't take on more than you're able for.'

'I knew you wouldn't let me down, Marissa,' said Séamus, but the ripple went beyond what was said.

I know. Thank you.

'This is all so very important,' Séamus said. 'And with energy work, it's also very important that you keep the relationship clean energetically. That you don't get mixed up in your client's energies, that you don't get too tangled in their story, especially if it's similar to your own, and you know that it will be. Like attracts like, this will keep you on your toes. You must be able to separate yourself out from your client, clear and cleanse your energy and, just like the soul-retrieval we did, give them back the pieces of themselves that they have given to you, because they trusted you and thought you could take better care of them then they could.'

'You must take back the pieces of yourself that sympathise with your client, that want to look after them, that want to continue to keep you in a co-dependent state, because some aspect of you believes that it's your job to heal the world, that you must heal everyone that comes to see you, that if you don't, then you have failed.'

They weren't expecting that. The mood became serious.

Séamus continued, 'You are not here to heal everybody. You are not here to heal the world. If you jump in where you're not wanted, you'll be taking a potential opportunity to learn away from your client. Learn by your mistakes. Anyone hear that before?'

They all nodded.

'Well, if you don't let your client learn, then they won't learn either. And this is great learning for *you*, because you must watch them make the mistakes that they are going to make.'

They breathed a sigh.

'Right. To reiterate, you won't be able to heal everyone that comes to your door. There will be a reason for that. It might not be anything to do with how good you are as a practitioner and everything to do with the journey your client is on. You are a side character in the play of their life, not a main character. They come and spend one or two hours in your company and then leave. You do your best, you do what you can, and then you separate yourself from them and leave them too. This is self-care.'

'So I want to teach you this, as the last thing we do on this apprenticeship. Take some space for yourselves now. Go on, I know yiz love each other madly like, but yiz need a little more space around your bodies for this bit.'

The group smiled and reorganised themselves so they weren't squashed in on top of one another. Some of them sat on the floor.

'Good. Now imagine a person. it could be a lover or friend, family member or work colleague. We'll focus on a person here, because this is useful for client work, and for any situation where you feel you're too tangled up with someone.'

'Woo hoo,' said Stephanie and everyone giggled.

I think I'll choose Matt. He didn't come up in the work with Zaad. Probably just as well he didn't – that turned out to be big work. Okay.

'Now, have yiz got someone in mind? Good. Visualise them and then allow your mind to clear, bring your body into stillness, slow your breath. Good.'

'Start with the energetic cords that bind you together. There will always be a connection, but a light silver thread is better than a heavy cord, one that's light and loose, not heavy and binding. Good.

'Now see how many cords there are between you, and how tangled they are. Now see them withering and dissolving away. See them falling away. Gone.'

Marissa imagined herself and Matt tangled up as if there were several balls of wool thrown together in a pile between them. She imagined winding the wool back round the balls, so that it became less messy. She didn't notice any tangible difference in how she was feeling, but it was fun to do.

'Séamus, I'm trying to do it with my mother,' said Finn, 'but it's just not going anywhere.'

'Well done, Finn, that's good work. Just seeing a cord that strong can be difficult to do. Can you change it at all? Colour, size, anything? It's been there since you were born, so it won't disappear that easily. Aah, I see many of you now understanding this. Good. So, for a client, it will probably snap and heal very quickly depending on how early you catch it, but for someone you know better and have known for longer, no, it won't be that easy, or straightforward. But by bringing your attention to this cord periodically, you can shrink it, dissolve it, change it so that it's not pulling you as much, or at all.

'Here's something you could try - can take out a shamanic knife and cut it.' He made a gesture of taking an imaginary knife out of his pocket and flicking it open. He made a cutting motion with his hand through the air. 'But again, it could repair itself behind your back, grow back when you're not looking, so you need to check periodically.'

Shamanic knife, oh my God! I think I have one of those, I've been using it. I have a shamanic jerkin with a pocket for the knife, too. Ha ha!

'All good, everyone done? Right. Then do that energy exchange with them, as we did before, only this time you're doing it for yourself. Scan your energy field and gather their energy up first.'

Marissa imagined Matt's energy in her energy field as blue. *Why blue? Strange, blue for a boy, that's so cliched, but that's what came up for me, so that must be it.* She allowed the images to reveal themselves in her mind and saw a small ball of blue energy inside her stomach. She used her imagination to push it outside of her body. It hovered there, not really going anywhere, she saw herself holding it in her hands. She then used it to draw out more blue energy from the rest of her body, until she had a medium-sized ball of blue energy gathered in her hands.

'Now cleanse it in your mind, visualise it getting brighter and lighter.'

Not so hard to do. Marissa imagined a small raincloud over the energy ball raining down crystal rainbow drops of water onto the blue ball of energy. She wanted a cleansing then, so she grew the raincloud and put it over herself, and felt the energy cleansing her, too. She shivered with the freshness of it. Then she connected to Reiki, drew Reiki down through her body and out her hands, and used her hands to cleanse the ball of light. The ball changed from a dark blue to a lighter colour and started to spin. It looked good.

Marissa smiled.

'Now visualise it travelling towards your person across space and time.'

Terry put up his hand.

'Terry?'

'How do you know if you're really doing this or if you're just making it up?'

'Well, it's a great question, Terry. Can you answer it for me?'

Terry shrugged his shoulders.

'Come on, you know you know the answer to this. Tell me! Tell us all.'

Terry blushed. 'Okay. I suppose if you feel better after doing it, then something has changed?'

'Yes, and?'

'And if they are different towards you, easier to be around, if the relationship improves, I mean, then something has changed?'

'Exactly. If they get the bill for the dinner out, instead of waiting for you to pay. That's how you know if it worked or not.' Séamus winked at the group.

'Now let's finish the process. Visualise the ball of light travelling across space and time and arriving in the energy field of the other person. Notice how they receive it, softening, smiling, feeling better.'

Marissa did that and imagined Matt sitting on the sofa in his flat with his feet up on the table, in T-shirt and shorts, the energy raining down on him and his face softening. She imagined him stopping worrying about her, him feeling more at ease in himself. That felt good to her.

'Good. Nearly finished this now. Ask your person's energy field, their higher self, to release any energy they may have that belongs to you. That could look like many different things depending on your relationship – but know that their higher self is always loving and kind and will never argue with you.'

Marissa imagined her own energy as pink and green, lifting up and out of Matt's body. He didn't seem to notice. *What! Why? Does he not miss me? Why doesn't he care if I take my energy back?*

'Wait a moment to make sure you've got all of it. See it forming in a ball over them, then visualise it coming to you, here in this room, across time and space.'

The room then felt very busy, very full, as if ten more people had showed up in their company.

'Wow, people, that's a lot of energy you've let other people take from you!' Séamus said. 'Anyone else feel that?'

They all nodded.

'Now let's clean it all up. You know how to do it.'

Marissa used her Reiki light to clear anything heavy and dull, anything that needed to go from the energy that she had just received.

'Now, last thing, allow your now cleansed energy to merge with your energy field, so that you take it back. It will go to where it's most needed.'

They sat in silence, the room stilled, and Séamus left them like that for a while.

Then he said, 'Well done. Very well done. That was five full minutes of silence.'

Wow, we're done? That was the most peaceful five minutes I've ever had. No wonder I have trouble sitting in silence. Olive would be proud of me!

'Self-care is silence,' said Séamus. 'Now you can see why. It's letting go of thoughts, our thoughts and other people's thoughts. Thoughts clutter your energy field. It's letting go of other people's energy, other people's emotional pain. Emotional pain can be loud and agitate you, uncomfortable, it can make it very difficult for you to be still. It's turning off the news, the external influences. They clutter your field up too, sharp and pointy energies, always listening in, always wanting to influence you.' He did a shiver.

'Self-care, in it's simplest form, is just being. Sitting with yourself, as you are in your wholeness, in the moment, with a total acceptance of all of the pieces of you. This is self-care. You can see it takes a lot of work to be able to do it. So if you can't sit still, know that you probably have some energy work to do first. I hope you continue to do this work, even if all you do is what we did today. Because if you do, it will keep your energy in good condition and you will be much happier in yourself and have so more to offer to the world.'

'Now, lads. Do it again and choose someone else in your mind.'

The room was silent as everybody worked. Marissa chose her mother this time. Some people referred back to notes, others just looked as if they were deep in concentration.

Fifteen minutes later, Séamus called them back to centre.

'Well done. You have your healing techniques – mapping the body, chakra clearing, going on the journey, getting the energy, finding a soul piece, blowing it in, and sealing up your client. But there's so much more you can learn. Shamanism is time travel, jumping timelines, changing your destiny, manifesting miracles. It's moving between worlds, speaking with the dead, visiting other planets. And working with the land, healing and cleansing the damage done by mankind. It gives you the key to unlock your best life, and the best life for others too. All of the healing that works with energy, anything that takes place in the quantum field, all of it is shamanism.'

'But you need time to embody all that I've taught you this year. You can't do it all in one go. If you want to come back and do more with me, I'll be starting an advanced medicine training in the autumn. Any questions?'

Séamus smiled and looked around the room. Of course there were questions!

'Séamus, what do we do with our medicine bundles? Are they really finished now?'

'Ahh, I was waiting for someone to ask me that. You may have seen the sacred inside of someone else's medicine bundle and compared it to your own, and felt short. Or felt proud that yours was more accomplished – I hope this is not the case. Everyone has their own medicine, everyone is different and that is to be expected. So what do you do with them? Have them with you for support. Have them hold space for you in the background while you work with clients. Place more sacred objects inside them as you grow and change, to mark your progress, milestones on the journey. Many different schools of thought use the bundles in many different ways. Me, I see it as a personal thing, something to hold space for you, something to come home to. So no, they are not finished yet, and they may never be finished, just as you are never finished growing. But as a group, in space and time, we are finished. We will include our medicine bundles in our closing ceremony.'

After a very animated twenty minutes, Séamus said, 'Now you have the techniques you've learned from me, you can start to charge your clients for sessions. It's up to you what you charge and how you do it.'

Just like Reiki.

'This isn't goodbye. No need for tears. I heard talk of pints up in Dublin someday, make sure you arrange a date for that before you scatter to the four directions. Now, let's stand in a circle before we close space. Bring your medicine bundle and place it in the centre of the circle, so they are all touching each other. Yes, you will have to push the sofa out, thanks Finn.'

They placed their medicine bundles gently in a pile on the floor and gathered in a circle together.

Séamus stood between Jenny and Zaad, he took their hands, and everyone else followed and closed the circle. He spoke.

'Thank you to the Monastery for holding us, for being such a wonderful healing, and learning, and teaching space. Thank you to the land beneath and around us for creating a safe space for this work.' He looked at each of them dead in the eye. 'Thank you, each of you, for showing up, for taking this to completion. You spread ripples out in the world, even if you never see another client, your energy has changed irreversibly, and that has an impact much further and wider than we will ever know. Together, let us say the closing prayer.'

They broke hands and faced North. There were tears running down Marissa's face as she repeated the closing prayer. Each word had such a weight to it, and she meant it so strongly. She couldn't believe this was the last day and the weekend was over, already. She looked at her friends. They seemed to be in a similar state to her.

What a good bunch of people. Friends for life, they're all amazing.

'And – we're done! See ya!'

Just like that. Wow.

CHAPTER THIRTY

Séamus's car had already left by the time the group stopped talking and went upstairs to finish packing and get their bags. A date had been set for a gathering, but it wasn't going to be for several weeks as they wanted everyone to be there and people had summer travel plans. It was okay though, they knew today wasn't goodbye and that made all the difference. The mood was still sombre, however, the realisation they would need to go back to 'real life' hung ominously around them all.

'Why did he disappear so quickly?' asked Saoirse while she and Marissa packed up their things.

'I don't know, maybe there's something going on for him,' suggested Marissa, as she closed her backpack and put her drum into her schoolbag. It didn't fit inside as easily this time. Had it expanded? She fastened the pouch on the last setting, but the drum was bursting out of the bag now. *I really must get a new bag. How could the drum have grown?*

She sat on her bed and looked out the window, not ready to leave just yet.

'Do you think we will ever be back here?'

'I don't know,' said Saoirse, coming over and sitting down beside her. 'Maybe, but it won't be the same, we won't be in the same group. But we will always have each other, and a place is a place is a place.'

They hugged.

'Where did you hear that?' asked Marissa. 'A place is a place is a place?'

Saoirse smiled. 'My dad. He used to say it to me when we were leaving family holidays and going home. I used to get very sad leaving, but he'd remind me that I was taking the most important thing home with me.'

'What was that?'

'Myself!'

'Ha, ha! Brilliant.'

Standing in the reception area, they all lingered on. Nobody was ready to leave, but the time was ticking and trains needed to be caught. For Marissa, there was still a long drive to Clifden, and a longer drive to Galway, then the train to Dublin. Stephanie offered to take her all the way to Dublin, Marissa was able to tell her that she really needed the space and time that the train ride offered to think about everything that had happened during the weekend. It felt good to be truthful, and she did accept a lift as far as the train station in Galway.

Finn came over, dragging Terry with him. 'Marissa,' he said in a low voice, pulling her aside.

'Yes?'

'I think we should try again. The three of us, we could arrange it. I know Terry is gonna be in Cork, and it really helped when we were touching you, but we could do it anyway, over the phone maybe, or we could it by text.'

'Why are you so keen?'

'I don't know. It's not finished, that's for sure. I feel I'm committed now. I really want to do it, and I want to show you what I saw last night in my dream.'

Last night? Oh yes, I remember now. I wonder why he's dreaming about the castle.

'Are we discussing our plans to release the soul cages?' asked Terry, hopefully.

'Yes,' said Finn with a serious look.

'Okay,' said Marissa, 'let me think about it. We should talk during the week, figure something out.'

'What about Saoirse?' asked Terry, looking at her standing by the door talking to Jenny and Stephanie.

'I don't think she wants to do it. Let's just do it with the three of us,' said Finn.

Terry thought for a moment before responding, 'Three is a magic number. Maybe it's better this way.'

Finn put his hand out. Terry grinned and laid his on top.

'Ha ha, okay!' Marissa laughed and put hers on top of the other two.

They all pulled their hands back in.

'Yes,' said Terry. 'For better or worse, we'll see what happens next.'

I don't like the sound of for worse. I don't think the boys really know what we're up against. I should end this now. But on the other hand, I might not get another opportunity to go there with back-up. Why can't I make up my mind?

'Okay, people,' Stephanie said, 'I don't want to break up our beautiful family, but I do need to get home.'

Liz, Saoirse and Marissa piled into Stephanie's car and they chit-chatted all the way to Galway. She had missed the train she had intended to get, but the next train was waiting on the platform.

'Thanks for the lift, Stephanie. I can't believe it's all over so fast.' Marissa pulled her bags out and smiled at the others.

'I know,' Stephanie said. 'Sure I'll see you at our gathering, bet the time will fly past.'

'Drive safely! Bye, Liz, bye Saoirse!'

'Bye!'

Marissa bought herself a can of Club Orange, a sandwich, Tayto and a chocolate bar, then climbed on board the train, getting a window seat. It was quite empty, she had a half hour before it was due to leave. She put her bags on the seat beside her to claim it, not wanting someone to sit there. Then she texted Matt, telling him she was on the later train. She placed her head against the window and closed her eyes, grateful to get some space for herself.

I won't be opening any of my chakras this time, that's for sure. Her head was busy, trying to separate the work she had done with Séamus from the journeys she had been on with Terry and Finn. *I have a bad feeling about taking the boys with me. I think we are going into deeper waters now. It was one thing doing it for fun, but they're so serious about this, I'm a little worried.*

She woke with a jolt when the train pulled out of Galway. She was tired, but also starving. She peeled herself away from the window, slowly removed the wrapping from her sandwich and took a bite. It didn't taste of very much, but the texture of the food in her mouth brought her back into reality. Swallowing it and feeling it travel down her oesophagus and into her stomach helped to bring her back into her body, back into the real world. *But what is real? We call this 'the real world', but I met Finn and Terry in the journey world. Maybe that's just as real as here.*

She watched the countryside roll past the window. It was a slow train, so it took an extra forty minutes, but she didn't mind. Enveloped in a heavy cloud of emotion, she closed her eyes once more.

'Parting is such sweet sorrow.'

She felt the presence beside her as the images started to form in her mind.

'You have some pretty good friends back there,' Thoth said.

'Yes, yes, I do.'

'You'd better be careful, though, you're entering deeper waters. I won't be there to rescue you if something goes wrong.'

'What could go wrong?'

'You can't be responsible for your friends. Even while they're travelling with you, they're still on their own.'

'Yes, I have been worrying about that. but Séamus said I shouldn't go alone.'

'That wasn't all he said. Did you listen to him?'

'He said a lot of things,' Marissa laughed.

'Yes, he did. Quite the showman, isn't he, but his heart is pure and his intentions are good.'

'Yes, I like him. I wonder what was going on for him this weekend. He seemed preoccupied.'

'We must stay out of business that doesn't belong to us.'

'True. Thoth?'

'Yes, Marissa?'

'What is my purpose? Here, I mean. And which world is real? This one with you, or the one I think I live in most of the time?'

'So many questions, Marissa,' said Thoth with a smile. 'Sometimes I forget that you're just starting out.'

Then they were in Dublin. *That felt so quick... Time really is relative. Did I meet Thoth just now? He never answered my questions...*

Marissa waited until most of the passengers had left the train before stepping out herself. And there he was, waiting patiently on the platform, with his soft face and his warm energy, his wide smile and his open arms. Matt. She fell into his embrace.

'I didn't know you'd be here! Were you waiting long?'

'I missed you. I wanted to see you. Yes, I was waiting ages, actually – I thought you were on the fast train. But hey, never mind, don't worry about it, I got to practise my Tai Chi while I was standing here! I don't think anybody saw me.'

Marissa ruffled his hair and hugged him tighter.

'And, it's Sunday, so I don't have to pay for parking.' Matt grinned.

'Ha, ha, you're a silly old bear.'

'Old bear? Charming!'

'It's a compliment, from *Winnie the Pooh*. You have to believe me.'

'I believe you,' he said, hefting her backpack up onto his back, then took her hand in one of his hands and her schoolbag in the other. They walked hand in hand out of the station to his car.

'Did you have a good time?'

'Oh yes! It was more than I could have hoped for. I'm still trying to make sense of everything that happened.'

'I imagine it will take some time.'

'Oh, yes! I'm glad I don't have to go to work tomorrow,' Marissa said, as they packed the car up and she got into the front seat. 'Are you staying over?'

Matt started the car. 'Of course!'

Marissa felt warm inside. 'Oh! I've nothing for dinner, so we need to stop at the shop on the way.'

'Or, we could get chips?'

'Oh great idea!'

Once home, Marissa lit a fire to take the dampness out of the flat, and Matt fed Tobermory, who looked scoldingly at Marissa before winding himself around Matt's legs.

'Is he angry with you for going away for the weekend?' joked Matt, enjoying the attention.

'Maybe he is angry, but probably not about that. I'm pretty sure I met him in my journey. Maybe he didn't approve of what I was doing.' Marissa felt the words slipping out of her mouth before she could censor them.

'What were you doing?'

'Oh, I was, erm, meeting Terry and Finn. We were experimenting to see if we could all be in the same journey together. It was fun! We even managed it.'

Matt was intrigued. 'That does sound fascinating. Did Séamus have you doing this?'

'No, it was something we wanted to do ourselves. Finn was a bird! Then Tobermory appeared, as a jaguar.' *That sounds okay, doesn't it? Sure that's all we did do, really.*

'How did you know it was him?' asked Matt, sitting down on the sofa and rearranging the cushions to make himself comfortable. The cat leapt up onto his lap and he continued to stroke him.

'He had the white streak across his head,' said Marissa, glaring at Tobermory. She sat down beside Matt. 'It *was* funny, though. Terry was there, dressed as a clown. He had make-up and a circus outfit.'

'I can easily see him like that,' said Matt with a grin.

Marissa gave him a dig.

Tobermory stood up and stretched, his back arching high into the air. He looked at Marissa, then walked confidently onto her lap, still looking at her. He he rubbed his head against her and she stroked him. She felt better then.

'He's forgiven you! It can't have been too terrible.' Matt smiled, then became more serious. 'Did you, did anything... nasty happen?'

'Nasty? At the workshop? No, it was great fun. We were very busy the whole time doing healing work, making new medicine stones and doing soul-retrievals. I can't believe it's all over already. Séamus is teaching again in the autumn, I think I'd like to do it.'

'Good. Hopefully all the mess from before is all over with then. Shall I go out to the chipper now? Chips and a spice burger for me!' He rubbed his stomach while smiling in anticipation.

'Yes, great idea, same for me too, thank you.'

Marissa got up early to see Matt off. He waved as he drove away. As he left, she cleared the energy between them, and it felt, calm. Walking back into her flat, it was like something was missing. *The feeling of heavy sadness! I don't feel it today!*

Marissa thought about going back to bed, but she was awake now, and had so much to think about.

Monday morning. It's my day off from office work, but it's not really a day off. I should do some work for myself for a change. It would be nice to be a little more organised.

She made a cup of tea, sat down at the small desk in her bedroom and switched on her computer.

Today's the day for me to finally make a website. Now I can offer psychotherapy, Reiki and shamanic healing, I'm ready to tell the world that I'm here. Yes, I do have a lot to do.

Out of habit, the first thing she did was open up her emails. As she read through her inbox, a name she saw in there surprised her. What surprised her most, however, was that her heart didn't leap with trepidation to see it. She didn't go into a spin or a panic. In fact, nothing jolted or unnerved her about that email whatsoever. It was just another email in her inbox. *How strange!* She opened it.

Dear Marissa,

I hope you're still using this email address, I'm writing on the off-chance. I want to get this off my chest as it's been on my mind for a very long time. I had a dream about you this morning and I knew I couldn't leave it any longer. You deserve an explanation, and I admit I treated you badly.

I'm sorry for the way I ran away. All I could think of was to get away from you. I didn't think about how you'd feel.

Now that time has passed, I can see it was my fault too. We weren't ready for each other. Perhaps I never would have been ready for you. It doesn't mean I didn't love you, I did. I still do. But I'm with Selena now, and we have two beautiful babies, and another on the way. I'm happy, happier than I've ever been in my life. I don't know, she's less complicated than you, life is mostly easy and good. I know who I am with her, sometimes with you I got confused.

Anyway. I just wanted to say sorry, that's all. I hope you forgive me, and I hope you find happiness too.

Best wishes,
James

Marissa stared at the screen, reading and rereading the email, searching between the letters, looking between the lines for the emotion that was supposed to hit her now, hit her in the stomach and make her bawl, bowl her over and knock her flat. But it didn't come. She simply sat there, sipping tea and reading, as if the email was from just anyone.

Wow.

Shouldn't I care more about receiving this note?

This is the one I've wanted for so long, and all I can think about right now is what I want my website to look like.

Four years in the making, four years of needing to hear these words, craving to understand why he left...

Life is mostly easy and good. She's less complicated than me.

I was too much of a challenge for him. He knows who he is with her... Yes, I did make it difficult for him at times. I guess some people don't sign up for a challenging life. I certainly did, though. I guess it affected him, too. That's fair enough.

I probably wouldn't be learning what I'm learning if we had stayed together. I don't think married life with James and a baby or three would have been enough for me.

He loves me.

I suppose I still love him too, in a way.

Marissa sought out, and then allowed herself to feel the love that she had buried deep inside her heart, for James. She didn't have too far to go to find it. She felt warm, then something burst open, like the liquid centre of a chocolate bursting through the sugar casing. The feeling trickled through her whole body, surprising her in its delicateness. It was a beautiful sensation, and there was a definite pressure release in her heart that went with it. She sat for a moment, relishing the sensation.

I wonder, do we always love the people that we love? I guess you can't turn off love without turning off a part of yourself. I don't want to turn off a part of myself ever again.

She felt his words on the screen, they were still there. She absorbed their energy. She knew not many people ever get an email like this. *So many never get this kind of closure. To know that he loved me, he just couldn't deal with my personality. This is true closure. It's good. I wonder now, have I healed this completely?*

In her mind, she tested herself with images of James and her together. No, no reaction. She then visualised the photograph that she had cried over the most, right when he left her. No reaction. *This is weird.*

She opened up Facebook in another tab on her browser and did a search for James, pulling up the images that were there and looked at him and his Selena, and his children. They looked good together, she was loath to admit it. She eventually found that exact photo that she always cried over, remembering herself late at night touching the screen, wanting to kiss him, slap him, scream at him. He looked so lovely in it, a bright, fresh smile, wide eyes, it captured the best of him. But this time, instead of feeling pain or anguish, all she felt was relief.

It's finished.

'It's finished!' She smiled. *I'm totally over him! And I'm really glad he's happy.*

She felt a pressing sense of urgency to reply.

No. I will reply when I'm ready to.

She got up to put some space between herself and the computer.

I wonder if this had anything to do with the work I did over the weekend, the soul-retrieval? Taking my energy back from him felt great, I hadn't realised he had so much of my energy still with him. Ah, that must be it – I've cleared my energy from his field, and he needed to get in touch with me right away! Amazing! This would be so useful to offer my clients. I'll make sure I put it on my website!

She still felt a pressing need to write back, but stopped herself once more. *I'll write back later. I had to wait four years for this email, he can wait a few hours.*

She made herself some breakfast, had a hot shower and dressed, then went back to her computer. Still, the email beckoned her to reply; the sense of urgency clambered over her like a small animal needing attention. She stopped what she was doing, took a breath, then mindfully and deliberately pushed it away.

No.

I will reply to you when I am ready to. I'm not making you wait for fun, or to anger you, I just don't feel like replying right now. Or maybe I won't reply at all. I have nothing to say. What do you want me to say? You're forgiven?

When she thought that, she felt a flush go through her body.

Yes, that's exactly what he wants. He's looking for absolution. He wants me to tell him that he is clean and clear and can go his way in the world as a free man.

Marissa felt a sense of power then, one she had never felt before. *I have power over James? No, I don't want that. I know power over someone can get me into trouble.*

She closed the computer.

It doesn't look like I will be getting any work done this morning. I need to go for a walk and clear my head.

Valeria was coming for Reiki later that evening and Marissa also had a booking from a woman called Judith, who had found her through her advert in the local shop.

Two people in a three-hour slot just so I can get the room ready, it's not economical. I need to get another space, and I really need to get myself a website.

As Marissa set up her Reiki room she still hadn't replied to James's email. The pressing urgency to respond was unavoidable now. Her 'small animal' had become much larger, and it had completely taken over her awareness.

Feck sake, why does this feel so urgent, so much need, just because he wants me to reply? Why should I be at his beck and call? Valeria's due in fifteen minutes and all I can think about is James!

She paced the room, trying to shift the feeling. It was as if James was sitting in her energy field now, laughing silently at her.

Okay, okay, I need to get this out of the way so I can focus completely on my clients. It's not fair to them, or to me.

She pulled out her phone and opened the email he had sent. She read it quickly one more time, then took a breath, and pressed 'Reply'.

> *Dear James,*
> *I must say it was a pleasant surprise to hear from you today.*
> *Yes, I forgive you. I have moved on. There is no need for*
> *either one of us to hold on to this now.*
> *I wish you all the best,*
> *Marissa*

It didn't look right, and sending it in a hurry wasn't her plan, but she felt pressed upon to send it as it was. *There was so much I wanted to say to him a year ago, but right now I don't know what to say. This seems so curt, after all the tears I cried, all the nights I lay awake, wishing he'd write to me...*

She looked at it again. *No, you know what? This is it. If I go any deeper, I'll be looking for emotion that just isn't there anymore, wanting to make him feel guilty about what he did just for the sake of it. I'm done with this now. I'm torturing myself, and I don't need revenge. James? We're well and truly over. Goodbye.*

She pressed 'Send', and the email disappeared.

She felt drenched in emotion. *Why do I feel like this? I thought I had healed it??*

She closed her eyes. *Dear angels, please come and help me, I don't want to fall into a trap and become stuck again, especially after doing all this healing work on myself.*

She visualised her energy field to see what was going on. It seemed okay, no, there was some stray energy sitting on her heart and her stomach, it was yellow and orange, there was a cloud of it around her head, too. *That's the colour that James's energy was when I worked with him in Clifden. Oh! He's been here on top of me all day. No wonder I haven't manged to get anything else done.*

She peeled the energy carefully off her body, gathered it into a ball and visualised it being cleansed.

'Thank you, James,' she said to the ball of energy, 'You taught me a lot. And now you can go.' She sent it back to him. She felt it leave, it helped, the urgency she was feeling, that crawling feeling all over her, that must have been it. But the emotion? It was still there, heavy and damp, and familiar. Now she knew it was most definitely her own.

If there's a part of me that still loves him, which there is, than there must be a part of me that is still upset. But which part of me? Is it the same part?

She imagined a knocking at her door and she saw in her mind's eye a younger version of herself standing there, sobbing. *Oh. I recognise her. I get it now.*

Come in, Marissa, it's okay.

Younger Marissa stepped into the room, apologetically. Marissa invited her to sit down in the chair, handed her tissues, then sat in the chair opposite her.

'Why are you so upset?' Marissa asked, tenderly.

'I don't know,' sobbed Younger Marissa. 'He still loves me, he said so in that email. Why did he leave me if he loves me?'

Marissa took a breath. Maybe she just needs some time to catch up?

'Yes, that's right he said he still loves you. But he isn't in-love with you, not anymore. And I'm not in-love with him. I'm happy for him with his wife and children - imagine, lots of mini-versions of James running around in the world - how cute is that!'

Younger Marissa smiled, sniffing back the tears. 'Yes, it is cute. Maybe we could meet him one day?'

'Maybe. Hey. You are loveable. And you are loved. I am loveable. I am loved. You are me, aren't you?'

Younger Marissa nodded.

'It's going to be okay. I'm, we're, doing great. We really are. And we have Matt now. But you know this already. So what is the problem, exactly? Tell me, so I can help you with it.'

Younger Marissa stopped crying and thought for a moment. 'I don't know, exactly. I've been sad for such a long time, I don't think I know how to be happy.'

Marissa smiled. 'Well, let's learn how, together.'

The images dissolved and the heavy feeling lifted and was replaced with a gentle calmness. Marissa breathed a sigh. She waited a moment, then drew the Reiki symbol for emotional healing around herself. Then she put one in the room, too, making sure she cleared the energy from the counselling chairs just to be sure.

The room felt still. Marissa's body was at ease. It was over for now, and if the emotion came back, she knew exactly what to do. And then he buzzer buzzed, snapping her back into the present moment. *Valeria.*

CHAPTER THIRTY ONE

It was time. He stretched out his limbs and pushed against the walls of his cocoon. This time he felt something give, something loosen. He pushed harder. There was a cracking noise, and then another and another, and with each crack he had more space to stretch and move. He spasmed as he straightened out his body. There was a louder craaack! *then fresh, cold water rushed in.*

He emerged. He was held by the water, the feeling of being free and held was delicious after all that time cooped up. He shook himself out then placed hesitant feet on the floor of the lake. He had feet! He wobbled for a moment, then propelled himself forward.

He felt a strange sensation, a pushing on his rib cage. Then he felt the weight of the water pushing on top of him, and a sudden urgency for air. He had to get up to the surface, he needed to breathe. Breathe?

He pushed himself off the lake floor and floated awkwardly up to the surface, his new limbs flailing, following the fanned beams of light from the sun. His eyes adjusted poorly to the change in light as the water became more translucent, filled with sunlight from above. Then, suddenly, with a crash, his head was above water. He gasped for breath, and felt something activate in his chest: his lungs!

He bobbed there for a moment to get his bearings. His legs were not much good for swimming. The lake gently pushed him towards the shore, as the land rose up to meet him he fell over and tumbled onto it. He had four stubby legs. Standing was his next challenge.

He was standing on the land. He did it! Now he could help her. Yes, now he could be with her more, help her more. But first, he was hungry, and needed to eat something. Yes, first food, then he would be ready, ready for anything.

'And can you make sure the printer has the new booklets and answer-sheets ready? Full colour, yes that's the latest version with the most up-to-date graph. Phew! Thanks. We need twelve of each of them – no, wait,' said Sarah to Siobhán, who was now her second assistant. 'Get twenty made, just in case. We never know who else may want to join us at the last minute. Better to have more than we need then not enough.'

Sarah was moving quickly up the ranks. The board of directors had approved her ECDL training course and she was going to London to present it to a prospective and very lucrative client. She had designed a quiz to go with the training course which put them out in front of the competition and she wanted the client to take the quiz, to get them more engaged with the material. Noreen thought it was an excellent idea and had given her a budget for it.

Marissa took the work that Sarah had given her back to her desk and made a plan to get through it so it would be ready before her deadline. *No chance of having lunch with Sarah this week. It's great, though. I'm delighted for her.*

Although work had become significantly more interesting, Marissa's mind drifted back to the evening before. She was missing something, she replayed the evening in her mind.

Both Reiki sessions had been straightforward. Valeria had been very chatty and had wanted to talk about her homeland while on the table, and Marissa simply worked around it as she didn't have the energy to push against it.

She'd also been expecting a text from Terry or Finn, thankfully nothing had come in from either of them.

When she got home, she wanted to spend some time reading and rereading the email from James, and the one she had sent to him. But when she was curled up in her pyjamas, ready to indulge herself, she simply didn't feel like it. It really was over. Instead, she put on a silly movie, made some popcorn and sat on the sofa with Tobermory curled in tight beside her. She felt a little sad, but mostly satisfied. She had checked on Younger Marissa, who was enjoying the popcorn and the movie, too. It felt good. She'd just pull a reassuring card to validate everything before going to bed. *That was my mistake. I should have just left it at that.*

'What do I need to know now?'

She pulled a card. *Raziel – Be aware, open your eyes.*

Ooh a new Angel! But be aware? Aware of what? She pulled another card for clarification and got *Sandalphon –Pay attention.*

I've never got these cards before. Their energy is very different, they feel pointed somehow. Not validating at all. What does it mean?

'Have you finished that work for me?' Sarah's breath was warm on the back of Marissa's neck.

Marissa jumped. 'Oh! Yes, hang on – there. Shall I email it?'

'Actually no, could you put it on a USB key for me? I'll take it with me. I've always wanted a reason to use one of those, with the office logo on it. They look so cool!' Sarah winked and patted the back of her freshly cut bob. '*I'm* going to London now, too! It's my turn!' She was practically singing.

'Yes, I know,' smiled Marissa, 'and your trip is paid for by the office, and you get to stay in a fancy hotel with the boss lady!'

'Isn't it great?' Sarah giggled. 'I won't have time for sightseeing or shopping, though.' She sighed. 'I never thought I'd be so excited about going to a meeting!'

'It's your project. I'm delighted you're able to present your work to a client, with Noreen there as back-up. And getting them to do the quiz is a brilliant idea. Bet they get half the questions wrong and want to take the lessons themselves, too. Well done! I'm really excited about it too. Promise you'll text me after and tell me how it goes. When's your flight?'

'Tomorrow morning. The meeting is at lunchtime and then we're taking the clients out for dinner. I'll be presenting at 3pm.'

'Ooh! Would you like me to send you distance Reiki so you're not nervous?'

Sarah considered it. 'I didn't know you could do that! Yes, why not? I'll probably be bricking it before the meeting. Knowing you're sending Reiki will help.'

Marissa took out her phone. 'I won't forget – I'll set an alarm right now. But Reiki or no Reiki, missus, you've nothing to worry about.'

Sarah smiled. 'Look at us!'

'I know! Don't forget to text and tell me all about it.'

When Marissa packed up her things to go home later that day, there was a text from Terry. Her heart leapt into her mouth.

What u up 2 tonite? u want 2 try journey by distance? :-)

She had been half-dreading this, yet was a little excited, too.

I do want to but Im nervous.. I'll phone u - Gimmie 5

She put her coat over her arm, switched off her computer and left the building, calling Terry as soon as she was outside the door. It was a balmy evening, the sun was bright, she didn't need her coat. *Why did I even bring it in with me to work today?*

'Hiya!' Terry said, brightly. 'Well? There are some souls trapped in cages, they cannot free themselves... Shall we help them get out?'

Hearing his voice reassured her. 'Yes, it does sound good. You're right - I don't know why I'm so worried. I think it's... Well, what happens if I get kicked out again, or you get stuck this time, or Finn? Is Finn even able to do it too?'

'I'll have to text him. Hang on, I think I can do it while I'm on the phone.'

Terry got cut off.

Marissa laughed, and walked to the bus stop to wait for her bus home.

Two minutes later, she was still waiting, and her phone was ringing.

'Sorry about that, guess I can't phone and text at the same time... Oh, hang on, here's a text back from Finn. Yes, he says he's on for it. So it's a threesome for tonight then.'

Excitement flashed through Marissa's body. *Okay, I do want to do this after all. Own it girl, own it.*

'No excuses now, Marissa, it will be great gas. Didn't you enjoy it the other night?'

'Yes. I don't know why I'm being so cautious. I guess I feel responsible for you both. And I remember how awful the pain was when I got kicked out of my journey. I'm hesitant in case that happens again.'

'Well I'm a big boy and so is Finn. Maybe you need a disclaimer? Okay, Here's one for you - I'm choosing to do this myself, and so is Finn. It will be good for you to have some company and both of us really want to do this.'

'Okay. I am owning it. Let's do it. What time?' Marissa felt prickles over her whole body, and something that felt like a rush of liquid over her. Was it relief? Or fear?

Her phone beeped. 'It's Finn, he says 8 o'clock tonight. That work for you?'

'Perfect. Phone me later so we can get an anchor point.'

Marissa hung up on Terry and texted Finn.

8 is good for all 3 of us. We need me as an anchor point. Leave it with me I'll figure something out by 8.

Good stuff – talk later :-), Finn

I don't know where Finn lives, he's in Dublin though, maybe he should come over to the flat? But Terry definitely can't, he's in Cork right now. Maybe we should wait until we can be together in real life to do this. Oh, here I go again, spirals of anxiety talking myself out of it. I'm sick of hearing myself going around in circles. Not today. I made the decision.

The bus arrived and it was full. She squashed herself into a standing space and managed to grab a railing. Everyone was sleepy from their day at the office, as the trip went on, Marissa found herself becoming agitated. Everyone was too close to her, she needed air and space, she couldn't breathe, she couldn't get off the bus fast enough.

She picked up food for dinner in the corner shop and soon she was sitting cross-legged on her sofa eating pasta. Tobermory sat beside her, looking disapprovingly, with the tip of his tail wagging in the air. Balmy evening air came through the open window in her little kitchenette. She also had the back door open, the sunshine spilled in through the doorframe, bathing her flat in light. It was her favourite time of year.

'What is it, baby? Do you want to come with us tonight to the castle? Me, Terry and Finn?'

Tobermory kept eye contact with her, but his pupils dilated and his tail stopped wagging. Still keeping eye contact, he stood up and stretched, arching his back, then delicately jumped onto the floor, stretching out his front legs, then his back legs. *The full yoga pose of the cat.*

'Is that a "yes" then?'

Tobermory mewed slightly aggressively.

Marissa's heart leapt.

'Have I got this right, Tobermory? You want me to invite you to come with us on the journey?'

Tobermory mewed again, still not breaking eye contact.

'Well,' said Marissa, as if talking to her cat was a normal day-to-day occurrence, 'I would love it if you came with us. As a jaguar?'

Tobermory looked at her for a moment longer, then walked away from her, into the bedroom.

Of course as a jaguar. Why would I even have the gall to ask him that? Marissa chuckled. *And he's not even called Tobermory. Well, he can blame James for that one!*

James... She pulled back, expecting the usual flash of emotion, but it didn't come.

'James, James, James, James,' she said out loud. *No, nothing.*

Tobermory came back into the living room cautiously, checking her out.

'I'm okay, baby, just checking I'm totally over him. That soul-retrieval is really powerful.'

Tobermory leapt up onto the window ledge and then out into the garden through the open window.

'Okay. I need to support myself on this journey tonight. What should I do? I've got my cat, sorry, my jaguar, and my two friends. Are we really going to break into that castle tonight and release those trapped souls?'

Marissa felt a thrill rush through her. *Aah, that's more like it. Let's enjoy this – it's a magical adventure. Life is amazing, really. I never thought, when I asked for my magic to come back, that there would be this much of it!*

'What else do I need to do?' she asked out loud. *I'll pull another card.* She used the same angel pack and wasn't surprised in the slightest when she got the same card: *Sandalphon – Pay attention. Now it makes sense. So many coincidences can't be coincidences after all.*

'Okay, I'm listening.'

She used sage and cleared the energy of her flat, got out her medicine bundle and her drum, then had an urge to take a salt bath. She looked at the time – it was already 7:30 and the boiler certainly didn't have enough hot water for a bath. *But it will be good to have one afterwards, to cleanse my energy.* She switched on the immersion.

Her phone started ringing and she jumped.

'Oh, hi! Mum!'

'Hello, love. We haven't seen you in a while, would you like to come to dinner tomorrow night?'

'I'd love to, Mum, but I'm working in St Mary's tomorrow, and then Cabra on Thursday. Friday could work. Can I bring Matt? I'll have to see what he's up to first.'

'Sounds good. I'll make a brisket! He likes his food.'

'Brisket? You've not made that in ages, Mum! Can you make Grandmama Lilly's recipe?'

Rose laughed. 'Yes, of course, that was my intention! And roast potatoes too.'

'And gravy? Matt will be there for sure!'

It was almost 8pm.

Marissa lit a candle and had her phone out on the table. A text came in:

Terry has invited you to join a group chat

Yes

She closed the back door and sat down on the sofa. Her candle was lit, she was as ready as she was going to be.

Are we ready? – F

Yes – M

Me 2! – T

Oh! Tobermory wants 2 come 2 – M

Who's that? – F

The black jaguar, that's my cat – M

ok! – T

Thats wild – F

yes I know, he was upset I didnt ask – M

Right on cue, Tobermory came over and sat on Marissa's lap.

He's here now, on my lap – M

So what about the anchor? – T

yes ok, let me go first, then I'll text when I'm there & u can find me – M

how? – F

Ok – back 2 the tree where we started the first time, remember? – M

Finn was a little slower to text than Terry, but they both said: Yes.

I'll wear my black armour – M

I'll b more discreet – T

ha ha – M

lol – F

I'll b a red bird – F

ok see u both there in a few – M

Marissa put the phone down in front of her. She took a few deep breaths and looked into the candle flame on the table, allowing it to dance in front of her eyes. She raised her hand to touch her ankh, felt her feet on the floor and Tobermory's claws in her leg.

'Ouch! Ouch! Tobes!! Okay, okay!'

She closed her eyes, went into her heart and into the room where she kept her weaponry and armour. She put on her chainmail suit, then her armour, allowing it to shrink to her body size. Then she took a long sword off the wall, and sheathed it, swung the sheath across her shoulders and placed it so the sword sat along her spine. It felt comforting to have it there. She strode out the small door, up the stairs and out into the space beside her lake. She looked down at the stony ground, there were footprints in the gravel, prints she didn't recognise. No time to waste.

She moved quickly through past the lakeside, into the forest beyond, and found her tree. Tobermory appeared beside her, he was a large graceful black jaguar, his white lightning streak gave away his identity. She smiled at him and he flicked his tail, he gave off a silent, yet confident air.

The tree wasn't happy. If it could have folded large heavy branch-like arms across the portal to prevent them from going in, it would have done so.

'You're taking your friends into danger,' said the tree, disapprovingly.

'I know, but they both said they wanted to go.' Marissa shuffled her feet, becoming agitated.

'Do you know the implications?'

'There are souls at risk, souls that we can save. I need to help them.'

'That's not quite how it works.'

Marissa sighed. 'Please? They're waiting for me.'

'If it's meant to be then go you must. And if you must, then it must be meant to be, otherwise you would not be here. So go. Just make sure you take the learning from this night.'

Marissa bowed gracefully. The tree's portal slowly opened. She and the jaguar walked confidently inside, down the stairs and out the other side.

When they emerged, Terry was already there, waiting for them. He was leaning against a large tree wearing a sparkling white suit. Large dark-coloured bell-shaped flowers were growing in clumps around the base of the tree, which was in it's full summer regalia of large, luscious, emerald green leaves. This forest had a different feeling to it than the forest where her dear friend the tree resided, but it was difficult to pinpoint exactly why.

'How did you get here first?' asked Marissa curiously, noticing several small golden orbs floating in and out of the flowers. They seemed very busy.

'Not sure. It was easy, though. Do you like my outfit?'

As Terry did a small twirl, his white suit changed colour, first to purple, then turquoise, then pink, then black.

He reached out and pulled a top hat out of nowhere. 'An outfit isn't complete without a hat,' he said, winking. He put it on, and grew a little taller.

'How do I know this is really you?'

'Who else could carry off an outfit like this?'

'It's really you.' Marissa smiled.

'Of course it's me, silly! Hey, you don't look too shabby yourself, missus. Love the fancy armoured suit, you look like a superhero.'

Marissa looked at herself. She had a deep red, almost black catsuit on, the same as before. Her ankh was visible around her neck, and smaller black ankhs were emblazoned on her cuffs, slightly larger ones down the side of her legs. She did a twirl, too. 'It was a gift from a goddess.'

'Well, she has good taste.'

Tobermory's large, powerful presence made itself known to them both. He had a golden collar around his neck with an ankh carved into it, almost matching Marissa's.

'We'll be safe with him on our side,' said Terry, patting him on the head. 'I wouldn't like to run into him down a dark alleyway, though.'

Tobermory snarled, showing bright white teeth.

'Exactly,' said Marissa with a shiver. I hope he really is my Tobermory!

They could hear the flapping of wings. 'Finn!' they both said at the same time.

Finn alighted on a branch. He looked at them both, his face fading in and out of the face of a medium-sized red kite. He had a large wingspan and strong, dark, clawed feet.

'Will you lead the way?' Marissa asked.

The bird settled for a moment. Finn's head dissolved completely into the sharp beak and keen eyes of the kite, then the bird rose up into the air, stretched his wings, circled his friends and flew away.

'Looks like that's our cue,' said Terry, and he headed out after the bird.

Marissa and Tobermory followed, through thicket and bush, forest and hedge, for what seemed like a long time, until they came to the almost familiar small cabin in the woods.

'Ooh, we're here,' said Terry excitedly, clapping his hands together.

They both went to enter the cabin, but Finn-bird swept in front of them and blocked the entrance. They stopped. Finn-bird flew up and down, as if signalling.

'Why can't you talk to us, Finn? This is a journey – I'm sure birds can talk in journeys, even telepathically?' said Marissa.

'Oh! I suppose you're right,' came back to them, not so much from Finn-bird saying the words but sending them.

'Can you hear him?' asked Terry.

'I think so.' Marissa turned to Finn-bird. 'What are you trying to say?'

Finn-bird was silent for a moment, then Marissa heard, 'The front entrance is a decoy. There's another way into the castle. Follow me.'

'It's a decoy?' said Terry. 'I don't like the sound of that. Do you think they're expecting us?'

'I hope not,' said Marissa with a shiver. She checked her sword was still in place. It was.

The two friends followed Finn-bird as he set off around the back of the cabin. He perched on a wall which was hidden by shrubbery. They worked their way along it, mapping it with their hands, brushing the vegetation aside as they looked for a way inside. Then he flew away.

'I'm glad this is a journey, otherwise I'd be knackered,' said Terry with a grin, brushing vines and flowers off a portion of the wall. 'I'm not that fit, although I know I look great.' He flexed his muscles. 'I only work out occasionally for photo shoots, and I've not had a decent session at the gym since Marrakesh.'

Marissa ignored him. She was tuning into the energies, trying to tune into her sense of knowing rather than handing all the navigation over to Finn. She had been here before, surely? She didn't like being a passenger on her own mission. Just then, on cue, Finn-bird came back, excited.

'Well?' asked Marissa, reminding him that he could speak.

'Oh yes! I found it! A way in. Come with me!'

They ran following Finn-bird, this door was quite a way away. Tobermory ran at their side. The closer they got to where they were going, the more difficult it became to run. The air around them was close and heavy. They slowed down, it felt as if they were carrying bags of sugar strapped to their arms and legs.

'If we had a saddle for him, it would be just dandy,' said Terry, out of breath.

Tobermory turned and snarled again, this time a little more strongly.

'Just kidding, just kidding,' said Terry, shrugging his shoulders.

Finn-bird led them to a point on the wall that was clear of shrubs and had a door in it. It felt like they were moving through treacle. They stopped and caught their breath.

'This doesn't feel right, and why are we out of breath?' asked Marissa, wiping sweat off her brow, then looking at it on her hand with a puzzled expression.

'I don't know, honey,' said Terry. 'Is it your journey or mine? This is all quite strange, if you ask me.' His voice quivered.

'Are you okay?' asked Marissa, turning to look at him. He was phasing out a little bit, not quite fully there. 'You don't seem yourself.'

'Maybe not.' Terry admitted. 'I was rather keen on coming here, but something does seem off just now. I'm not so sure I want to be here anymore.'

As Marissa looked at him she noticed his clothing was starting to change colour again. The colours weren't as vibrant as before, it shifted into swirls of mucky brown and mustard yellow.

'I'm not changing the colours,' Terry said, 'it's doing it by itself.'

Finn-bird alighted on Terry's shoulder, and the suit appeared to settle back to a dark brown, Terry seemed much more solid again.

'Thanks, pal,' said Terry, weakly.

Tobermory was pawing at the door in the wall. He pressed or pushed against something and a door opened. He went inside.

'Guess we have to follow him...' said Terry, not at all enthusiastic now.

Marissa looked at Terry with Finn-bird on his shoulder and smiled. 'He suits you!' she said.

'Yes. I was a pirate in a past life, or so I've been told.'

They went through the door without speaking.

'This isn't at all what I expected,' said Terry as they stepped into a bright white corridor with lots of doors off it.

The floor was white tiles, the walls and doors painted white and the ceiling was white tiles too. Large fluorescent lights flickered as if the lightbulbs were faulty. It looked more like a hospital than a castle.

'This looks nothing like what I expected. What do we do? Where do we go to now?'

Marissa felt covered in heavy sludge. She felt the need to get the hell out of there, and fast. But she couldn't move. Tobermory sat down beside her and pressed into her. They heard wails and screams from behind the closed doors, the three friends were in a real predicament.

'This is like an insane asylum,' said Terry with a shiver. 'It reminds me of where I spent the summer when I was nineteen. Horrid place.'

The white doors all flipped around at the same time, there were mirrors on their opposite sides. The corridor started twisting onto itself and the tiles slowly turned into mirrors, too.

'Now I really don't like it here,' said Terry, shivering. 'I have a thing about a hall of mirrors.' Finn-bird looked like a cartoon scribble of a bird with Finn's face instead of a bird's face.

Marissa shivered. 'I'm with you. Let's get out of here.'

They turned to leave, and everything froze, including them. Dark, malicious laughter rose out of every corner of the room, out of the ceiling and the floor. Marissa felt sick. She recognised the disembodied laugh. It was him.

Tobermory was looking at himself in one of the mirrors. He was reflected back as a small black kitten.

Then they unfroze, as if they were given a chance to run. The urge to run filled them all with a need to move. But where should they run to? It was now a closed corridor. Marissa felt disoriented and became panicked.

'Which way is out?'

The friends raced up and down the corridor, trying all the mirrored doors, but each time they tried one, they saw something different reflected in it, some trauma or incident related to one of them which dissolved into the fiery face of the demon laughing at them.

His laughter became stronger, his face in each door, his energy filling the corridor. Then the corridor began to spin, around and around, throwing them to the ground.

They held on to each other for dear life. Finn-bird started to shake, then he turned into Finn, then he disappeared completely.

'Finn!' Marissa screamed, distraught.

Then the spinning stopped and everything went dark.

'You didn't think we would make it that easy for you, did you?' said a honey-coated male voice.

Marissa shivered. It was him, his voice. It was etched on her memory, branded into her soul. It infused through her completely, making her feel like she was nothing.

'You thought you could just swan in here, and what? Rescue lost souls?' He started to laugh again. It was terrifying. 'What are you going to do now, Marissa? Kill me with your sword?'

Marissa had no idea. She and Terry were clinging on to each other. Tobermory was standing over them both, hackles up, teeth bared, but there was no body there to attack.

Then Terry disappeared with a POP, just like Finn.

'I see you brought your little friends with you, this time. How sweet.'

Then she heard a roar. It was feint, but a definite roar nonetheless.

The lights went on and Marissa was outside on a hill, alone. Standing on a battleground after the battle. Dead bodies were strewn everywhere and a wake of vultures picked at their bones, tore at their flesh. One of them stopped eating, turned, and looked at her dead in the eye.

She jumped. She was in her flat in Dublin. She felt terrible, sticky, as if she was covered in slime. She wasn't in pain this time, thank God.

'Shit! Terry! Finn!'

She texted them both.

Are u ok? Are you there?

Tobermory was there. He looked up at her from the floor, his pupils small pinpricks. His face looked hot and squashed, and his fur was matted on one side. He seemed exhausted. Marissa scooped him up and held him to her chest, nuzzling her face into his neck.

'Baby, baby are you okay?'

The phone beeped. *Terry! Thank God!*

I'm here, I'm ok. Are u back now? That was strange, shall I phone?

Yes, please phone

The phone rang.

'That journey turned into an episode of *Dr Who*. Are you back?' Terry's voice was tense and nervous.

'Yes, I'm back, I think I'm okay. What did you see at the end of the journey?'

'Everything went black, and then white. And your grand jaguar turned into a kitty cat.'

'Yes, that's pretty much what I saw too. My cat, is shaken up, he's here with me now. But where's Finn? He hasn't texted.'

'Uh, I don't know. He hasn't texted me either. It was pretty cool though, wasn't it?'

'I'm getting worried...'

'Wasn't it cool, though?' Terry was brightening up as he spoke to her. 'You know, if we keep going with this, we could really figure this out and free those trapped souls.'

'Terry! Stop! Didn't you hear him? What he said?'

'Who, Finn?'

'Jeeuz Christ, no.' In a quieter voice she said, 'The demon.'

'Demon? The demon was there?'

Marissa was silent.

'No, I didn't see him, or hear him at all.'

'But he *was* there, and he said that he wasn't going to make it easy for us.'

'It felt easy enough to me, I met you at the tree, we had a laugh, Finn showed up as a bird, we went for a walk and found a castle – hey that castle looked just like the one in Wizard of Oz! We found a way inside but we ended up in some sort of shopping mall. So strange! We were in the changing rooms looking for Finn for ages, I don't know what happened to him. One minute he was there, the next he was gone.'

'Terry?'

'Yes?'

'Were you in a hospital for the whole summer when you were nineteen?'

After a pause, Terry said quietly, 'How did you know that? I've never told anyone about that.'

'You told me. In my journey. And the place we ended up in terrified you, you said it reminded you of the hospital and you didn't want to be there.'

'I don't remember that at all. Finn disappeared, your cat turned into a kitten, and everything went black, and then white. That mall we were in though, it was so fancy, much fancier than the one in Dundrum. Did you see all those mannequins? They were quite creepy though. I wonder where it was?'

Marissa took a breath. With a curt tone she spoke, pronouncing each word very clearly. 'I wasn't in a shopping mall.' Then she felt her stomach turn with an acute rush of anxiety over Finn.

Terry registered what she was saying. 'Oh. Okay. I'll get off the phone now then and phone Finn right away.' He had dropped his playful tone of voice.

'Thanks.'

Marissa hung up, hugging Tobermory to her chest, still. She waited to hear back from Terry, watching the minutes ticking past. Images of the demon's face swam before her eyes. She pushed them away with the strength of her will. *Finn. I need to know he's okay.* She focused on giving Reiki to her cat, who started to look like himself again. *Sorry baby, this was a total mess, I won't do it again.*

After three minutes of Reiki Tobermory leapt off her lap, went to his favourite spot on the armchair, curled up into a tight ball and went to sleep.

Terry texted back:

he's not picking up the phone, OMG

'OMG' is right. What if the demon got Finn? Terry saw something different from me. I wonder at what point we split out of our journey. Maybe Finn wasn't in our journey at all. But I wonder if, oh my God, what if he was, and the demon put him inside one of those jars? Shit! Finn doesn't have Isis to set him free... This is terrible, and it's all my fault. What do I do? I'll have to go back into the journey to see if he is okay.

She texted Terry: I'm going back 2 get Finn

He phoned her straight away.

'Going back? How can you do that? I can't come with you, I'm too distracted and won't be able to focus. Back where, anyway? It doesn't even look like we went to the same place. You shouldn't go back on your own. And for all you know, he might have ended up in, well, Timbuctoo, instead of a shopping mall. Check him in real life instead. Do you know where he lives?'

'No, I don't have an address for him. Shit, shit, shit, we should have thought about this before we went. He still hasn't replied in the group chat, or to me.'

'And he's not getting his phone. What the hell has happened to him?'

Flashes of anxiety and a sinking feeling hit Marissa's stomach, she felt dizzy and the room started spinning. It tasted like the onset of a panic attack. She remembered how reluctant the tree was to let them go in the first place. *I should have listened.*

She hung up the phone and got up and walked around her flat, back and forth, then opened the back door, went outside and got hold of her breathing. *I sat outside here with Finn only a few days ago. I hope he's okay. Why didn't I think to get his address?*

The phone buzzed another text. *Finn!* She picked it up. *Shit, it's Matt.*

Hi love, how r u doing? U ok?

I can't text him back now. I'll have to pretend I didn't see it.

She texted Terry again.

Who would have his address? I could go to his house and check him

He's still not picking up. Maybe Saoirse has his address – T

This is awful – M

What else can we do? – T

Marissa texted Saoirse.

While waiting for a reply, she remembered the immersion for her bath was still on. She switched it off, the boiler was roasting hot. *Pity to waste all that hot water.* She ran the bath for herself, she knew she needed to clean her energy after that debacle. She poured in lots of Epsom salts, then poured herself into it.

Lying there in the hot salty water, she was able to catch a hold of her breath, and slow it down. Her body relaxed and she closed her eyes. Distorted images of the demon's face moved before her: him in her dream, him as Scott Taylor, him as Martin, even as Cheryl Bryant. She pushed them away. *I'm stronger than this.*

She sat up in the bathwater and washed her face. She did a body scan, checking her energy from head to toe. She was in Dublin and she wasn't in pain. And Terry was okay. But where was Finn? She sank back into the hot water again, sloshing some of it out onto the floor.

Finn is okay. I know he is. He has to be. And if Terry wasn't in the same journey as me, it's even less likely that Finn was. It will all be fine. No, he's not fine, is he? Has Saoirse texted me back yet? Oh, I left the phone in the other room. Feck sake.

She got out of the bath and went to get her phone, leaving a trail of water behind her.

There was a text from Terry.

Still nothing?

I'm trying to stay calm – M

Its been over an hour – T

Then a text from Saoirse. *Finally.*

Hi Marissa, no, I don't have it. why do you need it?

Shit, shit, shit, shit.

CHAPTER THIRTY TWO

Marissa had a fitful night's sleep. Not knowing whether Finn was lost to the demon wasn't conducive to sleeping well. When she woke, she was sure she had visited Thoth and spent time with him and a small blue dragon in Egypt, but she couldn't remember anything about it. *Strange...*

At 5.30am she got out of bed, got a drink and took it back to bed with her. She was wide awake now, and cold. So cold. She started to shiver under the covers. She put on socks, but it didn't seem to help. *I have to do something. Hey, I know what, I'll do a soul-retrieval! Yes! That's what I need to do, why didn't I think of it before?*

Tobermory was awake at her feet, looking at her. His fur looked less matted, but still he wasn't back fully to himself. Marissa nuzzled into him gently and kissed him, not wanting to disturb him too much.

'Tobermory, I'll do a soul-retrieval for you first.'

She couldn't focus, or tune into him. Her shivering got worse, with effort she got her cardigan and put on a beanie, and climbed back into the bed with a second blanket and wrapped her covers around her. Lying there curled into a ball under the covers shivering, she thought about what she could do. *Am I sick? It's like having flu. Maybe I need to do my own energy first. That's what they say about the oxygen masks on the plane... Okay, me first then.*

She brought her awareness into her heart, then stretched it outwards, to sense if her energy was trapped anywhere. It took a few moments, once she located something she relaxed a little and the intensity of her shivering went down a notch. There it was – a pull. She was drawn to something outside herself. *That must be me! But it's so heavy!*

She imagined casting a fishing line and hooking into it, then visualised winding it back to herself. But it was so heavy, the fishing line wasn't strong enough to shift it. *What do I need to do?* She imagined the fishhook growing to the size of an anchor, and the fishing line getting stronger, thickening until it became a cable, hooked onto some kind of motor. That's it. She watched as the motor pulled the cable, hauling the weight back to herself.

As it came closer, her shivering reduced, and she began to feel slightly warm. She took off her beanie. It felt as if she was pulling a huge weight into the bedroom. Now it was right there beside her, a solid mass of something on the bed.

Oh! My angels, can you help me? Raziel? Sandalphon? Should I be asking you for help? Is this my energy?

She felt a full body 'yes'. *So how to get it back inside me, then?*

She imagined the solid heavy energy was like a glacier, melting and trickling onto the bed, dripping slowly drop by drop into her body. *Yes!* It started to work. As the glacier melted, it left behind bits of debris which she burned in the violet flame. She was breathing more deeply now, she took off the top blanket, her body heat was stabilising. She felt stronger, more lucid. She was back. The morning sun was spilling in under the curtains and over the bed. Her sense of purpose had returned.

Now I need to do this for Terry, Finn and Tobermory.

Tobermory stretched and climbed down off the bed, scratched his claws on her rug, then curled into a ball on top of her clothes on the floor and went back to sleep. *He seems better, maybe his energy came back with mine?*

Marissa checked his energy field and saw images of dancing mice, butterflies and grassy fields. She laughed. *I think he's okay. I'll go and check on Finn now.*

She lay there for a while, figuring out how to connect to Finn, especially as she didn't know where he was. *The time and space symbol from Reiki! Of course!*

She drew it over the bed, then imagined herself stepping through it and into Finn's bedroom in the house where he lived.

It looked like a typical bedroom – it was messy, clothes were strewn everywhere and the curtains were shut, but some light was trickling through them, too. Finn lay face down in the bed, breathing shallowly. His covers were jumbled around him and Marissa could hear light snores coming from where his head lay on the pillow.

I hope this is right. If it is, then he's okay.

She did some Reiki on him, and he stirred in the bed and shifted onto his side. She approached, put the covers over him and sat down on the bed.

His soul pieces, a soul-retrieval.

She set her intention and asked for Finn's soul pieces to come back to him. She didn't want to go out and find them, so she willed them to come to her, instead. After a moment, what looked like orbs floated into the room, all different shapes, sizes and colours. They were like soap bubbles with images inside. There was one of Finn as a small boy playing football, and there was another with a red bird inside it.

Yes, this must be it. *There was one of him being smacked in the face by a girl.* Ha, ha, that's Finn, alright.

The orbs floated gently onto Finn's body and popped when they touched him, and were absorbed. The room filled with colour. Finn's breathing eased and his body relaxed into a deeper sleep. Marissa stood over him and closed the Reiki session, then stepped back through the time and space symbol into her room.

'Wow,' she said out loud. 'That was cool. Okay. I'm pretty sure he's okay. I know that was real. I can stop worrying now, Tobermory.'

She got up and got Tobermory some food. He followed her into the kitchen, winding in between her legs.

'You earned that, baby cat, you made such a cute kitten.'

Tobermory glared at her then tucked into his breakfast.

'Ha, ha.'

Marissa made herself a cup of tea and got back into bed. It was still early, there was still time to do a soul-retrieval for Terry before she had to get up for work.

The room felt full of energy. Marissa sipped her tea and focused her intention: to go through time and space to Terry and get his soul pieces back for him. She drew the time and space symbol and imagined herself stepping through it to be with him right now, wherever he was.

What?!

She saw a large, dark skull and crossbones.

She pushed at it, to get through it, but no, she couldn't move forward, the crossbones moved with her, blocking her every attempt. Then the skull started laughing at her.

This is a symbol of death, isn't it? But I know he's not dead.

She tried again, gently this time, to push through, but the bones were solid and determined, even when she tried to move around them, skirting clockwise, then counter-clockwise. The more she tried, the more strongly they pushed back.

Maybe I'm not allowed to do this for him. I know I didn't ask permission, but I did take him with me.

'I came with you willingly, darling,' she heard him say in her head. 'And no, I don't need you to do a soul-retrieval for me. I'm perfectly fine just as I am. But thank you for thinking of me all the same.'

That sounded just like Terry. It has to be him.

'Okay, sorry, I just wanted to help.'

'Yes, Marissa, but sometimes your help is not needed, or wanted.'

She felt a little hurt by that, and pulled away, brought her awareness back into her room, closed down the time and space symbol, and sat there thinking until it was time to get up for work.

At 8:30 she was at the bus stop when the group chat beeped a text.

It's Finn! Thank God!

Oh guys, sorry. I fell asleep, had phone on silent & missed all ur calls and texts. I'm fine. I feel gr8 today actually. Good long sleep I must have slept thru whole thing ha ha

Marissa was fuming.

Not funny Finn, not funny at all. I didn't know where u were, u disappeared & i couldn't find u – M

Finn, u put the heart crossways in both of us. U really fell asleep? Ha ha u really had us going, fell asleep, ha ha ha! – T

Ha ha you thought I was taken ha ha so funny yeah I'm good. Do it again tonight?

Both Terry and Marissa texted back: NO!

As the work day unfolded Marissa reasoned that it could have been so much worse. It was clear, however, that it was too risky to attempt anything like that, ever again.

Were they really there in the journey with me at all? I know Terry insisted on going there, and we did see some similar things at the start of it, according to what he said.

And it could be fun if we didn't have such a serious mission. Maybe we could just do it one more time?

No. But those souls are still trapped... I'll go myself. I'll go as Tori! Yes! Going as Marissa was a mistake. I can see that now. Tori is powerful, strong and resourceful, and she knows what she's doing, I was Marissa last night and I was confused, weak. I had a sword but I didn't know how to use it. How stupid is that?

Thank goodness it wasn't any worse. I have to be Tori in these journeys from now on. But how do I do that?

She played with ideas of how to jump in and out of being Marissa, then Tori, throughout her day at the office. As she worked, she imagined herself shifting into the feel of being Tori, being a taller, harder-limbed, warrior woman. *Warrior woman making coffee, warrior woman reading emails... Ha, ha, you wouldn't catch Tori in an office job.*

St Mary's was two bus trips away and her reason that day for leaving work early. She grabbed a sandwich and crisps and ate them on the way. *Warrior woman eating crips on the bus. Ha, ha, ha, this doesn't get old.*

Deep down, however, she knew she did need to figure this out. She hadn't felt any strong connection to Tori since the workshop.

Oh well, got to focus on my clients now.

There was a note at reception from Audrey, letting her know that Lucy had moved on and wasn't in St Mary's anymore.

Oh! We were going to try Reiki. Funny how each time Reiki came up, Lucy was so keen to try it, but we never managed it. Maybe it just isn't for her. Or maybe she's not supposed to get it from me.

Marissa looked at the intake sheet for the night. The new receptionist was much more organised, and Marissa was now getting client sheets with more information. Tonight, Loretta was coming first, then Sorcha, then someone new, named Emma. *I hope it's an easy, straightforward evening. I really am so tired.*

She took a few moments to get her bearings in the room, to reorganise the chairs and table, and to light a candle. She stood in silence and said the prayer to open sacred space, reminding herself of the boundaries of the work she was supposed to be doing there.

It's counselling, so no funny stuff. Feels good to say the prayer, though.

She sat and breathed, pushing all the adventures of the last few days out of her mind so she could be fully present for Loretta, who walked into the room all sunshine and light. She wore jeans, a clean tee-shirt and cardigan, and had her hair cut short, in a way which really suited her. She sat down in the chair opposite Marissa and smiled.

'You look great, Loretta. You must have had some sleep since last week!'

'Ha, ha! Hi, Marissa, I've had a good week, thank you – the first good week in a long time. I'm getting my life together. Feels like it, anyway. Since I let Barry see the kids, I've been able to breathe again.'

'That's wonderful. I love your hair! What would you like to talk about tonight then?'

'Thanks, yes, she did a good job on it. I thought it would help my self-confidence. I've been thinking about this a lot. That's what I want to talk about - my self-confidence has been shattered. I think that's why I was so reluctant to let Barry see the children, because I thought I was letting myself down by giving in to him. But I can see now that this runs deeper. I feel I let myself down a lot. Can we talk about this?'

'Of course. When you say "let yourself down", what do you mean exactly?'

Loretta took some time to think about it. Marissa had an urge to map her energy, to check her for bindings, to make sure she was clear and bright. *No. Not tonight. This is psychotherapy, a pleasant change from energy work. Loretta didn't sign up for energy work.* An image of the giant skull and crossbones she'd seen earlier that morning came into her awareness. *She didn't give her permission, either. That's what that means. So I will sit here, and be separate from her, and listen to her. She is over there, and I am over here, and we are just talking about her self-confidence issues.*

With that thought, something inside Marissa relaxed. *Oh, I've been on alert all day. I didn't realise. Interesting.*

As Loretta spoke about her old teacher at school putting her down in front of the class and her best friend doing better than she did in the exams, Marissa felt the world around her was a real and tangible place. She became drawn into Loretta's story of her first date, of how her mother said Barry would never be interested in her, yet he was, and of how she felt. *This is real. The journey I just did with Terry and Finn, it's hard to know what part of that was real, or if any of it was real at all.*

She looked at Loretta again and saw the lines on her face, the callouses on her hands, the bitten fingernails, and the hard look she had under the façade of friendliness.

All Loretta knows is this world, this place, and it hasn't treated her well. It's been hard on her and it's made her hard. But I know there's more to life than what's here, in front of us. I can see the magic in the layers beneath. But she can't. I wonder what would change in her if she could see the world the way that I do?

Marissa had shifted her physical body so that she was mirroring the way Loretta was sitting. After forty minutes, she realised that the part of her that wanted her to forget the shamanic landscape had become stronger.

This is something that I need to look at in myself. Is this part of me telling me the magic isn't real because life is easier without it? I don't think life is easy, not for anyone, but maybe it's simpler without the magic? All I need to worry about then, is making sure I fit in. But when I change gears and talk to a client, when I don't do energy work, it's like I change shape and a different programme takes over. It isn't me. I don't like it. It took over before, and I forgot who I was. Maybe Loretta has forgotten her magic the way I did.

'Sorry, Loretta, I don't mean to interrupt, but we only have a few minutes left, and I want to ask you something, something you haven't brought up yourself.'

'Yes, okay. What?' Loretta looked straight at Marissa, but it seemed hard for her to focus.

Marissa cleared her throat. 'Who are you?'

Loretta stiffened. 'What do you mean? I'm Loretta, aren't I?' She looked at Marissa as if she had two heads.

'Well,' Marissa replied, 'if you weren't called Loretta, and you had to tell me who you were, what would you say?'

Loretta looked even more confused.

'It's like that saying, "a rose by any other name would smell as sweet". "Rose" is a name for a particular type of flower - if the flower was called something else, it would still have the same qualities – beauty, smell, petals... "Loretta" is your name, but it doesn't describe your values, who you actually are.'

Loretta relaxed a little bit. 'I have no clue what you're talking about!'

'Okay, well let's look at it this way then. Maybe I'm not saying it well. You've been telling me about stuff that happened to you, and it's real stuff, some of it terrible, all of it important to you.'

'Okay.'

'But it's stuff that happened to you, it isn't you. You're carrying the stories of what happened and deciding who Loretta is, based on those stories.'

This is interesting, wonder where I'm going with this...

'Okay...'

'But if you weren't called Loretta, or if you weren't allowed name yourself at all, how would you describe yourself?'

'I don't know?'

'And if, on top of that I was to, say, wave a magic wand and suddenly you were to forget all the stories of the things that happened to you, then wouldn't that release you?'

'Release me? From what?'

'From the energy of those stories. Wouldn't it free you from the stories you tell yourself around how clever, how beautiful or how worthwhile other people think you are? If you had never known what they said, or cared what they said, or compared yourself to their idea of you, what would be different about you?'

'Oh. That's strange. I've never thought of that before.'

'Okay. Let's take a step backwards for a moment. If I was to give you a rose, and we didn't know what it was called, then what would we do?'

'Well, we'd look at it, I suppose. Smell it, touch it, admire it.'

'Yes, we would admire it, talk about it's qualities, the ones that we see right in front of us. Good. And if we were to look at you the same way, with no labels, no stories, just you, as you are right now in this moment, would you feel the same way about yourself?'

There was a pause.

'What if we admired you the way we would admire a rose?'

Loretta shivered. 'Ooh, I don't think I could do that, be admired.'

'Why not?'

'Well, isn't that bad?'

'Says who? We would do it to a rose and not think it was bad. What's the difference?'

Silence again.

'This isn't a test, Loretta, it's just something I thought of, actually, right now. You know what I think?'

Loretta shook her head.

'I think we are trained to think the worst of ourselves. I think it's ground into us from the moment we are born. And we try to fit in, to make ourselves an acceptable shape, one that people tell us we need to be, we forget who we actually are. If it's bad to admire ourselves, be proud of ourselves, how can we encourage ourselves, or try something new, or feel confident doing anything?'

'I suppose.'

'It seems clear to me now. We're wired to look for risks, right? And we become wired to look for our faults, yes?'

'Yes, I think I understand now.'

'If we are always looking for risks, and faults, then we never really see or acknowledge what is good. Being admired, or acknowledging that we're good at something, isn't reinforced. It's "bad" to do those things. All the stories you told me, the one's that you're holding the energy of, they're reinforcements of the bad stuff. You've been told you're not pretty, not smart enough, not good enough. Nobody has told you you're amazing, clever, or beautiful.'

'My dad did a few times while I was growing up. And Barry did, but I knew it was just 'cos he wanted something from me.'

'Ah, but he wanted it from you, not from some other girl.'

'True.'

'So you were told from time to time how good you are at something, or how beautiful you are? But you didn't tell me that. Maybe it wasn't as important to you as the bad stuff is? But it is more important, really. I reckon if you want to increase your self-confidence, you need to start changing what you are telling yourself. Yes?'

'Oh. I have to do that? Where do I start with it?'

'Maybe look at what you choose to believe. What stories are you replaying over and over again? Ask yourself what it would feel like if you allowed yourself replay the good stuff, too. Even a little bit? Anyway, we've come to the end of our session. Try it? And tell me about it next time. Will you do that?'

'It sounds really difficult.'

'Yeah, it will be, because you'll see how often you knock yourself. But it's difficult to be confident when you keep knocking yourself.'

'I think I understand. Okay, I'll give it a go. I suppose you're right. If I am to be confident in myself, I have to start reinforcing what I'm doing right, instead of reminding myself all the time of what I'm doing wrong.'

'Exactly. You've got it now. I don't think the change will happen overnight, but it's a good start.'

'Thanks.'

Marissa stood and stretched, then rearranged the cushions and clapped a few times to disperse the energies in the room. *It's true, though. We keep telling ourselves how stupid we are, then we think that we are stupid. Why do we do this to ourselves?*

There was a knock on the door. Sorcha was standing there.

'Hi! Come in! Nice to see you again.'

Sorcha came in and took the chair Marissa had just been sitting in. She was wearing the same outfit she had worn the week before, blue jeans and a dirty white hoodie top.

'What would you like to talk about with me tonight?' asked Marissa, sitting down in the other chair and bringing her full attention into the session.

Sorcha's face lit up. 'That game we played last week, with me and Adam, it really helped. I felt much better this week. I only texted him fifteen times. He actually replied once too!' Then her face fell. 'There's no chance he's getting back with me, though. He says he's met someone else and wants me to leave him alone.'

Marissa recalled the work they had done together the previous week. From what she could gather, using the Gestalt chair technique to talk to Adam seemed to have prolonged the conversation rather than helped to close off the relationship. *Maybe I should have used that soul-retrieval technique instead. I guess I can't get away from the shamanic work.*

'There's something else we could try, if it's okay with you, something that might help your body realise that the relationship is over.' *Yes, that's a nice way of saying it, and I could do it as a visualisation with her, so it would fit better into the psychotherapy session.* Marissa got a flash of excitement. *Finally! A way that I can combine the energy work with psychotherapy.*

Sorcha looked disappointed. 'I was hoping you could help me figure out how to get him back.' She crossed her legs and arms and looked like a five-year-old about to throw a temper tantrum.

Dammit. Okay, I can't push her if she's not ready. It's not fair to her.

'Okay, Sorcha, you just told me that he said he'd met someone else. Why do you think he'd come back?'

'I don't believe a word of it – he's just saying that to put me off.'

Try a different tack, I think.

'Why are you here in St Mary's?'

Sorcha was quiet. Then she touched her face, rubbed her jaw, as if recalling some pain or other.

'Did he hit you?'

Sorcha nodded and her eyes filled up with tears. 'Yeah, lots.'

'Then why do you want to get him back?'

Sorcha started to cry. 'I love him. I can't stop thinking about him, I dream about him, I miss him so much, it really hurts.' She looked up through the tears, mascara running down her face. 'It hurts so bad in here.' She pounded her heart with a closed fist.

Marissa got her the tissues and waited until the tears abated. *soul-retrieval would help, it really would...*

She pulled back. 'I understand that it hurts. But it doesn't sound as though he was good for you, if he hit you.

Sorcha blew her nose and wiped her face on her sleeve. By some miracle the mascara didn't mark the hoodie. Marissa was impressed.

'I know you're here to talk to me,' she said, 'and I want to help you feel better. The two-chair technique we tried last time was to help you get some closure on the relationship, not to open it up again.'

Sorcha sniffed, then asked, 'What's closure?'

'Closure is something that's needed when a relationship doesn't feel finished. The idea of the two-chair technique is to allow you to feel that everything that needs to be said has been said. It makes you a little more content with the ending.'

'But I've been talking to him all week, using that technique,' Sorcha protested, 'and he's told me loads about work and his new friends, and he's never mentioned a new girlfriend. That's why I don't believe him.'

Ah, okay, this makes sense now.

'Sorcha, what you've been doing is talking to your projection of Adam. It's not really him. You might be carrying a piece of Adam in your energy, and you put it in the chair and talk to it, and it talks back to you. But in actuality, it's you, talking to yourself. And this part of you didn't know that Adam had a new girlfriend, because it wasn't really him.'

But I know this isn't completely true, because I didn't make up all that stuff about Dad that time with Ronan. I'm pretty sure I didn't make it up. Dolores would say the energy is connected, so Adam's energy would know he had someone else. Maybe Sorcha is holding on to it so tightly that it can't leave. And she isn't clear in her own energy, so she can only hear herself, and not what his energy is saying. Yes! That makes more sense now.

Sorcha was shocked. 'So you mean I was talking to myself all week? He didn't hear any of it?' She looked very cross now.

'Oh dear. Maybe I didn't explain the technique well enough. I seem to remember we jumped right into it after you told me Lucy recommended it for you.'

Sorcha was blushing bright red now, holding her breath, and her hands were making fists, as if she was getting ready to punch something. *Not me, I hope.*

'Look, stop a moment. Breathe. Let's figure this out.'

Sorcha breathed out.

'Okay. You're a grown woman, and so am I. I would never do anything to hurt you deliberately, and I'm sorry the technique didn't work for you.'

Sorcha relaxed a little and her face regained its natural colour. 'Yes, you're right. I'm a grown woman.' She sank back into the chair. 'I guess I got carried away.' Emotion flooded her face once more as she kept speaking. 'Some part of me was hoping it was really him I was taking to, and I supposed I was pretending it was, and it rekindled something in me.'

A moment passed. Marissa stayed silent, willing her to continue.

'When I was texting him all those times, I know a part of me almost didn't want him to reply. I didn't want him to confirm that I was making this all up in my head.'

'It's good that you can recognise this, well done.'

There was another moment of silence, then Sorcha added, 'When he told me he had a girlfriend I was, well, shocked. Angry. Devastated.'

Marissa took a moment before responding. 'I understand. We all have inner child parts that want to be loved. Maybe that was your inner child playing the game of chairs with you, and nothing to do with Adam at all.'

'What do you mean?'

'Your inner child, it wants to be loved. Maybe it latched onto Adam, needing his love, and a child loves to play games too. So it sounds like your inner child was having fun, in a twisted sort of way, digging deeper into your wounding, searching for the love it craves. But you won't find it in the wound. The wound needs to heal. You yourself can love your inner child, though. You can give it what it wants.'

'How do I do that?'

'You start by telling your inner child how great it is, how sparkly and magical it can be.' *This sounds very much like what I said to Loretta just a few moments ago, but it's a totally different issue. Or maybe it isn't that different?*

Sorcha sighed. 'That sounds like a lot of hard work. And I don't know how to do it.'

'Let me help you. That's what I'm here for. It's not that difficult, not really. Close your eyes. Yes, that's good. Do you want another tissue?'

'I'm okay, thanks.'

'Okay. Now, imagine somewhere you liked to go as a child. Did you go to the seaside?'

'Yes, I love the sea. My dad would take us out to Howth when we were little and we would walk along the pier and watch the fishing boats.'

'That sounds lovely. Imagine you're in Howth. What does it look like?'

'We would go to a rhododendron forest too, in Howth, when the flowers were out. They're probably out now actually, or soon.'

Sorcha's countenance lifted as if a heavy weight had been taken off her shoulders. She kept talking.

'It's so beautiful there. With all the flowers, it's like being on a tropical island. The flowers are so pretty – pinks and purples, reds, and the green leaves. Some of those plants are twice and three times as big as I am! There's one there that grows up the face of a cliff wall. It's amazing to see it. When the wind blows, it blows the petals, and it's like it's raining colours onto you. It's really magical. That's a secret hidden place where Dad would take me, just the two of us. I used to love running around there, laughing, and we'd hunt for the gravestone in the middle, then he'd help me climb up to the top of it, and I'd dance and he'd clap! That's my best memory.' She opened her eyes. 'Have you been there?'

'No, it really must be a secret hidden place – I've never even known about it. I'll have to go and see it for myself.'

'Oh yes! You really should, it's just fabulous. On a sunny day, when you're there, it's like being on a tropical island.'

'I think we're getting off-track now. Can we go back to your inner child?'

Sorcha smiled, then nodded and settled back into her chair, closing her eyes and seeming much more at ease.

'Okay, you're in the hidden tropical forest filled with flowers, running around and laughing. How old are you?' Marissa got an image of a little Sorcha filled with joy and love for her father. She heard a voice in her mind say, 'Five.'

'I'm about five years old.'

Marissa felt prickles up and down her spine. Getting the age right felt good. She could almost see Sorcha at five, but had trouble imagining big trees with tropical pink flowers on them in Ireland. Really? Sure it didn't matter, not for the purposes of the visualisation.

'Okay, you're there too, adult Sorcha, watching little you running around in delight and laughing. Can you see it?'

Sorcha was still smiling and she nodded her head, then giggled, 'I forgot how much fun it was to go here.'

'Now, if you're able to, can you give little you a hug? Tell her she's great?'

'She is great! Look at her run! So fast! She's so happy too, she's no clue the world can be such an awful place.'

'But it can be an amazing place too.'

Reluctantly Sorcha admitted, 'Yes, you're right. Maybe I've forgotten that too. I've caught up with her now. She's lying on the ground laughing, refusing to get up! I'll lie down beside her.' She stayed with the images for a moment.

'Ah, I'm holding her hand and we're both looking up into the trees. There's a light breeze and the flowers are shaking. It's raining petals down onto us. It's beautiful.'

Something in the room got softer then.

'How does your heart feel now, Sorcha?'

'Better. It doesn't hurt as much now.'

'Can you give little Sorcha a hug?'

'Okay, yes.'

After spending some time with little Sorcha and giving big Sorcha work to do during the week so she could reconnect with little Sorcha, Marissa cleared the energy in the room and waited for her next client.

As she sat there, she reconnected to her current puzzle: how to become Tori. She imagined Tori's body – longer, leaner and harder than her own. She imagined Tori stepping into her body; she could almost see Tori's foot stepping into her own foot, Tori's knee melding with her own, then into her other foot, and other knee. She was just about to imagine Tori's hips sitting into her own hips as if Tori was going to sit into her body, when there was a loud knock on the door. She jumped and the images vanished.

'Hi, I'm Emma.'

A large woman stood at the door. She had light brown hair scraped into a messy tangled ponytail, wore jeans and a tee-shirt. She looked to be in her early thirties, and like many of the women in St Mary's, she had an air about her as if she had had a hard life.

'Hi, Emma, nice to meet you. Come in.' Marissa shook off the feeling of Tori, but a stretching feeling stayed with her, as if Tori really had come into her for a moment and stretched her out a bit.

Emma lumbered into the room. Marissa stood, but stayed by her chair, so Emma took the opposite one. They both sat down.

Marissa took a moment to register Emma's presence. Then she opened the session.

'I'm here to help you with whatever is on your mind today,' she said. 'Anything you say will be kept confidential, between us, here in this room. Unless I think you're at risk to yourself, then I'll have to tell my supervisor.'

Contracting in St Mary's was different from Cabra as she didn't know exactly how many sessions she'd have with each client. *And I've still not had a proper supervision session with Audrey. I really do have to pin her down and organise that. Once again I'm falling behind with my hours.*

'Right,' said Emma, looking very uncomfortable, as if she wanted to leave already.

'What would you like to talk about with me this evening?' asked Marissa, trying not to sound too tired. Her lack of sleep the night before was catching up with her. She noticed there was a new smell in the room, something heavy and pungent. *Ah Jaysys, Emma has some bad BO. Oh dear.*

'Dunno.'

They sat together for a few moments, Marissa trying not to be disgusted by the heavy smell that was becoming hard to ignore. She tried to breathe through her mouth so she didn't smell it, but that was too obvious.

Emma shifted in her seat.

I've got to do something about this, it's too distracting.

Marissa got up and walked to the back of the room and opened a window. The fresh air diluted the smell slightly and made the room more tolerable.

Marissa sat back down and turned to Emma. 'There must be something you'd like to talk about with me, something I can help you with?'

Emma scratched her head and her finger caught in the tail-end of a loose piece of hair from her ponytail. She pulled on it, then opened her bobbin and her hair spilled out. She gathered it together, loose bits and all, twisted it into a knot and tied it up tightly on the top of her head.

Marissa waited, becoming more and more uncomfortable with every passing minute.

Eventually, an air of resignation, Emma said, 'I seen some bad tings.' She paused. 'My life, it's been one bad ting after another.'

Marissa waited for more, not wanting to prompt her.

'So I'm here, in St Mary's,' Emma said. 'To get away from them, like. My family, you know, like. They did some bad tings. Yeah. They said I should talk about it, to you, like. Audrey said.'

Marissa nodded.

Emma was silent again.

'Was there anything in particular you wanted to share with me?'

'Where do I start?' Emma started to laugh.

First sessions are always awkward. I need more patience. And she needs to take a shower, badly. Okay, I've got to make more of an effort here.

'You can start anywhere you want – in the middle, at the end...'

'How can you start at the end? I'd like a happy ending, so I would. But I suppose it's not ended, not yet anyway.'

'You're right, we are here right now, so your life is not over yet.'

'True, dat. Very true. I'm still here.'

'Let me help you – tell me where did you grow up?'

'With me Ma, and me Da in the caravan on the sites. I've six brothers and five sisters. They're not all blood, only three of them are blood. But we're close, very close. Might as well be. Six families livin' together, all of us kids runnin' around like mad feckers.'

'We moved around a lot too, never stayin' in one place for long. So I missed a lot of school, like. Didn' go to school for a year or two. Didn' like school, me. Yeah. Me Da, he'd bring home loads of mad stuff. Once he brought home a VCR, you know one of those tings you can watch with the tapes?'

Emma told Marissa some of her personal history. There had been violence and laughter, loyalty and betrayal. Once she warmed up to Marissa she relaxed and showed an eloquence of thought that hadn't been apparent before. She knew right from wrong, and had gotten into trouble many times, trying to do the right thing. She thought St Mary's would be somewhere she could take space away from her family, and get help to make a clean go of life. By the time the hour had come to a close Marissa had begun to have admiration for this woman. *You really can't judge a book by its cover.* She was almost reluctant to close the session, only that she was so tired.

'Emma, we have come to time. It's been very interesting meeting you and I'm grateful you felt you could talk to me and tell me a few things about your life.'

Emma smiled. She seemed much more present in the room. 'Thanks for listening like. Yeah, I don't usually talk so much. I guess a lot of tings have happened to me, eh?'

'Yes, and I know that you've not told me everything. I'll be here next week if you want to come back. We could talk more. But you don't have to tell me any more details if you don't want to. Instead, we can look instead at how I can help you feel more confident, or happier, or how to reframe something that happened to you so that it doesn't hurt you so much.'

'How did you know some of dis stuff was hurtin' me?'

'You look as if you're carrying it around with you, the pain of it. I see it in your eyes.'

'Yeah, suppose I do carry it. Thanks for dat. Dat helps a lot.'

'Maybe if you want to, you can leave some of your pain here, in the room with me?'

'What will you do with it?'

Marissa smiled. 'Why, I'll explode it for you, of course.'

Emma smiled back. 'Ha, ha. Dat sounds great. Yes, please, and thank you.'

'You're very welcome. See you next time.'

CHAPTER THIRTY THREE

By the time she got home after her sessions it was late. Exhausted, she went straight to bed and slept thought the night, not remembering her dreams.

Tobermory woke her early in the morning, mewing, sticking his nose in her eye, and sitting on her chest. At 6:30 Marissa got up and let him outside, rubbed her eyes and put on the kettle. Sarah and Noreen were still in London, they wouldn't be in the office till tomorrow. She had some flexibility and wasn't feeling in a rush to get into the office for 9am.

She took her tea outside. *The air was sweet with pollen and warm from the southern wind. It was going to be another beautiful day.*

A walk in Stephen's Green before work? Could I do it? It isn't on the way to work, I'd need to take a different bus from there, but I could make it to my desk by 10 and nobody would notice. And I could get a doughnut and coffee...

Her heart set on her diversion, she took a long hot shower, ending with a blast of cold water to close her pores, put on her favourite summer dress and put together a smaller handbag, placing her fully charged phone inside.

Cabra tonight. Must remember my sage. She dropped the sage in, and her bottle of Aura Soma too.

She touched the golden ankh around her neck. She still hadn't taken it off since she'd got it in London. She put on a long cardigan, grabbed an umbrella, locked the flat and set off for the bus stop.

There was a slight chill in the air but her white cardigan kept it off her arms. The sky was clear but for a few white fluffy clouds. *A perfect day!*

She saw a bus approaching so she ran for it. There were only two people waiting at the bus stop, and the bus was mostly empty.

She hopped on, tapped her travel card and went upstairs to find a seat at the front. Sleepy, well-dressed people were dozing around her, but she was bright-eyed, enthusiastic and awake.

Okay. I'm going to merge with Tori now. It almost worked last night. I'll try again.

The bus bumped its way over the canal and down Richmond Street, then Camden Street, and it was difficult to concentrate.

I'll do it when I get to the park. It's too messy here.

Marissa watched for her stop then, holding the handrail tightly, twisted her body down the steep spiral staircase and waited for the double doors to open so she could alight onto the street.

The bus drove away. Traffic was building up beside her. She waited for a clear space and hopped out into the road, dodging a bicycle to make it across to the other side. She ducked into George's Street Arcade, enjoying the smells and sounds of the marketplace as it woke up, the happy chatter of the merchants as they anticipated a good day's trade.

A few moments later she was on Grafton Street, and there, on the corner, was the doughnut shop. Closed.

Her heart fell. *Well, I guess I could get a coffee somewhere else.* She looked at the time on her phone. *No, they should be open by now... Oh, wait!* She could see there was a woman inside the kitchens at the back. She brought out a large tray of doughnuts and placed them in the cabinet, saw Marissa there and smiled, then approached the door, flipped the sign and invited her in. Marissa's heart rose.

I got too attached to this. I need to keep an eye on that. It's only coffee and a piece of fried dough covered in sugar, for goodness' sakes!

Marissa gratefully ordered an americano, choose a doughnut, paid and left. The satisfaction she felt when walking towards the Green reminded her of crossing off something on a to-do list. She walked through the main gate into Stephen's Green and followed the path until she came to her favourite spot, the bandstand-like deck by the duck pond. The sunshine was strong now, hot on her face; she took her cardigan off and draped it over her handbag, which she placed on the floor of the deck. She stood looking at the reflection of the sun on the pond.

I remember the first time I saw Séamus was on a YouTube video that he filmed here. And now I've just finished his apprenticeship. What a year this has been! A trip to Peru, money from Uncle Lou, learning Reiki, meeting Matt! Finishing my diploma. Letting go of James. Totally letting him go. And new friends too – Saoirse, Terry, and the gang... I've done so much. And there's more to do – Dolores is running the Seichem, there's Reiki 3, and college too, I must sign up for the degree course.

She sipped her coffee and bit into the creamy goodness of the doughnut she had chosen. *Mmm. I still need a website, to find a room for more client work, and I want to do the next workshop with Séamus.* Savouring every morsel, allowing the sugary sweetness to melt on her tongue, washing it down with the hot liquid... *Delicious. Maybe it's okay to be attached to coffee and a sugary thing. I know the spiritual path is about non-attachment, but I'm only human.*

The ducks came out, looking for crumbs, but the doughnut had been eaten. Marissa crumpled the bag and stuffed it into a nearby bin, then licked the last of the sugar off her fingers. She closed her eyes, placing her weight equally on both feet. *Now, Tori, come to me. I want to merge with you.*

She visualised a hard warrior woman standing in front of her, flicking her hair back over tanned shoulders. *No, that's Wonder Woman from the TV show. Come on, Marissa, stop messing about!* She felt a presence beside her and opened her eyes. There was nobody there, but the sense of the presence remained.

'Tori? Is that you?'

She felt an affirmation. Not knowing quite what to say next, she tried to connect to this being that was supposedly a part of herself. Or was she part of her?

'That's your problem right there.'

She heard the voice strong and clear inside her mind. It gave her goosebumps.

'What do you mean?' she responded in thought.

'"Supposedly"? I'm "supposedly" a part of you? Or am I a part of you? You haven't claimed me yet. How can we merge if you think we're separate?'

Marissa thought about this for a moment. 'I suppose I'm a little scared of you. Of becoming you. I don't know what it means. To be you, I mean.'

She got a sense of Tori laughing. *'I didn't know what it meant to be you, either. You have a lot to deal with. Much of it, I would have no time for. Being human isn't all it's cracked up to be. It's difficult. But I see how far you have come. You have earned my respect.'*

Marissa felt this was a great honour, but was still hesitant. 'You're serious? You respect me?'

'Yes. I couldn't do it – be at the beck and call of others, be dumped upon with fear, other people's pain, have to feed that body of yours, sleep and earn money. Doing something you don't like so you can spend time doing something that you do like for a few moments of gratification. No, it's hard. No wonder so many of you don't like it here and want to go home.'

'Home?'

Tori smiled. *'Yes, your soul's home. You forget that so many of us find it too hard to wear a human suit. It feels pain, it's heavy and slow, and you can't be in many places at once, or change your shape.'*

'But I've been changing my shape.'

'Outside your body you have, yes, your light body. You are getting a good handle on that. Also something I admire – not many people can do this as easily as you. With the awareness that you've been cultivating you are getting better at it, too. More refined. I understand why you want to go back to the demon to free those spirits. It's exciting, and more compelling than anything you'd experience here in your human suit. You are wise not to do it without me. Your friends, well, that was something else. That bird! So funny! He's a nice boy. Much more exciting than your Matt. Or your James.'

This took Marissa by surprise. Finn was good looking, and since the soul-retrieval at the workshop, he had been much easier to be around. But no, she was getting off the subject here.

'I love Matt, He's good for me, he looks after me and understands.'

'But you've been hiding things from him, haven't you? You haven't told him about this, or about me, not really. And you haven't shared a journey with him.'

'No, but I could, I guess. I just don't want him to worry about me.'

'What makes you think he would be worried? Maybe he would enjoy. Maybe he would come and help you, too.'

'Maybe. Yes, you're right. I'll tell him about it.'

'It's up to you. I'll let you be the judge of human matters.'

Tori faced Marissa in a warrior pose, strong and tall.

'Now, are we going to merge or what? Claim me.'

Marissa looked at her. All of this was in her mind's eye, but it felt very real. It seemed like a turning-point. If she claimed this warrior as part of herself, what would change for her? Would she become too powerful? Would she lose her grip on reality? Would everyone hate her? What would it mean?

'Oh, so many questions! No wonder Emelda loses her patience with you!'

Marissa laughed and softened.

'We will figure it out together, as it arises, yes?' said Tori.

'Yes.'

Tori stepped forward, and Marissa softened her body and closed her eyes.

'We merge now.'

Tori turned her back to Marissa, then stepped back, putting her left foot into Marissa's left foot. Marissa felt a rush of energy through her body. Tori put her right foot into Marissa's right foot, and then sank backwards slowly, matching knee for knee, hip for hip, spine for spine. She leaned back into Marissa, and Marissa felt herself grow taller. She felt solid, peaceful. Something shifted in her heart, a hard thing deep in the centre of it liquified and spilled over, giving her relief. She stayed with the sensation, grateful that she had the time and space to give it attention.

As she solidified into herself, she became more aware of her surroundings. The colours around her were sharper. People were walking through the park – mothers with baby carriages, men and women in bright suits with briefcases, walking briskly by. And standing here, on the deck, for the first time in her life, she felt complete. *Yes, that's what it is. I feel complete. I belong to myself. I have everything I need right here.*

Her heart was at ease, completely at ease, for the first time in her life. All those questions she had had just a moment ago melted away. There was no anxiety at all in her body. She felt clear and focused. She didn't need anything. No need, for anything. Where's Tori? I am Tori. She smiled, then gathered up her cardigan and bag and stood there for a moment longer, getting her bearings. *It's hard to describe this feeling.* As she moved, it was as if she left a long silken carpet of light behind her.

She strolled through the park emanating pure light, it billowed out from her as if it were a bridal train. The light she left behind her seeped through the land, touching each blade of grass, each petal, insect and butterfly; lifting it, healing it, soothing it. As she walked past people her light rippled right through them, lifting the dross of the day-to-day life off their shoulders, clearing their auras, opening their hearts. Babies stopped crying and smiled, clouds of depression dissolved away, arguing couples remembered that they loved each other. Someone who had lost hope was renewed, a poet sitting on a bench finished his poem, and a little girl throwing bread to the ducks on the duckpond knew for certain that she was made of magic. Marissa glided gracefully towards the bus stop, not knowing the effect her bliss was having on people, and she didn't need to know.

She was going to be later for work than she had planned, but she didn't mind. She had a sense of inner knowing that it would be fine, that the bus would be there when she arrived at the bus stop and nobody would question her when she walked across the office to take a seat at her desk. And she got to the bus stop and there was the bus, just as she knew it would be. She took a seat downstairs, enjoying the sensation of the ripples of light which flowed from her as they reached out and beyond the confines of the bus and into the city.

Marissa Tori Rosenthal. Tori Marissa Rosenthal.

Marissa sat at her desk, doodling her name in a notebook while her computer woke up. *How does this change me? Who I am? What I do? Maybe it doesn't change anything at all.* She opened her emails and started to go through each one, checked her 'to do' list for the day, and began to cross some of the items off.

The day flew past. She felt switched on, in flow. Everything was sorted quickly. She even tied up some loose ends for Sarah that hadn't come together before London. *I might have arrived late, but I've done more work this morning than I've done all week.*

At lunch, Marissa-Tori found a bench near work to sit on in the sunshine, ate her sandwich then closed her eyes to check in with herself.

I'm still her, still me, still whole. If she is in me, then I am just me, just now. She felt an inner knowing that all was well, then was pulled to visit her guides by the lake. *I'll go via my tree.*

She brought her awareness into her body and was pleasantly surprised by how quickly she could do it. With each out-breath, she dropped down a little further into herself, until she was completely in her heart. The sounds of the street around her faded as she brought her whole awareness inside herself.

Here, she felt something was different – the clutter was gone, a large mess had been cleaned up. Her inner sanctum was no longer a wasteground, no longer strewn with tangled briars and thorns of half-baked ideas and unfinished symphonies. It had metamorphosed into a library with everything categorised and shelved in perfect order. Marissa remembered having once used filing cabinets, opening one of them to see the universe inside, but now she couldn't store her knowledge in deep dark drawers, it had to be out in the light, in the open, on large wooden shelves where it was much easier to access the information.

Something deep within expanded at this discovery, like a lotus flower reaching petals upwards to the sun, opening and opening, and opening again, layers upon layers. She smiled. The library, the books of paper, the slivers of life that once came from a tree, on shelves that were also from trees, danced before her eyes. Much better this way. She stepped back from it all and watched as it shrank down, twisting itself into itself for easier storage. It became more familiar then, the shape of it, eventually dissolving into the form of her own dear medicine tree, her axis mundi, a portal to the many shamanic worlds.

'Through you I can access all wisdom and learning,' said Marissa, with a deep knowing.

'Yes, that is correct,' said the tree, smiling, 'for I am the Tree of Knowledge.'

'Ha, ha! Of course you are!' said Marissa, laughing out loud, with her eyes still closed. She didn't care if anybody noticed her.

'You get closer to the truth with every passing day,' said the tree, and nodded to acknowledge her newfound strength.

Marissa smiled.

Wanting closer contact with the tree, she placed one of her hands onto its trunk and saw her hand dissolve into it. She got a start and pulled back. Her hand was hers once more. She tried again, placing her hand up against the trunk. Again it dissolved into the tree.

'Why?' she asked.

'I am part of you and you part of me. We are one.'

'I think I understand.'

'Then you know nothing,' said the tree and started to laugh. 'A little knowledge is a dangerous thing.'

Marissa placed her hand on the trunk once more, but this time it remained separate from the tree.

'In time, in time. So, are you here to visit me, or is there someone else calling to you?' asked the tree, with a knowing smile.

Marissa felt bad. She never had visited just to see the tree. She really should sometime.

'Emelda and Grandmother?' she asked.

'And your dragon,' said the tree.

'Dragon?'

The tree opened and she fell into it, falling, falling, spiralling, not sure if she was going down or up. The vortex carried her until she fell out of it and onto the stony beach beside the lake.

She stood up and looked around. The mountain stood there proudly, snow-capped and strong.

'Ausangate,' she whispered, and felt its strength flowing into her.

'Yes,' whispered the mountain, 'It is I and I am here and always, with you.'

Marissa smiled, looking towards the beautiful mountain, which seemed to lean in towards her, as if to bow to her. 'Thank you.'

She placed her hand on her heart, then offered light from her heart to the mountain.

'I am always here and always with you, also,' said a voice.

Marissa turned around. It was Emelda in her full regalia, wearing a long colourful dress, a headdress with feathers on it, and many necklaces. Her face looked younger. She was radiating joy.

'Emelda!' Marissa ran to her and put her arms around her, pulling her in and giving her a big hug.

Emelda hesitated, then she smiled and hugged Marissa back, then gently stepped away.

'Okay, okay. Too much for me, too much.'

Marissa smiled. 'I'm so happy to see you. It's like you and the mountain, you are my heart.'

'Like your heart? Yes. Like it. I like that.'

Grandmother Medicine Woman walked up from the lake. She was also in full regalia, wearing a long black robe, and many coloured necklaces, different in texture to those Emelda wore. Her hair was long and sliver, and free from adornments. She had no hat on. It was unusual to see her thus. She seemed much older, but her beauty shone through and she smiled, her wise old eyes glistening.

Marissa felt a warmth from inside gushing up with love and joy. 'My beautiful Grandmother Medicine Woman. Hey, you never did tell me your name!'

'Yes, you are correct, I never did!' Grandmother Medicine Woman cackled and laughed. It sounded like a bubbling stream.

Emelda laughed too. 'Old woman, you like your secrets,' she said, then turned to Marissa. 'She also never tell me!'

Marissa laughed and felt very connected to both the women. It was a beautiful moment.

Emelda and Grandmother Medicine Woman were still looking at her, then they looked at each other and nodded in approval.

'I see you have expanded,' said Grandmother Medicine Woman, looking Marissa up and down.

Marissa turned to the women. 'Tori and I had a chat together, earlier today. We have merged.'

'Ah. This part of your process, then, is over. You are both Marissa, and Tori, both here and often both over there too.'

'Often over there? Where do you mean?'

'In the other world, the world where you cannot see us. But we see you there, remember?' said Emelda.

'Ahh, yes. The world of no privacy. I do remember. But what shall I call myself here? I am Marissa there, but here I could be Tori? Or Marissa Tori? Or am I Tori-Marissa?'

The women laughed.

'Does it matter what you call yourself? Did you not say that to one of your clients only the other day?'

'Yes, I suppose I did.'

'Well then. You are you, no matter what you call yourself.'

'Yes, that is what I felt, as well.'

She noticed on the stony lakeside ground there were large, unusual footprints in the gravel, just like the ones she did not recognise the last time she was there. She was just about to ask about them when there was a roar, a loud roar that bounced off the mountain and back again.

Marissa wasn't afraid. She stood taller, became alert, stretched her senses, spilling her awareness out around her.

'Ahh! Here he comes, our old friend in his new body. Look! He is so strong and brave, even though he is still a baby.' Now he is ready to follow you into the next part of your journey.'

A turquoise and blue dragon trundled over, taking his own sweet time, clumsy on elephantine feet. His head was too large for his body, limbs awkward and flailing about. He looked more like a dinosaur than a dragon, he was the size of a donkey. He seemed apologetic about his appearance, ashamed of himself. He nuzzled against Marissa, then cocked his head to one side and looked at her quizzically. He felt familiar to her. Then she remembered.

'It was you, wasn't it, in the hall of mirrors. You rescued me once again didn't you.'

He perked up, eyes bright and looked at her, almost cat-like. It was a resounding 'Yes!'

'Thank you so much. I owe you my life.' She flung her arms around his neck and hugged him awkwardly. He shivered with delight.

She stepped back and he roared with joy, it rang through her, reverberating through the mountain and bounced back again, several times.

He looked shocked at the volume, perhaps he had not intended it to be as loud. He was apologetic once more. All three women laughed, then he did a little dance and they laughed once more.

'You still have some growing to do, I think,' said Marissa. ' Yet I have the feeling you will become very much stronger. I am so pleased to have a friend like you. Thank you my beautiful friend. I'm excited to see you grow.'

The dragon nodded, butted into her gently, then padded away like a big Golden Labrador. He ran awkwardly into the lake and splashed about, drinking water and spitting it out in rainbows. It was quite beautiful and funny to watch.

'He's still getting used to his new shape,' said Emelda, smiling like a proud mama. 'Once a water baby, always a water baby. But this dragon will breathe fire one day, once he completes his first shedding.'

'He has such a good heart,' said Marissa, still feeling grateful, while fascinated by the shape and colours of the dragon as he frolicked in the water. His glistening armoured scales were so similar to the scales of her beloved sea serpent, yet it was difficult to appreciate they were the same being.

'Everything changes and everything stays the same,' said Emelda, turning back to Marissa. 'We see you soon, yes?'

'Yes,' said Marissa, a cold breeze licking against her neck, raising goosebumps on her arms, bringing her back to her body on the bench in Dublin.

She stretched and stood. She had left her cardigan at her desk, so she slowly made her way back to the office.

A few hours later, she was setting up the room in Cabra. She could still feel Frances's energy in there, though she hadn't actually seen her this time. The room felt smaller than before, but she could have been imagining that. She kept checking Tori was with her, then reminded herself that she *was* Tori.

But what does that actually mean?

She sat down and wondered about William. He hadn't contacted her for Reiki, and he wouldn't be coming tonight, as they had finished. But that portrait on the wall, his face was not in it. *He left a feather there. Finn isn't the only one who can turn into a bird. I'm sure he got away.*

She drifted.

Aisling had been trapped and she'd let her out; it was only when she'd let someone else out that she'd felt that kick. *But I'm Tori now, so I'm stronger, faster, more experienced. And I don't want Terry or Finn holding me back. I should go myself, just me. That was my mistake. They held me back. I should see what I can accomplish on my own. And free more of those people.*

She remembered the event in London – the audience, the chains, the chanting. 'Scott, Scott, Scott...' *Chanting like they had lost their minds. Lost their souls.* Something solid in her shifted. *One step at a time, but this is the next step. Yes. I will go back.*

The buzzer sounded.

'Niamh!'

Marissa got up and pressed it, and stood there until Niamh arrived at the door.

Breathless, she said, 'Hi, Marissa! Sorry I'm a little late. What a week I've had! Wait till I tell you!'

Marissa stood out of the way and a very hyper Niamh came inside and sat down in the chair with her back to the door, still chatting away. Marissa sat in the opposite chair, giving her some space to unwind.

As Niamh continued to talk in a very animated fashion, Marissa said the opening sacred space prayer silently in her mind, then imagined herself drawing Reiki symbols for emotional healing, mental clarity and the power symbol. She drew them all big, in the centre of both chairs, and imagined them expanding outwards until they filled the room with light. As the energies settled, so did Niamh. She seemed less panicky now.

'So I tried the meditation, the one from YouTube, and then I was wide awake all night. I thought I saw dancing creatures in my room. It was really strange and scary, but I also kind of liked it.'

Marissa did a double-take – *What did I miss?* – then said, 'Sorry, Niamh – you tried what meditation?'

'An energy healing one. Remember our first session? You said you did healing on my energy. So I thought, *Why not do more?* and I spent ages looking up videos on YouTube, watching them all. Actually, now that I think about it, I probably watched three or four in a row that night.'

'No wonder you are hyper! Seeing dancing shapes in your room? Was this just last night?'

Niamh blushed. 'Did I do something wrong?'

'That's too many, all at once. Do you know who the people were that were in the videos? I mean, had you seen them before?'

'No, should I have?'

'That late at night? Oh yes, oh my goodness, yes!'

Marissa got prickles on the back of her neck and felt Thoth come into the room. His presence stood beside her, as if he was waiting patiently to hear what she was going to say next.

'What do I say to her?'

'I think you're doing well. Keep going, just be gentle with her, remember she's new to all of this.'

'Okay.'

'Niamh, you have to be careful when it comes to choosing a healer. You don't know who anyone is on YouTube and their motivation for making videos like that. Some healers don't always have your best interest at heart. They could want to break down your boundaries and take your energy. When you're tired, especially late at night, you are vulnerable. Oh, and they can also infiltrate your dreams and break into your mind that way. You have to be more discerning.'

Niamh looked shocked. 'Oh! That sounds terrible. I didn't know that could happen! I thought all healers just wanted to help, but I guess, like anything, yes. It makes sense. There are bad doctors out there too. You're right, I should have thought more about it.'

'Sorry to be so blunt. I suppose I should expect most people have not had that experience, or don't think this way. I just get upset to see it. Would it be okay if I check your energy field to make sure that you're clear? When exactly did you do this?'

'A few days ago. I have been a little jumpy since. But some amazing things have happened – that's what I wanted to tell you about.'

'Can I check you first?'

'Okay, yes, good idea.'

Niamh stopped talking and Marissa unfocussed her eyes, sent her senses outwards and felt into her energy field. She picked up something, but it was illusive.

'Thoth, can you check for me? Is that something you can do?'

'Yes, I will check her.'

Niamh jumped in her chair 'I felt something tickle me,' she said. 'Was that you checking me?'

'Actually, no, I asked one of my guides to do it just now, as I didn't pick up anything wrong and I wanted to be doubly sure. It was probably him.'

'A guide? Like a tour guide?'

Marissa sensed Thoth laughing. 'Yes, I suppose it's similar to a tour guide, but he's a spirit guide, a tour guide of the spirit world.'

'How insulting'

'I didn't mean to insult you!'

'Ah, sure I'm only winding you up. It is rather funny. She did have a tear in her auric field, and some stray energy did get inside. I repaired it and cleared it for her.'

'Thank you so much.'

'Okay, Niamh, you are clear now, but you weren't clear. Listen to me. There are people out there who aren't what they say they are. Not all spiritual teachers are good people, and not all of them are experienced enough to realise when they're doing harm. Some healers would rather heal other people than do their own healing work, and it's like stirring around dirty water instead of clearing and cleansing it and making it drinkable.'

'Nice image, and well said.'

'Thank you!'

Niamh took it in. 'How can you tell the difference? Between healers?'

'Well, it's difficult to tell when you start out. I made mistakes too, and I probably will still make some. But you can be aware that this is a thing that can happen. So I guess if you're going to a healer in real life, you could get a testimonial from someone who already went to them? But on YouTube, you would need to check out the videos, preferably during the day, at a distance, to feel if they are good or not for you. Not late at night when you're tired!'

'I have booked a workshop...It's in the Angel Shop. It's a card-reading workshop. I'm so excited, oh I hope the person will be good?'

'I'm sure if Mairead lets them work out of her shop they'd be good. I'd be interested in going to that, too!'

'Oh, would you? I can give you the information, if you like. Hang on, I have it here.'

Marissa had to stop herself.

I can't go to the same workshop as my client, can I? She pulled it back.

'It's okay Niamh, I can find out myself later. Thanks for the inspiration!'

'Yes, okay.'

'So, to recap, you watched three or four YouTubes. And had a wild night with dancing shapes in your room, then you signed up for a card-reading workshop. But you'll be more careful now.'

Niamh nodded and smiled.

'Okay then. Check-in time. How has your anxiety been? This is session five of our cycle of six, so I also need to see if you're happy to finish next week with me.'

'Oh. Yes. Yes, my anxiety hasn't been a problem this week. I've had another problem – that's what I wanted to tell you about. But I think yes, we can finish next week, that's fine with me.'

'Noted. Now tell me what happened.'

'Remember the homework you gave me, to imagine putting down other people's bags?'

'Ah yes, I remember. To put down the emotional pain that you're carrying for someone else.'

'Yes, that's it. Well, I tried it. Because I really want to feel better. Anyway, I put down my mother's bags, I stuck with that, with her. It was still difficult to do, but after a few days, I found myself able to walk away and leave them there. I felt so proud of myself! Then I did it again, the next day, just to see, and I got so upset and angry with myself, as I was carrying them all again!'

'I started to cry. I was very frustrated. So then I imagined myself building a bonfire, a huge one, and I put all her bags onto it and I screamed at her, not really at her, but in my mind. I burned them all. I felt different then. I slept well that night. That was last Saturday.'

Niamh took a breath.

'I know this is weird. But on Sunday, the morning after I did the bonfire thing, Mum came into my bedroom and started yelling at me. She woke me up and threw my stuff onto the floor! Literally, she took books off my shelves and threw them on the floor, then swept everything off my desk onto the floor too. She went totally crazy. I couldn't believe it. I didn't recognise her. I was sitting up in the bed watching. I couldn't speak. It was terrible.'

'Wow, that's powerful,' said Marissa, not wanting to break Niamh's flow.

'Then she marched out of the room, leaving it in a mess. It took me ages to get up and clean it up. I went downstairs, worried she'd still be mad, but she was in the kitchen making herself some breakfast like nothing had happened. She even asked me if I wanted some. It was so weird.'

'And you didn't mention the books? Or ask her what was going on?'

'No, I was afraid she'd lose the plot again. But my anxiety started up around it. Ahh yes, that's why I looked for a meditation, and then I had the idea of finding an energy one. And that's when I was up all night. I couldn't settle down again but I feel fine now. What do you think happened?'

'Wow that's dramatic alright. I'm really glad you're feeling better now, and that your anxiety has settled. Let's look at this together. We did the work here, you putting down your mother's emotional pain, but when you left, you kept picking it up again, yes?'

Niamh nodded.

'Okay. So then you became frustrated because you'd put her emotional pain down, but some part of you would keep picking it up again, yes?'

'Yes. And when I got angry, I didn't pick it up, I burned it all in the fire. But it wasn't a real fire, was it?'

'At some level, energetically, it was.'

There was silence for a moment.

Then Niamh said, 'Maybe my mother felt it and got angry at me, because I wouldn't carry her emotional pain anymore. Only she got angry at me in real life.'

'And maybe she didn't understand why she was angry, and it was easier for her to just pretend it never happened,' suggested Marissa.

'So what should I do?'

They sat for a moment thinking about it.

'Well,' suggested Marissa, 'have you picked her emotional pain back up again since you burned it all in the fire?'

'No. I kept checking. When I looked this morning, I wasn't carrying any of it. I felt quite happy with myself, actually.'

'Interesting. Has your mother reacted again?'

'No, it was only that one time.'

'Maybe she's used to it now?'

'Maybe. Yes, that's probably it.'

'Then perhaps you don't need to do anything. Keep checking you've not taken it back on again, and she will settle, and so will you. Then you could look at who else's pain you're carrying.'

'Oh. That's a good idea.'

'And don't watch brand new YouTube meditation videos before going to bed!'

'I'll never do that again! Thanks, Marissa!'

After her next two clients, Christina and Kevin, Marissa got the bus back to her flat.

Christina seemed nice. Her relationship of five years had just ended and she really wanted a baby. She was feeling hopeless, as she thought time was ticking and she wouldn't find anyone. She wanted to talk about the possibility of bringing a baby up on her own. Marissa mostly listened, it was a refreshing change from the deep work she had been doing of late.

Kevin was having trouble at work. He was close to retirement age so he just wanted to stick it out for two more years. Marissa pinned down what it was that was giving him trouble, namely he could do the job well, but it was the relationships in the office that were difficult. There was a new manager and they were having communication issues. She had given him some coping strategies and new ways to talk with his colleague and he said he would try it and report back the following week. He was very grateful to get something new to try.

So many people are unhappy, so many people working through difficulties. I'm glad I'm able to help. She looked the window at people as the bus passed them by, wondering if every single one of them was going through some sort of issue, and if they were getting help or not. *Probably not getting help. I know I'm very reluctant to ask for help.*

'That's for sure.'

'Tori?'

No response.

'Oh, of course, she's in me now. Is that you, Thoth?'

No response.

'Bear?'

No response.

I never closed the space, or cleared myself!

She visualised herself in the centre of the room in Cabra, clapping her hands loudly and saying the closing space prayer. Then she brought her awareness back to her body on the bus and did a scan of herself. She didn't feel clear.

It was her stop so she got off the bus and walked the few minutes back to her flat. She let herself in. Tobermory took one look at her and ran away.

Oh. I guess I need to clear my own energy now.

She sat on the sofa and worked on her own energy. After a minute or two, Tobermory came back and sat up in her lap. He looked at her and brushed up against her, mewing.

I wonder whether he picks up on my energy. I bet he does. It feels like he's telling me I'm not finished working on me, yet. Ok, time to ask for help.

She sank back into the sofa and called on her angels, asking them to help her cleanse her energy. She imagined herself standing under a tropical waterfall, with crystal water spilling over her body, washing away any debris she might have picked up from her clients. *Or from the room itself, it still felt damp. What is Frances doing in there?!*

It was too late to text Eli, but she did it all the same.

Eli – Remember you said you had a friend that might have a room I could use? Is it still available?

It's a good time to finish in Cabra. Niamh's last session is next week, and I don't think Kevin or Christina need me, they just need to talk to someone. I could finish up in Cabra next week... Finish in Cabra – I'll have to sit with that. Maybe not yet. I really should give them proper notice.

She checked her text had sent, then got up to fix a snack for Tobermory and to make some toast and tea for herself.

A text came in from Matt:

Meet u at ur parents tmrow, working late – I'll go straight there. Looking forward 2 seeing U x

She smiled and texted him back: looking forward to seeing EWE TOO :-)

CHAPTER THIRTY FOUR

Sarah's London trip had been a resounding success. The office was buzzing as everyone rallied around her to celebrate her first European EDCL sale. Work ended early that day as Noreen bought everyone a drink at their local pub.

'To Sarah! Onwards and upwards!' she said as she raised her glass to Sarah, who turned beetroot red. Everyone was looking at her and smiling.

Come on, Sarah, own it.

Sarah straightened up and held her ground, then raised her glass in turn. 'Onwards and upwards!'

Everybody clapped. It was one of the best days at work for a long time.

Sarah wasn't going home anytime soon. Marissa said her goodbyes and left so she wouldn't be late for dinner. She ran through the raindrops, deciding not to get the bus as it wasn't such a heavy shower.

It was strange meeting Matt at her parents' house, rather than somewhere beforehand. And he was already there, very comfortable chatting away with Rose and Bernie at the dinner table drinking tea, and talking about their favourite restaurants.

'Hello, love,' all three of them said to Marissa at the same time. She did a double-take, and so did they. It was quite funny.

'Your hair is wet,' said Rose, 'go get a towel and dry it in the bathroom? You can use my hairdryer if you want, you know where it is.'

Marissa dried herself off and a few minutes later she had sat down at the table with the others.

'How was your day?' Matt asked with a grin. He was loving it.

Rose laughed, then said to Bernie, 'Come on, love, let them have a few moments to catch up with each other. You can help me take the brisket out of the oven.'

They disappeared into the kitchen, but not before Bernie had given Marissa a hug.

'This is so strange, I don't think I'll ever get used to it,' she whispered to Matt as he embraced her too.

'It is nice, though, isn't it?' he said. Marissa could see that he was tired. He'd had a long day at the garage. 'Your brother is on his way over,' he added, 'so all the family will be here.'

Marissa took a long look at him. '*You're* my family.'

Matt smiled as Rose came back in with the gravy boat. They could hear Bernie carving the meat with his new electric carving knife.

Then the doorbell rang, and Marissa got up. 'I'll get it,' she said.

Carol had trouble walking from the doorway into the kitchen. Eli supported her and she flopped down on the sofa.

'Hello, everyone! I feel like a whale. This baby is so big now.'

She looked radiant.

'When are you due?' asked Marissa, getting her a glass of water.

'Three weeks' time. It can't come soon enough.'

Eli helped her take off her jacket. She was wearing a dark brown dress which clung tightly to her body, emphasising her large pregnant belly. Her hair was shining, eyes were bright and her skin was completely clear. For all intents and purposes, pregnancy suited her. Bernie said as much.

'Except it's so bloody awkward,' she complained. 'Oooh, I've got those cramps again. What did they call them? Bramton Hicks?'

'Braxton Hicks. Just breathe, you'll be okay, they will pass in a minute.'

Carol's face darkened and she focused on her breath, then something lifted and she smiled.

'It's like a practice run for the real thing,' said Eli. 'We've already been to the doctor about it. He says there's nothing to worry about, it's normal.'

Marissa had never seen Eli so attentive to anyone. It was nice, and he was enjoying it.

'Yes, I remember those,' said Rose. 'It means your body is getting ready to give birth.' She looked Carol up and down. 'Three weeks, you say? I think this baby is like its father, impatient, She will be here sooner than you think.'

'Impatient? It can bloody wait, I'm not ready for it yet!' Eli chuckled nervously.

'Doesn't matter what *you* want, son, babies get whatever *they* want, when they want it.' Bernie looked at Marissa, then back to Eli. 'And not much changes, I must say.'

'Now, now, dear, they're much less demanding now they're grown up,' Rose soothed.

'I wouldn't say so. They can just get some stuff for themselves now.'

Eli and Carol left around 8:30, as Carol needed to go to bed. Bernie took out a bottle of port and offered Matt a glass, and he couldn't say 'no'. After the second glass of port, he and Marissa made their excuses, Matt flagged down a taxi (it was still raining) and they joined Sarah in town, to help her celebrate. She was already out clubbing.

They sat close together in the back seat of the taxi on the way into the city. The rain pelted down heavily on the taxi roof, it was good to be inside.

'We've not been clubbing together before,' said Marissa, following the path of a raindrop with her finger on the window as it trickled down to the bottom.

'There's lots of things we haven't done together yet,' said Matt, leaning in and kissing her on the cheek. 'I'm looking forward to all of it.'

The next day, Marissa was hung over. Too much vodka and dancing had given her a sore head, and sore feet, but she had really enjoyed herself, and Matt had liked her dancing style. She liked dancing with Matt. Merging with Tori had made her a little more *risqué*, and Sarah had noticed this, and with wide eyes clapped her on as she danced solo to one of the summer's hit songs.

It had thankfully stopped raining, so they had walked through town afterwards and got a kebab and chips, chatting and laughing together. Sarah didn't mind being the odd-one-out, she hadn't been chasing men that night although she had had plenty of offers.

'This feels good, I'm in control, and I can save myself for someone I like.'

"Someone who deserves you, like Vincent?" suggested Marissa.

"Maybe," said Sarah shyly, with a glimmer in her eye.

Marissa lay in bed while Matt made breakfast.

'Oh my head hurts!'

'You're just not used to the alcohol,' he said, laughing, as she played the damsel in distress, flinging one arm across her forehead with her hair fanned out on the pillow. 'Come on, you need a full Irish to snap out of it, but you've not got the ingredients here. I'll nip down the shop and get some. Can I use your key?'

'I swear my head *really* hurts!' Marissa protested. 'I'm not pretending.'

'Key?'

'In my bag,' she said, pointing to it on the desk.

Matt opened it and fished out the key.

'I should get one cut for you,' Marissa said, absentmindedly.

'Really?' said Matt.

'Well, why not? It's probably about time!'

He sat down on the bed and scratched his beard, thinking.

'Why? What's wrong with that?' she asked, dragging herself and her spinning head up into a sitting position.

'Well, it's just weird, that's all. I was going to ask you later today, when you were more awake, if you wanted the keys to my place. You got there first.'

Marissa laughed and pulled herself up to a sitting position. 'Well, okay! We can have each other's keys. It would be nice. I like the thought of you being able to let yourself in whenever you want to.'

'Me too. But my place is so far away from your work.'

'And mine from yours.'

They were silent for a moment, then they looked at each other.

I'm walking the path of non-attachment, but I do need to tread carefully. What would Tori do? She fizzled. *I am Tori!*

'Hey, Matt, I can't make any decision with a hangover and an empty stomach,' she said with a smile.

'Right on it,' he said, grinning back at her, grabbing his coat and running out of the door.

They spent a rainy day together, resting in her flat, watching videos and talking. They went out for an early movie, and got dinner at their favourite bistro.

At the back of Marissa's mind she hankered to journey and test her new consolidated strength, but Matt's presence, although it wasn't an intrusion, didn't give her space to do it. And she loved his company. *Just enjoy being with him for now. If we ever move in together, I'll have to figure out how to do this with him around. But right now, I can wait.*

Matt left Marissa's flat on Sunday around lunchtime. They were still avoiding the subject of moving in together, but agreed to each make a spare set of keys to swap, which felt like a good next step.

Marissa opened the back door and all the windows to let the air in. Sunshine spilled in too, seeping into every nook and crevice, it was nice after the few days of rain. She put on some music and danced while she cleaned the flat from top to bottom, stripped the bed and emptied out the hearth, setting a fire for next time.

Tobermory watched from his chair, flicking his tail slightly, his eyes on her every move. She turned to him and danced for him, then approached him and made as if to pick him up, but he yammered at her and shot out the back door.

'Ha, ha! Silly cat, doesn't like dancing.'

Once the flat was clean, fresh covers were on the bed and the laundry was in the bag for the laundrette, Marissa made a cup of strong coffee, grabbed her notebook and pen, and sat in the garden in the sun.

She flicked through the notebook pages as a cautious Tobermory returned and curled up by her feet. 'That's okay, kitty, no more dancing. For now, anyway.'

What am I looking for? She blushed, embarrassed by the immaturity of some of the things she found scribbled in there. *Have I changed that much?*

She found a page where she had drawn an image of her bear. *Bear! Where are you?* She felt outwards for him, but he was nowhere to be found. Something inside her felt reassured, though, as she sensed Thoth coming to speak to her.

'Power animals are different from spirit guides.'

She unfocused her eyes and reached out her senses to find him. *I can connect better when I set a landscape to speak in.*

Thoth stood there in her mind's eye, wearing a lab coat, with two beakers in his hand. He was looking at a chemistry experiment that was set up on a bench.

I've been here before...

Marissa looked around. Thoth's white lab coat transformed into a deep purple velvet cloak with gold symbols and constellations embedded into it. Ah yes, the alchemical laboratory. I've not been in here for a while.

'Oh, but you have. Tori plays in here all the time. Just because your human brain doesn't recognise or remember something doesn't mean your soul hasn't been here or done that. You are multidimensional, visiting many places at the same time. You're just not aware of all of it.'

'And Bear?'

'Yes, Bear was always a part of you. As soon as you became more confident in yourself, he merged with you. That's why you can't find him, it was part of that process.'

'I miss him. But I feel his strength in me. And Tori's strength too.'

'Stop categorising it or separating it in yourself, it is all you.'

Thoth pulled a small elaborate glass vial from a pocket on the inside of his cloak, opened the copper stopper and added one drop of the elixir to the experiment on the table. The liquid in the experiment turned black. He nodded with approval, stoppered the vial and pocketed it.

'We have been working on this experiment for many years,' he said. 'You and I. It looks like it's almost ready.'

H – Human?

'So my human form thought she'd met you for the first time only a few weeks ago, but we have known each other for eons?'

Thoth smiled. 'Yes, exactly. The human is a complex object wrapped in simplicity. It's a beautiful creation, but too attached to its identity. If you stepped away from your ego self, and from who you think you are, you would see how much more of you there is.'

Marissa watched as the black liquid started separating into seven different colours, one for each ray of the sun, and decanting into seven small vials, one for each colour.

'Now, it's nearly time. Isis wants to see you again. We will meet tonight in her chambers.'

Thoth put a stopper on each of the seven vials and collected them all together, then placed them into the pocket on the inside of his velvet cloak.

Marissa opened her eyes, sipped her coffee, felt the ground beneath her feet. Then she went inside.

That night, wrapped in fresh sheets, Tobermory by her side, Marissa journeyed in her sleep.

She was in a long corridor. Thick, heavy, ancient doors lined either side of it. All of them were locked.

She started pounding on one with her fists. 'Open, God dammit!'

The door opened inwards and she fell into a room. Isis was standing there, laughing at her.

'What an elegant entrance for my finest warrior! Had you forgotten you have a key?' She smiled and pointed at the ankh around her neck.

Marissa's hand went up to it. 'Ah, okay. No, I didn't realise.'

'Well, you still have some integrating to do. Come in.'

Marissa followed Isis to a long table which was covered in a white tablecloth and laid with lavish food on golden plates. Fruit spilled over large bowls, fish lay on platters, steaming bowls of grains were mixed with raisins and flatbreads, sauces and dips. Solid gold knives and forks and brushed cotton napkins lay ready nearby.

Isis sat the head of the long table and Marissa sat on her left. At her feet wound the large black jaguar that was Tobermory. He sat down and pressed his weight into Marissa's side, so she felt his presence at every moment.

'Your friends, they are very sweet, but do cause trouble,' said Isis, pouring herself a long drink from a tall decanter.

'Friends?'

Isis placed a white bowl with a golden rim in front of Marissa and poured water into it until it was completely full. Marissa looked into the bowl, and after a moment, images revealed themselves. She saw a red bird. She shrank.

'Ah. Those friends. What are they doing without me?'

She saw Terry in his circus regalia in the forest, the bird on his shoulder, walking quickly, then running, then running frantically, trying to outrun something that was terrifying them. He screamed.

Marissa's heart jumped and the images disappeared. 'Are they still there now? Are they okay?' Anxiety licked at the edges of her senses, but it didn't take her over. She breathed out and willed herself to be calm.

Isis didn't look pleased. 'They are not accomplished. They don't have the abilities, or the foresight. This was last night. I don't want to be always cleaning up your mess. You must speak with them.'

'Are they safe?'

'For now, yes, they are safe.'

Servants came and placed wine and plates of food in front of Isis and Marissa. There were murmurings and talking, the rest of the guests came into focus. She could see Thoth at the other end of the table. He raised a glass of red wine and nodded to her, smiled, then drank. Others were there too. She had a sense of scholars, warriors, wise people, some she knew but she wasn't sure where from. Most of them were completely new to her.

Isis tapped her fork on her glass and the talking stopped. 'He moves once more, through his many vessels.'

Isis waited for the table die down. 'All of you who have humans working with you can empower them with a drop of the elixir from the Ray they have pledged their allegiance to. Thoth will give you the elixirs now.'

Thoth stood, placing the seven small vials on the table. He spoke in an authoritative voice that Marissa had not heard before.

'Master El Morya, I bring to you Liquid Blue, the Power of God.'

A tall man rose from the table, went to Thoth, took the elixir, bowed in thanks and sat back down.

'Kuthumi, for you, Liquid Yellow, the Wisdom of God.'

A dignified dark-skinned man in elaborate clothing stood and went to Thoth, who handed him the yellow vial. He bowed and sat down.

'Liquid Pink, the Love of God, for Paul the Venetian.'

A pale, light-skinned, effeminate man wearing purple and gold brocade, took the pink vial, bowed and sat down.

'White, the Purity of God, for Serapis Bey.'

Serapis Bey's power filled the room as he stood up. He was more than eight feet tall and wearing white and gold Egyptian robes. He took the vial, placed it in an inside pocket, bowed, then returned to his place at the table.

Thoth continued, 'Liquid Green, the Truth of God, for Hilarion.'

Hilarion stood, another powerful masculine presence, wearing gold and green. He received the vial gratefully and sat back down.

'Purple, the Peace of God, for Lady Nada.'

Lady Nada appeared in beautiful peach-coloured robes, the essence of roses surrounding her. She took the vial and sat back down in her place.

'And Essence of Violet, the Freedom of God, for Saint Germain.'

Saint Germain stood to receive this vial, his long purple robes sparkled with glistening gold threads woven in.

Marissa recognised his energy.

Thank you for protecting me with your violet flame.

He nodded at her as he returned to his place, putting his hands in prayer position to acknowledge her gratitude.

'Strengthening the light that shines through humanity will help shatter the old grid and shift consciousness to create their new-dimensional light body,' Thoth said. 'We must hold space for Gaia as we build the fifth-dimensional light grid so humanity can rise during the Age of Aquarius.'

They all stood, and those with vials held them up to the light that came in through the ceiling, so that each vial threw colourful sparkles and orbs onto the wall. It felt very special and Marissa felt honoured to be present at such a moment.

Isis leaned in and whispered to her, 'This is nothing, you should have seen my coronation!'

A ripple went through Marissa's body. 'I think I was there.'

Isis raised an eyebrow. 'Yes, of course, you have merged, and it is almost complete. Well done. Excellent.'

All at the table were silent once more. They sat down. The food had disappeared and the tablecloth had been removed. The thick wooden table was now laid out for strategy and war. For the first time Marissa noticed there were weapons hanging on the wall.

Everybody's focus was now on the centre of the table, the images of of Terry and Finn running through the forest played in a loop. The panic on Terry's face was very upsetting to see.

'We must clear them from our path,' Thoth said. 'We cannot move forward until this is taken care of. They have been noticed, and tracked back to us. Particularly this one.'

Terry. *Marissa felt the seriousness in the room.* Oh, Terry! What have you done?

'I will go to them,' she said. 'It's my fault for involving them in the first place.'

There were murmurings, then Kuthumi said, 'That will be much appreciated. We cannot afford further setbacks. I offer my services to you if they are required.'

There was a feeling of assent in the room.

'Now go,' Thoth said. 'We all know what we need to do, and we will meet back here when the mission is complete.'

Mission?

Marissa woke in her bed, disoriented. It was 5am. 'Terry!'

She turned to look for Tobermory, but he wasn't there. She reached for the light and switched it on. Blurry-eyed, she felt for her phone and checked her texts. No, nothing there from anybody. And it was too early to text or call either Terry or Finn. She turned over and faced the window.

'It will be fine. I know it will.'

CHAPTER THIRTY FIVE

A few hours later Marissa had fallen into a deep sleep. Her phone was ringing, she woke up in a flutter and answered it, blurry eyed, not having seen the caller ID.

'Terry? Finn? Oh! Eli! Are you okay?'

'Carol's gone into labour. I'm a wreck!' She heard the mixture of excitement and nervousness in his voice. She sat up in the bed.

'Isn't it too early?'

'Oh, sorry! Did I wake you up?

'Yes, no, I mean for the baby. Too early for the baby.'

'Oh! Yes. I guess those Braxton Hicks were the real thing.'

'I hope it will all be okay.'

'Yeah, the doctors seem pretty confident the baby is a good size. Must be cos of Mum's chicken soup. How are you doing?'

'I'm okay. I'm awake now. Hey, shouldn't you be in with Carol? Holding her hand or something?'

'I am with her, I just needed to get out for a few minutes.' In a hushed tone Eli admitted, 'I'm phoning you as an excuse to get out of the labour ward. Nobody told me it would be this stressful, and I don't even have to give birth to it.'

'Would you like me to send Reiki to Carol and the baby? And maybe some to you too, for your stress levels?'

'Yes please, that would be great. Oh shit, got to go, it will be any minute now. I'll text you later.'

Marissa looked into the phone as Eli hung up, as if that would help her see him and Carol. *Wow, Eli is going to be a dad. I can't picture him pushing a baby in a pram.*

She closed her eyes and connected to Reiki, drew the opening time and space symbol and visualised Carol in a hospital bed holding a bundle of baby, smiling and at peace. *A girl! Lovely!* Marissa felt the

Reiki flowing from her to Carol, and then saw Eli in her mind's eye, sleeping in the chair beside them, hair matted from sweat, but a peaceful look on his face. *That's good.* She kept going for a while, then texted Matt.

Hey Carol has gone into labour, exciting!

He texted right back: Eli must be brickin it! He'll b a great dad. Have a good day! phone me later?

sure. love u xx

'No, move that over there, and I like the white rose here, and can you make the background a little more purple? Yes, I like that. That's great!'

'If you want to update the website yourself, here's how you do it.'

'Thanks, that would be so useful to learn.'

Marissa had met up with Hugh, Tim's brother, who was a web designer. They were sitting in a café and in exchange for lunch and a small fee, he was showing her how to buy a website domain and install WordPress. He helped her lay out the pages and links that she wanted, and she watched as he created a simple website for her to use as a shopfront for her healing practice.

'And this is the editor. It's just like a word processor. You can type in this window here, look, when you press "Update", then refresh that tab – yes, that's it – then you see the website is updated.'

'Oh! That's so easy!'

Hugh smiled. 'Here's how you add a picture, so you can do this yourself when you get back home. It's a good idea to have a photo of yourself on there so people have a face to put to your name.'

Marissa nodded. 'Good idea. Thank you so much. I didn't think this would be so easy!'

'I know. People get away with charging so much money for something that's really simple. It's so much cheaper this way – you own the domain name now, and the hosting package is cheaper than one of those monthly subscriptions. And you can change the website yourself if you need to. Tim said you'd need to learn everything, but it seems you've got the hang of it now.'

'Wait a minute, let me just try it once more. Click here to open the editor, change this text here, then press this button, and... Hey presto! The website is updated! Wow, brilliant.'

'The hard part is choosing the name and the colour scheme, but you've done that. It looks good!'

Marissa had thought long and hard about what domain to choose. Many of the websites for therapy had pretty names that didn't actually mean anything. She felt that if she chose a pretty name, she might change her mind a year or so down the road. She'd worked long and hard to become herself, and she felt more like herself now than before, so MarissaRosenthal.com felt exactly right for her. It would stand the test of time. She knew that the website and colours could change as she changed, but her name would be the same no matter what.

'The birth of my website, and my niece has just been born today, too! It's a good day for new beginnings!'

'Congratulations!' said Hugh, looking at his handiwork. 'This looks great and you know how to change it if you need to. But if you make a mistake or want something bigger, like adding a page or something, you can let me know. Or you can look for a tutorial on YouTube. Hey have you thought of setting up a YouTube channel? I could help you with that too, if you want.'

'Eh, no, I think the website is enough for me for now. Thanks, though.'

Marissa went to the hospital to visit Carol, the baby and Eli. The small private room was filled with flowers and Rose and Bernie were already there. It was a small space, she didn't want to stay long. She kissed Carol's forehead and left a small teddy bear in the cot for the baby, who was scooped up into a bundle on Rose's knee.

'Isn't she adorable?' said Rose.

'So, are you going to be "Gran" or "Granny"?' asked Marissa, smiling.

'I'll let the baby decide when she's old enough to speak,' said Rose, cooing to the baby, who was sleeping with her thumb stuck in her mouth. She looked very serious and her eyes were tightly shut.

There was a commotion at the door, then an older man and woman appeared, filling the doorframe. 'Carol! Aww, Henry! Would you look?' *That must be Carol's mother.*

This was only the third time Carol's parents had met with Eli's parents. Eli snapped awake and stood up straight away.

Carol's father came in and proffered his hand first to Eli, and then to Bernie, who took it and shook it enthusiastically. Marissa slid out from between all the people, mouthed 'Good luck, see you later,' to Eli and left.

She had three clients booked into her Reiki room for that evening. Marissa felt calm and collected, until she remembered the image Isis had showed her of Terry and Finn, and then she felt the anxiety lapping at her feet, threatening to build up and overwhelm her. She had tried to tune in to find them earlier that day, but to no avail, and worse, her texts to them had not been answered.

I really must get Finn's address, so I can check on him in person.

There were a few minutes before her first client arrived. Once she had set up the room, she connected in and felt the presence of Saint Germain.

'Oh, hello again! I feel closer to you now that I've actually met you.'

'You met me a long time ago. Haven't we been working together this long while?' The voice rippled through Marissa's body; she knew she wasn't making this up.

'Of course. I'm still catching up with myself, figuring it all out.'

Marissa opened her bottle of Saint Germain Aura Soma and smiled to herself as she poured a drop into her hand, rubbed her hands together then smoothed the energy of the room to neutralise anything that needed to go before her clients came.

'Thank you.'

She imagined she could see Saint Germain bowing to her in return.

The buzzer buzzed and Marissa walked through the main hall to meet her client. Standing there was a very tall and thin, somewhat dishevelled gentleman with blue tortoiseshell glasses and a pleasant demeanour.

'Thomas?'

'I'm here for the Reiki. Am I in the right place?'

'Yes. I'm Marissa, come on in.'

Marissa led Thomas to her Reiki room and invited him to hang his jacket on the hook on the back of the door. He had found her through her advert in the local shop.

'Please sit down. Have you had Reiki before?'

'Yes, a few years ago when I was staying at a hotel – in Sligo, I think it was. It was very pleasant. I found it very helpful in settling my stomach and sending me to sleep. I've been having sleeping problems lately, you see. I thought this could help me.'

Marissa nodded. 'Shall we set an intention for the session to help you sleep better?'

'Oh, what a good idea! Yes, please. Intention. Hmmm. I'd also like to have more energy and not lose my rag at work. I've got a short fuse these days, no idea why.'

'Grand. Let's spend a moment connecting to the intention. Good. Now if you'd like to take off your shoes and lie down up here on the plinth, the energies and I will do the rest.'

After about fifteen minutes, Thomas was snoring lightly. Marissa had her hands on his crown. She felt her guides standing behind her. *Who is here?* She got an image of Serapis Bey. He put his hands over her hands as she worked and the Reiki flowed in twice as fast. She became a little lightheaded and started giggling, just stopping herself in time before she disturbed her client.

Serapis Bey stepped back and moved to Thomas's feet, while Marissa held his head. Thomas took a deep breath in and out, stretched, and sank into a deeper relaxed state.

Marissa had a sudden flash of Terry and Finn and saw their panicked faces in her mind. She looked down at Thomas on the plinth. *He won't notice if I go looking for them now, will he?* She looked at the small clock. *It won't take me long. Okay, I'll just be a minute.*

She gathered herself, and focused her mind on the image Isis showed her, as uncomfortable as it felt, she wanted to use it to help her track them down. Thomas jumped under her Reiki hands, snapping her out of it. He settled again, and this time she didn't place her whole attention on Terry, but left some of it for Thomas. *There, that's better.*

The images of Terry were in soft focus now.

Thomas was stirring again. She realised every time she took her mind away from him, his body seemed to notice. *This isn't fair to Thomas, he's here for Reiki, so I'll give him Reiki. I'll try to phone Terry quickly in between sessions. There must be a reason he's coming in so strongly to me right now.*

The rest of the session with Thomas was slow, it felt like every minute lasted an hour. Marissa kept checking the time, Thomas didn't seem to notice. Then it was over. Thomas was very grateful and wanted to stay and talk, but Marissa had to close the session or she'd not have time to ease her mind.

Terry answered on the third ring.

'Oh, thank God you got the phone.'

'Marissa? You okay?' Terry's lilting voice sounded just fine.

'Yes, but I was worried about you. You never replied to my texts.'

'Oh? I didn't? I thought I did. Maybe I did in my head! I'm good, Had a great day in Cork, even went out for an afternoon pint with my dad. We've not done that in years.'

'Okay. I can't talk now, I've got a client coming. Just wanted to see if you were okay.'

'No idea why I wouldn't be okay, but okay, my dear, I'm perfectly fine, thank you. We must get together soon. Hey, I'll be up in Dublin at the weekend – do you want to meet up? Hey, how about we get Finn too, and try to journey again together?'

'I'll think about it, Terry. Right now it doesn't feel like a good idea.'

'Well, think about it. You know I'm keen to, anyway. Easier when we are in the room together. See ya for a pint either way, I hope.'

'Okay. Bye.'

'Byeeee!'

Marissa hung up the phone and the buzzer sounded for her next client almost right away. It was Valeria. *I like Valeria. It's nice to have a regular Reiki client.*

Valeria was wearing a beautiful summer dress, her hair was loose and she had a smile on her face.

'Hello again, Marissa. Last week I dreamed of my family, and I remembered what you told me, to go through the Earth and back up again to see them, And I did it! In my dream! They were so happy to see me, they had a party, and we laughed and cried together. It was so beautiful.'

She slipped her sandals off, slid up onto the plinth and lay down.

'They told me all of their news! It was so funny. I think my brain made up a lot of it, remembering stuff from letters and messages. A friend of mine I haven't seen in many years was also in my dream. She came to the party. I was so happy to see her, I cried. She cried too. I woke up from that dream feeling so loved and special.'

Marissa opened the space and began to work on Valeria as she continued to speak.

'Just like you said, I came back to Ireland the way I had travelled home, through the Earth and up from the land. I didn't feel separate, but can you check that I did it correctly?'

'Of course, I would be happy to check, and to make sure you didn't bring anyone back here with you this time!'

She lifted her head up from the pillow to look at Marissa. 'Ha, ha, yes, that might be what happened! Because my friend, the same exact one from my dream, she contacted me a few days later, saying she had had a dream about me and she needed to get in touch. After all this time! It must be coincidence, right?'

Valeria rested her head back down on the pillow once more.

'I wonder, though, did we have the dream together? The same dream? Because she said it took her a day to get my email address from my mother, so when she wrote to me, it was two days after her dream,'

Valeria sat up again in excitement, 'which means that she could have dreamed the same thing at exactly the same time as me! What do you think?'

Marissa smiled, waiting for Valeria to lie back down again, which she did. She had moved down to Valeria's feet and was debating whether to put her hands on her naked legs and feet or over them. *Summertime dresses and sandals, this has never been an issue before. Should I bring socks for my clients? Ah, I know, a blanket.* She got a light blanket and put it over Valeria's legs, then placed her hands heavily onto her feet, which were now under the blanket. That was good.

'I will have to think about that one, Valeria,' she said thoughtfully. 'I haven't experienced it myself, dreaming the same dream as somebody else, but I suppose, how would we know, unless we actually spoke about it with that person?'

'It is interesting, no?'

'Yes, indeed it is. What if we went into one another's dreams all the time, and we just didn't know it? That could be funny.'

'Maybe I'll try it sometime with my sister. We could decide to meet in our dreams and see if we actually could.'

'You could always try, but it might not work out the way you expect.' *You can meet in the same journey, so why not meet in a dream?*

Marissa carried on working, moving around Valeria's body while Valeria chatted enthusiastically. *Are you feeling the Reiki at all? Do you even need it? Sure, what does it matter, you're here, and it's nice to see you so happy compared to how you were when we first met.*

Valeria was still talking. 'It would make a great story, don't you think, friends meeting in their dreams? What would they talk about in dreams that they couldn't talk about in real life?'

Marissa thought about this. 'Maybe they are in love, and they've never told each other in real life because they've been too scared, but in the dream they feel free and don't know that it's more than just a dream.'

'Oh, how wonderful! That would make an incredible movie, wouldn't it? Two people who were too shy to speak to each other in real life, but were passionate lovers in their dreams! Ha, ha!'

'I would watch that movie for sure,' said Marissa with a smile, as she finished up the session.

Valeria was still in the throes of her imagination. 'Maybe they are not even friends in real life at all! They see each other in a café and remember the same dream, but they are too shy to speak! Or they are on the bus and they both remember what they did the night before, but they can't look each other in the face because they are afraid to say "hello"!'

Valeria took the small blanket off her legs and gracefully slid off the plinth, sliding her feet into her shoes.

'This was fun, Marissa, and I will have fun thinking about all the possibilities. Maybe I will ask my friend if she dreamed she went to the party.'

'Well, I suppose that's the only way you'll find out!' Marissa took the money. 'But, Valeria, many people don't remember their dreams, so she might have been in your dream, but she may not remember.'

'Ah, what an interesting layer to add to our movie! Maybe I will write it myself. I will put your name on the credits and invite you to the opening night.'

'I will be delighted to come.'

As she was about to leave, Valeria turned around, her face alight. 'I will accept the Oscar for best original screenplay and say "thank you" to Marissa and "thank you" to the Reiki!'

They both laughed and Valeria skipped out of the door.

For the first time since she had started working in her Reiki room, Marissa had a third client. She was a little concerned as it meant her next client was going to be a half-hour over her allocated time for the room. It was the only way she could fit her in.

It will be fine, she told herself, nobody comes in here after I do. And it's a woman, so I will feel safe even though it's so late.

She cleared the energy from Valeria's session and spread St Germain through her energy field, preparing for her next person.

That was fun, the movie idea. I wonder how many people have amazing ideas for stories and films and never write them, or nver get the money to make them. And yet there are so many poor-quality movies and books that get huge backing ... and sequels! It's almost as if they want to keep the good stuff from being made, in case it gives us bigger ideas for our lives.

The buzzer buzzed and she walked to the front door to meet her.

'I'm here for Reiki?'

'Sandy?'

'Yes, that's me.'

'Come on in.'

Sandy was a slim woman in her forties. Her hair was braided into a long French plait, she wore a white linen suit and was carrying a briefcase. Marissa walked her to her Reiki room and offered her some fresh water, which she accepted gratefully.

'I've been working late and not sleeping well,' she said. 'I thought the Reiki might help me unwind.'

'Are you planning to go straight to bed after the session?'

Sandy nodded.

'Is there any area on your body that you'd like me to focus on?' *Oh I've never asked that before, how interesting!*

'I've been having stomach issues, IBS and bloating. It just won't settle. I've been working crazy hours lately, though, and not having proper meals, just eating on the run, so that's probably not helping.'

Marissa smiled. 'Probably not. Shall we get started? Can you take off your shoes?'

She helped Sandy up onto the plinth.

'Don't worry if you fall asleep while I'm working on you,' she said. 'It's okay. All you have to do is relax.'

'That might be a problem,' said Sandy. 'I've not been able to relax in a long time.'

Marisa covered her with a blanket, drew the open time and space symbol and began to flow Reiki through her body and into her. She was in flow from having had two clients already, but soon she realised that the Reiki didn't seem to be penetrating Sandy's energy field at all. It was unusual to feel the Reiki had nowhere to go.

Even under the blanket Marissa could see that Sandy was stiff. She looked at her body in more detail. Sandy's shoulders were tight and high up towards her ears, her breathing was short and quick, and her feet were splayed in two different directions. Her knees had buckled and her pelvis didn't seem to be in the right position at all.

'Are you in pain?'

'Yes, I am. My body hurts everywhere.'

'Can we do some breathing together? Just to try to see if it helps?'

Sandy opened her eyes quizzically.

'It's just that your breathing is very short and shallow, and the Reiki doesn't seem to be going into you. It might be because you're so stressed, you're pushing it away.'

Sandy thought for a moment. 'Yes, maybe I am. I've been trying so hard to relax, and trying so hard to get my work done, I think it's taken its toll on my body. I have scoliosis, so that doesn't help either.'

Okay, that could explain why her body looks twisted up.

Marissa breathed long, deep and slow. 'Can you copy my breathing and breathe with me?'

'I'll try.'

Sandy made some effort to change her breathing pattern. Marissa was patient and they tried it for about ten minutes, but although she continued to flow Reiki through her own body, it didn't flow into Sandy's.

Then finally something in Sandy released, her body jumped and both women got a fright! They laughed, then Sandy's shoulders softened a little and her legs weren't as tight as before. But the Reiki was still not penetrating.

'I have an idea,' said Marissa, 'now that you're a little more relaxed. Can you do a visualisation for me?'

Sandy nodded her head. She was getting sleepy now and she looked ready for bed.

'Imagine you're a house, and you're boarded up. You've got boards on the windows, locks on the doors, and nobody is getting inside. Are you a big house or a small house?'

Sandy thought for a moment. 'I'm a small house.

'Good, okay. Now I'd like you to look around. What's there that's making you feel so unsafe you have to board up the windows and doors?'

'Oh? Well, nothing really.'

'Do you have a garden?'

Sandy thought again for a moment. 'Yes, I have a lovely front garden with roses growing around the front door, and the back garden is long and has decking, furniture and a small stream going through it at the back.'

'That sounds idyllic.'

'It's my parents' house actually. That's where I grew up. I always wanted a house like that. The stream makes it very special.'

Marissa felt something ease in Sandy's body as they spoke about the house.

'So ... the sun is out, in your mind's eye, and it's a beautiful, soft day. You want to air the house and let the light in, so you take the boards off the windows. Is that okay?'

Sandy nodded.

'Do you feel able to do that?'

'Yes, and I'm opening the back door, and now the front door too.'

Sandy sighed, a long sigh that came from somewhere deep within her. Her body soaked up the Reiki then, it was thirsty for it, pulling it from Marissa almost as quickly as she could give it. Marissa laughed.

'What's funny?'

'Your body craves the Reiki, but you weren't letting it in. You are now – that visualisation helped a lot.'

'Oh? That's interesting.'

'What is your house like now, in your mind?'

'It's strange – it's grown a little, got bigger. And a bit brighter too.'

'Ah, good. I'll work now for the last twenty minutes of the session, and you can relax. Let's see what happens.'

Sandy drifted off to sleep after five minutes of absorbing Reiki. Marissa was able to work on her stomach then, and as she placed hands over her belly, she had an image of her bowels being all twisted up too. She visualised them untwisting, telling them it was safe to untwist, and then Sandy's stomach made a large growling noise. *That's funny.*

Marissa kept going for another ten minutes, as, as Sandy seemed to need it. Then she closed the session. Sandy was fast asleep. It was a quarter to ten.

With a firm touch, Marissa rubbed Sandy's arms and legs to bring her back to the room.

Sandy was groggy, but she opened her eyes and smiled. 'That was wonderful,' she said, sitting up.

She did look much better. Marissa helped her off the plinth and over to the chair, where she could put her shoes back on.

'It's so late!' Sandy said apologetically. 'I'm sorry to keep you.'

'No, it's fine. It took a long time to get you started, and your body really needed the Reiki.'

'I feel a lot better now. Sandy stretched and rotated her shoulders. 'Yes, I do feel much better.'

She paid Marissa and got up to leave. 'Thank you.'

'Sandy, can I make a suggestion to you?'

'Sure.'

'Can you make time every evening to relax?'

'Oh, I do!'

'Yes, good. When you're relaxing, can you use the images we worked with tonight? The images of the house?'

'Oh?'

'Yes, because that really helped your body relax. When you took the boards off the windows and opened the back door to let the light in, your body took down some of its protection and armour and let the Reiki in. So in essence you were telling your body it was safe to relax. Keep going with it. Maybe it will help you sleep better.'

'That's a great idea, and I will certainly try it, and I will come back again too. Thanks, Marissa.' Sandy reached into her handbag, pulled out €20 and handed it to Marissa. 'Thank you so much. Here's a tip.'

Marissa took the money. It felt a bit strange to do so, but she decided to accept it gracefully. 'Thank you.' She walked Sandy to the door and closed it behind her. *I suppose I'd tip my hairdresser if they did a good job on my hair. Maybe this is the same thing.*

She packed up the plinth and put it under the stairs, shut down the sacred space and put her things into her pack, then walked home. It was after ten, still bright and she felt good. *I won't be so happy doing this in the winter when it's dark. Guess I'll have to get used to it, I do like being able to help people, and it's so interesting, each session is totally different.*

Oh! Carol! And the baby!

She got into her flat, put the kettle on and texted Eli.

Are you awake? How are you? How's baby & Carol?

Eli phoned. His voice was almost a whisper. 'It's all good. I'm home now, alone. Feels so strange to be a dad and not to have the baby here with me. I can't wait to go bring them home tomorrow.'

'Tomorrow! That's quick!'

'Yes, apparently it was an easy natural birth, though nothing about it looked easy to me. And they want the bed, so they're sending them home.'

'That's fabulous. I'll have to come and visit you all when you're all settled in.'

'Come tomorrow! I might need you!'

'Ha, ha! Do you have a name yet?'

'We really thought it was going to be a boy. So, no name yet, just "baby".'

'So exciting, a brand-new person in the world. New beginnings. I wonder what she will be like.'

'Me too! I hope I do a good job of being a dad.'

'I'm sure you'll be great.'

CHAPTER THIRTY SIX

Marissa had a hot shower to wash the energy of the client sessions off her body and help her unwind before going to bed. She got into bed in fresh pyjamas and thought about Terry and Finn. *I know Terry sounded good on the phone, but maybe some of his soul is stuck in the forest.. I'll go check.*

Tobermory leapt up onto her bed and onto her lap, looking straight at her.

'I'll be careful, I promise. What? Do you want to come too?'

Tobermory mewed and placed his two front paws on Marissa's chest, pushing her back into the bed with his head.

'You don't want me to go?'

Tobermory sat on her chest and started to purr.

'You're a strange cat altogether,' said Marissa with a grin. 'Just a quick check on them. Isis wanted me to stop them from interfering. In exactly what, though, I have no idea.'

She closed her eyes, slowed down her breath and brought her awareness into her heart. It had been three days since she had merged with Tori, yet so many things had happened to distract her from going back to release the souls in the jars.

I wonder if that's the universe keeping me from doing something it doesn't want me to do. Or maybe it's a test to see how much I mean it, am true to my word... Of course I'm true to my word. I might make mistakes, but don't we all?

She checked in with her body. It felt limber and light and she felt connected and strong. *It feels good to feel good. It makes such a change from before. I wonder what is different about me now that Tori and I have merged that allows me to feel this way?*

She took a few more breaths. *Sorry, Tobermory, I really need to check on Terry and Finn. It's been long enough, and Finn is terrible with texting, so I'll go check on him first.*

She visualised Finn, imagining the energy cords that ran between them – long thin cords of pale yellow energy going out from her sacral chakra into time and space... She visualised herself getting smaller, then walking along one of the energy cords towards Finn. It seemed very long, and then she lost touch with it. She felt groggy and a little damp. While the bigger part of herself was still there in the bed, some aspect of her was with Finn now, but she couldn't reach either of them.

Strange, where is he? And where did that part of me go? Now I really need to go and find him and get that part of myself back too. What would Tori do? It feels as if I'm separating from her too. She closed her eyes again and visualised herself merging once more with Tori.

She imagined her armour, she imagined herself holding a weapon, some sort of javelin. She saw herself jumping onto that energy cord and sliding down it as if it was a waterslide.

Down and down she went. It corkscrewed around and she followed it until she was spat out onto a forest floor, landing like a cat on all fours.

There on the ground she saw a round shield. She picked it up, felt the weight of it in her hand. She felt as though she was now ready for battle. Are we at war?

Senses alert, she walked through the forest looking for either Finn-as-man, or Finn-as-bird. A small blob of orange yellow light bobbed out from the glades, circled around her, then merged with her. A part of myself coming back... But there's no sign of Finn.

As she moved through a thicket, she felt eyes on her from behind the bushes and trees. She hunkered down, then had the idea of whistling, and lo and behold, bounding out of the bush came her large black jaguar with a golden collar around its neck. She smiled as it started to run ahead, then she ran alongside it, following the pull of her intuition.

They were running for what felt like a long time. They ran out of the forest and onto a track, then into a deserted white city. The buildings were a mix of old and new, tower blocks and pantheons. Most of them were ruined, crumbling. They reminded Marissa of ancient Greece, but there was something distorted about the architecture, it was sinister. As she walked she studied her surroundings and saw gargoyles in each of the older style buildings. Headless statues lined the streets. The large and important buildings seemed to have been burned down, or hit by incendiary devices.

In a wide space which could have been a market square, Marissa saw a large red bird with a black breast shackled to a post. It was perching on a beam, its feathers were dishevelled as if it had stopped caring about its appearance, and it looked exhausted. A thick black ring was welded around one of its ankles; attached to that was a heavy chain which was pinned to a metal box, which was screwed into the post below. That bird wasn't going anywhere soon, and it knew it. The fight had completely gone out of it.

Marissa approached it cautiously, so not to upset it, and looked into its eyes. She got a fright, its eyes looked human. She wasn't sure if it was Finn, it had the look of someone who was depressed, who had lost hope. There was hardly any soul essence there at all. Depression is soul loss?

Marissa focused on the ring clamped tight around the bird's leg. The javelin was no good, she needed something smaller to cut through it. She patted herself down looking for her shamanic knife.

Tori must have some kind of knife on her, come on.

She felt for pockets and found one on her hip. There was an oblong disk inside with a button in the centre. She pulled it out and pressed the button, and a hooked knife popped out. Ah, perfect.

She approached the bird and it pulled back, raising its wings to scare her off.

'Finn? Is this you? It's me, Marissa.'

Was this Finn, or not? Either way, its resolve withered, its wings came down and it cocked its head on one side.

Maybe it isn't Finn. I'll release it anyway.

Marissa made clicking and tutting noises to soothe the bird as she looked at the ring and tried to figure out how to cut it off. The bird settled and began to chitter chatter and sway on its feet.

Then she discovered there was a lock on the back of the clip. Ah, great. *She was able to pick it open with the point of the knife.*

The red bird, now free, grew to three times its previous size, twisted into itself and transformed into a large vulture with nasty eyes that looked accusingly at her.

Marissa's hackles went up and she took a big step backwards, clutching her shield, preparing to defend herself if it was to attack.

In a loud, cawing, scraping voice, the bird crowed, 'Pieces of eight, pieces of eight, you are trespassing. It is not your place to be here. Go now, before we come and get you.'

Marissa started. That sounds familiar, where have I heard that before?

The bird repeated itself loudly. 'Go now, before we come and get you.'

Then she heard a deep cackling laugh. 'We come and get you, we come and get you, we come and get you...'

She was filled with terror.

Everything went black.

Dazed and confused, Marissa rubbed her eyes. The room was dark now, she switched on the light. She made the Reiki power symbol above her bed, then hopped out and got her medicine bundle and her drum, just to have them close by.

'Pieces of eight, pieces of eight? What is that, and where do I remember it from?' She lay back in the warm bed, keeping the light on, trying to sort out her memories. Tobermory, still sleeping, pressed against her.

I should visit my memory library! Of course. Marissa kept her eyes open as she dropped down into her heart and went to the tree.

The tree raised a sleepy eyelid then one of its branches turned into an arm and reached up into a higher branch, pulling down a book of memories. It opened to a page where Marissa could see herself in Clifden, in the room with Terry, going on a journey with him, for him, but not telling him all that she saw.

'Ah yes, of course, then we turned into mermaids. I told him about the mermaids, but I never told him about the vulture. And here it is, almost a year later. It's a warning. But for me, or for him?'

She turned to the tree, but it had already vanished.

She was wide awake now. It was after midnight and she needed some air. She got out of bed and threw on her cardigan and slippers, opened the back door, brushed off her deckchair and sat down. Tobermory leapt up onto the wall and was gone into the night.

I must be okay if he's not sticking around.

An echo of the malevolent laughter of the demon rippled through her body, but she didn't shrink from it. *It's a memory, he isn't here. And I must be getting closer if he's laughing at me. If that wasn't Finn, was it a decoy? Or was it Finn? It's too confusing.*

She looked up at the constellations. The night was partially cloudy and as usual it was difficult to see the stars with all the light pollution from the city. *If this was Clifden then I could see the sky. Clifden! Maybe...*

She closed her eyes and imagined herself at Clifden.

She stood outside the door of the big house, wearing her pyjamas and cardigan. She walked around the back and found Finn sitting by the fire pit, crying. Her heart opened, and relief flooded through her body.

'Ah, there you are!'

Finn looked up at her gratefully. 'I've been here for days!'

'But you texted me?' This must be a missing soul piece.

This must be a missing soul piece.

She sat down beside Finn and he gathered himself together.

'You were right,' he said. 'This is too big for us, we can't just mess about because we feel like it. I'm out now, I won't be doing any of this again.'

She wanted to give him a hug, he looked so like a little lost boy. She smiled and he sniffed and wiped his nose and tears on his sleeve.

'I can help you get home again, if you want?'

'Yes, please. It took all my strength to get here. I came looking for you and Terry. But you weren't here. Until now.' He sighed, then in a lower voice, cracking with emotion, he said, 'I tried everything to get home, but I couldn't figure out how. I was hoping someone would find me. Thanks, Marissa.'

She reached out and took his hand, and he gave it to her. They sat together, holding hands for a moment in silence. And as she looked at him, she noticed something drifting in and out of focus in his energy field, in his hip. It looked metallic, and was possibly the reason why he was stuck here.

'Finn, I think I need to do some energy work on you before you can go home. There's something not right. You must have picked up something on your travels.'

She had an image then, of a different Finn talking to her, as if he was speaking to her on the phone. 'Yes, you're right. I didn't want to bring this intrusion home with me. My sister, she's very sensitive to energy. I also didn't want that thing, you know, him, to find her. I kept this part of myself here, but I didn't know what to do next.'

Ah, that makes more sense. Finn is well able to get home himself.

She looked at him. 'Do I have your permission to work on you?'

'Okay,' he said.

'I feel I need to do an extraction on you right here. Can you lie down on the grass?'

Finn lay down. Marissa didn't have her pendulum or any of her tools with her. Oh well, this is a journey, so I can use my hand as the pendulum. Handy! Ha, ha!

She moved her hand up and down over Finn's body and was drawn back to his hip, where she had seen the metallic thing rippling earlier. It was right inside his body, deep into his pelvis. She sat there looking through the layers of his being into the wounded part.

This is a journey, so I can see what it is, show me. Show me.

The layer that represented Finn's jeans dissolved away around the wounded area so she could see his left hip bone. There was a metallic object protruding out of it. The skin around it was rotting, black, bruised and discoloured. She looked deeper, through his skin, following the metallic object. It looked like part of an anvil. She could see now that it was wedged deeply into his pelvis. It looked as if it had been hammered in. She recoiled. It didn't bear thinking about.

'It hurts,' said Finn apologetically. 'Hurts more now that you're looking at it.' He tried a grin, but it was more of a grimace. 'I knew there was something wrong, but didn't know exactly what it was.'

'Okay,' said Marissa. It looked so awful she really wanted to cry, but she knew she couldn't work on Finn when she felt that way. She shifted into counselling mode, where she was able to hold space for anything that the client might bring up without feeling it herself, making herself larger for emotions to have plenty of space to rush in and out without affecting her.

There, that's better. Now I can refocus on the work at hand.

She examined Finn's body again, and after a moment she asked it directly, 'Is there anything more I need to see?'

A few more bits and scraps of black metal appeared throughout his body, some deep inside, some protruding through skin. Finn shivered at the sight of them.

Marissa began by plucking out the smaller protruding bits. She placed them on the ground beside her. They melded together like mercury, forming a metallic rock.

She looked at it, then willed it to turn into a magnet, which it did. She then picked it up and ran it over Finn's body, using it to pull out all the shards and shrapnel. The magnet enlarged slightly each time a piece of metal made contact with it. She avoided his hip altogether.

Then she was finished, all was left was the larger piece in his pelvis. It was enmeshed so deeply into his pelvic bone she could see that the bone had already started to grow around it and she didn't want to just pull it out the way she had done with the other pieces.

She placed the magnet down on the ground. It didn't seem to be attracted to the piece in the hip bone anyway.

How do I take this out without hurting him? Can one of my guides come and help me?

She immediately felt strong presences behind her. She turned and there were El Moyra, Kuthumi and Serapis Bey. All of them arriving at once took her by surprise.

'Hi, guys! Ha, ha!'

They all smiled.

'Can you help me with Finn?'

They raised up the small elixirs that Thoth had given to them. 'We can use these to help your friend,' said El Moyra.

'Finn is a light bearer?'

They nodded.

'Wow, that's so interesting!'

Kuthumi spoke. 'One drop of this elixir from each of us onto the metal will melt it down, then his body can heal itself. This is a representation of him, it will hurt his incarnation only slightly. We will each place a drop on the metal, if you remove yourself.'

Marissa nodded. 'Thank you.'

She stood out of the way and each master placed one drop from their personal vials onto the metal intrusion in Finn's pelvis. Finn didn't seem to notice the masters, but he did appear to feel the effects of the droplets. His body stiffened and his left leg jerked each time a droplet fell on him.

'How come he can't see you?'

Serapis Bey said, 'We are at a frequency you have access to, but he does not.'

Another mystery unveiled.

The masters stepped back from Finn and the four of them watched as the three drops of liquid merged, blended, then infused into the metal in his hip. The metal started to hiss. It changed colour, turning mustard and green, muddy brown, then suddenly white, then red, and then it dissolved completely, appearing to burn a hole in Finn's body. The magnet on the ground beside him also dissolved completely. There was nothing left of that harmful material, whatever it was.

Finn's skin looked burned and bloody and there was a large hole where most of his pelvis used to be. Marissa was holding her breath, not knowing what to do next, when Lady Nada appeared, stepping in from behind the group. She smiled at Marissa, then bent down, placing both of her hands over the hole in Finn's pelvis. Marissa watched as the bone grew back, the organs within healed, the blood vessels joined back up and the muscle plumped up healthy and pink. Then Finn's skin closed over, unscarred and unblemished, then his jeans closed over that. He was in perfect health once more.

'Thank you so much,' said Marissa. Grateful tears ran down her face.

Lady Nada stepped back, and the four masters smiled at her, acknowledging her gratitude.

Kuthumi spoke once more. 'We are here to help. We are at your service. We didn't have time to talk with you earlier; the Great Goddess is always in such a rush, always so busy. But it is our pleasure to come anytime, and aid you when needed.'

Marissa smiled gratefully and the four beings of light nodded in thanks, became transparent and disappeared.

Finn was moving around on the ground, making noises.

'Hey, hey, take it easy, that was a big operation.'

He grimaced, then pulled himself up onto his elbows and raised his head off the ground. He looked down at his body and wiggled his hips. 'That feels so much better. Thanks, Marissa. You're a powerful healer.'

'I had quite a bit of help.' She smiled.

'I think I could go home by myself now,' he said, getting up from the ground.

'Let me just check you once more, okay? Just to be sure.'

She did a scan of his body with her hand once again as a pendulum.

'This is fun, I like doing it this way,' she said, flexing her fingers. 'It means I'll always have my pendulum with me!'

Finn laughed. 'You're always wanting to be at the ready. Thanks, Marissa, I really appreciate you coming to find me.'

He gave her a hug then disappeared.

Marissa felt a wide empty space where there had been several very powerful beings of light only a few moments ago. She took some time to consolidate herself. It had been an emotional experience, but one, thankfully, that had turned out in her favour.

I keep drifting in and out of feeling like I'm Tori. I'm more Marissa than Tori. Maybe I should just stop worrying about it. Ahh, now I understand what Thoth meant. Either way, it doesn't matter, she's me and I am her, doesn't matter what I call myself, it's all me. *Something inside her heart, eased.*

The house felt particularly peaceful. She had always liked Clifden, especially around the fire pit.

And there I was thinking I'd never be back here again! Ha, ha!

She looked up at the back of the house and saw a spirit family looking out of the window at her, smiling. She waved at them and they waved back. I guess not everybody wants to be rescued.

She checked her own energy field, then allowed all the images to dissolve away behind her eyes.

Then she was home, in her deckchair, outside in her courtyard. She shivered. It was cold. She opened her eyes. The sun was coming up.

'Oh my God, I was gone all night!'

She went inside and checked her phone. It was 5am.

I can still grab a couple of hours' sleep before I have to get up for work.

CHAPTER THIRTY SEVEN

Marissa was bleary-eyed while grabbing her third coffee of the morning. Her body felt heavy and it was difficult to focus, but going into the office had been worth it. Finn had written a long text to the group chat that morning. She knew now for a fact that he was safe, and his text was the validation she needed.

Hi guys, sorry I didn't text u. I lost 2 days of my life somewhere, don't know where. I'm ok, feel better 2day, but not going 2 do this again, srry. Gud luck with soul cages, let me no how it goes 4u. Finn.

The relief she felt when that text came in was so great, her head was spinning.

I knew there was something wrong. It's good now, it's clear, he's okay and I can move on.

But Terry wasn't so happy. He had written back straight away:

Oh. At least yr ok. Mind urself.

Marissa could pick up the disappointment behind his words.

I want to be clear this is over now.

That's fair enough Finn, thank u for doing all you did 2 help, its best this way.

Cheers M. Maybe get a pint together soon – F

There was no reply from Terry. It stuck like a piece of food in her gut, not hearing from him. His emotional state hung around her all morning like a bad smell. She knew how he was feeling, she didn't need further validation around that.

After lunch she went back to her desk, but she couldn't focus. Even after all the fresh air and food, she wanted to go to sleep. Her bones felt heavy. She sent an email to Sarah:

Sorry, I'm not well. I need to go home and sleep it off, whatever this is.

Sarah came around to her desk right away.

'Are you okay? What's wrong?'

Marissa looked up from the desk. 'I just didn't sleep last night, probably the last few nights, and need to catch up with myself. I'll be grand tomorrow.'

'Okay, no problem, I was worried in case, you know, you were having a panic attack or something. It's not been long since you've been back from Clifden and we haven't had a chance to catch up.' She turned to go, then changed her mind. 'Oh, by the way, congrats on being an aunty! Very cool. Do they have a name yet?'

'I think they're going with Leia. Not sure how they'll spell it, though.'

'Oh, that's a lovely name!'

Marissa smiled. 'Eli always was a *Star Wars* fan. As long as his next child isn't called Chewy!'

'*Star Wars*? Never seen it!'

'Really? You really should, you know.' Marissa smiled. 'So it's okay for me to go home?'

'Yes, of course. We really should make some time to catch up. I'm so busy now with work, though. I've almost finished the first part of my management diploma, I just need to finish the assignment and I'll have a management certificate!'

'Wow. Amazing woman. Congratulations!'

'Go home!'

Marissa got home by 3 o'clock and climbed dutifully into bed. But she was awake now. It had just been the soporific office environment that had been putting her to sleep. Or maybe it had been Terry's emotional state. Either way, the journey home on the bus had woken her up and the excess caffeine of the day had finally kicked in. So now she was wide awake and had a few hours before Matt arrived. They were going to visit Carol and Eli to see the baby, with no parental interruptions this time – *I need to get used to there being three of them!* – and Matt wanted them to go to their favourite bistro for dinner afterwards.

She got up, washed her face, and went into the living room. *Something isn't closed, I need to travel. What do I need to do? I know, I'll go and see the goddess, and maybe the masters again, to get to know them better. They'll know what to do.*

That felt good. She got comfortable on the sofa, holding her medicine bundle on her lap and placing her drum beside her. When she was ready, she closed her eyes.

There was a loud, irregular dripping noise. *That's the tap in the kitchen. No, I can't travel with that annoying me.*

She got up, tightened the faucet and sat back down again.

Now I'm too cold.

She got up, found a throw and put it over her shoulders.

When she sat down again, her phone buzzed. It was Eli, asking if they could bring some bread, milk and Hob Nobs with them when they came over. She agreed, then put her phone on silent.

She sighed, relaxed her body and sank into the sofa, feeling it supporting her.

Yes, okay, now I can go.

Then there was a knock at the door.

'Jesus Christ! What is going on?'

She waited for the person at the door to leave, but the knocking persisted, so she put her bundle and drum aside and got up to answer it. It was Michelle from upstairs.

'Hi! Sorry to bother you. I'm away tonight for a week. I know it's sudden like, but there was a cancellation on a sun holiday. Can you look after my flat?'

Marissa smiled. 'Sure, I've got the keys. No problem.'

'Ah, you're a star. And if I freak out about the immersion, will you remind me I've turned it off?'

'Ha, ha! Of course. Go, have fun.'

Once Michelle had left, Marissa stood with her back to the door. *What do I need to do to clear the energy of my flat so that I won't be disturbed again?* She looked at the time. *I need about forty minutes so I can journey, and then be back in time for Matt.*

She paused for a moment, then connected to the Reiki light and drew it down. She waited to feel it flood through her body, then she Reiki-ed the floor, ceiling and walls, her bedroom and the bathroom too, then stopped. She felt into the energy of the room. It felt good, and she felt a little better too. She drew the power symbol in the centre of the room and imagined it getting bigger until it enveloped the entire flat. Then she sat down on the sofa and breathed for a few moments, centring herself.

She felt a nudge to draw a card – two cards, one from each pack. *It's been a while, so why not?* She reached in under the table, brought out both packs and opened them up. As she shuffled the cards from the shamanic oracle, a card jumped out of the pack and fell on the floor. She picked it up. *Vulture – Purification.* Her heart leapt to see the vulture again. He was bald, and he didn't seem evil, he seemed purposeful. *I suppose someone has to do that work. Maybe he's not so bad after all? I need to know more.* She got the booklet from the box and read the text:

> *Vultures can dissolve and transform many poisons. They are the totem of Nekbet, Egyptian goddess of nature, childbirth, death and rebirth. Your difficulties are temporary, yet essential for a greater purpose. Trust Vulture to guide you through this time.*

These cards never cease to amaze me. 'Egyptian' – is the vulture related to Isis? Maybe he was sent by her? As scary as that vulture was in my journey, the card tells me what I needed to hear today. 'Temporary yet essential' difficulties – that makes them easier to manage.

She pulled out the angel cards. *I wonder who I'll get with the angel cards, maybe Metatron?* She shuffled the cards, cut and drew a card. Raziel – Mysteries. *Oh! Hi Raziel. Well, I have learned a lot lately. Yes, I suppose it fits.*

Marissa took a moment to connect to Archangel Raziel. She felt a large presence sweep in and surround her. Then there was a loud thump and a tapping noise, and she jumped in her chair with fright and opened her eyes. Tobermory was at the window, pawing to get in.

She looked at her phone. It was getting late. *Matt will be here soon, there really isn't enough time for a journey now. All that preparation and I just can't journey. So many distractions! Maybe I'm not supposed to journey now.*

The large angelic presence dissolved away. She heaved herself up off the sofa and let the cat in. *I need some tea.*

Kettle on, Marissa sighed and switched her phone back on too, giving up trying to journey. *Probably just as well. I'm so tired still from last night.*

As soon as her phone found the network, it rang. It was Matt.

'Hi! I couldn't wait to see you. I've been trying to phone you - I'm almost at your flat – are you home yet?'

'Actually, yes, I've been home for the last few hours. I was tired, so I left work early.'

'Oh? Why were you tired? Are you okay?'

'Yeah, I just couldn't sleep. I'm fine.'

'Okay. I'll see you soon. Can I stay tonight?'

Marissa smiled. 'That would be lovely, yes.'

'Great, see you in a few!'

Marissa couldn't journey with Matt there, she was too easily distracted and she knew it. *It's not meant to be today, is it? I'm just going to have to phone Terry. This is wrecking my head.*

He picked up on the second ring.

'Girl, it took you long enough.'

'Hi, Terry, I meant to call you earlier...'

'And I meant to call you, too. We're good. You and me. Hey, listen, I'm in Dublin at the weekend, let's meet on Saturday afternoon after my shoot. Are you free? We should regroup. I've not felt right since the last journey, and now that Finn's out, well, we need a new plan.'

Marissa checked her diary. Meeting him face to face was the best plan. 'Saturday's perfect. Come to my place and we can figure it all out.'

'Okay, honey, great. I've got to go. See you soon, kiss, kiss.'

Terry hung up the phone, and there was Matt at the door. *Life is moving fast, that's for sure.*

Matt had bought a small teddy bear for new-borns and had it wrapped in pink paper with a little yellow bow. They gave it to

Eli with bread and milk, and two packets of Hob Nobs, one with chocolate and one without.

Eli looked exhausted but happy. 'Hey, you've come at a good time, it's quiet in da house. Thanks for the stuff. I'll let Carol open the present. Come in!'

Carol was lying on the sofa with the sleeping baby on her chest. 'Shh,' she said as they entered the room.

'Ohmygosh! Isn't she tiny? And so cute!' Marissa went over to see Leia.

'What a beautiful little thing,' said Matt.

'She didn't feel very small when she was coming out of me,' said Carol in hushed tones, with her eyes still closed.

The baby was wearing a white babygro and was swaddled tightly in a blanket.

'Can she breathe okay, wrapped so tight?'

'I know, it seems very tight, doesn't it? Rose did it before she left, told me the baby would sleep better if she was wrapped like that. She's been quiet, so I'm leaving her in it!'

Carol made to sit up.

'No!' said Marissa. 'Don't get up, rest. You both must be exhausted.'

Matt went into the kitchen to help Eli. They brought out some tea and leftover lemon cake that Carol's mother had made.

'All the parentals were here,' said Eli as he placed the cake down on the table. 'It got quite tiresome, but at least they all behaved themselves.'

The cups knocked off the spoons and knife, making a clattering sound. The baby stirred. Everybody froze, but she didn't wake up.

Eli smiled. 'I'm still getting used to this.'

'It's only been a few hours,' said Matt in a fractionally louder voice than the others. Carol and Eli seemed worried, but again, the baby didn't seem bothered. 'They sleep through anything if they're really sleeping, don't be so worried,' Matt said. 'And I think they like to hear people's voices in the background, sure she's been hearing you guys talking the whole time she was in Carol's tummy. It's comforting.'

He helped himself to a generous slice of cake, then changed his mind and handed it to Marissa, who took it gratefully and sat on the sofa.

Eli pulled up a dining-room chair and joined them, while Matt cut another slice of cake for himself.

'How do you know so much about babies?' Eli asked, almost afraid to use his normal voice.

'My sister has three,' Matt said to Eli and Carol in his normal voice, 'almost all grown up now. I helped her for a while when they were babies. They're not as fragile as you think. You won't break her, I promise.' He smiled, and the tension was broken.

'We have heaps of food, do you want to stay for dinner too?' asked Carol. She began stroking the baby's back. The baby sighed and wiggled a little, and went into a deeper sleep.

Matt winked at Carol and she smiled. She began to reorganise herself on the sofa so she could be more comfortable.

'Thanks,' said Marissa, 'but we have a reservation at the bistro. Mmm, this cake is good!'

'It's my favourite,' said Carol, gently lifting the baby off her chest while continuing to stroke her back. She sat up slowly. 'Ouch, it still hurts. I had to get three stitches.'

'Do you want tea?' asked Eli.

She nodded. Eli poured her some, and gently took the baby from her and held her in the crook of his arm, smiling proudly.

'She's cool, isn't she?'

Marissa peered into the baby's face. 'Yes, very cool. Don't ask me who she looks like, though, she looks just like a baby to me.'

Eli laughed. 'I suppose the good thing about having her early is that I won't have to dash out at 3am looking for chopped herring!'

Carol stuck her tongue out. 'That was only the one time, and you were the one who suggested it.'

Eli blushed. 'Aww, go on. It was funny, though.'

Matt grinned. 'When Gwen was pregnant, she wanted anchovies. She doesn't like them normally, but with every pregnancy she needed to have them when she was coming close to term.'

'Bodies are amazing,' said Marissa. 'They know what they need.'

'I suppose so,' said Carol, 'though I don't know why they'd need anchovies, or chopped herring!'

'Protein from the fish? Or salt?' suggested Matt. 'Leia is a great name. *Star Wars*?'

Eli nodded.

'I just like the name,' said Carol with a smile. She was sitting up properly now, she took the last slice of cake for herself.

'Eli, while we're here,' Marissa said, 'I know this is off-topic, but did you ever manage to speak to your friend about that therapy room? For me?'

'Oh no, I never did. Was too busy! But I'll get around to it over the next few days. Nice website, by the way. I took a look at it. Well done.'

'Thanks. Hugh helped me, Tim's brother. Tim from work. He taught me how to update it too. He was very helpful.'

'You want a new room?' asked Matt.

'Yes. Sorry I didn't tell you before. I think it's time. There's someone in the room in Cabra ahead of me – Frances – and the energy is kind of damp in there after she's finished. I never have enough time now to clear the energy. And Sam, well, he's fixed in the other space till the end of the year. I thought I'd see if I could get a new space. Just for me. Especially now that I can offer shamanic healing sessions as well.'

Matt looked impressed. 'Great idea. Yes, you have a lot to offer now.'

'Clearing energy, though, what's that?' asked Carol, looking at Eli with the baby. He was cooing and preening with Leia in his arms. She smiled.

'Oh, yes, well, I've come to learn that my clients discard heavy emotional energy,' Marissa explained. 'Even the ones that just come for counselling - that's why they come to counselling really, to release their emotions. But the emotions stay in the room after the clients leave, and I feel them. After a while, the room needs to be cleared out. Nobody ever taught me that in college, but I do find that it's becoming a very important part of what I do.'

Carol seemed interested. 'What's a heavy emotion?'

Marissa was delighted to talk about her work. 'An emotion like sadness, grief or anger. Emotions are energy really, but they do hang around, and they are messy too.'

'I'd imagine so.' Carol said. 'How about this room? Does it feel like it needs to be cleared?'

Marissa tuned into it. 'Actually, it does. It feels like there are about 20 people in here!'

Carol smiled. 'With all the parents coming and going, I've noticed the room feels stuffy or something, even after they've gone.'

'Yes, that could be it, alright. Stuffy! Do you want me to clear the room for you now?'

Eli looked up at Marissa. 'Are you going to use your Reiki?'

'Hey! I sent it to you to help you calm down during the birth when you phoned me in a panic, remember?'

Carol turned to Eli. 'You were on the phone to your sister while I was giving birth to our baby?'

Eli blushed.

'Was he really in a panic?' Carol asked Marissa quietly with a smile.

She nodded in response. Eli looked caught out.

'I think it's sweet, actually,' said Carol to Eli, who seemed relieved. 'And much better than taking an "urgent business call" in the middle of my labour.'

'I did my best.'

'You did. It's all good.'

Eli changed the subject. 'So, you want a new room to work from – how many days a week were you thinking of taking it for?'

'Maybe two or three days a week? As much as I love Sarah and what she's doing now at work, they don't really need me there all the time and she has her own personal assistant. I could reduce my days and she wouldn't miss me too much. That would give me a good stretch of time in a healing room.'

'What days were you thinking of?' asked Eli.

'I already take off Mondays, so maybe Fridays too? Then I'd be in the office Tuesday, Wednesday and Thursday and could use my room Friday Saturday Sunday and Monday. I could have clients on the weekend! That would be great, if I could manage it, and of course, if Noreen was okay with it.'

Eli raised an eyebrow. 'You *know* Noreen will be okay with it.'

'Yes, she's been very accommodating.'

'When will you get time off?' asked Matt, concerned. 'If you're working on the weekend? You always tend to overdo it.'

'Yes, maybe I won't see anyone on Sundays as a rule. But Saturday could be a good day for clients, especially if they're working 9-5.'

Marissa sighed. 'I'll figure it out. Promise. Just don't forget to ask for me Eli, yes?'

'Sure, sis, no problem.'

'Now can you clear the heavy energies out of the room for me?' asked Carol. 'I'm sure they're not good for the baby, so can you show me how to do it as well, so I can do it next time?'

'It would be my pleasure.'

An hour later, Marissa and Matt were sitting at a candlelit table, drinking wine. Their conversation was easy and relaxed, and Marissa didn't feel she had anything to do or anywhere to go, so she could easily be in the moment. *Taking a night off is good for me, and yes, I need to make sure I don't overdo with the clients too.*

The food was lovely. When the waitress took away their plates, Matt reached into his pocket and pulled out a bunch of keys on a loop, with an angel wing keyring. He put them on the table where Marissa's plate had been.

'My flat, for you. This one here, that's the back door. I don't think we've gone out that way. I'll show you next time you're over.'

Marissa's heart did a flip as she reached into her handbag and pulled out the keys that she had made for Matt. She did as he had done and placed them on the table.

'And my flat, for you. I think you know which key is which. It's quite straightforward.'

She hadn't put a keyring on them, they still had the plastic label from the shop attached.

They looked at each other.

'I love the keyring,' Marissa said. 'Wish I had thought of doing something like that.'

Matt smiled. 'It's another milestone for us.' He lifted his glass in a toast. They drank.

They walked home arm in arm. When they reached Marissa's flat, she encouraged him to use his keys, which he did, after some fumbling around with the middle lock.

'Aha! There's a trick to this door,' he said.

'Yes, it's quite old, this building. It has many fiddly things about it, but I love it here.'

They entered and hung up their coats.

'I know you love it here,' Matt said. 'It has a lovely feeling to it, and you have the back garden too. That's difficult to get. Lots of the flats around Dublin don't have gardens.'

'How do you know?'

Matt was silent.

'Have you been looking for a new flat?'

'Not for myself, but yes, I've had a little look, just out of curiosity.'

'Oh. Okay.'

Marissa lit the fire. It wasn't cold, but they liked the cosiness of it. They sat cuddled up together on the sofa and watched as it crackled into life.

Matt noticed the Vulture card still out on the table. He picked it up and studied it.

'What an awkward-looking fellow! God wasn't paying attention when he made a vulture, was he? Seems he gave it the leftovers from the other birds.'

'I'm not sure I'm a fan of vultures,' said Marissa, taking the card from him and looking at the artwork again. 'But their medicine must be good, or they wouldn't be included in the pack.'

A moment passed, and Marissa put the card back down on the table again. 'It's strange,' she said. 'A vulture came to me in a journey and then he came to me again through the cards, as if he was following me from one reality into another. Can they do that?'

Matt took a moment to answer. 'I guess the cards are as close to a vulture in this reality as you're going to get in Ireland. It would be very strange to see a vulture at your window here! I know angels can leave feathers behind,' he said slowly. 'I watched a show on psychic mediums – you know, people that can talk to the dead. They said you can see people you love as butterflies and robin redbreasts when they die. They come to tell you that they're okay.'

'That's beautiful. Don't they leave coins too? I remember now, when my Grandfather Archie died, I was seeing copper pennies everywhere.'

'That must have been a while ago – we don't have so many copper pennies anymore.'

'I know. Isn't it terrible?'

'Yes, sometimes the new things aren't as good as the originals.'

Marissa leaned into Matt. 'You're a good old original to me.'

'Ha, ha, not funny.'

'I like it.'

She kissed him.

'What about Eli as a dad? That's wild, isn't it?'

'He'll settle into it,' said Matt, 'and maybe *be* less wild, I guess.'

'He has to buckle up and get serious and all, look after his family,' said Marissa matter-of-factly.

'Maybe. Or maybe not. If you're a dad, you can still have fun, you know,' said Matt.

'How would you know?' giggled Marissa.

'Well, I suppose I don't know for sure, but maybe I'd like to find out someday.'

CHAPTER THIRTY EIGHT

Marissa rolled over into the warm spot where Matt had lain. He had already left for work, and it was almost time for her to get up too. She felt bereft again, but this time she took a moment to use the technique she had learned in her workshop, so she wouldn't be missing him so deeply during the day. After a few moments, something in her chest lifted and she felt the deep ache inside her shrink down to nothing. *I wish everyone knew how to do this. It makes life so much more bearable.*

As she was brushing her teeth, in her mind's eye she got a flash of Terry running through the forest again and got a sick feeling in her stomach. She really had to check on him. *I know he's coming on Saturday, but that doesn't mean he hasn't left a part of his energy somewhere in limbo, like Finn, or worse... I don't want to think of what could be worse right now.*

She stood at the mirror with toothpaste dripping down her chin and closed her eyes, reaching out for Terry in all directions.

Where is he? She remembered he had said he was fine, but she had a feeling deep inside that this wasn't the case. *Am I making it worse by going back to that image Isis showed me? What if I energise it each time I remember?* She let the image go, but tried reaching out for Terry again while she was dressing. This time it felt as though her arms were tied behind her back. She was in a tight straitjacket and couldn't move.

Shocked, she opened her eyes. Her actual arms were free. *Of course they are. What is going on? What's going on with Terry? Why isn't he allowing me to connect to him? Why won't he let me help him?*

Work felt heavy and slow. It felt heavy and slow more and more these days, particularly since Marissa had decided she wanted to get a dedicated healing space. *I hope Eli has made that call!* She was happy to leave early to catch the two buses across town to St Mary's.

Loretta had decided not to come back. Marissa had someone new, as well as Sorcha and Emma. *I guess it was too difficult for Loretta to go where we were planning to go together. I hope she's okay, it's strange not saying goodbye to her. I really would like to have closure with people. I guess Mr Blakemore was right, though, it's a rare thing. Maybe when I'm in my own place, but actually, no, I don't think that will really make any difference. They can always cancel, or just don't come back. I suppose it's part and parcel of being a therapist.*

Marissa lit the candle and cleared the energy of the room, then sat and waited for her new client, Debby, to arrive.

There was a hesitant knock on the door.

'Come in. Debby?'

'Hi. Yes, that's me.'

'Come, sit down, choose a chair. It's nice to meet you. We have as many sessions as you need together. Anything you say is confidential, unless I think you're going to hurt yourself, then I need to tell my supervisor. Otherwise, whatever you say to me stays between us.'

'Okay. Thanks.' Debby sat down. She was about seventeen, dark skinned, long dark hair. She looked very small in herself, as if she had shrunken down.

'How are you? What would you like to talk about?'

There was silence for a moment while Debby got her bearings.

'I'm okay.' She took a breath and added, 'No, actually, I'm not okay. That's why I'm here. I don't know if you can help. I feel sick all the time, nervous.'

'Maybe I can help with this. Can you describe the feelings to me?'

Debby nodded. 'It's there all the time, in the background. Jittery. But sometimes it gets bad, I get the shakes, and I feel as if I'm going to vomit. And I don't know why – there's no reason for it that I can see.'

'You're telling me that you feel anxious most of the time?'

'Anxious. Yes, that's the word for it.'

'Is it like butterflies trapped in your stomach? The nausea?'

'Yes! That's it! It's like trapped butterflies in my stomach. How did you know?'

'This is more common than you may think. And I have a technique I can teach you that will help. Here, let me show you.'

Marissa taught Debby the mindfulness technique – feeling your feet on the ground, breathing slowly and being in the moment. Asking yourself 'What do you see? What do you hear? and How do you feel? Debby calmed down significantly and left her first session happy, resolving to try the mindfulness technique every time she was anxious. If she remembered, she would make a note of what triggered it to get worse, so she could bring that into her next session.

Sorcha came into the room soon after Debby had left with a skip in her step, wearing a pink hoodie and a pair of bleached jeans with a hole in the knee. She had her hair cut into a short bob which looked great. She sat down, crossed her arms and legs, and looked straight at Marissa.

'Hi!'

'Hi, Marissa! I've had a great week this week! Thank you so much!'

'Tell me about it!' said Marissa with a smile. 'I love your hair!'

'Thanks! Well, I've moved back with Mum. So I'm only coming here for classes, and for you.'

'What is that like?'

'It's great, especially as I've been minding little Sorcha, remember, from last time? It's nice to have Mum around. She can look after me, and I can look after little me!'

I'm not sure that was the plan. I need to know a little more.

'Okay, how is it going for you?'

'It's been really fun. I took little Sorcha to the beach, and to the cinema, and we went shopping.' She pulled on her pink hoodie and pointed to her jeans. 'Do you like what we got?'

'Very nice.'

'We've been staying up late, little Sorcha and me, I mean, and eating snacks, and dancing lots! It's the best fun!'

'And you've been doing classes too? Which classes did you do this week?'

'Actually, little Sorcha didn't want to go to the classes, so we watched TV instead.'

'So you're saying you've had great fun because you've let your inner child do anything she wanted?'

Sorcha blushed.

'I think you know that it's not really supposed to work that way, yes? You need to keep doing the important things that your inner child doesn't necessarily want to do too. And mind your inner child while you're doing those, of course. It's about finding balance between doing what your heart wants, doing what your head wants and doing the things that your body needs.'

Sorcha sank back into the chair. 'That sounds like too much hard work.'

'Yes, it can be work, and it can be difficult at times, but if you have the fun too, then you have the balance.'

Sorcha frowned.

'It's all learning, for you and for little Sorcha too. But as you mention you've moved back in with your mother, I'm wondering, does big Sorcha forget she's a grown-up when she moves back home?'

Sorcha looked shocked. 'What do you mean? How could I forget that?'

"Well, are you sleeping in the same room you slept in while you were a child?'

'Actually, yes.'

'Does it look the same as it did?'

'Yes, Mum hasn't changed a thing.'

'Is it possible you've regressed? What do you think?'

'What's "regressed"? Is it bad?'

Marissa smiled and toned down her voice. 'It's not necessarily bad, no. It could be a coping mechanism, or an automatic response to a familiar environment. You grew up in that room, so you were a child in there, and you're spending a lot of time, maybe too much time, with your inner child at the moment, so maybe you're regressing a little bit. Slipping, so to speak, from adult you to child you. How does this sound to you? Is it true?'

Sorcha thought seriously before answering. 'In a way, yes, I suppose it could be true. I don't like being responsible for myself, but I suppose it's better than being a child again. But what do I do? I'm trying to get everything right, doing what you say, doing what Mum says, and what Audrey has set out for me. It's too much to do.'

'So you've regressed to being a child who also has things she doesn't like to do and would much rather play and have fun instead.'

'Yes! Exactly.' Sorcha stretched out in her chair with a satisfied air, like a child who had just got her own way.

There was a pause.

I've got to turn this around. She seems totally disempowered. Yes, that's it, she is disempowered!

'Sorcha, do you realise that as an adult, you're allowed to say "no" to things?'

Sorcha looked interested.

'It sounds as though there are a lot of people telling you what to do right now.'

'For sure.'

'But you don't *have* to do what people tell you when you're an adult. Being grown up can be, well, really fun at times.'

'I guess.'

'From what you've told me, it sounds as though you have too many demands on your time and you're just not ready yet for them all. Or maybe you don't even need to do some of these things. Would this be the case?'

'Oh yes. Some of the things they want me to do are things I know I *should* do, like helping Mum with the housework. The classes – some of them are okay, but some are boring.'

'Can I talk to Sorcha the adult right now? And see what she has to say?'

'But I *am* her, aren't I?'

'You do sound more like her right now, alright. Let's breathe together for a moment.'

They took some deep breaths.

'Does your mum have another room in her house that you can sleep in so you're not living in your old bedroom?'

'Actually, there is a guest room.'

'What if you were to move in there? Then you could be adult Sorcha who is moving back home for a while to get herself sorted, instead of little Sorcha who has come back home and wants her mum to mind her and do all the things for her.'

'I hear what you're saying now. I understand. Yes, Mum has been making my dinner and telling me to turn off my light at night time to go to sleep. That's regressing. I can decide what time I go to sleep at, and I can make my own dinner too. I've allowed this to happen. Yes, you're right.'

'Well done for seeing it. It's very hard to admit when you're regressing, or to see behaviour that isn't ideal and own it. It looks like you and your mother have fallen back into an old pattern. Shifting those patterns is such an important part of, well, being an adult.'

Sorcha smiled.

'See, you can do this. You're well able. How do you feel now?'

'Not as overwhelmed as before. I like what you said a minute ago, that adults can say "no" to things.'

'What would you like to say "no" to?'

Sorcha thought for a moment. 'Well, to my mother treating me like a child. She's defo doing that, and I did just slip back into it, didn't I?'

'Like I said, it's good that you've noticed. Making a new pattern can be difficult though, being recognised as an adult by your parents can take a bit of work. Perhaps moving into the guest room would help her remember that you're a grown-up.'

Sorcha scratched her head. 'It's funny that I don't feel grown up, even though I'm twenty-six.'

'I understand. I'm not that much older than you, and some days I feel like a little girl too. Maybe you have to work a little bit harder to remind yourself that you get to choose now what you do in your life, choose how people treat you, and choose how you treat them too.'

'I was beginning to do that. When I left Adam the first time, I chose not to let him treat me badly, but I kept going back to him anyway.'

'Maybe that was little Sorcha feeling afraid that if she left him nobody else would love her?'

Sorcha was silent for a moment. Then her face filled with emotion and a tear ran down her cheek. After another moment, she said, 'Oh my God, Marissa, you hit the nail on the head. Yes, that was exactly what that was. I can see it now.'

Wow, what an epiphany!

Less flushed now, Sorcha continued, 'I don't want little Sorcha to destroy my life. So what do you think, if I keep working with her, with that part of me, I mean, and learn how to say "no", and have a balance between work and fun, will that fix me?'

'I don't think we are ever fixed,' Marissa replied, 'we just find new things we need to work on. But yes, I think what you're saying is a very good plan for now.'

Sorcha smiled.

'Just remember that you, big Sorcha, loves little Sorcha forever, no matter what. Tell her that you will never abandon her and always give her what she needs. But not always what she wants!'

She nodded.

'This means that you never have to compromise yourself to get love from someone else, whether it's a man, or your family, or anybody else. As long as big you can love little you, you've got a really good foundation for the rest of your life.'

Emma was her last client for the day. *Emma, Emma, which one is Emma...? Oh, yes! Emma.*

Marissa opened a window, just in case, and sat down to wait for Emma. She arrived ten minutes late and not as pungent as the week before, but the BO wafted through the room as she walked in and took her seat.

'Hi, Marissa.'

'Emma, hello! How was your week?'

''Twas strange. Remember what you said about explodin' the tings that was hurtin' me? You said you'd do it for me, like?'

'Yes, I do remember that.'

'Well, this week, I spent lots of the week goin' backwards.'

More regression?

'How do you mean, "going backwards"?'

Emma squirmed with obvious discomfort.

'Take your time, there's no rush. And you don't have to tell me if you don't want to.'

'Yeah, but I *do* want to. It's just hard.'

A few more moments passed.

'Did you explode more of the stuff that was hurting you? Did you do it yourself, I mean?'

Emma nodded.

'What was that like?'

Emma sat up. 'It was bloody great. I blew up bucketloads. Truckloads. But then I couldn't stop eatin'. That's what I mean by goin' backwards. I have an eatin' disorder, I never said it to ya.'

'Okay,' said Marissa sitting up straighter in her seat, 'do you want to talk about it with me now?'

'Heck yeah, that's why I brung it up. I'm bulimic – I eat loads, then vomit it up. Been doin' it for years. But this week, I just ate loads. Didn't make meself sick, I mean. I've not done dis in years. Jus' eatin' like dat.'

'Do you know what triggered it?'

'Whas a trigger? Like a gun?'

Marissa smiled. 'What exactly was it that caused you to eat lots this week?'

'Dunno. Tink it was blowin' up all me pain. I felt good from dat. Too good, maybe.'

Marissa nodded her head. 'Do you think, Emma, that you might have been punishing yourself for feeling good?'

She shook her head. 'No. No way. I don't do dat. Well, maybe sometimes, but no, not this time. I dunno wha' it was made me do it.'

Marissa thought for a moment. An image appeared in her mind of Emma with a cupboard instead of a stomach. She was taking dark, heavy weights and stones out of the cupboard and placing them on the ground beside her, then blowing them up. Then she put food inside the cupboard to fill the space. *That's so interesting! Thank you.*

'I think I might know why you've been eating, Emma.'

'Really? Do tell. Beats me. It's so annoyin'. Even now I'm thinkin' 'bout pizza and cake. It's a struggle not to eat. When I do eat, I get relief, but only for a few minutes.'

'It's been very difficult then, has it?'

'Oh yeah, worst ever. I really don't understand it. Hope you've got some clue for me.'

'I think I might do. So, you've been carrying a lot of pain, and you've been exploding it, the way I did last week.'

'Yep.'

'So maybe – just think about this as a possibility – you're used to carrying pain. So when you don't carry it anymore, you feel, well, lighter.'

'Yeah, I was feeling lighter alright, but I didn't lose any weight.'

'I know. It was your energy body that felt lighter, not your physical body.'

'Energy body?'

'Exactly. You are made of energy – your soul, your emotions, your thoughts, they're all made of energy.'

'But what's this then?' Emma held out her arm and pulled on the fat that was dangling below the bone.

'Yes, that's weight, but it's blood, muscle, fat and bone. They're made of energy too, but they're physical. I'm talking about the life inside you. Like, say, if you were dead, you'd leave your body, right? The blood, muscle, fat and bone would still be there, but there'd be no life-force flowing through them. The blood wouldn't flow, it would just congeal; there'd be no heartbeat, because there'd be no life making your heart beat.'

'Okay, so this isn't about my body at all den?'

'No, I don't think it is.'

'Oh, dat's good. Ha, ha. Maybe I'm not goin' backwards after all.'

'No, I don't think you are. This is something new.'

'So why did I eat then, what has it to do wit energy?'

'Exploding the emotions was you working with energy. You felt lighter, but your body felt unstable, so it thought it needed food to feel heavier again. But you didn't actually need it.'

'I don't understand.'

Marissa saw an image of a ship at sea and heard the word 'ballast'.

'I'll try to explain this in a different way. Do you know what ballast is, Emma?'

'Nope.'

'If a boat is going out to sea, it needs to be a certain weight, so that the sea doesn't topple it over, yes?'

'Okay, I can see dat.'

'So imagine a boat filled with cargo. It goes to shore, unloads the cargo and becomes lighter.'

'Right.'

'Then it has to go home, so either it gets filled with new cargo which weighs it down, or it gets filled with ballast. Boats have a ballast tank that is filled with water to make the boat heavy, so it is safer travelling in a storm. The wind won't knock it over, or the waves. Not as easily, anyway.'

'Dat makes sense.'

'So you're the boat and you just unloaded a cargo of heavy pain.'

'Aah, I git it now. I see it. Okay. So my body wanted something else to stay heavy, so it wouldn't topple over. But what would topple it over?'

'I don't know, maybe life? Your body released energy and wanted something heavy to replace it, so it thinks that energy will topple it over.'

'I wonder what that is. It kind of half makes sense to me.'

'Me too. But I know those things you told me last time weren't small things, they were very big things that happened to you, so perhaps your body just didn't feel safe to suddenly explode all of that emotion all at once. Maybe after talking tonight to me, it will settle down over the next few weeks as you get used to not feeling so heavy in yourself.'

'I hope so.'

'Maybe the best thing you can do, next time you get an urge to eat too much, is to ask yourself if you are hungry. If your body says "no"...'

'Ha, ha, my body just wants the food. It never tells me if it's hungry or not.'

'You don't feel hungry?'

'Nope, haven't felt hungry in years.'

'You're disconnected from how your body feels?'

Emma raised an eyebrow. 'I guess so.'

'Do you want to work on this with me? We could spend the next few sessions on it, if you like.'

Emma smiled. 'Could we? I would like to get hold of this in meself.'

'Sure. We absolutely could.'

'So what do I do this week, like?'

'Well, if you don't know if you're feeling hungry or not, you could start asking yourself, to get your body ready to feel hungry again. Maybe it will remember how to do that if you keep asking it if it's hungry. But that's not going to solve the energetic imbalance you're experiencing right now.'

'Probably not.'

'So, if you remember, you can ask about hunger. In the meantime, maybe just let your body do what it wants to do, but before you start eating too much, you can ask yourself if you feel safe in the world.' *That's a great idea!*

'Do I feel safe in the world? Ha, ha! No, never did.'

Marissa took a breath. *I need to slow this down a little bit.*

'I know you've seen lots of bad things, and had violence in your life, so your body possibly doesn't feel safe, even when you are. Maybe your weight then, the energetic weight as well as your physical weight, helped you feel safe. And your body translates that to physical weight, and makes you want to eat too much food. There's a lot here to process, Emma. We won't do it all today. Where would you like to start?'

'Well, the hungry thing is interesting. Wonder if I stopped eating until I felt hungry I would recognise the feeling.'

'That is something you could work on, for sure.'

'Yeah, I'll do that. I won't eat if I'm not hungry, then if I'm hungry, I can eat! Brilliant. Thanks, Marissa, see you next time.'

CHAPTER THIRTY NINE

I can't believe it's Thursday already and I've still not been able to journey, either to check Terry or to visit Isis. This is so frustrating!

Marissa turned in her bed and looked at the clock. She had an hour before she needed to get up for work.

I'll try again now.

She found her lapis lazuli crystal, held it in her hand and closed her eyes.

There was a party in the forest, with birthday cake and celebrations. The tree was laughing and clapping its hands, Emelda and Grandmother Medicine Woman were there, and so was the little blue dragon.

'Dragon! You're in the forest! That's fantastic!'

'Yes, isn't it wonderful?' said Emelda, grabbing Marissa's hand and spinning her around to music that she couldn't hear. She laughed and hugged her guide, she felt like a good friend.

'Come, come, have some cake!'

Marissa looked at the party table. There were lots of treats there. She saw pink muffins, took one and bit into it. It was lovely – a hint of strawberry and just the right amount of whipped pink icing.

'What are we celebrating?'

'Our Dragon's first time in the forest.'

'Oh I didn't miss it! How wonderful!'

The dragon did a little dance, then clambered over to the table and started pulling on the table cloth, pulling the food over towards himself so he could reach the chocolate cake.

'Can he have cake? Well I don't see why not.' Marissa went over to him, gave him some cake and rubbed his head. His eyes were sparkling, he looked very grateful.

'Marissa!'

Grandmother Medicine Woman came over with her arms outstretched and they embraced.

'Marissa, look at you. You're a warrior, a storyteller, a healer. We're celebrating you today, not the dragon.' She flicked her fingers at Emelda, as if to negate what she had said.

'I don't want the girl getting big-headed!' Emelda said defensively.

'It is a good-sized head that she has, much more sensible now,' Grandmother Medicine Woman said, 'and very much on her way to becoming who she truly is. We are proud of you, Marissa, and are taking the time to congratulate you on your successes and wish you well in your endeavours.'

'Thank you,' said Marissa, puzzled. She really had wanted to go and visit Terry, and this seemed like another way the universe was trying to distract her.

'Very clever,' said Grandmother Medicine Women. 'Yes, you got it. Now go, it's time for your job.'

Marissa was back in her flat. It was indeed time to get up for work. She laughed. It was nice to see her guides. She had a big space in her heart for all of them.

'And we do for you too,' she heard echoing in her mind.

I guess it is my job, and healing is my work.

Marissa's job passed the time of day, and then she went to Cabra, to do her work.

CHAPTER FORTY

Finally, it was Saturday. Terry was coming to Marissa's flat and they were going to sort it all out. Well, no, not really. They were going to go on a journey to The Soul Cages, to release souls. Marissa knew it, Terry knew it, but they had not said it explicitly to each other. Marissa cleared the whole afternoon for it, and got cake, because ... cake.

She had had enough of trying to connect and journey and being pushed out, kicked out or distracted by something right in front of her. They had to knock this thing on the head one way or another.

At noon her doorbell rang. Terry stood at the door, breathless and excited, holding an umbrella in one hand and fresh flowers in the other.

'Marissa!'

He swanned into the flat, put his things down on the sofa and opened out his arms, looking for a hug.

Marissa held onto him for a moment longer than usual.

'Hey! It's nice to see you too!'

She pulled away. 'Flowers! How beautiful. Thank you.' Marissa got a vase and unceremoniously put them into it, then placed them on the coffee table. Bright, large yellow daisies, pink roses and white spray, the flowers glowed with life.

'Yes, they were a gift from an admirer, but they suit you much better and I certainly don't want to bring them back to Bruce.' Terry winked. He wore a white flannel T-shirt with a collar and a crocodile badge sewn onto it, cream sailing shorts and white deck shoes with white ankle socks.

Marissa laughed. 'Of course they're not for me!'

Terry raised an eyebrow, 'I'll bring some for you specially next time, promise. You like the outfit?' he asked, spreading his arms wide and doing a twirl.

Marissa put his umbrella into the stand behind the front door and studied him. 'Not sure.'

'Not my usual attire, I know. I've come straight from the marina, we got all the shots early, thank goodness, because I was coming here by hook or by crook. Do you have any coffee? I'm dying for a cup.'

Marissa put on the kettle for coffee and organised the cake while Terry made himself comfortable.

'Oh what kind? Chocolate? I'll have some, yes please and thank you!' Terry sat down and flamboyantly crossed one leg over the other, then swapped them. He seemed a little anxious.

I don't know if I'm nervous or excited to see him.

Tobermory went over to Terry and rubbed up against him, then leapt into his lap. It seemed to calm him a little. Terry laughed.

'Aha, there you are, you brave jaguar cat! What a majestic creature you are – in shamanic worlds, that is! Ouch! And in this world too, oooh you are rather sensitive aren't you!'

Marissa brought the plates, milk and sugar out to the table, looking at Terry all the while to see if he seemed like his whole self after their last adventure. Her nerves, if that's what they were, hadn't settled at all. In fact they were getting worse. *Skull and cross-bones, he shut me out – why?*

'Ha ha,' said Terry, stroking Tobermory's back. 'It's like he understands everything I'm saying!'

'Yes, I think he does understand more than he lets on, it's strange, but kind of cool as well.' She went back to concoct the coffee.

'It's strange, isn't it, how he can be a jaguar over there and just a little kitty cat here,' Terry said, moving to Tobermory's head. Tobermory twitched his tail, seemingly insulted.

Marissa said, 'I don't think he likes your tone. He's more than just a little kitty cat to me.' She remembered how he knocked down a whole shelf of books to rescue her from whatever curse she had been under at the time. 'He's a great friend, I really appreciate him.'

She brought the French Press and two mugs out to the table. 'I heard that cats can see energy, maybe that's why he seems to understand what I say, half the time anyway.' Marissa cut some cake and offered it to Terry on a plate.

He took it from her. 'Thanks.' Turning to Tobermory, he said, 'Well, cat, I have great respect for you. I apologise if you feel insulted. Will you come with us on our journey today when we go?'

Tobermory's tail stopped twitching. He stood up and stretched, arching his back, not seeming to care that he was still on Terry's lap.

'Ouch! He stuck his claw in! That's twice now!'

'He's making his point.' A laugh burst through Marissa's tight lips. She couldn't help herself.

'Ha ha! That's hilarious' They both laughed, the tension easing between them. Tobermory hopped down gracefully from the sofa then leapt up onto the window ledge, where he turned and sat, looking quizzically at them both.

'So shall we go rescue these souls then?' asked Terry, brushing away cake crumbs.

'We said we'd talk about it, sort it out, but it looks like you've decided already.'

'Yes, I thought we both did? How could we not? We must!'

Marissa sighed. She knew she wanted to do it, but the weight of dread hung heavily on her shoulders. 'Okay then. Let's do it together.' She turned and looked at her cat. 'Tobermory, will you come with us?' She breathed out her anxiety and turned to Terry, 'I think it would be good if he came. We need the extra protection.'

I actually think we shouldn't go. Let's just talk and eat cake and drink coffee. Wow I'm really split again, why can't I pull myself together and make a decision?

'Thanks for the coffee,' Terry said excitedly. 'I'm ready to go right now though. I've been dying to do this all week with you. Every time I've tried to go on my own, it's been a nightmare. Literally! I found myself in a dark forest, I got lost in a labyrinth, I was in a deserted white city.'

'Oh! I was in a deserted white city too! I found a bird tied to a post and I thought it was Finn, but it wasn't – I wondered what that place was. And you were there too! How interesting. I ended up back in Clifden, in my journey, and Finn was there. I was so relieved. I did a healing on him and then he went home, himself. He was very badly wounded, I didn't want to say in the group chat...'

'Fair enough, it's difficult to know how a text would go down. I much prefer face to face. Anyway, Finn is safe and home, and officially out of the game. It's just the two of us now.'

Tobermory mewed.

'Okay then! The three of us – a perfect number. Shall we go? What do we need to do to prepare?'

Marissa felt a sick feeling once more in the pit of her stomach. She pushed it away. *It's now or never.* She cleared the energy of the room, lit a candle, and she and Terry stood together to say the opening prayer.

Terry nodded. 'The energy here feels good.'

Marissa got her medicine bundle and put it on the table beside them.

'Oh, I never thought of doing that! What a good idea!'

'Shall we go?'

They sat on the sofa holding hands and closed their eyes.

Terry giggled. 'Sorry, I always get giddy when I'm doing something serious.'

'Okay.'

They sat in silence.

'We need an anchor,' Terry said.

'Oh yes, I forgot.'

'Where are we going to meet?'

'When I'm in doubt I always go to my tree. Let's go there. I'll introduce you.'

'Great! I'm excited. Let's go!'

Marissa closed her eyes again, softened her focus and felt Tobermory settle into her lap. *Good. Thank you for coming with us.* She felt him relaxing into her as she brought her awareness into her body and travelled down into her heart, then Terry's phone rang and gave her a fright.

'Terry!'

'Oh, shit! Sorry. Hang on.' He switched it off.

'It's been like this all week,' said Marissa, becoming frustrated.

'I know, for me too. It's as if the universe doesn't want us to go.'

'I don't understand why. Aren't we doing something good?'

'Okay, here we go again. Phone off this time? Mine is off.'

'Yes, it's off.'

Marissa focused on her breathing. In and out, and down. In and out, and down... *Ah, that's better.*

She was in, and still holding Terry's hand. They were standing together in front of her tree. Tobermory was there too, he was more cat than jaguar but he had his golden collar around his neck. Terry looked like a pixie. He was wearing green shorts, a green tee-shirt and a green hat, had short cropped hair and little pointy ears.

'You look adorable,' said Marissa, smiling.

'Why, thank you, ma'am,' he said and bowed to her. 'Are you going to introduce me to your friend?'

'Great Tree of Wisdom, this is Terry.'

The big old tree opened one large wide eye, and then the other. 'I was waiting for you both. You travel once more together. And this time, so be it.'

It stretched its limbs, then a door opened in its trunk and they went in.

As they went down the stairs Marissa noticed her body changing into that of a warrior. She became leaner, taller, and her red/black armour appeared. Her javelin was in three parts, strapped to her back in some sort of travel sack. It feels much better than a sword, I'll take it. *Tobermory shifted into his jaguar shape, tall and graceful, his golden ankh collar around his neck, the lightning silver streak on his head glistened. Terry stayed the same.*

'I look cute. I don't need to change.'

Marissa laughed. The tree spat them out into a dark, familiar forest. Sinister shapes lurked behind tall crooked trees. There was a hissing on the wind.

'This is the place,' said Marissa. She turned to Jaguar and asked, 'Which way do we go?'

The jaguar stood still for a moment, sensing, then started to move.

'Oooh, this is exciting!' said Terry, jumping for joy and running after him.

Jaguar led them through the forest. Eyes watched from behind dark trees as they ran and jumped over fallen logs, swung on vines over streams and pushed through thickets until they came to the familiar space with the small ramshackle cabin that led to the castle.

This time the cabin was hung with fairy lights and it looked beautiful. Terry went straight up to the door, but Marissa pulled him back.

'Wait! Shh! We have to see if anyone is here first.'

'Oh, right. Right, okay.'

I'm regretting this now. This looks too pretty. Is it a trap? Honey to call us inside?

They hid by the cabin door for a moment.

'Nobody's in there,' said Terry confidently. 'I'm going in. The Soul Cages are calling me.'

He walked in proudly and Marissa had no choice but to follow. Jaguar stayed outside.

'Oh my gosh, look! So many of them.'

The inside of the cabin was very different from the outside. It was much larger than they expected, it looked like it went on for miles and miles. There were no fairy lights inside here, instead there were shelves filled with jars. There was no end to them. Each jar had a withered being inside, floating like a trapped firefly with its fire dying. It was overwhelming to see so many all in one place.

Terry placed his fingers on the glass of the nearest jar and a spark ignited, but it didn't stay lit for long.

'They're dying!' Terry exclaimed, his voice cracking with emotion. 'We have to set them free!'

What happened next happened so quickly Marissa didn't have time to react. Terry opened a jar, then another, then the third jar sucked him in and the stopper sealed itself shut on top, and he was gone.

'Terry! Where are you? TERRY!!'

Marissa panicked. She couldn't see which jar was his, there were so many, and everything was blurring before her eyes...

She pulled herself out of the journey. There was Terry, still on the sofa with her, but his eyes were closed and he was pale and shaking. She prised her fingers out of his hand and placed her hands on his shoulders and shook him, but he didn't respond. His mouth was just making little bubbles and he wasn't present in his body at all.

'Oh no! Terry! Terry! Come back to me!'

Marissa looked for Tobermory, but he was asleep in her lap. She prised him off and onto the sofa and tried to get back into the journey, but she couldn't get in.

The sun was going down.

'But we only just went a few moments ago! It can't be that late already!'

She looked at the phone. It was 8.30pm.

'What? What happened?'

Terry was still breathing but when she touched his face, it was cold.

'What should I do?'

She had the phone in her hand, so she rang Séamus.

'Hello, it's Séamus. Can't get the phone right now. You know what to do – leave a message.'

No, I can't. I can't tell him this in a message.

She hung up.

I'll try him again in a few minutes. Oh God.

Terry was shivering now so she put the kettle on and filled a hot water bottle and put it in his lap, then wrapped him in a blanket. She checked his heartbeat.

'Phew, still there, but what do I do?' *What do I do??* 'Please, anyone? Help me!'

She felt a dark, heavy presence in the room. Suddenly it tore her from herself, stretching her out in all directions. Fear – terror – was rippling through her, yet somewhere deep inside she was calm.

Is it him? Here? Again?

'Yes, it is I. I have come to see you again, Marissa Tori Rosenthal.'

Marissa was glued to the spot. The demonic presence approached her and grabbed her arm,

and suddenly they were in the medieval landscape where she had found herself many times before, the place where she had seen people shackled and barefoot on cobblestone streets. She was wearing the white jerkin and long trousers. She couldn't release herself from the demon's grip.

He looked at her and smiled. He seemed quite reasonable. He didn't look like Martin, or Scott, he looked like an ordinary man, a businessman, but he had hot fire deep in his eyes. His voice, when he spoke, had a strong magnetic pull. He did not need to speak loudly to be heard.

'You have seen me many times in many different guises, Marissa, in many women and men, and you will see me again. You may not always have recognised me, but I am expert in deception. You have much to learn.'

She was beginning to regain her sense of self. This is really happening. Snap out of it and deal with him, work with him.

'Yes, work with me, good. That's what we all need to do, work with each other. We can do it, you know, light can work with dark, and dark can work with light. We both have a purpose, you see. We cannot survive without each other. Let me show you, and in return for this, I will release your friend, Terry. Yes?'

Marissa stopped struggling. She really had no choice. 'Yes.'

'Then come with me.'

CHAPTER FORTY ONE

They walked along a cobblestone street where people were being lined up in shackles and chains, whipped and driven along the street into carts.

'Why?'

'People are strange creatures, Marissa Tori Rosenthal. I do believe you are learning this for yourself. Some of them choose this, willingly.'

'William?' she asked, remembering.

'Your William, ah yes, the bird. Very clever. You are becoming quite the thorn in my side, Ms Marissa. This talk together is long overdue.'

'He didn't want to do it...'

'He told you he didn't want to, but did he tell you the full truth of it? Or just what he wanted you to know? Did he tell you he enjoyed torturing those "poor souls" as you call them?'

Marissa thought for a moment. 'Actually, he did admit to that, yes.'

'Good. So you were paying attention.'

They walked past scenes of poverty and suffering, preachers preaching and throngs of people shouting 'Amen!' to the sky and bowing down on their knees on the cobblestones.

When they lifted themselves up, Marissa could see their faces were withered and bony. There was no light in their eyes, no life-force shining through.

'They sell their souls for a moment of happiness,' laughed the demon, pointing to the crowds. 'It's not just Scott Taylor that collects them for me, though he does a mighty fine job. I have many priests and preachers on my team, if you want to call it that.'

'How can they call themselves priests and preachers if they work for you?'

'Why not? Aren't we all just looking for the next best thing? Wanting something more than what we have? I can offer that too.'

'But what's in it for them?'

'Why, Marissa, I thought you'd never ask.' The demon stopped walking and smiled at her, then he waved his hand.

Three gargoyle-like creatures brought over a heavy gilded table and two matching chairs, placed them down by the side of the road and ran away.

'Would you like to sit?'

Before she could think, Marissa sat on the chair nearest to her and the demon sat on the other. The gargoyles came back with asymmetrical trays piled high with food and drink and laid it all out on the table.

Marissa shook her head. She didn't like losing control of her body, and she most certainly didn't want to accept anything from this creature.

'Rather wise, perhaps, considering how much you know about me,' he smirked. 'But no, I have no bone to pick with you, my dear girl. I would understand, of course, if you didn't trust me, but we are colleagues, compatriots, so to speak.'

'What do you mean? How could that be possible?'

The demon raised an eyebrow. 'Haven't you figured it out yet? We both work for the same, shall I say, being.'

Marissa was flooded with shock. 'What? We work for the same being?'

The demon laughed, reached for an elegant, triangular, wrought iron and glass decanter and poured a drink into a matching glass. He poured one for Marissa too. The dark liquid settled into the tall, triangular glasses and a silver vortex appeared in each one, spinning slowly, counter-clockwise. Both the glasses and the decanter had a silver triangular seal emblazoned upon them depicting a tight black spiral, which also ran counter-clockwise. They looked sinister, yet familiar.

'You should try it,' he said, tapping his glass with his long finger, smiling. 'It's the best that money can't buy. And you might need a drink by the time we're finished here.'

As he drank, Marissa was able to get a better look at him. He had neat black hair, blue eyes and was wearing a blue suit, white shirt and yellow tie. He looked like a businessman in his thirties, he could have been the CEO of a very successful company. He had a yellow handkerchief sticking slightly out of his breast pocket and cufflinks at his wrists with symbols on them. He looked very smart, very attractive.

'Are you really a demon?' she asked, eyeing a pink muffin that had appeared on the table.

'Yes. You like pink muffins, don't you?'

Marissa blushed. 'Have you been watching me this whole time?'

'Well, of course. You had to prove yourself a worthy adversary, and you didn't, not really. But the fact you are still here, talking to me now, is noteworthy. You have gone up in my estimation.'

'Was that you in the counselling room? And in my bedroom?'

He held his hand up. 'Guilty as charged.'

Laughing, he leaned forward and rested his hands on the table. Marissa could see the symbols on his cufflinks were identical to the sigil she had been drawing in the Scott Taylor book that she had burned.

'Yes, back to Scott again,' he said, 'one of my highest-ranking officers. He's an initiate of many lifetimes. He spent time in the School Hermetica studying those sigils and then had that particular one impregnated into his books. Between the lines, of course. Bewitching. Quite ingenious, really.'

Ah, this makes sense now.

'You can keep your thoughts to yourself if you like, but I can hear them all the same. Just like those blasted angels can.' He took another sip of his drink. 'Scott's personal stamp, Ha! What a work of absolute genius. Imagine, they queue up to receive it! Ha! People! So foolish and stupid, they have no idea what they are consenting to. Scott, or Balthezolimew, as we know him here, is in-line to become a magus of the fifth degree. He has certainly earned it, but it is not up to me whether to bestow that rank upon him. He will be exalted in His name.'

The pink muffin was looking more and more tempting but Marissa held herself back. It was a nice distraction from the conversation which was becoming overwhelming. Then she heard the echo of what the demon had just said repeating in her mind.

'No idea what they are consenting to? So they consent to him taking their souls? Or part of their souls?'

'Yes, indeed,' said the demon, taking another sip from his glass. 'That's exactly how it works. Make a wish, say the affirmation, there's consent right there, good enough as, anyway. Watch it in a movie, read it in a book, say it out loud - it's all the same to me.'

He put the glass down. His drink was now purple and was hypnotising to look at; the vortex spiral of silver spinning slowly through it gave the appearance of being alive. She was sure she had seen that glass before.

'Are you sure you don't want any?' he asked. 'It really is quite delicious, very special. No? Alright. More for me then. Here's the upshot – this whole system runs on consent. That's what we are here to discuss. You need to have a better understanding of it all. You can't take anyone from me who has consented to their fate. End of.'

Marissa remembered releasing the souls back in the cabin. 'They can't all know they've consented! And what they've consented to!'

'Perhaps not. Yet they sell their souls in exchange for pleasure, material objects, fame – all the worldly things that only mean something in the lower dimensions. More fool them, more kudos for me.'

The liquid in the glass was orange now, the silver spiral still swirling inside.

'But you, dear Marissa, do not seem interested in those things. You choose the path of light wholeheartedly, no matter what pain it may bring. And I am the other path. Both paths are painful, to be honest, you just choose whether to experience the pain now or later, that's all. We complement each other, no?'

Marissa shivered. Isis called him a bastard.

'Ah, the Great Goddess, my sister Isis. Always wanting her way with her devotees. Yes, the Great Narcissist. The narcissist and the bastard! Of course it's all a distortion. Everything is just a matter of opinion. Who's to say whose truth is really true? She isn't short of a few material objects – she has everything she ever wanted.'

Marissa wasn't happy to have her great goddess insulted.

'Now, now,' the demon soothed, 'we all have our opinions and our different perspectives. We never really know whose side anybody is on until they meet their end. Then, they are judged. For even the lightest of lightworkers have their very own deep, dark secrets. There's no such thing as a white witch, my dear. They just hide things better than most of the others do. From themselves, too. But even those secrets will come out in the end, for you cannot hide the darkness when the light shines upon it, isn't that right?'

Marissa remembered what her grandmother used to say: 'When you change your old lightbulb for a brighter one, you see more dirt. If you don't want to clean, don't fix the light!'

'Lovely woman, your Grandmother Lilly. I liked her. She liked her whiskey when nobody was looking. Great sense of humour too.'

'Don't tell me she...'

He smiled again. 'Your Grandmama Lilly, no, she wasn't one of mine. She knew all about consent. I tried, really I did, but my hands were tied when it came to her. Ha, ha, my hands were tied! But yes, they were. Do you get the picture yet?'

'I think so. You have to choose. Light or dark. Work now or pay later.'

'Yes!' He slapped the table. 'You've got it. The truth is the truth, even if you don't like it, no matter how uncomfortable it makes you. And that's where we slip in. Discomfort and vulnerability are so easy to manipulate. Your truth is not The Truth and it probably never will be. And ordinary life – well, there is plenty of distraction there to keep you from any sort of truth, especially if you don't want to know. Wilful blindness, they call it. Humans are very good at convincing themselves of anything. Especially when it comes to one of the biggest lies of all.'

'And what's that?'

'That everyone is entitled to be happy. Ha! Entitlement! Happiness! Both of these concepts created by our side, of course.'

Marissa thought for a moment. This is too straightforward. No, it can't be right. *'What about Martin? He didn't choose to have you use his body, did he?'*

'Consent is a many-edged sword, my dear. And we are tricky, tricksters, we like to play tricks to get our way. Some aspect of him did consent, or I wouldn't have been able to manipulate him. Simple as that.'

Marissa took some time to absorb this.

'What if they change their minds? People? Are you allowed to change your mind?'

'Are you sure you don't want that muffin? It's your favourite. I've got doughnuts too – your other guilty pleasure.'

The pink muffin was bigger and brighter than before, luring Marissa to it. She caught the scent of strawberry icing, but pulled herself back. At that, the demon's helpers brought out a huge tray of doughnuts, all different flavours, and placed them on the table beside the muffin. They looked very out of place in the medieval surroundings.

'Can I not tempt you?'

Marissa laughed. 'Is this to distract me? You have been watching me. You tempt to get consent too, I presume. Wear a person down where they are vulnerable and take their consent when they have no strength left to say no – that's downright evil. But you didn't answer my question. What if someone chooses the dark, or the light, and then changes their mind?'

'It's all in the contracting, my dear.'

'I remember someone talking to me about contracts before,' said Marissa.

'Yes. It can be quite boring, and one must be an expert in it, as it can get very complicated. Even at our end, we often use intermediaries to work through the contracts, as even we cannot tell, at times. Both sides can be as tricky as each other. We usually simply assume and step in, and if nobody interjects, well, then we chalk it up as another little victory. As they say, it's easier to ask for forgiveness than for permission. But we are honourable, if pinned to the post, that is.'

He sipped his drink.

'How do you contract with the darkness if you're not aware you're doing it?'

'What a fascinating conversation! I didn't expect this at all. Been eons since I spoke to anyone who was reasonable.' The demon seemed to relax a little. 'And there I was, on guard myself, waiting for you to make the first move. Waiting for you to attack me. Perhaps that was Tori's aspect; Marissa's aspect brings a calmness to the table, a level-headedness. Hmm. Yes, you two do belong together. What a formidable, and now reasonable, opponent you are turning out to be.'

He smiled. 'And I certainly am not going to take it personally that you won't partake of my repast.' He motioned to a helper to remove some of the food, which was then taken away, except for the plate with the pink muffin.

'You sound genuinely interested in how all this works,' the demon said.

'I am.'

'I will answer your question then. People make choices all the time, don't they?'

Marissa nodded.

'Each choice, big or small, is a light choice or dark choice. Each choice has a weight, and they all add up, just like calories. A moment on the lips, but your hips don't lie. And neither does your soul. We know everything that has been chosen, just as the other side does. Just as both sides can hear your thoughts and see your actions and your inactions. Inaction is also a choice.'

'I think I understand,' Marissa said. 'It's weights and balances, like savings in the bank, isn't it?'

'Yes, exactly. There is a scoreboard of sorts somewhere, I suppose. When it comes down to it, you can make as many little dark choices as you wish, but you may be able to, shall we say, redeem yourself at the last moment with one big, choice of the light, if you care to see it that way. And of course you can make 'light' choices until the day before the day you die, and on your deathbed you can do something so ostentatiously bad that it wipes out all of the light that you've earned and puts you back to square one.'

Marissa nodded.

'I do believe that's why people love that book, A Christmas Carol,' said the demon. 'It gives them hope, blasted story! Practically gives people permission to act like bastards all their lives and then switch sides at the last minute. Very irritating when that happens.'

'But who puts the weight to the choices?'

'Not humans, not us, and not the angels either. And not the Church. Religion is another distraction designed to confuse, I believe it was invented by both sides at some infamous conference or other. Talk about a contradiction! I've preferred to stay away from that one.'

He laughed, then stretched out his legs and drained his glass.

'I do like that, yes – banking, accounting, weights and measures. It's refreshing to speak to someone intelligent. It can be more complicated than you think, however, as you're never balanced out across one lifetime. You're not contracted for just one lifetime either, so you're born with the balance of previous lifetimes. In the black, or in the red, so to speak, before you even get started. Little babies innocent? Ha! Not a chance. You have the opportunity to go one way or the other for eons, until the final judgement.'

'Final judgement sounds so ...final.'

'Well, yes, that is the idea. It hasn't happened yet. I believe everybody will get it at the same time. Then I'll be out of a job. And so will you.'

'That is complicated,' said Marissa. 'Probably too much for my brain to work out, say, if it came to a client wanting to weigh in.'

'Ha, ha – yes, that's good, a weigh-in. Like those weight-loss TV shows. A friend of mine invented those. Great idea, reached so many people on so many levels. Television is a fabulous modus operandi for consent. Movies too. Break through the emotion, get the vulnerability and wham, you're in!'

'That's sneaky,' said Marissa lightly, shocked to find she was enjoying the conversation.

'Television can put a real wedge in, and radio too. Repetitive lyrics delivered through music wear you down and break through barriers over time. Repeat a lie often enough and people start to believe it. We have done such wonderful things with subliminal messaging. Anyway, I digress. The Creator wants you to choose him in every moment. It's the angel's role to make sure that you do, my role to make sure that you don't. He wants to know who really, truly wants Him. Who would sacrifice comfort for Him. Most people won't, and don't. So we get the majority. We get along quite nicely. It can be too easy for us at times, and incredibly disappointing for them.'

'Yes, that makes sense now. Thank you for explaining it.'

'Oh! Thanks to me? How refreshing. Nobody has thanked me, well, perhaps ever.'

There was a moment of silence between them.

'You're still eyeing that muffin. Go on, try it. It's wonderful - trust me.'

'Ha, ha. Trust a demon?'

'Why not? You trust angels that you haven't really met, not to the same extent that you've talked to me. How do you know what they are and what they really think of you? Aren't we just the same beings with different luminosities?'

Raziel – Mystery. This is a mystery unfolding.

'Raziel, now he's quite a character. I lost a substantial amount of money to him in a card game once.'

'Maybe next time, for the muffin.'

'And a card game?'

'Now that I'd like to see.'

'Yes, it is quite an experience. We are very similar, you know, angels and demons. We do the same job, just at different frequencies.'

He sat forward and rubbed his hands together.

'Time is moving on, and I've got souls to claim. Let's call it quits, yes? You are choosing the light, and your contract has been picked through and there are no holes, so my hands are tied once more when it comes to you. But your little friend Terry, he doesn't know what he wants. He is a mysterious one, indeed. He could still be mine, if we play our cards right.'

Marissa reeled. 'Oh God, Terry! Please, what can I do to save him?'

'Ah, and there I was thinking you'd forgotten all about him.'

Marissa's presence floated back towards her flat to check Terry's body, but the demon pulled her back into the journey.

'Not yet, little one, don't go just yet. For if you go now, Terry could be trapped in his worst nightmare forever. For he was born into his lifetime with quite a number of, say, debts in our favour.'

'He did say he was haunted by The Soul Cages.'

'Soul Cages – yes, I like that description.'

'Why do they haunt him?'

'Terry once was a fisher of souls, for us. No wonder that story haunts him. He was a pirate, smashing ships to send their souls to hell in exchange for bounty – gold, incense, spices, silk, all the good things in life. Ah, the irony, good things that send you straight to hell. Anyway, he was reckless and cared little for other people's lives. He died with a grand hoard of gold and nobody to share it with.'

'Ah. Pieces of eight.'

'Exactly.'

'But he's not a pirate now, not in this lifetime. He wouldn't hurt anyone, not Terry.'

'How do you know? He's hurt plenty through his lack of attention and self-centredness. But in this lifetime he does have an opportunity to redeem himself. Perhaps that is why he's drawn to healing work this time. The quickest way to earn points is to help someone else heal. That's why we have so many healers on our side – they think they're going back to the light, but they've not really made the commitment. They like what they like a little too much.'

'Your Terry isn't quite, as you say, in complete alignment with the light. Not just yet. It may only be a matter of time before he slips into the dark ways once more. We may only need to tempt him a little to get him back.'

Marissa thought of the pink jacket that Terry's friend Ed had stolen from the photo shoot and how Terry was often thinking that way himself, taking risks. Wasn't he wearing the clothing from the shoot today? Had he stolen it? But he was so intuitive, and such a gifted healer. And he was her friend. He was. She loved him. She didn't want to give up on him, not yet, not ever.

The demon spoke then, in Terrys voice. 'Oh, Marissa, darling, you really are naïve, aren't you, for someone who comes across as so accomplished? What you see in Terry, that's just the tip of the iceberg.'

This sent hot prickles down Marissa's body. She got her head together. 'Look, I understand Terry has to make his own choices. I love him, but if he chooses darkness, then it's his karma.'

'Yes, karma. That's right.'

'But I'm not going to give up on him, and he hasn't chosen you yet, not technically. So if you take him now, that's just wrong.'

'Not the right argument there, my girl. Try again?'

'I dragged him into this, so he is under my care, and I do not consent. Please release him.'

'Please?' The demon raised an eyebrow. 'Interesting.'

Marissa remembered then. 'You said if I listened to you, you'd release him.'

In response, the demon expanded in the chair, his face became distorted and his eyes fiery as he looked at Marissa, mouth wide, as if he was going to scream at her. But this time she didn't flinch. She looked him square in the eye and held her ground.

'I know I am in the right. That was our contract. I listened. Now release Terry.'

The demon shifted back into his human form, a little ruffled. 'One more for them, one less for us.' He shrugged, regaining his composure. 'But that's just for now. There are always more fish in the sea. And we haven't quite finished with Terry yet.'

'Take me to him.'

The demon rose from the table. In the pleasant speaking voice he had been using earlier, he said, 'This has been an experience, Marissa,' and held out his hand.

'For us both,' she replied, hesitant to take it. She decided to nod, instead.

He pulled his hand back in.

'I shall see you again.'

'I'm sure you will. It's been enlightening. Thank you.'

There was a flash, then Marissa was back in the cabin filled with jars.

Tobermory was there, in jaguar form, looking very happy to see her return. He licked her hand and rubbed his head against her leg. She needed a moment to get her bearings.

'I'm okay,' she said to him. 'I'm okay, love. It's fine. Let's get Terry and get the hell out of here, no pun intended.'

She looked along the shelves, this time with a different eye. All these souls made choices. If I was to release them, I'd override those choices and tip the balance of light and dark. I think I understand now.

She saw a jar with no dust on the stopper. Ah, freshly sealed. *It was brighter than the ones around it too. She peered into it and there was a pixie in there.*

Terry! And he isn't tired out yet, thank God!

She opened the stopper and the light flew out, flew around her twice, then transformed into Terry, who fell into her arms.

She caught him and held him, then hugged him and breathed in his scent. 'It's you, it's really you! You're okay!'

Terry took a few moments to stand up. He looked different, somehow, like the fight had totally gone out of him.

'I thought I was a goner, Marissa, I really did,' he whispered. 'I thought there was no hope and that was it.'

'Let's go home.'

Marissa took his hand and walked him out of the cabin and back to the tree. They emerged at the other end of the portal to find the tree looking at them with admiration.

'Go, take the boy home, and we will speak later, child,' it said.

Marissa nodded.

And then she was back in her flat. Beside her, Terry had colour back in his face, although he was still shivering. He opened his eyes. She held him.

'Oh my God, Marissa, what the hell was that? What happened?'

'Here, you need to warm up.'

Terry's hot water bottle had gone cold. Marissa prised it out of his arms and put the kettle on to refill it. She got her duvet off the bed and wrapped him in that, too. She was also cold. She lit the fire and went and put on another jumper. It was almost 11pm.

'Never again,' Terry said. 'Never again. That was horrendous. Absolutely *horrendous*. But you rescued me. How did you do that?'

'Ah, sure I went to see a man about a dog,' said Marissa with a grin.

'You look different, girl. I mean, look at you. I didn't notice before.'

'Are you okay?'

'Yes, I feel okay now, not completely okay, but the feeling is coming back into my fingertips. Could I trouble you for some tea?'

'Oh yes, no trouble.'

Marissa put the kettle on again as Terry slowly came back to life. She brought him a cup of tea with three spoons of sugar stirred into it.

'I don't think I'll be much good for pints later,' he said with a weak smile, cradling the cup in his hands.

'Sure, the pubs are almost closing now anyway.'

'Wha'? No way!'

'Yes, it's very late. Look you're here, you're okay, and that's the most important thing. Pints can wait.'

'But Bruce can't! I've got to run.'

'You're not going anywhere till you've drunk that tea, then I'm happy to let you go.'

After she had bundled Terry into a taxi and saw him off, Marissa thought back over her discussion with the demon. *From what he told me, Tori would have just fought him, but I brought something new to the table. Maybe all we need to do is talk to each other and come to some arrangement. Tori needed me in order to be complete. It wasn't just me that needed her.*

She climbed into bed and fell asleep almost right away, and into a dream.

'That demon you met is one of the more decent ones. You held your ground. I knew you would. Well done.'

Thoth was sitting on a white bench which faced the sea. It was a bright sunny day, the sky was blue and it reflected turquoise on calm waters. Marissa sat down beside him.

'The darkness sometimes oversteps the line and must be kept in check. I'm glad it worked out this way. We must not interfere with the grand plan, for that is still pushing ahead, and we are on schedule.'

'What plan?'

Thoth turned to her. 'The ascension of humanity. That begins now. The key opened the door on the Lion's Gate last year, 2012.'

'Oh yes, the year the world was supposed to end. I remember that. But it never ended, did it?'

'Actually, it did end, it ended several times. We had to adjust the timelines to avoid the annihilation that was planned. But we were successful.'

'Isn't that overstepping the line?'

'Would you rather be dead?'

'Well, no.'

'See this whole thing as an experiment. As we move closer to humanity having awareness of their own spiritual aspect, we gain awareness of other worlds and other beings, beyond even what we thought we knew. We have much to learn, too. What I know for sure is that you are needed, you're part of the first wave. There's so much to do.'

'Is that what the seven elixirs are for?'

'Yes, it's all connected.'

'And what do I have to do?'

'You're already doing it. Keep up with your studies, help anyone that needs help, find a few like-minded people on the ground that can validate your experiences, and stay connected to me and to your other guides. It may be difficult to hear us from time to time, and there will be times of no contact as there will be planetary interference. That is to be expected.'

'Okay, I will do my best.'

They sat looking at the sea for a while.

'Thoth?'

'Yes?'

'The demon, he said the Great Goddess Isis was a narcissist. I didn't like that.'

Thoth smiled. 'We all have our opinions and our perspectives. History is written by the victors, and of course all gods and goddesses have their faults as well as their powers, just like humans have their eccentricities. We must be discerning as to who we believe.'

'Yes, some of what he said made so much sense, why didn't you tell it to me instead of him?'

'We are all interested in humanity's progress through this current time. It's never been done before, humanity and spirit creating something new together. Perhaps it was the connection with him that was important for you. Either way, you've done something that's never been done before. Well done again.'

'It's exciting.'

'Yes, it will be very exciting, but very challenging too. Make sure you practice slowing down.'

'Olive told me to do that. I know I don't do it often enough.'

'Time will change too – your perception of chronological time will be different.'

'I think time is already different,' Marissa said. 'I've noticed that on my travels, days can feel like weeks and a few minutes can feel like hours.'

'It works the other way too – a year can pass by in minutes. Don't hold on to anything.'

'Ah yes, the path of non-attachment.'

'Exactly. I will be here if you need me. Ciao, Bella.'

'Bye, Thoth, see you soon.'

CHAPTER FORTY TWO

Several weeks later.

Marissa was dead. Her poor body was torn to bits, strewn over the forest floor. Pieces of hair and scalp, bone and sinew lay decomposing on mossy ground. Her stomach and intestines had been ripped out, tangles of guts and organs unceremoniously piled into heaps.

Marissa sighed.

Looking at the devastation, she realised this time she could find nothing salvageable. Her heart fell.

Her ravaged body parts began to melt, slowly dissolving into the earth. Nothing remained but for a glowing light which hovered above the ground. The light of her consciousness had not gone out.

'I'm still here!'

Marissa floated upwards, looking around as if saying goodbye to herself. Then she willed herself through the forest like a will-o-the-wisp until she found a familiar clearing.

There, hidden amongst the bushes was her dear friend, the wise old tree. She relaxed then, and gently hovered towards him. She spoke, using the telepathic voice of her mind.

'Hello, lovely tree. I seem to have lost my body completely. What do I do? Can you help?'

The tree stirred, large eyes which were embedded in its trunk opened slowly and his familiar smile widened in welcome. Marissa's heart, if she still had one, opened.

'It's all part of the journey my dear,' said the tree, yawning. 'Sometimes we have to go deeply into the dark places to find the pieces of ourselves.'

It sounded familiar. 'I think you said this to me before?' said Marissa.

The tree chuckled. 'Ahh, yes I am sure of it. We often need to hear something more than once before we listen to it. But I do believe you actually understand what I am talking about this time.'

'Yes, perhaps I do.' Marissa laughed too.

The tree laughed louder this time and turned to look directly at her, its wise eyes filled with love and compassion. 'You certainly have been dismembered,' it said, still laughing. 'Congratulations!'

It certainly did seem very funny. The tree continued to speak.

'You have an opportunity now to rebuild yourself completely.' The tree stretched out its branches, then enlarged in size. Marissa's light glowed more strongly in response. She felt herself solidifying. She looked at her hands, arms and body as she grew back into herself. Her body reappeared. It held a soft glow, and her feet didn't quite touch the ground the same way that they did before.

'Ah, there you are,' said the tree. 'You're not quite finished yet though. Because you are indeed, still alive. We awaken, we learn, we grow and transform, then we expand. We stay like that for a time, and then we do it all again. There is always more learning for us to do, even if we believe we know everything. We never, ever do. So well done, and onto the next.

+++

Marissa entered her new healing space in the city centre. It was clean and bright, above a shop on a busy street, but it was soundproofed so she didn't hear much to distract her. Strong sunshine poured in through the large window and she looked with pride at the two brand-new counselling chairs that she had bought. She adjusted the painting on the wall. The sunflowers in a field were the embodiment of hope, vibrancy and light, and that's what she wanted her clients to focus on.

She cleared the room with sage, but it didn't really need it. She opened her brand-new phone, found the compass and faced North, then called in the Four Directions, Earth and Sky to open a sacred healing space.

Her plinth was out and decked with fresh blankets, and there was plenty of space to move around it. She had water and brand-new tumblers, and a dedicated stereo with music for her Reiki sessions.

This was her space – well, okay, half hers; she was sharing it with Eli's friend – but it was her space for half the week, and she would build up to taking it full time once she'd given her notice in to Noreen. Two full days a week in the healing room and three in the office felt good enough for now.

Her first client was due shortly – Rebecca. She was the first psychotherapy client that she had obtained, under her own steam. Olive had recommended a new supervisor and she was going to pay for supervision herself, so she would not only get more counselling hours for her diploma, but she'd also have enough supervision hours to meet the requirements. It was a relief, and she was delighted with her decision.

She gave the room a final once-over. Matt had given her fresh flowers in a beautiful glass vase. He thought of all the small details, and she was touched by his kindness. She was also pleased to have something from him in her space; the vase would stay long after the flowers had withered.

She connected to Reiki and drew the power symbol and the symbols for emotional healing and mental clarity. She was excited about the Reiki Master-level workshop the following weekend. Matt would be doing it with her. Then she was taking a 'Divination and Paths of Destiny' class with Séamus two weekends after that. Not in Clifden, but in his room in Dublin. All the gang was going to be there, it would be a reunion. And if all that wasn't enough, she'd finally enrolled for the psychotherapy degree, and it was starting soon, so there was one more year of college with those friends too, to look forward to.

She looked at the clock. There was just enough time for her to go to the bathroom before her first client arrived. The bathroom was freshly painted and there was a framed quote on the wall, 'You can't get flowers without a little rain,' which felt appropriate. The room was freshly stocked with clean towels and toilet roll, and a vanilla scented oil diffuser she got as a gift from her mother.

Marissa used the toilet, flushed and went to wash her hands. She noticed the mirror above the sink was fogged up. *That's strange, it's not hot in here.* She peered at it, puzzled as to where the condensation was coming from. Then a large water droplet ran down the glass, getting larger as it picked up more condensation, and splashed into the sink. Then there was another.

Wait, what's this?

A letter 'E' slowly appeared on the mirrored glass, as if a child was writing it with thick, clumsy fingers. It was coarse and large, but clear and unmistakable. Marissa froze as the letter 'D' appeared beside it. Then came a 'W' and an 'A'. Then it stopped for a moment. *No, wait, there's an 'R' and there's a 'D'.* Then it did stop. A name was right in front of her, as clear as day: 'EDWARD.' It was unmistakable.

Marissa's whole body went cold. Ice cold. She could hear the buzzer buzzing, but it took a few moments for her to register what it was.

Look at this. Should I wipe it or leave it? If the client needs the bathroom, it looks so weird. I need to wipe it. But who would believe me if I told them what happened? I wouldn't believe it myself... I know, I'll take a picture and I'll have to think about it later.

The buzzer sounded again. Marissa had to get it, it was definitely her client, but first she took her phone out of her pocket and took a quick photograph of the glass before wiping it clear and quickly washing her hands. She caught her breath and went to get the door, trying to still her beating heart.

Rebecca was in her twenties and had come for counselling. Marissa felt her body thawing as she greeted her and welcomed her to into the room, all the while trying to push aside what she had just seen. It didn't feel real, but she had the photograph as proof. She poured some water for them both and invited Rebecca to choose a chair. It felt like her phone was burning a hole in her pocket.

'This is a lovely room. It feels really cosy in here,' Rebecca said.

Marissa sat down, beginning to shake as her blood began to thaw. She pressed her feet into the ground and it eased her symptoms. *I spoke to a demon, for God's sake, I can do this.* She imagined herself growing bigger, she had shrunk in a moment of weakness. *Yes, that's better.* The shaking eased and she brought her awareness back to the room. She smiled at Rebecca.

'Thank you. I just moved in, you're actually my first client here.'

'Oh! I hope it goes well for you.'

'Me too! Well, it's lovely to meet you Rebecca, welcome to my healing space. We can have as many sessions together as you want. I'd just like you to let me know when you'd like to finish up, so that we can have a proper closing session. I think we should check in every few sessions anyway, so we can make sure you feel you're getting value for your time here. It also helps me learn how to be better help to you, if we spend some time together talking about how you feel the sessions are working out. Is that okay?'

'Yes, that sounds reasonable.'

'Good.' Marissa relaxed now, she felt the warmth coming back into her body as she took the drivers seat. *Hey, this is a big deal, my first contract for my first psychotherapy client. It's worthy of celebration.*

She went on. 'I'd also like to let you know that everything you say here is confidential, except if I believe there is a risk that you're going to self-harm, or harm someone else, I will need to talk to my supervisor.'

Rebecca looked concerned. 'No, I'm not going to do that.'

Marissa smiled again. 'I have to say it up front, just so you know from the beginning of our relationship where we stand with each other.'

'Okay, makes sense.'

'Great.' Marissa loved being able to do the contract her own way. It was exciting, her attention was now fully back in the room.

'Now all that's out of the way, we can begin. What would you like to talk to me about tonight?'

Rebecca was silent for a moment, then her face filled with emotion, her cheeks flushed and she looked at the floor. Her eyes glistened and tears formed.

'Take your time,' said Marissa. *She must be holding all that emotion inside herself. It's good for her to get it out.*

Rebecca began to speak, choosing her words carefully. 'My dad, he died unexpectedly. It's been a few months now, but I'm still very upset about it. Mum said it might help me to talk to someone, 'cos I'm so worried about her, I won't tell her how I'm doing in case it upsets her even more. I came here for her, really. But now that I'm here, I think it might help me.'

'I understand. If you've never come to counselling before, it can be difficult enough without having something upsetting on your mind as well.'

Rebeca nodded. Marissa handed her a box of tissues and she took one and wiped her eyes.

'Would you like to tell me about him?' Marissa was fully present now, in therapist mode, giving her full attention to her client.

Rebecca smiled and a large tear ran down her cheek and splashed onto her skirt.

'Yes, I would,' she said. 'I loved him very much. His name was Edward.'

2057

Marissa eased her shawl on over her coat. Cold, blustery days like this slowed her down and the damp seeped into her bones. *Irish weather never did agree with me.*

Walking back to her house on the road she had often travelled down as a child, she shuffled along, slowing even more once she noticed there were leaves and puddles on the path. *Slow down, old woman, you don't want to slip.*

She stopped to catch her breath and get her bearings, and caught her reflection in the glassy surface of the puddle next to her. Her heart flipped for a moment and she peered in closer... *Must be my eyes playing tricks on me.*

There, in the puddle, was Marissa, aged seventeen, in school uniform, peering up at her. Their eyes met. A doorway to the soul, a slice out of time and space.

Something inside her clicked and she smiled. *Ah, yes, I remember this moment. And now we come full circle. There is magic in the world, after all.*

She smiled to see the girl, her shocked seventeen-year-old self, pulling back. She looked again, and there she was, reflected, silver hair, wizened face, seventy two years young and counting. The seventy two year old, looking just like Grandmother Medicine Woman without the regalia, leaving seventeen year old Marissa to wonder what the hell was going on.

She smiled. *She knew it was me all the time. She knew it was real. Oh, if she only knew what we got up to next!*

Great Spirit of the North, we come to you and ask for the strength and power to bear what is cold and harsh in life. We honour our ancestors who have also received the winds that truly can be overwhelming at times. Support us and warm us as we do our work, hold us as we release the patterns that are holding us back and place them into the fire.

Great Spirit of the East, direction of birth, of the sunrise, of hope and faith. We turn to you to help us fly above our problems, to bring in light to the darkest places, to show us the direction of the next mountain that we need to climb. Support us and lighten our way as we choose to walk on this pathway of healing, so we may rise to be the best that we can be.

Great Spirit of the South, spirit of growth and compassion, of fertility and warmth. We come to you to you to support us as we shed our skins and leave the old controlling ways behind. Unwind from us what is no longer needed and teach us the way of compassion and beauty, so we can walk softly and leave no footprints behind.

Great Spirit of the West, direction of death, of the sunset, of powerful medicine that goes beyond this lifetime. Teach us to live better lives, to be unafraid of death, to lift off the heavy chains that hold us back, support us as we transform our darkness into light, and help us bring that light to others.

Mother Earth, you are our true mother for you have given birth to all of the creatures in our world, the finned and the feathered, the two-legged, four-legged and many-legged. The trees and the oceans, the mountains and the valleys.

We honour you and all of your children, all of our relations. Teach us how to treat you better and remind us that we all share the same blood.

Father Sky, you look down upon us and see our true potential. You know the things that we do not know. We ask you to come and hold this space as we remember the truth of who we are. For we are not alone, we are all connected in this great universal family. Thank you for the chance to sing this song of life for one more day.

Great Spirit of the North - we thank you for offering us your strength, your power. We honour you, we honour those that came before us and those that will come after us. We release you now, with great gratitude.

Great Spirit of the East - we thank you for lending us your wings, for showing us the way. We are humbled in your presence, we see how far we have come, but we acknowledge we have much further to travel. We release you now with great gratitude.

Great Spirit of the South - we thank you for helping us shed our skins and transform into the beings that we are becoming. We endeavour to continue with the process of healing and growth. We release you now with great gratitude.

Great Spirit of the West - we are humbled to have been in your presence, reminding us to have great appreciation for each moment of every day of our lives. We see life everlasting in everything around us. We release you now with great gratitude. Ho!

Oh magical Mother, oh mystical Father, thank you for holding us as we do our healing work. We peel the illusion from our eyes and see the world as it really is, to know and experience the interconnectedness of all things. With majesty and grace we offer ourselves in service, to follow the beauty way, the path of light. And to walk gently upon you and leave no footprints, only light. And so it is.

Made in the USA
Middletown, DE
17 March 2023

26906007R00336